SEAN WALLACE is the founder, publisher and managing editor of Prime Books. In his spare time he has edited or co-edited a number of projects including three magazines *Clarkesworld Magazine*, *The Dark* and *Fantasy Magazine*, and a number of anthologies including *Best New Fantasy*, *Japanese Dreams*, *The Mammoth Book of Steampunk*, *People of the Book*, *Robots: Recent A. I.* and *War and Space: Recent Combat*. He has been nominated a number of times for Hugo Awards and World Fantasy Awards, won three Hugo Awards and one World Fantasy Award, and has served as a World Fantasy Award Judge. He lives in Germantown, MD, with his wife, Jennifer, and their twin daughters, Cordelia and Natalie.

Friends of the
Houston Public Library

D0192389

The Mammoth Book of

Warriors and Wizardry

Sean Wallace

ROBINSON

RUNNING PRESS
PHILADELPHIA · LONDON

ROBINSON

First published in Great Britain in 2014 by Robinson

Copyright © Sean Wallace, 2014 (unless otherwise stated)

The moral right of the author has been asserted.

*All characters and events in this publication, other than
those clearly in the public domain, are fictitious
and any resemblance to real persons,
living or dead, is purely coincidental.*

All rights reserved.
No part of this publication may be reproduced, stored in a retrieval system, or transmitted, in
any form, or by any means, without the prior permission in writing of the publisher, nor be
otherwise circulated in any form of binding or cover other than that in which it is published and
without a similar condition including this condition being imposed on the subsequent purchaser.

A CIP catalogue record for this book
is available from the British Library.

ISBN 978-1-47211-062-6 (paperback)
ISBN: 978-1-47211-076-3 (ebook)

Typeset in Plantin Light by Hewer Text UK Ltd, Edinburgh
Printed and bound by CPI Group (UK) Ltd, Croydon, CR0 4YY

Robinson
is an imprint of
Constable & Robinson Ltd
100 Victoria Embankment
London EC4Y 0DY

An Hachette UK Company
www.hachette.co.uk

www.constablerobinson.com

First published in the United States in 2014 by Running Press Book Publishers,
A Member of the Perseus Books Group

All rights reserved under the Pan-American and International Copyright Conventions

*This book may not be reproduced in whole or in part, in any form or by
any means, electronic or mechanical, including photocopying, recording,
or by any information storage and retrieval system now known or
hereafter invented, without written permission from the publisher.*

Books published by Running Press are available at special discounts for bulk purchases in
the United States by corporations, institutions, and other organizations.
For more information, please contact the Special Markets
Department at the Perseus Books Group, 2300 Chestnut Street,
Suite 200, Philadelphia, PA 19103, or call (800) 810-4145, ext. 5000, or e-mail
special.markets@perseusbooks.com.

US ISBN: 978-0-7624-5466-2
US Library of Congress Control Number: 2014939682

9 8 7 6 5 4 3 2 1
Digit on the right indicates the number of this printing

Running Press Book Publishers
2300 Chestnut Street
Philadelphia, PA 19103-4371

Visit us on the web!
www.runningpress.com

CONTENTS

INTRODUCTION

Warriors and wizardry: two of the most enduring and resonant archetypes in fantasy.

The warrior – tracing back to ancient heroes such as Gilgamesh, Arjuna, Beowulf and Gesar, through mid-era institutions like knights, steppe horsemen and samurai, to the modern Western fantasy warrior, in its variants "high" and "low", Aragorn and Conan. Perhaps it's a facet of human nature to admire strength and steadfastness. But the warrior archetype also includes everyday figures rising to meet warrior challenges, such as David, Marjuna and Joan of Arc; an earning of the warrior strength and steadfastness through grit and courage.

The wizard seems to represent an opposite: not brawn but brains; not physical strength but mental acumen; knowledge, manifested as corporeal power and often – but not always – wisdom. Perhaps the wizard arises as a synthesis of the supernatural transformations performed by gods in myth and the venerable societal presence of institutions such as shamans, elders and early thinkers, inventors and alchemists; evolving from human figures of myth such as Daedalus, Väinämöinen and Xuanzang as well as sorcerous semi-divine figures such as Hunahpu and Xbalanque, the djinn and Sun Wukong, through Merlin and Morgan le Fay to the modern Western fantasy wizard Gandalf. Perhaps the wizard arises from the facet of human nature to admire knowledge and ability to perform the supernatural, but also to mistrust or fear it.

But as fantasy fiction developed into its own genre, the modern Western forms of warrior and wizard have come to dominate the depiction of these archetypes. Although well known and popular, these narrow representations fail to span the universal variety of these archetypes; the range of cultures and variations in which tales of warriors and wizards have been told – ancient epics of India, China, Mongolia, mid-era sagas of the Mayans, Norse, Finns and Arabia, to name a mere few.

Enter the current fantasy short-fiction movement, with its nuanced focus on character and its eye for diverse takes on archetypes and portrayal of traditionally under-represented cultures and perspectives. The short-fiction format provides the current fantasist with a compact and intensified space in which to present, explore, deconstruct or subvert. The prevalence of these archetypes across human culture provides a rich panoply of warrior and wizard traditions to examine; to use to recast the predominant forms or offer under-represented ones, while at once reveling in the enduring allure that makes these archetypes yet resonant.

The stories in this volume represent the best of this current fantasy short-fiction exploration of universal warriors and wizardry. They are inspired by cultures from around the globe, including medieval Arabia, dynastic Egypt, Imperial China, tribal Europe and feudal Japan, as well as other fantastical worlds that defy categorization. They feature characters of traditionally and non-traditionally represented gender, orientation, origin, society and class. They focus not on these characters' exploits or might but on their human condition, what it means to be who they are: Yoon Ha Lee's surgeon who must cut free legendary warriors trapped in the paper of manuscripts, to defend his conquered moon; Benjamin Rosenbaum's bereaved villager who summons the courage to combat bizarre necromancies in pursuit of the abomination that razed his home; Mary Robinette Kowal's shaman whose magical power manifests from having his wife strangle him near to death; N. K. Jemisin's narcomancer, who slips into a land of dreams in order to free the dying from their souls.

Or the stories pair a warrior and a wizard together: Saladin Ahmed's duo of grumpy old ghost-hunter and earnest young swordsman ascetic; Richard Parks's duo of world-weary insightful samurai and reprobate priest; Chris Willrich's duo of thief (a "low" warrior) and poet (what is a poet if not a wizard of words?); Benjanun Sriduangkaew's dual protagonists not in concert but at odds: an expatriate sorcerer clashing with the warrior sent to arrest her and seize the bones of her dead golem daughter.

All these stories not only offer examinations of varied cultures, nuanced characters, and perspectives both traditionally represented and not, but do it while telling a great tale; entertaining, captivating, moving. They use the warrior and wizard archetypes as a starting point to delve into human culture and investigate the human condition. And, in showing us varied characters and diverse cultures and worlds, also teach us something about ourselves and our own. Which may be the greatest wizardry of all.

Scott H. Andrews
Editor-in-Chief, *Beneath Ceaseless Skies*

SMALL MAGIC

Jay Lake

The power of an oath, thought Alain, *is a terrible thing.* Here he was freezing on the northern frontier, a dozen summers from the last days of his youth, bound by two silver pennies pressed into his fist the day he took the Duke of Bourne's service.

Unlike most soldiers, he still had the pennies, somewhere, as yet unspent on whores or wine.

Alain would probably die here. Everybody had to die somewhere. Alain just wished he had been smart enough to die at home in bed. Where it was warm. Instead of standing brevet corporal to a pair of drunken serjeants, wondering what he would eat during the coming winter. All because he'd sworn by his name, over silver.

"Last supply caravan was, what, eleven months ago?" Serjeant Odilo, who chewed a local weed he claimed granted him visions of paradise, hawked a clustered wad into the dust. His lips were stained deep blue, as if he were a berry farmer forever sampling his crop. Odilo reminded Alain of some ape from the deepest south, cringing with unspoken pain, captive forever in invisible chains of duty.

"Been all four seasons," said Alain, staring at the clotted indigo wad of spit and leaves. Autumn was drawing to a close. Supply was on the minds of every trooper in the First Century.

Once, the army had seemed better than a narrow life on a little farm with some girl he'd known since childhood. Now, still not even thirty summers old, he felt broken-backed in the Duke's service. His life had washed him upon this northern shore guarding only seabirds and seals and whatever lurked bright-eyed in the night outside the flickering, fading circle of their watch fires.

The long, narrow harbor below the cliffs on which the soldiers dwelt was beautiful, winter and summer. It never quite froze, because of the warm waters flowing from the smoking flanks of Mount Abaia to the north and east. In winter, snow blanketed the rocky shores and highlighted the struggling firs along the steep cliffs. Summer brought wildflowers like a shattered rainbow, smeared across the earth with a smell of honey and grass so strong as to make the mules mad.

The captain's theory was that the Duke of Bourne had once meant to keep ships in the harbor, to guard these northern waters, and they, First Century of the Fourth Battle of the IV Legion, were sent to guard the landing from the Ice Tribes in their northern fastness. The subaltern had been silent on the matter since long before Alain arrived, preferring to live alone in the foothills to the east. Odilo and his brother serjeant Severus argued about everything from horses to women to the weather, but they wouldn't discuss First Century's years-long deployment either.

"Us as takes the Duke's coins do His Grace's bidding," Odilo was fond of saying over fire and wine. "No questions asked, no duties shirked."

Alain was hard-pressed to see what duties they might be shirking. The watchtower had been abandoned by the engineers after laying the foundation courses. One old derrick remained, that Alain and some of the other men had restored to working order the previous summer, just for something to do. A few loose blocks of dressed stone inhabited the camp, mostly tables now, that presumably the First of the Fourth were keeping safe from marauders.

Some of the younger men – recruits from the last few waves of reinforcements, including the final squad that had brought Alain four years earlier – liked to say they were there to be trained, strengthened, until they grew to champions to be summoned back to the Duke's Own Guard clothed in honor and glory. But Alain sometimes found eider-fletched arrows broken in the woods that told him a different story, along with soft-soled prints from shoes worn by no soldier of the Duke.

Alain believed that the absent subaltern trafficked with the Ice Tribes who live to the north, and that the Ice Tribes watched their Century's little camp. He had never understood what those strange men wanted.

"I saw powerful magic," said the captain. "Once."

The First Century gathered around a smoky evening fire, each man's face flickering into a goblin mask.

"Small magic, too," the old man continued. "The hardest kind. Anyone with talent can call a storm or set a raging fire, but to hold the flame in your hand, or make the water dance, now that's rare."

Odilo smacked his lips, then found his voice. "Begging your pardon, sir, but magic's mostly good for tearing a man's guts out and scaring the kiddies into their graves. Nothing but dark purpose, perfect and evil. Can't fight it, can't live with it."

"And there you're wrong." The captain's teeth gleamed yellow in the firelight, shaped by his smile. "Every work of magic has a flaw, a fault, some loophole from perfection. Otherwise the gods would not permit it to be. The greater the work, the greater the flaw, if it can be found. Small magic has small flaws."

After a moment of fire-crackling silence, the captain continued. "It can be of good purpose, too. I saw a wizard on a battlefield down near Southgate, when I was a trooper in the Army of the Black. Light cavalry, my first enlistment, before I was commissioned.

"We swept across a field just before dawn, aiming to get up in some high trees and screen the flank of that day's advance. There this fellow was on the field below us, his face all aglow like those jellyfish our harbor gets in the spring. My serjeant sent me out of cover to see what the lay was." The captain's smile widened. "I was disposable, you might say, in those days."

The men dutifully laughed.

"Anyway, there this little wizard was, barely tall as my shoulder, in robes I wouldn't hang on a beggar, and he had a man's life in his hands." The captain shook his head. "Don't know how else to put it.

"He had this little misty ball, no bigger than a child's head. Though I was on a horse thirty feet away, I could see a whole world inside, a baby in its nappies, a boy plucking apples, dinners and fairs and going for a soldier and his whole life until he was struck down by a spear that previous day on our battlefield.

"So I says to the wizard, 'What are you about, man? There'll be killing here soon.' And he looks at me the way a lamb looks at the slaughterman with the hammer and says with that slippery wizard echo in his voice, 'If I can only put one back into the world, my victory is still greater than your entire army.'"

The fire crackled for a while, silence of the night the only response to the captain's story, until Odilo spat again. "Did you run the little sharp-tongue through? Can't trust them wizards."

The captain just looked sad, then bid the men good evening and shuffled off to his hut.

"Alain, get *up*," hissed Odilo, hitting him again.

Until the frosts came, Alain often forsook the hut he shared with three other soldiers to sleep atop the abandoned foundation courses of the tower. It kept him closer to the stars, and slightly diminished the influence of the blackflies. He hoped.

Alain glared at Odilo through sleep-clouded eyes, seeing dawn's barest stain above the mountains to the east. "Wha . . . ? I don' ha' mornin' watch."

"Captain's dead," Odilo said quietly. No lip-smacking this morning. "His heart, maybe. Don't look like he been killed or nothing. But still as a stone, and not much warmer."

Amid a profound twinge of sadness – no father to his men, still the captain did serve as something of a befuddled uncle – Alain found his voice, and his curiosity. "I'm a brevet corporal, you're the serjeant. Why are you waking me?"

"I've sent a runner south." Odilo glanced over his shoulder, shaking his head.

Alain understood what he meant – no messages of theirs had been answered for almost a year.

The serjeant returned his glare to Alain. "I need someone to get the subaltern. He's in command of the Century now. Likely he won't throw rocks at *you*." Odilo's voice was suddenly low and sly. "You talk to him sometimes. I know it."

Alain realized Odilo was frightened. Of command? Of being abandoned?

It didn't matter.

The subaltern would not come, not if the Duke of Bourne himself appeared to deliver the orders in person. The subaltern had fled his life, remaining connected to the Century only by the tenuous thread of habit, and lack of sufficient ambition to move farther inland on his own.

"I'll go, but he won't help," Alain warned, discharging his final duty to the captain in one sentence.

"Someone's got to do it," Odilo hissed. Fear leaked from him like steam from a kettle.

Alain said nothing more, but brushed the chilly dew out of his boots with the warm underside of his blanket. Odilo moved off in the morning twilight, adrift, searching for purpose.

There were three eider-fletched arrows in the lintel of the subaltern's snug little cabin, and the door stood open, badly splintered. Alain jabbed at it with his spear, not afraid of marauders within – had they still been present they would not have let him approach this close – but of what portions of the subaltern might remain behind the door.

The wood creaked wide open, innocent of menace. Alain stepped in, feeling as if he were the barbarian, come to pillage civilization's last outpost.

Although over time he and the subaltern had exchanged careful, quiet nods in the forests of aspen and birch that lay inland north and east of the Century's encampment, Alain had in fact never spoken to the officer. As far as he knew, no one had, except possibly the captain. Who had other, more grave concerns to occupy him now.

The cabin was almost spotless inside. The silvery birch floor was polished clean as a deck in the Duke's fleet – Alain was on a ship once, briefly. Its perfection was marred only by a spray of blood and three fresh cuts.

Blows of an ax, from the look of the thing, Alain told himself.

There was almost no furniture, only a little frame bed slung with knotted ropes, a stool and a tiny table. Leaves, roots and vegetables hung from the ceiling. The embers of a fire still smoked in the little hearth. A flag with the Ducal insignia hung on one wall. Except for the blood and the ax scars, the cabin was unmarred. Unlooted. Intact.

"They took nothing but the subaltern," Alain whispered to Serjeants Odilo and Severus.

The three of them huddled on a wind-whipped point of rock jutting out over the bay far below. The men called it "The Leap" because every now and then someone did so, launching himself into the next cycle of life with a long, slow dive. It was one of the few places where a conversation could be guaranteed private, as there was no cover anywhere near. A brown gull hung in the wind, eyeing them in hope of fish heads or bread crusts.

"Go to Darknesh," muttered Severus, long-ago veteran of one of the stranger religions to be found in Bournemouth, with the scars to prove it. His cheeks were flushed, his words already slurred from early drinking.

Odilo glanced from Severus to Alain and back, over and over like a squirrel between two nuts. *Odilo would be comical,* Alain thought, *if not for the desperation in his face.*

"We should retreat," Odilo said, smacking his lips as blue spittle leaked down his chin. "Break the camp, march the Century back to North Coast Keep."

Ten days' march south and west, North Coast was where the Fourth Battle had its headquarters. Superior officers, discipline, all the things a good soldier shunned.

But a man wouldn't have to do his own thinking there. Or bury his own dead.

"North Coasht," Severus said, then grunted. "Bashtards shor'-measured our oil rash-en lasht year. Never did nothin' fer ush."

"Your runner will come back with orders," Alain said, filled with a sense of urgency, a new-found loyalty to the captain somehow inspired by the dead man's story about the grubby little wizard on the battlefield. "We should stand with our mission."

"What mission?" Odilo's voice peaked in panic before settling into his accustomed jeer. He spat out over the harbor, the brown gull diving after the wadded leaves. "Captain never told us nothing 'cept sit tight. Well, we sat tight. Now you want us to swivel around here on our asses, out of supply, waiting for the snows to come. A couple of weeks, the road back to North Coast will be waist-deep in mud, a couple of weeks after that, snow up to our earlobes. If'n we want to leave, we got to leave now."

Alain shrugged. "You're the serjeant. I'm just a corporal." Afraid to meet Odilo's eye, he looked out at the gull, returned to hanging in the wind. "But I'm staying."

The subaltern might need someone to come home to, even if he came in small pieces.

The First Century decided to bury their captain that coming evening, on the south side of their camp. The warm side. There was a squabble when no one could find the banners. Alain knew the Ducal standard was at the subaltern's cabin, but he kept his mouth shut, praying for the little wizard to come before cold dirt and pine needles filled the captain's face forever.

Each man in the Century dug at least a shovelful from the grave, which resulted in a scooped-out bowl in the soil. It was a kind thought, but Alain hated the shallow pit that was created, so he stripped to his trousers and dug the grave properly from the bottom of the pit, working with a fury born of frustration. It made for a huge trench. Exhausted, he finally climbed out.

"Planning to lay us all in the ground together?" Odilo asked as Alain cleaned the shovel and gathered his clothing.

Alain tried to smile. "A great man deserves a great grave."

Odilo spat. "He wasn't a great man. He was a jumped-up clerk turned out to fight in some war what couldn't get his old job back after. They kept him around and made him an officer 'cause he could read and write."

Alain could read and write, some – his childhood village had had a progressive priest who served a gentle god – but this didn't seem the time to mention that. "He was great to me," said Alain, thinking again of the grubby little wizard and the small magic of restoring a man's life.

★   ★   ★

When First Century marched out of their camp to lay the body to rest, wrapped in a sheet from the captain's cot, they found another eider-fletched arrow. This one was point down in the bottom of the grave, still quivering, though no one saw it fly and the woods were hundreds of yards away.

Without a word, Alain scrambled down into the grave, plucked the arrow from the turned earth, snapped it in two and climbed back out to lay the halves atop the captain's winding sheet. The men of the Century cheered, even Serjeant Severus. Then they rushed through the funeral, each eager to get to serious drinking and plotting their escape from this northern perdition.

The little wizard never came.

In the morning, eight men were gone, with their gear and somehow – against all common sense where the noisy beasts were concerned – one of the camp mules. Serjeant Severus was also among the missing, though his gear was still present.

Odilo would send no one after the deserters, but was willing to turn out a desultory search effort for Severus. Alain went to The Leap, where he spotted Severus floating in the bay far below.

At least he assumed it was Severus. A man was there, wrapped in an old tunic the color of bayberries, just as Severus wore lounging around the camp. His head seemed to be missing, although perhaps Severus was simply riding low in the water.

After some thought, Alain told Serjeant Odilo.

"Quiet, fool," Odilo said, smacking his lips. He had been chewing his weed like a mule ate hay, this last day or so. "Let the men search. I'll prepare our withdrawal."

Alain was overcome with a wave of stubborn pride. "So when Benno and Faubus and the others left, it was desertion, but now we're going to withdraw?"

"This is *orders*," Odilo said, pressing his puffy, blue-stained nose right into Alain's face.

"We already have orders, serjeant."

"You want to stay here and die at the hands of the Ice Tribes, fine with me. You've got Severus's squads now, *corporal*. Orders is half yours." Odilo spat between Alain's feet, then stalked away.

The Century's encampment surrounded the foundation courses of the unfinished tower. They were protected on three sides by wooden hoardings backed with clay, erected years before in best army fashion, though these were now mostly overgrown with beans and melon vines. Fields of hardy crops stretched around the hoardings. The fourth side was open to the cliff over the water, with gaps between the ends of the hoardings and the cliff large enough to drive a wagon through at each end.

First Century even had an old cannon, a lion-mouthed thing originally captured from the Onyx Navy far to the near-mythical south. It was spoil of some battle, handed from unit to unit and officer to officer until like the men it had finally washed up here on this northmost shore. There was a small pile of shot, rusted together, and four kegs of what was alleged to be powder, though no one in the Century seemed to know what to do with the stuff.

Alain organized some of the younger men to wrestle the cannon into the inland-facing gap between the hoarding and the cliff. He readied one of the unit's two wagons to block the other gap, while Serjeant Odilo supervised a loading up of the second wagon for the march south.

Neither of them had actually issued orders. Rather, each quietly made his intentions known, and some silent democracy of soldiers voted in successive pairs of booted feet, until the Century had divided itself around two heads, like a worm cut in half and left to regrow.

It was no surprise to Alain that most of Odilo's men chose to go with the serjeant, while most of Severus's men stayed with him. Alain was polite enough to leave Odilo's way clear. Odilo was smart enough not to comment on the folly of Alain's cannon.

Late that afternoon, as the Southron cannon was mounted in place and the departing wagon had been fully loaded, a rider appeared out of the trees a quarter mile inland, to the east. He

was a small man on a small horse, the animal grubby white
with shaggy hair, the man grubby brown wrapped in shaggy
furs.

Alain and Odilo found themselves side-by-side at the east-
facing hoarding. The weather had turned suddenly colder and
damper, and their breath curled and mingled together, nature
seeking to reunite the Century by some sympathetic magic.

"What do you think?" Odilo finally asked as the rider
approached at an insolently slow canter.

"I don't know yet," Alain said, looking carefully to see if any
heads were dangling from the rider's saddle.

The newcomer carried a tall pole with a small wooden circle
or wheel mounted across the top, from which dangled a forest
of dark horsetails. He was clad entirely in furs, only his face
visible, which glistened with smeared-on fat.

"Hai," said the rider.

"What's your business here?" Odilo demanded.

"I've come to ease your sorry lives," the rider said in aston-
ishingly good Wentish, the language of the duchy.

A herald of sorts, then, Alain thought.

"The chief of our chiefs requires this place for his use," the
rider went on. "You are invited to depart before his armies
come scouring."

"I—" Odilo began to say, but Alain elbowed him in the ribs
and spoke over him. "The Duke's army moves at no one's beck
save His Grace's own."

"You do not need this place," said the rider. "Your men do
nothing here but grow fat and tired. Go south, to your warm-
lands and your women, and leave our cold places to us."

"Fat and tired we may be, but here we'll stay," Alain shouted.
"Now begone and tell your little chief we will not surrender to
him."

"Nobody said nothing about *surrendering*," Odilo muttered
in a pained voice, but the rider was already cantering away.

That night around the fires, the silent democracy of soldiers
finally found its voice. "We'll all die here – for what?" "They
killed the captain, too, some ice wizard's work." "Magicked the
subaltern years ago." "Eating Serjeant Severus's liver even

now, I warrant you." "That Alain's crazy, and too big for his boots." "Odilo's a coward – we got a job to do."

At dawn the loaded wagon creaked away west and south, accompanied by the irritated complaints of mules, the shuffling of dozens of feet and one spitting serjeant. Alain stood atop his lion-mouthed cannon, facing northeast where the enemy doubtless waited, wondering what had ever possessed him to stay.

After the sun had broken above the shoulder of Mount Abaia into an icy clear day, Alain turned to find that over half the Century had stayed with him.

"Well," he said, "pull that last wagon around to block the other exit, and let's have men on the hoardings. A show of strength is what's called for here, and a show of strength is what we'll have."

As they bustled to their work, Alain again felt pride in being a soldier, for the first time in years. He recalled the Ducal standard in the subaltern's cabin. "I'm off to scout a bit. Hold fast, and see if some one of you can't manage to load this cannon up."

The men of the Century cheered as Alain walked into the woods, toward their enemy.

He found the cabin without challenge – there were no Ice Tribesmen in evidence. The arrows were gone and the door was shut, but Alain simply pushed in.

The flag was still there, but so was a large man in furs. Enormous, in fact, for an Ice Tribesman. His resemblance to the herald was passing at best, bald head tattooed with runes, a necklace of fingerbones around his neck. He sat on the subaltern's lone stool, staring at Alain with an expression of mild amusement that broadened to a yellow-toothed grin.

"You're their shaman," Alain said without preamble, ignoring the chill stab of fear in his heart. He was careful not to make any quick motions with his spear.

"How tell?" asked the tribesman in thickly accented Wentish. His voice was a braying rasp, with a strange echo underneath as if he spoke from two places at once. What the captain had called "a slippery wizard echo".

"Who else would be in here? And *someone* killed the captain." Alain leaned his spear against the doorpost. "Besides, you've got charms and fetishes."

"All Ice Tribe got charm fetish," said the shaman. "Big power, big pain. You go home now."

"This is my home. His Grace told me to come live here, and here I live." Well, actually, some clerk had told him, but it was the Duke's will, however indirect.

"Big magic in north. Big working, go home, danger you." The shaman mimed fangs and snarled. "Call snow demon, steal you heart. Many rider cross you grave. You go now, you safe."

Demons. The Ice Tribes were going to summon demons and bring their armies rampaging southward. The chill stab in his heart twinged again, the ordinary private magic of fear. His own death was close at hand, and the death of thousands more if the tribes swept southward behind their demons.

All the more reason to stand fast, to show the Ice Tribes that the Duke's men were brave and true.

Alain recalled the captain's story of the grubby little wizard and his small magic. "Big magic, sure. Call lightning. Send us storms. I've no doubt your snow demons could eat us like sausages." He stepped past the shaman, pulled the Ducal standard down from the wall. "We have some small magic of our own, oaths and loyalty. And I know a secret about small magic and big magic."

With that, Alain nodded at the shaman, wrapped the flag over one arm, took up his spear again and left. He saw no one on the walk back to the encampment, but he hadn't really expected to.

At the walls, the men were pointing to a wispy thread of smoke in the distance, far to the southwest along the coast. Alain knew it had to be Odilo's wagon burning, the serjeant and his men as dead as Severus and the captain, but he just shrugged when the younger men asked him what the fire might mean.

The older men looked grim and said nothing.

"Me, I was a sailor betimes," Michel said to Alain out of the corner of his mouth later that day.

Alain was fascinated. Was this fantasy, or secret history? Michel was a little man with a Southgate accent who'd never had much to say. "We've both lived in this place for four years," Alain said. "This is the first time you've brought that up."

"Jumped ship," Michel said. "Land is safer, always."

Even now? Alain wondered, but he did not say it. Instead, he waved at the lion-mouthed cannon, glowering in ancient, corroded brass. "You ever fired one of those things?"

Michel shook his head. "I seen 'em do it."

Alain smiled. "Then you're our master gunner. Get to work loading it." He named off three men to help Michel.

All evening whooping riders galloped back and forth in front of the hoardings, glinting shadows in the stormy darkness. A cold wind brought both snow and lightning – a rare mix – the thunder rolling over the encampment so loud and long that some men bled from the ears. Alain went from man to man, touching shoulders, telling them this was not an attack, only a stoking of the fire of their fear.

Six more men deserted that night, but at dawn their bodies lay below the hoardings amid the Century's trampled fields of turnips and rye, riddled with eider-fletched arrows. There was an odd beauty to the scene, men and arrows and ruined plants all dusted with snow to highlight their frailties and lend grace to their wounds.

If Alain's men had been archers, he would have salvaged the arrows, but the bodies were perhaps a better lesson. He realized that he was starting to think like an officer.

He hated that.

That afternoon, ranks of horsemen poured out of the woods. They all rode shaggy ponies, like the herald had, though Alain could see scraps of battle kit and armor from all over the Western Principate, not to mention further south and east. *There must be many deserters here*, Alain thought. *Who would join the Ice Tribes?*

The subaltern, perhaps. But why?

These horsemen rode to battle, not to terror like the night before. They pulled up in loose ranks, semi-circles of horses, lances couched, bows at the ready. The grinning shaman and the herald rode forward, their ponies dancing sideways beneath Alain's hoardings.

"Go away, little magic," said the shaman in his thick accent.

Holding his horsetail banner, the herald inclined his head slightly, and said in his very good Wentish, "We will not ask again. Great projects stride the ice, and you are as the winter hare before the hungry wolf."

Alain waved his hand in a prearranged signal. The arm of the old derrick swung up, the Ducal insignia breaking free over the Century's little encampment. His forty-two men lined the walls and stood ready by the lion-mouthed cannon, facing hundreds and hundreds of the Ice Tribesmen. "Our magic is the magic of our Duke. It is a small magic, but it wields a mighty fist. You shall not have our post unless you take it from us."

The grinning shaman and the herald held a whispered conversation. The shaman's grin was reduced somewhat, and the herald looked sour. "You must leave this place," said the herald. "It is necessary. There has been a bargain."

Aha, thought Alain. *Magic strides the ice, indeed.* As the captain had said, all great magic had a loophole, a condition of sorts. The Ice Tribes could not work their rite to summon the snow demons unless the Duke's men peacefully surrendered the post.

It was so simple. All he had to do to defeat them was stand in place. "I have made no bargain but my oath to His Grace," Alain called out as the men of the Century muttered to one another.

The herald stamped his horsetail banner into the ground. "Then we will make a new bargain now."

Alain laughed, his heart soaring with the gulls overhead. "My oath's little magic is stronger than your great one." He dropped his hand in the next signal. "I care *this* for your magic and your demands."

Nothing happened. The army of Ice Tribesmen stared expectantly, while somewhere on the hoardings, one of the Century began to giggle.

"The cannon is a failure," Pietro whispered under his breath to Alain. The grinning shaman laughed, while the herald looked even more sour. Alain watched him heft his horsetail banner, ready to dip it and signal the charge, having no doubt the herald would be first against the hoardings. This was no herald, this was a chief, perhaps even the chief-of-chiefs.

"Aha!" said Michel distinctly nearby, and the lion roared. There was smoke, and fire, and horses screamed while men cursed and dirt flew and horsetail banner span from its shattered staff as Alain's laugh returned to him and he thought, *Captain, you are avenged,* and he looked into the sky to see an eider-fletched arrow hanging there, riding the wind like a gull, only it became larger and larger, looming bigger than the harvest moon over the horizon until darkness struck him with sharp pain and all the thundering noise of battle.

Alain found himself in the subaltern's cabin, wrapped in the Ducal standard, which was stiff with dried blood. His head hurt, a fierce pounding above and between his eyes. His face was crusted with dirt, and he coughed mud as he awoke. It took him quite some time to clear the dirt from his mouth. Groggy and slow, he rose from the little rope bed, discovered that he was fully booted and clothed, and stumbled out the splintered door.

The woods were quiet. Not the strange quiet of a thousand men holding still, but the normal quiet of marmots and badgers and hares and hawks and squirrels and half a hundred other birds and animals. The day was crisp and cold, but clear. He stumbled toward the encampment, wondering what had become of the Century. Many horses had passed through these woods recently.

The encampment was ravaged, hoardings peppered with arrows, but the derrick still stood behind the wooden walls. *They did not burn the camp,* Alain thought. *We won.*

The ruins of the lion-mouthed cannon were there, burst to shards, surrounded by six fresh graves. Alain saluted Michel, then carefully – for his body ached almost as much as his head – climbed on to the foundation course of the uncompleted tower to stand on the cold stone where he had slept away the summers. He still wore the Ducal standard like a cape, but the wind was so chill Alain was not tempted to hoist it once more on the derrick.

No one remained in camp. The last wagon was gone.

"What am I doing here?" he asked a brown gull hovering nearby.

The bird dipped, cut across the wind to circle him, and cried once. Inside the keening of the gull, Alain found a bubble of . . . memory? Imagination? A little wizard in shabby robes, his face aglow with a ball of wispy light in his hands, and a bitter young soldier marching forever down empty roads.

"I must have died easy," Alain said to the gull, the captain's last story in his mind, "if I am the one he was able to put back into the world."

The little wizard's voice slipped into Alain's ears, so different from the braying rasp of the grinning shaman of the Ice Tribes, yet with the same uncanny echo. "For me to bring you back, it doesn't matter how you died. It only matters how you lived. Their great magic broke upon the rock of your little oath."

"But why?" Alain asked his memories.

There was no answer, except perhaps for the constancy of his loyalty. Small magic, the hardest kind, as the captain had said.

Wrapped in his Duke's flag, Alain went out to pick the last few raddled turnips from the trampled fields. He would stand firm here in the camp, following the small magic of his oath, until someday he was relieved.

KING RAINJOY'S TEARS

Chris Willrich

A king of Swanisle delights in rue
And his name's a smirking groan.
Laughgloom, Bloodgrin, Stormproud we knew
Before Rainjoy took the throne.

– Rainjoy's Curse

It was sunset in Serpenttooth when Persimmon Gaunt hunted the man who put oceans in bottles.

The town crouched upon an islet off Swanisle's west coast, and scarlet light lashed it from that distant (but not unreachable) place where the sunset boiled the sea. The light produced a striking effect, for the people of Serpenttooth were the desperate and outcast, and they built with what they found, and what they found were the bones of sea serpents. And at day's end it seemed the gigantic, disassembled beasts struggled again toward life, for a pale, bloody sheen coated the town's archways, balustrades, and rooftops. Come evening the illusion ceased, and the bones gave stark reflection to the moon.

But the abductor meant to be gone before moonrise.

From the main town she ascended a cliffside pathway of teeth sharp as arrowheads, large as stepping-stones. The teeth ended at a vast, collapsed skull, reinforced with earth, wood, and thatch, bedecked with potted plants. There was a door, a squarish fragment of cranium on hinges, with a jagged eyeslit testifying to some ancient trauma.

Shivering in the briny sea-wind, Gaunt looked over her shoulder at the ruddy sunset rooftops. She did not see the hoped-for figure of a friend, leaping among the gables. "Your last chance to help, Imago," she murmured. She sighed, turned, and knocked.

Blue eyes, dimly glowing, peered through the eyeslit. "Eh?" wheezed a harsh voice. Gaunt imagined in it the complaints of seagulls, the slap of breakers.

"Persimmon Gaunt," she answered. "A poet."

"A bard?" The voice snorted. "The king exiled those witch-women, ten years gone."

"I am not a bard! My tools are stylus and wax, paper and quill, not voice and memory. I have the distinction of being banished by the bards, before the king banished them."

Gaunt could be charming, particularly in such a setting: her specialty in verse was morbidity, the frail railing of life against merciless time. Serpenttooth suited her. More, she suited Serpenttooth, her fluttering auburn hair a wild contrast to her pale, angular face, the right cheek tattooed with a rose ensnared by a spiderweb.

But these charms failed. "What do you want, poet?"

"I am looking for the maker."

"Maker of what?"

"Of this."

She lifted a small, corked bottle. Within nestled an intricate, miniature sailing ship fashioned of bone. Its white sails curved in an imaginary wind; its banners were frozen in the midst of rippling. Yet the ship was not the extraordinary thing. There was water below it, not bone or glass, and the water moved: not the twitching of droplets but the roiling of a shrunken corner of the sea. It danced and flickered, and the ship heaved to and fro, riding the tiny surge.

Gaunt waved the bottle in various directions, but the ship cared nothing for gravity, forever hugging its tiny sea.

"Exquisite," Gaunt murmured, and not for the first time.

"A trinket," sniffed the other.

"Trinket? For four years these 'trinkets' have been the stuff of legend along the coast! And yet their fame does not travel further. Most who own such bottles – sailors, fishermen, pirates, and all their wives, lovers, and children – will not sell at any price. It's said these folk have all lost something dear to the sea."

"Nothing to do with me."

"There is more." Gaunt unstoppered the bottle. "Listen. Hear the sound of the sea. Hear the deep loneliness, and the deep romance. To know it is to know mischievous waves, and alluring shores. To brush raw fingertips against riches and fame. To wrap scarred arms around hunger and harm. To know the warm fantasy of a home long abandoned, and the cold acceptance of a five-fathom grave."

And there was a susurrant murmur from the bottle which held all these things, and more, which Gaunt, too chill already, would not say. There came a long answering sigh from behind the door. It blended with the murmur, and Gaunt could not distinguish them.

Weakly, the voice said, "Nothing to do with me. Go."

"I cannot. When an ... associate of mine procured this item, he found the private memoirs of the owner. We know who you are, Master Salt."

A pause. "You are base thieves."

Gaunt smiled. "Imago would insist he is a refined thief, I'm sure. And our victim was a dying lord who had no further use for the bottle."

"What do you want?"

"I bring you greetings," Gaunt said, "from your own maker."

There was silence. The door opened on creaking hinges. A figure stepped aside, and Gaunt entered.

The room resembled a captain's cabin, though it filled a sea serpent's skull, not a vessel's stern. Two oval, bone-framed windows overlooked the ruddy sunset sea. Underneath, shutters covered twin ventilation passages to the skull's nostrils. Nearby, a spyglass rested atop a bookcase of nautical texts. But the other dozen bookcases cradled dozens of ships-in-bottles, each bearing its own churning, miniature sea. Half-constructed vessels listed upon a vast table, pieces scattered like wreckage.

Gaunt plunked her bottle upon the table, ship sailing forever ceilingward.

Master Salt bent over it. "The *Darkfast Dreamweaver*. Fitting. Named for a great philosopher-thief of Ebontide." A smile sliced his face.

He was built like a sea barrel, yet possessed delicately shimmering blue skin. His bald head resembled a robin's egg gleaming with dew. "Her crew captured the hatchling of a Serpent of the Sunset. Quite a story. But they overfed the child, to keep it from thrashing. It outgrew its bonds, fed well indeed."

He nodded at the shelves. "Lost ships, all of them. I see their profiles in my dreams. Hear their names on the morning wind."

"They are astonishing. The king will be enthralled."

"Him," muttered Salt. "He neglected me, my sisters. Left us eight years in our tower, because we dared remind him he had a soul. We resolved to seek our own lives."

Gaunt said, "Now your exile is ended."

"Not exile. Escape."

"Surely you cannot abandon him," Gaunt persisted, "being what you are."

"If you know what I am, poet, you should fear me. Inhuman myself, I read the sorrow behind human eyes."

His gaze locked hers. Gaunt shivered as though a westerly wind scoured her face, but could not look away.

Salt squinted, then smirked. "You say I abandon? I see what you've left behind. You forsook the bards for the written word. And now you even neglect your art . . . for the love of a thief."

Master Salt's eyes changed. One moment they glowed a pale blue; then they resembled blue-sheened, mirrored glass. Yet the person reflected in them was not Gaunt, nor was the moment this one. Instead she beheld a scene from an hour ago.

A man leapt to and fro upon buildings of bone. There was a strange style to his movements. Though he chose his destinations in a boyish rush, his rooftop dance obeyed a strict economy, as though an old man carefully doled out a youth's energy. When he paused, Gaunt could see the two scars of his lean, ferret-like face, one made by steel, one by fire. He gazed out from Master Salt's eyes as if searching for her. Then he leapt to a new height.

"The thief Imago Bone, your lover and sometimes your mentor, prancing about on bone rooftops. Suppose he couldn't resist." Salt blinked his eyes back to their former, glowing state.

"But you knew he might be gone for hours. Impatient, you continued alone."

Gaunt's breathing quickened. She found she could not evade Master Salt, nor lie. "Yes. For all Bone's skill . . ."

". . . he is a boy," Master Salt said. "Yes, I see. I can taste sorrows, poet. Imago Bone's life is an accident, is it not? Bizarre magics stretched his adolescence nearly a century. Only now is he aging normally. He is a great thief; but he is a child in many ways. You fear for him. You are as often his guardian as his student. An unlikely pair, following foolish quests."

"They are not foolish." Gaunt shivered, staring into the shimmering blue eyes. "Not all . . ."

"Quests are excuses, poet. You must live as you wish. As I have done. You do not need bards, or Imago Bone, or King Rainjoy to justify your wanderlust."

Gaunt imagined she felt the tug of the trade winds. Or perhaps it was the clatter of a horse beneath her, the taste of bow-spray from a river canoe, the scent of a thousand fragile mountain wildflowers.

"A true wanderer," Salt said, "needs no nation, no captain, no hope of gold to answer the siren lure."

And Gaunt wondered, why had she tried to refashion Bone and herself as heroes, when they could simply travel, drink in the world?

But no, this quest was not foolish. She must resist Salt's words. "There . . . will be war," she stammered, "unless Rainjoy can learn compassion . . . And he never can, without you."

"I see also," Salt said unmoved, "why you help him."

Gaunt lowered her eyes.

"Abandon that guilt, poet. Abandon all that imprisons you! Leave this quest; join Bone as a thief if it suits you, or shirk him as well – either way, seize your freedom, and do not abuse mine." Salt lifted his hand to Gaunt's mouth. "I did not ask to become a someone, any more than humans do. Yet here I am, and I will set my own course. I will hear the sea, and trap its cries."

Now Master Salt scraped a thumbnail against the tip of an index finger, and a blue droplet fell against Gaunt's lips. As the salty tang kissed her, she imagined the rocking of a deck underfoot, heard the songs of seamen raising sail, smelled the stinging brine upon the lines. Her heart skipped once and her eyelids drooped, as she slipped toward a dream of adventure in distant waters, not merely losing her existence, but casting it aside like soiled clothes.

But then from somewhere came Imago Bone's easy voice. "You should listen to him, Gaunt," Bone said. "He makes perfect sense."

With a start, Gaunt opened her eyes. Bone crawled through the passage leading to the dragon-skull's nostrils, face blue from the cliffside winds and sweaty from carrying his many pouches of esoteric tools: ironsilk lines, quicksap adhesive, a spectrum of camouflaging dyes.

As Master Salt turned, Bone sprang to the bottle sheltering the miniature *Darkfast Dreamweaver*. The thief shattered it against the table's edge.

Salt cried out.

So did the broken bottle.

The miniature ocean within the glass spilled on to the dirt floor, foaming and dwindling like a tendril of surf dying upon shore. A chorus of drowning sailors arose, dimly, like an old memory. Then water and voices were gone.

"Curse you," spat Master Salt, and the spittle boiled upon the table, and gave a sound like maddened seagulls as it vanished. He seized the thief, pressing pale-blue thumbs against Bone's throat, thumbs that grew foam-white even as Bone went purple.

"Allow . . ." the thief gurgled, "allow me to introduce . . ."

"No," said Master Salt.

"Rude . . ." Bone's voice trailed off, and he flailed uselessly in Salt's grip.

Bone had saved her. Bone was friend, lover, companion on the road. Nevertheless Gaunt hesitated one moment as he suffocated; so much poetry did the shelves of bottles hold, they might have cradled densely inked scrolls from ancient libraries.

But she knew what she must do. She shut her eyes and yanked.

The shelves toppled, shattering glass, breaking small ships, spilling the trapped substance of Master Salt. The room filled with the despairing cries of lost sailors.

Master Salt shrieked and released Bone, who crumpled, hacking saltwater. Salt knelt as well, trying to clutch the tiny oceans as they misted into nothingness. His knees crunched glass and crushed ships.

Gaunt trembled with the destruction she'd caused. But soon the sailors' voices faded to dim wailing, and she regained her voice.

"Dead sailors move you?" she asked. "Expect more. War is brewing. To prevent it, King Rainjoy will need the compassion he lost. The compassion you bear."

"You speak of compassion? You, who can do this?"

"These voices are of men already lost. But if war comes, they will seem just a drop in a surgeon's pail."

Salt lowered his head.

"I will go," he said at last. "If only to prevent your crushing more dreams."

Imago Bone rose with a look of gratitude, put his hand upon Gaunt's shoulder.

"I regret I did not arrive sooner," he whispered, then smiled ruefully. "The skeletal rooftops, they beckoned . . ."

"We'll talk of it later," Gaunt said. "No one can help being who they are." She leaned against him, but could not bear to look at him, nor at Master Salt, who gathered broken ships, tenderly, bone by scattered bone.

"The first is found," sighed the man upon the ivory chair.

An older man, shuffling through the chamber of mists, stopped and coughed. "Majesty?"

"Persimmon Gaunt. And her companion thief." The voice was dim and flat. "They have found the first. Soon, all will be well."

"The reports I bring, ah, belie such optimism." The older man scuttled closer. His robes fluttered with no regard to the drafts. "The nobles, hmm, demand war with the Eldshore, if you cannot secure an alliance by marriage. I suggest you build ships, raise troops." He raised a wrinkled hand before the king's nose, then snatched at something only he could see.

He inverted the hand, revealing an enfleshment from the king's memory, the tiny image of a red-haired woman, proud and bejeweled. She spat in the king's direction. Her voice rose dimly: *You are cold, with no soul within you. You shall never have me.* Turning on her heel, she stalked off the palm and into nonexistence.

"Eldshore's princess *will* marry me," said the king, "once I am a better man. Once *they* make me a better man."

"Strange, mm? – that you can sense their doings while I cannot."

Mirthlessly, the king smiled. "You may have made them, sorcerer, but they belong to me."

"Do not hope for too much, my king. War is in the air."

"When you are here, Spawnsworth, the air smells of worse. Leave your reports and go."

When the older man had retreated up a staircase, the king said in a toneless voice without conviction, "I *will* feel again."

From the staircase descended the sounds of tortured things.

The journey to Lornbridge took two weeks, but they felt like two years to the thief Imago Bone.

Master Salt spoke only in grunts. Surely thousands of subjects were capable of grunting for their king; why should Rainjoy need this entity in particular?

Gaunt walked as though shouldering a treasure chest of guilt (Bone often pictured metaphorical treasure chests, feeling deprived of real ones) and there was a distance in her eyes even as she lay nights upon his shoulder.

So it was a relief, finally, to risk his neck reaching a well-guarded noblewoman noted for feathering suitors with arrows.

Seen through tall grass, the battlement looked sickly and moist in the moonlight. (Bone's cloak, after a treatment of saps and powders, matched it.) He slithered beside it, scrambled halfway up, paused for heavy bootfalls to pass, then scurried atop. Time for one gulp of manure-scented air, then he was over the other side, hurling a ball of sticky grain as he dove.

He thudded on to a haycart exactly as the pigpen filled with squealing. By the time the guards investigated, the animals would have devoured the evidence. He slipped into courtyard shadows.

This was more like it: sparks of danger against the steel of brilliant planning. A shame he wasn't stealing anything.

My beloved's doing, Bone thought as he climbed atop a stable. When they met he was a legend, perhaps the greatest second-story man of the Spiral Sea. (The higher stories went of course without question.) Though she could pay little, he'd accepted enormous risk recovering a manuscript of hers from a pair of sorcerous bibliophiles, a task that had required another book, a tome of the coldest kind of magic. That matter concluded, he'd undertaken an absurdly noble quest, the accursed tome's destruction.

Absurd nobility impressed Persimmon Gaunt.

Bone smirked, reversed his cloak to the side stained with berry juice, then leapt from the stable roof on to Duskvale Keep itself, clinging to irregularities in the russet stone. His slow corkscrew toward the highest window allowed him time to review six months of inquiries along the Spiral Sea, a process garnering nothing but scars, empty pockets, and a list of enemies who wouldn't at all mind the damnable book for themselves.

Half jesting, half desperate, Bone had proposed consulting the court wizard of Swanisle.

He'd expected scowls. Swanisle was notorious for persecuting the bards of its county Gaunt (a society of women compared to witches, and similarly treated) formerly by burning, today by exile. He'd assumed Persimmon left with her teachers, would seethe at the thought of returning. But she had assented with a strange look.

Bone should have worried more at that look.

Distracted by such thoughts, Bone froze upon hearing a bright *swish*. Presently, from afar, came a dim *thunk*.

Lady Duskvale was firing off correspondence.

There was not one keep at Lornbridge but two, separated by the narrow, abysmal Groangorge. Westward stood Duskvale Keep and eastward rose the sandstone tower of Mountdawn. For generations, Gaunt had explained to Bone, the youth of Duskvale and Mountdawn had swooned for each other, sighing and pining across the impassable deep.

Then, four years ago, the keeps' masters paupered themselves constructing a bridge. The fortresses became one small town. Not merely did a stone span connect the castle; dozens of hundred-foot ropes, cables, and pulleys twisted overhead with messages, squirrels, nobles' drying underwear.

Yet today the bridge was guarded, the ropes cut, the youth forbidden to mix.

Swish.

Thunk.

Bone smirked and climbed beside the topmost window.

"Oh, why does he not write me?" he heard a voice exclaim.

Bone craned his head. "Perhaps because—"

"Ay!"

An arrow shot past, a roll of paper wound upon the shaft.

This time there followed no *thunk* but a dim clatter upon the stone bridge.

"Perhaps," Bone said, heart pounding, "because he is not as good a shot as yourself. Though I am pleased even you must aim."

"Who are you?" the voice demanded.

Bone crouched upon the sill, and bowed. "Bone: acquirer of oddities."

Lady Duskvale regarded him with hawk-dark eyes framed by stern cheekbones and black rivulets of hair. "Do you plan mischief? I warn you, I will tolerate mischief with but one man, and he I fire arrows at. For you I have a knife for stabbing, and lungs for screaming."

"I have no wish for mischief, stabs, or screams."

"Are you . . . are you a messenger from Lord Mountdawn?"

"Better than that, my lady. I am Bone. I and the poet Gaunt have come to comfort Lornbridge. May I enter?"

"I would be more comforted with you outside."

"Even a footpad's foot may fall asleep."

"One moment." She nocked an arrow, drew, and aimed. Then she backed into the room. "All right."

Bone leapt inside. "I admire your caution – and more, the strength of your arm – but it is not thieves at your window you must fear. It is the embodiment of sorrow."

She raised her eyebrows, and Bone helped himself to a chair beside a small table serviceable as a shield. He drummed his fingers upon it. "Consider, my lady. In your father's day, these keeps were famous for romance. Men and women pined hopelessly from across the gulf. But that has changed."

"You mock me, thief?" Duskvale's fingers quivered upon the bowstring, as did Bone's upon the table. "Of course it has changed."

"Explain."

"Very well, though my arm grows weaker. Four years ago my father and old Lord Mountdawn, rest their souls, heard identical whispers in their sleep, imploring them to build the bridge. For a time all was glorious. Yet if there are whispers now, they implore weeping. Bravos duel for damsels, spurned paramours hurl themselves into the gorge. Only I and my love, young Lord Mountdawn, are spared these frenzies, for we are calculating and circumspect."

A carrier pigeon fluttered through the window, alighting upon a perch near Duskvale. She regarded it and Bone, then sighed and set down her bow. (Bone released a long breath.) Removing a note from the pigeon's foot Duskvale read, "'Soon I must fight my way across the bridge to your side. Each arrow is a caress, but I would kiss the calluses of the hand that fired it. Dear one! Alive or dead, my bloody hide arrives in the morning!'" She looked up in vexation. "You are interrupting a private conversation, you know. Explain your purpose."

"Are you aware," Bone asked, "that your monarch was once called the Weeping King?"

"Rainjoy?" she mused. "I heard Father say as much. A sensitive boy crushed by the crown's weight, weeping at the consequences of all commands." She crushed Mountdawn's note. "Men can be overwrought at times. But the king has changed. Now they call him Rainjoy the Stonefaced. What does it matter?"

"Did your father speak of the Pale Council?"

"Everyone knows of them," Duskvale said impatiently. "Rainjoy's wise advisors. They came from far away and never went among the people. But the people loved them, for they counseled compassion, and kept the king's cruel wizard at bay. But they departed four years ago and this is of no consequence and my beloved is about to die for me."

"Hear this: the Council did not come from a far land, nor did they return there. One member dwells nearby."

"What?"

"They are creatures of magic, my dear, born of a bargain between Rainjoy and his wizard."

"What bargain?"

"That Rainjoy, so wracked by conscience he could not function as king, should weep but three more tears in his life. Yet those tears would be given human form, so when Rainjoy wished he could safely seek the insights of sorrow."

Duskvale fingered her bow. "Impossible."

"No, merely quite ill-advised. I've met one such tear. Another dwells here. We will need your help, and your paramour's, to snare it. Tell me, do you retain builders' plans for the bridge?"

In the end it was the sincerity in Bone's eyes, or (more likely) the desperation in Duskvale's heart, that bade her send a pointed message to Mountdawn and then summon servants to make certain preparations. Bone was relieved not to relate stealing her father's ship-in-a-bottle and rifling his memoirs. For it was Lord Duskvale who had owned the faux *Darkfast Dreamweaver*, its surging in harmony with the whispers of Lornbridge.

Soon the moonlight found the thief whistling, strolling across that great stone arch. At midpoint he squeezed a tiny sack of quicksap, which he smeared full across his gloves then applied to his shoes.

He descended the bridge's side, enjoying the brisk mountain air, the churning murmur of the river far below, the tickle of vertigo. Presently there came a *swish* from the west and a *thunk* to the east.

At this signal Bone crawled underneath the span, hairs pointing toward watery, rocky doom. Where the plans indicated it would be, he discovered a square opening. He crawled inside.

Blue light surrounded him. "Who?" called a bleak voice, like a hollow wind through a shattered house.

The chamber was like a monk's cell, a cold stone sitting room with a few books (with such titles as *Ballad of the Poisoned Paramour* and *The Tragickal History of Violet Swoon*), some decoration (withered roses), odd mementos (lockets with strands of hair inside), and a lamp (bearing not oil but a pale-blue liquid glimmering like glacial moonlight).

"I had gambled," Bone said, shedding his gloves, "you would not wish to miss the romantic play of light upon the river. I am Imago Bone," he added, changing his shoes, "and I bring greetings from the king."

The quicksap discarded, Bone gazed upon Rainjoy's tear. She resembled a spindly, large-eyed maiden in a white shift. She shimmered gently in the blue light, reflecting and echoing it. Her long white hair fluttered and frayed, blending into the chamber's dim mists.

She regarded Bone with incomprehension. "Rainjoy abandoned us."

"He would enjoy your counsel again."

"I cannot give it. I am not his anymore, a slave, nameless . . . now I am Mistress Mist. This is my home. There must be love in the world, you see. Lonely were these keeps, but I whispered of this bridge, and they are lonely no longer. Still do I whisper of love."

"You whisper of more than that. Men and women have perished."

"*I* do not slay them," Mist answered sadly. "In my presence they sense what purest love could be, and how far short they fall." She frowned at Bone. "But you – why are you here? When your true love is elsewhere, waiting and worrying. Why while your precious moments with me? Do you abandon her for me? Do you betray?"

A chill enveloped him; he could not evade those eyes.

He thought of Persimmon Gaunt. Of course he would not betray her for this apparition. And yet – was he not flippant, unheedful of her? His dallying upon the rooftops of Serpenttooth nearly caused her death. Did he not repay devotion with childish disregard? Was he not cruel?

He did not deserve her, he realized, nor life. Better to end his existence now, than risk wounding her further. Bone yearned for the abyss at his back.

But even as the impulse for annihilation took over, his old lust for living cried out. He could not prevent his leap, but he

modified the angle and, falling, grasped the ironsilk strand
fired by Lady Duskvale.

The thread bent, rose, bent, held. It sliced his palm, and he
trembled with the urge to release it, dash himself to bits far
below. Fortunately the impulse weakened away from Mist.

He saw Gaunt leaning over the bridge's side. "I am sorry . . ."

"What?" she shouted.

He shook his head, cried instead: "Pigeon!"

Gaunt raised her arm. From the Mountdawn side of the
chasm a pigeon fluttered to alight upon Bone's shoulder, a
poem of Gaunt's affixed to its leg. Bone shrugged the bird
upward and it fluttered into the hidden chamber. Presently
Bone heard a sad voice, reading.

> *Love floating skyward is earthly no longer*
> *Braced with selfishness, ardor is stronger*
> *On solid ground let rest love's wonder –*
> *And so your bridge we break asunder.*

"Picks!" Bone shouted, and at once there sang a chorus of
metal biting stone.

"No!"

A large silvery blob, like a pool of mercury ignorant of gravity, flowed from beneath the bridge and oozed upward to the
span. Blue light rose from that spot, and, although Bone could
not see her, he heard Mist shout, "I concede! The bridge will
be mute without me. Please do not break it. Keep it, and find
love if you can. I will go."

A voice like lonely seabirds answered, "They snared me
likewise, sister. For we cannot destroy as they do."

"Yes, brother. They ruin themselves, and each other. We
only awaken their sorrow."

"But the last tear will defeat them, sister. The last is the
strongest of all."

"The second is found," said the king in the room of mists.

Framing the ivory throne, twin pillars of rainwater poured
from funnels and spilled into a pool with a swan's outline,
wingtips catching the water, nose aimed at the throne's foot, a

drain where the heart should be. Just as they believed distress strengthened the spirit, the royal house of Swanisle believed chill weather quickened the flame within a man.

The king rose, undressed, and waded in, his pensive expression unchanged.

From beside the throne his companion said carefully, "This poet is, ah, resourceful."

"Of course. She is a bard of Gaunt."

"Mm. Never forget, majesty, her ilk caused you great pain."

The king shivered in his pool. It gave him a look that resembled passion. "Great pain. And great wonder. I remember how every spider in its shimmering, dew-splattered web was an architect of genius to be cherished, not squashed. I remember a defiant spark in the eyes, a stony strength in the limbs of every maiden men declared ugly. I remember the disbelieving child in the faces of condemned men, a child whose mind might yet encompass creation, were that infinite head still upon that foreshortened neck. I remember knowing these things, Spawnsworth, but I can no longer *feel* them. But *they* will help. Soon."

"Soon," the wizard murmured, scratching his chin. His robe quivered, jerked, as though pained by needlepricks.

Nightswan Abbey formed the outline of a soaring bird, and, although its crumbling bulk no longer suggested flight of any kind, the music pouring from its high windows did much to compensate.

A crowd of the young and elderly gathered beneath the sanctuary windows every evening to hear the sweet polyphony, as the purple sunset kissed the first of the night's stars. The sisterhood could sing only within these walls; all else would be vanity. Even so, during the last four years their music had rekindled some of Nightswan's fame, long dimmed in this age of grim, conquering kings.

It was as if those hundred mortal throats conjured the spirit of the Swan Goddess of the Night and the Stars, she who plunged into the sun, seawater glistening upon her wings, to cool its fire and make the earth temperate and fit for life, she whose charred body fell back into the sea, to become Swanisle.

The music ceased and the listeners drifted away, murmuring to one another – all save four, who slipped among the bushes. Soon, two re-emerged, one casting a line to a window, the second glancing backward. "They will not flee," Gaunt whispered. "They are contemptuous, certain their sister will humble us. I am uneasy."

Bone shrugged. "We will handle her. We've seen worse, we two."

Gaunt did not reply.

They ascended to the vast sanctuary, slipping behind the winged marble altar of the Swan. In the pews a lone nun prayed. Her white cap, cut in the outline of a swan, enhanced the rich darkness of a robe embroidered with tiny stars. The intruders made hand signals: they would pause until she departed.

Then the nun looked up, her face still shadowed by her hood, and sang in a voice sweet as any of the abbey's chorus, yet with an unexpected pain, as though a delicate aperitif were served too hot. The first stanza was muted, but her voice rose with the second:

> *King Stormproud fell to war's caress,*
> *Left Swanisle to his boy,*
> *Who had not learned to love distress:*
> *Soft-hearted was Rainjoy.*

Gaunt gave Bone a sharp look, listening.

> *His shivering toes just touched the floor*
> *When he claimed his father's chair.*
> *When the sad queen's heart would beat no more*
> *He tore his silky hair.*

The nun rose. The intruders hid themselves behind the onyx, speckled pulpit as she approached the altar, still singing.

> *Yet when a wizard of county Gaunt*
> *(Spawnsworth was his name)*
> *Tried his wicked strength to flaunt*
> *The boy king's heart took flame.*

> *For all Gaunt's fear, and all its horror*
> *Marched as Rainjoy's foe.*
> *Enfleshment was the wizard's lore –*
> *To fashion warriors from woe.*

The sister knelt where the wine was kept, the wine that symbolized the goddess's blood, shed to make all life possible. She cast a surreptitious glance over her shoulder. Her face was a pale, dimly glowing blue, growing brighter as she sang.

> *Rainjoy led his armies north,*
> *Felled the work of Spawnsworth's hands,*
> *Yet surely more would soon ride forth*
> *Till they conquered all his lands.*

> *Now the bards of Gaunt were rightly known*
> *To clasp old secrets to the breast.*
> *So the army overturned every stone*
> *Till the king beheld the best.*

The nun passed her hand over the wine vessel, and shining droplets fell into the dark liquid. They quickly dimmed, and the wine appeared as before.

> *"Gaunt's ancient thanes," King Rainjoy spoke,*
> *"The very land would quick obey.*
> *To free it from the wizard's yoke*
> *I must know Gaunt as did they."*

> *The woman said, "What you seek takes years,*
> *A lifetime spent in Gaunt,*
> *A knowledge born of woe and tears,*
> *Not a young man's morning jaunt."*

> *"My father died on Eldshore's strand.*
> *My mother died of loss.*
> *A wizard makes to seize my land –*
> *This die I'll gladly toss."*

At last Gaunt could stand waiting no more, and stepped forward. The nun ceased singing, caught her breath.

Gaunt curtsied. Meanwhile Bone leapt forward, tumbled, rolled, and stood where he blocked the nun's best retreat. He bowed low, eyes upon her.

In a hot, dusky voice more evocative of tavern than tabernacle, the nun said, "You are agents of the king, I take it?" She raised her head, showing a weary blue face and sapphire smile like a dagger-cut. "I've sensed my siblings being gathered."

"You are correct. I am Persimmon . . . of Gaunt. A poet. This is my companion, Bone. We bear Rainjoy's plea for your help. He must marry Eldshore's princess to stop a war, but she refuses. She senses Rainjoy feels no sorrow, knows no compassion."

"A wise woman." The tear laughed, one sharp, jarring note. "I am Sister Scald. You are a poet of Gaunt? Did Gaunt's bards train you, before Rainjoy exiled them?"

"They did," Gaunt said, "before exiling me."

Glimmering eyes widened. "Did you learn 'Rainjoy's Curse'?"

"Yes," Gaunt said. And she did not sing, but continued Scald's song in speech.

> *She led him then, where doomed ships had lunged*
> *At cliffs where white foam churned;*
> *To chasms where young suitors plunged;*
> *To pyres where bards had burned.*
>
> *She wooed him with rhymes of sailors drowned,*
> *And songs of lovers dead,*
> *And poems of bards long in the ground,*
> *Until she wooed him to her bed.*
>
> *Into a fevered dream he fell*
> *Of the web that snares all lives –*
> *One soul's joy breeds another's hell.*
> *One suffers, and one thrives.*

He woke to slaps: For bedding her so,
She offered jibe and taunt.
He trembled chill as she did go;
For now he knew the soul of Gaunt.

And when the nightmare horde returned,
Raised from Gaunt's old pain,
He told it, "Sleep, for I have learned:
Let the land swallow you again."

The warriors melted into earth
And the wizard quick was seized.
Spawnsworth said, "O king of worth,
How might you be appeased?"

Rainjoy trembled. "I feel each death.
All paths shine slick with blood.
I cannot bear to end your breath."
The mage swore fealty where he stood.

A king of Swanisle delights in rue
And his name's a smirking groan.
But in Rainjoy endless tears did brew
And he longed for eyes of stone.

Scald's voice bit the silence. "He has those eyes now. The bards gave him knowledge of all life's woe, but Spawnsworth tricked him out of his tears. For a time he still consulted us, but who willingly seeks out sorrow? At last he consulted us no more. He became the sort of king Spawnsworth could control."

"He senses what he's lost. Serve him again."

"I serve others now."

Bone broke in. "Indeed? Your brother served others with bottled grief, your sister with a bridge of doomed desire. We threatened these contrivances; the tears surrendered. I say good riddance."

"You mock their work, thief?" Scald seized Bone's chin, locked eyes with his. "I see into your soul, decrepit boy. You've begun aging at last, yet you fritter away your moments impressing this foolish girl. And you," she released Bone, snatched Gaunt's ear, "you forsook the glory of voice and memory for clumsy meanderings of ink. Now you neglect even that dubious craft following this great mistake of a man." Scald stepped back, dismissing poet and thief with a wave. "What a pair you are, what a waste of wind your love! Who are you to lecture me?"

Shivering, Gaunt looked away, toward the tall windows and bright stars. But she replied. "I will tell you, tear of Rainjoy. I was a girl who saw the boy king rescue county Gaunt from the creatures who tore her family to bits. I was a bard's apprentice who loved him from afar. And when my teacher boasted of how she granted his request by breaking his spirit, I knew I'd follow her no more."

She looked at Bone, who regarded her wonderingly. "I'd not guard secret lore in my skull, but offer my words in ink, telling of grief such that anyone could understand. I would tarry in graveyards and let tombs inspire my verse. For if the bards hoarded living song, I would peddle the dead, written word." Gaunt returned her gaze to Scald. "When Spawnsworth made an end to Rainjoy's weeping, the king's first act was to exile the bards. And how I laughed that day. Come, tear. You cannot shame me. I will repay my teachers' debt."

"You surprise me," Scald said, "but I think you will not take me. I have no bottles, no bridge to harm. My substance passes into the sacramental wine, inspiring the sisters' music. Would you destroy all grapes in the world?"

"I do not need to." Gaunt gestured toward the door.

Scald turned, saw a cluster of black, star-speckled habits underneath white swan hats.

A nun with a silver swan necklace stepped forward, old hands trembling. "We have listened, Sister Scald. Gaunt and Bone sent warning by carrier pigeon that they would seek a king's tear this night, unaware we'd knowingly given you sanctuary. I have been torn, until this moment. I might defy even Rainjoy to honor our pledge, Scald . . . But you have meddled with our sacraments. You must go."

"Oathbreaker," Scald snarled. She looked right and left. "All of you – all humans are traitors, to yourselves, to others. Listen then, and understand."

And Scald sang.

This song was wordless. It was as though the earlier music was simply the white breakers of this, the churning ocean, or the moonlit fog-wisps crossing the lip of this, the crevasse. Now the cold depths were revealed. They roared the truth of human treachery, of weakness, of pain.

Before that song the humans crumpled.

"No . . ." Gaunt whimpered, covering her face.

"Nothing . . ." whispered Bone. "I am nothing . . . not man, not boy. A waste . . ."

Somehow, Bone's anguish bestirred Gaunt to defy her own. "You are something." She wrenched each word from her throat like splinters torn from her own flesh. "You are not a waste."

The sisters knelt, some mouthing broken regretful words, some clawing for something sharp, something hard, to make an end. But Gaunt raised her head to the singer. "Scald . . ." It should have been a defiant cry, but it emerged like a child's plea. "Look what you do, to those who sheltered you . . ."

Scald's eyes were hard, lifted ceilingward in a kind of bitter ecstasy. Yet she looked, and for a time watched the nuns cringing upon the stone floor.

She went silent.

She walked to one of the high windows. "I am no better than you," she murmured. "I sense my siblings, like me born of regret. It seems we cannot escape it." Scald removed her swan cap and lowered her head. "We will go."

Gaunt helped Bone to his feet. He clutched her shoulders as though grasping some idea rare and strange. "Why did you not tell me," he said, "of your family?"

She lowered her gaze. "When you suggested Spawnsworth might deal with that accursed tome we've locked away, Bone, I believed his skills were not appropriate and his character untrustworthy. But I realized we two might somehow repay the debt I felt to Rainjoy. It was a deception, Bone, one that deepened with time. I feared you would be angry."

He nodded. "Perhaps later. Now I am merely glad there is still a Gaunt to perhaps be angry with. It is done. For better or worse, we've recovered Rainjoy's tears."

She met his look. "Are they, Bone? Are they Rainjoy's? Or are they more like grown children? I think, whatever their faults, they have seized control of their existence. I think they are people." She scowled in frustration. "I fear Scald is right; I am never consistent."

"You cannot deliver them up, now, can you?"

She shook her head. "Forgive me, Bone. We've gained nothing."

"I disagree." He leaned forward, kissed her.

Startled, she kissed him back, then pulled away. "You are changing the subject! You can never focus on one thing; you are forever a boy."

"Fair enough, but I say you are the subject, and you are what I've gained. I know you better, now. And I would rather know you better, Persimmon Gaunt, than plunder all the treasure-vaults of Brightcairn. Though I'd cheerfully do both."

She gaped at him. "Then . . . you have your wish. Whatever Scald may think of us." She gazed at the bent figure beside the window. "To risk losing you three times this journey – it makes me care nothing for how odd is our love, our life. It is ours, and precious."

"Then, my dear," Bone said, "let's discuss how we'll evade the king's assassins, when we break our pledge."

"How precious . . ." Gaunt murmured, still watching Scald, and her eyebrows rose. "No, we will not break it, Bone! We will fulfill it too well."

A storm frothed against King Rainjoy's palace, and the hall of mists felt like a ship deck at foggy dawn. Salt, Mist, and Scald stepped toward the ivory throne, knelt beside the swan pool. Behind the Pale Council stood Persimmon Gaunt and Imago Bone.

Upon the throne, the king studied his prodigal tears.

"So," he said.

The tears blinked back.

"Gaunt and Bone," said the wizard Spawnsworth from beside the throne, his cloak twisting as though with suppressed annoyance. "I, ah, congratulate you. You have accomplished a great deed."

"Not so difficult," Bone said easily. "Send us to fetch the morning star's shyer cousin, or the last honest man's business partner, and we might have surrendered. These three were not so well hidden." He smiled. "Anyone might have found them."

"Whatever," Spawnsworth said with a dismissive wave. "Your, um, modesty covers mighty deeds. Now, majesty, I would examine these three in private. They have dwelled apart too long, and I fear they might be, ah, unbalanced. It might be years before I dare release them."

The tears said nothing, watching only Rainjoy.

"Yes," Rainjoy murmured, staring back, agreeing to something Spawnsworth had not said. "Yes, I would . . . speak with them."

Before the sorcerer could object, Gaunt said, "Alas, my king, Spawnsworth's fears are quite justified. I regret where duty leads."

With that, she drew a dagger and stabbed Sister Scald where her heart ought to have been.

By then Bone had sliced the glistening throats of Master Salt and Mistress Mist.

The king's tears lost their forms, spilling at once from their robes, flowing like pale-blue quicksilver into the swan pool, where they spiraled down into the drain and were lost to sight.

"What?" King Rainjoy whispered, shaking, rising to his feet. "What?"

"It was necessary, majesty," Gaunt said. "They had become mad. They meant you harm."

"We suspected," Bone said, "that only in your presence could they die."

"Die," echoed Rainjoy. He sank back on to the throne.

Spawnsworth had gone pale, his cloak twitching in agitated spasms. But his voice was calm as he said, "I will wish to investigate the matter, of course . . . but it seems you have done the kingdom a great, ah, service. It is not too late, I would say, to consider a reward. You sought my advice?"

Rainjoy cradled his head in his hands.

"Alas," said Gaunt, her eyes on the king, "our time with the tears has been instructive regarding your art. It is powerful, to be sure, but not suited to our problem. No offense is meant."

Spawnsworth frowned. "Then gold, perhaps? Jewels?"

Bone swallowed, but said nothing.

"My king," said the sorcerer, "what do you . . ." Then he bit his lip.

Rainjoy wept.

"My king," repeated Spawnsworth, looking more non-plussed than when Salt, Mist, and Scald vanished down the drains.

It was little more than a sparkling wetness along the left eye, a sheen that had barely begun to streak. Rainjoy wiped it with a silken sleeve. "It is nothing," Rainjoy said, voice cold.

Gaunt strode around the pool and up to the throne, ignoring Spawnsworth's warning look. She touched Rainjoy's shoulder.

"It is something," she said.

He stared at her wide-eyed, like a boy. "It is simply . . . I let them go for so long. I never imagined I would lose them forever. They did not obey."

"Oh, my king," Gaunt said, "my dear king. Tears cannot obey. If they could, they would be saltwater only."

He held up the sleeve, dotted with a tiny wet stain. "I have tears again . . . I do not deserve them."

"Yet here they are. Listen to them, King Rainjoy, even though these tears are mute. And never be parted from them."

The king watched as Gaunt returned to Bone's side. The poet gave the thief one nod, and Imago Bone offered the king an unexpectedly formal bow, before the two clasped hands and walked slowly toward the door. Rainjoy thought perhaps he heard the thief saying, *Your penance, Gaunt, will consist of a six-city larcenous spree, which I shall now outline,* and the poet's answering laugh. Perhaps she cast a final look back, but the mists embraced her, and he would never be sure. He regretted it, that he'd never be sure.

"I am sad, Spawnsworth," he said, wondering. "I do not sense life's infinite sorrow. But I am sad."

But Spawnsworth did not answer, and the light in his eyes was not nascent tears but a murderous glint. He stalked up the stairs.

In his tower there twitched a menagerie of personifications: howling griefs, snarling passions, a stormy nature blustering in a crystal dome, a dark night of the soul shrouding the glass of a mirror. In places there lurked experiments that twitched and mewled. Here a flower of innocence sprouted from the forehead of a gargoyle of cynicism. There a phoenix of renewal locked eyes forever with a basilisk of stasis.

Spawnsworth arrived in this sanctum, teeth grinding, and began assembling the vials of love's betrayal and friendship's gloom, the vials he would form into an instrument of revenge upon Gaunt and Bone.

There came a cough behind him.

He whirled and beheld three shining intruders.

"We are not easily slain, as you should know," Master Salt said. He opened a cage.

"We, clearly, are more easily forgotten," said Mistress Mist. She unstoppered a flask.

"But we will see you never forget us," said Sister Scald, pushing a glass sphere to shatter against the floor. "We believe you could use our counsel. Ah, I see there are many here who agree."

As his creations swarmed toward him, it occurred to Spawnsworth that the many grates in the floor, used to drain away blood and more exotic fluids, fed the same sewers as those in the hall of mists. "You cannot do this," he hissed. "You are Rainjoy's, and he would never harm me."

"We are Rainjoy's no longer," the tears said.

He turned to flee, and felt his own cloak tremble with excitement and spill upward over his face.

Of the many voices heard from the sorcerer's tower that hour, the one most human, the palace servants agreed, was the one most frightening. When they found Spawnsworth's body in the room of empty cages, all remarked how the face was contorted with sorrow, yet the eyes were dry.

A RICH FULL WEEK

K. J. Parker

He looked at me the way they all do. "You're him, then."

"Yes," I said.

"This way."

Across the square. A cart, tied up to a hitching post. One thin horse. Not so very long ago, he'd used the cart for shifting dung. I sat next to him, my bag on my knees, tucking my feet in close, and laid a bet with myself as to what he'd say next.

"You don't look like a wizard," he said.

I owed myself two nomismata. "I'm not a wizard," I said. I always say that.

"But we sent to the Fathers for a—"

"I'm not a wizard," I repeated, "I'm a philosopher. There's no such thing as wizards."

He frowned. "We sent to the Fathers for a wizard," he said.

I have this little speech. I can say it with my eyes shut, or thinking about something else. It comes out better if I'm not thinking about what I'm saying. I tell them, we're not wizards, we don't do magic, there's no such thing as magic. Rather, we're students of natural philosophy, specializing in mental energies, telepathy, telekinesis, indirect vision. Not magic; just science where we haven't quite figured out how it works yet. I looked at him. His hood and coat were homespun – that open, rather scratchy weave you get with moorland wool. The patches were a slightly different color; I guessed they'd been salvaged from an even older coat that had finally reached the point where there was nothing left to sew on to. The boots had a military look. There had been battles in these parts, thirty years ago, in the civil war. The boots looked to be about that sort of vintage. Waste not, want not.

"I'm kidding," I said. "I'm a wizard."

He looked at me, then back at the road. I hadn't risen in his estimation, but I hadn't sunk any lower, probably because that wasn't possible. I waited for him to broach the subject.

By my reckoning, three miles out of town, I said, "So tell me what's been happening."

He had big hands; too big for his wrists, which looked like bones painted flesh-color. "The Brother wrote you a letter," he said.

"Yes," I replied brightly. "But I want you to tell me."

The silence that followed was thought rather than rudeness or sulking. Then he said, "No good asking me. I don't know about that stuff."

They never want to talk to me. I have to conclude that it's my fault. I've tried all sorts of different approaches. I've tried being friendly, which gets you nowhere. I've tried keeping my face shut until someone volunteers information, which gets you peace and quiet. I've read books about agriculture, so I can talk intelligently about the state of the crops, milk yields, prices at market, and the weather. When I do that, of course, I end up talking to myself. Actually, I have no problem with talking to myself. In the country, it's the only way I ever get an intelligent conversation.

"The dead man," I prompted him. I never say *the deceased*.

He shrugged. "Died about three months ago. Never had any bother till just after lambing."

"I see. And then?"

"It was sheep to begin with," he said. "The old ram, with its neck broke, and then four ewes. They all reckoned it was wolves, but I said to them, wolves don't break necks, it was something with hands did that."

I nodded. I knew all this. "And then?"

"More sheep," he said, "and the dog, and then an old man, used to go round all the farms selling stuff, buttons and needles and things he made out of old bones; and when we found him, we reckoned we'd best tell the boss up at the grange, and he sent down two of his men to look out at night, and then the same thing happened to them. I said, that's no wolf. Knew all along, see. Seen it before."

That hadn't been in the letter. "Is that right?" I said.

"When I was a kid," the man said (and now I knew the problem would be getting him to shut up). "Same thing exactly: sheep, then travelers, then three of the Duke's men. My grandad, he knew what it was, but they wouldn't listen. He knew a lot of stuff, Grandad."

"What happened?" I asked.

"Him and me and my cousin from out over, we got a couple of shovels and a pick and an ax, and we went and dug up this old boy who'd died. And he was all swelled up, like he'd got the gout all over, and he was *purple*, like a grape. So we cut off his head and shoveled all the dirt back, and we dropped the head down an old well, and that was the end of that. No more bother. Didn't say what we'd done, mind. The Brother wouldn't have liked it. Funny bugger, he was."

Well, I thought. "You did the right thing," I said. "Your grandfather was a clever man, obviously."

"That's right," he said. "He knew a lot of stuff."

I was doing my mental arithmetic. *When I was a kid* – so, anything from fifty-five to sixty years ago. Rather a long interval, but not unheard of. I was about to ask if anything like it had happened before then, but I figured it out just in time. If wise old Grandfather had known exactly what to do, it stood to reason he'd learned it the old-fashioned way: watching or helping, quite possibly more than once.

"The man who died," I said.

"Him." A cartload of significance crammed into that word. "Offcomer," he explained.

"Ah," I said.

"Schoolteacher, he called himself," he went on. "Dunno about that. Him and the Brother, they tried to get a school going, to teach the boys their letters and figuring and all, but I told them, waste of time in these parts, you can't spare a boy in summer, and winter, it's too dark and cold to be walking five miles there and five miles back, just to learn stuff out of a book. And they wanted paying, two pence twice a year. People around here can't afford that for a parcel of old nonsense."

I thought of my own childhood, and said nothing. "Where did he come from?"

"Down south." Well, of course he did. "I said to him, you're a long way from home. He didn't deny it. Said it was his calling, whatever that's supposed to mean."

It was dark by the time we reached the farm. It was exactly what I'd been expecting: long and low, with turf eaves a foot off the ground, turf walls over a light timber frame. No trees this high up, so lumber had to come up the coast on a big shallow-draught freighter as far as Holy Trinity, then road haulage the rest of the way. I spent the first fifteen years of my life sleeping under turf, and I still get nightmares.

Mercifully, the Brother was there waiting for me. He was younger than I'd anticipated – you always think of village Brothers as craggy old fat men, or thin and brittle, like dried twigs with papery bark. Brother Stauracius couldn't have been much over thirty; a tall, broad-shouldered man with an almost perfectly square head, hair cropped short like winter pasture, and pale-blue eyes. Even without the habit, nobody could have taken him for a farmer.

"I'm so glad you could come," he said, town voice, educated, rather high for such a big man. He sounded like he meant it. "Such a very long way. I hope the journey wasn't too dreadful."

I wondered what he'd done wrong, to have ended up here. "Thank you for your letter," I said.

He nodded, genuinely pleased. "I was worried, I didn't know what to put in and leave out. I'm afraid I've had no experience with this sort of thing, none at all. I'm sure there must be a great deal more you need to know."

I shook my head. "It sounds like a textbook case," I said.

"Really." He nodded several times, quickly. "I looked it up in *Statutes and Procedures*, naturally, but the information was very sparse, very sparse indeed. Well, of course. Obviously, this sort of thing has to be left to the experts. Further detail would only encourage the ignorant to meddle."

I thought about Grandfather: two shovels and an ax, job done. But not quite, or else I wouldn't be here. "Fine," I said. "Now, you're sure there were no other deaths within six months of the first attack."

"Quite sure," he said, as though his life depended on it. "Nobody but poor Anthemius."

Nobody had asked me to sit down, let alone take my wet boots off. The hell with it. I sat down on the end of a bench. "You didn't say what he died of."

"Exposure." Brother Stauracius looked very sad. "He was caught out in a snowstorm and froze to death, poor man."

"Near here?"

"Actually, no." A slight frown, like a crack in a wall. "We found him about two miles from here, as it happens, on the big pasture between the mountains and the river. A long way from anywhere, so presumably he lost his way in the snow and wandered about aimlessly until the cold got to him."

I thought about that. "On his way back home, then."

"I suppose so, yes."

I needed a map. You almost always need a map, and there never is one. If ever I'm emperor, I'll have the entire country surveyed and mapped, and copies of each parish hung up in the temple vestries. "I don't suppose it matters," I lied. "You'll take me to see the grave."

A faint glow of alarm in those watered-down eyes. "In the morning."

"Of course in the morning," I said.

He relaxed just a little. "You'll stay here tonight, naturally. I'm afraid the arrangements are a bit—"

"I was brought up on a farm," I said.

Unlike him. "That's all right, then," he said. "Now I suppose we should join our hosts. The evening meal is served rather early in these parts."

"Good," I said.

Sleeping under turf is like being in your grave. Of course, there are rafters. That's what you see when you look up, lying wide-awake in the dark. Your eyes get the hang of it quite soon, diluting the black into gray into a palette of pale grays; you see rafters, not the underside of turf. And the smoke hardens it off, so it doesn't crumble. You don't get worms dropping on your face. But it's unavoidable, no matter how long you do it, no matter how used you are to it. You lie there, and the thought crosses your mind as you stare at the underside of grass; is this what it'll be like?

The answer is, of course, no. First, the roof will be considerably lower; it'll be the lid of a box, if you're lucky enough to have one, or else no roof at all, just dirt chucked on your face. Second, you won't be able to see it because you'll be dead.

But you can't help wondering. For a start, there's temperature. Turf is a wonderful insulator: keeps out the cold in winter and the heat in summer. What it doesn't keep out is the damp. It occurs to you as you lie on your back there: so long as they bury me in a thick shirt, won't have to worry about being cold, or too hot in summer, but the damp could be a problem. Gets into your bones. A man could catch his death.

It's while you're lying there – everybody else is fast asleep; no imagination, no curiosity, or they've been working so hard all day they just sleep, no matter what – that you start hearing the noises. Actually, turf's pretty quiet. Doesn't creak like wood, gradually settling, and you don't get drips from leaks. What you get is the thumping noises over your head. Clump, clump, clump, then a pause, then clump, clump, clump.

They tell you, when you're a kid and you ask, that it's the sound of dead men riding the roof-tree. They tell you that dead men get up out of the ground, climb up on the roof, sit astride the peak, and jiggle about, walloping their heels into the turf like a man kicking on a horse. You believe them; I never was quite sure whether they believed it themselves. When you're older, of course, and you've left the farm and gone somewhere civilized, where it doesn't happen, you finally figure it out: what you hear is sheep, hopping up on to the roof in the night, wandering about grazing the fine sweet grass that grows there, picking out the wild leeks, of which they're particularly fond. Sheep, for crying out loud, not dead men at all. I guess they knew really, all along, and the stuff about dead men was to keep you indoors at night, keep you from wandering out under the stars (though why you should want to I couldn't begin to imagine). Or at least, at some point, way back in the dim past, some smartass with a particularly warped imagination made up the story about dead men, to scare his kids; and the kids believed, and never figured it was sheep, and they told their kids, and so on down the generations. Maybe you never figure it out unless you leave the farm, which nobody ever does, except me.

As a matter of fact, I was just beginning to drift off into a doze when the thumping started. Clump, clump, clump; pause; clump, clump, clump. I was not amused. I was bone-tired and I really wanted to get some sleep, and here were these fucking sheep walking about over my head. The hell with that, I thought, and got up.

I opened the door as quietly as I could, not wanting to wake up the household, and I stood in the doorway for a little while, letting my eyes get used to the dark. Someone had left a stick leaning against the doorframe. I picked it up, on the off chance that there might be a sheep close enough to hit.

Something was moving about again. I walked away from the house until I could see up top.

It wasn't sheep. It was a dead man.

He was sitting astride the roof, his legs drooping down either side, like a farmer on his way back from the market. His hands were on his hips and he was looking away to the east. He was just a dark shape against the sky, but there was something about the way he sat there: peaceful. I didn't think he'd seen me, and I felt no great inclination to advertise my presence. If I say I wasn't scared, I wouldn't expect to be believed; but fear wasn't uppermost in my mind. Mostly, I was *interested*.

No idea how long I stood and he sat. It occurred to me that I was just assuming he was a dead man. Looked at it logically, far more likely that he was alive, and had reasons of his own for climbing up on a roof in the middle of the night. Well, there's a time and a place for logic.

He turned his head, looking down the line of the roof-tree, and lifted his heels, and dug them into the turf three times: clump, clump, clump. (And that was when I realized the flaw in my earlier rationalization. Three clumps; always three, ever since I was a kid. How many three-legged sheep do you see?) At that moment, the moon came out from behind the clouds, and suddenly we were looking at each other, me and him.

My host had been right: he was purple, like a grape. Or a bruise; the whole body one enormous bruise. Swollen, he'd said; either that or he was an enormous man, arms and legs twice as thick as normal. His eyes were white; no pupils.

"Hello," I said.

He leaned forward just a little and cupped his hand behind his left ear. "You'll have to speak up," he said.

Words from a dead man; a purple, swollen man sitting astride a roof.

"Tell me," I said, raising my voice. "Why do you do that?"

He looked at me, or a little bit past me. I couldn't tell if his mouth moved, but there was a deep, gurgling noise that could only have been laughter. "Do what?"

"Ride on the roof like it's a horse," I said.

His shoulders lifted; a slow, exaggerated shrug, like he didn't know what a shrug was but was copying one he'd seen many years ago. "I'm not sure," he said. "I feel the urge to do it, so I do it."

Well, I thought, one of the great abiding mysteries of my childhood not quite cleared up. "Are you Anthemius?" I asked. "The schoolmaster?"

Again the laugh. "That's a very good question," he said. "Tell you what," he went on, "come up here and sit with me, so we can talk without yelling."

In the moonlight, I could make out the huge hands, with their monstrous overripe fingers. How tight the skin would have to be, with all that pressure against it from the inside. Breaking a neck would be like snapping a pear off a tree.

"Let me rephrase that," I said. "Were you Anthemius? When you were—"

"Yes," he said, speaking quickly to cut off a word he didn't want to hear. "I think I was. Thank you," he added. "I've been trying to remember. It's been on the tip of my tongue, but somehow I can't seem to think of any names."

The approved procedure for coping with the restless dead is, essentially, what Grandfather did; though of course we make rather more of a fuss about it. The approved procedure should, needless to say, be carried out in daylight; noon is recommended. Should you chance to encounter a specimen during the night, there are two courses of action, both recommended rather than approved. One, you draw your sword and cut its head off. Two, you challenge it to the riddle game and keep it talking all night, until dawn comes up unexpectedly and strands it like a beached whale in the cruel light.

Commentary on that. I am not a man of action. I don't vault on to roofs, I don't carry weapons. One of the reasons I left the farm in the first place was I have trouble lifting even moderate loads. So much for option one; and as for option two . . .

Also, I was curious. Interested.

"What happened to you?" I said.

"You know, I'm really not sure," he replied; and the voice was starting to sound like a man's voice, my ears were getting the hang of it, the way my eyes had got used to the dark. "I know I was out in the snow and I'd lost my way. I got terribly cold, so that every bit of me hurt. Then the pain started to ease up, and I sort of fell asleep."

"You died," I said.

He didn't like me saying that, but I guess he forgave me. "I remember waking up," he said, "and it was pitch dark and terribly quiet, and I couldn't move. I was very scared. And then it occurred to me, I wasn't breathing. I don't mean I was holding my breath. I wasn't breathing at all, and it didn't matter. So then I knew."

I waited, but I hadn't got all night. "And then?"

He turned his head away. No hair, just a bulging purple scalp. A head like a plum. "I was terrified," he said. "I mean, I had no way of knowing." He paused, and I have no idea what was passing through his mind. "After a long time, I found I could move after all. I got my hands up against the lid, and I pushed, and I could feel the wood burst apart. That scared me even more, I thought the roof, I mean all the earth on top of me, I thought it'd cave in and bury me." He paused again. "I was always frightened of tight places," he said. "You know."

I nodded. Me too, as it happens.

"I guess I panicked," he went on, "because I kept pushing, and I somehow knew that I was incredibly strong, much stronger than I'd ever been before, so I thought, if I push hard enough. I wasn't thinking straight, of course."

"And then?" I asked.

"Pushed right up through the dirt and into the moonlight," he said. "Amazing feeling. The first thing I wanted to do was run to the nearest farm and tell them, look, I'm not dead after all." He stopped; he'd said the word without thinking. "But then I thought about it; and I still wasn't breathing, and I couldn't actually *feel* anything. I could move my hands and feet, I could stand upright and balance, all that, but – you know when you've been sitting a long time and your feet go numb. It was like that, all over. It felt so strange."

"Go on," I said.

He didn't, not for a long time. "I think I sat down," he said. "I don't know why I'd have done that; standing up didn't make me tired or anything. I don't feel tired, ever. But I was so confused, I didn't know what I was supposed to do. It all felt wrong." He lifted his heels slowly and let them drop; clump, clump, clump. "And while I was there the sun started to come up, and the light just sort of flooded into my head and bleached everything away, so I couldn't think at all. I guess you could say I passed out. Anyway, when I opened my eyes I was back where I'd started from, lying in the dark."

I frowned. "How did you get back there?"

"I just don't know," he said. "Still don't. It always happens, that's all I know. When the sun comes up, my mind washes away. If I've gone any distance, I know I have to get back. I run. I can run really fast. I know I've got to be back – home," he said, with a sort of breaking-up laugh, "before the sun comes up. I've learned to be careful, to give myself plenty of time."

He was still and quiet for a while. I asked, "Why do you kill things?"

"No idea." He sounded distressed. "If something comes close enough, I grab it and twist it till it's dead. Like a cat lashing out at a bit of string. Reflex. I just know it's something I have to do."

I nodded. "Do you go looking . . . ?"

"Yes." He mumbled the word, like a kid admitting a crime. "Yes, I do. I do my best to keep away from where there might be people. It's all the same to me: sheep, foxes, men. I'd go a long way away, into the mountains, if I could. But I have to stay close, so I can get back in time."

I'd been debating with myself, and I knew I had to ask. "What were you?" I said. "What did you do?"

He didn't answer. I repeated the question.

"Like you said," he replied. "I was a schoolteacher."

"Before that."

When he answered, it was against his will. The words came out slow, flat; he spoke because he had to. "I was a Brother," he said. "When I was thirty, they said I should apply to the Order, they thought I had the gift, and the brains, and the application and the self-discipline. I passed the exam and I was at the Studium for five years. Like you," he added.

I let that go. "You joined the Order."

"No." The flat voice had gone; there was a flare of anger. "No, I failed matriculation. I retook it the next year, but I failed again. They sent me back to my parish, but by then they'd got someone else. So I ended up wandering about, looking for teaching work, letter-writing, anything I could do to earn a living. There's not a lot you can do, of course."

Suddenly I felt bitter cold, right through. Took me a moment to realize it was fear. "So you came here," I said, just to keep him talking.

"Eventually. A lot of other places first, but here's where I ended up." He lifted his head abruptly. "They sent you here to deal with me, am I right?"

I didn't reply.

"Of course they did," he said. "Of course. I'm a nuisance, a pest, a menace to agriculture. You came here to dig me up and cut my head off."

This time, I was the one who had to speak against my will. "Yes."

"Of course," he said. "But I can't let you do that. It's my . . ."

He'd been about to say *life*. Presumably, he tried to find another way of phrasing it, then gave up. We both knew what he meant.

"You passed the exams, then," he said.

"Barely," I replied. "207th out of 220."

"Which is why you're here."

His white eyes in the ash-white moonlight. "That's right," I said. "They don't give out research posts if you come 207th."

He nodded gravely. "Commercial work," he said.

"When I can get it," I replied. "Which isn't often. Others far more qualified than me."

He grunted. It could have been sympathy. "Public service work."

"Afraid so," I replied.

"Which is why you're here." He lifted his head and rolled it around on his shoulders, like someone waking up after sleeping in a chair. "Because – well, because you aren't much good. Well?"

I resented that, even though it was true. "It's not that I'm not good," I said. "It's just that everyone in my year was better than me."

"Of course." He leaned forward, his hands braced on his knees. "The question is," he said, "do I still have the gift, after what happened to me? If I've still got it, your job is going to be difficult."

"If not?" I said.

"Well," he replied, "I suppose we're about to find out."

"Indeed," I said. "There could be a paper for the journals in this."

"Your chance to escape from obscurity," he said solemnly. "Under different circumstances, I'd wish you well. Unfortunately, I really don't want you cutting off my head. It's a miserable existence, but . . ."

I could see his point. His voice was quite human now; if I'd known him before, I'd have recognized him. He had his back to the moon, so I couldn't see the features of his face.

"What I'm trying to say is, you don't have to do it," he said. "Go away. Go home. Nobody knows you came out here tonight. I promise I'll stay away until you've gone. If I don't show up, you can report that there was no direct evidence of an infestation, and therefore you didn't feel justified in desecrating what was probably an innocent grave."

"But you'll be back," I said.

"Yes, and no doubt they'll send someone else," he said. "But it won't be you."

I was tempted. Of course I was tempted. For one thing, he was a rational creature; with my eyes shut, if I hadn't known better, I'd have said he was a natural man with a heavy cold. And what if the gift did survive death? He'd kill me. I had to admit it to myself: the thought that I could get killed doing this job hadn't occurred to me. I'd anticipated a quick, grisly hour's work in broad daylight; no risk.

I'm not a coward, but I appreciate the value of fear, the way I appreciate the value of money. I'm most definitely not brave.

I saw something in the moonlight, and said (trying not to talk quickly or raise my voice): "I could go back to bed, and then come back in the morning and dig you up."

"You could," he said.

"You don't think I would?"

"Not if we'd made an agreement."

"You could be right," I said. "But what about the farmers? You've got to admit—"

At which moment, the Brother (who'd come out of the back door, crawled up on the roof behind him, and edged down the roof-tree toward him until he was close enough to reach his neck with the ax he'd brought with him) raised his arms high and swung. No sound at all; but at the last moment, the dead man leaned his head to one side, just enough, and the ax-blade swept past, cutting air. I heard the Brother grunt, shocked and panicky. I saw the dead man – eyes still fixed on me – reach behind him with his left hand and catch the swinging ax just below the head, and hold it perfectly still. The Brother gasped, but didn't let go; he was pulling with all his strength, like a little dog tugging on a belt. All his efforts couldn't move the dead man's arm the thickness of a fingernail.

"Now," the dead man said. "Let's see."

The delay on my part was unforgivable, completely unprofessional. I knew I had to do something, but my mind had gone completely blank. I couldn't remember any procedures, let alone any words. *Think*, a tiny voice was yelling inside my head, but I couldn't. I heard the Brother whimper, as he applied every scrap of strength in a tendon-ripping, joint-tearing last desperate jerk on the ax-handle, which had no effect whatsoever. The dead man was looking straight at me. His lips began to move.

Pro nobis peccatoribus – not the obvious choice, not even on the same page of the book, but it was the only procedure I could think of. Unfortunately, it's one I've always had real difficulties with. You reach out with your hand that is not a hand, extend the fingers that aren't fingers; I'm all right as far as that, and then I tend to come unstuck.

(What I was thinking was: so he failed the exam, and I passed. Yes, but maybe the reason he failed was he didn't read the questions through properly, or he spent so long on Part One that he didn't leave himself enough time for Two and Three. Maybe he's really good, just unlucky in exams.)

I was mumbling: *Sol invicte, ora pro nobis peccatoribus in die periculi*. Of course, there's a school of thought that says the magic words have no real effect whatsoever, they're just a way of concentrating the mind. I tend to agree. Why should an archaic prayer in a dead language to a god nobody's believed in for 600 years have any effect on anything at all? *Ora pro nobis peccatoribus*, I repeated urgently, *nobis peccatoribus in die periculi*.

It worked. It can't have been the words, of course, but it felt like it was the words. I was in, I was through. I was inside his head.

There was nothing there.

Believe me, it's true. Nothing at all; like walking into a house where someone's died, and the family have been in and cleared out all the furniture. Nothing there, because I was inside the head of a dead man; albeit a dead man who was looking at me reproachfully out of blank white eyes while holding an ax absolutely still.

Fine; all the easier, if it's empty. I looked for the controls. You have to visualize them, of course. I see them as the hand-wheels of a lathe. It's because I had a holiday job in a foundry in Second Year. I don't know how to use a lathe. What I mostly did was sweep up piles of swarf off the floor.

Here is the handwheel that controls the arms. I reached out with the hand that is not a hand, grabbed it and tried to turn it. Stuck. I tried harder. Stuck. I tried really hard, and the bloody thing came away in my hand.

It's not supposed to do that.

I re-visualized. I saw the controls as the reins of a cart, the footbrake under my boot that was not a boot. I stamped on the brake and hauled back hard on the reins.

I haven't got around to writing that paper for the journals, so here it is for the first time anywhere. The gift does not survive death. Nothing survives. The room was empty. And the handwheel only broke off because I'm clumsy and cack-handed, the sort of person who trips over cats and breaks the nibs of pens by pressing too hard.

I heard the Brother gasp, as he jerked the ax out of the dead man's grip. The dead man didn't move. His eyes were still fixed on mine, right up to the moment when the ax sheared through his neck and his head wobbled and fell, bounced off his knee and tumbled off the roof into the short grass below. The body didn't move.

I know why. It took ten of us, with an improvised crane made of twelve-foot-three-inch fir poles, to get the body down off the roof. It must've weighed half a ton. The head alone was 200-weight. Two men couldn't lift it; they had to use levers to roll it along the ground. There was no blood, but the neck started to ooze a milky white juice that smelt worse than anything you could possibly imagine.

We burnt the body. We drenched it in pine-pitch, and it caught quite easily and burnt down to nothing; not even any recognizable bits of bone. The white juice flared up like oil. They rolled the head over to the slurry-pond and pitched it in. It went down with a gurgle and a burp.

"I heard you talking to it," the Brother told me. For some reason, the word *it* offended me. "I guessed you were using a variation on the riddle game, to keep it distracted till the sun came up."

"Something like that," I said.

He nodded. "I shouldn't have interfered, I'm sorry," he said. "You had the situation under control, and I could have ruined everything."

"That's all right," I said.

He smiled, as if to say, it wasn't all right but thanks for forgiving me. "I guess I panicked," he said. Then he frowned. "No, I didn't. I saw a chance of getting in on the act. It was stupid and selfish of me. You'll have to write to the prebendary."

"I don't see why," I said mildly. "The way I see it, your actions were open to several different interpretations. I choose to interpret them as courage and resourcefulness. I could put that in a letter, if you like."

"Would you?" In his face, I saw all the desperation and cruelty of sudden, unexpected hope. "I mean, seriously?"

"Of course," I said.

"That'd be . . ." He stopped. He couldn't think of a big enough word. "You've got no idea what it's like," he said all in a rush, like diarrhea. "Being stuck here, in this miserable place with these appalling people. If I can't get back to a town, I swear I'll go mad. And it's so cold in winter. I hate the cold."

You can sleep in the coach, Father Prior said when I tried to make a fuss about the timetable. I didn't say to him, have you ever been on a provincial mail-coach, on country roads, at this time of year? A dead man couldn't sleep on a mail-coach.

I slept, nearly all the way; on account, I guess, of not having had much sleep the night before. Woke up just as we were crossing the Fulvens bridge; I looked out of the window, and all I could see was water, moonlight reflected on water. Couldn't get back to sleep after that. Too dark to read the case notes, which I'd neglected to do back at the farm. But I remembered the basic facts from the briefing. These jobs are all the same, anyhow. Piece of cake.

The coach threw me out just after dawn, at a crossroads in the middle of nowhere. Somewhere up on the moors; I'm a valley boy myself. We had cousins up on the moor. I hated it when they came to visit. The old man was deaf as a post, and the three boys (mid-to-late thirties, but they were always *the boys*) just sat there, not saying a word. The mother died young, and I can't say I blame her.

They were supposed to be meeting the coach, but there was no one there. I stood for a while, then I sat on my bag, then I sat on the ground, which was damp. I heard an owl, and a fox, or at least I hope it was a fox. If not, it was something we never got around to covering in Third Year, and I'm very glad I didn't see it.

They arrived eventually, in a little dog-cart thing; an old man driving, a younger man and the Brother. One small pony, furry like a bear.

The Brother did the talking, for which I was quite grateful. He was one of the better sort of country Brothers: short man, somewhere between fifty and sixty, a distinct burr to his voice but he spoke clearly and used proper words. The boy was the younger man's son, the older man's grandson. He'd been fooling about in a big oak tree, slipped, fell; broken arm and a hideous bash on the head. He hadn't come around, and it had been a week now. They had to prize his mouth open with the back of a horn spoon to get food and water in; he swallowed all right, but that was all he did. You could stick a needle in his foot half an inch and he wouldn't even twitch. The swelling on the back of his head had gone down – the Brother disclaimed any medical knowledge, but he was lying – and they'd set the arm and splinted it, for what that was worth.

I thought, better than killing the restless dead. One of my best subjects at the Studium, though of course we did all our practicals on conscious minds, with a Father sitting a few feet away, watching like a hawk. I'd done one about eighteen months earlier, and it went off just fine; in, found her, straight out again. She followed me like a dog. I'd been relieved when Father Prior told me; it could've been something awkward and fiddly, like auspices, or horrible and scary, like a possession. Just in case, I'd brought the book. I'd meant to mug up the relevant chapter, either at the farm or on the coach, but I hadn't got around to it. Anyway, it had to be better than that empty place.

It was quite a big house, for a hill farm; sitting in the well of a valley, with a dense copper-beech hedge on all four sides, as a windbreak. Just the five of them in the house, the Brother said: grandfather, father, mother, the boy, and a hired man who slept in the hayloft. The boy was nine years old. The Brother told me his name, but I'm hopeless with names.

They asked me, did I want to rest after the journey, wash and brush up, something to eat? The correct answer was, of course, no, so I gave it.

"He's in here," the Brother said.

Big for a hill farm, but still oppressively small. Downstairs, the big kitchen, with a huge table, fireplace, two hams swinging like dead men on gibbets. A parlor, tiny and dusty and cold.

Dairy, scullery, store; doorway through to the cow stalls. Upstairs, one big room and a sort of oversized cupboard, where the boy was. I could just about kneel beside the bed, if I didn't mind the windowsill digging in the small of my back.

The hell with that, I thought, I'm a qualified man, a professional, a Father; a wizard. I shouldn't have to work in conditions you wouldn't keep pigs in. "Take him downstairs," I said. "Put him on the kitchen table."

They had a job. The stairs in that house were like a bell tower, tightly coiled and cramped. Father and grandfather did the heavy lifting, while I watched. It's an odd thing about me. Sometimes, the more compassion is called for the less capable I am of feeling it. I offer no explanation or excuse.

"He shouldn't have been moved," the Brother hissed in my ear, just loud enough so that everyone could hear. "In his condition—"

"Yes, thank you," I said, in my best arrogant-city-bastard voice. I couldn't say why I was behaving like this. Sometimes I do. "Now, if you'll all stay well back, I'll see what I can do."

I looked at the boy, and I could remember the theory perfectly, every last detail, every last lecture note. His eyes were closed; he had a stupid face, fat girly lips, fat cheeks. If he lived, he'd grow up tall, solid, double-chinned, gormless; the son of the farm. Pork fat and home-brewed beer; he'd be spherical by the time he was forty, strong enough to wrestle a bullock to its knees, slow and tireless, infuriatingly calm, a man of few words; respected at the market, shrewd and fat, his bald patch hidden under a hat that would never come off, probably not even in bed. A solid, productive life, which it was my duty to save. Lucky me.

Theory; theory is your lifeline, they used to tell me, your driftwood in a shipwreck. I reminded myself of the basic propositions.

To recover a lost mind, first make an entrance. This is usually done by visualizing yourself as a penetrating object: a drill bit, a woodpecker's beak, a maggot. The drill bit works for me, though for some reason I tend to be a carpenter's auger, wound in with a brace. I go in through the spiral flakes of waste bone thrown clear by the wide grooves of the cutter. I assume it's from some childhood memory, watching Grandad at work in the barn. You're not really supposed to use personal memories, but it's easier, for someone with my limited imagination.

Once you're in, first ward, immediately, because you never know what might be waiting for you in there. I raised first ward as soon as I felt myself go through. I use *scutum fidei*, visualize a shield. Mine's round, with a hole in it at twelve o'clock so I can see what's going on.

I peered through the hole. No nasty creatures with dripping fangs crouched to pounce, which was nice. Count to ten and lower the shield slowly.

I looked around. This is the crucial bit, and you mustn't rush. How long it takes depends on the strength of your gift, so naturally I take ages. The light gradually increases. First things first; get your bearings. Orientate yourself, taking special care to get a fix on the point you came in by. Well, obviously. If you lose your entry point, you're stuck in someone else's head forever. You really don't want that.

I lined up on the corners of a ceiling, drawing diagonal lines and fixing on their point of origin, measuring the angles with my imaginary protractor (it's brass, with numbers in gothic italic). One-oh-five, seventy-five; repeat the numbers four times out loud, to make sure they're loaded into memory. Fine. Now I know where I am and how to get out again. One-oh-five, seventy-five. Now, then. Let the dog see the rabbit.

I was in a room. It's nearly always an interior; with kids, practically guaranteed it's their bedroom, or the room they sleep in, depending on social class and domestic arrangements. In all relevant essentials, it was the room upstairs I had him carried down from. Excellent; nice and small, not many places to hide anything. So much easier when you're dealing with a subject of limited intelligence.

I visualized a body for myself. I tend not to be me. With children, it's usually best to be a nice lady; the kid's mother, if possible. I'm not good enough to do specific people, and I have real problems being women. So I was a nice old man instead.

Hello, I said. Where are you?

Don't worry if they don't answer. Sometimes they do, sometimes they don't. I walked around the bed, knelt down, looked under it. There was a cupboard; one of those triangular jobs, wedged in a corner. I opened that. For some reason, it was full of the skins and bones of dead animals. None of my business; I closed it. I pulled the covers off the bed, and lifted the pillow.

Odd, I thought, and touched base with theory. The boy must still be alive, or else there would be no room. If he's alive, he must be in here somewhere. He can't be invisible, not inside his own head. He can, of course, be anything he likes, so long as it's animate and alive. A cockroach, for example, or a flea. I sighed. I get all the rotten jobs.

I adjusted the scale, making the room five times bigger. Go up in easy stages. If he was being a cockroach, he'd now be a rat-sized cockroach. If he was being a rat, of course, he'd be cat-sized and capable of giving me a nasty bite. I used *lorica*, just in case. I looked under the bed again.

I visualized a clock, in the middle of the wall opposite the door. It told me I'd been inside for ten minutes. The recommended maximum is thirty. Really first-rate practitioners have been known to stay in for an hour and still come out more or less in one piece; that's material for a leading article in the journals. I searched again, this time paying more attention to the contents of the cupboard. Dried, desiccated animal skins: squirrels, rabbits, rats. No fleas, mites, or ticks. So much for that theory.

I visualized a glass jug, to represent my energy level. You can use yourself up surprisingly quickly and not know it. Just as well I did. My jug was a third empty. You want to save at least a fifth just to get out again. I visualized calibrations, so as to be sure.

Quick think. The recommended course of action would be to visualize a tracking agent (spaniel, terrier, ferret), but that takes a fair chunk of your resources; also, it burns energy while it's in use, and getting rid of it takes energy, too. I drew a distinct red line on my measuring jug, and a blue line just above it. The alternative to a tracker is to increase the scale still further; twenty times, say, in which case your cockroach will be a wolf-sized monster that could jump you and bite your head off. I was still running *lorica*, but any effective ward burns energy. If I found myself with a fight on my hands, I could dip below that essential red line in a fraction of a second. No, the hell with that.

I visualized a terrier. I'm not a dog person, so my terrier was a bit odd; very short, stumpy legs and a rectangular head. Still, it went at it with great enthusiasm, wagging its imaginary tail and making little yapping noises. All around the room, nose into everything. Then it sat on the floor and looked at me, as if to say, Well?

Not looking good. My jug was half-empty, I'd used up my repertoire of approved techniques, and found nothing. Just my luck to get a special case, a real collector's item. Senior research fellows would be fighting each other for the chance of a go at this one, but I just wanted to get the job done and clear out. Wasted on me, you might say.

I vanished the dog. Quick think. There had to be something else I could try, but nothing occurred to me. Didn't make sense; he had to be in here somewhere, or there'd be no room. He couldn't be invisible. He could only turn himself into something he could imagine – and it had to be real; no fantasy creatures the size of a pinhead. At five times magnification, a red mite would be plainly visible; also, the dog would've found it. Tracking agents, even inferior ones visualized by me, smell life. If he was in here, the dog would've found him.

So . . .

As required by procedure, I considered abandoning the attempt and getting out. This would, of course, mean the boy would die; you can't go back in twice, that's an absolute. I'd be within my rights, faced with an enigma on this scale. The failure would be noted on my record, of course, but there'd be an annotation, *no blame attaches*, and it wouldn't be the first time, not by a long way. The kid would die; not my problem. I'd have done my best, and that's all you have to do.

Or I could think of something. Such as what?

They tell you: be wise, don't improvise. If in doubt, get out. Making stuff up as you go along is mightily frowned on, in much the same way as you're not encouraged to fry eggs in a fireworks factory. There's no knowing what you might invent, and outside controlled conditions, invention could lead to the

Cartographic Commission having to redraw the maps for a whole county. Or you could make a hole in a wall, which is the worst thing anybody can do. At the very least, I'd be sure to end up in front of the Board, facing charges of unauthorized innovation and divergence. Saving the life of some farm kid would be an excuse, but not a very good one.

I could think of something. Such as . . .

There's no such thing as magic. Instead, there's the science we don't properly understand, not yet. There are effects that work, and we have no idea why. One of these is *spes aeternitatis*, a wretchedly inconsistent, entirely inexplicable conjuring trick that no self-respecting Father would condescend to use. That's because they can't get it to work reliably.

I can.

Spes aeternitatis is an appearances-adjuster. You can use it to find hidden objects, or translate lies, or tell if a slice of cake or a glass of wine's got poison in it. I do it by visualizing everything that's wrong in light blue. It's a tiny little scrap of talent that I've got and practically everybody else hasn't; it's like being double-jointed, or wiggling your nostrils like a rabbit.

I closed my eyes and opened them again, and saw a light-blue room. Everything light blue. Everything false.

Oh, I thought; then, one-oh-five, seventy-five, and I started lining up diagonals for my escape. But that wasn't to be, unfortunately. The room blurred and reappeared, and it was all different. It was my room; the room I slept in until I was fifteen years old.

He was sitting on the end of the bed; a slight man, almost completely bald, with a small nose and a soft chin, small hands, short, thin legs. I'd put him at about fifty years old. His skin was purple, like a grape.

"You were wrong," he said, looking up at me. "The talent survives death."

"That's interesting," I said. "How did you get in here?"

He smiled. "You practically invited me in," he said. "When I heard that fool behind me, with the ax, I looked at you. You felt sorry for me. You thought: is he not a man and a Brother? Or words to that effect. I used Stilicho's transport, and here I am."

I nodded. "I should've put up wards."

"You should. Careless. Attention to detail isn't your strongest suit."

"The boy," I said.

He shrugged. "In there somewhere, I dare say. But we aren't in his head, we're in yours. I've made myself at home, as you can see."

I looked around quickly. The apple box with the bottom knocked out, where I used to keep my books; it was where it should be, but the books were different. They were new and beautifully bound in tooled calf, and the alphabet their titles were written in was strange to me.

"My memories," I said.

He waved his hand. "Well rid of them," he said. "Misery and failure, a life wasted, a talent dissipated. You'll be better off."

I nodded. "With yours."

"Quite. Oh, they're not pleasant reading," he said, with a scowl. "Bitter, angry; memories of bigotry and spite, relentless bad luck, a life of constant setbacks and reverses, a talent misunderstood. You'll see that I failed the exam the second time because, sitting there in Great School, I suddenly hit on a much better way of achieving *unam sanctam*; quicker, safer, ruthlessly efficient. I tried it out as soon as the exam was over, and it worked. But I got no marks, so they failed me. I ask you, where's the sense in that?"

"You failed the retake," I said. "What about the first time?"

He laughed. "I had the flu," he said. "I was practically delirious, could barely remember my name. Would they listen? No. Rules. You see what I mean. Bad luck and spite at every turn."

I nodded. "What happens to me?"

He looked at me. "You'll be better off," he repeated.

"I'll stop existing. I'll be dead."

"Not physically," he said mildly. "Your body, my mind. Your fully qualified licensed-practitioner's body, and a mind that saw how to improve *unam sanctam* in a half-second flash of intuition."

It says a lot about my self-esteem that I actually considered it, though not for very long. Half a second, maybe. "What happens now?" I asked. "Do we fight, or . . . ?"

He shrugged. "If you like," he said, and extended his arm. It was ten feet long, thick as a gatepost. He gripped my throat like a man holding a mouse, and crushed me.

I guess I was about 70 per cent dead when I remembered: I know what to do. I drew a rather shaky second ward; he closed his fingers on thin air, and I was standing behind him.

He swung around, roaring like a bull. He had bull's horns sticking out of his forehead. I tried second ward again, but he got there before I did, grabbed my head, and smashed my face into the wall.

Just in time, I remembered: there is no pain. I used Small Mercies, softening the wall into felt, and slipped through his fingers. I was smoke. I hung above him in a cloud. He laughed, and fetched me back with *vis mentis*. The back of my head hit the floor, which gave way like a mattress. I became a spear, and buried myself in his chest. He used second ward and was on the other side of the room.

"You fight like a first-year," he said.

Which was true. I clenched my mind like a fist; the walls closed in on him, squashing him like a spider under a boot. I felt him, like a nail right through the sole. Back to first ward, and we stood glowering at each other, in opposite corners of the room.

"You can't beat me," he said. "I'll wear you down and you'll simply fade away. Face it, what the hell have you got to live for?"

Valid point. "All right, then," I said.

His eyes opened wide. "I win?"

"You win," I said.

He was pleased; very pleased. He grinned at me and raised his hand, just as I got my fingers around the handle of the door and twisted as hard as I could.

He saw that and opened his mouth to scream. But the door flew open, knocking me back. I closed my eyes. The door was, of course, the intersection of two lines drawn diagonally across the room, at 105 and 75 degrees precisely.

I opened my eyes. He'd gone. I was in the boy's room, the room upstairs. The boy was sitting on the floor, legs crossed, hands under his chin. He looked up at me.

"Well, come on," I snapped at him. "I haven't got all day."

*   *   *

They were pathetically grateful. Mother in floods of tears, father clinging to my arm, how can we ever thank you, it's a miracle, you're a miracle-worker. I wasn't in the mood. The boy, lying on the kitchen table under a pile of blankets, looked up at me and frowned, as though something about me wasn't quite right. A quiet, analytical stare; it bothered the hell out of me. I refused food and drink and made father get out the pony and trap and take me out to the crossroads. But the mail won't be arriving for six hours, he objected; it's cold and dark, you'll catch your death.

I didn't feel cold.

At the crossroads, huddling under the smelly old hat father insisted on giving me, I tried to search my mind, to see if he'd really gone. There was, of course, no way he could have survived. I'd opened the door (Rule One: never open the door) and he'd been sucked out of my head out into the open, where there was no talented mind to receive him. Even if he was as strong as he'd claimed to be, there was no way he could have lasted more than three seconds before he broke up and dissipated into the air. There was absolutely nothing he could have done, no way he could have survived.

The coach arrived. I got on it, and slept all the way. At the inn, I got a lamp and a mirror, and examined myself all over. Just when I thought I was all clear, I found a patch of purple skin, about the size of a crab apple, on the calf of my left leg. I told myself it was just a bruise.

(That was a year ago. It's still there.)

The rest of the round was just straightforward stuff: a possession, a small rift, a couple of incursions, which I sealed with a strong closure and duly reported when I got back. Since then, I've volunteered for a screening, been to see a couple of counselors, bought a pair of full-length mirrors. And I've been promoted; field officer, superior grade. They're quite pleased with me, and no wonder. I seem to be getting better at the job all the time. And I'm writing a paper, would you believe? Modifications to *unam sanctam*. Quicker, safer, much more efficient. So blindingly obvious, I'm surprised no one's ever thought of it before.

Father Prior is surprised but pleased. I don't know what's got into you, he said.

THE WOMAN IN SCARLET

Tanith Lee

It was always one way when he met them, on the long roads, high lands, low lands, rich or not, at the little villages, in the towns, too, and in the slim white cities, even there, or under the green roofs of forests, or on a seashore washed by the sea empty of most things but air and light. "*Look*," he noted them whisper, the men, the women, the children, the slaves. "Do you see him? He is a *Sword's Man*." Sometimes they would follow him a short distance. If not, they stared till he was out of sight. Occasionally, not that often, they might approach, more likely send a servant after him. Otherwise, the approach came from strangers still unseen, who had heard tell of him, or sensed his arrival, like a season. The men generally wanted straightforward help, rescue, or to train some rabble of an army, or teach their sons to fight. The women usually required him to murder somebody. Then again, men and women both now and then wanted him for other things. To show him off, display him, to bed him or own him, if only for a night. He said No more times than he said Yes, to all the requests. But for the beds it was always No. They should remember, and they did, but hoped he might forget. He was wedded to his Sword. All his kind were. Married to her, and her possession, never theirs.

"Coor Krahn, must you be going?"

"I must."

"Can't I tempt you to remain a handful more days? There's the horse I spoke of . . . why don't you come and see if you like it?"

"I walk where I go, Lord Juy. It keeps me fitter."

"Oh that. You're fit as three men. Stay for the dinner tonight. It's my daughter's birth-feast."

"My work's done here, Lord Juy. My thanks, but I'll be on the road by noon."

"She's restless," said the rich aristocrat, half contemptuous, and half jealous, frowning, admiring, uneasy, "is she?"

"Maybe."

"Tell me her name again."

Coor Krahn did not like to say his Sword's name to others, but also he did like to. He stayed in two minds on this. "Sas-peth," Coor Krahn said, unsmiling, his black eyes burning up, so Lord Juy slightly recoiled. "Sas-peth Satch."

"And that other name she has – no, don't say that one. I recall that one. And why she has it. It's a good name, Coor Krahn. And you are a mighty Sword's Man. Now, because of your skills, my lands stretch to the Black River. I'm grateful. The slave will bring your fee. It's as we agreed."

"I never doubted that," said Coor Krahn. He bowed and turned his back upon Lord Juy. (They both understood he had referred not to a lord's honor but to a Sword's Man's power and rights.)

A few minutes later a slave came, and presented the wallet of gold, crawling on his knees.

The Sun was high over the scaled towers of Juy's mansion as Coor Krahn turned on to the road out of the valley.

The wallet was stowed in the leather pack across his back. No sane man in half a world would ever dare to try to steal it. Nor any of the ornaments a Sword's Man wore, nor any piece of his armor or arms.

At Coor Krahn's side, she hung from the belt of red leather in her scarlet silk scabbard. Although young still, he had walked so long, so many years, with that feel of her beside him, that to walk without her would have seemed like lameness. And in the same way, to sleep without her lying along his body and under his hand, like death.

"Sas-peth," he murmured once, as he walked up from the glowing valley, "Sas-peth Satch." But now he smiled, to himself, or to her. He often spoke a little to her, though he never spoke very much to other men, and to women, less.

*   *   *

Tonight he dreamed of her.

In the dreams he saw her in her spirit shape, which naturally was female. But also, in dreams, she put on flesh and blood. They were walking in a night garden, high on a roof above a city, perhaps Curhm-by-Ocean, or Is-lil in the north. Slender and dark, the sculptured trees rose from stone pots, and a stone lion, polished smooth as water, held the round orange Moon between his ears.

Coor Krahn could smell a perfume, like a spice, which in her woman shape the Sword had put on. Her hand rested lightly on his arm. Her face too was powdered pale, as the faces of aristocratic women always were. (Although in other dreams, when she strode or rode with him into battle, she was tawny as any peasant boy.) Her long hair looked smooth as the lion, as night water. She wore her color, as she always did, deep red, bordered with flame red. Her eyes were black as his own.

"Why are you up here, Lady Sas-peth?" he asked her courteously. He was unfailingly formal, when first addressing her, even when, as in some dreams they did, they lay down together.

"There is the sea," she said, pointing her narrow finger away across the houses and the temples, to a curving line of fine white fire, which described waves breaking on the city stones. This was Curhm then, yet it had a look more of Gazul, which rose by a desert.

"Do you wish to go to the sea, Sas-peth?"

"No. Away from the coast."

"Tell me then, where shall we go?"

Then she turned her narrow, perfect face and gazed at him. Her gaze was not like that of any woman he had ever met, highborn or lowly. Nor, for that matter, like the gaze of any man.

"At this time, I grow tired of our wandering about, Coor Krahn. Let us rest soon."

In the dream he was startled. But she sometimes made him start. During the first dream in which she had bared her breasts and kissed him and drawn him down, he had been amazed, so amazed that it amounted to fear, until, presently, everything was lost in her.

"Then – then, lady, we'll rest a while. Where would you wish our rest to be?"

"Some small place," she said, idly now, more womanly. She glanced away, and smiled secretively, as sometimes she did before they coupled. But she drew her hand from his arm, and the long tail of her scarlet sleeve slipped over his wrist, cool as a snake. "The next small place, perhaps."

"It will be some upland village . . ." he said, almost protesting. She did not reprimand him.

Instead, she drifted off, crossing over the face of the Moon, moving away through the garden, until she vanished behind the trees.

He woke, disturbed slightly, and lay thinking of the memory of her, her shadow-silhouette against the face of the Moon.

But under his hand, she lay silent now, and steel hard, out of her scabbard.

"Whatever you wish, Sas-peth Satch. As always. I am your warrior, master of all but you. Your slave, Sas-peth."

He had slept that night under the pines and sobe trees of a little wood, and in the morning, when he walked out of the wood, he could see nothing below but the track and the sloped shoulders of the hills. At once he felt relieved, and wondered at himself. In the past, now and then, she had come to him asleep and told him they must do certain things, take a certain direction or avoid another. So far as he knew, no loss had ever resulted from his obedience. Why should it? A Sword could only bring her warrior good; fame, wealth and kudos, through lawful battle, which was the reason for his life.

He walked on, along the hills, she at his side.

Coor Krahn had been born in a poor town, whose name meant Pigs City. Undoubtedly pigs were kept there, and provided the mainstay of the town's economy. Coor Krahn grew up in a thatched house-hut, one of three belonging to the town's overseer, and overlooking five courtyards, each full, like all the town courtyards, and the town streets, of pink and gray pigs.

When Coor was nine, some Sword's Men entered the town. The overseer had himself called them, because Pigs City was experiencing conflict with a neighboring brigand across the river. (There had been trouble for months, and one night part of the town burned – Coor remembered well the cries and shrieks, the streaming metallic flames, and the odor of roast pork – that in later years he realized was not all attributable to unlucky pigs.)

Waiting on his father the overseer's table, with several other older sons, Coor was dazzled and astonished by the four warriors, the Sword's Men. They blazed in the greasy torchlight in their mail and ribbed plates of armor. These carapaces had been decorated with chasings and bosses of gold and silver so intricate they seemed embroidered there, while jewels blinked and gleamed like coals, or witch's eyes of glacial ice. The men were tanned to bronze, their hair long, braided or worn tied high, as the tails of the horses they had brought. One had a scar across his cheek that pulled his face that side always into a grin. It was a wonderful scar, and he was rightly proud of it, sometimes fondling it, and he had given it a name: The Moon's Tooth, which Coor never forgot, though afterward he forgot the names of all four men.

Their Swords also had names, and these names Coor forgot as well, but for perhaps another reason – they daunted him so. Slanting from the belts of their men, as the warriors sat at the overseer's dinner, each Sword leaned in her scabbard of silk over leather over steel over velvet, and force swirled from them. The Swords were four queens, four enchantresses, and this was made most plain. A cup of hot wine was set before each Sword, which drink her Sword's Man never touched, also a platter with a little of the best meat, and a flower laid on it, as if for a great lady.

Within a single day, the Sword's Men had settled the brigand across the river. His head, and those of his two lieutenants, were fixed on poles by the wooden town gate, for everyone to delight in. The heads had not even quite rotted down to the skulls when Coor ran away from Pigs City and followed the road the Sword's Men had taken, eastward, to Curhm.

He had seen the warriors paid in silver and gold coins, all the town could spare. It was not that which made him run after them. He knew they, and their kind, maintained the fabric of law and justice across the sphere of lands too great for him, then, ever to imagine. It was not that either. Coor was strong and healthy and bored almost to a stone with pigs, and of course the men, their magnificence, had impressed everyone. Nor was it that. It was the swirl of half-seen lightning, the presence, the essence of the four Swords, and of one in particular. He learned after this was not quite unheard of. The Sword had "flirted" with him, as an empress might, leading him on just a short way, to bring him to awareness of his fate. She had been sheathed in jade silk. Not recollecting her outer name, he had yet some idea she was also called for something green, but that inner name her Sword's Man had never revealed. Any more than Coor, when once he had become a Sword's Man at the Sword-School of Curhm, would much reveal the inner name of Sas-peth Satch. For the inner name was given mostly at the first meeting, awake or in dream, after the man was wed to her. Only those you allowed to hire you, or were close to you in other ways, had a right to hear it. And then, generally, they – like Lord Juy – were too afraid to speak it aloud.

The Sword-School was harsh. It needed to be, to slough off quickly those who had mistaken their destiny. Some few died in their first months. Not many. Most simply failed and went home, or to other vocations. Sad, bitter even, but resigned. Only now and then one who failed killed himself. There was one of those during Coor's second year. This boy, called Fengar, threw himself from the top of the Sun Wind Temple, and died on the pavement below, an offering to the wind goddess.

Coor had known, or believed he had known, he too would rather die than fail.

But he did not fail, he did extremely well. He rose straight, like a star, as if all of him, body, mind, and spirit, had already been honing itself, unsuspected, for this work.

At first his teachers were stern with him, zealous in case he should turn out only to be a star which burned up and fell. But after five years at the School, they were stern in another way, harsher if anything, to hammer him flawless.

From a yokel of the low lands, just able to scratch his name, he became educated and fined. He learned not only the arts of the warrior, but some of the knack of a scholar, able to read and to write, and of a courtier, who can speak and behave gracefully, unless provoked. No Sword's Man ever had a wish to insult through ignorance, for any unwise enough to anger him he would be able to destroy. But these were material things.

In his seventeenth year, the mystery began to be taught him.

This was the mystery of the Sword, the core of the ethos of a Sword's Man. Until reckoned ready, the apprentice owned no sword of any type. The blades he fought with and learned by were common property. But now the night approached when the School would give to Coor his own individual weapon. Not a sword, but a Sword. An artifact which had been forged for him alone, occultly, hidden from all but its makers. In other hands, it was not yet female, only he would wake it to its feminine life, and to its power.

At phases of the Moon, junctures of the zodiac, the concealed artisans of Curhm-by-Ocean created a Sword for Coor, as they, or their forebears, had done, through a thousand years, for every Sword's Man of that School.

First came the ceremony that made Coor a warrior. Before it he was starved a month of food and sleep, and drawn by draughts of midnight herbs and tart, transparent smokes, into some other state, half from his body, which in turn seemed eccentric, wilder, and curiously less finite than he had ever known it. In this strange condition, he viewed eternity, the unimportance of everything else, and its contrasting utter necessity, for trivia held the seeds of different, higher matters, to be discovered only after death.

Thirty-one endless days and limitless nights Coor lived in this mode. On the evening of the thirty-second day, as stars dewed the twilight over Curhm, they led him to his wedding.

A Sword's Man stayed celibate. That is, he was faithful only to his Sword. Although female, it was his phallus. Yet it – she – and only she – might make love to him. And her only might he ever take. She would lie at his side, in his arms, every night. And in dreams, if by his courage and his genius in combat he made her care for him, then she would give him pleasures no human woman ever could.

Coor, now named Coor Krahn, stood naked in the unlit dark of that huge granite chamber, and when they brought her to him, his steel mistress, without a scabbard, naked too, his sex rose hard, and he shook as if meeting at last his one true love.

He made his vows. In the luminous darkness, he thought he heard the Sword faintly singing at each resonance of his voice.

Then as he gazed at her, a hooded man was there, and as always he did, with exaggerated gentleness, lifting Coor Krahn's left forearm, made a long thin cut in it with a virgin razor.

The blood ran out and dripped away and away, ruby beads, and finally they brought his Sword, to drink his blood, and as she drank, he kissed her, her silken skin of steel, for the first time.

When he did so, his erection faded and sank down. But he was appeased; as if he had reached a climax, and that energy was spent. While from the lessening of his flesh, vast vitality seemed to burst back through him. And in that moment, he knew the Sword's inner name.

After the marriage, they took him to a couch, where he was to lie down and hold her, and sleep, and have the beginning dream.

The wine was drugged, and he slept instantly.

He found himself on a mountaintop, among the white, cold snow, under a sky glittering light, without color. But the Sword stood before him, and she was a woman, and clothed in red, and so he knew he had been right in the name. Touching his body lightly with pearl fingers just above the heart, the Sword spoke to him in her woman's voice, while her beauty scorched him like the fiery sky.

"I am to be called Sas-peth Satch. Say my name."

"Sas-peth . . . Sas-peth Satch, my lady."

"My inner name you may also speak, since I informed you at our kiss, and you heard me."

Then he said that name, and she nodded, and the dream was gone. After this he slept for a hundred hours.

Waking he remembered as they always did, and both the names. Sas-peth Satch was The Woman In Scarlet.

When it appeared, five days after she told him of it in the garden dream, the "small place" turned out to be attractive enough.

The hill itself was terraced for agriculture, and brilliant as if carved from emerald. There were fields, and yards of vines. A river, crystalline and thin in spots as a rope, threaded all through, and sallow willows hung over it, and then an orchard of ash-plums, and hyacinth trees.

The town was prosperous. Having reached the wide main street, which had been paved, he looked through to a second hill, and there was a lord's mansion on it, with dragon-tinted roofs. Had the Sword brought him here for war? It seemed unlikely. Even the people on the street (who stared after him in the usual way) looked otherwise carefree.

Coor Krahn went to the inn. The slave by the door was well fed and went down on his knees, smiling, to welcome a guest.

The inn master saw to the care of a Sword's Man personally. It was his pert wife, eyeing Coor Krahn in a fashion he knew quite well, who said to him, "And why can you be here, a great Sword's Man, in *our* peaceful little pond?"

"I'm on my way somewhere," he answered. When she tried to improve on this, he did not reply, and sat as if thinking, until she left him alone.

The day passed with sunlight and the mooing of cows in the water-meadows. As evening stole through, Coor Krahn heard the inn filling up below, and kept to his chamber. They would be discussing him sufficiently as it was.

Lanterns lit in the courtyard. Moths danced. Cool breezes blew the veils of night, and a firefly winked on and off by the well.

He was restless. He did not know why he was here. Did she mean him to stay here for sure; as she had said to *rest* here, and as the inn slut had said, in this peaceful little pond? He was young, not yet thirty. Sufficient time for restful dawdling in a decade or so.

"Why have you sent me here, Sas-peth?" he asked her softly, as she went up and down with him across the room. "Why must I loiter? Do *you* aspire to loiter – to rest – *you*? Or were you only playing a game with me?"

He thought, if he slept, he might dream of her and then she would tell him why, or what she really wanted. Or even that she had been testing him, his loyalty to her that she had never, in any case, doubted. And that tomorrow they would go on, away from here.

But when he fell asleep it was late. The youthful Moon had sailed over, and the town was silent as a grave. And he only dreamed, incredibly, as he seldom did, that he was once more living in Pigs City. The change was, in this dream, he was a man full grown, yet not a warrior. He was the overseer, since his father and the other sons were all dead. He was sitting in a courtyard, with pigs everywhere, seeing to a judgment of some errant wife. She looked, of course, exactly like the pert wife of the inn master, who had tried to interest him earlier.

When he woke, dawn was ahead of him, the sky beyond the window like a peach. He caressed the steel skin under his hand, his wedded wife, the Sword.

"Perhaps, lady, I need some sign from you. Pardon my asking it of you. But I'm foxed. I don't understand. Perhaps give me some sign today, why it is you truly want to remain in this *small place*. Have I mistaken it? Was it some other town you had in mind? Guide me, Sas-peth Satch. Or maybe I'll have to go on anyway, a little distance, to make sure I didn't mistake your meaning."

When he said this, a shudder went over him. The dawn was cold, despite its flush, and he had thrown off the blanket. But it was not because of that. He felt his words had been dismissive, a threat that he would have his own way in spite of what the Sword wished. And that could never, must never be.

"Whatever you want, lady," he said.

As he got up, his limbs seemed stiff. For a second he caught sight of the ghost of some man's old age. But Coor Krahn was young, and in a moment was as he had been. He put himself, his character, on again, like his clothes.

But buckling on the belt of the Sword, for the first time in his life, it slipped through his fingers. He caught the scabbard before it met the ground. The Sword had not been in the scabbard, or the omen would have perturbed him more.

At noon, an elaborately dressed servant was waiting for him downstairs.

"From my master, I bring you greetings, Sword's Man. And this modest trinket."

Coor Krahn accepted the modest trinket – a broad silver armband set with several clear gems – such tokens were frequent enough. He thought, Now I shall discover why I was brought here. He said, "What's the name of your master?"

"The Lord Tyo Lionay."

Coor nodded graciously. Of course, he had never heard of him.

Lord Tyo's house was very fair, not large, but exquisite in all apparent detail. Beyond, elaborate gardens ran down the hill, and next there was Lord Tyo's game park, full of spotted antelope, blond foxes, and rare tigers whose eyes were blue.

The aristocrat met Coor Krahn in a marble yard. It had a marble cistern of water, where great gold and black carp swam, or put up bold heads to look at them – at which Tyo laughed, and fed them dainties, and stroked them, too. A nightingale sang by day, in a mulberry tree of purple fruit.

"How may I assist you, Lord Tyo?"

Tyo only smiled, and the servant refilled their cups.

"I need nothing, Sword's Man. I have no enemies. Nor any war-goals: I possess already almost everything I want."

Coor did not frown, though he suspected now duplicity. Tyo was handsome, perhaps a year or so younger than himself. Tyo's manner was frank and charming.

"Then, my lord, you're too generous. If you require no service from me, I'm uneasy at accepting your gift."

"Please keep the armlet. I collect such things – it's my pleasure to gift them. Your service to me you perform in allowing me to meet with you. I'd heard much of you, Coor Krahn, your valor and ability."

"You're again too generous, Lord Tyo."

"Then permit my excess. Dine with me – stay in this house, and lie soft for once. There are many diversions here. I also collect curious creatures . . . and there are lovely women, if you incline to them."

Coor Krahn did frown. He said, "I am a Sword's Man. When you heard of me, had you never heard that?"

"And married to the blade? Naturally. But surely that isn't always so . . ."

Coor Krahn felt a low dull anger. (In his mind he remembered the falling empty scabbard.) Did this lordling dare insult him? "With myself, Lord Tyo, always it is so."

"Forgive my ignorance, then. I'm sorry to have offended you, my noble guest. But stay and dine."

"I'm bound elsewhere."

As Coor said this, the Sword lay heavy at his thigh. He was very conscious of her. No, he was not bound elsewhere, for she had bound him here. But why – for this? To bear with this rich fool and his rich fool's whims?

"Must you hurry on your road? Is it an urgent mission?"

Now Coor did not answer, scorning a lie.

And his silence, Lord Tyo Lionay took, it seemed willfully, for agreement.

He dreamed of the Sword that night, when he slept on the silken bed, at Tyo's mansion. A girl had come to bathe him, a lovely girl indeed, with skin like cream and hair like night rain. But he sent her out. After this, and the heavy food and wine, sleep and the dream came swiftly.

Sas-peth Satch lay by him on the bed in Tyo's house. She was naked as a Moon, and at once put her hands upon him, watching him as his excitement mounted, playing his body like her instrument until orgasm released him with its death.

"You see that I reward you," said Sas-peth then.

"Yes, my lady. I'm rewarded beyond all treasures."

"Then you will cease your argument with me."

"I'd never argue against you, Sas-peth."

"But you have."

"How have I?"

"You resist my will that you remain here."

"Ah, lady," he sighed. "*Here?*"

"Here."

"In this house?"

She said nothing.

"If you demand it, I shall. But won't you tell me—?"

She rose, and stood, garbed suddenly again, in the facile way of dreams (and magic) in her scarlet garments. She turned her face aside from him. For a second she seemed to him nearly evasive. "Do you question me still?"

"Not your *right* to command me, lady, only the reason. A warrior isn't made for much of such a life. Perhaps with me – not even for a single day. To *lie soft*, and eat and drink over and again, and talk and talk – to tell stories of his acts that sound like boasting, to listen constantly to some lord's worthless chat – *he* jabbers like some farmgirl—"

Between one word and the next, she was gone. Like the firefly by the well, her glow winked out, and he lay alone in the dream, and waking, under his hand her steel was that of an icicle, so his palm seemed stuck to her and scalded by her coldness.

"How have I angered you, Sas-peth, Sas-peth Satch?"

He knew. He had resisted. She was his empress; he must obey.

Coor Krahn turned over sullenly to his left side, letting go of her as sometimes – rarely – had happened in sleep. He lay with his back to her, and in the marble court below the nightingale sang on, like a clockwork engine, itching inside his brain.

"May I see it? – pardon my clumsiness – may I see *her*? I mean, the Sword?"

It was the second day here. Coor looked at Lord Tyo, who stood there, mannerly, groomed and good looking, ingenuous perhaps, or merely stupid.

"A warrior doesn't give over his Sword to any man but his brothers, his master, or his smith."

"I meant, evidently, that you should hold her, but perhaps I might look. Her power's very glamorous. It attracts me."

"Let me enlighten you, my lord. What you ask is like wanting a squint at my prick." Coor Krahn had intended uncouthness. But Tyo only put back his head and laughed. Coor Krahn said ironly, "She is only drawn out for me, in privacy. Unless I draw her to kill. If another man sees her, as you ask to do, she must taste his blood."

Tyo gazed straight in his eyes. Tyo's eyes were steady and pure.

"If that's the price, I would pay it. I take it you mean a sip, not my life's blood. I've heard of this custom, I believe. Yes, why not."

The provision of the blood – a sip, as the wretch had said – had been made of necessity. There could come certain occasions when, as Coor had mooted, a Sword must be drawn outside the need of war. For repair, or before a peer. Then the Sword's Man himself did not give her his own blood. Some fitting other was selected, by the warrior, his School or the smith, one who reckoned himself honored to be used, and would wear the scar of her bite with colossal pride.

"Again, I've offended you, my dear," said Tyo familiarly, and Coor wished to slap him like some silly slattern fumbling him at an inn.

"You make light of what is profound," said Coor Krahn.

"Not I. I'm caught in the web of her fascination. Soon you'll be gone. I must take up again my restricted life. Do you really grudge me this? Oh then, I'll say no more."

A board game was brought. They ate ash-plums, and played it, as if it mattered.

In Coor Krahn a fury was rising like a storm. It began in him on the second day at the mansion, by which time anyway he was already sick of the place and everything it held. The decorative food curdled in his belly, the nightingale hurt in his ears. The tamed beasts that strolled about the marble corridors, and lay sunning themselves in Tyo's park – where his lordship did not even hunt them – seemed to be other versions of Coor Krahn, also trapped and tamed, his teeth grown sticky from candies. Ten days and nights went like this. All alike. Music was played them, girls rippled in lascivious dances, board games were set for table-wars, intellectual verses read out. The lord and Coor rode and dined, and talked, and talked, and separated only to sleep. Tyo was affectionate and nearly deferential, so that Coor came to believe this lord found him most amusing. Not one dream came to Coor, not one dream of her, to tell him what he should do. Except, alone with her one night, he said, "Let me go from here, my lady. Or I must go from here – without your letting me." And in the dark spaces of sleep after this, he thought he caught a glimpse of her, faint as a candle flame, miles ahead and carried away from him. And he followed in vain.

*   *   *

Perhaps the eleventh night arrived, or the twelfth; twelfth – the number it was sometimes believed was unlucky. He had that day ridden all over the park (as if searching for escape) and the tigers had watched with lolling tongues. In sleep he saw Sas-peth walking under the Sun with a tiger, which had red eyes, not blue. And he followed, but now not in vain, although he did not instantly catch up to her.

If it was the fool's park they were in, he was not sure. But it was a park, cultivated, the trees grown for effect, pruned to ardent shapes that obscured no possible vista.

He came on Sas-peth Satch again suddenly. She waited under a cedar, and the tiger was gone. She looked away and away, and when Coor spoke to her, she did not reply, or turn to him. And then he realized that another was there with her, someone that he, Coor Krahn, could not see, so that at first he took the vague figure only for a shadow – although Sas-peth, in dreams, cast no shadow at all.

"Here I am," she said, "do you see?" But not to Coor Krahn.

The shadow-figure became a little less vague. It held out its arm, and Sas-peth put her hand on this arm.

Who is this that she touches?

Then there was nothing there, and she looked back at Coor Krahn, and her face was expressionless as she said to him, "I have not called you to me, Coor Krahn. What do you want? Must I forbid you, like a child, to follow me at such times?"

She had been communing with some spirit of her own kind, he reasoned. He felt shamed, and begged her forgiveness. But she merely looked away once more, and then he woke, and the fury stirred blindly inside him, like thunder under a hill.

Still, time passed. It hurt him, each wasted hour an injury. But why was the hurt so much? It was a pleasing place, this small place. No, it was a hell for him. Sleeping or waking, here he was, with this pampered lord fool, like the lord fool's slave. And the fool wanted a look at the naked Sword, and would pay in fool's blood . . .

*   *   *

They were in the marble courtyard when the fury burst, staining the air, and the aura of Coor Krahn's soul, with a black shot by fire.

But Lord Tyo did not seem to notice. Urbanely he toyed with an ivory gamepiece, smiling on.

"*Then*, my lord, if you *say* no more, *I* say as you did, *why not?*"

Stunned, bewildered, Tyo blinked at him.

And Coor Krahn put his right hand over on to the hilt of his Sword.

When he touched her she was like some electric thing. Sparks flew up inside his arm, but he wrenched her from the scabbard with a noise like a rusty scream, and in the air she blazed and rang, slicing the light of day like gauze. The whole landscape seemed to gasp and petrify in awe. The Sun, wounded, trickled sparkling on her blade's edge. And Tyo stared up at her, where the Sword's Man had lifted her high into the sky. Tyo was white, he was trembling. He said softly, "So beautiful she is. Better than any jewel. Better than anything, even a woman dressed in lilies."

"Yes, so she is. Better than anything." The rage now had remade Coor Krahn. He was remote and in control of himself. It was like a battle-anger, and yet, not quite. "She's thirsty, too. Are you ready?"

"Yes."

"So brief a word. Only one? I thought you'd talk more. Bare your arm for her, then."

Tyo rent his sleeve. Expensive sequins spun off like tears, or like the blood to come.

Coor Krahn slit the aristocrat's skin with great delicacy, being careful not to cut too deep, as he longed to do, careful not to shear off his foul and hated head.

Tyo made no sound. The blood welled up, and Sas-peth Satch drew herself along, by means of Coor Krahn's grip, all the flat of her shining blade, until she was scarlet from hilt to tip.

And in that moment, as once before, long ago, Coor Krahn knew her secret.

He snatched her off, and in that same movement, she dropped from his hand, his fingers nerveless. She fell away from him. She fell at the feet of Tyo Lionay.

Tyo whispered, "What – what is it? Pick her up, man. She's not some stick – she's a Sword."

"Pick her up? No, let her lie there."

"What are you thinking of, Sword's Man? Have you gone mad?"

"Yes. It could drive me there."

"*Take her up.*"

"You take her." Tyo gaped at him, his color oddly coming back from shock, though he swayed like an uprooted tree. "You take her, Tyo Lionay. It's you she's chosen."

"This is madness."

"I told you, perhaps it is. But now I see. Why she sent me here. She *smelled* you, like the fruit trees. I should have seen through her, she showed me often enough, in her own woman's way."

"Coor Krahn—"

"Don't speak my name to me, you thing of shit. Take her and keep her. Here's the scabbard too." It went down by her, on the marble, with a crack. "Keep her with your other collected stuffs. Take her to bed at night. See what you dream."

And turning, he left Lord Tyo, still somehow standing, among the scattered Sun on gold and red, and above the faithless Sword that had named herself The Woman In Scarlet, since she must always be sheathed in blood.

Only when he reached the city of Gazul did he stop for as long as a day and a couple of nights. And then he left Gazul and went on, into the desert beyond.

Events had happened before that, during three months of travelling. He had been called for by a pair of lords, to fight for them. He said No. But then a peasant village had entreated him to rid them of a local tyrant, showing him the bodies of four young men whipped to death. So there Coor had paused for an afternoon. He had had to ask them for a sword. It was a rough old thing, some tarnished heirloom of the village overseer, but it did his work well enough. He saw then, with a deep bitterness, that it was his own skill in combat, as much as any weapon, which gained results.

Afterward, they begged him to keep the sword. They said they would be vainglorious, telling others they had given the sword to a Sword's Man whose own blade was currently under repair. (They were so restricted in their knowledge, they had not faltered at his lack of his Sword, and concocted this explanation from spontaneous ingenuity.)

He accepted the old sword, and refused other payment. He left the slain tyrant for them to tear in ritual pieces and bury in twenty different unmarked graves. (The man had been a monster.) Inasmuch as he could feel anything, save his bitterness and insane agony, Coor was not sorry to have helped the village.

The ugly old sword was quite good, quite reliable. At another place, after another fight, he had it new-surfaced and strengthened, and made a little heavier, to suit him. Here at the smith's, no one offered comment. Only the smith's boy asked anxiously if he should find a worthy man, so the drawn sword could taste blood. Coor Krahn did not answer. It was the smith who shut the boy's mouth with a glare. Even fancied up, it was sufficiently obvious this sword was not any sort of Sword.

Coor Krahn did not speculate on how others regarded the facts. Probably they invented halfway logical tales, as the village had. The Sword's Man's true Sword was being mended or specially garnished. Instead of impatiently awaiting her, he had journeyed on, and would then go back to collect her. Or maybe some of them realized he had lost his Sword, supposed she was broken, or taken from him, perhaps even dishonorably. But where they required his talents, and he gave them, no one expressed an opinion.

He slept under trees, under hills, in caves, at the wayside. He would not go in to sleep in any house, hovel, or palace.

There was, in the third month, a woman in a town a few miles from Gazul. She was a paid girl of the streets, but clean and pretty and young. When she spoke to him he went with her through the back alleys to her tiny dwelling. He had lain with only one, and that in dreams. This girl was limber and cunning, and scented with jasmine, but although he could rise up and enter her gate, though he could ride her well enough that she sobbed and melted like warm honey, there was no resolution for him. He could not reach it. And at last he pretended, as she herself might normally have done.

She would not presently accept payment, not, she said, because he was a warrior, but because of the pleasure he had given her. She vowed too, on a mighty god, she would tell no one he had lain down with her. "Tell any you like," he said. "Tell them, Coor Krahn had you." And then she shrank from his face.

There were never any dreams save the dreams any man might have, save once. Then he did dream, he thought, that far off he saw her – saw *her* – Sas-peth. She was standing up in water, like the sea, the waves shattering round her in white mirrors. But she was a woman only to her hips, and from there she was only a Sword, her female center locked in steel, impenetrable. And her face was averted from him, and anyway at a distance.

Gazul was closing the gates when he reached them. It was night, but a city night, thick-starred with lit windows and gaudy paper lanterns. He stayed that night, and the following day and night. He entered nowhere, not even an inn. He wandered the streets, the marketplace, and was stared at, and he heard the mutter: *Look! A Sword's Man.* But then he heard them saying, But whose sword is that? Never his. That old battered black cleaver. What can that be about? Of course this was a city. They were sophisticated and had no manners. Next morning, when the gates were opened, he walked away.

Look! Look! He thought he heard them cheeping. *There he goes into the waste land. What is he at? Why? Why?*

Oh, I could tell you, he thought.

And then, when he looked back, and Gazul was only a smudge of Sun on the horizon, and the barren Earth, powdered with dust, unrolled before him like existence, he wept. The tears were hard as bits of marble to shed. They tore his eyes and lay salty on his face like blood.

He sat under a lean, crippled tree and crumbled the dry dirt in his fingers.

Coor Krahn recalled the first Sword he ever saw, the Sword in the jade scabbard, when he was nine, at Pigs City. He had learned then that such a blade was always capable of seducing another, man or boy, of leading him on. But she did not then give herself to him. She stayed faithful to her husband. Only his Sword, only Sas-peth Satch, The Woman In Scarlet, had betrayed her bonded warrior.

He thought he might as well sit there, in the dust, under the tree, until he died. He drew the black sword, which was sexless, not even male, and laid it down. Coor told the sword he was sorry, and thanked it for its service. He would bury the sword, it deserved that much. But first Coor Krahn would use it to cut his veins.

However, he had not slept for two nights and two days. He fell asleep before he could pick up the black sword again.

She came to him in the night.

The desert, in the dream, was gilded by faint fires. A round Moon of red amber was nailed in the sky above.

Sas-peth had been brought here apparently in a roofed litter, tasseled and draped with silk, by slaves, and these all waited for her some way off. She wore her scarlet, and many jewels. Her hair was elaborately dressed.

"Coor Krahn," she said, "say my name to me."

He looked at her. He paused, and then said, "Your name is *The Bitch*."

Her face did not alter. He had never seen her angry, only stern for battle. While during love, she had been amorous, sly, coaxing. Never passionate, or tender.

"Why are you here?" he said.

"What do you believe the reason might be?"

"To show me he adorns you with silk and jewelry. Does he wear you to war, too, that little boy, Tyo?"

"There are no wars in Tyo's place."

"Rest there, then. Rest and rust."

"Shall I come back to you?" she asked, surprising him, jolting his heart to the core. "What would you do?"

"How can you come back, unless I go and fetch you, Sas-peth? Do you want me to fetch you? Want, then."

"You will do without me? How?"

He said nothing.

"And now," she said. "Imagine I were to say, I am here to show I am ready to be with you again."

"I would say, Sas-peth, that I won't have you."

"Even in your dreams? Even as a woman? Even in love?"

It was an awful thing to know, as Coor knew it, that to take to her again would be worse even than when he had been robbed of her.

Coor Krahn, in the dream, shut his eyes and commanded himself: "*Wake* now."

But when he opened his eyes, he was still in the dream with her. And now she stood naked, pale as ivory, her hair combed down and down.

"No, Sas-peth," he said, "it was Tyo you wished to have. Fill his dreams, not mine. Let him wear away his spirit on your edge. In all the lands, I never heard a story of one such as you. Did I shame you in combat? Did I fail you? Did I abuse the poor, insult the helpless? Was I a drunkard, a cheat, a coward – was I a weakling or an idiot? Or *unchaste*? Go out of my dream, you whore."

She turned away. It seemed to him then, in all his dreams of her, she had so often, just like this, turned from him, hiding, masking herself in his trust or his lust. Worse than that, in his respect for her.

"What life will you have," she said, "without me?"

"What life indeed."

"It was a passing desire," she said, head turned, strands of her fine hair blowing like smoke against the Moon. "A momentary, weightless thing, to be with that other one, to live another way. But only for a while, a little minute. And perhaps, I tested you." (He knew she lied.)

Bluntly he said, "What could he give you?"

"Nothing," she said softly, the woman Sas-peth.

"And that," said Coor Krahn, "is all now you will get from me."

Then she turned back, and she was beside him, lying against him on the dust, her arms wound round him and her lips on his. "I have been everything to you," she said. "I am your life."

"So you are. I see it now, Sas-peth. I'd thought I would have to die, and I was wrong in that."

He held her fast with his left arm, and with his right hand, drew up the old black genderless sword, which had come into the dream with him, as it seemed for this purpose. Coor Krahn drove the sword into her, up through her belly into her heart.

Her head curved back, and she looked at him, his Sword. She looked at him a long while, not speaking, until her eyelids fell like two white petals.

Raising his face from hers, Coor Krahn saw a lion standing on the desert, the red Moon between its ears. Eventually it vanished, but Sas-peth Satch did not. She lay heavy as lead in his arm until he let her go, and woke at last.

With sunrise, he buried the black sword, as he had promised.

In the Sword-School of Curhm-by-Ocean, he was questioned all the days of three more months, terrible questions on and on, over and over. They examined his dreams too (in none of which did she appear). They drugged him and beat him and starved him and made him drunk. And in the end, when they were sure he had not lied, they made him well again, scoured out like a shell. That day he was brought a new Sword that had been made randomly for him, or for one in his predicament. It was one of only twelve hoarded at any given time, in a secret store against such a need as his own. Coor Krahn was told, and it was the elderly master who told him, so he should grasp it could not be false, that, though it had not often come about, the thing which had happened with him, yet, along the years, still it was clandestinely known. He was not the only one to die this death.

The new Sword was male. It had no name, was his to name. It was a slave, not an empress, but a mighty slave, headstrong, gorgeous, and dangerous as that other slave who might rebel, fire.

Once Coor had come to know it, and wore it at his side, and walked with it, he met it in a dream. In the flesh it was himself, but younger, and a little less, and a little more crazy. It – he – laughed, the new Sword, clowning, amusing Coor. Coor Krahn called it, therefore, Coor's Brother.

Then the master took Coor Krahn half a mile down to a small room in the rock below the School's temple, and showed him a horrible thing, which was a line of narrow vitreous boxes.

These were the graves of some twenty-five or twenty-six or -seven Swords, mostly broken in pieces. And the last of the metal corpses was Sas-peth Satch. But she was pierced tidily right through, not mutilated. She had kept her glamour. Even ruined, she was beautiful, peerless.

"He sent her here to us," the master said, "Lord Tyo Lionay. He found her lying so on his floor one morning. She'd cut him as she fell. He will always carry the scar. He knew enough to want her, and enough to know what had been done. He sent jewels with her, rubies and pearls. Removed, as you see. He begs your forgiveness."

"He will never have that," replied Coor Krahn, without interest. Then he said very low, "But is she dead? Yes. She's dead. I see she is. Sas-peth, better than rubies and pearls."

The sword shone, even without light. In memory he gazed again at the closing of her petal lids, her smooth hair poured in the dust. He murmured to himself, "Perhaps."

FLOTSAM

Bradley P. Beaulieu

Strange how one can be so close to freedom, yet still wish for death. Freedom: the water below the bowsprit I rested on; water that would welcome me with open arms had I so chose; water that I had loved so much, but now found to be mocking, perhaps more so among the closeness of the harbor.

I began to shift backwards to escape the water's call when two sets of footsteps crept on to the forecastle deck behind me. I shrugged my shoulders tight, wishing them to be gone, anticipating the humiliation to come.

"It doesn't wear clothes," a young male said.

"Yes, never has." This, the captain's niece, present from the moment we docked to the moment we left again.

The boy giggled. "You can see its poop-hole."

"I told you!"

I despised that the humans' sense of decency had worn off on me, but still I turned to hide my privates from them. Twenty years with another culture would do this to even the most antithetical society.

The boy gasped, and his heart beat faster. "What happened to its eyes?"

"They're just glossed over, see? He's a shaman. They're born with no eyesight."

Not strictly true, I thought, but close enough to the truth.

The boy's footsteps came closer. "Looks like rotted cheese."

"Told you." The girl came closer as well. Though she feigned confidence, I could hear her heartbeat catching up to her brother's. The coarse skin of her hand ran along the smoothness of mine. Her touch brought some feelings of

resentment, but the simple reminder of youth and its innocence shadowed such thoughts.

"Come here," she said. "His skin's like an eel."

The boy's sweat mingled with the dead-fish smell of the
harbor. His footsteps receded.

"Scared as a mouse," the girl said with feigned disgust, yet
she backed away quickly, too.

From the quarterdeck, a liquid voice rose above the gulls
and creaking wood of ships at dock. "Necra. What are you
doing?" Captain Hoevin's long stride echoed over the main
deck towards us.

The children scuttled to one side. "Nothing, Uncle Hoevin,"
the girl said.

His steps halted a few paces short of me. "Nothing indeed.
The yeavanni are not pets, least of all Khren here."

"Yes, Uncle."

"Off with you now. We're nearly ready to depart."

Just then, a thundering crack pealed over the harbor. The
concussion struck a moment later – long before I had a chance
to cover my ear-pads. The pain of it coursed through me, and
only long breaths later did it recede to a dull pain.

"Go, I said!"

The children's scattered footsteps left the forecastle
deck and diffused into the maelstrom of other sounds and
the ringing in my own ears. The captain shifted slowly to
the gunwale.

He didn't speak for some time. "We need to talk, Khren."

"Perhaps we do, Captain."

"You've heard the cannons, no doubt."

He knew that I did, so I said nothing.

"The new sightings are nearly complete, and the fleet's
ready to set sail. Tonight."

Still I said nothing. I was unsure where the human wished
to take the conversation.

"Your . . . race. You've been an immense help to us over the
years. And despite whatever advantage the king may have
taken, *I* appreciate it. You've saved my men a dozen times.
More."

His words shed from me like water slipping over yeavanni skin.

"Well. The king decided to wait until now to give his latest request. We're to fight through the blockade to the south. They're ready to tear down the walls of Trilliar, and we cannot allow it."

A low laugh escaped my throat. As with most humans that hear such sounds, the captain's heart quickened. "You mean *you* will fight, Captain."

"No, Khren. You will fight, too."

"I will not. Our atonement does not include battle."

The captain's fingers drummed against the wooden railing. He smelled of rum and garlic. "He's offered to free you of your commitment if you do this."

My response died in my throat. What simple words Hoevin had spoken . . . but what promise they held. "The king would forgive us?" My own question barely made sense to me.

"Yes. One battle – provided we win – is the last service he shall require from you. From all of you."

I turned from the captain, unable to be near him any longer, and crawled further up the bowsprit. I opened my mind to the water; how I longed to drop into its arms and return to my people, return to those I had come to believe were lost to me forever. But at what price? The king would have us kill when death is what delivered us to him in the first place.

Behind me, the captain shuffled some steps away. "Think on it, Khren. Think of your home, your people."

Waves lapped against the hull of the ship. The sounds beckoned me, begged me to join them among the waters, to swim with them and follow my brothers home. But my stomach soured at the captain's words – they had the taint of deception and corruption upon them. Fight for us, and be freed, they said. But kill, and lose our eternal salvation. Such urges tempted while trapped within this mortal shroud.

With a broken heart, I turned from the water and shimmied up the jib-line to the foremast. I stayed as far away from the water as I could, for I didn't know if I could resist the calls of the sea much longer.

I felt the night breeze as it tugged the ship against the ocean current below. A school of dolphin splashed through the waves on the portside; a few strays played to starboard as well. I leapt free of the bowsprit and dove into the water, unable to resist its call any longer.

The cool water met me, and I rejoiced in a deep dive below the ship's keel. A large dolphin nudged my back. I could feel the waves of its escape before me. I pursued, catching up easily until the beast tired of my simple chase and sped off into the deep. In my prime, I could keep up with schools of dolphin, but as twilight touched the ocean of my life, I could only rely on their sympathy.

The ship's motion, ahead and above, washed over me. The trickle of the dolphin pod did the same, but it came staccato, as opposed to the deep bass of the ship.

Something else lingered nearby – behind and below. I turned and felt for the presence, unsure of the source – but I had an inkling. I sent a bellowing call through the water; a moment later, a haunting reply was returned. Another yeavanni, and this one I was not so sure I wanted to speak to.

I felt the yeavanni swim nearer, heard the trickle of its movement through the deeps. He stopped nearby and performed a slow pirouette. *At least he still shows respect*, I thought.

"Khrentophar," he began, "it is good to have you near."

"And you, Iulaja."

We swam together, trailing the ship by a half-league.

"I bring news," Iulaja said, "though I'm sure you've heard some of it already."

I was pleased to feel the link between us build. I could feel his concern over the humans' battle. "Of the war? Yes, I know of it."

"I've come from the other ships, and the queen before that." An eagerness overcame Iulaja then. A joy.

"The queen wishes us back, does she?"

Confusion touched him for only a moment. "Yes, as do the other shaman. They have agreed to fight this human battle, and be done with them."

Sorrow overcame my heart. "They have all agreed?"

"Yes, all of them, Khrentophar. All but you."

I couldn't speak for a moment. *All of them?* "You asked them before coming to me."

Iulaja's mind echoed his embarrassment. "You would have convinced them otherwise, Khrentophar. Our villages would have you back home. I would step down so that you might return to your proper place."

We swam in silence for a time, catching up to the ship. A school of greyridge whales harrooned their song into the night. Iulaja drove before me and brought me to a halt. His anger soured the water between us.

"Do you wish to talk like the humans, still and unmoving? Have you become so like them that you wish to stay until your dying day?"

"In truth, Iulaja, I would welcome my dying day. These humans lay foul on my tongue, ring with clangor in my ears, drive coral under my skin. If Yeavan, in her divine guidance, would summon me to the depths, I would rejoice and sing so that all the yeavanni could hear." I began swimming again, forcing Iulaja to keep pace. "Yet I will not lose my place in her land to further the goals of these land-ridden beasts."

The water turned colder.

"You have paid a score times the deathbond price. Twenty years, Khrentophar! The sinking of their ship was an *accident*. *They* stumbled on to *our* lands in a hurricane."

"A hurricane we summoned."

"As a ritual to our Goddess! I don't understand why, but I believe she wanted them dead. Those humans care nothing for Yeavan; they don't bow to her will, nor does she have dominion over them or we would have had you back long before now. Do you truly think she wished for this to happen after Khuum Livva, her holiest day?"

"I think, Iulaja, *shaman* of our people, *keeper* of her faith, that she will guide us as she sees fit. I cannot willingly murder for them. I will not."

Iulaja turned away in heat and anger. He swam to one side and turned back. "Then you can stay with them, Khrentophar, though it rots my heart to see it so. Farewell."

"Begone, traitor," I said to him.

Iulaja's echoes trailed off and were lost among the din of the dolphin pod.

"Begone, dear Iulaja," I said to the sea. "May she keep you well."

The ship had pulled ahead, but I caught up to it quickly. I dove up from beneath the prow and leapt from the water to grasp the bowsprit and swing around. I dropped down to my typical, folded pose, hating the simple fact that I *had* one.

A heartbeat from behind startled me. The distinctly human rhythm was small, frail. No human man had such a signature. I could not at first remember who it belonged to, but it came to me shortly.

"Come out, girl. It's no use hiding from someone blind to the world."

After a moment, I heard her tentative footsteps sidle up the gunwale.

"I don't think your uncle would approve."

Her heartbeat sped up. So impressionable, these humans.

"Please don't tell him. I wanted to go to war. I wanted to help fight the enemy."

She *wanted* to? My heart wept at such a statement. How can they still live when even their children hunger to kill?

"What would make you want such a thing, child?"

"They killed my father. He was a captain, like Uncle Hoevin."

"Why don't you search for a way to reconcile instead?"

The girl seemed taken aback, for she said nothing for a long time. "Because they killed him." Her voice was tentative, but it grew stronger the more she talked. "They killed everyone on the ship, even those they took hostage."

"And peace? When will that come?"

"When I have revenge. Then we can have peace."

I laughed; again the girl's heart raced as she stepped away. "Yes, child. That is the way of your world, isn't it?"

"I don't understand."

"No, you wouldn't. I should call your uncle." Before she could plead for my silence, I continued. "Go. I won't tell. Perhaps if you see war with your own eyes, you won't be so quick to embrace it. Go."

She took two steps back, but then her feet turned. "Can I talk to you more? Will you tell me what you meant?"

Tell her? Among the rotted places of my heart, a clear note rang out. Teach a human child. Is this what Yeavan had in store for me? Have I endured twenty years of heartache to bring them into her fold? As quickly as the note had sung out, it was smothered by the drums of war.

"We will see, child. We will see."

Long after she had hidden herself beneath the canvas of the rowboat, I pondered her words.

On the fourth day from port, the sun warmed my back as I lounged on the bowsprit, smelling the sea.

A brass bell rang three times, cutting through the wind. I clapped my hands over my head and hunkered down tightly.

The thunder of a cannon broke the calm, rattling my head despite my meager protection. Far to the starboard side, the splash of the cannonball broke a wave, and again further away, and more times as it skittered over the sea's surface.

"That's enough, men," Captain Hoevin called. "Secure the cannons."

A league or more behind us, another cannon peal broke over the waves. Twelve other ships had joined the fleet in the last two days, and according to the captain, the other seven would be joining us shortly. We were now only a half-day's sail from the besieged city of Trilliar.

The minds of my fellow shaman called from the other ships – two were ahead, on the flagship and another gargantuan vessel, and the others behind. With each that came nearer, the bond between us strengthened.

The captain had found his niece, Neera. She had been allowed to stay, for with the battle so near and the city at such need, the captain could no longer justify returning home. To my surprise, she had kept her promise, returning to speak to me several times each day. She asked of my home and the other yeavanni villages on the far side of the sea. She asked how I could manage without eyes, how I could talk with the other shaman, how I could control the seas. All of these I answered as best I could, and in truth, my heart rejoiced at the chance to speak of Yeavan and her ways.

Even if the girl never learned, never believed, it was an outpouring that had been damming up inside me for years. Too many years, I thought. So many that the speaking of such things brought back a yearning such as I hadn't felt in a long time.

My proud words of faith to Iulaja felt hollow to me now. In the bowels of my mind I had to admit that, had the enemy appeared before me right there and then, I might have slaughtered them all simply to go home. Iulaja had a point, after all. Yeavan did not speak of ritual with other races. What were human lives to her? Did we not war with our enemy, the salazaar? Did Yeavan not sanction such actions when necessary? Ah, but there lies the rub: this felt too much like murder, instead of defending our people.

Footsteps padded over the forecastle deck, and I broke the contact with my brothers and sisters, perhaps embarrassed at the relationship I had fostered with the human girl.

"Uncle says the battle will begin tomorrow."

"Yes."

"Will you fight?" she asked, spoken like she was unsure what she wanted the answer to be.

"No, child, I will not."

She stepped to the gunwale and tapped something metal against the wood of the rail.

"That's probably best," she said, "seeing as you want to fall to Yeavan's arms."

I laughed. The girl's heartbeat, to her credit, barely rose. She'd become more accustomed to yeavanni sounds over the last few days.

"And you? Do you still wish for revenge?"

Her tapping ceased. "I don't know. I'm still angry."

"Mortals can expect no less."

"There are still times when I wish them dead."

"The mind wanders, child. You cannot hope to still all such thoughts. What of revenge?"

"No. I guess I don't want it anymore." She laughed. "I won't even see the battle in any case. Uncle has me in the cook's larders for the whole thing."

"That's for the best, I would think."

We lapsed into silence, and I breathed the sea air deeply. Below, the sound of something small breaking the water's surface hid among the breaking waves. I closed my eyes, and opened myself up to the sea. The object tasted metallic.

"What did you wish for, child?"

Her heart skipped. "I thought you couldn't see."

"The sea sees much for these dead eyes."

"I . . . I wished for the enemy to break before we reached Trilliar. I don't want to see war anymore."

As if devouring the girl's naive thoughts, a brass bell's clanging broke the silence. I had been with this ship for two decades, and never had it rung with the nervous fervor I heard then. But, then again, never had we been in true battle. Across the sea, bells rang from the other ships.

"Enemy flags, Captain. Ten degrees to port, coming round the cliffs."

The ship came to life, men moving about, some climbing through the rigging above. Rope creaked and sure feet pounded their way to their stations.

"How many?" the captain called.

"Over a score or I'm a king's fool."

Neera moved to port and hopped up on the railing. Her heart beat faster than the bell had rung. "How soon?" she asked.

"Depends whether the fleet runs or not."

"How close are the other ships?"

I opened myself to the other shaman. At the edge of our awareness, the other seven approached. "An hour if we turn to meet them."

Heavy boots climbed up the forecastle stairs. Neera moved out along the bowsprit and grasped my hand. The contact surprised me, but it was oddly touching as well. No human had ever held my hand in such a way.

"He'll send me away now. Good luck."

"May she preserve you, child."

"Neera!" Captain Hoevin bellowed. "Get your mischievous hide below decks!"

Neera gave one last squeeze before shimmying back to the deck. Her footsteps receded as the captain's approached.

"One hour if we turn around, Captain," I said.

Words died on his breath, and he paced for a few moments. "With their ships, I don't think we have that much time. Will you help us?"

"I will relay information from the other shaman and the sea, but that is all."

"We need you. Your inaction could cause more deaths than fighting."

"No, Captain; that is fool's logic. I will not take responsibility for a conflict I never began."

The captain heaved a great sigh. "I hope you change your mind, Khren, even if it's only for Neera's sake." His bootsteps grew softer as I considered his words.

For Neera's sake. Odd how one can wish for death and friendship in the same breath. Did I care for Neera so much to actually *consider* his proposal?

I leapt from the bowsprit to dive deep into the cold sea. The water welcomed me again, but I paid it little mind. Our fleet began turning to cover the distance to the trailing ships. I swam ahead, wondering how the next few hours would unfold. The enemy was not so far off that I couldn't sense them; the watchman had been right: twenty-four ships. The sea held them in its light grip, allowing them to slip through its currents to come ever nearer. I could sense the eagerness of those onboard.

Something tainted the waters, though – a taste I hadn't felt in . . . years, yet I couldn't place it. Too faint it was, but foul just the same. I began to swim forward when I felt one of my brothers dive into the sea ahead. Behind, a sister-shaman joined us, and I moved to meet them. Unlike Iulaja, my brethren merely swam with me, knowing they could not change my mind. I nearly opened my mouth to convince them to shun this course, but their anger rose with the unspoken thought, so I remained silent.

The enemy closed the distance faster than they should have been able to. Much faster. The taste like sour blood returned to my tongue, stronger. I scrambled amongst my memories for understanding.

The enemy's lead ship turned starboard to bring its cannons to bear. Together, our small group called the sea to protect us from the imminent cannon blasts. Moments later, the first of them rang out, booming through the sea around us. The sour taste became pronounced, like I had opened my mouth to a goblet full of blood.

Salazaar.

Our sworn enemy had joined battle with the enemy humans. They rode the ships – I could feel them now, each one a torch held against the cold surface of my mind. Another cannon boomed over the ocean. As the cannonball was loosed, a salazaar infused it with fire, lending it explosive strength, which released when it struck near my ship. I exhaled relief when I realized it had struck wide.

My brother and sister had already begun weaving. They swam in a complex circle, moving closer to our own ships to come between them and the enemy. More shaman dove into the waters behind us. They swam with energized fervor towards the dancing globe. Some called to me, but most spurned my presence and added their anger to the swirling call of sea and sky. Above the water, storm clouds gathered as more enemy ships brought their cannons to bear.

Our own ships, perhaps realizing that they could not outrun the salazaar-assisted sails of the enemy, turned to bring their cannons to bear as well. An entire barrage sounded from two enemy ships. I heard them claw into our flagship. Fire from the salazaar shed flame over the decking and masts.

My fellow shaman danced in a large, writhing globe, circling ever tighter. A current pushed harshly at one of the enemy ships, turning it about, despite what its rudder might wish. The same happened to the ship nearest it. The first tentative lightning strike rang down from the stormy sky, tearing into a third ship.

Our own ships fired back, and the new cannons broke one of the enemy ships. From this strike could I feel the first enemy deaths – perhaps from cannon shot, perhaps from the shredded wood as the shots struck home, perhaps drowning after being flung unconscious from their ship. The reason mattered not at all; I wept for them just the same. Even the salazaar. When the first one died, I wished, as I always had, that our peoples could have patched our indescribable differences.

But I must be honest. There was hatred, too. A small part of me relished the idea of the vile lizards dying. Indeed, as the water began to heat from their efforts, I found myself urging my brothers on.

Above us, the water's surface began to hollow until forming into a bowl, limiting the depth we had to work with. Our circle of shaman broke and began swimming away, but it was too late for some. The furthest behind, the most visible, was whisked into the air. Immediately, I felt fire ring across the distance from three separate ships and strike the hovering yeavanni.

Her death throes echoed across all of our minds, but it was followed quickly by the second and third. I could feel the glee with which the salazaar dealt their death.

I pleaded to my Goddess, *Yeavan, how can you allow this? Please, oh please, stop this insanity.*

I swam, afraid for my life. Afraid of being flung into the air like a salmon caught for the spit. The salazaar released their water-hollow, which sucked us back towards the center. The seabed churned around us, sending rock and coral to biting against our skin.

Our brothers from the other part of the fleet had arrived, though. They swam in a shaman-circle a league away, and a water spout pulled up from the sea, twisting and writhing into the sky. This they let loose on the nearest ship before drawing another from the cold depths. Iulaja was among them. I could feel his scorn as he wove his magic. His hatred soured perhaps more than the salazaar taint.

My own group of shaman regrouped and began weaving once more. They asked me, begged me, to help, and still I resisted.

The rock below us split, opening a deep channel. In moments, the water around the shaman dance flashed an incredible heat. The circle broke apart, and three more yeavanni lives were lost to the boiling sea.

Cannon peals rang above, and death's specter took more and more lives on both sides. Three salazaar used the winds to leap from their ships on to one of ours – Captain Hoevin's. I could feel their fire rip into the men aboard. With a fear I couldn't quite explain, I dug through the water towards my ship. What I planned to do, I had no idea. But I remember how striking it was that a sense of loyalty had sprung up inside me.

I reached the ship and leapt up from the water to the bowsprit. Only two of the salazaar remained. The heat from their flame touched nearly all of the sails. I nearly blacked out from the intensity.

Captain Hoevin screamed from the quarter deck. "Reload, men. Quickly, by God!" I heard him run forward and the sound of his rapier coming free came just before another salazaar blast raked the quarter deck. Ten men screamed, including Captain Hoevin.

"No!" I screamed, impotent in my rage.

The next blast, I could tell, was directed especially towards the captain. I followed his maniacal shrieks as he ran across the main deck. The distinct sound of steel biting flesh rose above it, and then a salazaar howl broke over the din.

His foul brother sent one more blast into the captain, and Captain Hoevin fell lifeless and burned to the deck. Another body fell: the wounded salazaar.

Neera's calls broke the relative silence that followed. "Uncle!"

"No, child! Don't go near him! Run!"

My warning had little effect, and by any measure, it was too late. Another blast from the remaining salazaar scoured young Neera as she ran. Her body struck the nearby gunwale with a thud, and a moment later, she splashed into the sea.

In that one instant – the instant I realized Neera's fate – I lost my tentative hold on my mind. A gurgle escaped my throat; a sound of pain and regret; a burst of hatred and revenge.

A warcall.

I leapt from the forecastle deck, pulling the strength of the sea with me. My leap took me on to the salazaar's back, and, though my hands and feet sizzled, I bore him to the ground and wrenched him over to face me.

The fetid beast began to speak, but my tightening forearm silenced him. I summoned the sea. For this waste of life, I needed but little, and it came eagerly in any case. A snake of water slipped up the side of the ship and over the railing. It slithered closer and reared up behind me. The salazaar felt fear. For one of the few times in my life, I dearly missed my eyesight. Seeing the look on his pitiful face as the snake dove down his mouth and nose would have been like fine wine to my parched throat. I slipped my handhold down to his shoulders now that the snake had ensured its entrance. It slipped through throat and lungs in an instant as a cacophony of burps and gurgles escaped the salazaar's throat. He could no longer breathe, but still he writhed.

I enjoyed every single moment of it.

His life was snuffed by the holy water nearly a minute later. I panted over him, wishing he had more to give me. No matter. There were more of his kind about.

I dove into the sea to rejoin my brothers and sisters. They had regrouped into one dance. There were few now, but I made one more. I swam around them, touching yeavanni flesh, coaxing more magic from them, and them from me. These podlings knew too little of death. I coaxed just the right dance from them, and together, we began a deadly ballet between water and air. We dragged the sea about the enemy ships. Our anger fueled the speed. Above, lightning rang down, snapping into salazaar and main masts, sails and rigging.

The lizards tried to pull us from the sea again, but we would no longer be caught off guard. We dove deeper, moved around the sea's hills and mountains, its tunnels and warrens. It mattered little where we danced from; the weave would still be as tight.

We called a storm, focusing solely on the enemy ships, but one yeavanni's anger touched the next. Their anger fed more, and it built and built until we thought we would burst from it. The storm scoured the sea about us. The whirlpool sucked the enemy ships down: one, two, now four and five of them gone.

A gale drove at the few ships that tried to escape. Waves lashed at those poor vessels. I pulled away from my brothers. I became the focus of their magic – the avatar to the god we had summoned. I rose above the sea on a water spout and brought the full fury of the storm and sea upon them. Six ships remained, then five, two, and finally the last had been wrecked from the power of Yeavan.

I turned about, feeling for more of them, but finding none. Where had they gone? Why could I kill no more?

Kill no more . . .

The geis over my mind began to clear. The destruction registered in a glacier crawl. *Dear Yeavan, what have I done?*

I dropped from the spout and fell listlessly into the water below. My sides tightened as I realized how large the storm had become, how dangerous – to everyone – it had grown in our thirst for revenge. Seven, perhaps eight of our ships had remained when I left my ship. Now, only two remained. Surely, several were wrecked from our own magic; the churning seas must have dragged seaman after seaman under the waves; dozens of lives snuffed by our thirst for salazaar blood. I swam about the ocean floor, wailing my sorrow to the seas around me.

It took me minutes to realize the state of the two remaining ships. One would surely founder, and the other would be a near thing. I swam quickly to the ship that might be saved, and asked Yeavan, in her grace, for one last favor. She granted this, and the water was staved from the cracks in the ship's hull. The humans inside began pumping the water out, and slowly, she began to regain her height.

My brothers joined me a short time later, though many of them felt loath to do it. *We've done enough for them*, their minds said.

"You can go home soon enough," I told them. "Give them this token, this bauble that means nothing to you."

They agreed and stayed until both ships were well enough to sail. But then they began to leave. One by one, the yeavanni shaman turned from the ships and began to swim home.

I waited until I was sure the human ships could make it without me, and then I turned away, too. But I didn't swim towards yeavanni seas. I swam towards the battle, towards the sight of my ship's sinking. I found her ruined hull in little time and searched around the remains of the once-proud ship.

I found Neera shortly after. She rested at the bottom, cupped by soft seaweed. I pulled her from the bottom and began swimming towards the departing ships.

Iulaja met me and blocked my way. "Leave her, Khrentophar. *They* fashioned this graveyard, not you. Let her rest among the other humans."

I floated nearer to Iulaja and touched his shoulder. "I will return to them, Iulaja. I owe her a deathbond."

"You . . ." His mind flared with disbelief. "None of them, not even her, deserves that. Drop her and come home."

"Yeavan protect me, but I cannot. I touched this child, Iulaja. Perhaps more of them can come to understand us."

"They will never understand us. *Never.*"

Odd, how freedom can change its meaning. I had once wished for nothing but death by the hands of my Goddess, to be free of human shackles. There, floating close to my brother, I wished only to live that I might pass on her ways.

Iulaja misunderstood my hesitation. His hand touched my shoulder, and he said, "Come, brother."

I pulled away. "I cannot."

He floated nearby for long seconds, and then his anger flared, and he swam to one side. "Begone, fool yeavanni."

I hugged Neera tight and swam away.

Long after I had left Iulaja, I heard his ever so faint words. "Begone, dear Khrentophar. May she hold you close to her heart."

A WARRIOR'S DEATH

Aliette de Bodard

The room was in the most opulent part of the sacred precincts, away from prying eyes. Rich frescoes made it seem larger than it was, and a fountain whispered its endless song, giving a pleasant coolness to the air. But the room was no longer peaceful: its sanctity had been defiled by the murder of the War-God's vessel.

The pale body lay on a makeshift altar of blood-spattered cushions, a gaping hole in its chest. It was a grotesque parody of the holiest sacrifice, and the vessel's heart was nowhere to be seen.

The War-God's high priest, Chamatl, knelt beside me. "We have touched nothing, Uzume."

"How long ago did this happen?"

He shrugged. "It happened today, that much is sure. He was still alive to receive the morning devotions."

I wondered why someone would commit such a sacrilege. The chest had been opened with several jagged cuts, nothing like the clean marks a priest's knife would have left. Gently, I raised the man's head. His eyes were open, his face twisted in a horrible grimace of pain, but his mouth was closed. According to Chamatl, no one had heard his death cries. He had died bravely, a true warrior.

And he was truly dead. Without the proper rituals for the sacrifice, the divine spark that had lived within him was rising back to the heavens – while the mortal part, torn from the divine, was making its way underground to the world of the dead. There would be no eternal reward, no ascension to godhood for the man who had offered his body as a vessel for the spirit of the War-God.

The dead man had pale hair, pale skin, and eyes the red-brown color of a deer's hide. I was unfamiliar with his race. Ten years had passed since my disgrace, and still I envied him for the honor that he'd been given. For failed warriors like me, for warriors who broke and ran on the battlefield, there was no reward, no chance of being chosen to host a god. All that was left to a disgraced warrior was the daily grind of the maize fields, a life spent alone with memories of battles.

I raised my gaze to Chamatl. "Who was he before the god took him?"

"I don't know," he said.

"Who offered him, then?"

Chamatl looked embarrassed. "Huracan, of the clan of Ertec, offered this sacrifice."

Ertec. "A merchant clan?" Had our city fallen so low?

Chamatl gazed at the frescoes. "There have been no wars this year, no warriors brought back as prisoners. It has been our sacred duty since the beginning of time to offer a vessel worthy to host the War-God, a foreigner . . ."

"Still, you could have had a war captain offer the vessel."

"I could have. But things went otherwise." Chamatl looked back at the dead man. "I trust you have seen what you needed to see? Come then. We will find a more pleasant place to speak."

We stood in the main courtyard of the sacred precincts, watching maidens practice the Dance of Deer. "Why did you want me to see this murder?" I asked.

"I need you to find who killed him. Discreetly."

"And the Festival of Renewal?" I asked. "The people will expect you to sacrifice this incarnation of the War-God so he can be reborn in the heavens and start the cycle anew. What are you going to tell Ahuatl?"

"We'll have someone ready to take his place," Chamatl said.

"In three months? I thought it took nine months of seclusion for the War-God to become fully incarnate in the body of the vessel, as it takes nine months for a child to be fully formed in the mother's womb."

"There are drugs we can use in desperate cases like these," Chamatl said. "I need to know who did this." His brow creased with worry. "The way the vessel was killed – a parody of sacrifice – implies an enemy attempt to cut us off from our god. To make Ahuatl fall."

Ahuatl. Despite my disgrace, I loved my city. I loved my people, the beauty of our stone buildings, and our language. I loved our methods of cultivation and our skill at healing the sick. "How do you know this is true?"

"Ahuatl is the greatest city in the world," Chamatl said. "We bring civilization to the barbarian countries. We give them our beauty and our skills. But not everyone loves Ahuatl as I do. There are rumors of unrest in the conquered provinces, and agitators are at work here in the city."

"The god will watch over us," I said.

Chamatl looked dubious. Behind him, the maidens had started another dance, to the measured beat of drums. "What matters to me is that Ahuatl goes on," he said. "I want the murderer brought to justice as a warning to the other agitators."

"Who are these agitators?"

Chamatl shook his head. The turquoise pectoral he wore jangled, rippling like the skin of a snake. "I don't want to unfairly influence your investigation. Go see Huracan. He'll tell you the identity of the fallen vessel."

"I see." Chamatl had his own ideas, then; people he desperately wanted to blame.

"If you do find out who killed him," Chamatl said, "I can use my influence to change your life."

"You have nothing I want."

"Not so," Chamatl said. "The vessel of the War-God must be a captured prisoner or a slave. But there are other gods you could host, Uzume."

My heart missed a beat. "You would give me this honor?"

"If you redeem yourself, yes," Chamatl said. "I can arrange for you to host the God of Spears. A minor god, to be sure, but still a god."

I took a sharp breath. That he would offer this to someone who was not a warrior . . .

To become a god. To merge with the divine nature, and come endlessly back to earth, incarnation after incarnation. To help guide and protect Ahuatl. My stomach felt hollow.

I saw the gleam of triumph in Chamatl's gaze. He had me, body and soul. And he knew it.

As I left the temple, I found myself drawn to a recent fresco of our pantheon, showing the War-God surrounded by His court. He was in the center, proud and savage; around Him was the Inner Circle; at His side, the God of Battles, crushing an enemy warrior underfoot. Beyond the Inner Circle stood the minor gods, modestly ornamented, gripping knives instead of swords. Each god's face had been painted over several times, to reflect the face of the latest vessel.

I scanned the painted faces, until I found one that was familiar.

Mixtal.

I clutched the golden pendant he had given me. A year ago, the high priests had chosen Mixtal to receive the essence of the God of Skirmishes. He had come to the maize fields to bid me farewell. I remembered the arrogant lift of his head when he delivered the news. He felt sorry for me, I saw it in his eyes, but when he left, he did not look back.

The pendant was a gift in memory of our friendship. Even though its sale would have kept me in luxury for a year, I clung to it as a reminder of what I had lost the day my courage failed me before the massed ranks of the enemy.

On the mural, the War-God dwarfed Mixtal. His face was wild with the fury of battle. With an enemy soldier under one foot, and a bloody sword in each fist, His expression was merciless; the battlefield was no place for pity. He would never understand my failure.

I released the pendant, felt its warmth against my chest.

Though I could not hope to be forgiven, I had always hoped I could redeem myself, and Chamatl was offering me a second chance. A chance at immortality. A chance to save my city.

I tore my gaze from the mural, and went to see Huracan.

* * *

The Ertec clan lived on the edge of the city, with little to distinguish their adobe houses from those of their peasant neighbors; the merchants of Ahuatl had long ago learned that an ostentatious display of wealth only angered the warriors and caused unrest. To keep the peace, the merchant class hid their luxurious gardens and comfortable rooms behind modest walls.

The opulence of Huracan's house surprised me. A two-storey building with an ornate door, it had walls frescoed with unsettling images of gods and goddesses presiding over human sacrifices: everything from beheadings to the skinning of strangled men.

Huracan himself was a tall, lean man. He received me without fuss in his inner courtyard, in the shadow of palm trees. I sipped ground cocoa beans mixed with water, enjoying their bitter taste – cocoa was a luxury far beyond my means.

"Your sacrifice is dead," I said.

"How?" Huracan had remarkable control of his face: his eyes flickered only briefly.

"Someone cut out his heart."

"That would be the usual way," Huracan said. "Although not the usual time."

He was taunting me. "He was murdered, in a mockery of the sacrifice."

"Just the heart cut out? No flute? No prayers?"

When the day for the Festival of Renewal came, the incarnation of the War-God would walk along the crowded avenues of the city, to the rhythm of sacred hymns. People would throw flowers before him; and when at last he reached the Red Pyramid, where he would be sacrificed, he would play melancholy, hollow notes on a flute of bone.

"No," I said. "The vessel was merely butchered, the War-God's manifestation incomplete."

"Poor Ralil. He wanted so much to become a god."

"He volunteered?"

Ralil. Ahuatl's warriors volunteered for the sacred duty of hosting the gods, but it was unheard of for a captured prisoner to offer himself.

"Ralil was reluctant at first, but the last time I saw him, he looked almost happy."

Happy. He shouldn't have been. What had happened to him?

I sipped my cocoa, slowly, treasuring the last of it. "Where did you get him?"

"I bought him in the marketplace because he looked healthy and strong." Huracan grimaced. My interrogation did not please him, yet he was compelled to answer. "Ralil was captured from Maenque."

Maenque. Once a year the War-God and His Court offered us their blood in sacrifice, and Ahuatl repaid them with the blood of conquered cities in minor ceremonies throughout the year. Maenque was among the last of Ahuatl's conquered cities, on the very edge of the western coast.

"Did Ralil have any relatives in Ahuatl?" I asked.

Huracan raised an eyebrow. "I offered him in sacrifice," he said. "I visited him to apprise myself of the progress of the god, but I did not keep a watch on his life." He sipped at his bitter cocoa. "He did have a countrywoman named Pochtli here in Ahuatl. She came to see him many times before he entered seclusion."

Pochtli. As a slave, she had served in the temple of the War-God; once freed, she had started weaving cactus fiber into loincloths for peasants. She had soon found herself at the head of several weaving workshops, making everything from rough clothes to fine cotton warrior-dress. There were rumors that, at night, the weaving workshops became meetinghouses for foreigners living in Ahuatl.

"Thank you," I said.

"My pleasure. Keep me informed, Uzume, will you?"

"I will do as I see fit," I said curtly. I owed this merchant nothing.

Huracan's gaze became chilly. "I am not without importance."

"Neither am I," I said.

"Ralil was my offering," Huracan said. "Do not dismiss me so lightly."

His offering. A mere merchant had offered the greatest sacrifice.

"Why were you chosen to make an offering?" The words came before I could stop them.

Huracan smiled. "Am I unworthy, then?"

I did not answer.

"Perhaps you do not like me, or my kind. But we have our uses," Huracan said. "Chamatl is an . . . acquaintance of mine. I recently completed a delicate mission for the Emperor, and as a reward, I was allowed to offer Ralil for sacrifice." Huracan must have seen my face, for he said, "Don't look so shocked, Uzume. We fight for the city in our own way, travelling to far-away places where people worship gods that do not understand the power of blood."

"You're a spy," I said. "Among other things."

Spies. That was no way to fight a war. You fought your enemy squarely on the battlefield, not through lies and knife stabs in the back. "How do you know Chamatl?"

"He buys books from me," Huracan said. Three rings glittered on his hand, each with a different stone: turquoise, obsidian, jade. "Foreign books about religion, mostly."

I sighed. One day Chamatl's curiosity would lead him into trouble with the Emperor. Chamatl believed in knowledge, devoured books, and took from them unorthodox views on religion and politics.

Though arrogant, Huracan appeared sincere. I saw no reason to trouble him further.

Pochtli's house was in the artisans' district. The streets echoed with the cries of birds kept for ornamental feathers, and the sharp chipping sounds of the workers making obsidian knives.

Pochtli kept me waiting and offered no refreshments. I sat in the courtyard of her modest house, and wondered how the War-God fared. Being torn from His flesh and sent back to the heavens must have been . . . unexpected.

At last, a slight woman entered the courtyard and glared at me, fists on her hips.

I bowed slowly, forcing a smile.

"You have no place here," said Pochtli. Her skin had a healthy tan from working under the sun, but her eyes were foreign, the same russet brown as Ralil's.

I kept my temper, but I stepped forward to loom over her. "I am Uzume, once a warrior of the Eagle Regiment. I come under the authority of Chamatl, High Priest of the War-God, who speaks for our Emperor."

Pochtli looked away and snorted. "What do you want?"

"Answers," I said. "Do you know Ralil?"

She wavered, as if trying to decide which lie to use. "Yes," she said finally. "I knew Ralil. From Maenque. He was a kinsman of mine."

"Was?" An odd thing to say; she could not know of his murder yet.

"Ralil embraced your religion when he was captured." She spat on the earthen floor of the courtyard. "He turned away from our gods and dedicated himself to yours."

I looked at the spit glistening next to my sandal, and wanted nothing more than to drag her before Chamatl for showing disrespect. But there was more at stake than my pride, so I said nothing. Ralil had embraced our faith. Perhaps this explained his enthusiasm for the sacrifice, but he had not shown such fervor at the beginning. "Are you sure Ralil was a believer?"

"Ralil accepted his fate as the vessel of a foreign god," Pochtli said. "What other explanation can there be?"

"Did he ever tell you he worshipped the War-God?"

"He didn't have to," Pochtli said. "I went to the temple to try to bring him back to reason. But he wanted to become a god. He said it was worth it." She spat again. "He said having a man from Maenque host a god of Ahuatl was in the best interest of our people. He spoke to me as if I were a fool not to share his beliefs."

Pochtli was lying. She would not meet my eyes. Her bitterness about her kinsman's conversion sounded genuine, but it gave her a reason to have arranged his death. "You hated Ralil for his choice?" I asked.

She watched me, gauging every nuance of my speech. "It's you I hate, Uzume. You and your *civilization*. What kind of civilization would steal our men and tear out their still-beating hearts, all in the name of a god who cares too little for his people, and too much for conquered land?"

"Ahuatl's patron deity is the God of War," I said. "We don't need Him to care for us; we need Him to lead us to victory."

She smiled joylessly. "You warriors all think the same. Ralil didn't understand either."

"You've been freed," I pointed out. "If you hate us so much, you should go back to your kinsmen."

"Maenque has been conquered, and my kinsmen grovel before you there, as well as here. I prefer to stay in Ahuatl."

"And try to destroy us?"

"Ahuatl deserves to fall," Pochtli said. "It will fall with or without my help. The only thing that keeps Ahuatl strong is conquest. Now that the whole of the known world belongs to your people, what will they do with it?"

"Do?"

She sighed. "The gods of Maenque do not feast on human blood. They do not require conquest. Our society is one of equals, and merciful rule. Ahuatl will fall before it."

I raised my hand to strike her, but Ahuatl does not punish those who speak their minds – only those who plot against it.

"You are on dangerous ground," I snapped. "Everything you say threatens Ahuatl. You have every reason to destroy the Feast of Renewal."

"I cannot be blamed for whatever happened to Ralil," she said.

"The man is dead. And you are a suspect in his murder."

"If Ralil is dead, good riddance."

"Did you kill him?"

"No," she said. She looked me with burning hatred. "Go away, Uzume. I told you, I have no need to make your city fall."

Pochtli despised us. Ahuatl had shown her mercy, and yet she dared to scorn us. She truly hated Ahuatl, she was happy that Ralil was dead, and she seemed quite capable of killing him. She had gone to the temple often enough to know its layout. She had access to obsidian blades in the nearby market. The knife-makers wouldn't remember her.

I left, determined to bring her to justice.

From Pochtli's house, I stopped to barter a maize cake from a shop, and ate it on the way back to the temple. In the sacred precincts, I interrogated every man, woman and child I could find – the servants, the priests, the maidens. They all knew that the War-God's vessel was dead, and they were frightened.

But none of them had seen Pochtli enter the precincts the day before.

Frustrated, I sat alone in a deserted courtyard to listen to the priests sing. They were teaching the sacred hymns, and the slow, measured rhythm of their verses lulled me into a trance.

I needed a witness to the crime, but the only witness I had was the War-God Himself. The thought frightened me; one did not summon a god with impunity, and our supreme god least of all. I was not keen on reminding the War-God of my existence, and my failure as a warrior.

Once, I had worn an elaborately embroidered cotton tunic, and a warrior's feather-headdress. At the Festival of Warriors, I garbed myself in jaguar skins, and went to the Great Plaza to join my regiment.

A maiden of the temple stepped forward to join me, wearing a ceremonial skirt with a pattern of reeds, and together we moved to the rhythm of the Dance of Serpents.

Now I wore a loincloth of cactus fibers, and I was alone.

I gripped the pendant Mixtal had given me so hard it bit into my skin, and my eyes filled with tears.

With difficulty, I composed myself, and the drone of the prayers washed over me.

"Lord, whose blood, freely given in sacrifice, renews our covenant, I call you. I have something that belongs to you." I lifted Mixtal's gold pendant so that it caught the light of the sun.

Only priests are allowed to summon the War-God, and so I dedicated my prayer to the God of Skirmishes. Mixtal.

The prayers of the priests receded, and silence flowed over me. I heard the faint cries of warriors launching themselves into battle, the low moans of enemies dying. The air smelled of freshly spilled blood. Mixtal was coming.

The God of Skirmishes coalesced and stood in the courtyard as if he had always been there, standing above me, watching me weep. He was tall, with bronzed skin, and he shone with a radiance that hurt my eyes and set my heart aflame. I wanted so much to be in his place.

"Uzume," he said. In his voice were the horns of battle.

I stood and bowed low. "Lord."

"Why have you called me?" he asked.

"I must request a favor, Lord."

The God of Skirmishes laughed. "You are not worthy."

His contempt nearly overpowered me; I fought the urge to abase myself before him, to beg for mercy, though I knew he had none to give. "Sacrilege has been committed in the sacred precincts. A man was murdered, and the War-God sent back to the heavens before his time."

"Indeed," said Mixtal. His eyes were filled with anger; he toyed with an obsidian knife as if I were the murderer to be brought to justice.

"I need to speak with Him."

"The War God has no time for you." The eyes of the God of Skirmishes were remote, expressionless. Mixtal remembered me, but I no longer meant anything to him. It should not have hurt me so much, to be unloved by the gods, but Pochtli's voice rang in my head: *a god who cares too little for his people, and too much for conquered land.*

I shook it off. I did not need the gods to love me; I needed them to be strong for Ahuatl. "If the War-God will not heed my words, then Ahuatl will fall," I said. "Whoever killed Him can kill again, and again. If this murderer is not stopped, the War-God could be kept from Ahuatl for centuries, until we have forgotten His very name."

The god did not move. At length he bowed his head a fraction. "I will speak to Him." And with that, he vanished.

I waited. The absence of the god was a welcome relief. I had not understood how overpowering he would be, how the mere sound of his voice would make me want to weep.

And then the War-God came. The courtyard was flooded with light, and a great shadow took shape at the heart of the radiance. I fell to my knees and bowed until my head touched the ground. I could not look at Him.

"Rise, my child," said the God of War. His voice was kind, unlike Mixtal's, yet it was heavy with the shout of warriors, the clash of swords on the battlefield, the cries of sacrifices on the altar as their blood spilled forth. It was more than I could bear.

With difficulty, I rose to my knees, averting my eyes. "My Lord, supreme above gods," I gasped.

"Behold Me," He said.

I raised my eyes. The War-God had both hands extended, as if in a blessing. He had the face of all His incarnations, of all the people we had conquered for Him. He wore a quetzal-feather headdress, and a tunic of imperial turquoise.

"Lord," I said. "Who works to bring the city down?"

"No one threatens Ahuatl," the War-God said.

"But someone killed your vessel," I said, confused. The god's voice echoed endlessly in my mind.

"It is of no consequence," said the War-God. "Always, I fall down to earth; always, I spill my blood to renew Our covenant. I cannot die. Do you doubt Me, Uzume?" His eyes, brimming with compassion, saw through my piety.

I shrivelled, as every petty thought in my head was exposed; from the moment I had accepted Chamatl's directive, I had been thinking not of Ahuatl's glory, but of my own ascension to godhood. It was not for the city I wanted to solve this crime, but for myself. A true warrior would have thought nothing of reward. I had again disgraced myself.

"No," I whispered, knowing I could not be forgiven for my failures. "I do not doubt You, my Lord."

He extended a hand over my head. "Go with my blessing, Uzume." The War-God gave me a look of pity, a look that absolved me of all guilt and shame, and then He vanished.

I sat paralyzed by disbelief, a peculiar feeling rising through me, suffusing me with warmth.

Though I had done nothing to deserve it, I had been forgiven, and it filled me with joy. A joy that should not have been. Mixtal, a lesser god, had treated me with contempt, as was his nature, yet the very God of War had shown pity. I knew, then, that something had gone terribly wrong with the protector of Ahuatl. He had become human.

After a long search of the sacred precincts, I found what I was looking for secreted deep in a midden not far from where Ralil had been killed. Filthy, it lay in my hand in seven pieces: bones that told their own story.

Chamatl was at his worship, piercing his earlobes with thorns. By the time he had finished offering blood to the War-God, I had recovered sufficiently from my interview with the two gods to present a blank face to him. But inwardly, I still shook, remembering the War-God's parting gaze.

Chamatl's eyebrows rose. "Uzume? I had not expected you so soon."

His face was painted the black of dried blood. It was unsettling. "I know who killed Ralil," I said.

"Indeed?" Chamatl's face was a careful blank.

I held out the fragments of the sacrificial flute, stained with dirt and Ralil's blood. "You hid them well, but not well enough."

Chamatl played it well; his tone was quiet, reasonable. "What are you talking about, Uzume?"

"Everything was done according to ritual," I said, my voice shaking. "You missed nothing."

"I did nothing."

"You did more than enough, Chamatl. Ralil played the flute in honor of the gods, you said the prayers, and then you cut him open. And Ralil ascended. Half-man, half-god."

"What makes you think I did this?"

"The tune," I said. "Only the high priest and the vessel of the War-God know the sacred song. Only you have the skill to make the sacrifice."

Chamatl would not meet my gaze.

I pressed him. "I will take this before the Emperor. I will tell him of your sacrilege."

At last, Chamatl said, "It's not easy to open a man's chest when there are no priests to hold him down. Even drugged, he struggled, and the cuts were not as clean as I could have wished." He spoke of this as he would have spoken about the weather.

"I saw the War-God," I said. "He *pitied me*. The War-God pitied me for wasting my life. You have tainted Him with Ralil's humanity." I had not dared believe that I could be right, that a high priest would commit sacrilege, but the determined look on Chamatl's face made me furious. "What have you done to us, Chamatl?"

"I did what needed to be done," said Chamatl. "I made Him human. There is a part of Ralil in Him now that will never go away."

"And Ahuatl will fall," I spat. "That was why Ralil was so glad to be sacrificed: he would make our gods weaker."

"You are wrong about Ralil," Chamatl said. "Before he was taken by the God, he spent five years serving Ahuatl. He came to appreciate the unity we have brought to the squabbling tribes of the world. He believed in an Ahuatlan empire. An empire of equals. He wanted to change things."

"Are you happy, Chamatl, now that things have changed?"

"War cannot hold an empire together," he said. "It is time for the War-God to become something else."

"He is a God of War," I snapped, reminded of Pochtli's words. "We need a strong, merciless god who can guide us into battle."

"Do we?" Chamatl said. "In other lands they have gods who do not endlessly demand blood, who encourage their people to live in peace."

"Your books have poisoned you," I said. "You are a priest of the War-God. Don't you see what you have taken from us?"

"Things had to change," Chamatl said. "We built Ahuatl on hatred, but nothing can last on those foundations. The age of conquest is gone, and merciful wisdom will serve us better now. We need a society of equals. If we have to spill more blood to mark our covenant, let it be the blood of the priests in their daily devotions, and the voluntary ascension of the sacred vessels."

I looked at him, at his eyes that shone with a cold certainty, and felt only anger. "Love? Caring? You lie to yourself, Chamatl. You feel nothing. Ralil existed only because he did your bidding. Pochtli is an inconvenience that must be removed."

"Do you care for her?" Chamatl asked.

That made me pause. I remembered Pochtli, her endless, sterile hatred of what we were. "No," I said at last, remembering how bitterness had filled her until it overwhelmed everything else. "But I pity her. She is blind."

"So are you," Chamatl said sadly.

"I would rather be blind than set myself up as the champion of compassion, and yet have none. I, at least, act according to my beliefs."

Chamatl's eyes shone with anger. "And tell me, Uzume, what is it that you believe?"

I said slowly, "That a warrior must lay down his life for the city if need be. That we must not think of sacrifices or rewards, but serve Ahuatl as best as we can."

"But you," Chamatl said, "have not fought battles for a long time."

"No," I said.

"Tell me." Chamatl spoke softly. "What have you achieved all those years, hating yourself?"

Strong words were on the tip of my tongue, begging to be flung in his face. And then I remembered Pochtli's hatred. I remembered Mixtal's distant eyes, the way they had wounded me like a knife stab. I remembered the War-God's gaze, how it had filled me with warmth, and I held back my outburst. "No," I said. "No."

I had achieved nothing with my life. On the maize fields, I had done nothing but dream of what I could not have. Like Pochtli, I had let myself become consumed with bitterness. *Hatred achieves nothing.*

"Ahuatl will not fall," I cried. "We are strong."

Chamatl did not answer. He was watching me, his face a mask, but I thought I could see, far underneath, the glimmer of compassion – the compassion he'd given to his god.

I hid my face in my hands, and let the memory of battles wash over me, but all I could see was the War-God's last gaze, the pity that had seared me to the core.

Chamatl said softly, "Let them lay this at Pochtli's door, Uzume. You will have your godhood, your ascension into the heavens. Only I can ensure this. The Emperor will not condone the sacrifice of a failed warrior unless I convince him otherwise." For the first time, there was despair in his voice. "Don't you see, Uzume? If we do not change, we *will* fall."

Gods take me, I saw it all too well. We were as strong as I had been, closed around a core of hatred. We were strong until the day something came to shatter our beliefs, and nothing was left to sustain us. "I will not help you do this," I said.

"You have no choice."

He was lying. The damage could yet be undone. The priests, if apprised of Chamatl's actions, could find a way to return the inhumanity of the War-God.

Did I wish for such a return?

I thought of Mixtal's remote gaze, which had showed no friendship, no pity. I thought of Ahuatl and the empire. Chamatl offered us a chance to build something truly great, and who was I to stand in the way?

I clung to the only thing that still made sense to me. "I know one thing," I said. "Whatever else happens, I will not let you sacrifice Pochtli for your vision. She is innocent."

"Innocent?" he said. "She would topple us all, given the chance."

"As would many others. You would kill her because she voices her opinion? Is that the foundation for your empire of equals?"

"You are not worthy to judge me," Chamatl snapped.

"You asked me to investigate," I said, thrusting the bloody fragments of the flute into his hands. "You asked me to choose. Let the War-God choose what is best for us. Let Him guide us, as He has always done. I will not stand in your way. But neither will I lie for you."

"What will you tell the Emperor?"

"I will admit failure, and go back to my maize fields," I said.

"You would disgrace yourself a second time?"

"Sometimes," I said, "the hardest thing is to know your own worth. I am not worthy of ascending amongst the gods."

Chamatl smiled bitterly. "A true warrior, Uzume. Proud and unbending to the end."

"No," I said, but I was still glad that he would call me a warrior. What a fool I was.

Chamatl shook his head sadly. "Your kind was always—"

"My kind." I sighed. "My kind is dead. The War-God's word is law among us, and you have made Him human. If He will no longer lead us into war, Ahuatl will not need warriors. In twenty years, hardly anyone will remember us."

"It needed to be done."

"Perhaps," I said.

I left Chamatl standing with the pieces of the broken flute in his hands, and as I exited the sacred precincts, I thought of our great battles, fading to meaningless murals within hidden temples. I thought of the new age that I had just helped usher in.

The sun was setting behind the platform of the pyramid, and the whole city of Ahuatl was wreathed in red light, from the stone temples to the tall adobe homes of the warriors, from the outer markets to the maize fields on the outskirts of the city. And it seemed to me, looking at the red orb sinking below the horizon, that it was like a great eye closing – but only to open in the morning, on a day more glorious than before.

A SIEGE OF CRANES

Benjamin Rosenbaum

The land around Marish was full of the green stalks of sunflowers: tall as men, with bold yellow faces. Their broad leaves were stained black with blood.

The rustling came again, and Marish squatted down on aching legs to watch. A hedgehog pushed its nose through the stalks. It sniffed in both directions.

Hunger dug at Marish's stomach like the point of a stick. He hadn't eaten for three days, not since returning to the crushed and blackened ruins of his house.

The hedgehog bustled through the stalks on to the trail, across the ash, across the trampled corpses of flowers. Marish waited until it was well clear of the stalks before he jumped. He landed with one foot before its nose and one foot behind its tail. The hedgehog, as hedgehogs will, rolled itself into a ball, spines out.

His house: crushed like an egg, smoking, the straw floor soaked with blood. He'd stood there with a trapped rabbit in his hand, alone in the awful silence. Forced himself to call for his wife Temur and his daughter Asza, his voice too loud and too flat. He'd dropped the rabbit somewhere in his haste, running to follow the blackened trail of devastation.

Running for three days, drinking from puddles, sleeping in the sunflowers when he couldn't stay awake.

Marish held his knifepoint above the hedgehog. They gave wishes, sometimes, in tales. "Speak, if you can," he said, "and bid me don't kill you. Grant me a wish! Elsewise, I'll have you for a dinner."

Nothing from the hedgehog, or perhaps a twitch.

Marish drove his knife through it and it thrashed, spraying more blood on the bloodstained flowers.

Too tired to light a fire, he ate it raw.

On that trail of tortured earth, wide enough for twenty horses, among the burnt and flattened flowers, Marish found a little doll of rags, the size of a child's hand.

It was one of the ones Maghd the mad girl made, and offered up, begging for stew meat, or wheedling for old bread behind Lezur's bakery. He'd given her a coin for one, once.

"Wherecome you're giving that sow our good coins?" Temur had cried, her bright eyes flashing, her soft lips pulled into a sneer. None in Ilmak Dale would let a mad girl come near a hearth, and some spit when they passed her. "Bag-Maghd's good for holding one thing only," Fazt would call out and they'd laugh their way into the alehouse. Marish laughing too, stopping only when he looked back at her.

Temur had softened, when she saw how Asza took to the doll, holding it, and singing to it, and smearing gruel on its rag-mouth with her fingers to feed it. They called her "little life-light", and heard her saying it to the doll, "il-ife-ight", rocking it in her arms.

He pressed his nose into the doll, trying to smell Asza's baby smell on it, like milk and forest soil and some sweet spice. But he only smelled the acrid stench of burnt cloth.

When he forced his wet eyes open, he saw a blurry figure coming toward him. Cursing himself for a fool, he tossed the doll away and pulled out his knife, holding it at his side. He wiped his face on his sleeve, and stood up straight, to show the man coming down the trail that the folk of Ilmak Dale did no obeisance. Then his mouth went dry and his hair stood up, for the man coming down the trail was no man at all.

It was a little taller than a man, and had the body of a man, though covered with a dark-gray fur; but its head was the head of a jackal. It wore armor of bronze and leather, all straps and discs with curious engravings, and carried a great black spear with a vicious point at each end.

Marish had heard that there were all sorts of strange folk in the world, but he had never seen anything like this.

"May you die with great suffering," the creature said in what seemed to be a calm, friendly tone.

"May *you* die as soon as may be!" Marish cried, not liking to be threatened.

The creature nodded solemnly. "I am Kadath-Naan of the Empty City," it announced. "I wonder if I might ask your assistance in a small matter."

Marish didn't know what to say to this. The creature waited. Marish said, "You can ask."

"I must speak with . . ." It frowned. "I am not sure how to put this. I do not wish to offend."

"Then why," Marish asked before he could stop himself, "did you menace me on a painful death?"

"Menace?" the creature said. "I only greeted you."

"You said, 'May you die with great suffering.' That like to be a threat or a curse, and I truly don't thank you for it."

The creature frowned. "No, it is a blessing. Or it is from a blessing: 'May you die with great suffering, and come to know holy dread and divine terror, stripping away your vain thoughts and fancies until you are fit to meet the Bone-White Fathers face to face; and may you be buried in honor and your name sung until it is forgotten.' That is the whole passage."

"Oh," said Marish. "Well, that sounds a bit better, I reckon."

"We learn that blessing as pups," said the creature in a wondering tone. "Have you never heard it?"

"No indeed," said Marish, and put his knife away. "Now what do you need? I can't think to be much help to you – I don't know this land here."

"Excuse my bluntness, but I must speak with an embalmer, or a sepulchrist, or someone of that sort."

"I've no notion what those are," said Marish.

The creature's eyes widened. It looked, as much as the face of a jackal could, like someone whose darkest suspicions were in the process of being confirmed.

"What do your people do with the dead?" it said.

"We put them in the ground."

"With what preparation? With what rites and monuments?" said the thing.

"In a wood box for them as can afford it, and a piece of linen for them as can't; and we say a prayer to the west wind. We put the stone in with them, what has their soul kept in it." Marish thought a bit, though he didn't much like the topic. He rubbed his nose on his sleeve. "Sometime we'll put a pile of stones on the grave, if it were someone famous."

The jackal-headed man sat heavily on the ground. It put its head in its hands. After a long moment it said, "Perhaps I should kill you now, that I might bury you properly."

"Now you just try that," said Marish, taking out his knife again.

"Would you like me to?" said the creature, looking up.

Its face was serene. Marish found he had to look away, and his eyes fell upon the scorched rags of the doll, twisted up in the stalks.

"Forgive me," said Kadath-Naan of the Empty City. "I should not be so rude as to tempt you. I see that you have duties to fulfill, just as I do, before you are permitted the descent into emptiness. Tell me which way your village lies, and I will see for myself what is done."

"My village—" Marish felt a heavy pressure behind his eyes, in his throat, wanting to push through into a sob. He held it back. "My village is gone. Something come and crushed it. I were off hunting, and when I come back, it were all burning, and full of the stink of blood. Whatever did it made this trail through the flowers. I think it went quick; I don't think I'll likely catch it. But I hope to." He knew he sounded absurd: a peasant chasing a demon. He gritted his teeth against it.

"I see," said the monster. "And where did this something come from? Did the trail come from the north?"

"It didn't come from nowhere. Just the village torn to pieces and this trail leading out."

"And the bodies of the dead," said Kadath-Naan carefully. "You buried them in – wooden boxes?"

"There weren't no bodies," Marish said. "Not of people. Just blood, and a few pieces of bone and gristle, and pigs' and horses' bodies all charred up. That's why I'm following." He looked down. "I mean to find them if I can."

Kadath-Naan frowned. "Does this happen often?"

Despite himself, Marish laughed. "Not that I ever heard before."

The jackal-headed creature seemed agitated. "Then you do not know if the bodies received . . . even what you would consider proper burial."

"I have a feeling they ain't received it," Marish said.

Kadath-Naan looked off in the distance towards Marish's village, then in the direction Marish was heading. It seemed to come to a decision. "I wonder if you would accept my company in your travels," it said. "I was on a different errand, but this matter seems to . . . outweigh it."

Marish looked at the creature's spear and said, "You'd be welcome." He held out the fingers of his hand. "Marish of Ilmak Dale."

The trail ran through the blackened devastation of another village, drenched with blood but empty of human bodies. The timbers of the houses were crushed to kindling; Marish saw a blacksmith's anvil twisted like a lock of hair, and plows that had been melted by enormous heat into a pool of iron. They camped beyond the village, in the shade of a twisted hawthorn tree. A wild autumn wind stroked the meadows around them, carrying dandelion seeds and wisps of smoke and the stink of putrefying cattle.

The following evening they reached a hill overlooking a great town curled around a river. Marish had never seen so many houses – almost too many to count. Most were timber and mud like those of his village, but some were great structures of stone, towering three or four stories into the air. House built upon house, with ladders reaching up to the doors of the ones on top. Around the town, fields full of wheat rustled gold in the evening light. Men and women were reaping in the fields, singing work songs as they swung their scythes.

The path of destruction curved around the town, as if avoiding it.

"Perhaps it was too well defended," said Kadath-Naan.

"Maybe," said Marish, but he remembered the pool of iron and the crushed timbers, and doubted. "I think that like to be Nabuz. I never come this far south before, but traders heading this way from the fair at Halde were always going to Nabuz to buy."

"They will know more of our adversary," said Kadath-Naan.

"I'll go," said Marish. "You might cause a stir; I don't reckon many of your sort visit Nabuz. You keep to the path."

"Perhaps I might ask of you . . ."

"If they are friendly there, I'll ask how they bury their dead," Marish said.

Kadath-Naan nodded somberly. "Go to duty and to death," he said.

Marish thought it must be a blessing, but he shivered all the same.

The light was dimming in the sky. The reapers heaped the sheaves high on the wagon, their songs slow and low, and the city gates swung open for them.

The city wall was stone, mud, and timber, twice as tall as a man, and great gates were iron. But the wall was not well kept. Marish crept among the stalks to a place where the wall was lower and trash and rubble were heaped high against it.

He heard the creak of the wagon rolling through the gates, the last work song fading away, the men of Nabuz calling out to each other as they made their way home. Then all was still.

Marish scrambled out of the field into a dead run, scrambled up the rubble, leapt atop the wall and lay on its broad top. He peeked over, hoping he had not been seen.

The cobbled street was empty. More than that, the town itself was silent. Even in Ilmak Dale, the evenings had been full of dogs barking, swine grunting, men arguing in the streets and women gossiping and calling the children in. Nabuz was supposed to be a great capital of whoring, drinking and fighting; the traders at Halde had always moaned over the delights that awaited them in the south if they could cheat the villagers well enough. But Marish heard no donkey braying, no baby crying, no cough, no whisper: nothing pierced the night silence.

He dropped over, landed on his feet quiet as he could, and crept along the street's edge. Before he had gone ten steps, he noticed the lights.

The windows of the houses flickered, but not with candle-light or the light of fires. The light was cold and blue.

He dragged a crate under the high window of the nearest house and clambered up to see.

There was a portly man with a rough beard, perhaps a potter after his day's work; there was his stout young wife, and a skinny boy of nine or ten. They sat on their low wooden bench, their dinner finished and put to the side (Marish could smell the fresh bread and his stomach cursed him). They were breathing, but their faces were slack, their eyes wide and staring, their lips gently moving. They were bathed in blue light. The potter's wife was rocking her arms gently as if she were cradling a newborn babe – but the swaddling blankets she held were empty.

And now Marish could hear a low inhuman voice, just at the edge of hearing, like a thought of his own. It whispered in time to the flicker of the blue light, and Marish felt himself drawn by its caress. Why not sit with the potter's family on the bench? They would take him in. He could stay here, the whispering promised: forget his village, forget his grief. Fresh bread on the hearth, a warm bed next to the coals of the fire. Work the clay, mix the slip for the potter, eat a dinner of bread and cheese, then listen to the blue light and do what it told him. Forget the mud roads of Ilmak Dale, the laughing roar of Perdan and Thin Deri and Chibar and the others in its alehouse, the harsh cough and crow of its roosters at dawn. Forget willowy Temur, her hair smooth as a river and bright as a sheaf of wheat, her proud shoulders and her slender waist, Temur turning her satin cheek away when he tried to kiss it. Forget the creak and splash of the mill, and the soft rushes on the floor of Maghd's hovel. The potter of Nabuz had a young and willing niece who needed a husband, and the blue light held laughter and love enough for all. Forget the heat and clanging of Fat Deri's smithy; forget the green stone that held Pa's soul, that he'd laid upon his shroud. Forget Asza, little Asza whose tiny body he'd held to his heart . . .

Marish thought of Asza and he saw the potter's wife's empty arms and, with one flex of his legs, he kicked himself away from the wall, knocking over the crate and landing sprawled among rolling apples.

He sprang to his feet. There was no sound around him. He stuffed five apples in his pack, and hurried towards the center of Nabuz.

The sun had set, and the moon washed the streets in silver. From every window streamed the cold blue light.

Out of the corner of his eye he thought he saw a shadow dart behind him, and, he turned and took out his knife. But he saw nothing, and though his good sense told him five apples and no answers was as much as he should expect from Nabuz, he kept on.

He came to a great square full of shadows, and at first he thought of trees. But it was tall iron frames, and men and women bolted to them upside down. The bolts went through their bodies, crusty with dried blood.

One man nearby was live enough to moan. Marish poured a little water into the man's mouth, and held his head up, but the man could not swallow; he coughed and spluttered, and the water ran down his face and over the bloody holes where his eyes had been.

"But the babies," the man rasped, "how could you let her have the babies?"

"Let who?" said Marish.

"The White Witch!" the man roared in a whisper. "The White Witch, you bastards! If you'd but let us fight her—"

"Why—" Marish began.

"Lie again, say the babies will live forever – lie again, you cowardly blue-blood maggots in the corpse of Nabuz . . ." He coughed and blood ran over his face.

The bolts were fast into the frame. "I'll get a tool," Marish said, "you won't—"

From behind him came an awful scream.

He turned and saw the shadow that had followed him: it was a white cat with fine soft fur and green eyes that blazed in the darkness. It shrieked, its fur standing on end, its tail high, staring at him, and his good sense told him it was raising an alarm.

Marish ran, and the cat ran after him, shrieking. Nabuz was a vast pile of looming shadows. As he passed through the empty city gates he heard a grinding sound and a whinny. As he raced into the moonlit dusk of open land, down the road to where Kadath-Naan's shadow crossed the demon's path, he heard hoofbeats galloping behind him.

Kadath-Naan had just reached a field of tall barley. He turned to look back at the sound of the hoofbeats and the shrieking of the devil cat. "Into the grain!" Marish yelled. "Hide in the grain!" He passed Kadath-Naan and dived into the barley, the cat racing behind him.

Suddenly he spun and dropped and grabbed the white cat, meaning to get one hand on it and get his knife with the other and shut it up by killing it. But the cat fought like a devil and it was all he could do to hold on to it with both hands. And he saw, behind him on the trail, Kadath-Naan standing calmly, his hand on his spear, facing three knights armored every inch in white, galloping towards them on great chargers.

"You damned dog-man," Marish screamed. "I know you want to die, but get into the grain!"

Kadath-Naan stood perfectly still. The first knight bore down on him, and the moon flashed from the knight's sword. The blade was no more than a handsbreadth from Kadath-Naan's neck when he sprang to the side of it, into the path of the second charger.

As the first knight's charge carried him past, Kadath-Naan knelt, and drove the base of his great spear into the ground. Too late, the second knight made a desperate yank on the horse's reins, but the great beast's momentum carried him into the pike. It tore through the neck of the horse and through the armored chest of the knight riding him, and the two of them reared up and thrashed once like a dying centaur, then crashed to the ground.

The first knight wheeled around. The third met Kadath-Naan. The beast-man stood barehanded, the muscles of his shoulders and chest relaxed. He cocked his jackal head to one side, as if wondering: is it here at last? The moment when I am granted release?

But Marish finally had the cat by its tail, and flung that wild white thing, that frenzy of claws and spit and hissing, into the face of the third knight's steed.

The horse reared and threw its rider; the knight let go of his sword as he crashed to the ground. Quick as a hummingbird, Kadath-Naan leapt and caught it in midair. He spun to face the last rider.

Marish drew his knife and charged through the barley. He was on the fallen knight just as he got to his knees.

The crash against armor took Marish's wind away. The man was twice as strong as Marish was, and his arm went around Marish's chest like a crushing band of iron. But Marish had both hands free, and with a twist of the knight's helmet he exposed a bit of neck, and in Marish's knife went, and then the man's hot blood was spurting out.

The knight convulsed as he died and grabbed Marish in a desperate embrace, coating him with blood, and sobbing once: and Marish held him, for the voice of his heart told him it was a shame to have to die such a way. Marish was shocked at this, for the man was a murderous slave of the White Witch: but still he held the quaking body in his arms, until it moved no more.

Then Marish, soaked with salty blood, staggered to his feet and remembered the last knight with a start: but of course Kadath-Naan had killed him in the meantime. Three knights' bodies lay on the ruined ground, and two living horses snorted and pawed the dirt like awkward mourners. Kadath-Naan freed his spear with a great yank from the horse and man it had transfixed. The devil cat was a sodden blur of white fur and blood: a falling horse had crushed it.

Marish caught the reins of the nearest steed, a huge fine creature, and gentled it with a hand behind its ears. When he had his breath again, Marish said, "We got horses now. Can you ride?"

Kadath-Naan nodded.

"Let's go then; there like to be more coming."

Kadath-Naan frowned a deep frown. He gestured to the bodies.

"What?" said Marish.

"We have no embalmer or sepulchrist, it is true; yet I am trained in the funereal rites for military expeditions and emergencies. I have the necessary tools; in a matter of a day I can raise small monuments. At least they died aware and with suffering; this must compensate for the rudimentary nature of the rites."

"You can't be in earnest," said Marish. "And what of the White Witch?"

"Who is the White Witch?" Kadath-Naan asked.

"The demon; turns out she's somebody what's called the White Witch. She spared Nabuz, for they said they'd serve her, and give her their babies."

"We will follow her afterwards," said Kadath-Naan.

"She's ahead of us as it is! We leave now on horseback, we might have a chance. There be a whole lot more bodies with her unburied or buried wrong, less I mistake."

Kadath-Naan leaned on his spear. "Marish of Ilmak Dale," he said, "here we must part ways. I cannot steel myself to follow such logic as you declare, abandoning these three burials before me now for the chance of others elsewhere, if we can catch and defeat a witch. My duty does not lie that way." He searched Marish's face. "You do not have the words for it, but if these men are left unburied, they are *tanzadi*. If I bury them with what little honor I can provide, they are *tazrash*. They spent only a little while alive, but they will be *tanzadi* or *tazrash* forever."

"And if more slaves of the White Witch come along to pay you back for killing these?"

But try as he might, Marish could not dissuade him, and at last he mounted one of the chargers and rode onwards, towards the cold white moon, away from the whispering city.

The flowers were gone, the fields were gone. The ashy light of the horizon framed the ferns and stunted trees of a black fen full of buzzing flies. The trail was wider: thirty horses could have passed side by side over the blasted ground. But the marshy ground was treacherous, and Marish's mount sank to its fetlocks with each careful step.

A siege of cranes launched themselves from the marsh into the moon-abandoned sky. Marish had never seen so many. Bone-white, fragile, soundless, they ascended like snowflakes seeking the cold womb of heaven. Or a river of souls. None looked back at him. The voice of doubt told him: you will never know what became of Asza and Temur.

The apples were long gone, and Marish was growing light-headed from hunger. He reined the horse in and dismounted; he would have to hunt off the trail. In the bracken, he tied the charger to a great black fern as tall as a house. In a drier spot near its base was the footprint of a rabbit. He felt the indentation: it was fresh. He followed the rabbit deeper into the fen.

He was thinking of Temur and her caresses. The nights she'd turn away from him, back straight as a spear, and the space of rushes between them would be like a frozen desert, and he'd huddle unsleeping beneath skins and woolen blankets, stiff from cold, arguing silently with her in his spirit; and the nights when she'd turn to him, her soft skin hot and alive against his, seeking him silently, almost vengefully, as if showing him – see? This is what you can have. This is what I am.

And then the image of those rushes charred and brown with blood and covered with chips of broken stone and mortar came to him, and he forced himself to think of nothing: breathing his thoughts out to the west wind, forcing his mind clear as a spring stream. And he stepped forward in the marsh.

And stood in a street of blue and purple tile, in a fantastic city.

He stood for a moment wondering, and then he carefully took a step back.

And he was in a black swamp with croaking toads and nothing to eat.

The voice of doubt told him he was mad from hunger; the voice of hope told him he would find the White Witch here and kill her; and thinking a thousand things, he stepped forward again and found himself still in the swamp.

Marish thought for a while, and then he stepped back, and, thinking of nothing, stepped forward.

The tiles of the street were a wild mosaic – some had glittering jewels; some had writing in a strange flowing script; some seemed to have tiny windows into tiny rooms. Houses, tiled with the same profusion, towered like columns, bulged like mushrooms, melted like wax. Some danced. He heard soft murmurs of conversation, footfalls, and the rush of a river.

In the street, dressed in feathers or gold plates or swirls of shadow, blue-skinned people passed. One such creature, dressed in fine silk, was just passing Marish.

"Your pardon," said Marish, "what place be this here?"

The man looked at Marish slowly. He had a red jewel in the center of his forehead, and it flickered as he talked. "That depends on how you enter it," he said, "and who you are, but for you, catarrhine, its name is Zimzarkanthitrugenia-fenstok, not least because that is easy for you to pronounce. And now I have given you one thing free, as you are a guest of the city."

"How many free things do I get?" said Marish.

"Three. And now I have given you two."

Marish thought about this for a moment. "I'd favor something to eat," he said.

The man looked surprised. He led Marish into a building that looked like a blur of spinning triangles, through a dark room lit by candles, to a table piled with capon and custard and razor-thin slices of ham and lamb's foot jelly and candied apricots and goatsmilk yogurt and hard cheese and yams and turnips and olives and fish cured in strange spices; and those were just the things Marish recognized.

"I don't reckon I ought to eat fairy food," said Marish, though he could hardly speak from all the spit that was suddenly in his mouth.

"That is true, but from the food of the djinn you have nothing to fear. And now I have given you three things," said the djinn, and he bowed and made as if to leave.

"Hold on," said Marish (as he followed some candied apricots down his gullet with a fistful of cured fish). "That be all the free things, but say I got something to sell?"

The djinn was silent.

"I need to kill the White Witch," Marish said, eating an olive. The voice of doubt asked him why he was telling the truth, if this city might also serve her; but he told it to hush up. "Have you got aught to help me?"

The djinn still said nothing, but he cocked an eyebrow.

"I've got a horse, a real fighting horse," Marish said, around a piece of cheese.

"What is its name?" said the djinn. "You cannot sell anything to a djinn unless you know its name."

Marish wanted to lie about the name, but he found he could not. He swallowed. "I don't know its name," he admitted.

"Well then," said the djinn.

"I killed the fellow what was on it," Marish said, by way of explanation.

"Who," said the djinn.

"Who what?" said Marish.

"Who was on it," said the djinn.

"I don't know his name either," said Marish, picking up a yam.

"No, I am not asking that," said the djinn crossly. "I am telling you to say, 'I killed the fellow who was on it.'"

Marish set the yam back on the table. "Now that's enough," Marish said. "I thank you for the fine food and I thank you for the three free things, but I do not thank you for telling me how to talk. How I talk is how we talk in Ilmak Dale, or how we did talk when there were an Ilmak Dale, and just because the White Witch blasted Ilmak Dale to splinters don't mean I am going to talk like folk do in some magic city."

"I will buy that from you," said the djinn.

"What?" said Marish, and wondered so much at this that he forgot to pick up another thing to eat.

"The way you talked in Ilmak Dale," the djinn said.

"All right," Marish said, "and for it, I crave to know the thing what will help me mostways, for killing the White Witch."

"I have a carpet that flies faster than the wind," said the djinn. "I think it is the only way you can catch the Witch, and unless you catch her, you cannot kill her."

"Wonderful," Marish cried with glee. "And you'll trade me that carpet for how we talk in Ilmak Dale?"

"No," said the djinn, "I told you which thing would help you most, and in return for that, I took the way you talked in Ilmak Dale and put it in the Great Library."

Marish frowned. "All right, what do you want for the carpet?"

The djinn was silent.

"I'll give you the White Witch for it," Marish said.

"You must possess the thing you sell," the djinn said.

"Oh, I'll get her," Marish said. "You can be sure of that." His hand had found a boiled egg, and the shell crunched in his palm as he said it.

The djinn looked at Marish carefully, and then he said, "The use of the carpet, for three days, in return for the White Witch, if you can conquer her."

"Agreed," said Marish.

They had to bind the horse's eyes; otherwise it would rear and kick when the carpet rose into the air. Horse, man, djinn: all perched on a span of cloth. As they sped back to Nabuz like a mad wind, Marish tried not to watch the solid fields flying beneath, and regretted the candied apricots.

The voice of doubt told him that his companion must be slain by now, but his heart wanted to see Kadath-Naan again: but for the jackal-man, Marish was friendless.

Among the barley stalks, three man-high plinths of black stone, painted with white glyphs, marked three graves. Kadath-Naan had only traveled a little ways beyond them before the ambush. How long the emissary of the Empty City had been fighting, Marish could not tell; but he staggered and weaved like a man drunk with wine or exhaustion. His gray fur was matted with blood and sweat.

An army of children in white armor surrounded Kadath-Naan. As the carpet swung closer, Marish could see their gray faces and blank eyes. Some crawled, some tottered: none seemed to have lived more than six years of mortal life. They held daggers. One clung to the jackal-man's back, digging canals of blood.

Two of the babies were impaled on the point of the great black spear. Hand over hand, daggers held in their mouths, they dragged themselves down the shaft towards Kadath-Naan's hands. Hundreds more surrounded him, closing in.

Kadath-Naan swung his spear, knocking the slack-eyed creatures back. He struck with enough force to shatter human skulls, but the horrors only rolled, and scampered giggling back to stab his legs. With each swing, the spear was slower. Kadath-Naan's eyes rolled back into their sockets. His great frame shuddered from weariness and pain.

The carpet swung low over the battle, and Marish lay on his belly, dangling his arms down to the jackal-headed warrior. He shouted: "Jump! Kadath-Naan, jump!"

Kadath-Naan looked up and, gripping his spear in both hands, he tensed his legs to jump. But the pause gave the tiny servitors of the White Witch their chance; they swarmed over his body, stabbing with their daggers, and he collapsed under the writhing mass of his enemies.

"Down further! We can haul him aboard!" yelled Marish.

"I sold you the use of my carpet, not the destruction of it," said the djinn.

With a snarl of rage, and before the voice of his good sense could speak, Marish leapt from the carpet. He landed amidst the fray, and began tearing the small bodies from Kadath-Naan and flinging them into the fields. Then daggers found his calves, and small bodies crashed into his sides, and he tumbled, covered with the white-armored hell-children. The carpet sailed up lazily into the summer sky.

Marish thrashed, but soon he was pinned under a mass of small bodies. Their daggers probed his sides, drawing blood, and he gritted his teeth against a scream; they pulled at his hair and ears and pulled open his mouth to look inside. As if they were playing. One gray-skinned suckling child, its scalp peeled half away to reveal the white bone of its skull, nuzzled at his neck, seeking the nipple it would never find again.

So had Asza nuzzled against him. So had been her heft, then, light and snug as five apples in a bag. But her live eyes saw the world, took it in and made it better than it was. In those eyes he was a hero, a giant to lift her, honest and gentle and brave. When Temur looked into those otter-brown, mischievous eyes, her mouth softened from its hard line, and she sang fairy songs.

A dagger split the skin of his forehead, bathing him in blood. Another dug between his ribs, another popped the skin of his thigh. Another pushed against his gut, but hadn't broken through. He closed his eyes. They weighed heavier on him now; his throat tensed to scream, but he could not catch his breath.

Marish's arms ached for Asza and Temur – ached that he would die here, without them. Wasn't it right, though, that they be taken from him? The little girl who ran to him across the fields of an evening, a funny hopping run, her arms flung wide, waving that rag doll; no trace of doubt in her. And the beautiful wife who stiffened when she saw him, but smiled one-edged, despite herself, as he lifted apple-smelling Asza in his arms. He had not deserved them.

His face, his skin, were hot and slick with salty blood. He saw, not felt, the daggers digging deeper – arcs of light across a great darkness. He wished he could comfort Asza one last time, across that darkness. As when she would awaken in the night, afraid of witches: now a witch had come.

He found breath, he forced his mouth open, and he sang through sobs to Asza, his song to lull her back to sleep:

> *Now sleep, my love, now sleep –*
> *The moon is in the sky –*
> *The clouds have fled like sheep –*
> *You're in your papa's eye.*
> *Sleep now, my love, sleep now –*
> *The bitter wind is gone –*
> *The calf sleeps with the cow –*
> *Now sleep my love 'til dawn.*

He freed his left hand from the press of bodies. He wiped blood and tears from his eyes. He pushed his head up, dizzy, flowers of light still exploding across his vision. The small bodies were still. Carefully, he eased them to the ground.

The carpet descended, and Marish hauled Kadath-Naan on to it. Then he forced himself to turn, swaying, and look at each of the gray-skinned babies sleeping peacefully on the ground. None of them was Asza.

He took one of the smallest and swaddled it with rags and bridle leather. His blood made his fingers slick, and the noon sun seemed as gray as a stone. When he was sure the creature could not move, he put it in his pack and slung the pack upon his back. Then he fell on to the carpet. He felt it lift up under him and, like a cradled child, he slept.

He awoke to see clouds sailing above him. The pain was gone. He sat up and looked at his arms: they were whole and unscarred. Even the old scar from Thin Deri's careless scythe was gone.

"You taught us how to defeat the Children of Despair," said the djinn. "That required recompense. I have treated your wounds and those of your companion. Is the debt clear?"

"Answer me one question," Marish said.

"And the debt will be clear?" said the djinn.

"Yes, may the west wind take you, it'll be clear!"

The djinn blinked in assent.

"Can they be brought back?" Marish asked. "Can they be made into living children again?"

"They cannot," said the djinn. "They can neither live nor die, nor be harmed at all unless they will it. Their hearts have been replaced with sand."

They flew in silence, and Marish's pack seemed heavier.

The land flew by beneath them as fast as a cracking whip; Marish stared as green fields gave way to swamp, swamp to marsh, marsh to rough pastureland. The devastation left by the White Witch seemed gradually newer; the trail here was still smoking, and Marish thought it might be too hot to walk on. They passed many a blasted village, and each time Marish looked away.

At last they began to hear a sound on the wind, a sound that chilled Marish's heart. It was not a wail, it was not a grinding, it was not a shriek of pain, nor the wet crunch of breaking bones, nor was it an obscene grunting; but it had something of all of these. The jackal-man's ears were perked, and his gray fur stood on end.

The path was now truly still burning; they flew high above it, and the rolling smoke underneath was like a fog over the land. But there ahead they saw the monstrous thing that was leaving the trail; and Marish could hardly think any thought at all as they approached, but only stare, bile burning his throat.

It was a great chariot, perhaps eight times the height of a man, as wide as the trail, constructed of parts of living human bodies welded together in an obscene tangle. A thousand legs and arms pawed the ground; a thousand more beat the trail with whips and scythes, or clawed the air. A thick skein of hearts, livers, and stomachs pulsed through the center of the thing, and a great assemblage of lungs breathed at its core. Heads rolled like wheels at the bottom of the chariot, or were stuck here and there along the surface of the thing as slack-eyed, gibbering ornaments. A thousand spines and torsos built a great chamber at the top of the chariot, shielded with webs of skin and hair; there perhaps hid the White Witch. From the pinnacle of the monstrous thing flew a great flag made of writhing tongues. Before the awful chariot rode a company of ten knights in white armor, with visored helms.

At the very peak sat a great headless hulking beast, larger than a bear, with the skin of a lizard, great yellow globes of eyes set on its shoulders and a wide mouth in its belly. As they watched, it vomited a gout of flame that set the path behind the chariot ablaze. Then it noticed them, and lifted the great plume of flame in their direction. At a swift word from the djinn, the carpet veered, but it was a close enough thing that Marish felt an oven's blast of heat on his skin. He grabbed the horse by its reins as it made to rear, and whispered soothing sounds in its ear.

"Abomination!" cried Kadath-Naan. "Djinn, will you send word to the Empty City? You will be well rewarded."

The djinn nodded.

"It is Kadath-Naan, lesser scout of the Endless Inquiry, who speaks. Let Bars-Kardereth, Commander of the Silent Legion, be told to hasten here. Here is an obscenity beyond compass, far more horrible than the innocent errors of savages; here Chaos blocks the descent into the Darkness entirely, and a whole land may fall to corruption."

The jewel in the djinn's forehead flashed once. "It is done," he said.

Kadath-Naan turned to Marish. "From the Empty City to this place is four days' travel for a Ghomlu Legion; let us find a place in their path where we can wait to join them."

Marish forced himself to close his eyes. But still he saw it – hands, tongues, guts, skin, woven into a moving mountain. He still heard the squelching, grinding, snapping sounds, the sea-roar of the thousand lungs. What had he imagined? Asza and Temur in a prison somewhere, waiting to be freed? Fool. "All right," he said.

Then he opened his eyes, and saw something that made him say, "No."

Before them, not ten minutes' ride from the awful chariot of the White Witch, was a whitewashed village, peaceful in the afternoon sun. Arrayed before it were a score of its men and young women. A few had proper swords or spears; one of the women carried a bow. The others had hoes, scythes, and staves. One woman sat astride a horse; the rest were on foot. From their perch in the air, Marish could see distant figures – families, stooped grandmothers, children in their mothers' arms – crawling like beetles up the faces of hills.

"Down," said Marish, and they landed before the village's defenders, who raised their weapons.

"You've got to run," he said, "you can make it to the hills. You haven't seen that thing – you haven't any chance against it."

A dark man spat on the ground. "We tried that in Gravenge."

"It splits up," said a black-bearded man. "Sends littler horrors, and they tear folks up and make them part of it, and you see your fellow's limbs come after you as part of the thing. And they're fast. Too fast for us."

"We just busy it a while," another man said, "our folk can get far enough away." But he had a wild look in his eye: the voice of doubt was in him.

"We stop it here," said the woman on horseback.

Marish led the horse off the carpet, took its blinders off and mounted it. "I'll stand with you," he said.

"And welcome," said the woman on horseback, and her plain face broke into a nervous smile. It was almost pretty that way.

Kadath-Naan stepped off the carpet, and the villagers shied back, readying their weapons.

"This is Kadath-Naan, and you'll be damned glad you have him," said Marish.

"Where's your manners?" snapped the woman on horseback to her people. "I'm Asza," she said.

No, Marish thought, staring at her. No, but you could have been. He looked away, and after a while they left him alone.

The carpet rose silently off into the air, and soon there was smoke on the horizon, and the knights rode at them, and the chariot rose behind.

"Here we are," said Asza of the rocky plains, "now make a good accounting of yourselves."

An arrow sang; a white knight's horse collapsed. Marish cried "Ha!" and his mount surged forward. The villagers charged, but Kadath-Naan outpaced them all, springing between a pair of knights. He shattered the forelegs of one horse with his spear's shaft, drove its point through the side of the other rider. Villagers fell on the fallen knight with their scythes.

It was a heady wild thing for Marish to be galloping on such a horse, a far finer horse than ever Redlegs had been, for all Pa's proud and vain attention to her. The warmth of its flanks, the rhythm of posting into its stride. Marish of Ilmak Dale, riding into a charge of knights: miserable addle-witted fool.

Asza flicked her whip at the eyes of a knight's horse, veering away. The knight wheeled to follow her, and Marish came on after him. He heard the hooves of another knight pounding the plain behind him in turn.

Ahead the first knight gained on Asza of the rocky plains. Marish took his knife in one hand, and bent his head to his horse's ear, and whispered to it in wordless murmurs: fine creature, give me everything. And his horse pulled even with Asza's knight.

Marish swung down, hanging from his pommel – the ground flew by beneath him. He reached across and slipped his knife under the girth that held the knight's saddle. The knight swiveled, raising his blade to strike – then the girth parted, and he flew from his mount.

Marish struggled up into the saddle, and the second knight was there, armor blazing in the sun. This time Marish was on the sword-arm's side, and his horse had slowed, and that blade swung up and it could strike Marish's head from his neck like snapping off a sunflower; time for the peasant to die.

Asza's whip lashed around the knight's sword-arm. The knight seized the whip in his other hand. Marish sprang from the saddle. He struck a wall of chainmail and fell with the knight.

The ground was an anvil, the knight a hammer, Marish a rag doll sewn by a poor mad girl and mistaken for a horseshoe. He couldn't breathe; the world was a ringing blur. The knight found his throat with one mailed glove, and hissed with rage, and pulling himself up drew a dagger from his belt. Marish tried to lift his arms.

Then he saw Asza's hands fitting a leather noose around the knight's neck. The knight turned his visored head to see, and Asza yelled, "Yah!" An armored knee cracked against Marish's head, and then the knight was gone, dragged off over the rocky plains behind Asza's galloping mare.

Asza of the rocky plains helped Marish to his feet. She had a wild smile, and she hugged him to her breast; pain shot through him, as did the shock of her soft body. Then she pulled away, grinning, and looked over his shoulder back towards the village. And then the grin was gone.

Marish turned. He saw the man with the beard torn apart by a hundred grasping arms and legs. Two bending arms covered with eyes watched carefully as his organs were woven into the chariot. The village burned. A knight leaned from his saddle to cut a fleeing woman down, harvesting her like a stalk of wheat.

"No!" shrieked Asza, and ran towards the village.

Marish tried to run, but he could only hobble, gasping, pain tearing through his side. Asza snatched a spear from the ground and swung up on to a horse. Her hair was like Temur's, flowing gold. My Asza, my Temur, he thought. I must protect her.

Marish fell; he hit the ground and held on to it like a lover, as if he might fall into the sky. Fool, fool, said the voice of his good sense. That is not your Asza, or your Temur either. She is not yours at all.

He heaved himself up again and lurched on, as Asza of the rocky plains reached the chariot. From above, a lazy plume of flame expanded. The horse reared. The cloud of fire enveloped the woman, the horse, and then was sucked away; the blackened corpses fell to the ground steaming.

Marish stopped running.

The headless creature of fire fell from the chariot – Kadath-Naan was there at the summit of the horror, his spear sunk in its flesh as a lever. But the fire-beast turned as it toppled, and a pillar of fire engulfed the jackal-man. The molten iron of his spear and armor coated his body, and he fell into the grasping arms of the chariot.

Marish lay down on his belly in the grass.

Maybe they will not find me here, said the voice of hope. But it was like listening to idiot words spoken by the wind blowing through a forest. Marish lay on the ground and he hurt. The hurt was a song, and it sang him. Everything was lost and far away. No Asza, no Temur, no Maghd; no quest, no hero, no trickster, no hunter, no father, no groom. The wind came down from the mountains and stirred the grass beside Marish's nose, where beetles walked.

There was a rustling in the short grass, and a hedgehog came out of it and stood nose to nose with Marish.

"Speak if you can," Marish whispered, "and grant me a wish."

The hedgehog snorted. "I'll not do *you* any favors, after what you did to Teodor!"

Marish swallowed. "The hedgehog in the sunflowers?"

"Obviously. Murderer."

"I'm sorry! I didn't know he was magic! I thought he was just a hedgehog!"

"Just a hedgehog! Just a hedgehog!" It narrowed its eyes, and its prickers stood on end. "Be careful what you call things, Marish of Ilmak Dale. When you name a thing, you say what it is in the world. Names mean more than you know."

Marish was silent.

"Teodor didn't like threats, that's all . . . the stubborn old idiot."

"I'm sorry about Teodor," said Marish.

"Yes, well," said the hedgehog. "I'll help you, but it will cost you dear."

"What do you want?"

"How about your soul?" said the hedgehog.

"I'd do that, sure," said Marish. "It's not like I need it. But I don't have it."

The hedgehog narrowed its eyes again. From the village, a few thin screams and the soft crackle of flames. It smelled like autumn, and butchering hogs.

"It's true," said Marish. "The priest of Ilmak Dale took all our souls and put them in little stones, and hid them. He didn't want us making bargains like these."

"Wise man," said the hedgehog. "But I'll have to have something. What have you got in you, besides a soul?"

"What do you mean, like, my wits? But I'll need those."

"Yes, you will," said the hedgehog.

"Hope? Not much of that left, though."

"Not to my taste anyway," said the hedgehog. "*Hope is foolish, doubts are wise.*"

"Doubts?" said Marish.

"That'll do," said the hedgehog. "But I want them all."

"All . . . all right," said Marish. "And now you're going to help me against the White Witch?"

"I already have," said the hedgehog.

"You have? Have I got some magic power or other now?" asked Marish. He sat up. The screaming was over: he heard nothing but the fire, and the crunching and squelching and slithering and grinding of the chariot.

"Certainly not," said the hedgehog. "I haven't done anything you didn't see or didn't hear. But perhaps you weren't listening." And it waddled off into the green blades of the grass.

Marish stood and looked after it. He picked at his teeth with a thumbnail, and thought, but he had no idea what the hedgehog meant. But he had no doubts, either, so he started toward the village.

Halfway there, he noticed the dead baby in his pack wriggling, so he took it out and held it in his arms.

As he came into the burning village, he found himself just behind the great fire-spouting lizard-skinned headless thing. It turned and took a breath to burn him alive, and he tossed the baby down its throat. There was a choking sound, and the huge thing shuddered and twitched, and Marish walked on by it.

The great chariot saw him and it swung toward him, a vast mountain of writhing, humming, stinking flesh, a hundred arms reaching. Fists grabbed his shirt, his hair, his trousers, and they lifted him into the air.

He looked at the hand closed around his collar. It was a woman's hand, fine and fair, and it was wearing the copper ring he'd bought at Halde.

"Temur!" he said in shock.

The arm twitched and slackened; it went white. It reached out: the fingers spread wide; it caressed his cheek gently. And then it dropped from the chariot and lay on the ground beneath.

He knew the hands pulling him aloft. "Lezur the baker!" he whispered, and a pair of doughy hands dropped from the chariot. "Silbon and Felbon!" he cried. "Ter the blind! Sela the blue-eyed!" Marish's lips trembled to say the names, and the hands slackened and fell to the ground, and away on other parts of the chariot the other parts fell off too; he saw a blue eye roll down from above him and fall to the ground.

"Perdan! Mardid! Pilg and his old mother! Fazt – oh, Fazt, you'll tell no more jokes! Chibar and his wife, the pretty foreign one!" His face was wet; with every name, a bubble popped open in Marish's chest, and his throat was thick with some strange feeling. "Pizdar the priest! Fat Deri, far from your smithy! Thin Deri!" When all the hands and arms of Ilmak Dale had fallen off, he was left standing free. He looked at the strange hands coming toward him. "You were a potter," he said to hands with clay under the nails, and they fell off the chariot. "And you were a butcher," he said to bloody ones, and they fell too. "A fat farmer, a beautiful young girl, a grand-mother, a harlot, a brawler," he said, and enough hands and feet and heads and organs had slid off the chariot now that it sagged in the middle and pieces of it strove with each other blindly. "Men and women of Eckdale," Marish said, "men and women of Halde, of Gravenge, of the fields and the swamps and the rocky plains."

The chariot fell to pieces; some lay silent and still, others which Marish had not named had lost their purchase and thrashed on the ground.

The skin of the great chamber atop the chariot peeled away and the White Witch leapt into the sky. She was three times as tall as any woman; her skin was bone white; one eye was blood red and the other emerald green; her mouth was full of black fangs, and her hair of snakes and lizards. Her hands were full of lightning, and she sailed on to Marish with her fangs wide open.

And around her neck, on a leather thong, she wore a little doll of rags, the size of a child's hand.

"Maghd of Ilmak Dale," Marish said, and she was also a young woman with muddy hair and an uncertain smile, and that's how she landed before Marish.

"Well done, Marish," said Maghd, and pulled at a muddy lock of her hair, and laughed, and looked at the ground. "Well done! Oh, I'm glad. I'm glad you've come."

"Why did you do it, Maghd?" Marish said. "Oh, why?"

She looked up and her lips twitched and her jaw set. "Can you ask me that? You, Marish?"

She reached across, slowly, and took his hand. She pulled him, and he took a step towards her. She put the back of his hand against her cheek.

"You'd gone out hunting," she said. "And that Temur of yours" – she said the name as if it tasted of vinegar – "she seen me back of Lezur's, and for one time I didn't look down. I looked at her eyes, and she named me a foul witch. And then they were all crowding round . . ." She shrugged. "And I don't like that. Fussing and crowding and one against the other." She let go his hand and stooped to pick up a clot of earth, and she crumbled it in her hands. "So I knit them all together. All one thing. They did like it. And they were so fine and great and happy, I forgave them. Even Temur."

The limbs lay unmoving on the ground; the guts were piled in soft unbreathing hills, like drifts of snow. Maghd's hands were coated with black crumbs of dirt.

"I reckon they're done of playing now," Maghd said, and sighed.

"How?" Marish said. "How'd you do it? Maghd, what *are* you?"

"Don't fool so! I'm Maghd, same as ever. I found the souls, that's all. Dug them up from Pizdar's garden, sold them to the Spirit of Unwinding Things." She brushed the dirt from her hands.

"And . . . the children, then? Maghd, the babes?"

She took his hand again, but she didn't look at him. She lay her cheek against her shoulder and watched the ground. "Babes shouldn't grow," she said. "No call to be big and hateful." She swallowed. "I made them perfect. That's all."

Marish's chest tightened. "And what now?"

She looked at him, and a slow grin crept across her face. "Well now," she said. "That's on you, ain't it, Marish? I got plenty of tricks yet, if you want to keep fighting." She stepped close to him, and rested her cheek on his chest. Her hair smelled like home: rushes and fire smoke, cold mornings and sheep's milk. "Or we can gather close. No one to shame us now." She wrapped her arms around his waist. "It's all new, Marish, but it ain't all bad."

A shadow drifted over them, and Marish looked up to see the djinn on his carpet, peering down. Marish cleared his throat. "Well . . . I suppose we're all we have left, aren't we?"

"That's so," Maghd breathed softly.

He took her hands in his, and drew back to look at her. "Will you be mine, Maghd?" he said.

"Oh yes," said Maghd, and smiled the biggest smile of her life.

"Very good," Marish said, and looked up. "You can take her now."

The djinn opened the little bottle that was in his hand and Maghd the White Witch flew into it, and he put the cap on. He bowed to Marish, and then he flew away.

Behind Marish the fire beast exploded with a dull boom.

Marish walked out of the village a little ways and sat, and after sitting a while he slept. And then he woke and sat, and then he slept some more. Perhaps he ate as well; he wasn't sure what. Mostly he looked at his hands; they were rough and callused, with dirt under the nails. He watched the wind painting waves in the short grass, around the rocks and bodies lying there.

One morning he woke, and the ruined village was full of jackal-headed men in armor made of discs who were mounted on great red cats with pointed ears, and jackal-headed men in black robes who were measuring for monuments, and jackal-headed men dressed only in loincloths who were digging in the ground.

Marish went to the ones in loincloths and said, "I want to help bury them," and they gave him a shovel.

FOX BONES. *MANY USES.*

Alex Dally MacFarlane

A fox's foreleg bones: humerus, ulna, and radius. Main use:
attack. Also used for treating colds and headaches.

The two imperial men were walking in an alarmingly accurate
direction.

"Let's go," Za said. With only a glance in the direction of
her basket, safely hidden among rocks where no one could see
it, she opened the fox-ear pouch she wore at her waist and
pinched ground foreleg bones from one compartment. *For
fur-bright fire*, she thought as she licked it from her fingers. She
made saliva to swallow it down. *For strength.*

Her brothers did the same, and together – full of power,
bursting with it like a rice-wine container over-full and leak-
ing – they descended into the gully and chased the imperial
men, with fire at their fingers.

The men had swords. Za and her brothers laughed and
circled them, marking how their eyes went wide.

"You're going to die," Za said in the Nu language – the
imperial language – and traced arcs of fire through the air with
her fingers.

"So are you," one of the men replied, "but only after giving
the emperor all your silver, little animal." He lunged at her, his
sword swinging sudden as a midwinter wind.

He fell, covered in Za's fire, and only screamed for a moment
before it burnt away his throat.

The other man died under her brothers' fire – but he
reached for something in his bags and hurled it into the air
before they finished killing him.

The siblings stood over the bodies, their power fading, and stared up as a white ball flew straight into the sky, far above the trees, and began to blaze like a small sun.

In the men's bags, they found a map that marked a village high in the hills.

"It's too close." Tou moved his finger marginally along the hilltop to where their village truly lay.

"Look." Za unfolded the map further and, with each piece of paper she exposed, she felt more and more sick. Villages dotted the high hills. "They're all too close."

From the mountains in the far north, where vast spirits kept the snow from ever melting, the green hills stretched out like numerous fingers towards the lowlands where the Nu lived. Only two hill-fingers away from theirs, a perfectly placed dot marked the village where Koua, Za's closest childhood friend, had gone to be married. Imperial men had been there, almost two years earlier – forcing the people of the village to reveal the location of their silver mine, forcing them to work it until their bones filled the empty tunnels.

"Take the bodies to the river," Za said. "Just in case that thing up there burns out before more of them can arrive. Then scout more, in case they weren't the only group. I'm going to see if I can find out any good information."

"How?" Tou asked, just curious –

– but Pao knew. "If you trust a word that comes out of that man's mouth, you deserve to join these men in the river!"

"He hates them almost as much as we do!" Za snapped back, wanting their mother's strength to smack him into silence.

"So he said! To win you over, to   "

"Enough," Tou said. "They will come anyway. If Za can convince that man to tell us anything useful, she should try."

"You're an idiot," Pao spat, but he didn't stop Za as she ran back to her basket, where her infant son was bundled with the bamboo shoots she had been harvesting.

She began the long walk downhill to the trade town, hating Pao, hating the Nu, trying to ignore her son's complaints at her long, jostling pace.

*Fox-skull. Many purposes, including the
acquisition of the fox's ability to see at night
and its strong senses of smell and hearing.*

Za had hunted the fox when she was still weak and sore from childbirth, but no one else would do it for a half-Nu baby.

"Perhaps it's for the best," her mother had advised as the boy, small from his premature delivery, cried feebly beside Za. "He will only last a few days. And because of his size, he has not hurt you."

As soon as night fell on the boy's second day and everyone slept, Za wrapped herself in clothes and gathered what she needed: her bow and arrows, her fox-ear pouch, her mortar and pestle. She touched her baby once on the forehead, gently, so as not to wake him, and set out into the snow that coated the ground in a fine layer like cotton.

Her pouch still contained fox-skull.

It cast the forest in a pale-grey glow. Za sniffed the wind. Foxes sometimes hid in winter, but they didn't hibernate. They needed to hunt too.

Za tried to put aside her mother's words. "It only works half the time, and who knows what his Nu blood will do? It probably won't work at all. He's small and sickly – let nature run its course."

"I want to try," she had said.

"Listen to wisdom for once in your life, child!" Temper had flared in her mother's voice – the same anger that had made her strike Za to the floor when she revealed the pregnancy, although later she had apologized with grief in her eyes. "Your life will be normal again. Don't you want that?"

In the snow, an hour's hard hike from her village, Za crouched. Something rustled. She nocked an arrow and waited, still as a rock, until she saw what her nose had found: a male fox, searching for food. Za drew the bowstring back and released, and her arrow struck it in the rump, only wounding. It ran off – slowly, dripping blood, and even sore, tired Za managed to follow it until she had a clear second shot.

She finished it with her knife and flayed it on the spot, rolled up the hide to carry home, and began stripping away the flesh. The hide would help to make her son's first jacket, she decided, and the flesh would go into a stew for herself, to restore her energy and enrich her milk. But before all that, she needed the bones.

Out of respect for the fox, she ground its bones there, setting her mortar and pestle in the snow and forcing her cold fingers to cooperate. First she ground the tail bones, murmuring the words her grandmother had taught her early in the pregnancy: *For a strong heart. For strong lungs. For strong arms and legs. For strength. For strength.* She poured the pale powder into a small pouch. Then she ground the other bones, separating them as use dictated, and picked up the hide and meat and set off home with steps full of fear: that the tail bones would not strengthen her son; or that they would, and her mother would hate her for it.

A fox's hindleg bones: femur, tibia, and fibula.
The speed that a sprinting fox longs for.

Further south, the hills were entirely cultivated, and the trade town sat among them like a curious outcrop of bare fat trees. Za followed a narrow path from an outlying village. On either side, terraces of rice and corn stretched up and down the hill: over a hundred large steps from the top of the hill to the valley, and again on the other side.

If she glanced north, the imperial men's orb still shone in the sky.

With several weeks until the next trade day, the town's streets were almost bare. Men and women worked in the surrounding fields while children helped or watched animals or played near their houses. A few people recognized her, with her half-Nu son; she hurried between the houses with their anger at her back.

She remembered liking this town.

At its far side, a house sat slightly apart from the others, identical in construction – walls of wood and a roof of dried banana leaves – but far smaller. Almost at its door she stopped, biting her fingers. She needed information. She didn't want to talk about anything else – she wouldn't let him. Fixing her village firmly in her mind – her grandparents, her parents, her littlest sister who liked to chase the chickens – she took one step forward, and another, and soon she stood outside the doorway, looking at the man bent over his paper with ink staining his fingers dark like indigo, as if she had never left.

Hello. I hate you. No I don't. Why was I stupid in the fertile part of my cycle?

"Why are there imperial men in the northern hills?"

The brush in Truc's hand clattered to the paper, ruining his words. "Za," he said, then thought better of whatever he'd wanted to ask first. Silence grew awkwardly between them. Her son stood up in the basket, trying to pull himself up to see over her shoulder, and Truc's agonized expression worsened. "He's mine?" he asked softly.

Za glared at him. *What other Nu man was I fucking?* The father couldn't be a Hma man – the differences between Hma and half-Nu babies were small, but they'd been pointed out enough that Za doubted anyone could miss them.

"Tell me about the imperial men," she demanded.

"What imperial men? Um, do you want to come inside? I have some soup and tea and . . ." His words withered. "Come inside, at least, Za, and sit down." Several stools sat by the wall, unused. If Za's shoulders had hurt less, if her feet hadn't needed to carry her to the town so quickly, she might have refused him. Instead, she stepped inside and gently put the basket on the floor beside her and sat on one of the stools, longing for the silent emptiness of the forest.

Truc stayed at his table, stiff-shouldered, not quite watching her or her son.

"You must know about them," Za said. "You're still one of them – someone would have come to you. What did you tell them?"

Sighing, he said, "They came to me with a map and asked me to confirm its details."

"A map." From among bundles of uncooked rice and freshly cut bamboo shoots and some corn she had traded in the last village for extra shoots, she removed the map: wet on the edges, from rainfall and her son's brief mouthy fascination, but unmistakable.

"Yes." Truc looked directly at her. "That orb in the sky is theirs. I assume that, when you took this map, one of them managed to set it off."

"You told them where to go." *Deny it,* she thought. Then, *Tell the truth.*

"No. I promise you, no. I told them nothing, even though they threatened me. I threatened back. They left. And now that orb is in the sky, confirming their suspicions." He sounded genuinely unhappy.

"What are they doing?"

"Looking for silver, of course, but that is not all. What I managed to get their leader to say indicated tensions in the imperial court – they need an enemy to fight for a while, and your secretive, silver-rich people suit their needs perfectly."

"Why? There's so many people in their empire."

"And they are busy fighting most of the others, too." Truc smiled wryly. "This is why I left, remember."

"I remember you saying that my people would be safe."

His meagre humour faded. "I thought you would be. That map . . . I don't know where they got that information."

"How do we stop them?"

"I don't know."

Two years ago, after the destruction of Koua's new village, he hadn't been able to answer. He had promised to think of ideas, to use his exiled life in ways that benefited the people of the hills – but Za's mother had been right. None of his fine ideals made a difference.

"Are there more of them?" she asked, because nothing mattered except getting information.

"Yes. A small detachment – about one hundred, I believe. They are probably in the hills north of here already."

One hundred imperial soldiers walking faster than she could, guided by the orb.

She stood up and took her son from the basket. "Goodbye."

"Za," he said as she turned, and he filled her name with an intensity of emotion that surprised her.

"I need to tell my people," she said without looking back. "I need to travel fast."

Many more questions hung in the air between them. She answered just one.

"His name's Cheu." She didn't tell Truc that sometimes, on days when she looked at her son's face and saw every small

way he differed from little Hma boys, she called him Fenh – a
Nu name, one of Truc's many.

Outside the town, she tied her son to her chest and swallowed ground hindlegs.

A fox's tail vertebrae. Used to sustain life.

Za breathed a story on to the ground tail bones:

"Long ago, all our people were created in the mountains, by
a great spirit who had already created many animals. When the
time came for the spirit to make people, a different animal
oversaw each of our births: foxes watched the first Hma man
and woman be stitched from the air, ants watched the first
Daren, snakes watched the first Pinoh, and so on.

"Many years later, the spirit grew weary of our company and
sent us away, and we moved south into the hills where we settled
comfortably and developed our own ways of life. Even we Hma
are different. Some of us, whose clothes are bright as every
flower combined, live in the same hills as many other people,
and are probably the most numerous. Some of us, whose clothes
are almost fully black and whose cheeks are tattooed with lines
as thin as hairs, live in small numbers in hills far to the west. We,
the only hill-people to live where snow sometimes falls, are scattered across many hills, always in the north, always hidden."

She pressed more powder to the baby's tongue.

I will make you fully Hma, she thought. *I will fill you with our
stories – then you'll have to be Hma, and this will work, and you'll
live, and everyone will stop hating you.*

Blinking away tears, she began another story.

*A fox's scapula. Pleasant when smoked with
tobacco. Said to promote health in the elderly.*

Za stopped at the last Hma village before hers, a place where
two rivers crashed together and bamboo grew thick-stemmed
on the shore. The white peaks of distant mountains hung in the
northern sky like clouds. She put away her fox-speed at the
village's edge and appeared in front of an old woman who sat
on a fence surrounding a small corn field.

"That's a good trick!" the woman said, grinning toothlessly. "Although I don't think your son likes it."

He still wailed against her chest.

"He's fine," Za said. The sudden stop had jarred her. She blinked, expecting the village to blur like the road behind her. She kept herself still.

"Will you be staying long?"

"No."

"What do you want to discuss then, little mountain one?"

The noises of the village and the eternal river wrapped around each other in a distant knot. Here, with only her son's quietening cries and the faint sucking of the old woman on her pipe, she didn't feel like she did in the village. She preferred being here. In the village they often derided her for sleeping with a Nu man, the girls with their Hma husbands and their first Hma children with perfect little Hma faces.

"Would you at least like a drink?"

"No." Za felt stable enough to talk. "My village is in danger. I have to hurry to them."

"The imperial men," the old woman said unhappily.

"What do you know about them?"

"They have been in this area, hunting silver." Anger simmered in her eyes, but sadness kept it from boiling. "We told them we don't know the location of any mines. We trade the silver for our corn, for our little chickens that hatch as easily as the sun rises. So they stole as much of our silver as they could, and moved on."

Za looked at the woman's jacket, so brightly stitched that she hadn't noticed how little silver adorned it – only two small discs, which would sit side-by-side if she fastened the jacket at her throat. And she wore just two narrow hoops of silver in her ears. Compared to her, Za felt like a silver mine. One thick band of stitched colour – red and white and yellow and black, and the russet of magic-rich fox fur – circled her indigo-dark jacket at her chest, and a row of silver discs ran above and below it. A similar design circled the end of both sleeves. Nothing decorated her dark trousers or boots, but thick bracelets clustered at her wrists and a large hoop hung from each ear. Even her son, whose jacket bore thick bands of fox fur for protection, owned more silver than the old woman.

Za's village knew a good silver mine, as bounteous as the summer sun. A sick suspicion clenched in her.

"You told them," she hissed.

"No." The old woman spoke firmly. "We don't know where you live, so how could we give them any details? They're far away, we said. They come to us but we don't go to them. And then, a month later, one of our men went hunting and never returned."

Of all the people of the village, a hunter would best be able to guess the village's location.

"We still don't know where he is," the old woman said. "Perhaps he lives, in one of the stolen mines. Perhaps his ghost wanders the mountains, lost."

Za shivered. "They're coming for us."

"That light in the sky is theirs, isn't it?"

"Too near."

Za realized she was holding on to her son, like a child with a new fur. *You will be safe*, she thought. *At least, from the Nu.* What would they do to a half-Nu child? Throw him into the forest with the other infants, too small to work in a mine, left to cry at pines and rocks for food? Keep him? Sneer at him, just like everyone else?

"He's a handsome child," the old woman said, smiling. "A year?"

"Almost." Za swallowed. "Thank you." She couldn't remember when someone had last complimented her child. She stroked his hair absently. "I have to go."

"Safe journeys, little mountain ones. I hope you impale many imperial soldiers on your claws."

Za grinned. "Oh, we will."

Some people stared as she jogged through the village, but the wind stole their words – she slid back into her fox-speed and ran with the forest blurring at her sides. She heard her son scream.

"Hush," she said, gasping, jarring again from fast to slow. "Please. We need to hurry."

The wails tore at her ears.

Za opened the pouch at her waist and frowned as, for the first time since the days after his birth, she fed him fox-bone. *At two years*, her grandmother had said. *Wait two years. It is powerful and dangerous; wait, unless the baby's life is in danger.* Well, it most likely was. The Nu would laugh as they tore the silver from his jacket and threw him aside. Stupid to think otherwise.

His eyes went wide and he inhaled as if trying to breathe all of the journey ahead.

"All you have to do is stay still," she told him, "and try to enjoy it." She felt very strange, talking to him like this. "Can you do that?"

He wriggled and stared into the forest, so Za re-bound him to her chest, facing out, and hoped he didn't get too many bugs in his eyes and mouth. Slitting her own eyes, she ran, and her son pealed with joy.

Fox hide. *Use varies depending on how it is stitched.*

Za sat nearly alone in her family's house, winding a long braided strip of fox hide around her son's head: one loop for every week he had lived so far and for every decade she hoped he would live. Ten weeks accumulated around his head, with its tufty dark hair. Soft as a fox cub's, Za thought. Ten decades – though none lived that long. He watched her, with dark eyes in a face that seemed to get plumper every day, slowly gaining the fat he should have got in her womb.

"For sixty healthy years," Za said, on the sixth loop.

No one joined them for this ritual, except for her littlest sister who sat just inside the doorway, crouched and wary. Misbehaving Bao, who ignored their mother's order.

Za didn't shoo her away.

"For seventy healthy years," Za said, on the seventh loop.

Her son watched her with such contentment, such a simple kind of happiness: fed and warm and full of fox-strength, wrapped in it tight as the linens, woollen blankets and the fur stitched with every protective strengthening thread Za knew. As she began the eighth loop, he made little noises of pleasure.

Her hands and her mouth worked, put magic into him, but she turned her head away.

At Bao's ten-week ritual, her extended family and almost everyone else from the village had crowded into their house or peered in from outside, through the door and windows. They had prepared a feast. They had sung and beat on the fox-hide drums brought out only for this day: small drums, with threads as white as snow and as grey as rocks criss-crossing the deep, rich russet of the fox. Ten weeks! They had hung ten amulets in the house, to keep the ten child-spirits sweet, and they had stamped ten times to send death away. Stay, ten-week baby! They had named her.

"For ninety healthy years," Za said, unable to keep the tremor from her voice. She imagined her family gathered around her son, and tears rolled over her face like an icicle melting.

"For a hundred healthy years."

She sewed the braid fast with sun-yellow thread, brought the thread round and round and round the join so that it bulged like a strange stone. She kept her hands steady, though her tears splashed on her son's face.

Her son, who needed a name.

Possibilities tangled in her head: Hma names, good names, beautiful names, Nu names. Little half-Nu boy who no one but her – and Bao, who remained by the door, probably just curious about a part of her life she couldn't remember – would acknowledge. Her mother wasn't even speaking to her anymore. A Nu name would suit him. Why couldn't he look Hma? Why couldn't the stories she'd poured into him with milk and powdered fox-bone, a uniquely Hma magic – why couldn't her milk, her fully Hma milk – why couldn't all of it make him Hma and not Nu?

Za picked up her son, held him out – to the family that wasn't there. Her hands shook. "Your name," she managed, before sobs replaced the name she'd picked at random. She thought, wildly, *I'll drop him and he'll die and my family will talk to me again.*

"What's his name?" a small voice said.

Old enough to want to be helpful, little Bao put her hands under Za's son, steadying Za's hands. Such a serious expression for a three-year-old's face.

"Your name," Za said softly, "is Cheu."

"Cheu!" Bao said excitedly. It was a common name; Za suddenly remembered that a boy Bao's age had that name. His parents wouldn't like her for this. Za decided she didn't care.

"Be strong, Cheu. Be brave, Cheu. Be loving, Cheu. Be healthy, Cheu."

Bao echoed her words as closely as possible and kissed Cheu's head afterwards.

He wouldn't tolerate being held up for much longer; his face scrunched and he cried for milk. Za returned to the edge of the room, where her blankets and cushions made a far more comfortable place to nurse, and rearranged her jacket around him. It didn't take long for Bao to grow bored of watching. The girl wandered away and Za was alone once again, with the fox hide around her son's head scratching uncomfortably at her chest and only the drip-drip of her tears for company.

Fox teeth. *For tearing enemies to pieces.*

"We must move the village," said Yi, the old woman who took charge in times of difficulty. She sat on a little wooden stool in the open space between houses, where early winter sun fell on the gathered villagers like an offering. Everyone stayed silent as she talked. "It was last done when my grandparents were children, also to escape the Nu. We must gather our possessions tonight and leave at first light tomorrow, and when the Nu soldiers arrive they will find only empty houses to burn to the ground. If they find our mines, they will have to work the silver themselves."

Or have other Hma work them, Za thought. *Or us, caught while we're fleeing.*

She bit her fingers, reluctant to speak out – to have the entire village stare at her, with her son fidgeting in her arms. But she couldn't let them agree to this.

"Mother-Yi, may I talk?"

When everyone stared at her, she did her best to ignore them, focusing on old Yi with her smile empty of teeth.

"Of course, child. You have brought us such valuable information. Speak up!"

Murmurs spread. Not everyone agreed with Yi's generosity. Za clutched her son tighter and spoke.

"They are only days behind us and I probably didn't take their only map. They know where our village is. With a hundred of them, they'll find it. And they'll find our trail – not even we can hide the movement of a whole village. A stray heel-print here, a dropped thread there, and they'll follow us into the mountains, and we'll never be able to live in safety.

"But if we kill them all, or send them running, by the time they try to find us again, our tracks will have faded. Winter is coming, in only a month or two. Perhaps the snow will fall again." And they would go into it, towards those higher reaches where people were no longer supposed to dwell, where mountains birthed icy winds and spirits slept. How far did they need to move to be safe forever? How far would the mountains let them?

"So keen to kill the people who are just like your baby's father!" one of the men exclaimed.

Laughter fell around her like slung stones.

Since her son's birth she had stayed away from the other people of the village, had split her time between household work and going far from the village on patrol. They laughed and she wanted to run back into the forest with her son, wanted to throw him aside and beg their forgiveness. Hated herself for both thoughts. Hated them.

Yi glared at the villagers and reached for her staff, no doubt to stamp it on the ground and demand their respect.

Someone mentioned trust and whether spreading her legs for a Nu man made her Nu too.

"Shut up!" Za screamed, and realized it had been Pao and that their mother had smacked him so hard he lay on the ground, moaning. "He's not—" He was. Little half-Nu boy, ugly little boy, from loose-legged Za. She felt it all, rattling around in her skin like knuckle-bones in a cup. "He's Hma!" she shouted, as Yi drew the conversation back to its main subject. Some people went quiet. "He's Hma! He's Hma and he's mine and I'm Hma, I fed him fox-bone, I told him all our stories while he drank my milk, and if you don't shut up you can drink my piss!"

Everyone stared at her in silence.

She shook, held Cheu to her chest, said, "Why don't you ever shut up?" And for once, they did.

Her mother put a hand on her shoulder. "I think Za is right. If we all flee together, they will follow us. Some of us must defend the rest – but not by killing them. We cannot. Count every healthy adult in the village who possesses enough skill and power with the fox-bones to fight, and you will not find fifty, or forty, or even thirty. We could surprise them, and then they would recover, and kill us, as our finite power fades.

"However, there is something else we can do: destroy their supplies, and perhaps kill a few of them, to put the fright in them. Without their supplies they cannot follow us. It will be dangerous and difficult, and perhaps each soldier sleeps beside their food . . ." Her voice faltered there, at the difficulty of their task. "But I think this is our best chance. And I will be honoured if Za is with us."

Whatever Pao might have said next was silenced by Tou, who kicked him in the ribs.

As the village agreed with Za's mother's plan, Za wiped away tears with the fox-fur on her sleeve and returned to the ground, tucked away among other people.

Later, her mother murmured angrily, "You are Hma, even if your son isn't, fully."

Za stroked his hair.

The village split in two, its very walls taken apart – small parts bound to backs, transported ahead to be the first walls, shelter for the young, the elderly, the infirm. Its nearby stores were opened and emptied, sacks of rice put on to two wagons, sacks of dried corn added to the wagons where possible, added to baskets and hefted by all but the weakest of the group who departed. The two buffalo, used to plough the lower-altitude rice terraces at certain times of year, were brought from their pens and tied to the wagons, touched fondly by passing people. *Be steady. Be strong.* The further food stores, kept separate from the village for safety, were not touched. In safer times, people would return and find what remained. Children accepted bags of pots, herbs, any spare clothes. Adults hefted baskets full of not just food but fabric, medicines, silver. The graves of the dead were honoured one last time.

The group who departed began their journey throughout the day: wagons and children and the elderly and infirm and adults who possessed little ability with the magic and some adults who did, protecting their mobile village.

Za watched Tou walk away with her son in a fabric-filled basket on his back. "Time to go," her mother said.

"Yes."

With pouches full of fox-bone, they left the village behind.

The forest opened to them like a fox-ear pouch and they pierced their tongues with teeth. They swallowed foreleg bones and hindleg bones and skull.

They spread out. The forest crunched under Za's feet and she knew it crunched under twenty-one other pairs of feet, knew that her mother ran nearby, that Pao and Xi ran together, her with a tiny child curled in her womb like a fleck of dust. This fight would determine the new lives of many, and Xi did not consider her new life more important than those, though she hoped it would survive.

Za bared her teeth, thinking of the village's future – and of her son, more distant with every step. She felt Tou, who had swallowed fox-skull to sense the forest around the fleeing villagers, holding him.

She knew when Xi killed a Nu scout, tearing his chest open before he even realized she stood in front of him. She knew when another scout fell, and another.

She knew when the first of their group found the army, camped on a flat place where, generations ago, their village had grown rice.

"There are small tents, for the soldiers," her mother said, and everyone heard despite the distances between them, "and bigger tents. Perhaps they contain supplies. We must burn them – and burn the small tents too, if possible, in case they also contain supplies, and because the soldiers will not survive the high-hill nights without them if they still pursue us."

At her wordless yell, they burst from the forest as one.

The first soldiers ran, terrified, and two of the larger tents shone in the night. But the soldiers regrouped, with weapons no one had anticipated. They gathered together to defend their remaining two large tents, holding swords like teeth, and threw gourds full of something that exploded and tore apart even fox-fast limbs. Za felt two deaths – brief agonies that left her gasping. Nearby, Xi screamed. Pao lay lifeless in his blood. The soldiers readied to throw more of their gourds, and Za dashed forwards, grabbed Xi, pulled her away to safety.

If only the fox-bones let them throw their fire like gourds, over the soldiers' heads, on to the tents.

"We need to lure them away!" Za's mother said.

Their group crouched among tents and the old ridges between rice paddies, holding themselves still, putting more fox-bone on their tongues. Xi's tears dripped on to her fingers and she chased the smeared bone with her tongue. Za hurt, too – she hadn't wanted Pao to die, hadn't wanted to see a former friend torn open. "We'll get them," Za whispered – to Xi, to all of their group. Movement. "Look. Those men by their tent." Not all of the soldiers were in big, safe groups after all. Za and Xi ran forward, pounced on three men, killing one of them – and dragged the other two away, towards the forest, and others ran out of cover to circle them, tracing fire-shapes in the air as if they planned to torture the screaming men all together.

Several soldiers broke away from the two groups. Shouts told them not to, but they ran forwards and they were captured too, or killed. Even more followed.

Za felt her mother and six others emerge from hiding, and in the fear and frenzy they reached the tents, and the fires began to warm the night. The soldiers scattered, afraid again, and the Hma ran through the camp, laughing, igniting the smaller tents. "Run south!" Za yelled at the soldiers who fled her fire. "Run south!" *And give us enough time to escape!*

Someone screamed.

Za knew that scream. It was as if Tou stood beside her, as if he had come down from the fleeing village, but—

No. *No.*

They slowed, they looked up into the hills, as if they could see clearly the ambush falling on their moving village.

They ran.

A fox's heels. Mixed with certain herbs, an abortifacient.

Throughout the pregnancy, Za knew where to find the necessary herbs: carefully dried, hanging from the ceiling. They wafted in the breezes that drifted through the house, as if beckoning her. Once, she tore off enough leaves and held them over a pot of boiling water, and imagined how easily the barely developed baby would leave her body. No half-Nu child.

When only she knew about the pregnancy, she had found happiness in the thought of a child, though it hadn't come according to her plans. But neither had Koua's death; neither had meeting Truc. She had accepted it. Then – shouting, fists, silence.

She didn't know what to do. She dropped the herbs to the floor.

She didn't decide and then it was too late, and her son came out of her, bringing with him a knifing hurt at the way his eyes folded more like a Nu than a Hma, the months of silence from her mother, the looks and the comments from her village all the way down to the trading town, from people who had always smiled at her.

A fox's pelvis. Used in several healing remedies.

Yi led the defence: burning bright with her fire, tearing away pieces of wall-wood and hurling them in flames at the soldiers. Others – old, young – clustered around her and in smaller groups, protecting anyone unable to fight.

Bodies lay along the ground like rocks.

Za's mother directed the returning group: encircle the attackers, kill as quickly as possible. "Do not look down. Later we will mourn the dead."

They all looked.

Two little girls lay on the ground. Not Bao. Za blinked away tears at the sight of such young deaths – and there were babies, too. But though she ran faster than storm-winds and left soldiers clutching their burnt throats behind her, she couldn't find Tou or Cheu.

Her father and grandparents stood with Yi, and Bao hid at their feet. Za circled around them, fending off soldiers, who scattered, finally outnumbered.

As her fox-bone ran out, as her senses and speed and fire-hot fingers returned to normal, the cold night fell on Za and she collapsed. "Cheu," she gasped. Around her, the village rearranged itself for the next few hours: healing those who could be saved, honouring those who could not.

Za's father brought a bowl of hot stew made with ground pelvis and helped her drink.

"Tou felt Pao die," he said, "and then they attacked us. He ran after some soldiers, away into the forest, and he hasn't come back."

"Cheu."

Her father stroked her hair. "He was with Tou."

Though every part of her body protested, stiff and sore, Za got to her feet.

"You need to rest, Za."

"No."

The forest kept its secret for so long that she stopped crying. She forced one foot in front of the other, knowing that eventually she would find their bodies, and bury them, and move on into the mountains with the rest of her village. Branches scratched her face. The cold ached in her fingers. Battle-wounds worsened; she limped, but she could still walk. The moon gave her poor light to see with. High above, the orb had finally dimmed, and the other soldiers hadn't carried a replacement – or it had been destroyed. Za managed to smile. Maybe the village had enough time now.

Something cried.

She looked to one side, at a dark shadow: a cave.

In it, still-breathing Tou curled unconscious around the basket. Cheu cried hungrily.

"Oh." Za sank to the ground, to pull him from the bundled cloths and silver and hold him close.

As the village moved into the whitening mountains, Za felt as though some looked at her and Cheu with mistrust as often as snowflakes fell around them. She carried a basket as heavy as anyone else's, she cried together with Xi at the memory of Pao's death, she hunted and cooked and sat with everyone else, turning hides into mountain clothes – yet the looks didn't stop.

Most of the time she walked with her mother, who out-glared them all, and stayed utterly silent.

Cheu babbled sometimes, apparently fascinated by the cold, exhausting, hungry process of fleeing. Wrapped in hide and spare fabric, nestled in a child's basket padded with pine needles for extra warmth, fed as much meat as she could spare, he didn't feel any of it. Za made sure of it.

No soldiers had attacked; with a week between the village and the ambush, many began hoping for safety. Many began to talk more decisively of where to build their new village. They needed to survive the winter, but then their lives could begin anew.

In a few months, Cheu's noises would be words. *Mama. Papa?* Za wrapped her arms around his basket, torn between shushing him – how they looked at her whenever he babbled, how they looked at him – and letting him practise his infant-babble.

He deserved better. And not just, Za thought, from the village. From her. That old woman had called him handsome. A handful of people looked at him differently. Limping Tou ruffled his short hair. Xi gave him pine cones to play with, snapping off some of the scales to make them look like people. Za's mother started smiling at him in the evenings, when he pottered around their fire pointing at sparks. Za's grandmother winked at him as she carried her remaining chickens.

One night, Za couldn't sleep for crying, so angry at herself.

The next morning, as she heaped snow over the ashes of their fire and hoisted her baskets on to her back and front, she began to sing to him. People glared at her. She flushed and fell silent. But as the village began to walk, they looked away; quietly, so that only Cheu could hear, she gathered up her courage and sang,

> *I ground the fox-bones*
> *for you,*
> *I hand-stitched the jacket*
> *for you,*
> *I walked into the mountains*
> *for you . . .*

WHERE VIRTUE LIVES

Saladin Ahmed

"I'm telling you, Doctor, its eyes – its teeth! The hissing! Name of God, I've never been so scared!"

Doctor Adoulla Makhslood, the best ghul hunter in the great city of Dhamsawaat, was weary. Two and a half bars of thousand-sheet pastry sat on his plate, their honey- and pistachio-glazed layers glistening in the sunlight that streamed into Yehyeh's teahouse. Adoulla let out a belch. *Only two hours awake. Only partway through my pastry and cardamom tea, and already a panicked man stands chattering to me about a monster! God help me.*

He brushed green and gold pastry bits from his fingers on to his spotless kaftan. Magically, the crumbs and honey-spots slid from his garment to the floor, leaving no stain. The kaftan was as white as the moon. Its folds seemed to go on forever, much like the man sitting before him.

"That hissing! I'm telling you, I didn't mean to leave her. But by God, I was so scared!" Hafi, the younger cousin of Adoulla's dear friend Yehyeh, had said "I'm telling you" twelve times already. Repetition helped folk talk away their fear, so Adoulla had let the man go on for a while. He had heard the story thrice now, listening for the inconsistencies fear introduces to memories – even honest men's memories.

Adoulla knew some of what he faced. A water ghul had abducted Hafi's wife, dragging her toward a red riverboat with eyes painted on its prow. Adoulla didn't need to hear any more from Hafi. What he needed was more tea. But there was no time.

"She's gone!" Hafi wailed. "That horrible thing took her! And like a coward, I ran! Will you help me, Doctor?"

For most of his life men had asked Adoulla this question. In his youth he'd been the best brawler on Dead Donkey Lane, and the other boys had looked up to him. Now men saw his attire and asked for his help with monsters. Adoulla knew too well that his head-hair had flown and his gut had grown. But his ghul hunter's raiment was unchanged after decades of grim work – still famously enchanted so that it could never be dirtied, and quietly blessed so that neither sword nor knife could pierce it.

Still, he didn't allow himself to feel too secure. In his forty years ghul hunting he'd faced a hundred deaths other than sword-death. Which deaths he would face today remained to be seen.

"Enough," Adoulla said, cutting off yet more words from Hafi. "I've some ideas where to start. I don't know if your wife still lives, young man. I can't promise to return her to you. But I'll try my best to do so, and to stop whomever's responsible, God damn them."

"Thank you, Doctor! Um . . . I mean . . . I hereby thank and praise you, and beg God's blessings for you, O great and virtuous ghul hunter!"

Does he think I'm some pompous physician, to be flattered by ceremony? A ghul hunter shared a title but little else with the haughty doctors of the body. No leech-wielding charlatan of a physician could stop the fanged horrors that Adoulla battled.

Adoulla swallowed a sarcastic comment and stood up. He embraced Hafi, kissing him on both cheeks. "Yes, well. I will do all I can, child of God." He dismissed the younger man with a reassuring pat on the back.

O God, Adoulla thought, *why have You made this life so tiring? And why so full of interrupted meals?* In six quick bites he ate the remaining pastries. Then, sweets in his belly and a familiar reluctance rising within him, he left Yehyeh's teahouse in search of a riverboat with painted eyes, a ghul, and a bride whom Adoulla hoped to God was still alive.

Raseed bas Raseed frowned in distaste as he made his way down the crowded Dhamsawaat street his guide called the Lane of Monkeys. Six days ago Raseed had walked along a quiet road near the Lodge of God. Six days ago he'd killed three highwaymen. Now he was in Dhamsawaat, King of Cities, and there were dirty, wicked folk all about him. City people who spoke with too much speed and too little respect. Raseed brushed dust from his dervish-blue silks. As he followed his lanky guide through the press of people, he dwelt – though it was impermissibly proud to do so – on his encounter with the highwaymen.

"A 'Dervish Dressed in Blue', eh? Just like in the song! I hear you sons of whores hide jewels in those pretty dresses."

"Haw haw! 'Dervish Dressed in Blue'! That's funny! Sing for us, little dervish!"

"What do you think that forked sword'll do against three men's spears, pup? Can your skinny arms even lift it?"

When the robbers had mentioned that blasphemous song, they had approached the line that separates life from death. When they had moved from rough talk to brandishing spears, they'd crossed that line. Three bodies now lay rotting by the road. Raseed tried not to smile with pride at the thought.

They'd underestimated him. He was six-and-ten, though he knew he hardly looked it. Clean-shaven, barely five feet, and thin-limbed as well. But his silk tunic and trousers – the habit of the Order – warned most ruffians that Raseed was no easy target. As did the curved sword at his hip, forked to "cleave the right from the wrong in men", as the Traditions of the Order put it. The blade and silks inspired respect in the cautious, but fools saw the scrawny boy and not the dervish.

That did not matter, though. Soon, God willing, Raseed would find the great and virtuous ghul hunter Adoulla Makhslood. If it pleased God, the Doctor would take Raseed as an apprentice. *If* Raseed was worthy.

But I am impatient. Proud. Are these virtues? The Traditions of the Order say, "A dervish without virtue is less than a beggar."

The sudden realization that he'd lost sight of his guide pulled him out of his reflections. For a moment Raseed panicked, but the lanky man stepped back into view, gesturing for him to follow. Raseed thanked God that he'd found a reverent and helpful guide, for Dhamsawaat's streets seemed endless. Raseed had been the youngest student ever to earn the blue silks. He feared neither robbers nor ghuls. But he would not know what to do if lost amidst this horde of lewd, impious people.

Life had been less confusing at the Lodge of God. But then High Shaykh Aalli had sent him to train with the Doctor.

"When you meet Adoulla Makhslood, little sparrow, you will see that there are truths greater than all you've learned in this Lodge. You will learn that virtue lives in strange places."

Before him, his guide came to a halt. "Here we are, master dervish. Just over that bridge."

At last. Raseed thanked the man and turned toward the small footbridge. The man tugged at Raseed's sleeve.

"Apologies, master dervish, but the watchmen will not let you cross without paying the crossing tax."

"Crossing tax?"

The man nodded. "And the bastards will charge you too much once they see your silks – they respect neither piety nor the Order. If you wish, though, I will haggle for you. A half-dirham should suffice. Were I a richer man I'd cover your tax myself – it's a sad world where a holy man must pay his way over bridges."

Raseed thanked the man for his kindness and handed him one of his few coins.

"Very good, master dervish. Now please stay out of sight while I bargain. I will return for you shortly. God be with you."

Raseed waited.

And waited.

Adoulla needed information. Ghuls had no souls of their own – they did only as their masters bade. Which meant that a vile man had used a water ghul in his bride-stealing scheme. And if there was one place Adoulla could go to learn of vile men's schemes, it was Miri's. There was no place in the world that pleased him more, nor any that hurt him so.

Though God alone knows when I'll get there. Adoulla walked the packed Mainway, wishing the crowd would move faster, knowing it wouldn't. Overturned cobblers' carts, dead pack animals, traffic-stopping processions of state – Dhamsawaat's hundred headaches hurried for no man. Not even when a ghul stalked the King of Cities.

By the time he reached Miri's tidy storefront it was past midday. Standing in the open doorway, Adoulla smelled sweet incense from iron burners and camelthorn from the hearth. For a long moment he stood there at the threshold, wondering why in the world he'd been away from this lovely place so long.

A corded forearm blocked his way, and another man's shadow fell over him. A muscular man even taller than Adoulla stood scowling before him, a long scar splitting his face into gruesome halves. He placed a broad palm on Adoulla's chest and grabbed a fistful of white kaftan.

"Ho-ho! Who's this forgetter-of-friends, slinking back in here so shamelessly?"

Adoulla smiled. "Just another foolish child of God who doesn't know to stay put, Axeface."

The two men embraced and kissed on both cheeks. Then Axeface bellowed toward an adjoining room, "The Doctor is here, Mistress. You want me to beat him up?"

Adoulla could not see Miri, but he heard her husky voice. "Not today, though I am tempted. Let the old fart through."

For one moment more, though, Axeface held him back. "She misses you, Doctor. I bet she'd still marry you. When're you gonna wake up, huh?" With a good-natured shove, he sent Adoulla stumbling into the greeting-room.

One of the regular girls, wearing a dress made of sheer cloth and copper coins, smiled at Adoulla. The coins jingled as she shimmied past, and he tried to keep from turning his head. *Just my luck*, he thought not for the first time, *that the woman I love runs the whorehouse with the city's prettiest girls*.

Then she was there. Miri Almoussa, Seller of Silks and Sweets, known to a select few as Miri of the Hundred Ears. Her thick curves jiggled as she moved, and her hands were hennaed. Adoulla had to remind himself that he was there to save a girl's life. "When one is married to the ghuls, one has three wives already," went the old ghul hunter's adage. *O God, how I wish I could take a fourth!*

Silently, Miri led him to a divan. She glared at him and brushed her hand over his beard, ridding it of crumbs he hadn't known were there. "You're a wonderful man," she said by way of greeting, "but you can be truly disgusting sometimes."

A man's slurred shouts boomed from the next room. Irritation flashed across Miri's face, but she spoke lightly. "Naj is usually so quiet. Wormwood wine makes him loud. At least he's not singing. Last week it was ten rounds of 'The Druggist, the Draper, and the Man Who Made Paper' before he passed out. Name of God, how I hate that song!" She slid Adoulla a tray with coffee, little salt fish, and rice bread. Adoulla popped a fish into his mouth, the tiny bones crunching as he chewed. Despite the urgency of his visit he was hungry. And Miri was not a woman to be rushed, no matter what the threat.

She continued. "Unlike *some* people, though, Naj can be counted on to be here every week, helping to keep me and mine from poverty. It's been a while, Doullie. What do you want?" She set her powder-painted features into an indifferent mask.

"I'm wondering, pretty one, if you've heard anything about a stolen bride in the Quarter of Stalls."

Miri smiled a disgusted smile. "Predictable! Of course you already have your gigantic nose in this nonsense! Well. For the usual fee plus . . . 5 per cent, I might remember something my Ears have heard."

"A price hike, huh?" Adoulla sighed. "You know I'll pay what you ask, my sweet."

"Indeed you will. We may be more than friends here and there, 'my sweet', but we're not man and wife. *Your* choice, remember? Our monies are separate. And this, Doullie, is about money. Now, according to my Ears . . ."

A name would've made Adoulla's task easier, but Miri's information was almost as good. A red riverboat with eyes painted on the prow had been spotted only two hours ago at an abandoned dock near the Low Bridge of Boats. And Hafi's wife may not have been the first woman taken by the ghul. Two of Miri's Ears said the ghul served a man, one said a woman, but none had gotten a close look.

Still, Adoulla had a location now. Enough to act on. And so, calling himself mad for the thousandth time in his life, Adoulla prepared to leave a wonderful woman's company to chase after monsters.

★   ★   ★

Raseed approached the well-kept storefront and allowed himself to hope. This was not Adoulla Makhslood's home, but after Raseed's "guide" had absconded, an old woman had led Raseed to this storefront, insisting that she had just seen the Doctor enter.

Raseed paused at the threshold. He had journeyed far, and if it pleased God he'd have a new teacher. *If* it pleased God. He took a measured breath and stepped through the doorway.

Inside, the large greeting-room was dim. Scant sunlight made its way through high windows. Tall couches lined the wall opposite the door, and a few well-dressed men sat on them, each speaking to a woman. And at the center of the room, on a juniper-wood divan, sat a middle-aged woman and an old man in a spotless kaftan. They stared as a massive man with a scar ushered Raseed in. Raseed looked at the man in white. *Doctor Adoulla Makhslood?*

It had to be him. He was the right age, though Raseed had expected the Doctor to be leaner. And clean-shaven. This old man had the bumpy knuckles of a fist-fighter. *Can this rough-looking one really be him?*

Raseed bowed his head. "Begging your pardon, but are you Doctor Adoulla Makhslood? The great and virtuous ghul hunter?"

The man snorted a laugh. "'Great and virtuous'? No, boy, you're looking for someone else. I'm Doctor Adoulla Makhslood, the best belcher in Dhamsawaat. If I see this other fellow, though, I'll tell him you're looking for him."

Raseed was confused. *Perhaps he's testing me somehow.* He spoke carefully. "I apologize for disturbing you, Doctor. I am Raseed bas Raseed and I have come, at High Shaykh Aalli's bidding, to offer you my sword in apprenticeship." He bowed and waited for the Doctor's response.

Old Shaykh Aalli? The only true dervish Adoulla had ever known? Adoulla had assumed that ancient Aalli had gone to meet God years ago. Was it really possible this Raseed had been sent by the High Shaykh? And might the boy be of some help? The Doctor sized up the five-foot dervish. He was yellow-toned with tilted eyes and a clean-shaven face. He looked like one who had killed but did not yet value life.

A scabbard of blue leather and lapis lazuli hung at the boy's waist. Adoulla smiled as he thought of the bawdy song that poked fun at an "ascetic" dervish's love for his jeweled scabbard. The tune was as catchy as the words were blasphemous. Without meaning to, Adoulla started humming "Dervish Dressed in Blue". The boy frowned, then bit his lip.

God help me, he looks so sincere. Adoulla sighed and stood, avoiding Miri's glare. "We'll talk as we walk, boy. A girl's life is in danger and time is short." He paid Miri her fee, mumbled his inadequate goodbyes, and herded the boy out on to the street.

A dervish of the Order. Adoulla decided he could not ignore the advantages of having such a swordsman at his side. After all, who knew what awaited him at the Low Bridge of Boats? He was easily winded these days, and he had no time to stop by his townhouse for more supplies. He needed help, truth be told. But first the boy had to be set straight.

"The name of Shaykh Aalli goes far indeed with me, boy. You may accompany me for now. But we're not in a holy man's parable. We're trying to save a poor girl's life and keep from getting ourselves killed. God's gifts and my own study have given me useful powers. But I'll kick a man in his fig-sack if need be, make no mistake. A real girl has been stolen by a real monster. God forbid it, she may be dead. But it's our job to help however we can."

The boy looked uncomfortable, but he bowed his head and said, "Yes, Doctor." That would be enough for now.

The thoroughfare the Doctor called the Street of Festivals was lined with townhouses separated by small gardens. A girl hawked purple pickles from a copper bowl. Raseed smelled something foul, but it wasn't the pickles.

Two houses down a human head had been mounted above the doorway.

The Doctor spat. "The work of 'His Greatness' the Khalif. That is the head of Nassaar Jamala. Charged with treason. He made a few loud speeches at market. Meanwhile, young brides are abducted by ghuls and the watchmen do nothing."

"Surely, Doctor, if the man was a traitor it was righteous that he should die," Raseed said.

"And how is it that *you* are a scholar of righteousness, boy? Because you're clean-shaven and take no wine? Shave your beard and scour your soul?" The Doctor squinted at Raseed. "Do you even need to shave yet? Hmph. What trials has your mewling soul faced, O master dervish of six-and-ten-whole-years? O kisser of I-am-guessing-exactly-zero-girls?"

The Doctor waved his big hand as if brushing away his own words. "Look. There are three possibilities. One, you're a madman or a crook passing yourself off as a dervish. Two, you are a real Lodge-trained holy man – which in all likelihood still makes you a corrupt bully. Three . . ." He gave Raseed a long look. "Three, you are the second dervish of the Order I've ever met who actually lives by his world-saving oaths. If so, boy, you've a cruel, disappointing life ahead."

"'God's mercy is more powerful than all the world's cruelties'," Raseed recited.

But the Doctor merely snorted and walked on.

As Raseed followed through the throngs of people, his soul sank. Despite years of training he felt like a small boy, lost and about to cry. His long journey was over. He had made it to Dhamsawaat. He had found the man Shaykh Aalli named the Crescent Moon Kingdoms's greatest ghul hunter.

And the man was an impious slob.

Doubt began to overwhelm Raseed. What would he do now? He knew that he needed direction – he wasn't so proud that he couldn't admit that. But what could he learn from this gassy, unkempt man?

And yet Raseed could not deny that there was something familiar about Adoulla Makhslood. A strength of presence not unlike High Shaykh Aalli's that seared past the Doctor's sleepy-seeming eyes. Perhaps . . .

He didn't realize he'd come to a halt until a beggar elbowed past him. The Doctor, a dozen yards ahead, turned and hollered at him to hurry. Raseed followed, and they walked on into the late afternoon.

It was nearly evening when they finally approached the abandoned dock near the Low Bridge of Boats. *There should be watchmen here, keeping the street people from moving in*, Adoulla thought. But neither vagrants nor patrols were in sight. *Bribery. Or murder.*

"Doctor!" The boy's whisper was sharp as he pointed out on to the river.

Adoulla saw it too: the red riverboat. He cursed as he saw that it was already leaving the dock. The owner had seen their approach – a lookout spell, no doubt. Adoulla cursed again. Then two figures stepped out from behind a dockhouse twenty yards ahead.

They were shaped vaguely like men, but Adoulla knew the scaly grey flesh and glowing eyes. *Water ghuls. And not one of them, but two!*

Adoulla thanked God that he had the little dervish with him. "Enemies, boy!"

The ghuls hissed through barb-toothed leech-mouths, and their eyes blazed crimson. It was no wonder Hafi had run from them. Any man in his right mind would have.

Adoulla dug into his kidskin satchel and withdrew two jade marbles. He clacked the spheres together in one hand and recited from the Heavenly Chapters.

"God the All-Merciful forgives us our failings."

The jade turned to ash in Adoulla's palm, and there was a noise like a crashing wave. The water ghul nearest him lost its shape and collapsed into a harmless puddle of stinking liquid, twitching with dead snakes and river-spiders.

The drain of the invocation hit Adoulla and he felt as if he'd dashed up a hill. *So much harder every year!*

The other ghul came at them. Raseed sped past Adoulla, his forked sword slashing. The creature snaked left. The boy's weapon whistled through empty air. The ghul drove its scaly fist hard into the boy's jaw. It struck a second time, catching Raseed in the chest. Adoulla was amazed that the boy still stood.

Regaining his own strength, Adoulla reached back into his satchel. He'd had only the two marbles but there was another invocation . . . *Where is that vial?* The ghul struck at Raseed a third time . . .

And the boy dodged. He spun and launched a hard kick into the ghul's midsection. Its red eyes registered no pain, but the creature scrabbled backward.

Adoulla marveled at the boy's speed. Raseed's sword flashed once, twice, thrice, four times. And Adoulla saw that his other invocation would not be needed.

Ghuls fell harder than men, but they fell all the same. The boy had finished this one. Its hissing shifted into the croaks and buzzes of swamp vermin. Its claws raked the air. Then, its false soul snuffed out, the thing collapsed in a watery pile of dead frogs and leeches.

Adoulla smiled at the puddle. *So he's not all bravado, then. Ten-and-six years old!* "Well done, dervish! I've seen stone-hard soldiers run the other way when faced with those glowing eyes. But you stood your ground and you're still alive!"

"It . . . it wouldn't die!" the boy stammered. "I cut it enough to kill five men! It wouldn't die!"

"It was a ghul, boy, not some drunken bully! Let me guess: for all your zeal, this is the first time you've faced one. Well, I won't lie. You did brilliantly. But our work isn't done. We've got to find that boat."

"Brilliantly," he said. Raseed sheathed his sword, trying not to feel pride. He had killed a ghul!

"Thank you, Doctor. I hope—"

He heard a noise from the dockhouse. To his surprise, a scrawny young woman stepped from the shadows. Except that there was not enough shadow there to have hidden her. *How could I not have seen her? Impossible!* The girl wore a dirty dress with billowy sleeves. Her face was a small oval, her left eye badly bruised.

"You killed them," she said. "You *killed* them!"

The Doctor smiled at her. "Well, not *killed*, exactly, dear. They never truly lived. But we stopped them, yes." He bowed slightly, like a modest performer.

"But he said they couldn't be killed! He swore it!"

The Doctor's expression turned grim. "Who swore it? Are you not Hafi's wife? Did these creatures not attack you?"

The girl frowned. "Attack me? I . . . he *swore*," she said dazedly. "They . . . gave me time." She shook her head, as if driving some thought away, and raised a clenched fist. As she did, Raseed saw that she held two short pieces of rope, one white, one blue. His keen eyes noted intricate knots tied at the end of each. The girl raised the white rope – tied with a fat, squarish knot – to her mouth.

"Damn it! Stop her!" the Doctor shouted. There was an unnaturally loud whispery sound as the girl blew on the white rope. As Raseed stood there confused, Adoulla's shout twisted into a scream. The Doctor hunched over, gripping his midsection in agony. He spoke around gritted teeth. "Get. Ropes."

The girl blew on the knot again, and Raseed heard another whispery puff-of-air sound. The old man screamed again and dropped to his knees.

Knot-blowing! Raseed had never seen such wicked magic at work, but he'd heard dark stories. He charged as he saw the girl raise the blue rope – tied with a small, sleek knot – to her lips. *That one's for me*, he realized. But Raseed was too swift. He crossed the space between them and palm-punched the woman flat on her back. The little ropes flew from her hand. Before she could get to her feet, Raseed's sword sang out of its scabbard. He held its forked tip to her throat.

The Doctor shuffled up beside him, panting and still wincing with pain. "Let her stand," he said, and Raseed did so. The Doctor's tone was hard but strangely courteous. "So. Young lady. Blower-on-knots. Were these *your* pet ghuls we destroyed?"

The girl sounded half asleep. "No. Pets? No. Zoud said that . . . said that . . ." She eyed Raseed's sword fearfully and trailed off.

The Doctor took a deep breath and gestured to Raseed, so he brought the blade away from the girl's throat. But he did not sheathe it.

The Doctor's voice grew infuriatingly gentle. "Let's begin again. What's your name, girl?"

The girl's eyes lost a bit of their glaze. She had the decency to look ashamed. "My name's Ushra."

"And who has hurt you, Ushra? The magus who made these ghuls? What's his name?"

The girl looked at the ghuls' puddle-remains. "He . . . my husband is called Zoud. He sent me to stop you while he got away. I'm his wife. First wife. I've . . . I've helped him catch others. Four . . . five now?"

Wickedness, Raseed thought. *This one deserves death.*

"Well, his girl-stealing days are over," the Doctor said. "Whatever's happened, we'll help you, Ushra, but we also need your help."

Raseed could not keep his disapproval to himself. "And why have you never run away, woman? Or used your knots on this Zoud?"

"I would never! I *could* never. You shouldn't say such things!" Ushra looked terrified, and for a moment Raseed almost forgot that she was a wicked blower-on-knots who had just made the Doctor helpless with her magic. For a moment.

"I must go back!" she said. "He'll find me. He'll make more ghuls! He'll feed my living skin to them! He did it with his stolen wives . . ."

The Doctor sucked in an angry-sounding breath. "We'll stop him, Ushra. Where is he going in that riverboat? Where can we find him?"

Raseed could not let this interrogation continue. "With apologies, Doctor, this one has worked wicked magics and must be punished. It is impermissible, according to the Traditions of the Order, to twist information from one who must be slain."

The Doctor threw his hands up. "God save us from fanatical children! We're not going to slay her. We're going to stop this half-dinar magus Zoud, and save Hafi's wife. Whatever your Shaykhs taught you, boy, if you wish to study with me you will—"

The puff-of-air sound again.

Another rope. She had another rope hidden in those sleeves! As Raseed thought it, his vision went black.

Blinded! It was so sudden that he cried out in spite of himself. He felt a soft hand on his face. Then his stomach twisted up and his mind stopped working properly. All around him was darkness and his thoughts seemed wrapped in cotton. *What is this? What foul magic has she worked on me?*

Raseed could not ask the Doctor, because the Doctor was not there.

*   *   *

Adoulla heard the puff-of-air sound again, and suddenly he was alone on the dock. The girl had disappeared and, along with her, Raseed.

Damn me for a fool! A whisking spell, no doubt, used to travel from the location of one object to another. Adoulla had seen such magic before – leaving an ensorcelled coin at home and carrying its counterpart to provide a quick escape – but he hadn't known knot-blowing could be used the same way. *She must have touched the boy, too.* The girl's power was great, if feral. Adoulla himself avoided such spells. It only took one bad whisking to break a mind, and the caster never knew when it was coming. No quick trip home was worth a lifetime of gibbering idiocy.

He had to find them, and fast. Praise God, he had a name now. A crude tracking spell, then. He would have a splitting headache the next day from the casting, but it was his only choice. Standing on the still-quiet dock, Adoulla dug charcoal and a square of paper from his satchel. After writing the Name of God on the front of the paper and "Zoud" on the back, he pulled forth a platinum needle, pricked his thumb, and squeezed one drop of blood on to Zoud's name. He rolled the square into a tube and placed it in his pocket. The mental tug he felt meant God had deemed Adoulla's quarry cruel enough to lead His servant to the man. He followed it eastward, the half-sunk sun at his back.

He cursed himself five times as he crossed Archer's Yard. Adoulla had shown mercy, and the girl had betrayed him. The dervish had been right. Adoulla was a soft old man who called for tea when he should be calling for the blood of his enemies. The Yard's hay training targets stood abandoned now, a few arrows still sticking out of them. To Adoulla's mind the arrows seemed accusatory fingers pointing at him – a fuzzy-headed fool whose weak heart had killed a boy of six-and-ten.

No. Not if he could help it. He had brought the boy into this mess. Now, if Raseed still lived, Adoulla would get him out of it.

Raseed awoke blindfolded, gagged, and bound. During his training he'd learned to snap any bonds that held him, no matter how well tied. But something was wrong here. He was bound not with rope or chain, but with some fiendish substance that burned hotter the harder he tried to escape.

His struggles caused him a slicing pain in his wrists and ankles, but for an uncontrolled moment he thrashed like a madman.

Calm yourself! He was disgusted at how easily he lost a dervish's dignity. He went into a breathing exercise, timing his inhalations and exhalations. The first thing was to figure out where he was. They had blindfolded him, which meant that the knot-blower's blinding curse was not permanent. *Praise God for that.* Adapting quickly, Raseed let his other senses take over. He heard the cries of rivergulls and a splashing sound against one wall. He smelled water and felt himself swaying. A boat. *Zoud's. The one we saw leaving.* Raseed was captive on a boat, and bleeding.

He wondered where the Doctor was. *I should not have listened to him. He is old and grown soft.* Raseed could have ended the girl's life and ought to have done so. Now it was too late. Impermissible panic began to rise in him.

Inhale . . . exhale. He would not feel fear. He would find a way out.

Suddenly Raseed heard a sobbing sound. A young woman crying as she spoke. "I'm sorry, holy man. So sorry. The whisking spell could have killed you."

Ushra. Perhaps a yard away from him. From the same direction he heard glass clink and smelled something acidic.

"What can I do?" the girl continued, her voice moving about. "I'm damned. I didn't want to be his wife, master dervish. He . . . he took me and he made me need him. But the things he did to the other wives . . ." The girl wept wordlessly for a moment, then took a deep breath. "Please don't scream," she whispered, pulling down Raseed's gag.

Talk to her!

Raseed felt that God was with him, for the words came quickly. "You can correct your wickedness, Ushra. You can make amends for your foulness. 'In the eyes of God our kindnesses weigh twice our cruelties.'"

She untied his blindfold, and Raseed blinked at the dim lantern-light. Ushra crouched before him, a long glass vial in the crook of her arm. The look on the girl's face gave him hope. "*Our kindnesses weigh twice our cruelties.*" The scripture echoed in Raseed's head.

"Zoud's gone now, master dervish, but he'll return soon. He left me to guard you." She took a breath and closed her eyes. "I know I can't fix everything. But I freed the girl, his new wife. That will weigh well with God, won't it?"

Raseed would not presume to speak for Him. He said simply, "God is All-Merciful."

The girl opened her teary eyes and spoke more swiftly. "He bound you with firevine. It can't be untied. I've poisoned it, but it'll take an hour to die. God willing, it'll die before he returns." More weeping. "I *am* foul, holy man. My soul is dirty. But, God forgive me, I want to live. I have to go. You don't know the things he can do, master dervish. I have to go."

Ushra went.

But she's freed Hafi's wife! Raseed praised God as he lay there captive, bleeding, alone.

The red riverboat had docked near the High Bridge of Boats. Adoulla found the hatch open and thanked God. He made his way into the cabins without being discovered, which meant that this Zoud was either blessedly overconfident or waiting for him. For a moment Adoulla half-hoped that he'd find Raseed and the magus's "wives" before Zoud found him.

But then, as he came to the threshold of a cabin that seemed impossibly spacious, he heard whistling. It was "The Druggist, the Draper, and the Man Who Made Paper", Miri's least-favorite song. *Not a good omen.*

The room *was* impossibly spacious, Adoulla realized. A magically enlarged cabin, grown to the size of a tavern's greeting-room. In a far corner the dervish lay bound on the floor. *Firevine!* Dried blood ringed Raseed's wrists and ankles.

Between Adoulla and the boy stood Zoud.

The magus was gaunt and bald with a pointed beard. Raseed's sheathed sword lay at Zoud's feet, and beside the magus stood an oaf whose size made his purpose obvious – *bodyguard.* There was no way Adoulla could reach the dervish before those two did.

Zoud, disturbingly unsurprised at Adoulla's entrance, stopped whistling and gestured toward Raseed. "He is in great pain."

Adoulla frowned. "Why stage this gruesome show for me?"

Zoud smiled. "Simple. I'm no fool – I know your sort. I don't want you as an enemy. Hounding me across the Crescent Moon Kingdoms on some revenge-quest. No. All I ask is your oath before God that you'll leave me in peace. I'd hoped to take the boy with me – the Order has enemies who'd pay well for a live dervish. But if you'll be reasonable you may walk off this ship, and we'll put the boy off as well. That's fair, isn't it? You've taken much from me already. My new wife. Even my first wife."

Ushra's not here? And Hafi's wife is free? How? Adoulla could find out later. What mattered now was that his options had just increased. In the corner behind the magus and his henchman, Adoulla saw a small flicker of blue movement. *Impossible!*

He smothered a smile and silently thanked God.

"So," Zoud said. "Do I have your oath, Doctor?"

Adoulla cleared his throat. "My oath? In the Name of God I swear that you, with your tacky big-room spells, are but a half-dinar magus with a broken face coming to him!"

Everything happened at once.

He heard a snapping noise and the boy was free. It was impossible to snap firevine. But Adoulla adapted quickly to impossibilities. As Raseed leapt to his feet Zoud darted behind his bodyguard and screamed, "Babouk! Kill!" The magus clapped twice.

Oh no.

The flash of red light dazzled Adoulla for a moment. But his eyes knew and adjusted to the glamour glimmer of a dispelled illusion well enough. Adoulla had to give this fool Zoud his due. The big bodyguard was gone. In his place was an eight-foot-tall cyklop.

This is not good.

A blue streak darted at the one-eyed, crimson-scaled creature. *Raseed!* The dimwitted monster grunted as the dervish barreled into it and knocked the mighty thing off its clawed feet.

Adoulla stood there for a stunned half-moment. *Half the monster's size, yet he topples it!* Dervish and furnace-chested cyklop wrestled on the ground until the monster wrapped its massive arms around the boy. Adoulla took a step toward the pair and shouted, "Its eye! One sword-stroke through its eye!"

Then he whirled at the familiar sound of blade leaving sheath. Zoud stood before him with a hunted look on his face and a silver-hilted knife in his hand. *All out of tricks, huh? And now you think to buy your freedom with a knife?* Adoulla cracked his knuckles and took a step toward the magus.

Raseed wriggled free of the cyklop's crushing hug. The monster pressed him again, closing its clawed hands around Raseed's fists. His wounds from the firevine burned, but he pushed the pain away.

As part of his training, Raseed had once wrestled a northern bear. This creature was stronger. Still, Raseed thought, as impermissible pride crept in, he would slay it. Then he'd know that he had fought a cyklop and won. He twisted his powerful arms, trying to get the leverage to free himself. But the cyklop held him fast. And the pain in Raseed's wrists and ankles grew worse.

Then he heard a small sound and his left hand blazed with pain. His little finger was broken. Another sound. His index finger. The rest would follow if he did not get free. But how?

The cyklop decided for him. Shifting, it hoisted Raseed aloft like a doll. The monster tried to dash Raseed's brains out on the floorboards.

Raseed twisted as he fell, somersaulting across the room. His sword hand was unharmed. He thanked God and forced away the pain of his wounds. He scooped up the blue scabbard, rolled to his feet, drew.

The cyklop grunted. It blinked its teacup-sized eye as Raseed rushed forward. With eagle-speed Raseed leapt, sword extended. He thrust upward.

With an earsplitting howl, the cyklop fell, blood seeping from its single eye. Watching the monster die, Raseed felt more relief than pride.

* * *

Adoulla charged Zoud, making sure that his robed shoulder was his opponent's most prominent target. A sneer flashed on Zoud's face. The fool thought Adoulla was blundering into his dagger-path.

The silver-handled blade came down.

And glanced off the blessed kaftan, as surely as if Adoulla were wearing mail. Zoud got in one more useless stab before Adoulla let loose the right hook that had once made him the best street-fighter on Dead Donkey Lane. With a girlish cry, the magus crumpled into a heap. Somewhere behind Adoulla, the cyklop howled its death-howl.

His tricks gone and his nose broken, Zoud lay bleeding at Adoulla's feet. The magus whimpered to himself like a child yanked from a good dream. Before Adoulla knew what was happening, Raseed was at his side.

"Magus!" the dervish said. "You have stolen and slain women. You dared demand an oath before God to cover your foulness. For you, there can be no forgiveness!" Raseed sent his blade diving for Zoud's heart. In a breathspace, the forked sword found it. The magus's eyes went wide as he gurgled and died.

Adoulla felt ill.

"What is wrong with you, boy? We had the man at our—" He fell silent, seeing the boy's firevine wounds.

Raseed narrowed his tilted eyes. "With apologies, Doctor, I expected Adoulla Makhslood to be a man who struck swiftly and righteously."

"And instead you've found some pastry-stuffed old fart who isn't fond of killing. Poor child! God must weep at your cruel fate."

"Doctor! To take God's name in mock is imper—"

"Enough, boy! Do you hear me? Fight monsters for forty years as I have – cross the seas and sands of the Crescent Moon Kingdoms serving God – then *you* can tell *me* what is 'impermissible'. By then, Almighty God willing, I'll be dead and gone, my ears untroubled by the peeps of holy men's mouths!" The tirade silenced the dervish, who stood looking down at the magus's bleeding corpse.

The problem was, Adoulla feared that the boy's way might be right. Adoulla thought of the girl, Ushra. And of Raseed's pain as the firevine had tortured him. And of Zoud's dead "wives". He sighed.

"Oh, God damn it all. Fine, boy. You're right. Just as you were about the blower-on-knots." Adoulla sat down with a grunt, right there on the bloody floorboards. He had fought a dozen battles more difficult than this over the decades, but he did not think he'd ever felt so weary.

Raseed spoke slowly. "No, Doctor. *You* were right. About Ushra, at least. She did what she did from weakness and fear of a wicked man. Yet I would've killed her." The dervish was quiet for a long moment. "It was her, Doctor. Ushra. She poisoned the firevine. She freed Hafi's wife. I'm ashamed to say it, but I must speak true – I wouldn't have escaped if not for her."

Adoulla was too tired to respond with words. He grunted again and clambered to his feet.

Yehyeh's teahouse buzzed with chattering customers. Raseed tried to ignore the lewd music and banter. Hafi and his tall, raven-haired wife sat with her grateful parents on a pile of cushions in the far corner. At a table near the entrance, Raseed sat with the Doctor, who was nursing what he had called a "God-damned gruesome tracking spell headache." Lifting his head from his hands slowly, the Doctor fixed a droopy eye on Raseed.

"How many men have you killed, boy?"

Raseed was confused – why did that matter now? "Two. No ... the highwaymen ... five? After this villain last night, six."

"So many?" the Doctor said.

Raseed did not know what to say, so he said nothing.

Adoulla sighed. "You're a fine warrior, Raseed bas Raseed. If you're to study with me, though, you must know your number and never forget it. You took a man's life yesterday. Weigh that fact! Make it harder than it is for you now. Remember that a man, even a foul man, is not a ghul."

Again, Raseed was confused. "'Harder', Doctor? I've trained all my life to kill swiftly."

"And now you will train to kill reluctantly. *If* you still wish an apprenticeship."

"I do still wish it, Doctor! High Shaykh Aalli spoke of you as—"

"People speak of me, boy, but now you've met me. You've fought beside me. I eat messily. I ogle girls one-third my age. And I don't like killing. If you're going to hunt monsters with me, you must see things as they are."

Raseed, his broken fingers still stinging, his wrists and ankles still raw, nodded and recalled the High Shaykh's words about where virtue lives. *Strange places indeed.*

A quiet settled over the table and Adoulla devoured another of the almond-and-anise rolls that Yehyeh had been gratefully plying him with. As he ate he thought about the boy sitting across from him.

He did not relish the thought of a preachy little dervish in his home. He could only hope the boy was young enough to stretch beyond the smallness that had been beaten into him at the Lodge. Regardless, only a fool would refuse having a decades-younger warrior beside him as he went about his last years of ghul hunting.

Besides, the dervish, with his meticulous grooming, would make a great house-keeper!

He could hear Miri's jokes about boy-love already.

Miri. God help me.

Raseed lifted his bowl of plain limewater and sipped daintily. Adoulla said nothing to break the silence, but he slurped his sweet cardamom tea. Then he set his teabowl down, belched loudly, and relished the horrified grimace of his virtuous new apprentice.

THE EFFIGY ENGINE:
A TALE OF THE RED HATS

Scott Lynch

11th Mithune, 1186
Painted Sky Pass, North Elara

"I took up the study of magic because I wanted to live in the beauty of transfinite mathematical truths," said Rumstandel. He gestured curtly. In the canyon below us, an enemy soldier shuddered, clutched at his throat, and began vomiting live snakes.

"If my indifference were money you'd be the master of my own personal mint," I muttered. Of course Rumstandel heard me despite the pop, crackle, and roar of musketry echoing around the walls of the pass. There was sorcery at play between us to carry our voices, so we could bitch and digress and annoy ourselves like a pair of inebriates trading commentary in a theater balcony.

The day's show was an ambush of a company of Iron Ring legionaries on behalf of our employers, the North Elarans, who were blazing away with arquebus and harsh language from the heights around us. The harsh language seemed to be having greater effect. The black-coated ranks of the Iron Ring jostled in consternation, but there weren't enough bodies strewn among the striated sunset-orange rocks that gave the pass its name. Hot lead was leaving the barrels of our guns, but it was landing like kitten farts and some sly magical bastard down there was responsible.

Oh, for the days of six months past, when the Iron Ring had crossed the Elaran border marches, their battle wizards proud and laughing in full regalia. Their can't-miss-me-at-a-mile wolf-skull helmets, their set-me-on-fire carnelian cloaks, their shoot-me-in-the-face silver masks.

Six months with us for playmates had taught them to be less obvious. Counter-thaumaturgy was our mission and our meal ticket: coax them into visibility and make them regret it. Now they dressed like common officers or soldiers, and some even carried prop muskets or pikes. Like this one, clearly.

"I'm a profound disappointment to myself," sighed Rumstandel, big round florid Rumstandel, who didn't share my appreciation for sorcerous anonymity. This week he'd turned his belly-scraping beard blue and caused it to spring out in flaring forks like the sculpture of a river and its tributaries. Little simulacra of ships sailed up and down those beard strands even now, their hulls the size of rice grains, dodging crumbs like rocks and shoals. Crumbs there were aplenty, since Rumstandel always ate while he killed and soliloquized. One hand was full of the sticky Elaran ration bread we called corpsecake for its pallor and suspected seasoning.

"I should be redefining the vocabulary of arcane geometry somewhere safe and cultured, not playing silly buggers with village fish-charmers wearing wolf skulls." He silenced himself with a mouthful of cake and gestured again. Down on the valley floor his victim writhed his last. The snakes came out slick with blood, eyes gleaming like garnets in firelight, nostrils trailing strands of pale caustic vapor.

I couldn't really pick out the minute details at seventy yards, but I'd seen the spell before. In the closed ranks of the Iron Ring the serpents wrought the havoc that arquebus fire couldn't, and legionaries clubbed desperately at them with musket-butts.

As I peered into the mess, the forward portion of the legionary column exploded in white smoke. Sparks and chips flew from nearby rocks, and I felt a burning pressure between my eyes, a sharp tug on the strands of my own magic. The practical range of sorcery is about that of musketry, and a fresh reminder of the fact hung dead in the air a yard from my face. I plucked the ball down and slipped it into my pocket.

Somewhere safe and cultured? Well, there was nowhere safer for Rumstandel than three feet to my left. I was doing for him what the troublemaker on the ground was doing for the legionaries. Close protection, subtle and otherwise, my military and theoretical specialty.

Wizards working offensively in battle have a bad tendency to get caught up in their glory-hounding and part their already tenuous ties to prudence. Distracted and excited, they pile flourish on flourish, spell on spell until some stray musket ball happens along and elects to take up residence.

Our little company's answer is to work in teams, one sorcerer working harm and the second diligently protecting them both. Rumstandel didn't have the temperament to be that second sorcerer, but I've been at it so long now everyone calls me Watchdog. Even my mother.

I heard a rattling sound behind us, and turned in time to see Tariel hop down into our rocky niche, musket held before her like an acrobat's pole. Red-gray dust was caked in sweaty spirals along her bare ebony arms, and the dozens of wooden powder flasks dangling from her bandolier knocked together like a musical instrument.

"Mind if I crouch in your shadow, Watchdog? They're keeping up those volleys in good order." She knelt between me and Rumstandel, laid her musket carefully in the crook of her left arm, and whispered, "Touch." The piece went off with the customary flash and bang, which my speech-sorcery dampened to a more tolerable pop.

Hers was a salamandrine musket. Where the flintlock or wheel mechanism might ordinarily be was instead a miniature metal sculpture of a manor house, jutting from the weapon's side as though perched atop a cliff. I could see the tiny fire elemental that lived in there peering out one of the windows. It was always curious to see how a job was going. Tariel could force a spark from it by pulling the trigger, but she claimed polite requests led to smoother firing.

"Damn. I seem to be getting no value for money today, gents." She began the laborious process of recharging and loading.

"We're working on it," I said. Another line of white smoke erupted below, followed by another cacophony of ricochets and rock chips. An Elaran soldier screamed. "Aren't we work-ing on it, Rumstandel? And by 'we' I do in fact mean—"

"Yes, yes, bullet-catcher, do let an artist stretch his own canvas." Rumstandel clenched his fists and something like a hot breeze blew past me, thick with powder. This would be a vulgar display.

Down on the canyon floor, an Iron Ring legionary in the process of reloading was interrupted by the cold explosion of his musket. The stock shivered into splinters and the barrel peeled itself open backward like a sinister metal flower. Quick as thought, the burst barrel enveloped the man's arm, twisted, and – well, you've squeezed fruit before, haven't you? Then the powder charges in his bandolier flew out in burning constella-tions, a cloud of fire that made life immediately interesting for everyone around him.

"Ah! That's got his attention at last," said Rumstandel. A gray-blue cloud of mist boiled up from the ground around the stricken legionaries, swallowing and dousing the flaming powder before it could do further harm. Our Iron Ring friend was no longer willing to tolerate Rumstandel's contributions to the battle, and so inevitably . . .

"I see him," I shouted, "gesturing down there on the left! Look, he just dropped a pike!"

"Out from under the rock! Say your prayers, my man. Another village up north has lost its second-best fish-charmer!" said Rumstandel, moving his arms now like a priest in ecstatic sermon (recall my earlier warning about distraction and excitement). The Iron Ring sorcerer was hoisted into the air, black coat flaring, and as Rumstandel chanted his target began to spin.

The fellow must have realized that he couldn't possibly get any more obvious, and he had some nerve. Bright-blue fire arced up at us, a death-sending screaming with ghostly fury. My business. I took a clay effigy out of my pocket and held it up. The screaming blue fire poured itself into the little statu-ette, which leapt out of my hands and exploded harmlessly ten yards above. Dust rained on our heads.

The Iron Ring sorcerer kept rising and whirling like a top. One soldier, improbably brave or stupid, leapt and caught the wizard's boot. He held on for a few rotations before he was heaved off into some of his comrades.

Still that wizard lashed out. First came lightning like a white pillar from the sky. I dropped an iron chain from a coat sleeve to bleed its energy into the earth, though it made my hair stand on end and my teeth chatter. Then came a sending of bad luck I could feel pressing in like a congealing of the air itself; the next volley that erupted from the Iron Ring lines would doubtless make cutlets of us. I barely managed to unweave the sending, using an unseemly eruption of power that left me feeling as though the air had been punched out of my lungs. An instant later musket balls sparked and screamed on the rocks around us, and we all flinched. My previous spell of protection had lapsed while I was beset.

"Rumstandel," I yelled, "quit stretching the bloody canvas and paint the picture already!"

"He's quite unusually adept, this illiterate pot-healer!" Rumstandel's beard-boats rocked and tumbled as the blue hair in which they swam rolled like ocean waves. "The illicit toucher of sheep! He probably burns books to keep warm at home! And I'm only just managing to hold him – Tariel, please don't wait for my invitation to collaborate in this business!"

Our musketeer calmly set her weapon into her shoulder, whispered to her elemental, and gave fire. The spinning sorcerer shook with the impact. An instant later, his will no longer constraining Rumstandel's, he whirled away like a child's rag doll flung in a tantrum. Where the body landed, I didn't see. My sigh of relief was loud and shameless.

"Yes, that was competent opposition for a change, wasn't it?" Tariel was already calmly recharging her musket. "Incidentally, it was a woman."

"Are you sure?" I said once I'd caught my breath. "I thought the Iron Ringers didn't let their precious daughters into their war-wizard lodges."

"I'd guess they're up against the choice between female support and no support at all," she said. "Almost as though someone's been subtracting wizards from their muster rolls this past half-year."

The rest of the engagement soon played out. Deprived of sorcerous protection, the legionaries began to fall to arquebus fire in the traditional manner. Tariel kept busy, knocking hats from heads and heads from under hats. Rumstandel threw down just a few subtle spells of maiming and ill-coincidence, and I returned to my sober vigil, Watchdog once more. It wasn't in our contract to scourge the Iron Ringers from the field with sorcery. We wanted them to feel they'd been, in the main, fairly bested by their outnumbered Elaran neighbors, line to line and gun to gun, rather than cheated by magic of foreign hire.

After the black-clad column had retreated down the pass and the echo of musketry was fading, Rumstandel and I basked like lizards in the mid-afternoon sun and stuffed ourselves on corpsecake and cold chicken, the latter wrapped in fly-killing spells of Rumstandel's devising. No sooner would the little nuisances alight on our lunch than they would vanish in puffs of green fire.

Tariel busied herself cleaning out her musket barrel with worm and fouling scraper. When she'd finished, the fire elemental, in the form of a scarlet salamander that could hide under the nail of my smallest finger, went down the barrel to check her work.

"Excuse me, are you the – that is, I'm looking for the Red Hats."

A young Elaran in a dark-blue officer's coat appeared from the rocks above us, brown ringlets askew, uniform scorched and holed from obvious proximity to trouble. I didn't recognize her from the company we'd been attached to. I reached into a pocket, drew out my rumpled red slouch hat, and waved it.

About the hats, the namesake of our mercenary fellowship: in keeping with the aforementioned and mortality-avoiding principle of anonymity, neither Tariel nor myself wore them when the dust was flying. Rumstandel never wore his at all, claiming with much justice that he didn't need the aid of any particular headgear to slouch.

"Red Hats present and reasonably comfortable," I said. "Some message for us?"

"Not a message, but a summons," said the woman. "Compliments from your captain, and she wants you back at the central front with all haste at any hazard."

"Central front?" That explained the rings under her eyes. Even with mount changes, that was a full day in the saddle. We'd been detached from what passed for our command for a week and hadn't expected to go back for at least another. "What's your story, then?"

"Ill news. The Iron Ring have some awful device, something unprecedented. They're breaking our lines like we weren't even there. I didn't get a full report before I was dispatched, but the whole front is collapsing."

"How delightful," said Rumstandel. "I do assume you've brought a cart for me? I always prefer a good long nap when I'm speeding on my way to a fresh catastrophe."

Note to those members of this company desirous of an early glimpse into these, our chronicles. As you well know, I'm pleased to read excerpts when we make camp and then invite corrections or additions to my records. I am not, however, amused to find the thumbprints of sticky-fingered interlopers defacing these pages without my consent. BE ADVISED, therefore, that I have with a spotless conscience affixed a dweomer of security to this journal and an attendant minor curse. I think you know the one I mean. The one with the fire ants. You have only yourself to blame. – WD

Watchdog, you childlike innocent, if you're going to secure your personal effects with a curse, don't attach a warning preface. It makes it even easier to enact countermeasures, and they were no particular impediment in the first place if you take my meaning. Furthermore, the poverty of your observational faculty continues to astound. You wrote that my beard was "LIKE the sculpture of a river and its tributaries", failing to note that it was in fact a PRECISE and proportional model of the Voraslo Delta, with my face considered as the sea. Posterity awaits your amendments. Also, you might think of a more expensive grade of paper when you

buy your next journal. I've pushed my quill through this stuff
three times already. – R

13th Mithune, 1186
Somewhere near Lake Corlan, North Elara

Rumstandel, big red florid garlic-smelling Rumstandel, that bilious reservoir of unlovability, that human anchor weighing down my happiness, snored in the back of the cart far more peacefully than he deserved as we clattered up to the command pavilion of the North Elaran army. Pillars of black smoke rose north of us, mushrooming under wet gray skies. No campfire smoke, those pillars, but the sigils of rout and disaster.

North Elara is a temperate green place, long-settled, easy on the eyes and heart. It hurt to see it cut up by war like a patient strapped to a chirurgeon's operating board, straining against the incisions that might kill it as surely as the illness. Our trip along the rutted roads was slowed by traffic in both directions, supply trains moving north and the displaced moving south: farmers, fisherfolk, traders, camp followers, the aged and the young.

They hadn't been on the roads when we'd rattled out the previous week. They'd been nervous but guardedly content, keeping to their villages and camps behind the bulk of the Elaran army and the clever fieldworks that held the Iron Ring legions in stalemate. Now their mood had gone south and they meant to follow.

I rolled from the cart, sore where I wasn't numb. Elaran pennants fluttered wanly over the pavilion, and there were bad signs abounding. The smell of gangrene and freshly ampu-tated limbs mingled with that of smoke and animal droppings. The command tents were now pitched about three miles south of where they'd been when I'd left.

I settled my red slouch on my head for identification, as the sentries all looked quite nervous. Tariel did the same. I glanced back at Rumstandel and found him still in loud repose. I called up one of my familiars with a particular set of finger-snaps and set the little creature on him in the form of a night-black squir-rel with raven's wings. It hopped up and down on Rumstandel's stomach, singing:

Rouse, Rumstandel, and see what passes!
Kindle some zest, you laziest of asses!
Even sluggard Red Hats are called to war
So rouse yourself and slumber no more!

Some sort of defensive spell crept up from Rumstandel's coat like a silver mist, but the raven-squirrel fluttered above the grasping tendrils and pelted him with conjured acorns, while singing a new song about the various odors of his flatulence.

"My farts do not smell like glue!" shouted Rumstandel, up at last, swatting at my familiar. "What does that even mean, you wit-deficient pseudo-rodent?"

"Ahem," said a woman as she stepped out of the largest tent, and there was more authority in that clearing of her throat than there are in the loaded cannons of many earthly princes. My familiar, though as inept at rhyme as Rumstandel alleged, had a fine sense of when to vanish, and did so.

"I thought I heard squirrel doggerel," our captain, the sorceress Millowend, continued. "We must get you a better sort of creature one of these days."

It is perhaps beyond my powers to write objectively of Millowend, but in the essentials she is a short, solid, ashen-haired woman of middle years and innate rather than affected dignity. Her red hat, the iconic and original red hat, is battered and singed from years of campaigning despite the surfeit of magical protections bound into its warp and weft.

"Slack hours have been in short supply, ma'am."

"Well, I am at least glad to have you back in one piece, Watchdog," said my mother. "And you, Tariel, and even you, Rumstandel, though I wonder what's become of your hat."

"A heroic loss." Rumstandel heaved himself out of the cart, brushed assorted crumbs from his coat, and stretched in the manner of a rotund cat vacating a sunbeam. "I wore it through a fusillade of steel and sorcery. It was torn asunder, pierced by a dozen enemy balls and at least one culverin stone. We buried it with full military honors after the action."

"A grief easily assuaged." My mother conjured a fresh red hat and spun it toward the blue-bearded sorcerer's naked head. Just as deftly, he blasted it to motes with a gout of fire.

"Come along," said Millowend, unperturbed. This was the merest passing skirmish in the Affair of the Hat, possibly the longest sustained campaign in the history of our company. "We're all here now. I'll put you in the picture on horseback."

"Horseback?" said Rumstandel. "Freshly uncarted and now astride the spines of hoofed torture devices! Oh, hello, Caladesh."

The man tending the horses was one of us. Lean as a miser's alms-purse, mustaches oiled, carrying a brace of pistols so large I suspect they reproduce at night, Caladesh never changes. His hat is as red as cherry wine and has no magical protections at all save his improbable luck. Cal is worth four men in a fight and six in a drinking contest, but I was surprised to see him alone, minding exactly five horses.

"We're it," said Millowend, as though reading my thoughts. Which was not out of the question. "I sent the others off with a coastal raid. They can't possibly return in time to help."

"And that's a fair pity," said Caladesh as he swung himself up into his saddle with easy grace. "There's fresh pie wrapped up in your saddlebags."

"A pie job!" cried Rumstandel. "Horses and a pie job! A constellation of miserable omens!"

His misgivings didn't prevent him, once saddled, from attacking the pie. I unwrapped mine and found it warm, firm, and lightly frosted with pink icing, the best sort my mother's culinary imps could provide. Alas.

Would-be sorcerers must understand that the art burns fuel as surely as any bonfire, which fuel being the sorcerer's own body. It's much like hard manual exercise, save that it banishes flesh even more quickly. During prolonged magical engagements I have felt unhealthy amounts of myself boil away. Profligate or sustained use of the art can leave us with skin hanging in folds, innards cramping, and bodily humors thrown into chaos.

That's why slender sorcerers are rarer than amiable scorpions, and why Rumstandel and I keep food at hand while plying our trade, and why my mother's sweet offering was as good as a warning.

In her train we rode north through the camp, past stands of muskets like sinister haystacks. These weren't the usual collections with soldiers lounging nearby ready to snatch them, but haphazard piles obviously waiting to be cleaned and sorted. Many Elaran militia and second-liners would soon be trading in their grandfatherly arquebuses for flintlocks pried from the hands of the dead.

"I'm sorry to reward you for a successful engagement by thrusting you into a bigger mess," said Millowend, "but the bigger mess is all that's on offer. Three days ago, the Iron Ring brought some sort of mechanical engine against our employers' previous forward position and kicked them out of it.

"It's an armored box, like the hull of a ship," she continued. "Balanced on mechanical legs, motive power unknown. Quick-steps over trenches and obstacles. The hull protects several cannon and an unknown number of sorcerers. Cal witnessed part of the battle from a distance."

"Wouldn't call it a battle," said Caladesh. "Battle implies some give and take, and this thing did nothing but give. The Elarans fed it cannonade, massed musketry, and spells. Then they tried all three at once. For that, their infantry got minced, their artillery no longer exists in a practical sense, and every single one of their magicians that engaged the thing is getting measured for a wooden box."

"They had fifteen sorcerers attached to their line regiments!" said Tariel.

"Now they've got assorted bits of fifteen sorcerers," said Caladesh.

"Blessed pie provisioner," said Rumstandel, "I'm as keen to put my head on the anvil as anyone in this association of oath-bound lunatics. But when you say that musketry and sorcery were ineffective against this device, did it escape your notice that our tactical abilities span the narrow range from musketry to sorcery?"

"There's nothing uncanny about musket balls bouncing off wood and iron planking," said Millowend. "And there's nothing inherently counter-magical to the device. The Iron Ring have crammed a lot of wizards into it, is all. We need to devise some means to peel them out of that shell."

Under the gray sky we rode ever closer to the edge of the action, past field hospitals and trenches, past artillery caissons looking lonely without their guns, past nervous horses, nervous officers, and very nervous infantry. We left our mounts a few minutes later and moved on foot up the grassy ridgeline called Montveil's Wall, now the farthest limit of the dubious safety of "friendly" territory.

There the thing stood, half a mile away, beyond the churned and smoldering landscape of fieldworks vacated by the Elaran army. It was the height of a fortress wall, perhaps fifty or sixty feet, and its irregular, bulbous hull rested on four splayed and ungainly metal legs. On campaign years ago in the Alcor Valley, north of the Skull Sands, I became familiar with the dust-brown desert spiders famous for their threat displays. The scuttling creatures would raise up on their rear legs, spread their forward legs to create an illusion of bodily height, and brandish their fangs. I fancied there was something of that in the aspect of the Iron Ring machine.

"Watchdog," said Millowend, "did you bring your spyflask?"

I took a tarnished, dented flask from my coat and unscrewed the cap. Clear liquid bubbled into the air like slow steam, then coalesced into a flat disc about a yard in diameter. I directed this with waves of my hands until it framed our view of the Iron Ring machine, and we all pressed in upon one another like gawkers at a carnival puppet-show.

The magic of the spyflask acted as a refracting lens, and after a moment of blurred confusion the image within the disc resolved to a sharp, clear magnification of the war machine. It was bold and ugly, pure threat without elegance. Its overlapping iron plates were draped in netting-bound hides, which I presumed were meant to defeat the use of flaming projectiles or magic. The black barrels of two cannon jutted from ports in the forward hull, lending even more credence to my earlier impression of a rearing spider.

"Those are eight-pounder demi-culverins," said Caladesh, gesturing at the cannon. "I pulled a ball out of the turf. Not the heaviest they've got, but elevated and shielded, they might as well be the only guns on the field. They did for the Elaran batteries at leisure, careful as calligraphers."

"I'm curious about the Elaran sorcerers," said Rumstandel, twirling fingers in the azure strands of his beard and scattering little white ships. "What exactly did they do to invite such a disaster?"

"I don't think they were prepared for the sheer volume of counter-thaumaturgy the Iron Ringers could mount from that device," said Millowend. "The Iron Ring wizards stayed cautious and let the artillery chop up our Elaran counterparts. Guided, of course, by spotters atop that infernal machine. It would seem the Iron Ring is learning to be the sort of opponent we least desire . . . a flexible one."

"I did like them much better when they were thick as oak posts," sighed Rumstandel.

"The essential question remains," I said. "How do we punch through what fifteen Elaran wizards couldn't?"

"You're thinking too much on the matter of the armored box," said Tariel. "When you hunt big game with ordinary muskets, you don't try to pierce the thickest bone and hide. You make crippling shots. Subdue it in steps, leg by leg. Lock those up somehow, all the Iron Ring will have is an awkward fortress tower rooted in place."

"We could trip it or sink it down a hole," mused Rumstandel. "General Alune's not dead, is she? Why aren't her sappers digging merrily away?"

"She's alive," said Millowend. "It's a question of where to dig, and how to convince that thing to enter the trap. When it's moving, it can evade or simply overstep anything resembling ordinary fieldworks."

"When it's moving," I said. "Well, here's another question – if the Elarans didn't stop it, why isn't it moving now?"

"I'd love to think it's some insoluble difficulty or breakdown," said Millowend. "But the telling fact is, they haven't sent over any ultimatums. They haven't communicated at all. I assume that, if the device were now immobilized, they'd be trying to leverage its initial attack for all it was worth. No, they're waiting for their own reasons, and I'm sure those reasons are suitably unpleasant."

"So how do you want us to inaugurate this fool's errand, captain?" said Rumstandel.

"Eat your pie," said my mother. "Then think subtle thoughts. I want a quiet, invisible reconnaissance of that thing, inch by inch and plate by plate. I want to find all the cracks in its armor, magical and otherwise, and I want the Iron Ring to have no idea we've been peeking."

ENCLOSURE: The open oath of the Red Hats, attributed to the Sorceress Millowend.

To take no coin from unjust reign
Despoil no hearth nor righteous fane
Caps red as blood, as bright and bold
In honor paid, as dear as gold
To leave no bondsman wrongly chained
And shirk no odds, for glory's gain
Against the mighty, for the weak
We by this law our battles seek

ADDENDUM: The tacit marching song of the Red Hats, attributed to the Sorcerer Rumstandel, sometimes called "The Magnificent".

Where musket balls are thickest flying
Where our employers are quickest dying
Where mortals perish like bacon frying
And horrible things leave grown men crying
To all these places we ride with haste
To get ourselves smeared into paste
Or punctured, scalded, and served on toast
For the financial benefit of our hosts!

13th Mithune, 1186
Montveil's Wall, North Elara
One Hour Later

Cannon above us, cannon over the horizon, all spitting thunder and smoke, all blasting up fountains of wet earth as we stumbled for cover, under the plunging fire of the lurching war machine, under the dancing green light of hostile magic, under the weight of our own confusion and embarrassment.

We had thought we were being subtle.

Millowend had started our reconnaissance by producing a soft white dandelion seedhead, into which she breathed the syllables of a spell. Seeds spun out, featherlike in her conjured breeze, and each carried a fully realized pollen-sized simulacrum of her, perfect down to a little red hat and a determined expression. One hundred tiny Millowends floated off to cast 200 tiny eyes over the Iron Ring machine. It was a fine spell, though it would leave her somewhat befuddled as her mind strained to knit those separate views together into one useful picture.

Rumstandel added some admittedly deft magical touches of his own to the floating lens of my spyflask, and in short order we had a sort of intangible apparatus by which we might study the quality and currents of magic around the war machine, as aesthetes might natter about the brushstrokes of a painting. Tariel and Caladesh, less than entranced by our absorption in visual balderdash, crouched near us to keep watch.

"That's as queer as a six-headed fish," muttered Rumstandel. "The whole thing's lively with dynamic flow. That would be a profligate waste of power unless—"

That was when Tariel jumped on his head, shoving him down into the turf, and Caladesh jumped on mine, dragging my dazed mother with him. A split heartbeat later, a pair of cannonballs tore muddy furrows to either side of us, arriving just ahead of the muted thunder of their firing.

"I might forward the hypothesis," growled Rumstandel, spitting turf, "that the reason the bloody thing hasn't moved is because it was left out as an enticement for a certain band of interlopers in obvious hats."

"I thought we were being reasonably subtle!" I yelled, shoving Caladesh less than politely. He is all sharp angles, and very unpleasant to be trapped under.

"Action FRONT," cried Tariel, who had sprung back on watch with her usual speed. The rest of us scrambled to the rim of Montveil's Wall beside her. Charging from the nearest trench, not a hundred yards distant, came a column of Iron Ring foot about forty strong, cloaks flying, some still tossing away the planks and debris they'd been using to help conceal themselves. One bore a furled pennant bound tightly to its staff by a scarlet cord. That made them penitents, comrades of a soldier who'd broken some cardinal rule of honor or discipline. The only way they'd be allowed to return to the Iron Ring, or even ordinary service, was to expunge the stain with a death-or-glory mission.

Such as ambushing us.

Also, the six-story metal war machine behind the penitents was now on the move, creaking and growling like a pack of demons set loose in a scrapyard.

And then there were orange flashes and puffs of smoke from the distances beyond the machine, where hidden batteries were presumably taking direction on how to deliver fresh gifts of lead to our position.

Tariel whispered to her salamander, and her musket barked fire and noise. The lead Iron Ringer was instantly relieved of all worries about the honor of his company. As she began to reload, shrieking cannonballs gouged the earth around us and before us, no shot yet closer than fifty yards. Bowel-loosening as the flash of distant cannonade might be, they would need much better luck and direction to really endanger us at that range.

I enacted a defensive spell, one that had become routine and reflexive. A sheen appeared in the air between us and the edge of the ridge, a subtle distortion that would safely pervert the course of any musket ball not fired at point-blank range. Not much of a roof to shelter under in the face of artillery, but it had the advantage of requiring little energy or concentration while I tried to apprehend the situation.

Rumstandel cast slips of paper from his coat pocket and spat crackling words of power after them. Over the ridge and across the field they whirled, toward the Iron Ring penitents, swelling into man-sized kites of crimson silk, each one painted with a wild-eyed likeness of Rumstandel, plus elaborate military, economic, and sexual insults in excellent Iron Ring script. Half-a-dozen kites swept into the ranks of the charging men, ensnaring arms, legs, necks, and muskets in their glittering strings before leaping upward, hauling victims to the sky.

"Hackwork, miserable hackwork," muttered Rumstandel. "Someday I'll figure out how to make the kites scream those insults. Illiterate targets simply aren't getting the full effect."

The cries of the men being hoisted into the air said otherwise, but I was too busy to argue.

The war machine lurched on, cannons booming, the shot falling so far beyond us I didn't see them land. So long as the device was in motion, I wagered its gunners would have a vexed time laying their pieces. That would change in a matter of minutes, when the thing reached spell and musket range and could halt to crush us at leisure.

"We have to get the hell out of here!" I cried, somewhat suborning the authority of my mother, who was still caught in the trance of seed-surveillance. That was when a familiar emerald phosphorescence burst around us, a vivid green light that lit the churned grass for a thirty-yard circle with us at the center.

"SHOT-FALL IMPS," bellowed Caladesh, which is just what they were; each of the five of us was now beset by a cavorting green figure dancing in the air above our heads, grinning evilly and pointing at us, while blazing with enough light to make our position clear from miles away.

"Here! Here! Over here!" yelled the green imps. The reader may assume they continued to yell this throughout the engagement, for they certainly did. I cannot find the will to scrawl it over and over again in this journal.

Shot-fall imps are intangible (so we couldn't shoot them) and notoriously slippery to banish. I have the wherewithal to do it, but it takes several patient minutes of trial and error, and those I did not possess.

Fire flashed in the distance, the long-range batteries again, this time sighting on the conspicuous green glow. It was no particular surprise that they were now more accurate, their balls parting the air just above our heads or plowing furrows within twenty yards. This is where we came in after the last intermission, with the enemy bombardment, the scrambling, and the general sense of a catastrophically unfolding cock-up.

Rumstandel hurled occult abuse at the penitents, his darkening mood evident in his choice of spells. He transmuted boot leather to caustic silver slime, seeded the ground with flesh-hungry glass shards, turned eyeballs to solid ice and cracked them within their sockets. All this, plus Tariel's steady, murderous attention, and still the Iron Ringers came on, fierce and honor-mad, bayonets fixed, leaving their stricken comrades in the mud.

"Get to the horses!" I yelled, no longer concerned about bruising Millowend's chain of command. It was my job to ward us all from harm, and the best possible safeguard would be for us to scurry, leaving our dignity on the field like a trampled tent.

The surviving penitents came charging up a nearby defile to the top of Montveil's Wall. Caladesh met them, standing tall, his favorite over-and-under double flintlocks barking smoke. Those pistols threw .60 caliber balls, and at such close range the effect was . . . well, you've squeezed fruit before, haven't you?

The world became a tumbling confusion of incident. Iron Ring penitents falling down the slope, tangled in the heavy bodies of dead comrades, imps dancing in green light, cannonballs ripping holes in the air, a lurching war machine – all this while I frantically tried to spot our horses, revive my mother, and layer us in what protections I could muster.

They weren't sufficient. A swarm of small water elementals burst upon us, translucent blobs the color of gutter-silt, smelling like the edge of a summer storm. They poured themselves into the barrels and touch-holes of Caladesh's pistols, leaving him cursing. A line of them surged up and down the barrel of Tariel's musket, and the salamander faced them with steaming red blades in its hands like the captain of a boarded vessel. The situation required more than my spells could give it, so I resolved at last to surrender an advantage I was loath to part with.

On my left wrist I wore a bracelet woven from the tail-hairs of an Iron Unicorn, bound with a spell given to me by the Thinking Sharks of the Jewelwine Sea, for which I had traded documents whose contents are still the state secrets of one of our former clients. I tore it off, snapped it in half, and threw it to the ground.

It's dangerous arrogance for any sorcerer to think of a fifth-order demon as a familiar; at best such beings can be indentured to a very limited span of time or errands, and against even the most ironclad terms of service they will scheme and clamor with exhausting persistence. However, if you can convince them to shut up and take orders . . .

"Felderasticus Sixth-Quickened, Baronet of the Flayed Skulls of Faithless Dogs, Princeling of the House of Recurring Shame," I bellowed, pausing to take a breath, "get up here and get your ass to work!"

"I deem that an irretrievably non-specific request," said a voice like fingernails on desert-dry bones. "I shall therefore return to my customary place and assume my indenture to be dissolved by mutual—"

"Stuff that, you second-rate legal fantasist! When *you* spend three months questing for spells to bind *me* into jewelry, then you can start assuming things! Get rid of these shot-fall imps!"

"Reluctant apologies, most impatient of spell-dabblers and lore-cheats, softest of cannonball targets, but again your lamentably hasty nonspecificity confounds my generous intentions. When you say, 'get rid of', how exactly do you propose—"

"Remove them instantly and absolutely from our presence without harm to ourselves and banish them to their previous plane of habitation!"

A chill wind blew, and it was done. The shot-fall imps with their damned green light and their pointing and shouting were packed off in a cosmic bag, back to their rightful home, where they would most likely be used as light snacks for higher perversities like Felderasticus Sixth-Quickened. I was savagely annoyed. Using Felderasticus to swat them was akin to using a guillotine as a mousetrap, but you can see the mess we were in.

"Now, I shall withdraw, having satisfied all the terms of our compact," said the demon.

"Oh, screw yourself!" I snarled.

"Specify physically, metaphysically, or figuratively."

"Shut it! You know you're not finished. I need a moment to think."

Tariel and Caladesh were fending off penitents, inelegantly but emphatically, with their waterlogged weapons. Rumstandel was trying to help them as well as keep life hot for the Iron Ring sorcerer that must have been mixed in with the penitents. I couldn't see him (or her) from my vantage, but the imps and water elementals proved their proximity. Millowend was stirring, muttering, but not yet herself. I peered at the towering war machine and calculated. No, that was too much of a job for my demon. Too much mass, too much magic, and now it was just 200 yards distant.

"We require transportation," I said, "Instantly and—"

"Wait," cried my mother. She sat up, blinked, and appeared unsurprised as a cannonball swatted the earth not ten feet away, spattering both of us with mud. "Don't finish that command, Watchdog! We all need to die!"

"Watchdog," said Rumstandel, "our good captain is plainly experiencing a vacancy in the upper-story rooms, so please apply something heavy to her skull and get on with that escape you were arranging."

"No! I'm sorry," cried Millowend, and now she bounced to her feet with sprightliness that was more than a little unfair in someone her age. "My mind was still a bit at luncheon. You know that flying around being a hundred of myself is a very taxing business. What I mean is, this is a bespoke ambush, and if we vanish safely out of it they'll just keep expecting us. But if it looks as though we're snuffed, the Iron Ring might drop their guard enough to let us back in the fight!"

"Ahh!" I cried, chagrined that I hadn't thought of that myself. In my defense, you have just read my account of the previous few minutes. I cleared my throat.

"Felderasticus, these next-named tasks, once achieved, shall purchase the end of your indenture without further caveat or reservation! NOW! Interpreting my words in the broadest possible spirit of good faith, we, all five of us, must be brought alive with our possessions to a place of safety within the North Elaran encampment just south of here. Furthermore – FURTHERMORE! Upon the instant of our passage, you must create a convincing illusion of our deaths, as though . . . as though we had been caught by cannon-fire and the subsequent combustion of our powder-flasks and alchemical miscellanies!"

I remain very proud of that last flourish. Wizards, like musketeers, are notorious for carrying all sorts of volatile things on their persons, and if we were seen to explode the Iron Ringers might not bother examining our alleged remains too closely.

"Faithfully shall I work your will and thereby end my indenture," said the cold voice of the demon.

The world turned gray and spun around me. After a moment of disjointed nausea I found myself once again lying under sharp-elbowed Caladesh, with Rumstandel, Tariel, and my mother into the bargain. Roughly 600 pounds of Red Hats, all balanced atop my stomach, did something for my freshly eaten pie that I hesitate to describe. But, ah, you've squeezed fruit before, haven't you?

Moaning, swearing, and retching, we all fell or scrambled apart. Guns, bandoliers, and hats littered the ground around us. When I had managed to wipe my mouth and take in a few breaths, I finally noticed that we were surrounded by a veritable forest of legs, legs wearing the boots and uniform trousers of North Elaran staff officers.

I followed some of those legs upward with my eyes and met the disbelieving gaze of General Arad Vorstal, supreme field commander of the army of North Elara. Beside him stood his general of engineers, the equally surprised Luthienne Alune.

"Generals," said my mother suavely, dusting herself off and restoring her battered hat to its proper place. "Apologies for the suddenness of our arrival. I'm afraid I have to report that our reconnaissance of the Iron Ring war machine ended somewhat prematurely. And the machine retains its full motive power."

She cleared her throat.

"And, ah, we're all probably going to see it again in about half an hour."

ENCLOSURE: Invoice for sundry items lost or disposed of in Elaran service, 13th instant, Mithune, 1186. Submitted to Quartermaster-Captain Guthrun on behalf of the Honorable Company of Red Hats, countersigned Captain-Paramount Millowend, Sorceress. 28th instant, Mithune, 1186

ITEM VALUATION:
Bracelet, thaumaturgical . . . 1150 Gil. 13 p.
Function (confidential)
Spyflask, thaumaturgical . . . 100 Gil. 5 p.
Function (reconnaissance)
Total Petition . . . 1250 Gil. 18 p.
Please remit as per terms of contract.

WATCHDOG – Actually, I picked up your spyflask when you rather thoughtlessly dropped it that afternoon. I did mean to return it to you eventually. These minor trivialities of camp life do elude me sometimes. I hadn't realized that the company received a hundred gildmarks as a replacement fee. Do you want me to keep the flask, or shall I write myself up a chit for the hundred gildmarks? I am content with either. – R

13th Mithune, 1186
Somewhere near Lake Corlan, North Elara

But they didn't come. Not then.

Afternoon wound down into evening. Presumably, the Iron Ring thought it too late in the day to commence a general action, and with all of their sorcerous impediments supposedly ground into the mud, one could hardly blame them for a lack of urgency. The war machine stood guard before Montveil's Wall, and behind it came the creak and groan of artillery teams, the shouts of orders, and the tramp of boots as line regiments moved into their billets for the night. The light of a thousand fires rose from the captured Elaran fieldworks and joined in an ominous glow, giving the overcast the colors of a banked furnace.

In the Elaran camp, we brooded and argued. The council ran long, in quite inverse proportion to the tempers of those involved.

"It's not that we can't dig," General Alune was saying, her patience shaved down to a perceptibly thin patina on her manner. "For the tenth time, it's the fact that the bloody machine moves! We can work like mad all night, sink a shaft just about the right size to make a grave for the damn thing, and in the morning it might spot the danger and take five steps to either side. So much for our trap."

"Have you ever seen a pitfall for a dangerous animal?" said Tariel, mangling protocol by speaking up. "It's customary to cover the entrance with a light screen of camouflage—"

"Yes, yes, I'm well aware," snapped General Alune. "But once again, that machine is the master of the field and may go where it pleases, attacking from any angle. We have no practical means of forcing it into a trap, even a hidden one."

"Has the thing truly no weak point, no joint in its armor, no vent or portal on which we can concentrate fire? Or sorcery?" said Vorstal, stroking the beard that hung from his craggy chin like sable-streaked snow. "What about the mechanisms that propel it?"

"I assure you I had the closest look possible," said Millowend. "It was the only useful thing I managed to do during our last engagement. The device has no real machinery, no engine, no pulleys or pistons. It's driven by brute sorcery. A wizard in a harness, mimicking the movements they desire the machine to make, a puppeteer driving a vast puppet. You might call it an effigy engine. It's exhausting work, and I'm sure they have to swap wizards frequently. However, while harnessed, the driver is still inside the armored shell, still protected by the arts of their fellows. It's as easy to destroy the machine outright as it is to reach them."

"How many great guns have we managed to recover since yesterday's debacle?" said General Vorstal.

"Four," said General Alune. "Four functional six-pounders, crewed by a few survivors, the mildly injured, and a lot of fresh volunteers."

"That's nothing to hang our hopes on," sighed Vorstal, "a fifth of what wasn't even adequate before!"

"We could try smoke," said Rumstandel. While listening to the council of war he'd added flourishes to his beard, tiny gray clouds and twirling water-spouts, plus lithe long-necked sea serpents. Life had become very hard for the little ships of the Rumstandel Delta. "Or anything to render the hull uninhabitable. Flaming caustics, bottled vitriol, sulfurous miasma, air spirits of reeking decay—"

"The Iron Ring sorcerers could nullify any of those before they caused harm," I said. "You and I certainly could."

Rumstandel shrugged theatrically. Miniature lightning crackled just below his chin.

"Then it must be withdrawal," said Vorstal, bitterly but decisively. "If we face that thing again, with the rest of the Iron Ring force at its heels, this army will be destroyed. I have to preserve it. Trade territory for time. I want 100 volunteers to demonstrate at Montveil's Wall while we start pulling the rest out quietly." He looked around, meeting the eyes of all his staff in turn. "Officers will surrender their horses to hospital wagon duty, myself included."

"With respect, sir," said General Alune, "you know how many Iron Ring sympathizers . . . that is, when word of all this reaches parliament they'll have you dismissed. And they'll be laying white flags at the feet of that damned machine before we can even get the army reformed, let alone reinforced."

"Certainly I'll be recalled," said Vorstal. "Probably arrested, too. I'll be counting on *you* to keep our forces intact and use whatever time I can buy you to think of something I couldn't. You always were the cleverer one, Luthienne."

"The Iron Ring won't want easy accommodations," said Millowend, and I was surprised to notice her using a very subtle spell of persuasion. Her voice rang a little more clearly to the far corners of the command pavilion, her shadow seemed longer and darker, her eyes more alight with compelling fire. "You've bled them and stymied them for months. You've defied all their plans. Now their demands will be merciless and unconditional. If this army falls back, they will put your people in chains and feed Elara to the fires of their war-furnaces, until you're nothing but ashes on the trail to their next conquest! Now, if that war machine were destroyed, could you think to meet the rest of the Iron Ring army with the force you still possess?"

"If it were destroyed?" shouted General Vorstal. "IF! If my cock had scales and another ninety feet it'd be a dragon! IF! Millowend, I'm sorry, you and your company have done us extraordinary service, but I have no more time for interruptions. I'll see to it that your contract is fully paid off and you're given letters of safe passage, for what they're worth."

"I have a fresh notion," said my mother. "One that will give us a long and sleepless night, if it's practicable at all, and the thing I need to hear, right now, is whether or not you can meet the Iron Ring army if that machine is subtracted from the ledger."

"Not with any certainty," said Vorstal slowly. "But we still have our second line of works, and it's the chance I'd take over any other, if only it were as you say."

"For this we'll need your engineers," said Millowend. "Your blacksmiths, your carpenters, and work squads of anyone who can hold a shovel or an axe. And we'll need those volunteers for Montveil's Wall to screen us, with their lives if need be."

"What do you have in mind?" said General Alune.

"A trap, as you said, is wasted unless we can guarantee that the Iron Ring machine moves into it." Millowend mimicked the lurching steps of the machine with her fingers. "Well, what could we possibly set before it that would absolutely guarantee movement in our desired direction? What challenge could we mount on the field that would *compel* them to advance their machine and engage us as directly as possible?"

After a sufficiently dramatic pause, she told us.

Then the real shouting and argument began.

14th Mithune, 1186
Somewhere near Lake Corlan, North Elara

Just before sunrise, the surviving Elaran skirmishers fell back from Montveil's Wall, their shot-flasks empty, their ranks scraped thin by musketry, magic, and misadventure in the dark. Yet they had achieved their mission and kept their Iron Ring counterparts out of our lines, away from the evidence of what we were really up to.

Behind them, several regiments of Elaran foot had moved noisily throughout the night, doing their best to create the impression of the pullback that was only logical. A pullback it was, though not to the roads but rather to a fresh line of breastworks, where they measured powder, sharpened bayonets, and slept fitfully in the very positions they would guard at first light.

We slept not at all. Tariel and Caladesh passed hours in conference with the most experienced of the surviving Elaran artillery handlers. Rumstandel, Millowend and I spent every non-working moment we had on devouring anything we could lay our hands on, without a scrap of shame. My mother's plan was a pie job and a half.

The sun came up like dull brass behind the charcoal bars of the hazy sky. Fresh smoke trails curled from the Iron Ring positions, harbingers of the hot breakfast they would have before they moved out to crush us. General Vorstal had reluctantly sentenced his men and women to a cold camp, to help preserve the illusion that large contingents in Elaran blue had fled south during the night. We sorcerers received our food from Millowend's indentured culinary imps, their pinched green faces grotesque under their red leather chef's hats, their ovens conveniently located in another plane of existence.

As the sun crept upward, the Iron Ring lines began to form, regimental pennants fluttering like sails above a dark and creeping sea. A proud flag broke out atop the war machine, blue circle within gray circle on a field of black. The symbol of the Iron Ring cities, the coal-furnace tyrants, whose home dominions girded the shores of vast icy lakes a month's march north of Elara.

By the tenth hour of the morning, they were coming for us, in the full panoply of their might and artifice.

"I suppose it's time to find out whether we're going to be victorious fools, or just fools," said Millowend. We had taken our ready position together, all five of us, and rising anxiety had banished most of our fatigue. We engaged in our little rituals, chipper or solemn as per our habits, hugging and shaking hands and exchanging good-natured insults. My mother dusted off my coat and straightened my hat.

"Rumstandel," she said, "are you sure now wouldn't be an appropriate time to rediscover that chronically misplaced hat of yours?"

"Of course not, captain." He rubbed his ample abdominal ballast and grinned. "I much prefer to die as I've always lived, handsome and insufferable."

My mother rendered eloquent commentary using nothing but her eyebrows. Then she cast the appropriate signal-spell, and we braced ourselves.

Five hundred Elaran sappers and work-gangers, already drained to the marrow by a night of frantic labor, seized hold of ropes and chains. "HEAVE!" shouted General Alune, who then flung herself into the nearest straining crew and joined them in their toil. Pulleys creaked and guidelines rattled. With halting, lurching, shuddering movements, a fifty-foot wood and metal tripod rose into the sky above the Elaran command pavilion, with the five of us in an oblong wooden box at its apex, feeling rather uncomfortably like catapult stones being winched into position.

We leveled off, wavering disconcertingly, but more or less upright. Cheers erupted from thousands of throats across the Elaran camp, and musketeers came to their feet in breastworks and redoubts, loosing their regimental colors from hiding. Our North Elaran war machine stood high in the morning light, and even those who'd been told what we were up to waved their hats and screamed like they could hardly believe it.

It was all a thoroughly shambolic hoax, of course. The Iron Ring machine was the product of months of work, cold metal plates fitted to purpose-built legs, rugged and roomy, weighed down with real armor. Ours was a gimcrack, upjumped watchtower, shorter, narrower, and wobbly as a drunk at a ballroom dance. Our wooden construction was braced in a few crucial places with joints and nail-plates improvised by Elaran blacksmiths. Our hull was armored with nothing but logs, and our only gun was a cast-iron six-pounder in a specially rigged recoil harness, tended by Caladesh and Tariel.

"Let's secure their undivided attention," said Millowend. "Charge and load!"

Tariel and Caladesh rammed home a triple-sized powder charge, augmented with the greenish flecks of substances carefully chosen from our precious alchemical supply. Rumstandel handed over a six-pound ball, laboriously prepared by us with pale ideograms of spells designed to ensure long, straight flight. Caladesh drove it down the barrel with the rammer while Tariel looked out the forward window and consulted an improvised sight made from a few pieces of wood and wire.

"Lay it as you like, then fire at will," said Millowend.

Our gunners didn't dally. They sighted their piece on the distant Iron Ring machine, and Tariel whistled up her salamander, which was taking a brief vacation from its usual home. The fire-spirit danced around the touchhole, and the six-pounder erupted with a bang that was much too loud even with our noise-suppression spells deadening the air.

Ears ringing, nostrils stinging from the strange smoke of the blast, I jumped to a window and followed the glowing green arc of the magically enhanced shot as it sped toward the enemy. There was a flash and a flat puff of yellowish smoke atop the target machine's canopy.

"Dead on!" I shouted.

We had just ruined a cannon barrel and expended a great deal of careful sorcery, all for the sake of one accurate shot at an improbable distance. It hadn't been expected to do any damage, even if it caught their magicians by surprise. It was just a good old-fashioned gauntlet across the face.

"They're moving," said Caladesh. "Straight for us."

The Iron Ringers answered our challenge, all right. It was precisely the sort of affair that would appeal to them, machine against machine like mad bulls for the fate of North Elara. Hell, it was just the sort of thing that might have appealed to us, if only our "machine" hadn't been a shoddy counterfeit.

"Forward march," said my mother, and I resumed my place at her side along with Rumstandel. This part was going to hurt. We joined hands and concentrated.

We hadn't had time to devise any sort of body harness for the control and movement of our device. Instead we had an accurate wooden model about two feet tall, secured to the floor in front of us. On this we could focus our sorcerous energies, however inefficiently, to move corresponding pieces of the real structure. Ours was, in a sense, a *true* effigy engine.

Imagine pulling a twenty-pound weight along a chain in hair-fine increments by jerking your eyebrow muscles. Imagine trying to push your prone, insensate body along the ground using nothing but the movements of your toes. This was the sort of nightmarish, concentrated effort required to send our device creaking along, step by step, shaking like a bar-stool with delusions of grandeur.

The energy poured out of us like a vital fluid. We moaned, we shuddered, we screamed and swore in the most undignified fashion. Caladesh and Tariel clung to the walls in earnest, for our passage was anything but smooth. It was a bit like being trapped inside a madman's feverish delusion of a carriage ride, some fifty feet above the ground, while a powerful enemy approached with cannons booming.

We had to hope that our Elaran employers had strictly obeyed our edict to clear our intended movement path. There was no chance to look down and halt if some unfortunate soul was about to play the role of insect to our boot-heel.

Iron Ring cannonballs shrieked past. One of them peeled away part of our roof, giving us a ragged new skylight. Closer and closer we stumbled, featherweight frauds. Closer and closer the enemy machine pounded in dread sincerity. Even fat and well-fed sorcerers were not meant to do what we were doing for long; our magic grew taut and strained as an over-filled water-sack. It was impossible to tell tears from sweat, for it was all running out of us in a torrent. The expressions on the faces of Tariel and Caladesh struck me in my preoccupation as extremely funny, and then I realized it was because I had never before seen those consummate stalwarts look truly horrified. Another round of fire boomed from the charging Iron Ring machine. Our vessel shuddered, rocked by a hit somewhere below. I tried to subdue my urge to cower or hide. There was nothing to be done now; a shot through our bow would likely fill the entire cabin with splinters and scythe us all down in an instant. In moments, we must also come within range of the wizards huddled inside the enemy machine, and we were in no shape to resist them. Luck was our only shield now. Luck, and a few seconds or yards in either direction.

"They're going," cried Tariel. "THEY'RE GOING!"

There was a sound like the world coming apart at the seams, a juddering drum-hammer noise, sharpened by the screams of men and metal alike. Everything shook around us and beneath us, and for a moment I was certain that Tariel was wrong, that it was we who'd been mortally struck at last, that we were on our way to the ground and into the history books as a farcical footnote to the rise of the Iron Ring empire.

The thing about my mother's plans, though, is that they tend to work, more often than not.

Given luck, and a few seconds or yards in either direction.

I didn't witness it personally, but I can well imagine the scene based on the dozens of descriptions I collected afterward. We had barely thirty more yards of safe space to move when the Iron Ring machine hit the edge of the trap, the modified classic pitfall scraped out of the earth by General Alune's sappers, then concealed with panels of canvas and wicker and even a few tents. A thousand-strong draft had labored all night to move and conceal the dirt, aided here and there by our sorcery. It wasn't quite a ready-made grave for the war machine. More of a good hard stumble of about thirty feet.

Whatever it was, it was sufficient. In clear view of every Iron Ring soldier on the field, the greatest feat of ferrothaumaturgical engineering in the history of the world charged toward its feeble-looking rival, only to stumble and plunge in a deadly arc, smashing its armored cupola like a crustacean dropped from the sky by a hungry seabird. A shroud of dust and smoke settled around it, and none of its occupants was left in any shape to ever crawl out of it.

Millowend, Rumstandel, and I fell to our knees in the cabin of our hoax machine, gasping as though we'd been fished from the water ten seconds shy of drowning. Everything felt loose and light and wrong, so much flesh had literally cooked away from the three of us. It was a strange and selfish scene for many moments, as we had no idea whether to celebrate a close-run tactical triumph, or the simple fact of our continued existence. We shamelessly did both, until the noise of battle outside reminded us that the day's work was only begun. Sore and giddy, we let Rumstandel conjure a variation of his kites to lower us safely to the ground, where we joined the mess already in progress.

It was no easy fight. The Iron Ringers were appalled by the loss of their war machine, and they had deployed poorly, expecting to scourge an already-depleted camp in the wake of their invincible iron talisman. They were also massed in the open, facing troops in breastworks. Still, they were hard fighters and well led, and so many Elarans were second-line militia or already exhausted by the long labors of the night.

I'll leave it to other historians to weigh the causes and the cruxes of true victory in the Battle of Lake Corlan. We were in it everywhere, rattling about the field via horses and sorcery and very tired feet, for many Iron Ring magicians remained alive and dangerous. In the shadow of our abandoned joke of an effigy engine, we fought for our pay and our oath, and as the sun finally turned red behind its veils of powder smoke, we and 10,000 Elarans watched in exhausted exaltation as the Iron Ring army finally broke like a wave on our shores, a wave that parted and sank and ran into the darkness.

After six months of raids and minor successes and placeholder, proxy victories, six months of stalemate capped by the terror of a brand-new way of warfare, the Elarans had flung an army twice the size of their own back in confusion and defeat at last.

It was not the end of their war, and the butcher's bill would be terrible. But it was something. It meant hope, and frankly, when someone hires the Red Hats, that's precisely what we're expected to provide.

In the aftermath of the battle I worked some sorcery for the hospital details, then stumbled, spell-drunk and battered, to the edge of the gaping pit now serving as a tomb for the mighty war machine and its occupants.

I have to admit I waxed pitifully philosophical as I studied the wreck. It wouldn't be an easy thing to duplicate, but it could be done, with enough wizards and enough skilled engineers, and small mountains of steel and gold. Would the Iron Ring try again? Would other nations attempt to build such devices of their own? Was that the future of sorcerers like myself, to become power sources for hulking metal beasts, to drain our lives into their engines?

I, Watchdog, a lump of coal, a fagot for the flames.

I shook my head then and I shake my head now. War is my trade, but it makes me so damned tired sometimes. I don't have any answers. I keep my oath, I keep my book, I take my pay and I guard my friends from harm. I suppose we are all lumps of coal destined for one furnace or another.

I found the rest of the company in various states of total collapse near the trampled, smoldering remains of General Vorstal's command pavilion. Our options had been limited when we'd selected a place to build our machine, and unfortunately the trap path had been drawn across all the Elaran high command's nice things.

Caladesh was unconscious with a shattered wagon wheel for a pillow. Tariel had actually fallen sleep sitting up, arms wrapped around her musket. My mother was sipping coffee and staring at Rumstandel, who was snoring like some sort of cave-beast while miniature coronas of foul weather sparked around his beard. In lieu of a pillow, Rumstandel had enlisted one of his familiars, a tubby little bat-demon that stood silently, holding Rumstandel's bald head off the ground like an athlete heaving a weight over its shoulders.

"He looks so peaceful, doesn't he?" whispered Millowend. She muttered and gestured, and a bright new red hat appeared out of thin air, gently lowering itself on to Rumstandel's brow. He continued snoring.

"There," she said, with no little satisfaction. "Be sure to record that in your chronicles, will you, Watchdog?"

The reader will note that I have been pleased to comply.

STRIFE LINGERS IN MEMORY

Carrie Vaughn

My father was a wise man to whom many came seeking advice. During his audiences I'd lurk behind his chair or fetch his cup, and they called me fair, even when I was little. I grew to be golden-haired and wary. I was destined for – something.

War overwhelmed us. The Heir to the Fortress was dead – no, in exile, nearly the same. The evil rose, broke the land over an iron knee, and even my father went into hiding.

Then he came.

I was eighteen. The stranger was – hard to say. He looked young but carried such a weight of care, he might have lived many lifetimes already. He came to ask my father how he might make his way along the cursed paths that led to the ancient fortress now held by the enemy.

My father proclaimed, "That way is barred to any who are not of the Heir's blood, but that line is dead. It is useless."

Our gazes met, mine and that stranger's, and I saw in him a shuttered light waiting to blaze forth. I gripped the back of my father's chair to steady myself.

The stranger and I knew in that moment what was destined to be, though our elders needed a bit more persuading.

So it came to pass that the stranger, Evrad – Heir to the Fortress, the true-blooded prince himself – took the cursed paths and led an army to overthrow the stronghold of his enemy and claim the ancient fortress as his own. He married the wizard's daughter and made her – me – his Queen. Happily, the land settled into a long-awaited peace.

The night after the day of his coronation and of our wedding we had alone and to ourselves. When the door closed, we looked at one another for a long time, not believing that this moment had come at last, remembering all the moments we believed it would not come at all. Then, all at once, we fell into each other's arms.

He made love to me as if the world were ending. I drowned in the fury of it, clinging to him like he was a piece of splintered hull after a shipwreck. Exhausted, we rested in each other's arms. I sang him to sleep and, running my fingers through his thick hair, fell asleep myself.

I had dreamed of this, sleeping protected by him. I had dreamed of waking in his arms, sunlight through the window painting our chamber golden, drawing on his warmth in the chill of morning.

Instead, I awoke to the sound of a scream. Evrad's scream. He thrashed, kicking me. I backed away, arms covering my head. Our blankets twisted, pulling away from the bed as he fought with them. When I dared to look, he had curled up, drawing his limbs close. He was trembling so hard I felt it through the bed.

"Evrad?" I whispered. He remained hunched over and shaking, so I reached for him. "Evrad. Please."

I touched his shoulder, the slope of it glowing pale in moonlight shining through the window. It was damp with sweat.

He flinched at the touch and looked at me, his eyes wide and wild. My stomach clenched – he did not seem to see me.

Then, "Alida?"

He came to life, returned to himself, and pulled me close in an embrace. I held him as tightly as I could, but my grip seemed so weak compared to his.

"Oh, my love," he said over and over. "I thought it was a dream: you, peace – you. I dreaded waking to find you weren't real."

"Hush. Oh, please hush. You're safe."

I said those words to him many times, on many nights. I kept hoping he would believe me.

Strife lingered in the memory of what we had suffered. He defeated an army of horrors, but the demons may yet overcome him.

He kept the nightmares well hidden. He always appeared to his men, his guards, his people as the hero, the savior, the King.

He looked the part, standing tall, smiling easily and accepting gracefully the adoration of hardened warriors and toddling children alike.

He turned his best face toward the people, keeping his secret soul hidden. But he could not hide it from me. So it fell to me to keep my best face toward him, to be strong for him, and hide my secret soul away.

One night, he came to our chamber carrying an arcane-looking bottle covered with dust, the cap sealed with wax.

"I will sleep through the night," he said in much the same way he'd once said he would defeat the dark army that threatened to overrun him. Liquid sloshed in the bottle when he set it on the table.

"What is it? Rare potion?"

"Rare whiskey," he said with a grunt. "Perhaps it will make me forget the shadows."

I pursed my lips, making a wry smile. "That will inspire sweet dreams, and not the comfort of my arms?"

"Oh, my love." He touched my cheek with all the tenderness I could hope for, though his face was lined with worry. I took his hands, locking their anxious movements in mine.

Once, we needed no words, but I could not read the thoughts that clouded his expression. During the war, he had been proud, his look keen and determined. I had never seen him so careworn.

He kissed my hands and went out of our chambers. At least he left the whiskey behind.

A month passed, then came the night I awoke alone.

Perhaps the stillness woke me. Midnight – the dark chill of night when he usually began sweating, trembling as if all the fears he had kept at bay during the war came on him at once – had passed and no screams woke me. I sat up, felt all around the bed, looked when my sight adjusted to the dark. I was alone.

I searched for him. Wrapping my cloak tight around me, I went along the battlements where I could see half the realm across the plains. I searched the stables, where he might have sought the calm influence of sleeping horses. I carried a lantern through stone corridors where no one had walked since Evrad claimed the fortress.

I found him crouched in a forgotten corner, arms wrapped around his head, face turned to the wall. He had managed to tie a cloak around his middle, but it was slipping off his shoulders.

A guard walking his post from the other end of the corridor found him at the same time. "My liege!" the man cried and rushed toward him.

I interposed, stopping him with a raised hand. "Please. Stay back." Turning to Evrad I said, "My lord? My lord, are you awake?"

I touched his shoulder. He looked at me. The lantern light showed his cheeks wet with tears. "Come, my lord. Let's go to bed." I helped him to his feet, like he was an old man or a child.

To the guard I said, "You will not speak of this. You will keep this secret." And what of the next night? And what of the night the guards found him before I did? I was a wizard's daughter but I still needed sleep. I needed more eyes. "You will help me keep this secret, yes?"

"Yes, my Queen. Oh yes." Wonder and pity filled his gaze. I remembered his face, learned his name, Petro. If I ever heard rumor of the King's illness, this man would answer for it.

We had fair nights. Some nights, he only whimpered in his sleep, in the throes of visions I did not want to imagine. Some nights, drunk on wine, we threw logs on the fire until it blazed, making the room hot, and we played until we wore each other out.

Other nights, I wore my cloak, took another in case he had lost his, and searched deserted corridors by lantern light. I always waited until I had put him back to bed and he slept before I sat by the fire and cried.

At last, weary and despairing, I departed in the shrouded hour before dawn. I used craft that my father taught me: how to move without sound, how to turn aside the curious gaze, how to not leave tracks. I left my own horse behind and took one from the couriers that would not be so quickly missed. I rode hard, turned off the main way, and found the forested path that led through ravine and glen to my father's valley.

After the war, he secluded himself in a valley beyond the line of hills where the city lay, a day's journey away. He said he wished to be out of reach of peaceful folk who would trouble him with petty complaints now that the great matters were over. He said he was finished dispensing wisdom for people simply because they asked for it.

What a gentle place. I had traveled with him when he came to live here, but my heart had been so full of the times, of the ache of war and separation from my beloved, that I hadn't looked around me. Water ran frothing down a rocky hillside and became a stream that flowed through a meadow of tall grass scattered with the color of wildflowers. Late sun shining through pollen turned the air golden. I could smell the light, fresh and fertile.

I made a mistake. I shouldn't have run away. Or better, I should have brought Evrad here, to this place.

The whitewashed cottage sat where the grass ended and trees began. Smoke rose from a hole in the roof.

My horse, breathing hard and soaked with sweat, sighed deeply and lowered her head to graze. I pulled off her tack, brushed her, and let her roam free. I left my gear by the cottage's door and went inside.

A fire burned at the hearth in the back of the cottage's one room. Near it were a kettle and all manner of cooking implements. A cot occupied one corner, a table and chair another, and the rest of the walls had shelves and shelves of books. My father sat in a great stuffed chair near the fire, wrapped in a blanket, gazing into a shallow bowl of water he held in his lap.

Quietly, I sat at his feet as I had when I was little.

"My Queen, is it?" he said. A smile shifted the wrinkles of his face. He was bald, but for a fringe of white hair.

"Your daughter still."

"No, I gave you away."

"Father . . ."

He sighed. "Why have you come here? What trouble drives you from your home?"

"Perhaps I only wish to visit you."

"I still have sight, girl." He touched the surface of the water in the basin and flicked his fingers at me, sprinkling me. I flinched, then hugged my knees.

He shook his head. "I was supposed to be able to leave the keeping of the world to its heirs."

"If you have your sight, then you know what is wrong."

"Tell me. I want to hear what you think is wrong."

I was Queen of this land, the destined love of the greatest of heroes, fortunate and blessed beyond reason, and he made me feel like a hapless child. Perhaps that was why the heroes in the stories were almost always orphans.

"The war haunts him," I said. "He has nightmares. He cannot sleep. He buries all this deep in his heart, but it is festering there. How long can he survive like this? I am afraid, more afraid than I ever was when he carried his sword against the enemy. I try to comfort him. I don't know what to do."

Grunting with the effort, he leaned over the arm of his chair to set the basin on the floor. "So, are you looking for a potion or a spell that will set all to rights?"

I hadn't thought of that, when I decided to come here. If there were such a thing I would gladly take it. But my coming here was selfish. I wanted to rest in the shelter of another, as tired as I was of *being* shelter for another.

"Or do you simply flee from what you do not understand?"

I could have cried, but I pretended to be strong. In a world where fate had ordered all our actions and brought us all to this point, I was terrified that it should leave us now. "The evil lingers. I thought he had defeated it for all time."

"He is battle-weary. That is no surprise. As for a cure? Time and care. I know no magic to speed it along. We must be vigilant. Each of us has a role in the war. Now, yours has come."

"But he is the warrior and King, I am just a—" I almost said any of a dozen things: woman, child, pawn, symbol. None of the stories prepared me to be anything else.

"He is King, so he must hide his fears. It falls to you, then, to keep him sane."

"This has been a mistake. Would the true Heir of the Fortress suffer so?"

"Would one who was not the Heir have survived to suffer so?"

"I cannot do this," I said, tears falling at last.

My father smiled and touched my hair with his arthritic hand. "He said the same thing to me before he departed for the last battle. I will tell you what I told him." He held my hand. His was warm and dry. "'That may be true,' I said. 'But you must try, because no one else will.'"

I pressed his hand to my face, wishing I was a child again, able to hide behind his chair and take no part in the worries of the world.

He continued, "You may have the hardest battle of all. No one victory will defeat this enemy. This is not a beast to slay and be done with."

"And no one will sing of my battles."

I slept curled in a blanket near the hearth that night – the first night in many I had not been awakened by sleepwalking or nightmare cries. I treasured the peace of the valley. In the morning, I sat in the meadow by the stream. Since settling at the fortress and into my life as Queen, I had seldom touched living earth or smelled grass and wildflowers warmed by the sun. Here, I could pretend none of it had happened.

My father joined me. He spent a long time settling to the ground, leaning on his cane. He'd never used a cane before. Too late, I reached to help him, to give him my arm to lean on. He'd never needed help before, so I didn't think of it. He spent time arranging his cane and robes around him, gazing over the dancing water.

"When will you return to him?" he said at last.

"I don't know." I had to gather my strength. I could spend the rest of my life gathering strength and still not have enough.

"Make it soon."

I'd been picking at grass, weaving something of a tangled wreath. I threw the mess of it into the stream. "If you don't wish me to stay, I can go elsewhere."

"I want you to go to your home. Your child should know his father."

"My—" I flushed, my whole body burning from my scalp to my bare toes. Then the expected movement: I put my hand on my belly. "You don't mean—"

He smiled, a cat-wise smile of secrets. "I still have sight. You – are still learning."

A child. Me – a child. My child. *His* child. Oh, have mercy. Forgive me.

"Father, I must go."

"Yes, you must."

I caught my horse, saddled her quickly, and fled in a whirlwind. I had galloped a mile when I pulled up suddenly – I was carrying a child. I should be more careful.

What would Evrad say? Perhaps he would sleep well, with a child in his arms.

Halfway back to the fortress, a thunder of hoofbeats galloped toward me. I waited for the rider to appear around the curve in the road. The horse was a snow-white charger, with a gold breastplate and gold fixings on his tack, tail flying, mane rippling. His rider pulled up hard, and his hooves raised dust as he skidded in the road.

I knew this stallion, and I knew the rider who jumped from the saddle and ran toward me.

As I dismounted I stumbled, my grip on the saddle keeping me upright. Here was my hero, my King, face uplifted, striding with strength and determination. Grim and fierce, as I had seen him ride to battle, as I had not seen him in weeks. I had not lost him to the war.

I would have run to meet him, but I had moved just a few steps away from my horse when he reached me. He caught me in his arms and held tight. His leather doublet pressed my flesh, his rough cheek brushed mine.

"I'm sorry," I cried again and again, weeping on his shoulder.

He made soothing noises. "Hush. It's enough that you're safe. I guessed where you had gone, and I meant to go and beg you to return. I meant to make promises – to tie myself to the bed so you wouldn't have to search after me at midnight anymore. To have my guards knock me unconscious every evening so I might sleep through the night."

I laughed. "No guard of yours would even try, my lord."

He touched my cheeks, wiping away tears. "I know you are a wizard's daughter. Your spirit is wild, free as the wind, and your will is strong. I have nothing that can bind you – but tell me you will never leave me again. Promise me."

Oh, how such words would bind me. Did he not know that words are nearly all that will bind a wizard, or his daughter?

"I promise," I said.

Men fight for symbols: a crown, a throne, lines on a map.

When he reclaimed the fortress and we married, our story ended but our lives didn't. None of the old stories prepared me for the battles I now fought.

I remembered the night he left my father's hall to meet the last battle, when all but I believed he was marching to his death.

I held him as long as I could. "I wish I could go with you. I wish I could do more than wait here for news."

"But you're already doing so much."

"What? What am I doing?" I said, smiling with wonder.

"You are the symbol of what we fight for: all that is beautiful."

Men fight for symbols. What do women fight for?

Again I wandered nighttime passages, my way lit by a dim lantern, searching. I moved slowly, some seven months along my child's time. I wore two cloaks and fur boots, because winter was upon us. On bad nights, when the terrors wrenched Evrad to immobility, he found dark passages and shivered there in the cold, fighting demons in his mind. I walked every corridor in the fortress and could not find him. Petro had not seen him either.

On bad nights, he hid in dark passages. This night was worse.

I found him on the battlements of the highest tower. A spire jutting above the sheer wall of the fortress, it served as a watch-tower and a place for message fires. He leaned on the stone wall, gazing straight down, a hundred feet to hard earth.

I caught my breath and swallowed a scream.

"My lord? Evrad," I said softly, my voice shaking. "What are you doing?"

He climbed to sit on the lip of the wall. He looked at me; his eyes were feral, shining. He trembled. Sweat matted his hair, and his face was pale, drained of blood. He wore only breeches and gooseflesh covered his arms.

If I reached for him, the gesture might push him over.

"Go back to bed. Why must you follow me?"

Because I loved him. Because I worried about him. Because it was my duty, and I must do it so the secret of his nighttime terrors did not spread. But I didn't say those things.

"I will follow you to the end of the world, over cliffs into fiery rifts that split the earth if I must. But I will follow you."

"Like the demons."

"I'm faster than demons. They will not reach you before I do."

"Will you follow me there?" He nodded over the wall to the long drop.

The moon shone near full, low in the sky, painting the land with shadows. Lurking behind each house and tower and city wall, stretching away from every rise in the land, every tree on the plain, black shapes reached toward the fortress.

"They whisper in my ear, *jump*. Oh, Alida."

My knees gave way and I sat on the stone, lurching with my swollen weight. I couldn't shutter the moon, to chase away the shadows.

"Evrad. What did you fight for? Did you fight for this, to cast yourself off a tower? Then they've won. The enemy is dead and gone, but will still win the war. It was all for nothing. What did you fight for?"

"I don't know anymore . . ."

"Me, Evrad! You fought for me! Now I am yours. You don't have to fight anymore. You've won."

He shook his head. "I'm not worthy of you. You deserve better. Someone who doesn't have nightmares."

I laughed, clapping my hand over my mouth because the sound was so acrid. "I deserve better? Evrad – you are the hero of the age, the king of legends. And I deserve *better*? Who do you think I am?"

He looked at me. His frown was long, unmovable. "You are everything."

I crawled toward him. "Come down from there, Evrad. Come to me." I stretched my hand to him. I had to be stronger than the shadows. My voice had to be more alluring. "Touch me. Just touch me."

A small goal, an easy quest, well within his reach. A slender hand, poised in the dark. He leaned, lips parted in an expression of longing.

He fell off the lip of the wall and into my arms.

"I don't want better. I don't want the hero and king. I want you." We sat for many hours, hugging each other against the cold.

I brought him to bed and wrapped myself around him. He shivered. I was not blanket enough against the cold.

"Do you see them? In the shadows on the wall?" he said. Candle flames flickered in a draft. The warped shadows of a cup, a candlestick, a comb danced and trembled all around.

"It's only light and dark."

"I know that – but I see memories. I see a thousand goblin warriors throwing themselves against the burning ramparts of the city. I see them pulling my men into the flames. And there's nothing I can do. I didn't destroy them. They're still here, watching us."

Almost I could see their red eyes and clawed hands. For all his army had saved, 10,000 men had perished in the war. Goblins shook spears which rippled like ocean waves above their heads. I had not been there, yet I could almost see. He lived with such visions in his waking mind. How did he endure?

I got up and blew out the candle, banishing the shadows. Returning to bed, I pressed myself against his back and whispered in his ear. "They're gone now."

He was crying.

Over time, we learned what sparked the grim memories. Bonfires. Shadows under a full moon. Then, our sons in armor. Oh, were his nightmares fierce after Biron's first day in armor. If I could have changed the world, altered the course of sun and moon, rewritten tales of destiny that had been put down by great unseen hands, our children would never have learned to fight. But they were the children of a King and must learn the ways of arms. Evrad insisted on this. Even after waking in the night and telling me that the faces of his men dying over and over in his dreams had changed, and were now the faces of our children.

Over time, nights became easier. With children to occupy him – first a son, then two daughters, and two more sons – he went to bed happy and weary. He did not notice the shadows so much.

Thus peace ruled the land for our children's time, and our children's children's time, and will rule beyond. Just like in the stories.

I sit by a window, my gray hair braided behind me, my withered hands resting on a worn blanket. Evrad is also old, but he wears his age, his gray, and his wrinkles like a prize. He still rides out, straight as a statue in the saddle, and I still wait for him.

Behind me, a door opens and closes softly. Our youngest son, Perrin, attempts to not disturb me. I don't have to look; I am my father's daughter, and I have acquired some of his sight over the years. My father is long dead.

Perrin comes to my chair and kneels on the rug. This puts him at the height he was as a boy. I look on him as if he is a boy come to beg a favor. But he is a man, with a beard and his father's bold eyes.

"Mother? I've almost finished. But I have one last question."

My other children have become warriors, diplomats, husbands, wives, parents, leaders, and healers. Perrin, while he dutifully learned swordplay and manners along with his siblings, has become none of these. He is a scholar, historian, chronicler. A bard.

He has been writing an account of the great War of the Fortress and the turning of the age. I've read parts of it – what he has seen fit to show me – and hardly recognize the events and trials I lived through. It reads like the old stories.

"Oh?" I say. "Why not just invent an answer? It won't sound any more outlandish than what's there already."

"I've written no lies—"

"No, of course not. But you've painted the truth with bold colors indeed." Gah, that's something my father might have said.

He looks away, smirking. Like I might have done, kneeling at my father's chair. "I have a question about a thing I am not sure even happened."

He paused, wincing in difficult thought, trying to speak – my son the bard, tongue tied. I might have laughed, but he looked to be in pain. Finally, he said:

"When I was young, quite small, a noise woke me, and I was afraid. I thought to go to your chamber to seek comfort. The passages were very dark. I crept along the walls like a mouse, fearful of losing my way in my own home. Then, I heard crying. I turned a corner and saw a lantern. In the circle of light I saw you and Father sitting on the floor. You held him in your arms, and he was crying. I thought his heart would break. And I realized – he was afraid of something, more afraid than I was or had ever been. That sight . . . terrified me. I ran back to my own bed. I trembled under my blankets until dawn, and never spoke of it until now.

"Tell me: What I saw – was it real? Did it happen?"

Evrad and I have even managed to keep our troubles from our children. Mostly. He walks in his sleep rarely these days. No reason anyone should know.

"Yes. It happened that night and many others. The horrors of that war have haunted him for many years. It may be that the enemy left him with such visions as revenge, as a final defiance. Or perhaps it is the price for victory." I shake my head. I have invented many excuses, but the simplest is probably the truest: his memory haunts him, and there is no one to blame.

I lean forward and rest my hand on Perrin's shoulder. "You must not write of this. You must not add this to your chronicle."

"But – it means the hero's journey is not ended. It adds all the more to his victory, that he has continued to struggle and continued to win—"

"The hero must be strong, more than human, and when he becomes King, his struggles should be over. *That* is the end of the story. That is the law of stories, Perrin, however else the rest of us must live. If people saw him any different – some spirit would go out of the world, I think. People would believe in him less." I sit back and take a tired breath.

"Believe in him less because he is human?"

"Just so."

I watch Perrin thinking. As a child, his questions went on longer than any of the others' did. He was the one who wanted to know why different birds had different songs, and why water could not flow uphill. He exhausted my ability to make answers. Even now, I hope he has no more questions.

"I understand, I think," he says at last. "The war ends, the age ends, the story ends."

"So the children can make their own stories."

He nods, and wonder of wonders I think he does understand. "One more question," he says, and I brace. "Which was harder? The battles leading into the new age, or the ones after?"

Strange. Looking back now, I only remember the ones after. The ones before happened to someone else, in another age.

I click my tongue and think of what my father might have said. "That's not a fair question. It doesn't matter which is harder, because no one will ever know of the battles after."

Shadows writhe across the floor and climb to the ceiling. They swim around the bed and my sleeping lord. One is like a laughing mouth, another like a reaching hand that touches the slope of his shoulder.

"Get away from him." I have drunk too much wine and my vision is spinning. I throw the cup. Wine flies in a spray of droplets across the floor. The silver cup drops with a ringing noise. The sound of swords striking or inhuman teeth gnashing in a cry of victory.

"He is mine!" I cry, standing. "You cannot have him."

Blood rushes in my ears like laughter. I want to scream, I open my mouth to scream, and then—

"Dear heart? What are you doing?" Sitting up, he rubs sleep from his eyes, his brow furrowed with curiosity.

"It's the light," I say in a fey mood. "You were right all along. The demons have come for us."

He searches the room, his eyes gold in the candle's glow. His face is calm, but he takes a trembling breath before saying, "It's only light. Come to bed."

"I must win you back. You fought a war and won. Now it's my turn. I will win you back!"

I clench my fists at my sides. My jaw trembles with an unsounded scream. My King watches me. Soon, the wrinkled brow eases, the tired face softens into a smile. To see him smile so, at night – but then, I must look amusing, in a rage, wine spilled around me, shift falling off my shoulders.

He says, simply as grass in summer, "I know you will. Come to bed, love."

I go to him, wrap my arms around him and kiss him, deeply, longingly. His hands press against me, inviting and warm. So warm.

He pulls away for just a moment. "I know how to chase away the shadows," he says, and blows out the candle.

A SWEET CALLING

Tony Pi

Red paper lanterns, strung high like persimmon moons, welcomed customers to the market street. I announced my next performance of the sugar opera to passers-by, hoping to draw the curious to my stall. But if the row of candy zodiac animals in front of me couldn't lure them in, perhaps my show would.

Taking a dollop of warm caramel, I fashioned a straw-thin spout and blew into it to inflate a bubble of sugar. An elderly couple stopped to watch, while two boys gaped in amazement as I pulled limbs and long ears from the hollow, golden shell to make a rabbit. Satisfied with my handiwork, I stuck the candy-hare on to a bamboo stick and dabbed on molasses eyes.

The elderly pair complimented me on the show and bought two caramel monkeys I had on display. I thanked them. I had arrived in Chengdu with very little money, but hoped to make a small profit by the end of the night. For each creation I sold at the festival, I earned a coin. Such was the simple life of a candyman.

Few customers, however, lingered as long at my stall as Lun the wheelwright. It wasn't my sugar figurines that caught the lad's eye, but the winsome lass ladling out *yuanzi* dumplings across the street.

"You want to win her heart, Lun?" I held the caramel rabbit forth. "Give her this. I guarantee she'll adore it."

Lun wavered. "I'm grateful, *Tangren* Ao, but suppose I say the wrong thing?"

"Courtship, like any craft, needs practice. Compare her to the moon; they love that. Quickly, before nightfall brings more admirers to her stall." I'd seen her turn away two suitors already, a willowy scholar and a brocade merchant with a fat purse.

The lad took the gift and trudged across the stone road, yielding to peasants, horse carts, and even a stiltwalker who passed before him.

I tried not to smile. I would surprise them both with a little magic when he showed her the rabbit: wrinkle its nose, waggle its tail. They'd dismiss it as a trick of the crimson light. But in sharing that moment of delight, perchance they'd fall in love.

Spring's a delicious time to meddle!

"Make a *lóng* next!" demanded the pesky boy, who had yet to buy anything.

"Dragons are hard, kid."

"Bet you don't know how," said his snotty friend.

"I said hard, not impossible. After my break, I'll show you."

I sat, shut my eyes, and hurled my senses into the sugar-rabbit across the way.

I spied through dotted eyes at the world grown vast. Lun's stammer thundered in my pulled-candy ears. The *yuanzi* girl's lips curled in a grand smile. But there came an odd cracking sound from near her soup-pot. The girl glanced down and shrieked.

Lun backed away but stumbled, and I – rabbit-I – fell from his hand. My vision spun, but I caught a glimpse of flames before the impact against the cobblestones shook me from the candy-shell and back into my body.

I blinked open true eyes.

A monkey shaped from fire hunched on top of Lun, setting his shirt alight. Lun grabbed for it but winced as he clutched only flame.

The crowd fled in panic.

"Roll, Lun!" I cried as I bolted into the street. "Smother the flames!"

Lun obeyed, but the fire monkey pressed its attack.

I grabbed the ladle from the *yuanzi* girl (with muttered apologies) and scooped soup from the pot, slinging the hot broth at the fire-beast. The splash doused only its tail, but before I could dip the ladle for more sweet soup, the monkey darted away with all-too-human strides.

"Lun! Are you all right? What happened?"

The lad winced and blew on the burns to his hands. They'd blister, but he was lucky his wounds hadn't been worse. "The fire under her pot just came alive! Is it because it's the Year of the Monkey?"

"Doubt it." It moved too like a man to be a wild spirit. Could it be an elemental conjuration under a puppeteer's sway?

The monkey clambered up the stiltwalker's wooden legs, its flaming paws raking the startled performer's flesh. Climbing on to the man's shoulders, the beast leapt on to a riddle lantern before the man toppled over.

People cried for the city guard.

I called to the frightened *yuanzi* girl. "Please, look after Lun!"

The girl remembered to breathe and hastened to Lun's side, concern clouding her face.

I dashed to the fallen stiltwalker and untied the stilts from his legs. Motes of burning paper rained down on us as the fire monkey leapt from one lantern to another, then another and another, until it landed on the thatched roof of the *yuanzi* girl's family teahouse. With mad glee, it set the thatch ablaze, and the flames regenerated its tail.

I cursed. Our troubles had just begun.

Lun raised the cry of "Fire!" while the girl screamed for everyone to get out. Patrons poured out of the teahouse, but those in nearby establishments heeded the call as well, knowing the blaze would eat through the row of wood and thatch buildings like a child through a skewer of candied haws.

Proprietors filled buckets with water from the bronze vats outside, but how could they tame the rooftop fire?

I left the stiltwalker and flitted between terrified citizens towards my stall. I saw the boys Pest and Snot run off with fists full of sugar zodiac animals, leaving only a pair of Oxen-on-a-stick and a half-gnawed Rooster in the dust. Greedy brats!

With the teahouse roof vigorously ablaze, the monkey hopped across a string of lanterns to my side of the boulevard and ignited a new fire. Wide streets normally prevented flames from leaping the gap, but tonight, a web of lanterns crisscrossed all of Chengdu. The monkey conjuration could travel the high paths and set fires wherever it pleased, and no man could hope to intercept it.

Even the animal seemed deliberate, as the abundance of the Monkey sign would cast suspicion on an angry spirit, or worse, someone who played with that shape.

Like a *Tangren* making candied monkeys in plain view of the teahouse.

Had the arsonist planned it all, choosing the Lantern Festival to wreak the most havoc without getting caught? But who'd harbor such calculated hatred, and how would I catch him?

The mystery taunted me like a devious lantern riddle, but I hadn't the time to mull over clues. I couldn't stand idly by while Chengdu burned.

My father had taught me the secret of sweet possession. Each generation of *Tangren* in my family would push the bounds of our magic the way we'd inflate a candy-bubble. Spying was our earliest power, then animation, and last year I discovered water-shaping. To fight the fires, I'd need that new skill now, and also water and golden caramel to conjure with.

With mandated fire stations every 300 steps, the fire-fighting force soon swarmed the street with buckets, but the number of blazes daunted them. Lun, with cloth-bandaged hands, pointed out the monkey to incredulous men.

At my stall, I pulled a glob of hot caramel from my pan. Years of practice making the scalding heat bearable as I palmed, twirled, and blew on the gooey lump to cool it.

To battle such hungry blazes spreading by rooftop, I'd need a storm's worth of water, maybe from the Jinjiang River nearby. The sun had set and the River Bridge Gate was shut, but I had no choice. I tucked a bamboo stick behind my ear and ran southward, rolling the sugar ball between my palms to keep it soft. In my haste I nearly collided with a dour-faced official who glowered and barreled past me, roaring orders to the fire-fighters.

The walls of Lesser City loomed ahead, too high to climb. But if I chose the right animal, it might be no obstacle at all.

Only twelve primal shapes could contain an elemental conjuration: the animals of the *shengxiao* zodiac, the foundation of every *Tangren* master's repertoire. Goat, Rabbit, Pig; Tiger, Horse, Dog; Snake, Rooster, Ox; Monkey, Dragon, and Rat.

I had to call the Dragon, rider-of-mists and bringer-of-rains, the most dangerous of all.

I shaped a hollow in the caramel with my fourth finger and stretched it funnel-long. Snipping away excess candy with a bite, I blew into the thin sugar-pipe, making the bulbous end expand, but this time I laced the breath with half of my soul like Iron-Crutch Li of the Eight Immortals.

My hands recalled the Three Joints and Nine Resemblances of the dragon-shape, drawing the soft shell long and plucking limbs, antlers, and frills of golden sugar. On the dragon's head I molded a *chimu* lump, without which it could not fly.

I twisted off the airpipe. Almost done save the final touch. Breaking the bamboo stick in two with my teeth, I jabbed a sharp point into the back of my hand and drew blood.

Dragons only come alive when you dot their eyes.

I settled on the dirt in the shadow of the wall, hoping my body would be safely hidden here, and called to the spirit of Dragon.

O Sacred Dragon, hear me! I, the insignificant Ao Tienwei, humbly ask your aid.

A voice like thunder echoed through my head. *You are not one of mine, Water Rat, though I know you from your tributes of art*, it said, calling me by the sign of my birth year. *What will you ask, and what will you give in return?*

Lord Dragon, Chengdu burns and I must quench the flames. Water I have in plenty, but not strength enough to fly. Legends tell of your dominion over water and sky. If you would lend me your power, I'd soar and save the city, bringing you new worship and reverence.

It considered it. *Your proposal pleases me, Water Rat. Fly with my blessings.*

A thousand thanks, Sacred One.

I lobbed the blood-eyed Dragon underhand into the air and cast my consciousness inside, becoming the small caramel creature. Starlight on my *chimu* lump pulled me towards the new moon sky, and I floated over the wall and down into the river.

I bobbed thrice before sinking into the frigid depths. I felt my sugar-body begin to dissolve, and welcomed the simultaneous sensations of drowning and fading. That was the trick to elemental possession; my first tries failed because I fought those fears when I should have embraced them. As my senses seeped from hardened candy into sweetened water, I asked the river to accept my offering in trade for a moat's worth of water. The river savored the candy and gave me what I asked, but left to me the shaping of the river-water.

I began molding the water into likeness of the candy-dragon. I'd never attempted so prodigious a conjuration before, a horse being the largest water-shaping I'd succeeded at. It took all my strength to merely break the surface with my water-dragon head, but as my manifestation took shape, Dragon power welled inside me and lifted me heavenward. As my sinuous body escaped the Jinjiang River, my undulations freed startled fish from my frame and threw them back into safe currents. I gave thanks to Dragon and flew, grander than any conjuration I ever dared.

Below, the gardens and pagodas grew small like tray landscapes, while the folk on the streets might as well be tiny dough figurines. I spiraled in the air to get my bearings. More the impression of a dragon than a detailed rendition, this grand manifestation was slow to respond to my thoughts, but it would have to do.

Points of red lantern lights dotted the city below, though the fires in Lesser City shone fierce through billowing smoke. I dove for the scene of the fiery devastation.

All along the street, blazes raged out of control. The *yuanzi* girl and her parents huddled by the overturned stall in front of the doomed teahouse, cradling a sign that boasted "fragrant tea from river water". A bandaged Lun fought alongside the others to put out what fires they could, while the magistrate in charge grabbed a snake-halberd and cut down a string of lanterns, hollering for other soldiers to do the same.

A handful of men saw my coming and cried out in astonishment. All turned to look, with some men thinking it best to flee, while others gaped in bewilderment and forgot their tasks.

I ignored the stares and twisted through the air, spewing river-water at the flames licking the sky. The blasts of water worked wonders at extinguishing blazes, but each spray diminished me by a like sum and rippled the veneer of my dragon-shape. I did my best to hold the dwindling manifestation together and surveyed the rooftops with liquid eyes.

There! The fire monkey hid in the high flames and blinding smoke of the brocade shop to my left, its flicking tail betraying its place. I angled my flight towards the demon, our eyes meeting at last. For good or for ill, the sorcerer now knew I pitted my magic against him.

I spat a cauldron-sized pearl of water at the monkey, but the agile beast vaulted out of the way on to an adjacent roof and raced across black tiles. I rushed through rising steam after it, but the monkey was too small and nimble to target with bursts of water.

In spite of my laggard reflexes, I could still fly faster than the beast could run. I overflew the beast and walled off its progress forward with watery coils, but the monkey grabbed the roof's edge and swung through the back window of a wineshop. I gave chase and spewed a great measure of water through the opening, but the monkey leapt out of a front-facing window as the flood struck. In single-minded pursuit, I threaded my body forcibly through the narrow frames, stripping more water from my manifestation. I emerged slimmer, overshadowing the market street where the fire monkey had landed between the magistrate and Lun.

The magistrate lowered his halberd and sliced at the fire monkey, while Lun hoisted his bucket and readied to throw.

Trapped between the fearless official and a wheelwright with a bucket of water, the fire monkey hesitated.

That moment of indecision was just enough time for me to gamble it all.

High above the trio, I purposefully shaped away my *chimu* lump and my ability to fly ended abruptly. I fell bodily on top of them, river-water overflowing the bounds of my dragon-shape as the conjuration collapsed. The impact sent my awareness tumbling out of the elemental conjuration.

For the first time, I lost all of my senses.

In the past, ending a conjuration meant my soul would fly back to my body. I had never been stripped of every sensation:

no sight, no sound, no pulse racing or hackles rising on the back of my neck.

Nothing but naked fear and solitude.

I tried picturing my body, from my dry eyes to the growl of hunger in my belly, from the itch between my toes to the sting of the wound on my hand.

But still I could not return.

Did I overreach myself, conjuring with too much water? What if I were trapped like this forever?

What I'd give to feel my heart pound in terror!

No, stop obsessing over *why* and think about *what-now*. I shouldn't let this predicament cool and harden into permanence while I fretted; I ought to shape the situation while it was malleable. I might be bodiless but I still had memory and thought, purpose and principle. If an escape didn't exist, I'd make one.

I remembered asking my father to teach me sweet possession when I was sixteen. Father was a difficult master to please, finding fault in my interpretations of the Dragon. "You must pay tribute to the animal with your artistry."

"But why?" I asked. "Paintings, sculptures, and calligraphy last. Candy figurines don't."

Father swatted the back of my head with his folding fan. "The sugar opera may be fleeting art, but it's no excuse to slacken! Show respect for the animals before you ask to wear their shapes, in particular the spirits of the twelve signs. Revere them, my son, lest they find cause to meddle in your affairs."

I took Father's lesson to heart. It took months of practice to render a Dragon to his liking, thereby completing a *Tangren*'s zodiac repertoire. At last, he consented to teach me the spying skill. "Always begin with taste," he said, handing me a golden Tiger impaled on bamboo. "Lick and burn the sweet flavor into your memory."

Taste, of course!

I meditated on the flavor of my family's secret sugar blend: brown layered on cane, dusted subtly with musk-flavored sugar. As the memory of that taste crystallized in my mind, I caught a tinge of it coming from beyond remembrance. I latched on to the taste and willed myself towards it.

My senses returned, though not to my body as I hoped, but back inside the rabbit-on-a-stick beside the toppled *yuanzi* stall. I wore a drenched and sticky hollow candy-skin, a small comfort compared to my own skin, but a skin nonetheless.

From this low angle, I could only see the hulking remnants of the stall on the paved road, but my rabbit ears revealed my surroundings in full. In the distance, fire-fighters chattered about the Water Dragon and the Fire Monkey battle as they threw water on to flames. I heard no urgency in the men's voices, which likely meant the fires were under control.

There would be legends told of this night, which ought to please Dragon.

Behind me, the magistrate questioned Lun and the *yuanzi* girl about the mysterious monkey. "And it attacked you without provocation?" he asked in a calm, scratchy voice.

"Yes, Magistrate Gongsun," Lun replied. "All I did was, um, offer candy to Miss Deng when the fire monkey crawled out. I stared, it stared, and then it jumped me!"

I animated the belly of the rabbit-shell and eased myself off the bamboo stick. The wall where I hid my body wasn't far by human scale, but at caramel-rabbit size it might as well be a *li* away. Perhaps if I invoked the Rabbit's speed . . .

"Candy, hmm? Tell me about this candyman," Gongsun urged.

"*Tangren* Ao?" Lun spoke my name with cheer. "He's a pleasant man, nosy but generous. He's from Ji'nan, I think."

"Did Ao make any monkey figurines?" Gongsun pressed.

"What? Surely you don't think he's behind the fires!"

I cursed my luck. The judge was right to suspect a human behind the arson, but did he have to suspect *me*?

"Answer the question, son," Gongsun said. "Monkeys or not?"

"Well, why wouldn't he in the Year of the Monkey? Magistrate, he saved me from burning alive. I'd rather believe he brought the dragon."

I was heartened to hear Lun defend me so.

"Perhaps, or perhaps not," Gongsun said. "Regardless, I have questions for him. Guards! Find this candyman."

If they brought my body back, I'd be spared the trek. On the other hand, I'd have to lie my way out of another charge of sorcery or flee the city.

"Magistrate, wasn't it just a duel between spirits?" Miss Deng asked.

"It might be, Miss Deng, but magic isn't the sole providence of gods and demons. I must consider all possibilities, including a magician with a vendetta against you or your family."

"A vendetta?" She sounded surprised.

"It burned your teahouse first. I do not doubt that it was personal. Any trouble with the gangs? Unpaid gambling debts?"

Miss Deng paused. "My father may love Constellation Dominoes, but he knows his limits."

"We shall see," Gongsun said. "What of this candyman? Did you know him?"

"No, he never crossed the street."

Gongsun sighed. "Try to remember everyone who came to your stall. If this arson is an act of planned revenge, the instigator is likely as meticulous and ruthless in covering up his crime. We must find him before he has that chance."

As Miss Deng recounted further details for Gongsun, I wondered if I might have seen my foe. But countless people had passed my stall since I set up shop this afternoon. It could be any of them.

Instead, I considered how the sorcerer might have enchanted the *yuanzi*-pot fire. An elemental conjuring required an offering in the shape of a primal animal. If his power were akin to mine, then he must have offered something in the shape of a monkey to that fire. But how?

I softened the rabbit-candy and hopped to the soup-pot apparatus, knocked over during the chaos. Among the bits of burnt wood lay the charred halves of a walnut-shell. They must have made that cracking sound I heard.

If an offering had been sealed inside, the flames would have to burn through the shell or melt whatever held the halves together. The sorcerer would have had time to flee the scene.

The small walnut couldn't fit a *Tangren*'s sugar animal. But perhaps a different kind of food offering, like a dough-figure, would suffice. A master of dough-sculpting could easily hide a tiny painted monkey in the hollow.

But one detail still puzzled me. The soup-pot apparatus sat on the ground, too low for anyone to easily feed a walnut to the fire without attracting attention. Surely Miss Deng would comment if someone tampered with the fire?

Unless the scoundrel responsible had been short.

I'd have noticed a dwarfish man among the street performers, but those kids – had Pest and Snot gone for *yuanzi*? I couldn't remember, but Miss Deng could have easily dismissed the antics of boys at her stall.

Of course, neither boy could be the arsonist. By the looks of them they were anywhere between nine and twelve years old, too young to plan arson. Besides, the monkey was setting fires at the same time they were running away with candy loot. The sorcerer must have bribed them to plant the walnut in the fire. And if the magistrate was right about the mindset of the arsonist, then the boys were in grave danger. A promise of more spoils would surely lure them into a trap!

Squishy footfalls grew loud behind me. I froze.

Giant fingers hoisted me by the ears in front of great, scrutinizing eyes. Magistrate Gongsun.

The Sichuanese man in his early fifties suffered his wet official's robes without complaint; the wing-tips of his black hat, once extending stiffly to either side, now sagged from the wet of river-water. "So this is the candyman's handiwork," he boomed.

Had he seen me move?

A guardsman raised a call. "Magistrate! We found the candyman unconscious by the town wall. What should we do with him?"

Gongsun glanced in that direction. "Lay him down by his stall and watch him."

My body! I reached for it with my mind but still couldn't grab hold. How close did I need to be?

If I squirmed out of Gongsun's hand, I could hop to my body and try to awaken, and if I did I'd tell the magistrate my fear for the children's safety. But would he believe my story? I had nothing but guesswork.

But maybe I *could* find solid proof. Those kids took so many sugar figurines that they couldn't possibly have eaten them all. If I could find one of those shells . . .

What had they taken? A fistful of Monkeys, a pair of Pigs, a Horse, and a Snake. I'd made only one Snake in recent days, as that sign never sold well outside its Year. Unless the boys ate it already, that was my best chance to find them.

I opened my awareness and sought caramel in the vicinity, reaching as far as the walls of Chengdu. My mind probed each instance like a tongue discerning a shape, hoping to find the serpentine candy. We'd hunt for secrets this way, my father and I. He never shied from using the dirt we uncovered to blackmail rich men.

When I located the Snake, my mind darted through the connection into its coils, but I left a thread of sugary taste so I could find my way back to Rabbit. Half-wound about a bamboo stick, I saw through dotted molasses that the older boy held me in his right hand and Horse in his left. The younger kid trailed behind him with a bundle of Monkey candy. I caught only dizzying glimpses of our surroundings awash in red light, like the shadowy foliage of a park or garden.

Snot tugged on Pest's sleeve. "Let's go home."

Pest stopped. "Not yet, brother."

"You go then," Snot said, his voice wavering. "I'm going home."

"Fine! I'll keep everything for myself," Pest said.

Snot ran off while Pest continued onward alone. A familiar pagoda loomed before us, and I realized where we were: the Flower-Strewing Tower. The sorcerer must have intended to watch the streets burn from the tower once he ended his conjuration.

I had to get Pest out of here now, but how? I hadn't blooded the Snake's eyes so I couldn't shape water, leaving me only this candy-body to defend him. But I could petition the spirit of Snake. *O Snake of Ten-Thousand Years! I, Ao Tienwei who did not give you proper notice, ask your help to save a life.*

I taste you, Tangren *Rat,* Snake answered. *What succor do you seek, and what losses will you suffer?*

A beardless man in the garb of a scholar emerged from the pagoda. His eyebrows were so sparse that I'd almost say he had none. He was one of the suitors that Miss Deng had rebuffed!

"Where's your brother?" the willowy scholar asked.

"The crybaby went home," Pest said. "I did what you asked. Where's my money?"

The man smiled. "I left the sycees in a pouch under that bench there. The gold's all yours."

No time to answer Snake. I softened and sprang off the bamboo, landing on the path between the scholar and the boy. They startled and backed away. I reared up, shaped and hardened caramel fangs, and mock-attacked Pest.

Frightened, the boy turned to run, but saw the stone bench and couldn't resist. With candy-horse still in one hand, he scrambled to the seat and fumbled under it.

There's nothing there, kid, run!

"So you were the water dragon, *Tangren*?" the scholar-sorcerer said in a low voice. "Stop interfering with my revenge."

He raised his foot and stomped down. I slithered away in the nick of time. *Grant me venom, Snake!*

My price—

The scholar started towards the kid.

Anything, Snake! I coiled and sprang for the man's ankle, sinking fangs deep into his flesh. The scholar cried out and stumbled.

So be it, Snake said.

Something flowed through my fangs into the scholar's blood.

I heard the rattle of rocks, then small footfalls receding. The kid saw through the sorcerer's lie at last.

I had no time to celebrate. Pillar-like fingers pulled and ripped me in two.

The shock again sent my consciousness reeling, but I caught the thread of sweetness and followed it back to Rabbit. My rabbit-self lay on the table at my stall. A towering Magistrate Gongsun stirred through the pot of cooling caramel beside me.

With Pest still in danger, I abandoned caution and leapt off the table, catching the magistrate by surprise. He grabbed for me but clawed only air as I landed on top of my body's chest.

But despite the closeness of my flesh, I could not return to it.

Gongsun knelt and reached for rabbit-me.

Always begin with taste, I decided, and scurried towards my human mouth. I burrowed between the lips and kissed the tip of my own tongue.

My awareness flooded back inside my body.

I pulled the candy out of my mouth and gasped for breath. The Dragon conjuration had taken too much out of me, and I struggled to sit up.

Gongsun raised a bushy eyebrow and extended his hand. "You and I have much to discuss, candyman."

I took his hand. "Magistrate, you must send men to the Flower-Strewing Tower, without delay." I said, nearly breathless. "The arsonist's a scholar with almost no eyebrows. Please hurry, before he catches the boy!"

"What boy? Explain."

Lun and Miss Deng saw me stir and came towards us, hand in bandaged hand. "So good to see you awake, *Tangren* Ao!" Lun said.

I smiled weakly. "Miss Deng, did a willowy scholar give you any gifts? Dough-figures, perhaps?"

"Master Shuai? Yes, he tried to give me several of the miniatures, but I refused them all," she answered. "I didn't want to encourage him. He's chased me since my hair-pinning ceremony two years ago."

"Shuai had a kid slip a magical figurine into your fire, but now the boy's a liability." I turned to Gongsun. "You must believe me, Magistrate. Find Shuai."

Gongsun stood and called to a group of halberdiers. "Go. Detain anyone at the Flower-Strewing Tower." The soldiers hastened away without question. "Stay here, *Tangren* Ao."

"I'm coming with you." My legs weak, I could only stand with Lun's help. "Thank you, Lun."

We left Miss Deng with her family on the market street and headed for the pagoda.

The halberdiers found the scholar Shuai trying to limp with a swollen foot away from the Flower-Strewing Tower. They held the cursing suspect at blades' point and called out to Pest.

The boy poked his head out from behind a clump of bamboo, still clutching Horse-on-a-stick in an iron grip. "Did you kill the snake?"

I grinned. "Don't worry. It won't be back." However, my smile faded when I realized I had no idea what Snake would demand of me.

With Shuai in custody and the boy safe under the soldiers' protection, Gongsun demanded answers. "Start from the beginning."

"I'll gladly answer all your questions, Magistrate, but only in confidence."

"Agreed."

Lun helped me to the tower on Gongsun's instructions. "Thank you, *Tangren* Ao," he whispered in my ear.

"No need, Lun. She likes you. All you needed was a little push." I was glad the candy-rabbit brought them together, even though things had turned out much differently than I expected.

"I meant the water dragon."

I pretended not to know what he was talking about. "You have a vivid imagination, lad."

Lun left with a crooked smile.

I couldn't lie to Magistrate Gongsun. I couldn't prove the scholar's guilt unless he understood how Shuai's magic and mine worked. I sat on the steps of the pagoda and recounted the night's events, and for the first time, spoke frankly about my power. As I revealed my secret, the burden of years fell away. Despite myself, my eyes brimmed with unshed tears.

At the end of it, Gongsun stroked his beard. "I believe you, though few others will."

"No one else must know."

"I agree. However, I still intend to bring Shuai up on charges of sorcery and arson. The boy's testimony will seal his fate, and I will crush him with the full force of the law."

Not what I wanted to hear, being a sorcerer myself, but nonetheless I bowed. "I, your insignificant servant, thank you."

"You have a strange and useful talent that ought not go to waste, *Tangren* Ao," Gongsun said. "Will you work for me? I will pay you well for it."

"And give up this sweet calling? The life of a *Tangren* is all I know."

"I am not asking you to abandon your trade. Stay in Chengdu. Learn the city. Help us rebuild. I only ask that, when I have need of you, you answer my summons. What say you?"

He surely knew how my magic could advance his career. For good or for ill, my fate was now entwined with his, so long as he demanded it. But what choice did I have? You should never anger a man who could sentence you to death. I felt as helpless as a rat caught in the coils of a—

"Your animal sign wouldn't happen to be Snake, would it?" I asked.

"Indeed," Gongsun replied. "How did you know?"

THE NARCOMANCER

N. K. Jemisin

In the land of Gujaareh it was said that trouble came by twos.
Four bands of color marked the face of the Dreaming Moon;
the great river split into four tributaries; there were four harvests
in a year; four humors coursed the inner rivers of living flesh.
By contrast, two of anything in nature meant inevitable conflict:
stallions in a herd, lions in a pride. Siblings. The sexes.

Gatherer Cet's twin troubles came in the form of two
women. The first was a farmcaste woman who had been
injured by an angry bull-ox; half her brains had been dashed
out beneath its hooves. The Sharers, who could work miracles
with the Goddess's healing magic, had given up on her. "We
can grow her a new head," said one of the Sharer-elders to Cet,
"but we cannot put the memories of her lifetime back in it.
Best to claim her dreamblood for others, and send her soul
where her mind has already gone."

But when Cet arrived in the Hall of Blessings to see to the
woman, he confronted a scene of utter chaos. Three squalling
children struggled in the arms of a Sentinel, hampering him as
he tried to assist his brethren. Nearer by, a young man fought
to get past two of the Sharers, trying to reach a third Templeman
– whom, clearly, he blamed for the woman's condition. "You
didn't even try!" he shouted, the words barely intelligible
through his sobs. "How can my wife live if you won't even try?"

He elbowed one of the Sharers in the chest and nearly got
free, but the other flung himself on the distraught husband's
back then, half dragging him to the floor. Still the man fought
with manic fury, murder in his eyes. None of them noticed Cet

until Cet stepped in front of the young man and raised his jungissa stone.

Startled, the young man stopped struggling, his attention caught by the stone. It had been carved into the likeness of a dragonfly; its gleaming black wings blurred as Cet tapped the stone hard with his thumbnail. The resulting sharp whine cut across the cacophony filling the Hall until even the children stopped weeping to look for the source of the noise. As peace returned, Cet willed the stone's vibration to soften to a low, gentle hum. The man sagged as tension drained out of his body, until he hung limp in the two Sharers' arms.

"You know she is already dead," Cet said to the young man. "You know this must be done."

The young man's face tightened in anguish. "No. She breathes. Her heart beats." He slurred the words as if drunk. "No."

"Denying it makes no difference. The pattern of her soul has been lost. If she were healed, you would have to raise her all over again, like one of your children. To make her your wife then would be an abomination."

The man began to weep again, quietly this time. But he no longer fought, and when Cet moved around him to approach his wife, he uttered a little moan and looked away.

Cet knelt beside the cot where the woman lay, and put his fore- and middle fingers on her closed eyelids. She was already adrift in the realms between waking and dream; there was no need to use his jungissa to put her to sleep. He followed her into the silent dark and examined her soul, searching for any signs of hope. But the woman's soul was indeed like that of an infant, soft and devoid of all but the most simplistic desires and emotions. The merest press of Cet's will was enough to send her toward the land of dreams, where she would doubtless dissolve into the substance of that realm – or perhaps she would eventually be reborn, to walk the realm of waking anew and regain the experiences she had lost.

Either way, her fate was not for Cet to decide. Having delivered her soul safely, he severed the tether that had bound her to the waking realm, and collected the delicate dreamblood that spilled forth.

The weeping that greeted Cet upon his return to waking was of a different order from before. Turning, Cet saw with satisfaction that the farmcaste man stood with his children now, holding them as they watched the woman's flesh breathe its last. They were still distraught, but the violent madness was gone; in its place was the sort of grief that expressed itself through love and would, eventually, bring healing.

"That was nicely done," said a low voice beside him, and Cet looked up to see the Temple Superior. Belatedly he realized the Superior had been the target of the distraught husband's wrath. Cet had been so focused on the family that he had not noticed.

"You gave them peace without dreamblood," the Superior continued. "Truly, Gatherer Cet, our Goddess favors you."

Cet got to his feet, sighing as the languor of the Gathering faded slowly within him. "The Hall has still been profaned," he said. He looked up at the great shining statue of the Goddess of Dreams, who towered over them with hands outstretched in welcome and eyes shut in the Eternal Dream. "Voices have been raised and violence done, right here at Her feet."

"S-Superior?" A boy appeared at the Superior's shoulder, too young to be an acolyte. One of the Temple's adoptees from the House of Children, probably working a duty-shift as an errand runner. "Are you hurt at all? I saw that man . . ."

The Superior smiled down at him. "No, child; I'm fine, thank you. Go back to the House before your Teacher misses you."

Looking relieved, the boy departed. The Superior sighed, watching him leave. "Some chaos is to be expected at times like this. The heart is rarely peaceful." He gave Cet a faint smile. "Though, of course, you would not know that, Gatherer."

"I remember the time before I took my oath."

"Not the same."

Cet shrugged, gazing at the mourning family. "I have the peace and order of Temple life to comfort me now. It is enough."

The Superior looked at him oddly for a moment, then sighed. "Well, I'm afraid I must ask you to leave that comfort for a time, Cet. Will you come with me to my office? I have a matter that requires the attention of a Gatherer – one with your unique skill at bestowing peace."

And thus did Cet's second hardship fall upon him.

The quartet that stood in the Superior's office were upriver folk. Cet could see that in their dingy clothing and utter lack of makeup or jewelry; not even the poorest city dweller kept themselves so plain. And no city dweller went unsandaled on the brick-paved streets, which grew painfully hot at midday. Yet the woman who stood at the group's head had the proud carriage of one used to the respect and obedience of others, finery or no finery. The three men all but cowered behind her as the Superior and Cet entered the room.

"Cet, this is Mehepi," said the Superior, gesturing to the woman. "She and her companions are from a mining village some ways to the south, in the foothills that border the Empty Thousand. Mehepi, I bring you Cet, one of the Temple's Gatherers."

Mehepi's eyes widened in a way that would have amused Cet, had he been capable of amusement. Clearly she had expected something more of Gujaareh's famed Gatherers; someone taller, perhaps. But she recovered quickly and gave him a respectful bow. "I greet you in peace, Gatherer," she said, "though I bring unpeaceful tidings."

Cet inclined his head. "Tidings of . . ." But he trailed off, surprised, as his eyes caught a slight movement in the afternoon shadows of the room. Some ways apart from Mehepi and the others, a younger woman knelt on a cushion. She was so still – it was her breathing Cet had noticed – that Cet made no wonder he had overlooked her, though now it seemed absurd that he had. Wealthy men had commissioned sculptures with lips less lush, bones less graceful; sugared currants were not as temptingly black as her skin. Though the other upriver folk were staring at Cet, her eyes remained downcast, her body unmoving beneath the faded-indigo drape of her gown. Indigo: the mourning color. Mehepi wore it too.

"What is this?" Cet asked, nodding toward the younger woman. Was there unease in Mehepi's eyes? Defensiveness, certainly.

"We were told the Temple offers its aid only to those who follow the ways of the Dream Goddess," she said. "We have no money to tithe, Gatherer, and none of us has offered dreams or goods in the past year . . ."

All at once Cet understood. "You brought her as payment."

"No, not payment . . ." But even without the hint of a stammer in Mehepi's voice, the lie was plain in her manner.

"Explain, then." Cet spoke more sharply than was, perhaps, strictly peaceful. "Why does she sit apart from the rest of you?"

The villagers looked at one another. But before any of them could speak, the young woman said, "Because I am cursed, Gatherer."

The Temple Superior frowned. "Cursed? Is that some upriver superstition?"

Cet had thought the younger woman broken in spirit, to judge by her motionlessness and fixed gaze at the floor. But now she lifted her eyes, and Cet realized that, whatever was wrong with her, she was not broken. There was despair in her, strong enough to taste, but something more as well.

"I was a lapis merchant's wife," she said. "When he died, I was taken by the village headman as a secondwife. Now the headman is dead, and they blame me."

"She is barren!" said one of the male villagers. "Two husbands and no children yet? And Mehepi here, she is the firstwife—"

"All of my children had been stillborn," said Mehepi, touching her belly as if remembering the feel of them inside her. That much was truth, as was her pain; some of Cet's irritation with her eased. "That was why my husband took another wife. Then my last child was born alive. The whole village rejoiced! But the next morning, the child stopped breathing. A few days later the brigands came." Her face tightened in anger. "They killed my husband while she slept beside him. And they had their way with her, but even despite that there is no child." Mehepi shook her head. "For so much death to follow one woman, and life itself to shun her? How can it be anything but a curse? That is why . . ." She darted a look at Cet, then drew herself up. "That is why we thought you might find value in her, Gatherer. Death is your business."

"Death is not a Gatherer's business," Cet said. Did the woman realize how greatly she had insulted him and all his brethren? For the first time in a very long while, he felt anger stir in his heart. "*Peace* is our business. Sharers do that by healing the flesh. Gatherers deal with the soul, judging those which are too corrupt or damaged to be salvaged and granting them the Goddess's blessing—"

"If you had learned your catechisms better you would understand that," the Superior interjected smoothly. He threw Cet a mild look, doubtless to remind Cet that they could not expect better of ignorant country folk. "And you would have known there was no need for payment. In a situation like this, when the peace of many is under threat, it is the Temple's duty to offer aid."

The men looked abashed; Mehepi's jaw tightened at the scolding. With a sigh, the Superior glanced down at some notes he'd taken on a reedleaf sheet. "So, Cet, these brigands she mentioned are the problem. For the past three turns of the greater Moon, their village and others along the Empty Thousand have suffered a curious series of attacks. Everyone in the village falls asleep – even the men on guard duty. When they wake, their valuables are gone. Food stores, livestock, the few stones of worth they gather from their mine; their children have been taken too, no doubt sold to those desert tribes who traffic in slaves. Some of the women and youths have been abused, as you heard. And a few, such as the village headman and the guards, were slain outright, perhaps to soften the village's defenses for later. No one wakes during these assaults."

Cet inhaled, all his anger forgotten. "A sleep spell? But only the Temple uses narcomancy."

"Impossible to say," the Superior said. "But given the nature of these attacks, it seems clear we must help. Magic is fought best with magic." He looked at Cet as he spoke.

Cet nodded, suppressing the urge to sigh. It would have been within his rights to suggest that one of his other Gatherer-brethren – perhaps Liyou, the youngest – handle the matter instead. But after all his talk of peace and righteous duty, that would have been hypocritical. And . . . in spite of himself, his gaze drifted back to the younger woman. She had lowered her eyes once more, her hands folded in her lap. There was nothing peaceful in her stillness.

"We will need a soul-healer," Cet said softly. "There is more to this than abuse of magic."

The Superior sighed. "A Sister, then. I'll write the summons to their Matriarch." The Sisters were an offshoot branch of the faith, coexisting with the Servants of Hananja in an uneasy parallel. Cet knew the Superior had never liked them.

Cet gave him a rueful smile. "Everything for Her peace." He had never liked them either.

They set out that afternoon: the five villagers, two of the Temple's warrior Sentinels, Cet, and a Sister of the Goddess. The Sister, who arrived unescorted at the river docks just as they were ready to push off, was worse than even Cet had expected – tall and commanding, clad in the pale-gold robes and veils that signified high rank in their order. That meant this Sister had mastered the most difficult techniques of erotic dreaming, with its attendant power to affect the spirit and the subtler processes of flesh. A formidable creature. But the greatest problem in Cet's eyes was that the Sister was male.

"Did the messenger not explain the situation?" Cet asked the Sister at the first opportunity. He kept his tone light. They rode in a canopied barge more than large enough to hold their entire party and the pole-crew besides. It was not large enough to accommodate ill feelings between himself and the Sister.

The Sister, who had given his name as Ginnem, stretched out along the bench he had claimed for himself. "Gatherers; so tactful."

Cet resisted the urge to grind his teeth. "You cannot deny that a different Sister – a female Sister – would have been better suited to deal with this matter."

"Perhaps," Ginnem replied, with a smile that said he thought no one better suited than himself. "But look." He glanced across the aisle at the villagers, who had occupied a different corner of the barge. The three men sat together on a bench across from the firstwife. Three benches back, the young woman sat alone. "That one has suffered at the hands of both men and women," Ginnem said. "Do you think my sex makes any difference to her?"

"She was raped by men," Cet said.

"And she is being destroyed by a woman. That firstwife wants her dead, can you not see?" Ginnem shook his head, jingling tiny bells woven into each of his braids. "If not for the need to involve the Temple in the brigand matter, no doubt the firstwife would've found some quiet way to do her in already. And why do you imagine only a woman could know of rape?"

Cet started. "Forgive me. I did not realize . . ."

"It was long ago." Ginnem shrugged his broad shoulders. "When I was a soldier; another life."

Cet's surprise must have shown on his face, for a moment later Ginnem laughed. "Yes, I was born military caste," he said. "I earned high rank before I felt the calling to the Sisterhood. And I still keep up some of my old habits." He lifted one flowing sleeve to reveal a knife-sheath strapped around his forearm, then flicked it back so quickly that no one but Cet noticed. "So you see, there is more than one reason the Sisterhood sent me."

Cet nodded slowly, still trying and failing to form a clear opinion of Ginnem. Male Sisters were rare; he wondered if all of them were this strange. "Then we are four fighters and not three. Good."

"Oh, don't count me," Ginnem said. "My soldier days are over; I fight only when necessary now. And I expect I'll have my hands full with other duties." He glanced at the young woman again, sobering. "Someone should talk to her."

And he turned his kohl-lined eyes to Cet.

Night had fallen, humid and thick, by the time Cet went to the woman. Her companions were already abed, motionless on pallets the crew had laid on deck. One of the Sentinels was asleep; the other stood at the prow with the ship's watchman.

The woman still sat on her bench. Cet watched her for a time, wondering if the lapping water and steadily passing palm trees had lulled her to sleep, but then she lifted a hand to brush away a persistent moth. Throwing a glance at Ginnem – who was snoring faintly on his bench – Cet rose and went to sit across from the woman. Her eyes were lost in some waking dream until he sat down, but they sharpened very quickly.

"What is your name?" he asked.

"Namsut." Her voice was low and warm, touched with some southlands accent.

"I am Cet," he replied.

"Gatherer Cet."

"Does my title trouble you?"

She shook her head. "You bring comfort to those who suffer. That takes a kind heart."

Surprised, Cet smiled. "Few even among the Goddess's most devout followers see anything other than the death I bring. Fewer still have ever called me kind for it. Thank you."

She shook her head, looking into the passing water. "No one who has known suffering would think ill of you, Gatherer."

Widowed twice, raped, shunned . . . He tried to imagine her pain and could not. That inability troubled him, all of a sudden.

"I will find the brigands who hurt you," he said, to cover his discomfort. "I will see that their corruption is excised from the world."

To his surprise, her eyes went hard as iron, though she kept her voice soft. "They did nothing to me that two husbands had not already done," she said. "And wife-brokers before that, and my father's creditors before that. Will you hunt down all of them?" She shook her head. "Kill the brigands, but not for me."

This was not at all the response that Cet had expected. So confused was he that he blurted the first question that came to his mind. "What shall I do for you, then?"

Namsut's smile threw him even further. It was not bitter, that smile, but neither was it gentle. It was a smile of anger, he realized at last. Pure, politely restrained, tooth-grinding rage.

"Give me a child," she said.

In the morning, Cet spoke of the woman's request to Ginnem.

"In the upriver towns, the headman's wife rules if the headman dies," Cet explained as they broke their fast. "That is tradition, according to Namsut. But a village head must prove him or herself favored by the gods, to rule. Namsut says fertility is one method of proof."

Ginnem frowned, chewing thoughtfully on a date. A group of women on the passing shore were doing laundry at the riverside, singing a rhythmic song while they worked. "That explains a great deal," he said at last. "Mehepi has proven herself at least able to conceive, but after so many dead children the village must be wondering if she too is cursed. And since having a priest for a lover might also connote the gods' favor, I know now why Mehepi has been eying me with such speculation."

Cet started, feeling his cheeks heat. "You think she wants . . ." He took a date to cover his discomfort. "From you?"

Ginnem grinned. "And why not? Am I not fine?" He made a show of tossing his hair, setting all the tiny bells a-tinkle.

"You know full well what I mean," Cet said, glancing about in embarrassment. Some of the other passengers looked their way at the sound of Ginnem's hair-bells, but no one was close enough to overhear.

"Yes, and it saddens me to see how much it troubles you," Ginnem said, abruptly serious. "*Sex*, Gatherer Cet. That is the word you cannot bring yourself to say, isn't it?" When Cet said nothing, Ginnem made an annoyed sound. "Well, I will not let you avoid it, however much you and your stiffnecked Servant brethren disapprove. I am a Sister of the Goddess. I use narcomancy – and yes, my body when necessary – to heal those wounded spirits that can be healed. It is no less holy a task than what you do for those who cannot be healed, Gatherer, save that my petitioners do not die when I'm done!"

He was right. Cet bent at the waist, his eyes downcast, to signal his contrition. The gesture seemed to mollify Ginnem, who sighed.

"And no, Mehepi has not approached me," Ginnem said, "though she's hardly had time, with three such devoted attendants . . ." Abruptly he caught his breath. "Ahh – yes, *now* I understand. I first thought this was a simple matter of a powerful senior wife plotting against a weaker secondwife. But more than that – this is a race. Whichever woman produces a healthy child first will rule the village."

Cet frowned, glancing over at the young woman again. She had finally allowed herself to sleep, leaning against one of the canopy-pillars and drawing her feet up on to the bench. Only in sleep was her face peaceful, Cet noticed. It made her even more beautiful, though he'd hardly imagined that possible.

"The contest is uneven," he said. He glanced over at the headwoman Mehepi – acting headwoman, he realized now, by virtue solely of her seniority. She was still asleep on one of the pallets, comfortable between two of her men. "Three lovers to none."

"Yes." Ginnem's lip curled. "That curse business was a handy bit of cleverness on Mehepi's part. No man will touch the secondwife for fear of sharing the curse."

"It seems wrong," Cet said softly, gazing at Namsut. "That she should have to endure yet another man's lust to survive."

"You grew up in the city, didn't you?" When Cet nodded, Ginnem said, "Yes, I thought so. My birth-village was closer to the city, and surely more fortunate than these people's, but some customs are the same in every backwater. Children are wealth out here, you see – another miner, another strong back on the farm, another eye to watch for enemies. A woman is honored for the children she produces, and so she should be. But make no mistake, Gatherer: this contest is for power. The secondwife could leave that village. She could have asked asylum of your Temple Superior. She returns to the village by choice."

Cet frowned, mulling over that interpretation for a moment. It did not feel right.

"My father was a horse-trader," he said. Ginnem raised an eyebrow at the apparent non sequitur; Cet gave him a faint shrug of apology. "Not a very good one. He took poor care of his animals, trying to squeeze every drop of profit from their hides."

Even after so many years it shamed Cet to speak of his father, for anyone who listened could guess what his childhood had been like. A man so neglectful of his livelihood was unlikely to be particularly careful of his heirs. He saw this realization dawn on Ginnem's face, but to Cet's relief Ginnem merely nodded for Cet to continue.

"Once, my father sold a horse – a sickly, half-starved creature – to a man so known for his cruelty that no other trader in the city would serve him. But before the man could saddle the horse, it gave a great neigh and leapt into the river. It could have swum back to shore, but that would have meant recapture. So it swam in the opposite direction, deeper into the river, where finally the current carried it away."

Ginnem gave Cet a skeptical look. "You think the second-wife *wants* the village to kill her?"

Cet shook his head. "The horse was not dead. When last I saw it, it was swimming with the current, its head above the water, facing whatever fate awaited it downriver. Most likely it drowned or was eaten by predators. But what if it survived the journey, and even now runs free over some faraway pasture? Would that not be a reward worth so much risk?"

"Ah. All or nothing; win a better life or die trying." Ginnem's eyes narrowed as he gazed contemplatively at Cet. "You understand the secondwife well, I see."

Cet drew back, abruptly unnerved by the way Ginnem was looking at him. "I respect her."

"You find her beautiful?"

He said it with as much dignity as he could: "I am not blind."

Ginnem looked Cet up and down in a way that reminded Cet uncomfortably of his father's customers. "You are fine enough," Ginnem said, with more than a hint of lasciviousness in his tone. "Handsome, healthy, intelligent. A tad short, but that's no great matter if she does not mind a small child—"

"'A Gatherer belongs wholly to the Goddess'," Cet said, leaning close so that the disapproval in his voice would not be heard by the others. "That is the oath I swore when I chose this path. The celibacy—"

"Comes second to your primary mission, Gatherer," Ginnem said in an equally stern voice. "It is the duty of any priest of the Goddess of Dreams to bring peace. There are two ways we might create peace in this village, once we've dealt with the brigands. One is to let Mehepi goad the villagefolk into killing or exiling the secondwife. The other is to give the secondwife a chance to control her own life for the first time. Which do you choose?"

"There are other choices," Cet muttered uneasily. "There must be."

Ginnem shrugged. "If she has any talent for dreaming, she could join my order. But I see no sign of the calling in her."

"You could still suggest it to her."

"Mmm." Ginnem's tone was noncommittal. He turned to gaze at Namsut. "That horse you spoke of. If you could have helped it on its way, would you have? Even if that earned you the wrath of the horse's owner and your father?"

Cet flinched back, too startled and flustered to speak. Ginnem's eyes slid back to him.

"How did the horse break free, Cet?"

Cet set his jaw. "I should rest while I can. The rest of the journey will be long."

"Dream well," Ginnem said. Cet turned away and lay down, but he felt Ginnem's eyes on him for a long while afterward.

When Cet slept, he dreamt of Namsut.

The land of dreams was as infinite as the mind of the Goddess who contained it. Though every soul traveled there during sleep, it was rare for two to meet. Most often, the people encountered in dreams were phantoms – conjurations of the dreamer's own mind, no more real than the palm trees and placid oasis which manifested around Cet's dream-form now. But real or not, there sat Namsut on a boulder overlooking the water, her indigo veils wafting in the hot desert wind.

"I wish I could be you," she said, not turning from the water. Her voice was a whisper; her mouth never moved. "So strong, so serene, the kind-hearted killer. Do your victims feel what you feel?"

"You do not desire or require death," Cet said.

"True. I'm a fool for it, but I want to live." Her image blurred for a moment, superimposed by that of a long-legged girlchild with the same despairing, angry eyes. "I was nine when a man first took me. My parents were so angry, so ashamed. I made them feel helpless. I should have died then."

"No," Cet said quietly. "Others' sins are no fault of yours."

"I know that." Abruptly something large and dark turned a lazy loop under the water – a manifestation of her anger, since oases did not have fish. But like her anger, the monster never broke the surface. Cet found this at once fascinating and disturbing.

"The magic that I use," he said. "Do you know how it works?"

"Dreamichor from nonsense-dreams," she said. "Dreamseed from wet dreams, dreambile from nightmares, dreamblood from the last dream before death. The four humors of the soul."

He nodded. "Dreamblood is what Gatherers collect. It has the power to erase pain and quiet emotions." He stepped closer then, though he did not touch her. "If your heart is pained, I can share dreamblood with you now."

She shook her head. "I do not want my pain erased. It makes me strong." She turned to look up at him. "Will you give me a child, Gatherer?"

He sighed, and the sky overhead seemed to dim. "It is not our way. The Sister . . . dreamseed is his specialty. Perhaps . . ."

"Ginnem does not have your kind eyes. Nor do your Sentinel brethren. You, Gatherer Cet. If I must bear a child, I want yours."

Clouds began to race across the desert sky, some as tormented abstractions, some forming blatantly erotic shapes. Cet closed his eyes against the shiver that moved along his spine. "It is not our way," he said again, but there was a waver in his voice that he could not quite conceal.

He heard the smile in her voice just as keenly. "These are your magic-quieted emotions, Gatherer? They seem loud enough."

He forced his mind away from thoughts of her, lest they disturb his inner peace any further. What was wrong with him? By sheer will he stilled the unrest in his heart, and gratifyingly the sky was clear again when he opened his eyes.

"Forgive me," he murmured.

"I will not. It comforts me to know that you are still capable of feeling. You should not hide it; people would fear Gatherers less if they knew." She looked thoughtful. "Why do you hide it?"

Cet sighed. "Even the Goddess's magic cannot quiet a Gatherer's emotions forever. After many years, the feelings inevitably break free . . . and they are very powerful then. Sometimes dangerous." He shifted, uncomfortable on many levels. "As you said, we frighten people enough as it is."

She nodded, then abruptly rose and turned to him. "There are no other choices," she said. "I have no desire to serve the Goddess as a Sister. There is none of Her peace in my heart, and there may never be. But I mean to live, Gatherer – *truly* live, as more than a man's plaything or a woman's scapegoat. I want this for my children as well. So I ask you again: will you help me?"

She was a phantom. Cet knew that now, for she could not have known of his conversation with Ginnem otherwise. He was talking to himself, or to some aspect of the Goddess come to reflect his own folly back at him. Yet he felt compelled to answer. "I cannot."

The dreamscape transformed, becoming the inside of a room. A gauze-draped low bed, wide enough for two, lay behind Namsut.

She glanced at it, then at him. "But you want to."

That afternoon they disembarked at a large trading-town. There Cet used Temple funds to purchase horses and supplies for the rest of the trip. The village, said Mehepi, was on the far side of the foothills, beyond the verdant floodplain that made up the richest part of Gujaareh. It would take at least another day's travel to get there.

They set out as soon as the horses were loaded, making good time along an irrigation road which ran flat through miles of barley, hekeh, and silvercape fields. As sunset approached they entered the low, arid foothills – Gujaareh's last line of defense against the ever-encroaching desert beyond. Here Cet called a halt. The villagers were nervous, for the hills were the brigands' territory, but with night's chill already setting in and the horses weary, there was little choice. The Sentinels split the watch while the rest of them tended their mounts and made an uneasy camp.

Cet had only just settled near a large boulder when he saw Ginnem crouched beside Namsut's pallet. Ginnem's hands were under her blanket, moving over her midsection in some slow rhythmic dance. Namsut's face had turned away from Cet, but he heard her gasp clearly enough, and saw Ginnem's smile.

Rage blotted out thought. For several breaths Cet was paralyzed by it, torn between shock, confusion, and a mad desire to walk across camp and beat Ginnem bloody.

But then Ginnem frowned and glanced his way, and the anger shattered.

Goddess . . . Shivering with more than the night's chill, Cet lifted his eyes to the great multi-hued face of the Dreaming Moon. What had that been? Now that the madness had passed, he could taste magic in the air: the delicate salt-and-metal of dreamseed. Ginnem had been healing the girl, nothing more. But even if Ginnem had been pleasuring her, what did it matter? Cet was a Gatherer. He had pledged himself to a goddess, and goddesses did not share.

A few moments later he heard footsteps and felt someone settle beside him. "Are you all right, Gatherer Cet?" Ginnem.

Cet closed his eyes. The Moon's afterimage burned against his eyelids in tilted stripes: red for blood, white for seed, yellow for ichor, black for bile.

"I do not know," he whispered.

"Well." Ginnem kept his voice light, but Cet heard the serious note underneath it. "I know jealousy when I sense it, and shock and horror too. Dreamseed is more fragile than the other humors; your rage tore my spell like a rock through spidersilk."

Horrified, Cet looked from him to Namsut. "I'm sorry. I did not mean . . . is she . . . ?"

"She is undamaged, Gatherer. I was done by the time you wanted to throttle me. What concerns me more is that you wanted to throttle me at all." He glanced sidelong at Cet.

"Something is . . . wrong with me." But Cet dared not say what that might be. Had it been happening all along? He thought back and remembered his anger at Mehepi, the layers of unease that Namsut stirred in him. Yes. Those had been the warnings.

Not yet, he prayed to Her. *Not yet. It is too soon.*

Ginnem nodded and fell silent for a while. Finally he said, very softly, "If I could give Namsut what she wants, I would. But though those parts of me still function in the simplest sense, I have already lost the ability to father a child. In time, I will only give pleasure through dreams."

Cet started. The Sisters were a secretive lot – as were Cet's own fellow Servants, of course – but he had never known what price they paid for their magic. Then he realized Ginnem's confession had been an offering. Trust for trust.

"It . . . begins slowly with us," Cet admitted, forcing out the words. It was a Gatherer's greatest secret, and greatest shame. "First surging emotions, then dreaming awake, and finally we . . . we lose all peace, and go mad. There is no cure, once the process begins. If it has begun for me . . ." He trailed off. It was too much, on top of everything else. He could not bear the thought. He was not ready.

Ginnem put a hand on his shoulder in silent compassion. When Cet said nothing more, Ginnem got to his feet. "I will help all I can."

This made Cet frown. Ginnem chuckled and shook his belled head. "I am a healer, Gatherer, whatever you might think of my bedroom habits—"

He paused suddenly, his smile fading. A breath later Cet felt it too – an intense, sudden desire to sleep. With it came the thin, unmistakable whine of a jungissa stone, wafting through the camp like a poisoned breeze.

One of the Sentinels cried an alarm. Cet scrambled to his feet, fumbling for his ornaments. Ginnem dropped to his knees and began chanting something, his hands held outward as if pushing against some invisible force. The Sentinels had gone back to back in the shadow of a boulder, working some kind of complicated dance with their knives to aid their concentration against the spell. Mehepi and one of the men were already asleep; as Cet looked around for the source of the spell, the other two men fell to the ground. Namsut made a sound like pain and stumbled toward Cet and Ginnem. Her eyes were heavy and dull, Cet saw, her legs shaking as if she walked under a great weight, but she was awake. She fought the magic with an almost visible determination.

He felt fear and longing as he gazed at her, a leviathan rising beneath the formerly placid waters of his soul.

So he snatched forth his own jungissa and struck it with a fingernail. Its deeper, clearer song rang across the hills, cutting across the atonal waver of the narcomancer's stone. Folding his will around the shape of the vibrations, Cet closed his eyes and flung forth the only possible counter to the narcomancer's sleep spell: one of his own.

The Sentinels dropped, their knives clattering on the rocky soil. Namsut moaned and collapsed, a dark blur among the Moonlit stones. Ginnem caught his breath. "Cet, what . . . are you . . ." Then he, too, sagged.

There was a clatter of stones from a nearby hill as the narcomancer's jungissa-song faltered. Cet caught a glimpse of several dark forms moving among the stones there, some dragging others who had fallen, and abruptly the narcomancer's jungissa began to fade as with distance. They were running away.

Cet kept his jungissa humming until the last of the terrible urge to sleep had passed. Then he sagged on to a saddle and thanked the Goddess, over and over again.

"A jungissa," Cet said. "No doubt."

It was morning. The group sat around a fire eating travel-food and drinking bitter, strong coffee, for none of them had slept well once Cet awakened them from the spell.

The villagers looked at each other and shook their heads at Cet's statement, uncomprehending. The Sentinels looked grim. "I suspected as much," Ginnem said with a sigh. "Nothing else has that sound."

For the villagers, Cet plucked his own jungissa stone from the belt of his loinskirt and held it out for them to see. It sat in his hand, a delicately carved dragonfly in polished blue-black. He tapped it with his thumbnail, and they all winced as it shivered and sent forth its characteristic whine.

"The jungissa itself has no power," Cet said to reassure them. He willed the stone silent; it went instantly still. "It amplifies magic only for those who have been trained in narcomantic techniques. This jungissa is the child of a stone which fell from the sky many centuries ago. There are only fifteen other ornaments like it in all the world. Three have cracked or broken over time. One was given to the House of the Sisters; one is used by the Temple for training and healing purposes; but only I and my three brother-Gatherers carry and use the stones on a regular basis. The remainder of the stones are kept in the Temple vault under guard." He sighed. "And yet, somehow, these brigands have one."

Ginnem frowned. "I saw the Sisters' queen-bee stone in our House just before I left for this journey. Could someone have stolen a stone from the Temple?"

One of the Sentinels drew himself up at that, scowling in affront. "No one could get past my brothers and me to do so.

"You said these stones fall from the sky?" asked Namsut. She looked thoughtful. "There was sun's seed in the sky a few months ago, on the night of the Ze-kaari celebration. I saw many streaks cross the stars; there was a new Moon that night. Most faded to nothing, but one came very near, and there was light in the hills where it fell."

"Another jungissa?" It was almost too astounding and horrible to contemplate – another of the Goddess's gifts, lying unhallowed in a pit somewhere and pawed over by ruffians? Cet shuddered. "But even if they found such a thing, the rough stone itself would be useless. It must be carved to produce a sound. And it takes years of training to use that sound."

"What difference does any of that make?" Ginnem asked, scowling. "They have one and they've used it. We must capture them and take it."

Military thinking; Cet almost smiled. But he nodded agreement.

"How did you see sun's seed?" Mehepi demanded suddenly of Namsut. "Our husband had you with him that night – or so I believed 'til now. Did you slip out to meet some other lover?"

Namsut smiled another of her polite, angry smiles. "I often went outside after a night with him. The fresh air settled my stomach."

Mehepi caught her breath in affront, then spat on the ground at Namsut's feet. "Nightmare-spawned demoness! Why our husband married a woman so full of hate and death, I will never understand!"

Ginnem threw a stern look at Mehepi. "Your behavior is offensive to our Goddess, headwoman."

Mehepi looked sullen for a moment, but then mumbled an apology. No hint of anger showed on Namsut's face as she inclined her head first to Ginnem, then to Mehepi. That done, she rose, brushed off her gown, and walked away.

But Cet had seen something which made him frown. Nodding to the others to excuse himself, he rose and trotted after her. Though Namsut must have heard him, she kept walking, and only when he caught her in the lee of the hill did she turn to face him.

He took her hands and turned them over. Across each of the palms was a row of dark crusted crescents.

"So that was how you fought the spell," he said.

Namsut's face was as blank as a stone. "I told you, Gatherer. Pain makes me strong."

He almost flinched, for that conversation had taken place in dreaming. But within the mind of the Goddess everything was possible, and desires often called forth the unexpected.

To encourage that desire was dangerous. Yet the compulsion to brush a thumb across her small wounds was irresistible, as was the compulsion to do something about them. Namsut's eyelids fluttered as Cet willed her into a waking dream. In it she looked down to see that her hands were whole. When he released the dream, she blinked, then looked down. Cet rubbed away the lingering smears of dried blood with his thumb; the wounds were gone.

"A simple healing is within any Servant's skill," he said softly. "And it is a Gatherer's duty to fight pain."

Her lips thinned. "Yes, I had forgotten. Pain makes me strong, and you will do nothing that actually helps me. I thank you, Gatherer, but I must wash before we begin the day's travels."

She pulled away before he could think of a reply, and as he watched her leave he wondered how a Gatherer could fight pain in himself.

By afternoon the next day they reached their destination. According to Mehepi, the brigands had attacked the village repeatedly to claim the mined lapis-stones, and the result was devastation on a scale that Cet had never seen. They passed an empty standing granary and bare fields. Several of the village's houses were burned-out shells; the eyes and cheeks of the people they saw were nearly as hollow. Cet could not imagine why anyone would vie to rule such a place.

Yet here he saw for the first time that not all the village was arrayed against Namsut. Two young girls with warm smiles came out to tend her horse when she dismounted. A toothless old man hugged her tightly, and threw an ugly glare at Mehepi's back. "That is the way of things in a small community like this one," Ginnem murmured, following Cet's gaze. "Often it takes only a slight majority – or an especially hateful minority – to make life a nightmare for those in disfavor."

Here Mehepi took over, leading them to the largest house in the village, built of sun-baked brick like the rest, but two stories high. "See to our guests," she ordered Namsut, and without a word Namsut did as she was told. She led Cet, Ginnem, and the two Sentinels into the house.

"Mehepi's room," Namsut said as they passed a room which bore a handsome wide bed. It had probably been the headman's before his death. "My room." To no one's surprise her room was the smallest in the house. But to Cet's shock he saw that her bed was low and gauze-draped – the same bed he'd seen in his dream.

A true-seeing: a dream of the future sent by the Goddess. He had never been so blessed, or so confused, in his life.

He distracted himself by concentrating on the matter at hand. "Stay nearby," he told the Sentinels as they settled into the house's two guestrooms. "If the brigands attack again, I'll need to be able to wake you." They nodded, looking sour; neither had forgiven Cet for putting them to sleep before.

"And I?" asked Ginnem. "I can create a kind of shield around myself and anyone near me. Though I won't be able to hold it if you fling a sleep spell at my back again."

"I'll try not to," Cet said. "If my narcomancy is overwhelmed, your shield may be our only protection."

That evening the villagefolk threw them a feast, though a paltry one. One of the elders drew out a battered double-flute, and with a child clapping a menat for rhythm they had weak, off-key entertainment. The food was worse: boiled grain porridge, a few vegetables, and roasted horsemeat. Cet had made a gift of the horses to Mehepi and her men, and they'd promptly butchered one of them. It was likely the first meat the village had seen in months.

"Stopping the brigands will not save this place," Ginnem muttered under his breath. He was grimly chewing his way through the bland porridge, as were all of them. To refuse the food would have been an insult. "They are too poor to survive."

"The mine here produces lapis, I heard," one of the Sentinels said. "That's valuable."

"The veins are all but depleted," said the other. "I talked to one of the elders awhile this afternoon. They have not mined good stone here in years. Even the nodes the brigands take are poor quality. With new tools and more men they might dig deeper, find a new vein, but . . ." He looked about the room and sighed.

"We must ask the Temple Superior to send aid," Ginnem said.

Cet said nothing. The Temple had already given the villagers a phenomenal amount of aid just by sending a Gatherer and two Sentinels; he doubted the Superior would be willing to send more. More likely the village would have to dissolve, its people relocating to other settlements to survive. Without money or status in those places, they would be little better than slaves.

Almost against his will, Cet looked across the feast-table at Namsut, who sat beside Mehepi. She had eaten little, her eyes wandering from face to face around the table, seemingly as troubled by the sorry state of her village as the Templefolk. When her eyes fell on Cet, she frowned in wary puzzlement. Flustered, Cet looked away.

To find Ginnem watching him with a strange, sober look. "So, not just jealousy."

Cet lowered his eyes. "No. No doubt it is the start of the madness."

"A kind of madness, yes. Maybe just as dangerous in its own way, for you."

"What are you talking about?"

"Love," Ginnem said. "I'd hoped it was only lust, but clearly you care about her."

Cet set his plate down, his appetite gone. Love? He barely knew Namsut. And yet the image of her fighting the sleep spell danced through his mind over and over, a recurring dream that he had no power to banish. The thought of leaving her to her empty fate filled him with anguish.

Ginnem winced, then sighed. "Everything for Her peace."

"What?"

"Nothing." Ginnem did not meet Cet's eyes. "But if you mean to help her, do it tomorrow, or the day after. That will be the best time."

The words sent a not entirely unpleasant chill along Cet's spine. "You've healed her?"

"She needed no healing. She's as fertile as river soil. I can only assume she hasn't conceived yet because the Goddess wanted her child fathered by a man of her choosing. A blessing, not a curse."

Cet looked down at his hands, which trembled in his lap. How could a blessing cause him such turmoil? He wanted Namsut; that he could no longer deny. Yet being with her meant violating his oath. He had never questioned that oath in the sixteen years of his service as a Gatherer. For his faithfulness he had been rewarded with a life of such peace and fulfillment as most people could only imagine. But now that peace was gone, ground away between the twin inexorabilities of duty and desire.

"What shall I do?" he whispered. But if the Sister heard him, he made no reply.

And when Cet looked up, a shadow of regret was in Namsut's eyes.

Ginnem and the Sentinels, who had some ability to protect themselves against narcomancy, took the watch, with Ginnem to remain in the house in case of attack. Exhausted from the previous night's battle and the day's travels, Cet went to sleep in the guestroom as soon as the feast ended. It came as no great surprise that his hours in the land of dreams were filled with faceless phantoms who taunted him with angry smiles and inviting caresses. And among them, the cruelest phantom of all: a currant-skinned girlchild with Cet's kind eyes.

When he woke just as the sky began to lighten with dawn, he missed the sound of the jungissa, so distracted was he by his own misery. The urge to sleep again seemed so natural, dark and early as it was, that he did not fight it. Perhaps if he slept again, his dreams would be more peaceful.

"Gatherer!"

Perhaps if he slept again . . .

A foot kicked Cet hard in his side. He cried out and rolled to a crouch, disoriented. Ginnem sat nearby, his hands raised in that defensive gesture again, his face tight with concentration. Only then did Cet notice the high, discordant whine of the narcomancer's jungissa, startlingly loud and nearby.

"The window," Ginnem gritted through his teeth. The narcomancer was right outside the house.

There was a sudden scramble of footsteps outside. The window was too small for egress, so Cet ran through the house, bursting out of the front door just as a fleet shadow ran past. In that same instant Cet passed beyond range of Ginnem's protective magic, and stumbled as the urge to sleep came down heavy as stones. Lifting his legs was like running through mud; he groaned in near pain from the effort. He was dreaming awake when he reached for his own jungissa. But he was a Gatherer and dreams were his domain, so he willed his dreamself to strike the ornament against the doorsill, and it was his waking hand that obeyed.

The pure reverberation of the dragonfly jungissa cleared the lethargy from his mind, and his own heart supplied the righteous fury to replace it. Shaping that fury into a lance of vibration and power, Cet sent it at the fleeing figure's back with all the imperative he could muster. The figure stumbled, and in that instant Cet caught hold of the narcomancer's soul.

There was no resistance as Cet dragged him into dream; whatever training the brigands' narcomancer had, it went no further than sleep spells. So they fell, blurring through the land of dreams until their shared minds snagged on a commonality. The Temple appeared around them as a skewed, too-large version of the Hall of Blessings, with a monstrous statue of the Dream Goddess looming over all. The narcomancer cried out and fell to his knees at the sight of the statue, and Cet took the measure of his enemy at last.

He was surprised to see how young the man was – twenty at the most, thin and ragged with hair in a half-matted mix of braids and knots. Even in the dream he stank of months unwashed. But despite the filth, it was the narcomancer's awe of the statue which revealed the truth.

"You were raised in the Temple," Cet said.

The narcomancer crossed his arms over his breast and bent his head to the statue. "Yes, yes."

"You were trained?"

"No. But I saw how the magic was done."

And he had taught himself, just from that? But the rest of the youth's tale was easy enough to guess. The Temple raised orphans and other promising youngsters in its House of Children. At the age of twelve those children chose whether to pursue one of the paths to service, or leave for a life among the laity. Most of the latter did well, for the Temple found apprenticeships or other vocations for them, but there were always a few who suffered from mistakes or misfortune and ended badly.

"Why?" Cet asked. "You were raised to serve peace. How could you turn your back on the Goddess's ways?"

"The brigands," whispered the youth. "They stole me from my farm, used me, beat me. I, I tried to run away. They caught me, but not before I'd found the holy stone, taken a piece for myself. They said I wasn't worthy to be one of them. I showed them, showed them. I showed them I could make the stone work. I didn't want to hurt anyone but it had been so long! So long. It felt so good to be strong again."

Cet cupped his hands around the young man's face. "And look what you have become. Are you proud?"

". . . No."

"Where did you find the jungissa?"

The dreamscape blurred in response to the youth's desire. Cet allowed this, admiring the magic in spite of himself. The boy was no true narcomancer, not half-trained and half-mad as he was, but what a Gatherer he could have been! The dream re-formed into an encampment among the hills: the brigands, settled in for the night, eighteen or twenty snoring lumps that had caused so much suffering. Through the shared underpinnings of the dream Cet understood at once where to find them. Then the dream flew over the hills to a rocky basin. On its upper cliff-face was an outcropping shaped like a bird of prey's beak. In a black-burned scar beneath this lay a small, pitted lump of stone.

"Thank you," Cet said. Taking control of the dream, he carried them from the hills to a greener dreamscape. They stood near the delta of a great river, beyond which lay an endless sea. The sky stretched overhead in shades of blue, some lapis and some as deep as Namsut's mourning gown. In the distance a small town shone like a gemstone amid the carpet of green. Cet imagined it full of people who would welcome the youth when they met him.

"Your soul will find peace here," Cet said.

The youth stared out over the dreamscape, lifting a hand as if the beauty hurt his eyes. When he looked at Cet he was weeping. "Must I die now?"

Cet nodded, and after a moment the youth sighed.

"I never meant to hurt anyone," he said. "I just wanted to be free."

"I understand," Cet said. "But your freedom came at the cost of others' suffering. That is corruption, unacceptable under the Goddess's law."

The narcomancer bowed his head. "I know. I'm sorry."

Cet smiled and passed a hand over the youth's head. The grime and reek vanished, his appearance becoming wholesome at last. "Then She will welcome your return to the path of peace."

"Thank you," said the youth.

"Thank Her," Cet replied. He withdrew from the dream then, severing the tether and collecting the dreamblood. Back in waking, the boy's body released one last breath and went still. As shouts rang out around the village, Cet knelt beside the body and arranged its limbs for dignity.

Ginnem and one of the Sentinels ran up. "Is it done?" the Sentinel asked.

"It is," Cet said. He lifted the jungissa stone he'd taken from the boy's hand. It was a heavy, irregular lump, its surface jagged and cracked. Amazing the thing had worked at all.

"And are you well?" That was Ginnem. Cet looked at the Sister and understood then that the question had nothing to do with Cet's physical health.

So Cet smiled to let Ginnem see the truth. "I am very well, Sister Ginnem."

Ginnem blinked in surprise, but nodded.

More of the villagers arrived. One of them was Namsut, breathless, with a knife in one hand. Cet admired her for a moment, then bowed his head to the Goddess's will.

"Everything for Her peace," he said.

The Sentinels went into the hills with some of the armed village men, after Cet told them where the brigands could be found. He also told the villagefolk where they could find the parent-stone of the narcomancer's jungissa.

"A basin marked by a bird's beak. I know the place," said Mehepi with a frown. "We'll go destroy the thing."

"No," Namsut said. Mehepi glared at her, but Namsut met her eyes. "We must fetch it back here. That kind of power is always valuable to someone, somewhere."

Cet nodded. "The Temple would indeed pay well for the stone and any pieces of it."

This set the villagers a-murmur, their voices full of wonder and, for the first time since Cet had met them, hope. He left them to their speculations and returned to the guestroom of the headman's house, where he settled himself against a wall and gazed through the window at passing clouds. Presently, as he had known she would, Namsut came to find him.

"Thank you," she said. "You have saved us in more ways than one."

He smiled. "I am only Her Servant."

She hesitated and then said, "I . . . I should not have asked you for what I did. It seemed a simple matter to me, but I see how it troubles you."

He shook his head. "No, you were right to ask it. I had forgotten: my duty is to alleviate suffering by any means at my disposal." His oath would have become meaningless if he had failed to remember that. Ginnem had been right to remind him.

It took her a moment to absorb his words. She stepped forward, her body tense. "Then you will do it? You will give me a child?"

He gazed at her for a long while, memorizing her face. "You understand that I cannot stay," he said. "I must return to the Temple afterward, and never see the daughter we make."

"Daugh—" She put a hand to her mouth, then controlled herself. "I understand. The village will care for me. After all their talk of a curse they must, or lose face."

Cet nodded and held out a hand to her. Her face wavered for a moment beneath a mix of emotions – sudden doubt, fear, resignation, and hope – and then she crossed the room, took his hand, and sat down beside him.

"You must . . . show me how," he said, ducking his eyes. "I have never done this thing."

Namsut stared at him, then blessed him with the first genuine, untainted smile he had ever seen on her face. He smiled back, and in a waking dream saw a horse running, running, over endless green.

"I have never *wanted* to do this thing before now," she said, abruptly shy. "But I know the way of it." And she stood.

Her mourning garments slipped to the floor. Cet fixed his eyes on them, trying not to see the movements of her body as she stripped off her headcloth and undergarments. When she knelt straddling his lap, he trembled as he turned his face away, his breath quickening and heart pounding fast. *A Gatherer belongs wholly to the Goddess*, that was the oath. He could hardly think as Namsut's hands moved down the bare skin of his chest, sliding towards the clasp of his loinskirt, yet he forced his mind to ponder the matter. He had always taken the oath to mean celibacy, but that was foolish, for the Goddess had never been interested in mere flesh. He loved Namsut and yet his duty, his calling, was still first in his heart. Was that not the quintessence of a Gatherer's vow?

Then Namsut joined their bodies, and he looked up at her in wonder.

"H-holy," he gasped. She moved again, a slow undulation in his lap, and he pressed his head back against the wall to keep from crying out. "This is holy."

Her breath was light and quick on his skin; dimly he understood that she had some pleasure of him as well. "No," she whispered, cupping his face between her hands. Her lips touched his; for a moment he thought he tasted sugared currants before she licked free. "But it will get better."

It did.

They returned to the Temple five days later, carrying the narcomancer's jungissa as a guarantee of the villagers' good faith. The Superior immediately dispatched scribes and tallymen to verify the condition of the parent stone and calculate an appropriate price. The payment they brought for the narcomancer's jungissa alone was enough to buy a year's food for the whole village.

Ginnem bid Cet farewell at the gates of the city, where a party of green- and gold-clad women waited to welcome him home. "You made the hard choice, Gatherer," he said. "You're stronger than I thought. May the Goddess grant your child that strength in turn."

Cet nodded. "And you are wiser than I expected, Sister. I will tell this to all my brothers, that perhaps they might respect your kind more."

Ginnem chuckled. "The gods will walk the earth before that happens!" Then he sobered, the hint of sadness returning to his eyes. "You need not do this, Gatherer Cet."

"This is Her will," Cet replied, reaching up to grip Ginnem's shoulder. "You see so much, so clearly; can you not see that?"

Ginnem gave a slow nod, his expression troubled. "I saw it when I realized you loved that woman. But . . ."

"We will meet again in dreams," Cet said softly.

Ginnem did not reply, his eyes welling with tears before he turned sharply away to rejoin his Sisters. Cet watched in satisfaction as they surrounded Ginnem, forming a comforting wall. They would take good care of him, Cet knew. It was the Sisterhood's gift to heal the soul.

So Cet returned to the Temple, where he knelt before the Superior and made his report – stinting nothing when it came to the tale of Namsut. "Sister Ginnem examined her before we left," he said. "She is healthy and should have little trouble delivering the child when the time comes. The firstwife did not take the news happily, but the elder council vowed that the first child of their reborn village would be cared for, along with her mother who so clearly has the gods' favor."

"I see," said the Temple Superior, looking troubled. "But your oath . . . that was a high price to pay."

Cet lifted his head and smiled. "My oath is unbroken, Superior. I still belong wholly to Her."

The Superior blinked in surprise, then looked hard at Cet for a long moment. "Yes," he said at last. "Forgive me; I see that now. And yet . . ."

"Please summon one of my brothers," Cet said.

The Superior started. "Cet, it may be weeks or months before the madness—"

"But it will come," Cet said. "That is the price of Her magic; that is what it means to be a true narcomancer. I do not begrudge the price, but I would rather face a fate of my choosing." The horse was in his mind again, its head lunging like a racer's against the swift river current. Sweet Namsut; he yearned for the day he would see her again in dreams. "Fetch Gatherer Liyou, Superior. Please."

The Superior sighed, but bowed his head.

When young Liyou arrived and understood what had to be done, he stared at Cet in shock. But Cet touched his hand and shared with him a moment of the peace that Namsut had given him, and when it was done Liyou wept. Afterward Cet lay down ready, and Liyou put his fingertips over Cet's closed eyes.

"Cetennem," Cet said, before sleep claimed him for the final time. "I heard it in a dream. My daughter's name shall be Cetennem."

Then with a joyful heart, Cet – Gatherer and narcomancer, Servant of peace and justice and the Goddess of Dreams – ran free.

GOLDEN DAUGHTER, STONE WIFE

Benjanun Sriduangkaew

For skeleton, steel and stone. For life, the edge of youth and command.

These are the things my daughter is made of. These are the things she leaves behind when the spell is gone and the wish is dead.

Sometimes I'd cup her chin and say that I wished her skin was like teak and her hair like the vestment of a crow, the natural shades of my lineage. And she would tell me, *I would have been ugly and despised to the one whose wish bought my provenance.*

Do you think me ugly, then?

Golem honesty, she answered. *You aren't beautiful. Neither are you ugly. And children, Mistress, must believe their mothers pretty – thus I do, imitating the limits and distortion of their perspective.*

I laughed. It was glorious to have a child such as she, frank and strange. A child that was old when we boarded the exiles' ship. A child my wife named Areemu, her last gift to me.

"Mistress Erhensa," someone says. They've been saying that for some time, in the belief that shock has deafened me and robbed me of a voice.

My brow to the window, Areemu's remains in my arms. The road outside is a black ribbon, wet-sharp with frost under the halo of my seahorse lamps. An empty road. This is not a season for visitors.

"Mistress Erhensa. The Institute of Ormodon is here to collect the golem."

A girl purchased her some 200 years past. A girl gold of hair and skin, eyes like the canals after a storm. "Tell them there is no golem."

"But there must be, Mistress Erhensa." This voice does not belong to my servant. "We detected the flux of its dissipation. I was dispatched immediately."

It's too dim for the glass to glare, and so I'm obliged to turn. The Ormodoni is ludicrously young, ludicrously freckled, and it is an insult they've sent this over a gray-haired officer. Her gaze severe, her shoulders high beneath the weight of pauldrons, her stance square despite the bulk of plating. Much too proud, before age has earned her the right.

"You must be tired from the journey," I say, rote. There's no journey – it is a step and a thought from the Institute of Ormodon to my domain, a requirement all practitioners must heed. Keep our doors open, or else. "We don't often have visitors. Lais will find you a room and supper if you want it. In the morning we will talk."

"I'm Hall-Warden Ysoreen Zarre."

"I'm sure you are." I did not ask.

"I am to bring your answer within the night."

"Expectations have a way of being thwarted, Hall-Warden Zarre. Your superiors will have to understand. Over breakfast, we may discuss the golem. Or you may depart now and we may discuss nothing."

Who defies Ormodon; delays its enforcers? Who dares? No one wise, but lately I am past wisdom.

"In the morning, then." Hall-Warden Zarre turns on her heels. "I look forward to it."

I watch her back and watch the door shut behind her, thinking again of the girl with the pale hair. A child with no real thought between one act and the next save her own pleasure. I consider the matter of remaking and redoing, of resurrection.

Her death is new. There is time. If one callow wish animated Areemu once, might not another bring her back?

* * *

Ysoreen's gums burn, acidic, with the residue of golem death. Unlike most officers she doesn't need Institute scryers to sense this. Gifted, they've always praised her; fine material for thaumaturgy. Instead she trained to understand golems, those double-edged creatures, those threats to Scre from within.

To think Erhensa – a foreigner living on sufferance – would treat an Ormodoni as she has; to think Ysoreen did not teach the sorcerer her place. This failure stays sour on her tongue and keeps her from tasting the foods. They are foreign: a tea red as garnets, pastry that crumbles at a glance, a smell of cardamom and tropical fruits. An island to the west, bordering turquoise sea under a gilded sky; so she's heard. She does not believe, for if there exists such a paradise, why would Erhensa be here? The reality would be a patch of territory off the coast, mired in gray silt.

But Erhensa's fancy has been given part-life in the piscine gazes blinking at her from between mosaic tiles, in the murals moving out of the corner of her eye. Figures in the distance balanced impossibly on the crests of tides; birds slashing through a burnished horizon.

Ysoreen sleeps against an unpainted wall, pulling the blankets over herself, breathing her own leathers and steel. Tomorrow she will confront; tomorrow she will demand. Ormodon assumes efficiency in its operatives, and she's armed to subdue wayward sorcerers. In this house she is no one's lesser.

She is up before dawn may warm the room and wake the fish. She straightens out the sheets and coverlets so no imprint of her may linger in the creases. She drinks from a bedside jug and rinses her mouth. When the manservant comes she is ready.

He takes her to the garden with its outland trees, its high walls of iron and lazuli. So high the world outside may not be seen; so high the house seems its own dominion, the islander its queen.

She comports herself like that too, as though the bushes are her throne and the scarlet ixora her maids. The sun glances off the darkness of her skin so she seems chiseled, more wood than life. Within the circumference of Erhensa's power, the rime stays out and the flowers thrive.

The sorcerer does not rise; barely stirs as Ysoreen approaches. In her lap is a clear casket holding loose gemstones, platinum filigrees, a fistful of thread.

Ysoreen points at the box. "I'll be taking that, Mistress Erhensa."

"This is a collection of baubles, nothing more."

"I am not unschooled." This specific golem is a common choice of study for its unusual construction, and she has read the manuscript of its creation; more than can be said of the islander. "Nevertheless it is law, and by law the golem never truly belonged to you. As all constructs it belongs to the Institute, and so does its material."

A smile on those thin, lined lips. "Technically I brought my golem with me when I came to Scre, but of course I've agreed to your laws. What do you do with their parts? It can't be avarice that drives you to collect – were this one baked of mud and silt you'd have demanded the same."

"Yours is not the place to question."

"As you will," Erhensa says. "Allow me to make you a gift, as amends for making you wait a whole night. Fox fur imparts excellent warmth and will make the season more tolerable."

Ysoreen's teeth click together. Protocols force her to accept tribute from any sorcerer, so long as the object inflicts no harm or malice. "Fox fur, in this weather?"

"I was hoping you would hunt. Inconsiderate of me to ask of a guest, but I'm no good at the business of tracking and conquering animal wits, a task that perhaps better suits you."

The insult needles, but Ysoreen does not react. She is stone, Erhensa less than wind.

I watch her through the bright, clear eyes of a fox. You see the world differently this way, closer to the ground, sight plaited from smells, nose to soil and snow. A fox's mind is so wide, made of simple geometry and immediate needs.

The fox sniffs and tosses its head. She comes.

I lied to the Hall-Warden: the hunt is no mystery to me. It is different here in a country that knows no frost, where predators and prey do not have to contend with a chill that would shrivel the lungs and bruise the cheeks. But there are certain principles in common, certain rhythms that aren't so unlike. A need for subtlety, a requirement for finesse.

Ysoreen Zarre disregards them all. Her boots stamp deep prints, and she marches without care for tracks or stealth. She is unerring in her pursuit, and though I make the fox give her a good and worthy chase, she never loses the sense of where it is, where it heads.

It is fleet, but she is fleeter. It is clever, but she is cleverer. It tires long before she does, heaving on its legs.

When she has pierced its side with arrows, is she aware I am watching? Her knife cuts abrupt and efficient, opening its belly: entrails steaming in the snow and flecking her gloved wrist.

The fox's vitals push their final beat, and my sight extinguishes in smears of blood and heat.

Erhensa nods when the manservant brings her the fur, cleaned and scented and brushed to a sheen.

Ysoreen sits by as the sorcerer works. "A description of the golem in your own words?"

"Your Institute is obsessed with cataloguing everything, reducing the world to verbiage. It's no way to be." Erhensa leans back into her cushions. "Her name was Areemu. It was something else once – a thing bleached as summer-beaten bone, frail as sun-baked clay – but when one takes on a child, it's correct to recast her a little."

"Golems are servitors, Mistress Erhensa. You do not call a shovel your daughter."

"Golems," the sorcerer says, "are vessels of wishes. When you're done building one it is as if you've given birth. When you take one in it is as if you've adopted new kin. You put so much of what you want into them, just as with offspring of the womb. Less blood, less mess. No less love."

Erhensa has threaded copper wire through the fur. She has quick, nimble fingers; Ysoreen finds herself entranced by their speed. She pushes away from that and jots into a little book. *Surrogate daughter.* "Who made the golem?"

"Have you ever wished for something fiercely, desperately, only to discover that the world does not contain it?"

"No."

"You must've led a perfect life. A loving family, a good wife."

"I've no more need for a wife than I do a second head – less, since a second head could guard my back."

Erhensa laughs. "So many ardor-notes must've crumpled under your heel. But Areemu, yes. There was a girl. A princess or the daughter of a puissant magistrate. She was beautiful, it is written. Eyes like the glaze of honey on scarab wings. A little like yours."

She's less than wind. But there's no stopping the rush of blood, no hiding the surge of heat. Like her mothers and sisters, Ysoreen is one of the best to have graduated from the Academy of Command. One of the best, save her unruly moods. She tries too hard, they told her; as long as she fights herself, as long as she pours effort into suppressing rather than understanding, she will be like this. "My eyes are no such thing. What would a princess want with a golem? She couldn't possibly lack for slaves."

"She wanted a lover."

"Then she must've been brutishly ugly." A relief; the thought of being compared to a hideous girl sits better on Ysoreen than the opposite.

"Hardly. Areemu could not lie, and she said the girl was so lovely she might stop the stars in their tracks. She had suitors uncountable. A duchess who wooed her with a gift of elephants and birds of paradise. An arctic queen who sent a chariot pulled by white tigers and an ice house that never melted. A witch who enchanted an entire aviary for her, so the birds would always sing and never die. To each the princess said no, and no again. She'd been told all her short life that she was perfect, and she would take nothing less than perfect for her consort."

The volume Ysoreen read was a golemist's manual: formulae and procedure rather than history. It doesn't mention from whence came the commission, whether there was a princess or whether she was coveted. Erhensa's tale may well be apocryphal. She records, all the same.

"Her mother sent for conjurers instead of suitors. The best thaumaturgists in the land and several lands surrounding. From east and west they came, from north and south they journeyed, to prove themselves supreme among their kind and make for her a paramour. One who would not betray, one who would be gallant to her always, one who would never weep come what may. What woman of mortal matter could do so much?"

Wish fulfillment, Ysoreen adds. It's a common motive to buy a golem; perhaps the most common. Surrogate parent. Surrogate child. And lovers, always lovers. Left unchecked half the nation of Scre would have been golems.

Erhensa shifts the fox away from her lap. Even her magic is alien. She has not murmured an incantation, dropped a pinch of powder or struck crystals together, but somehow she's liberated a triangle of fur from the rest. A perfect isosceles, as though measured with ruler and ink. "The true challenge was volition. She did not want a mute toy which would come when called, say yes when asked, kiss her when pressed. The princess wanted to be loved back truly."

"Not likely," Ysoreen says. "Golems don't have emotions. They can pretend, if it's inscribed into their cores. Nothing more."

"I'm glad you know so much about golems. It is enlightening. They must give you a peerless education that you may know such subjects better than practitioners."

"I have made golems my study."

"Is that so? Ah, it seems I've run out of feathers. Will you bring me some? I'm a stranger to the way of winged things, the difficulties of ensnaring and capturing. An owl will do, Hall-Warden. Something gray, with a coat like velvet."

You see the world differently as a bird, so much closer to the sky. Thought is like the center of a yolk, sloshing within a brittle shell. Bones so light, sinews so lean.

I reach from the inside and make this one a girl.

The confoundment is partial; her shoulders flare into wings rather than arms, and her stare remains amber, dark-seeing and immense. Feathers give her modesty, shrouding her skull in place of human tresses.

She flits from branch to branch. Hardly any skin on her; hardly any hip or breast. Ysoreen sees through the guise, as she must. Does she pause, does she hesitate? For the length of a blink.

The fox was fast, but it was a slash of red on sunlit snow. The girl-owl is gray nearing black and the moon is a half-lidded eye. The Hall-Warden must keep her gaze trained skyward; keep her feet firm on the wet mulch.

The owl grins down and laughs into her wings.

In the end she falls too, an arrow's fletching in her belly, for Ysoreen does not permit herself failure. The Hall-Warden stands over the girl who is slowly reverting to an owl. Her knuckles drag over her face, and this time her knife is not so swift.

She makes small noises in her throat as she dismembers and flays. The knife-point plunges into the owl-girl's eyes, and my sight burns out in a flash of steel and moonlight.

Ysoreen jolts into a morning so white it blinds her and for a moment she pants into the glare, blinking down tears.

The smell of blood clings. There is no help for it; she fills the brass tub and strips. The lidded jug is warm and the water steams, an enchanted courtesy. When she sinks into the bath the scent of foreign flora rise. Citrus. Her mind drifts and snags on the thought of Erhensa's fingers. Long, elegant, tapered like candles.

She pulls herself up short and out of the bath. The sorcerer turned an owl into a woman to do – what? Annoy and disturb. Quickly she dresses, slotting and strapping on the armor. When the manservant comes only the stains on the floor where water has dripped mark Ysoreen's indulgence.

Erhensa is busy with the charm, sewing feathers into the lattice of copper wire and fur. Her needle flashes, disappearing and reappearing. "It'll be a fine thing. Not so often do I make these with such attention, with such fresh ingredients."

"Using magic against an Ormodoni officer is misconduct that merits execution."

"Putting on slightly unusual clothes is enough to have me put in chains, Hall-Warden Zarre, so must we go over such tedious minutiae? No harm was done and none was meant."

Anyone else Ysoreen would have cut short and confronted with the exact penalties for their offense. She'd have disabled them and brought them to the Institute, there to be stripped of their properties and status, there to be fettered and their magic ripped out. The crime warrants that and more.

Instead she kneels in the grass, where each blade comes up to her shoulder and casts a stripe on her cheeks. Why allow Erhensa to believe that the owl moved her. It was only a bird.

"Permit me to continue where I left off," says Erhensa. "Areemu was the labor of two sisters, a goldsmith and a carpenter who dabbled in alchemy. They wouldn't have recognized a formal axiom if it sank teeth into their ankles. A convocation of scholars, and they were bested by a pair of tradeswomen." Erhensa's mouth curves, wicked. "Imagine the insult of it."

Ysoreen's lips twist as though yoked to the islander's amusement. She straightens them at once.

"They made her out of the most delicate filigrees but also gave her a spine extracted from a rare and special ore: strong as steel but weightless, lustrous as silver but untarnishing. They enameled her skin and shielded her joints in diamonds. For might she not be the princess's knight as well as her darling?"

Made for combat, Ysoreen writes. It matches the two sisters' journal. Anywhere, anytime, there's always a thaumaturgist investing in the idea of an army that knows no pain or disobedience.

"Areemu was presented before the court. The princess had been taught: you are the fairest and none may compare, you are the moon and the stars while all else are candlelight. Yet here Areemu shone, a sun." Erhensa sets the charm down. "You had too little sleep, didn't you?"

Because she dreamed, all night, of a girl who was a bird. She dreamed of driving the blade into eyes too enormous, of tearing out a heart too small and holding it in her fist still beating, always beating. A clot of nausea, a tactile memory. "It is nothing. I'm the mistress of my flesh and it my slave, not the other way around."

"Body and mind should walk in harmony, as friends or sisters." Erhensa reaches across and strokes Ysoreen's forearm. The touch goes through fabric; a tug at her arteries. The queasiness recedes. "Take this as my apology."

Ysoreen looks down at the sorcerer's hand. Those fingers,

that skin the shade of oak. She swallows, and when her breath stutters she knows that she's stayed too long, has let Erhensa under her skin. Symptoms of immaturity, she's always said of her peers in scorn. *She* is above it.

"Tomorrow I leave." Her words do not stumble. "With the golem's parts."

"It was pleasant to break my solitude. You will not think of it so, but you kept an old woman company, and that's a fine, gracious thing."

"You are not so old as that."

"I forget that in your country the grayness and bruises of age descend like anchors on a fraying rope. As soon as the first blush of adolescence is past, the flesh puckers and creases while the tendons wither. It's the winter, which bleeds you of vigor. It's the food, which lacks spice and so does not arm your livers." The sorcerer tips her head back. "Where I'm from the grandmothers keep hold of their resilience and dignity long after their heads are white."

"Why did you leave?" Ysoreen says before she can clinch shut the strings of her curiosity.

"A callow conviction that my will was the sun around which the world must revolve. I offended a woman of prominence and supremacy. And so, as the dusk of my life approaches, I'm severed from my kin and clan, to wait for the end in a land with ice for marrow, which delights only in conquest. A land that loathes me."

"You could've wedded."

"I could have." A deep chuckle. "I thought you said a wife was less use than a second head?"

"I meant – for myself."

The charm inches toward completion. Topaz beads glitter in the velvet of feathers and fur. "Do you want no one to grow old with? It can be difficult to weather alone the decades when your vision dims and your reason fades."

"Then," Ysoreen says, "I'd have to marry a woman at least ten years my junior."

"Or one to whom age does not mean weakness." Erhensa lifts the triangle and exhales upon it.

Ysoreen imagines that breath against her cheek.

★   ★   ★

It is death to sway the mind of an Ormodoni. When I entered Scre, that was one of the compulsions I bowed to, and it slithered into me where it abides even now, a snake of spite and abasement. But it is not Ysoreen's thoughts that I pluck at, nothing so coherent as picture or language. It is only a look through warped glass. Enough to see that her dream is a bucking beast of russet and soot, snarled with longing.

I wake her, and the dream falls apart like muscle tearing under a machete.

She answers the door in armor. Always she wears it; refuses to be seen without. Despite its protection she flinches at the sight of me. Have I struck too harsh with my trick; have I sundered her courage?

"I wanted to finish my account of Areemu."

It is to her credit that she is instantly alert. "As you wish." Perhaps reminded of courtesy a young woman owes one her mother's age, Ysoreen takes my elbow. Her grip tenses then relaxes, firm.

To my library, where the talisman simmers in the symbols of my country, the symbols of Sumalin. Laminated petals captured at their prime: the liveliest purple, the tartest yellow, the purest white. The seeds of papayas that will never grow here. The shells of tortoises that won't survive this cold. My shelves strain with volumes from home, paper and wood, alloys and mosaics. More than any treasure, I've guarded these, some brought with me on that exiles' ship, others purchased and amassed over my banishment. I've become known as the madwoman who'll trade jewels for books, so long as they are from the island of my nativity.

Ysoreen conducts me to my seat with a courtier's gravity, the way they do in high-ceilinged Institute halls. She unfolds my shawl, draping it over my shoulders. Then she steps away, hands clasped behind her.

"Where were we? Yes. The presentation of Areemu. She did not yet live, and if her eyes were clear jewels they did not yet see. It was this unlife that made her bearable to her prospective mistress: it was still possible to think Areemu a doll, satellite rather than sun. Seizing Areemu's shoulders, the princess ordered that she live. This manner of waking shaped Areemu;

prepared the facets of her logic. She would have made a fine instructor at your Institute. No human mind is keener; no pupil a quicker study."

Ysoreen stiffens. Her teachers ought to be proud of her, their Hall-Warden, so strict and strictly adherent to their every code. "What have you taught her?"

"Any skill or discipline she cared to learn. Astronomy, painting, horticulture."

"What else was she like?"

"This."

The door opens and Areemu steps through.

A glance too long or a thought too weighty will scatter her, this shimmer in the cold. But Ysoreen Zarre will not be able to tell that. Areemu seems as solid as either of us; more, for we are merely suet and fluids while she is – was – harder elements, sturdier substance.

My daughter is holding a dress I trained her to sew, and in this art she exceeded me: a marvel of sleek fabric and wave-patterns, embroidery of tails and shark pectorals to honor my ancestral land. Laughing soundlessly Areemu shakes out the gown to show me her work.

Ysoreen's attention is held fast by my mirage daughter. I know then that I will have Areemu back. I will have my daughter back and the chambers of my house will echo no more; the chambers of my heart will brighten again.

"Your gift will be finished by noon tomorrow. I will be sorry to see you go."

"If I—" Ysoreen has turned to me, but her thoughts are looped tight around Areemu. "If before I leave I ask you a question, will you give me a true answer?"

"You are of Ormodon." I know what the question will be.

"Not that. I want . . . an answer that is not obliged. If such a thing is possible."

"I will give you your answer," I say, folding that memory of Areemu to myself, lustrous as the best nacre-silk.

It is the code of Ormodon to be true to the self. *Hold your soul before a convex glass each dawn*, her superiors said, *and study it without mercy. Let no secrets elude your gaze, for it is their way to suppurate. Instead, mine every last one to find its strength; hammer the metal of your secrets until it is supple and strong. With this, sheathe your will. Your desires shall not be weakness but armor for the weapon of your mind.*

This is what she has not mastered, her one flaw. This is what she must master now.

Before, it was simple to sort her small wants, her transient hopes, into those that might be acted upon and those that might not; those that she could do without and those she could not. What is prohibited, what may be obtained. None of them was ever so tangled as this.

It doesn't have to be. Erhensa will say yes. Marriage to an officer is better than gold, and Ysoreen can give the islander everything. Elevation, if Erhensa wishes it. Unquestioned right to live where she does; do as she pleases.

A daughter who lives and grows, to help Erhensa forget the golem. They'll need a blood-rite and a willing womb. There's never a shortage of refugee women who will take on the burden; it earns them three years of wanting for nothing and a chance at citizenship.

Ysoreen doesn't wait. She passes the manservant in the corridor, who gives berth and stammers that his mistress is in her study, does the Hall-Warden not require directions, does she . . .

"She knows the way." Ysoreen finds herself laughing, her steps buoyant. An aviary of possibilities in her chest.

Erhensa looks up, and Ysoreen fancies that her mouth flexes toward a smile. There is a circle of color in the sorcerer's irises that she hasn't noticed before, the shade of good citrines, and she marvels at this newfound clarity.

"A question, you promised." Erhensa's voice is a caress.

The cautious eagerness of that. And why not? Those glances, those gestures. Ysoreen gathers herself and goes to one knee before the sorcerer. Bolder than she feels, she clasps Erhensa's hand; savors with a frisson the texture of it, soft-rough, calluses. "Mistress Erhensa, I'd like your leave—"

"Yes," Erhensa exhales. "Of course, yes."

Ysoreen's thoughts teeter and tip over. Momentum alone drives her to complete her sentence. "Mistress Erhensa. With your leave I would court you, and at a later date ask to be yours in marriage. Would you have this?"

But the answer is yes, already; her throat needs not dry, her heart needs not race – hunter chasing prey – after her desire.

Except Erhensa's fingers do not knit into hers; except Erhensa does not clasp her face or bend to kiss her. All she says is, "Oh, Hall-Warden," before she frees herself from Ysoreen.

On her knee still, Ysoreen swallows, breathless. She does not— "You are saying no?"

"I believed you would ask an entirely different question, and it is that which I answered. The shape of your moods, the direction of your temperament. I couldn't be surer."

Her armor jangles – too loud – as she comes to her feet, quick as the burn of shame. Quicker. "But I thought . . ."

"I was a fool, singular in my purpose." Erhensa shakes her head. "Hall-Warden, you've a future ahead of you, a ribbon that spools incandescent around the core of your spirit and station. What could you want with an immigrant sorcerer as old as I?"

"The heart doesn't *think*." Ysoreen sets her fists against the hard metal at her back, glad for the cuirass. It fortifies her composure; keeps her formal. Her words are in the rhetorical mode of the Institute. "It told me it found beauty in you. It told me that it wants. I obey, for if it is fulfilled then my intellect and humors will both come to benefit. If it goes unfulfilled, as it now does, then I will have lanced it and bled it of any authority over me."

"An odd philosophy, but it surely is superior to repression, which is universally hopeless. I did not mean to mislead you."

Ysoreen does not clutch at her breast, which throbs and roils with the terror of having been laid bare. "What did you mean to accomplish?"

"It doesn't matter."

"I say it does." Her control asserts, piecemeal, as much habit as discipline.

"And I may not deny a Hall-Warden." Erhensa's wariness returns, and it is as if the last three days never happened. "Areemu was animated by a specific wish, with the shape and tune of a certain age. Her components remember that still – not for long, not forever, but for now."

"I would," Ysoreen snaps, "never consider a golem wife."

"Matrimony wouldn't have been necessary. Only your passion was required. It is moot, in any case. You will take Areemu, I suppose."

"Yes." Her palms are clammy, her pulse yet unsteady.

"You said golems are your study. Tell me this, would it have worked?"

"With a specific ritual, known only to its creators. But that is moot."

Erhensa sets the casket into her arms, the fox-owl talisman around her neck. "Good day, Hall-Warden Zarre."

Ysoreen grips the case; thinks of dashing it to the ground. Yet what purpose will it serve? The glass will shatter, but the bars and stones: those need the solar furnace, a proper disposal.

She makes a perfunctory bow. She leaves; she flees, outpacing her humiliation.

My daughter then is gone, the last dream and echo of her. Only in the weave of my recall does she live, and that will diminish as age devours its due. I may create a skein of my memory, and each strand would be so vivid, so near solidity. Except to whom will I leave that; who will treasure Areemu's images? Who will treasure our long talks of home; who will find meaning when I ask Areemu, *Do you remember the taste of coconut, the sweetness of palm sugar?*

Perhaps the Hall-Warden is right that I should've wedded. No woman of Scre in their frosted arrogance would have looked at me. In the refugee camps, however, I could have found women far closer to Sumalin than to this nation where winter's children reign. It is how unions are frequently made among Scre tradeswomen too poor or uncomely. Any life would be better than in the camps, and I present a far loftier prospect than being a potter's spouse, a cobbler's concubine.

It is futile to contemplate. This is not a choice I may make in faith, for all that I would give a desperate woman succor and she would give me companionship. For that paltriness I will not betray my nuptial vows, made on a sun-drenched day beneath palm shades, my bride and I heavy with a wealth of pearls we dived for.

We could have grown old side by side. There would have been daughters, sharp and spirited. One might have gone to the palace a handmaiden or magistrate, and another still might have honed herself to discipline not unlike Hall-Warden Zarre but tempered with the kindness of our sun.

Instead my wife gave me Areemu, hastily purchased and dearly paid for. There was no time for any other token; no time to spare for the conception of a flesh daughter. Neither of us broke that day when I turned my back to Sumalin and my face to the sails. Areemu at my side, wearing the pearls my bride and I had meant to pass to our children.

Age means possibilities trampled in our wake. Age means a serpent behind us heavy with ashes, while the length ahead gets ever shorter and each path we did not take comes back to hiss and bite, filling our veins with venom. That is life: a corpse that weighs us down, a beast that gobbles us up.

I've not turned all of Areemu over. It will work, the Hall-Warden said. So there is a way. Where there is one, others must exist; there is no destination with just a single road toward it.

The largest ruby, red as rambutan shell. Within its facets the last of her life wheels, an orrery of pinpoints in slow orbits. Slower by the day. When it stops entirely she will be beyond revival.

Night or day I keep it by me, as if by the warmth of my skin I may incubate it and hatch Areemu. Night or day I scheme and toil; were I a witch in certain tales sung out in the prairie, I would be hunting down pet foxes and toddlers for their eelish kidneys, their slippery brains. But I am not a story, the nearest village and its clutch of toddlers is too far, and in this matter foxes are of no use.

If blood is spilled, it is my own. If carving out my lungs would avail her life, then I would plunge the knife into my breast and call it fair.

Golemry has never ignited my passion, and I've taken it up only after Areemu entered my guardianship. Braving the intricacy of her structure humbles and infuriates – I am no artisan; have never been a prodigy. There once existed a record of Areemu's making, each step inscribed with zealous faith from the first notion, the first sketch; the sisters were meticulous and rightly proud. A decade or so after acquiring Areemu, the princess had this manuscript destroyed and all copies incinerated. Areemu was hers alone; must remain unique. So thorough she was, and so ruthless. No shred of it survives.

The shadow of her malice haunts. The poison of her sneer, long-dead, stiffens the tendons of my wrists.

Areemu's life dims by the hour.

When the gate flares I am alert – intensely alert, for the ruby's inner orrery succumbs more rapidly now, and I may not waste even an hour on sleep.

The gating sounds as the noise of wave against rock: a sound of home, a sound absent from this land. I am prepared. Who can tell the caprices of a spurned heart; who may say what will bud from a soil of rage?

She grips not her blade or a sorcerer's whip but the casket of Areemu's parts and a collection of papers. Ysoreen has been weeping. On skin like hers it shows. Small surprise that in this country they try so very hard not to cry.

"Hall-Warden, the hour is late. My servant is resting, and I fear I haven't readied any sweetmeats to share."

"Hang the sweetmeats." Her voice is hoarse, her hair disheveled. It doesn't look as if she has been getting any more rest than have I. "I came for something else."

"Yes?" She must have noticed that Areemu's core is missing. The consequence will not be light on me. It will not be open to appeal.

"I couldn't conquer my thoughts of you. I couldn't extricate myself from them – from you." Ysoreen inhales. "I cannot permit this to be. One way or another I must have resolution."

"It will pass, Hall-Warden." In a year or two she'll look back and marvel that she ever felt so fiercely.

"I know myself, Mistress Erhensa. This will lodge deep in me, a splinter under the scar. It will prick when I least expect and bleed me from the inside. It will make me weak." She thrusts the casket at me. "Will you allow me the chance to visit you a suitor?"

I laugh even as my power tautens in readiness. "You aren't very good at courtship."

"I've never felt the need to practice." Ysoreen looks up, down, away. "It's inexact. It's illogical."

"Come here, Hall-Warden."

We are neither of us at ease, at trust; a truce hovers between us but it is cobwebs, it is slivers, it will come apart at a murmur. She approaches, and there is a look about her that she wore when she chased that fox, that owl.

The casket is between us when I clasp her jaw – and she flinches, for now her hands are trapped and her head is in my grip; if I am not half so hale as she nor a fraction so vital, still I am not weak. Ysoreen's face is broad, eyes deep-set beneath a scuffed brow. A blunt, decisive nose; it is this part of her that I kiss. My halfway offering.

Her eyelids flutter, rapid, against my cheeks. "In the Institute's archives there is a copy of the sisters' manuscript."

Now it is my rhythms which stutter, flung out of cadence. The pages she carries. "Is there. Is it—"

"I told you, golems are my study. I know how to reawaken your daughter."

I kiss her again, on the lips. It is more calculation than passion, more necessity than desire. In my place any other would've done the same. She goes rigid then pliant, mouth ajar and hot with want. Her clutch at my back, this side of bruising; the taste of her tongue tart.

She is the first to draw away. Though her breathing has gone to rags, there's a wariness to the tightness of her jaw. Perhaps she is aware – cannot escape – the fact this is a bargain where we put our goods on the table and haggle over the price. Kisses for a resurrection. So cheap; my merchant aunts would've shown pride.

Ysoreen gathers herself. "Your need, to fuel the wish. My youth, to replicate the conditions of the original animation. The golem's first name before the princess, before *Areemu*. The one you don't know." Hunger has ruddied her cheeks. She wants more than kisses; will have more than touches. "The sisters loved her enough to give her a name, to provide a means to restore her."

My fingers are already on the casket's clasps. Ysoreen gives way – though does she notice I open the case with greater zeal than when I parted her lips? Does she recognize I pry and tug at it as I never did with her armor?

Recalling Areemu's shape is simple. It's in the material, in the core, and when I evoke that remnant the pieces slot together, clicking, singing.

In a moment she is complete, sapphire irises shut, platinum limbs corded with strength. Her loveliness does not move the Hall-Warden, whose gaze is for me alone.

"You'll have to tell me," I say. "I don't read the manuscript's language." Practice alone allows me to control my tone; when you've used your voice as an instrument for this long, it is second nature to play it precisely.

"I'll read it aloud. You're familiar with the rite? I will be the princess's substitute."

The spell is no hardship either. Merely words, merely a rearranging of potential cupped within Areemu – this has never been difficult; it is the infusion of autonomy that eludes. I could always have had my daughter back a mannequin: no words but that of a parrot's, no motion but that of routine. But with the sisters' original formulae, their original words . . .

My puissance envelops Areemu's frame, shimmering strands, cat's cradle. Ysoreen takes Areemu's fingertips – hesitates, before anointing each. It is more grudgingly still that she kisses Areemu's golden lips and pours Areemu's true name into that inanimate throat.

They wait for the golem to stir. According to the sisters' instructions it will take until midday, and so Erhensa asks Ysoreen to share her bed.

She follows the sorcerer, her pulse like a wound. When she sheds her armor and not much else Erhensa crooks a lopsided smile. "You will wear the rest to bed?"

"I don't think of you as a . . . a courtesan. I'm not . . ." That pathetic. Or that honest. A transaction with a courtesan or a refugee would have been frank.

"I do not invite you to think of me so. But don't speak ill of paid companions, pricey ones in your marble brothels or elsewise. Some do it because they've no alternatives or because the laws of Scre confine them to the camps. Some do it for they want to, and that's their choice as much as mine is to practice power, as yours is to administer the curbing of it."

So Ysoreen takes off more until she is down to a shift. Under the sheets she lies on her side, Erhensa at her back, a fistful of sheet between them.

As the moth-lamps dim Ysoreen shuts her eyes, though she knows she will find no peace. Too many hours lie between her and dawn. Too much want lies between her pride and the ambush of Erhensa's offer. There's more than one bed in this house, and she could have refused.

Once, her hand – intent, accident, between – finds Erhensa's. It is a contact so brief, brushing her knuckles, brushing the inside of her wrist. Ysoreen thinks that this will do; the lust has been sated and she can move past it, a return to the liberty of ambition, the clarity of a rise through Ormodoni ranks.

It does not do. It does not suffice.

In the dark, Erhensa's chin against her shoulder. "Your flesh is iron. They train you to make a weapon of your body, don't they?"

Ysoreen listens for the sounds of winter night. Hoots and howls. She evaluates the virtue of silence. "What of it?"

"I'm making a decision."

"On what?"

"Later," the sorcerer whispers, "when Areemu lives again."

A terrible epiphany. This islander possesses control, a true ease of being. That is what drew Ysoreen: this thing she does not have.

They remain in the warmth of furs together long after dawn.

They hear her steps, first, and the chiming of her joints. When the door parts this is what Ysoreen sees: a wrist that gleams, a tress that glitters. The golem looks at them both, and says wonderingly, "Mother?"

Erhensa's voice frays, the first faltering of her faultless poise. Ysoreen makes herself absent.

If her daughter's return made her weep, Erhensa has already wiped away the tears. She has changed to a layered, beaded skirt she says is of her home. "Sumalin," she says, naming that island far to the west at last, a name that's never appeared in documents of her past.

The golem is gone to roam the premises, bright-eyed and eager to move again.

"My mothers did not call me Erhensa," the sorcerer says, distant. "They wove other things into my name, the aspects of Sumalin. Sand like turmeric, sea like emeralds. Girls like the sun."

"Blinds when looked at, burns when touched?"

"I didn't realize you had a sense of humor, Hall-Warden." Erhensa's gaze refocuses, here and now. "Will Ormodon not punish you for reassembling a golem, your family not shun you for wanting an immigrant spouse?"

"I was authorized to take the manuscript, and my family is ... unconventional." All too happy to accept a powerful sorcerer into their own, foreign or not. "I had no intention of throwing everything away to pursue you."

"How determined are you on cleaving a path to the top?"

Ysoreen never mentioned that. Her skin prickles. Erhensa has read more than just her moods. "I mean to join First Command."

"A long way from Hall-Warden." The islander holds out her hand. "We each know where the other stands, don't we?"

"When I'm First Command – perhaps Tactician Prime – what will you want of me, as a late wedding gift?" Ysoreen takes the hand; finds it as warm as Sumalin might be. Women like the sun.

"Passage to Sumalin. A visit or two. As wife to one of the First Command I'll enjoy certain immunities – but not as the spouse of anyone lesser. You do not know my home, but I will tell you that it does not fear Scre."

"Every nation fears Scre. And when I ascend so high, with you my wife, you'll forfeit your home. You'll be Scre truly, Sumalin no longer."

Erhensa thumbs the warped pearls on her skirt. "I will see the shores of my birth, barred to me otherwise. That will suffice."

Ysoreen purses a kiss over Erhensa's knuckles, their texture to her a rough thrill. "An exchange is all we'll ever have?"

"I cannot promise love. Not immediately. Perhaps never, perhaps slowly, perhaps before the season thaws. I believe that I'll grow fond of you."

"Even though this is how it begins?"

"We begin in honest negotiation. Marriages have been knotted over less, over worse." A smile, to soften what they have, what they don't yet have. "At my age it will not be passion like the monsoons, ardor like the waves."

"Teach me that," Ysoreen says against the skin of her island bride-to-be. "Teach me to master myself, and I'll do anything for you."

"Very well. Let us begin."

Outside, in the summer of Erhensa's power, a golem-daughter lifts her voice in song.

EFFIGY NIGHTS

Yoon Ha Lee

They are connoisseurs of writing in Imulai Mokarengen, the city whose name means *inkblot of the gods*.

The city lies at the galaxy's dust-stranded edge, enfolding a moon that used to be a world, or a world that used to be a moon; no one is certain anymore. In the mornings its skies are radiant with clouds like the plumage of a bird ever-rising, and in the evenings the stars scatter light across skies stitched and unstitched by the comings and goings of fire-winged starships. Its walls are made of metal the color of undyed silk, and its streets bloom with aleatory lights, small solemn symphonies, the occasional duel.

Imulai Mokarengen has been unmolested for over a hundred years. People come to listen to the minstrels and drink tea-of-moments-unraveling, to admire the statues of shape-shifting tigers and their pliant lovers, to look for small maps to great fortunes at the intersections of curving roads. Even the duelists confront each other in fights knotted by ceremony and the exchange of poetry.

But now the starships that hunt each other in the night of nights have set their dragon eyes upon Imulai Mokarengen, desiring to possess its arts, and the city is unmolested no more.

The soldiers came from the sky in a glory of thunder, a cascade of fire. Blood like roses, bullets like thorns, everything to ashes. Imulai Mokarengen's defenses were few, and easily overwhelmed. Most of them would have been museum pieces anywhere else.

The city's wardens gathered to offer the invading general payment in any coin she might desire, so long as she left the city in peace. Accustomed to their decadent visitors, they offered these: Wine pressed from rare books of stratagems and aged in barrels set in orbit around a certain red star. Crystals extracted from the nervous systems of philosopher-beasts that live in colonies upon hollow asteroids. Perfume symphonies infused into exquisite fractal tapestries.

The general was Jaian of the Burning Orb, and she scorned all these things. She was a tall woman clad in armor the color of dead metal. For each world she had scoured, she wore a jewel of black-red facets upon her breastplate. She said to the wardens: What use did she have for wine except to drink to her enemies' defeat? What use was metal except to build engines of war? And as for the perfume, she didn't dignify that with a response.

But, she said, smiling, there was one thing they could offer her, and then she would leave with her soldiers and guns and ships. They could give her all the writings they treasured so much: all the binary crystals gleaming bright-dark, all the books with the bookmarks still in them, all the tilted street signs, all the graffiti chewed by drunken nanomachines into the shining walls, all the tattoos obscene and tender, all the ancestral tablets left at the shrines with their walls of gold and chitin.

The wardens knew then that she was mocking them, and that, as long as any of the general's soldiers breathed, they would know no peace. One warden, however, considered Jaian's words of scorn, and thought that, unwitting, Jaian herself had given them the key to her defeat.

Seran did not remember a time when his othersight of the city did not show it burning, no matter what his ordinary senses told him, or what the dry pages of his history said. In his dreams the smoke made the sky a funeral shroud. In waking, the wind smelled of ash, the buildings of angry flames. Everything in the othersight was wreathed in orange and amber, flickering, shadows cinder-edged.

He carried that pall of phantom flame with him even now, into the warden's secret library, and it made him nervous although the books had nothing to fear from the phantoms. The warden, a woman in dust-colored robes, was escorting him through the maze-of-mists and down the stairs to the library's lowest level. The air was cool and dry, and to either side he could see the candle-sprites watching him hungrily.

"Here we are," the warden said as they reached the bottom of the stairs.

Seran looked around at the parchment and papers and scrolls of silk, then stepped into the room. The tools he carried, bonesaws and forceps and fine curved needles, scalpels that sharpened themselves if fed the oil of certain olives, did not belong in this place. But the warden had insisted that she required a surgeon's expertise.

He risked being tortured or killed by the general's occupation force for cooperating with a warden. In fact, he could have earned himself a tidy sum for turning her in. But Imulai Mokarengen was his home, for all that he had not been born here. He owed it a certain loyalty.

"Why did you bring me here, madam warden?" Seran said.

The warden gestured around the room, then unrolled one of the great charts across the table at the center of the room. It was a stardrive schematic, all angles and curves and careful coils.

Then Seran saw the shape flickering across the schematic, darkening some of the precise lines while others flowed or dimmed. The warden said nothing, leaving him to observe as though she felt he was making a difficult diagnosis. After a while he identified the elusive shape as that of a girl, slight of figure or perhaps merely young, if such a creature counted years in human terms. The shape twisted this way and that, but there were no adjacent maps or diagrams for her to jump to. She left a disordered trail of numbers like bullets in her wake.

"I see her," Seran said dryly. "What do you need me to do about her?"

"Free her," the warden said. "I'm pretty sure this is all of her, although she left a trail while we were perfecting the procedure . . ."

She unrolled another chart, careful to keep it from touching the first. It appeared to be a treatise on musicology, except parts of it had been replaced by a detritus of clefs and twisted staves and demiquavers coalescing into a diagram of a pistol.

"Is this your plan for resistance against the invaders?" Seran said. "Awakening soldiers from scraps of text, then cutting them out? You should have a lot more surgeons. Or perhaps children with scissors."

The warden shrugged. "Imulai Mokarengen is a city of stories. It's not hard to persuade one to come to life in her defense, even though I wouldn't call her *tame*. She is the Saint of Guns summoned from a book of legends. Now you see why I need a surgeon. I am given to believe that your skills are not entirely natural."

This was true enough. He had once been a surgeon-priest of the Order of the Chalice. "If you know that much about me," he said, "then you know that I was cast out of the order. Why haven't you scared up the real thing?"

"Your order is a small one," she said. "I looked, but with the blockade, there's no way to get someone else. It has to be you." When he didn't speak, she went on, "We are outnumbered. The general can send for more soldiers from the worlds of her realm, and they are armed with the latest weaponry. We are a single city known for artistic endeavors, not martial ones. Something has to be done."

Seran said, "You're going to lose your schematic."

"I'm not concerned about its fate."

"All right," he said. "But if you know anything about me, you know that your paper soldiers won't last. I stick to ordinary surgery because the prayers of healing don't work for me anymore; they're cursed by fire." And, because he knew she was thinking it: "The curse touches anyone I teach."

"I'm aware of the limitations," the warden said. "Now, do you require additional tools?"

He considered it. Ordinary scissors might be better suited to paper than the curved ones he carried, but he trusted his own instruments. A scalpel would have to do. But the difficult part would be getting the girl-shape to hold still. "I need water," he said. He had brought a sedative, but he was going to have to sponge the entire schematic, since an injection was unlikely to do the trick.

The warden didn't blink. "Wait here."

As though he had somewhere else to wait. He spent the time attempting to map the girl's oddly flattened anatomy. Fortunately, he wouldn't have to intrude on her internal structures. Her joints showed the normal range of articulation. If he hadn't known better, he would have said she was dancing in the disarrayed ink, or perhaps looking for a fight.

Footsteps sounded in the stairwell. The woman set a large pitcher of water down on the table. "Will this be enough?" she asked.

Seran nodded and took out a vial from his satchel. The dose was pure guesswork, unfortunately. He dumped half the vial's contents into the pitcher, then stirred the water with a glass rod. After putting on gloves, he soaked one of his sponges, then wrung it out.

Working with steady strokes, he soaked the schematic. The paper absorbed the water readily. The warden winced in spite of herself. The girl didn't seem capable of facial expressions, but she dashed to one side of the schematic, then the other, seeking escape. Finally she slumped, her long hair trailing off in disordered tangles of artillery tables.

The warden's silence pricked at Seran's awareness. *She's studying how I do this*, he thought. He selected his most delicate scalpel and began cutting the girl-shape out of the paper. The medium felt alien, without the resistances characteristic of flesh, although water oozed away from the cuts.

He hesitated over the final incision, then completed it, hand absolutely steady.

Amid all the maps and books and scrolls, they heard a girl's slow, drowsy breathing. In place of the paper cutout, the girl curled on the table, clad in black velvet and gunmetal lace. She had paper-pale skin and inkstain hair, and a gun made of shadows rested in her hand.

It was impossible to escape the problem: smoke curled from the girl's other hand, and her nails were blackened.

"I warned you of this," Seran said. Cursed by fire. "She'll burn up, slowly at first, and then all at once. I suspect she'll last a week at most."

"You listen to the news, surely," the warden said. "Do you

know how many of our people the invaders shot the first week of the occupation?"

He knew the number. It was not small. "Anything else?" he said.

"I may have need of you later," the warden said. "If I summon you, will you come? I will pay you the same fee."

"Yes, of course," Seran said. He had noticed her deft hands, however; he imagined she would make use of them soon.

Not long after Seran's task for the warden, the effigy nights began.

He was out after curfew when he saw the Saint of Guns. Imulai Mokarengen's people were bad at curfews. People still broke the general's curfew regularly, although many of them were also caught at it. At every intersection, along every street, you could see people hung up as corpse-lanterns, burning with plague-colored light, as warnings to the populace. Still, the city's people were accustomed to their parties and trysts and sly confrontations. For his part, he was on his way home after an emergency call, and looking forward to a quiet bath.

It didn't surprise him that he should encounter the Saint of Guns, although he wished he hadn't. After all, he had freed her from the boundary of paper and legend to walk in the world. The connection was real, for all that she hadn't been conscious for its forging. Still, the sight of her made him freeze up.

Jaian's soldiers were rounding up a group of merry-goers and poets whose rebellious recitations had been loud enough to be heard from outside. The poets, in particular, were not becoming any less loud, especially when one of them was shot in the head.

The night became the color of gunsmoke little by little, darkness unfolding to make way for the lithe girl-figure. She had a straight-hipped stride, and her eyes were spark-bright, her mouth furiously unsmiling. Her hair was braided and pinned this time. Seran had half-expected her to have a pistol in each hand, but no, there was only the one. He wondered if that had to do with the charred hand.

Most of the poets didn't recognize her, and none of the soldiers. But one of the poets, a chubby woman, tore off her necklace with its glory's worth of void-pearls. They scattered in all directions, purple-iridescent, fragile. "The Saint of Guns," the poet cried. "In the city where words are bullets, in the book where verses are trajectories, who is safe from her?"

Seran couldn't tell whether this was a quotation or something the poet had made up on the spot. He should have ducked around the corner and toward safety, but he found it impossible to look away, even when one of the soldiers knocked the pearl-poet to the street and two others started kicking her in the stomach.

The other soldiers shouted at the Saint of Guns to stand down, to cast away her weapon. She narrowed her eyes at them, not a little contemptuous. She pointed her gun into the air and pulled the trigger. For a second there was no sound.

Then all the soldiers' guns exploded. Seran had a blurry impression of red and star-shaped shrapnel and chalk-white and falling bodies, fire and smoke and screaming. There was a sudden sharp pain across his left cheek where a passing splinter cut it: the Saint's mark.

None of the soldiers had survived. Seran was no stranger to corpses. They didn't horrify him, despite the charred reek and the cooked eyes, the truncated finger that had landed near his foot. But none of the poets had survived, either.

The Saint of Guns lowered her weapon, then saluted him with her other hand. Her fingers were blackened to their bases.

Seran stared at her, wondering what she wanted from him. Her lips moved, but he couldn't hear a thing.

She only shrugged and walked away. The night gradually grew darker as she did.

Only later did Seran learn that the gun of every soldier in that district had exploded at the same time.

Imulai Mokarengen has four great archives, one for each compass point. The greatest of them is the South Archive, with its windows the color of regret and walls where vines trace out spirals like those of particles in cloud chambers. In the South Archive the historians of the city store their chronicles. Each book is written with nightbird quills and ink-of-dedication, and bound with a peculiar thread spun from spent artillery shells. Before it is shelved, one of the city's wardens seals each book shut with a black kiss. The books are not for reading. It is widely held that the historians' objectivity will be compromised if they concern themselves with an audience.

When Jaian of the Burning Orb conquered Imulai Mokarengen, she sent a detachment to secure the South Archive. Although she could have destroyed it in a conflagration of ice and fire and funeral dust, she knew it would serve her purpose better to take the histories hostage.

It didn't take long for the vines to wither, and for the dead brown tendrils to spell out her name in a syllabary of curses, but Jaian, unsuperstitious, only laughed when she heard.

The warden called Seran back, as he had expected she would.

Seran hadn't expected the city to be an easy place to live in during an occupation, but he also hadn't made adequate preparations for the sheer aggravation of sharing it with legends and historical figures.

"Aggravation" was what he called it when he was able to lie to himself about it. It was easy to be clinical about his involvement when he was working with curling sheets, and less so when he saw what the effigies achieved.

The Saint of Guns burned up within a week, as Seran had predicted. The official reports were confused, and the rumors not much better, but he spent an entire night holed up in his study afterward estimating the number of people she had killed, bystanders included. He had bottles of very bad wine for occasions like this. By the time morning came around, he was comprehensively drunk.

Six-and-six years ago, on a faraway station, he had violated his oaths as a surgeon-priest by using his prayers to kill a man. It had not been self-defense, precisely. The man had shot a child. Seran had been too late to save the child, but not too late to damn himself.

It seemed that his punishment hadn't taught him anything. He explained to himself that what he was doing was necessary; that he was helping to free the city of Jaian.

The warden next had him cut out one of the city's founders, Alarra Coldly-Smiling. She left footsteps of frost, and, where she walked, people cracked into pieces, frozen all the way through, needles of ice piercing their intestines. As might be expected, she burned up faster than the Saint of Guns. A pity; she was outside Jaian's increasingly well-defended headquarters when she sublimated.

The third was the Mechanical Soldier, who manifested as a suit of armor inside which lights blinked on-off, on-off, in digital splendor. Seran was buying more wine – you could usually get your hands on some, even during the occupation, if your standards were low – when he heard the clink-clank thunder outside the dim room where the transaction was taking place. The Mechanical Soldier carried a black sword, which proved capable of cutting through metal and crystal and stone. With great precision it carved a window in the wall. The blinking lights brightened as it regarded Seran.

The wine-seller shrieked and dropped one of the bottles, to Seran's dismay. The air was pungent with the wine's sour smell. Seran looked unflinchingly at the helmet, although a certain amount of flinching was undoubtedly called for, and after a while the Mechanical Soldier went away in search of its real target.

It turned out that the Mechanical Soldier liked to carve cartouches into walls, or perhaps its coat-of-arms. Whenever it struck down Jaian's soldiers, lights sparked in the carvings, like sourceless eyes. People began leaving offerings by the carvings: oil-of-massacres, bouquets of crystals with fissures in their shining hearts, cardamom bread. (Why cardamom, Seran wasn't sure. At least the aroma was pleasing.) Jaian's soldiers executed people they caught at these makeshift shrines, but the offerings kept coming.

Seran had laid in a good supply of wine, but after the Mechanical General shuddered apart into pixels and blackened reticulations, there was a maddening period of calm. He waited for the warden's summons.

No summons came.

Jaian's soldiers swaggered through the streets again, convinced that there would be no more apparitions. The city's people whispered to each other that they must have faith. The offerings increased in number.

Finding wine became too difficult, so Seran gave it up. He

was beginning to think that he had dreamed up the whole endeavor when the effigy nights started again.

Imulai Mokarengen suddenly became so crowded with effigies that Seran's othersight of fire and smoke was not much different from reality. He had not known that the city contained so many stories: Women with deadly hands and men who sang atrocity-hymns. Colonial intelligences that wove webs across the pitted buildings and flung disease-sparks at the invaders. A cannon that rose up out of the city's central plaza and roared forth red storms.

But Jaian of the Burning Orb wasn't a fool. She knew that the effigies, for all their destructiveness, burned out eventually. She and her soldiers retreated beneath their force-domes and waited.

Seran resolved to do some research. How did the warden mean to win her war, if she hadn't yet managed it?

By now he had figured out that the effigies would not harm him, although he still had the scar the Saint of Guns had given him. It would have been easy to remove the scar, but he was seized by the belief that the scar was his protection.

He went first to a bookstore in which candles burned and cogs whirred. Each candle had the face of a child. A man with pale eyes sat in an unassuming metal chair, shuffling cards. "I thought you were coming today," he said.

Seran's doubts about fortune-telling clearly showed on his face. The man laughed and fanned out the cards face-up. Every one of them was blank. "I'm sorry to disappoint you," he said, "but they only tell you what you already know."

"I need a book about the Saint of Guns," Seran said. She had been the first. No reason not to start at the beginning.

"That's not a story I know," the man said. His eyes were bemused. "I have a lot of books, if you want to call them that, but they're really empty old journals. People like them for the papers, the bindings. There's nothing written in them."

"I think I have what I came for," Seran said, hiding his alarm. "I'm sorry to trouble you."

He visited every bookstore in the district, and some outside of it, and his eyes ached abominably by the end. It was the same story at all of them. But he knew where he had to go next.

*　　*　　*

Getting into the South Archive meant hiring a thief-errant, whose name was Izeut. Izeut had blinded Seran for the journey, and it was only now, inside one of the reading rooms, that Seran recovered his vision. He suspected he was happier not knowing how they had gotten in. His stomach still felt as though he'd tied it up in knots.

Seran had had no idea what the Archive would look like inside. He had especially not expected the room they had landed in to be welcoming, the kind of place where you could curl up and read a few novels while sipping citron tea. There were couches with pillows, and padded chairs, and the paintings on the walls showed lizards at play.

"All right," Izeut said. His voice was disapproving, but Seran had almost beggared himself paying him, so the disapproval was very faint. "What now?"

"All the books look like they're in place here," Seran said. "I want to make sure there's nothing obviously missing."

"That will take a while," Izeut said. "We'd better get started."

Not all the rooms were welcoming. Seran's least favorite was the one from which sickles hung from the ceiling, their tips gleaming viscously. But all the bookcases were full.

Seran still wasn't satisfied. "I want to look inside a few of the books," he said.

Izeut shot him a startled glance. "The city's traditions—"

"The city's traditions are already dying," Seran said.

"The occupation is temporary," Izeut said stoutly. "We just have to do more to drive out the warlord's people."

Izeut had no idea. "Humor me," Seran said. "Haven't you always wanted to see what's in those books?" Maybe an appeal to curiosity would work better.

Whether it did or not, Izeut stood silently while Seran pulled one of the books off the shelves. He hesitated, then broke the book's seal and felt the warden's black kiss, cold, unsentimental, against his lips. *I'm already cursed,* he thought, and opened the covers.

The first few pages were fine, written in a neat hand with graceful swells. Seran flipped to the middle, however, and his breath caught. The pages were empty except for a faint dust-trace of distorted graphemes and pixellated stick figures.

He could have opened up more books to check, but he had already found his answer.

"Stop," Izeut said sharply. "Let me reshelve that." He took the book from Seran, very tenderly.

"It's no use," Seran said.

Izeut didn't turn around; he was slipping the book into its place. "We can go now."

It was too late. The general's soldiers had caught them.

Seran was separated from Izeut and brought before Jaian of the Burning Orb. She regarded him with cool exasperation. "There were two of you," she said, "but something tells me that you're the one I should worry about."

She kicked the table next to her. All of Seran's surgical tools, which the soldiers had confiscated and laid out in disarray, clattered.

"I have nothing to say to you," Seran said through his teeth.

"Really," Jaian said. "You fancy yourself a patriot, then. We may disagree about the petty legal question of who the owner of this city is, but if you are any kind of healer, you ought to agree with me that these constant spasms of destruction are good for no one."

"You could always leave," Seran said.

She picked up one of his sets of tweezers and clicked it once, twice. "You will not understand this," she said, "and it is even right that you will not understand this, given your profession, but I will try to explain. This is what I do. Worlds are made to be pressed for their wine, cities taste of fruit when I bite them open. I cannot let go of my conquests.

"Do you think I am ignorant of the source of the apparitions that leave their smoking shadows in the streets? You're running out of writings. All I need do is wait, and this city will yield in truth."

"You're right," Seran said. "I don't understand you at all."

Jaian's smile was like knives and nightfall. "I'll write this in a language you do understand, then. You know something about how this is happening, who's doing it. Take me to them or I will start killing your people in earnest. Every hour you make me wait, I'll drop a bomb, or send out tanks, or soldiers with guns. If I get bored I'll get creative."

Seran closed his eyes and made himself breathe evenly. He didn't think she was bluffing. Besides, there was a chance – if only a small chance – that the warden could come up with a defense against the general; that the effigies would come to her aid once the general came within reach.

"All right," he said. "I'll take you where it began."

Seran was bound with chains-of-suffocation, and he thought it likely that there were more soldiers watching him than he could actually spot. He led Jaian to the secret library, to the maze-of-mists.

"A warden," Jaian said. "I knew some of them had escaped."

They went to the staircase and descended slowly, slowly. The candle-sprites flinched from the general. Their light was almost violet, like dusk.

All the way down the stairs they heard the snick-snick of many scissors.

The downstairs room, when they reached it, was filled with paper. Curling scraps and triangles crowded the floor. It was impossible to step anywhere without crushing some. The crumpling sound put Seran in mind of burnt skin.

Come to that, there was something of that smell in the room, too.

All through the room there were scissors snapping at empty space, wielded by no hand but the hands of the air, shining and precise.

At the far end of the room, behind a table piled high with more paper scraps, was the warden. She was standing side-ways, leaning heavily against the table, and her face was averted so that her shoulder-length hair fell around it.

"It's over," Jaian called out. "You may as well surrender. It's folly to let you live, but your death doesn't have to be one of the ugly ones."

Seran frowned. Something was wrong with the way the warden was moving, more like paper fluttering than some-one breathing. But he kept silent. *A trap*, he thought, *let it be a trap*.

Jaian's soldiers attempted to clear a path through the scissors, but the scissors flew to either side and away, avoiding the force-bolts with uncanny grace.

Jaian's long strides took her across the room and around the table. She tipped the warden's face up, forced eye contact. If there had been eyes.

Seran started, felt the chains-of-suffocation clot the breath in his throat. At first he took the marks all over the warden's skin to be tattoos. Then he saw that they were holes cut into the skin, charred black at the edges. Some of the marks were logographs, and alphabet letters, and punctuation stretched wide.

"Stars and fire ascending," Jaian breathed, "what is this?"

Too late she backed away. There was a rustling sound, and the warden unfurled, splitting down the middle with a jagged tearing sound, a great irregular sheet punched full of word-holes, completely hollowed out. Her robe crumpled into fine sediment, revealing the cutout in her back in the shape of a serpent-headed youth.

Jaian made a terrible crackling sound, like paper being ripped out of a book. She took one step back toward Seran, then halted. Holes were forming on her face and hands. The scissors closed in on her.

I did this, Seran thought, *I should have refused the warden.* She must have learned how to call forth effigies on her own, ripping them out of Imulai Mokarengen's histories and sagas and legends, animating the scissors to make her work easier. But when the scissors ran out of paper, they turned on the warden. Having denuded the city of its past, of its weight of stories, they began cutting effigies from the living stories of its people. And now Jaian was one of those stories, too.

Seran left Jaian and her soldiers to their fate and began up the stairs. But some of the scissors had already escaped, and they had left the doors to the library open. They were undoubtedly in the streets right now. Soon the city would be full of holes, and people made of paper slowly burning up, and the hungry sound of scissors.

WEARAWAY AND FLAMBEAU

Matthew Hughes

Raffalon clung to the wall of Hurdevant's keep, the adhesive on his palms holding him tight to the gray stone. Above him, no more than arm's reach above his head, the hinges of the small window creaked again. A moment ago, someone had opened the left-side panel; now it was the right's turn. Logically, the next event would be the poking out of a head. Raffalon would be discovered, if he hadn't been already, and the consequences would not redound to his credit.

Raffalon's profession was the transfer of valuables to his possession without consultation or consent of their owners. He'd been practicing it since boyhood and had become quite good at wall-scaling, lock-tickling, and ward-hoodwinking. He was particularly versed in the art of the rapid exit when circumstances turned adverse.

In order to avoid such exits, he preferred to choose his own targets; but he was not averse to hiring out his hard-won skills to others, so long as they met his fee. And provided that the proposed operation's level of risk fitted the thief's definition of acceptable.

Neither condition applied to the present situation, however. The risk of at least one thing going wrong, he had calculated when informed of the nature of the mission, approached near certainty. Worse, he was about to incur the enmity of Hurdevant, whose reputation for stringency had led his fellow magicians to dub him Ironhand – and he wasn't being paid so much as a bent sequint.

The griptight on Raffalon's left hand was losing its strength. He pulled it free and spat into the palm, reactivating its adhesive power, then pressed it again to the wall. In a few moments, he would need to do the same to the right hand, unless by then he was already being consumed by a blast of flame from the wizard's wand, or carried off by a summoned demon to its smoky lair, there to be used for unspeakable purposes.

A thief's credo is to avoid capture and punishment by any means necessary. But Raffalon had added a corollary to that code: when all is lost, at least go out with a bold face. He now set his features into as intrepid an arrangement as he could manage, and turned his gaze upward. He found himself staring, as expected yet hoped against, into the uncompromising visage of Hurdevant the Stringent.

"And there you are," said the wizard, as if continuing a conversation.

"Indeed," said Raffalon, seeing nothing to be gained by dissembling.

"Come up the rest of the way and through the window. I have disabled the spell that guards it."

Raffalon spat on a hand again and used the griptight to climb another arm's length. "Was it, by any chance, Bullimar's Differentiating Portal?"

Hurdevant snorted. "For a small window set high in a tower? Of course not. It was Pilasquo's Pinch."

"I don't know that one," the thief said, working his way up to the window sill.

The magician explained that, once Raffalon was halfway through the window, its frame would have closed upon his middle, squeezing it so tightly that he would have resembled one of those wasps whose thorax and abdomen are connected by a narrow tube of chitin.

"It won't do that now?" the thief said, one leg over the sill.

"No, now get in here."

Raffalon dropped to the stone floor of the tower. He scowled when he saw that the small, circular room was empty – another element of the operation that the one who had sent him into peril had got wrong.

"What made you think I would use the Bullimar?" Hurdevant was saying. "It's for doors. Especially for hidden trapdoors."

The thief was too disgusted to answer. A moment later, he

realized that Hurdevant was not accustomed to wait for responses to his queries. The soles of his feet became convinced that they were in contact with live coals. Hopping about, though instinctive, brought no relief. "Glabro!" he managed to shout.

The magician made a subtle gesture and the burning stopped. "Glabro Malaprop?" he said, and his grim lips almost achieved a smile. "You're another one of his?"

"Not by choice, I assure you!" Raffalon scuffed the soles of his climbing boots against the stone floor in an attempt to cool his feet. The action had no great effect, but the burning sensation was gradually subsiding of its own accord.

"But Glabro sent you? And told you that the window would be warded by the Bullimar?" The wizard snorted again; Raffalon was beginning to think it was a characteristic action. "Feckless scantbrain," Hurdevant concluded. "What made you give credence to . . ."

But then a suspicion further clouded the grim face. He sketched an invisible figure in the air and Raffalon saw an arrangement of lines of green light, some straight, some curved, come to hover before the magician's eyes. After a moment, the thief realized that he was seeing a schematic of Hurdevant's estate. His captor studied it a while then wiped it away with a wave of one long-nailed finger.

"It occurred to me," the wizard said, "that you might be a diversion. But, no, Glabro does not rise even to that lowly rung on the ladder of cunning." He pulled his nose then stroked its end, apparently as an aid to thought. "I presume you were after the Sphere of Diverse Utility again?"

"I have never been here before," Raffalon.

"I am lumping you in," said the wizard, "with all the other thimblewits and donnydunces Glabro has sent since I won the Sphere from him – quite legitimately – in a contest of skill."

"He seemed to think you had bested him unfairly," Raffalon said.

"Well, that's precisely the problem with the poor dolt: he only seems to think." The wizard clapped his hands to signal that a new chapter was about to open. "Now, what to do with you?"

"May I suggest—"

"You may not." Hurdevant spoke a syllable and moved three fingers in an unusual way. Raffalon's power of speech deserted him. "I sent back the last one inverted, wearing his innards on his outside. It doesn't seem to have made a useful impression."

The captive waggled eyebrows and pointed fingers at his mouth to signal that he had a suggestion. The wizard gave him back control of his tongue and Raffalon said, "Perhaps I could bear him a verbal message? A stern lecture and an unambiguous warning not to test your patience in future?"

"I have," said the wizard, "no patience. If I did have any, I would not waste a scrap of it on Glabro." He thought again then raised both eyebrows and a finger. "Do you know, you present me with an opportunity. I've been experimenting with a synthesis of Ixtlix's Sprightly Wearaway and Chunt's Descending Flambeau."

"I'm not familiar with either," said Raffalon. "I would be delighted to hear about them. Especially from one with such a fine speaking voice."

Hurdevant returned the thief a dry look. "You seek to delay the moment. Also you offer flattery, to which, unfortunately for you, I am immune." He gathered up the skirts of his robe and said, "I will need to refresh my memory. We will go to my library."

He crooked a finger and said an obscure syllable. Immediately, Raffalon's feet followed Hurdevant out of the door. The two men descended a spiral of stone steps to another level of the manse, then wove their way through a maze of corridors until they came to a strongly barred door carved to resemble the face of a fierce creature with inset ivory fangs. It was only when the wizard set his hand to the portal's latch, causing the thing's nose to twitch, that Raffalon realized this was no carving; it was an actual boldruk, enslaved and dragged up from the second plane, compressed into the dimensions of a door. Had the thief approached it without Hurdevant's protection, the fiend would even now be digesting his bones.

Beyond the boldruk was a high-ceilinged room, the walls lined with shelved books of many shapes and sizes, bound in a plethora of materials, from cloth of gold to dragonhide. Some of their spines were lettered in scripts Raffalon could identify only as ancient.

Hurdevant crossed to a high shelf and took down a small libram bound in yellow chamois, then stooped to lift a large folio of parchment sheets clapped between wooden boards. He carried them to a lamplit table and opened both, flicking through pages until he found what he sought. As he set himself to memorizing the words and gestures of power, the lamp dimmed and shadows encroached. Raffalon smelled a sharp tang of ozone and saw the wizard's hair lift slightly from his head while his eyes changed color several times.

"There," said Hurdevant, closing the books. He looked at the captive and rubbed his palms together. "Once both spells are operating, I'll have to send you to Glabro. That means a third cantrip, but I'll just use a simple sending spell. The fluxions should adjust themselves."

The wizard turned to a mirror hanging between two bookcases and touched its frame here, there and a third place. "Now to find out where Glabro is." A moment later, he said, "Ahah, there he is, in his pitiful excuse for a garden."

"What will happen to me?" said Raffalon.

"Ixtlix's Sprightly Wearaway causes you to dance a comical jig until you expire of exhaustion. Chunt's Descending Flambeau consumes you in a brightly burning flame, from the top down. Together, they should make quite a spectacle. And the sight of two spells in combination must remind Glabro that I will always be one too many for the likes of him."

He ordered Raffalon to step away from an armchair upholstered in pale leather – "It was my father's," he said. "Literally. I don't want him scorched." – and mused aloud that the thief had done him a favor by appearing just when he was ready to test the conjoined spell. He had been planning to use a reanimated corpse, but said that their lack of *ardor vita* meant they never burned as hotly as did a living man.

And, as a bonus, the circumstances allowed the wizard to put an elbow in Glabro's eye – an activity in which he delighted.

Raffalon made a last try. "Perhaps, in gratitude for my having done you all these services, we could dispense with the dancing and burning?"

Hurdevant returned him a disparaging look. "But that would negate your contribution. Do you not see the logic?" He rubbed his hands again and said, "First the Sprightly Wearaway, then the Descending Flambeau, then the sending. I'll say goodbye now."

Raffalon made to protest, but the wizard again silenced him. Hurdevant assumed a precise posture then uttered the mantra of the dancing spell, meanwhile raising his arm only to bring it down in a long sweep as he came to the final syllables, two fingers pointing at his target.

The thief experienced a sensation as of tiny bubbles effervescing through his flesh, an unbearable inner tickling. His knees bent and he leaped into the air. No sooner did his feet reconnect with the carpet than he began to execute high kicks and daring saltations, left, right, left, and right again, while his arms alternately flew up over his head then descended so that his palms could smartly smack his buttocks.

The wizard declared the effect to be excellent. Then he gathered himself, took a new stance, and began to intone Chunt's Descending Flambeau. Raffalon could not hear the oral part of the spell over his own heavy breathing and rump-slapping, but the gestural component was impressive. It concluded with a rapid rolling of one wizardly hand over the other and a double snap of thumb and middle fingers. At that point the thief's hair burst into flame.

Instantly, Hurdevant spoke two short words and struck his knuckles together. Just as instantly, Raffalon was no longer in the magician's library. But neither was he in Glabro's garden, surrounded by the other wizard's erotic topiary. Instead, he was . . . nowhere.

Around him, as well as above and below, was a featureless gray void. He turned and twisted – or at least thought he did; without visual referents, he could not be entirely sure – but on all sides there was nothing to see.

It was a moment before the thief realized he was no longer kicking and slapping. Nor, he found when he touched his scalp, was his hair on fire. *Well, that's good news*, he thought, although he would reserve judgment on his overall situation until he had more facts to work with.

He looked again in all directions, then realized that, in this place, direction might be a meaningless term. He tried listening, but heard nothing. Nor was there any scent, and the air had no taste when he extended his tongue.

It was at that point that another realization came: there could be nothing to sniff or taste because there was no air. When he moved a hand from side to side, he felt no breeze stir the hairs on its back. Moreover, it occurred to him that he was not breathing. Nor needed to.

He wondered if he were dead. But his new environment matched none of the several hells and four paradises that had ages ago been identified by astral travelers. Raffalon's knowledge of the nine planes – two below his own, and six above – was not extensive, but he was sure that none of them consisted of undifferentiated noneness.

Wherever he was, he was better off than he would have been had Hurdevant succeeded in sending him, cavorting and blazing, among Glabro's artfully pruned bushes and shrubs – probably igniting a few before he expired. But, having acknowledged that fact, he saw no need to settle for it.

What I need, he told himself, *is to get out of here and into somewhere that's an improvement.* At that thought, his mind conjured up an image of a tavern he favored when he was in funds – the Badge and Buckle, it was called – where the ale was never frowsty and the barmaids were liberal in all the ways that mattered.

As he contemplated the mental picture of the place it occurred to him that he was seeing a simulation that was a good deal sharper and more detailed than his imagination could usually achieve.

I'm not imagining it, he realized, *I'm seeing it.* The how and why of it completely eluded him, but Raffalon was more given to practicalities than theoretical constructs. If he could see it, perhaps he could get to it.

He reached out, but the picture – if it was a picture – was beyond his grasp. He tried to stride toward it, but his legs moved without moving him. He swept his arms before him as if he were stroking through water, but there was nothing to push against, and he made no progress.

Frustrated, he hung in the emptiness. But a thief's mind, though not as subtle and capacious as a wizard's, is not without the ability to make connections. *I thought of the Badge and Buckle, and there it was. What if I think of moving toward it?*

He did. And did.

Now it was as if he were just outside the tavern's tap room, which was at the moment mostly empty. Raffalon had chosen mid-afternoon as the optimum time to invade Hurdevant's tower, reasoning that the wizard might well be occupied in his workroom, distracted by wizardly endeavors. That was less than an hour ago, and the tavern had not yet attracted the usual supper crowd, many of whom would stay on to become the usual all-night-carousal crowd.

He examined the scene: a couple of grim-and-bitter drinkers, nursing their tankards and grievances through the day; a dust-smeared traveler making a meal out of whatever was left over from the lunch menu; Boudin the barman, busy behind his counter with preparations for the evening rush; and Undula, the older of the two barmaids, cleaning off a table in the far corner.

He reached out and his hand encountered its first resistance since he had popped into this nonplace. It felt like a wall; but when he pressed, it seemed to give a little, like the side of a tent stretched taut between poles and pegs.

I thought of the Badge and Buckle, and there it was, Raffalon said in his mind. *I wanted to move toward it and I did. What if I now will myself to be there?*

His first thought was to seek to burst the membrane that separated him from the tavern. But before he could concentrate on doing so, some part of his mind warned that, once broken, such a barrier might not be reparable. And who knew what might then ensue? Perhaps the tavern, the town, the realm, and all the worlds beyond might pour through into the emptiness. That couldn't be a good result.

Instead, he focused on the tap room, then on him in it. As the thought crystallized, he felt a tingle along the front of his body, a sensation that then passed all the way through him to exit from his back and buttocks. And when it had passed, he was standing in the Badge and Buckle.

Only the traveler had noticed his sudden appearance, and the man quickly averted his eyes as sensible strangers do when confronted by events that are none of their business. Boudin looked up from a stack of glasses and said, "Raffalon! What'll it be?"

"Something strong," said the thief, seating himself at an empty table, his back, as always, to the wall. "I have some thinking to do."

Raffalon was a thoroughly schooled thief, having served a full apprenticeship under Gronn the Shifter and being then duly accepted into the Ancient and Honorable Guild of Purloiners and Purveyors. He had since added twelve years' experience to his training and was thus well versed in the complexities of his art. But when an opportunity presented itself, he did not disdain to ply the simple technique of in-out-and-away. It was his grasping of such an opportunity that led him to become the unwilling servant of a minor magician who called himself "Glabro the Supernal", but who was more widely known by the sobriquet Hurdevant had used: Malaprop.

The thief had been walking the back alleys, looking for possibilities, when he happened to pass Glabro's house. He saw that the small door to the rear courtyard was half-open. On the tiles just within lay a bulging satchel. Next to it, propped against the door jamb, was a staff of the kind foot-travelers use. The picture was clear: someone had been about to depart on a journey, but remembering at the last moment something left behind, had stepped back into the house, leaving staff and luggage at the gate.

Raffalon stopped, looked both ways along the alley, then into the courtyard. Both were empty. He stooped and opened the satchel, rummaged within. His fingers touched a dense, smooth object even as his eye caught the gleam of gold. He seized the prize and stood up to depart.

Or such was his intent. What actually happened was that the golden thing refused to budge from its hiding place. Reasoning that it must be far heavier, and thus even more valuable, than he had supposed, the thief applied both hands to the task. But still, he could not lift the thing.

Frowning, he bent his legs – Gronn had always taught that a sprung back was the reward of an unthinking burglar – and sought to take a better grip. That was when he discovered that he could not remove his hands from the prize. He was still squatting and tugging fruitlessly when Glabro glided smoothly out of the rear door of his house, pointed a black rod at him and said something that made Raffalon's world go dark.

He awoke to find himself in the wizard's workroom, his hands no longer stuck to the bait, but his limbs stapled to the stone wall by iron brackets. His trousers were down around his knees and the wizard was fastening something about those parts of himself that Raffalon – indeed all sensible men – most carefully guard from sudden impacts.

Glabro straightened, saw that his captive was fully with him again, and said, "Jhezzik, a brief half-squeeze."

Instantly, Raffalon knew a pain the like of which he had never encountered before, and which he was certain he never wanted to encounter again.

"I see I have your attention," the wizard said.

"Every jot," the thief assured him.

"Excellent. Then here's what you will do for me." In a few short sentences, he explained that the thief would go to the manse of Hurdevant and gain entrance to the tallest tower, in whose topmost room he would find an object called the Sphere of Diverse Utility – he showed an image – which Hurdevant had unjustly wrested from its rightful owner, Glabro.

To ensure that the thief undertook the mission without delay, the sprite known as Jhezzik would accompany him there and back again. "Although it will not go in with you," Glabro said. "Hurdevant's grinnet would sniff it out right away and come rushing to seize it – which would be as unpleasant for you as for Jhezzik. So it will see you there then wait for you to emerge with the Sphere. And, of course, accompany you back here."

Raffalon began to protest on several counts: Hurdevant's defenses were unbreachable; he was known to be unremittingly watchful; the Guild had a mutual non-interference agreement with the Ancient and Worthy Council of Wizards and Thaumaturges. He got no further before Glabro bade Jhezzik intervene.

"As for the defenses, he uses Bullimar's Differentiating Portal. I will teach you a counter-word to nullify it. You will go just after lunch, when he putters in his workroom. None will know of it, save you and I." When Raffalon attempted a fresh argument, he added, "And, of course, Jhezzik."

Thus did Raffalon find himself clinging to the wall of Hurdevant's tower when the wizard opened his window. Which led to his unexpected passage through the gray noneness. Which had delivered him to the Badge and Buckle, where he now sat, sipping a second beaker of strong arrack, his thinking done and his plan set.

He called to Boudin behind the bar. "Is that boy about, the one who washes pots? I have an errand for him."

Shortly after, for the promise of a coin, the lad raced off toward Glabro's house, a sealed note in his pocket.

The thief was still nursing his second arrack when Glabro entered the tap room. The wizard gave the place a suspicious eye, but seeing nothing to threaten him, he advanced to sit at Raffalon's table. He peered at the man opposite from a number of angles before saying, "Why are you intact?"

"Instead of inside-out, like your last operative?"

"Hurdevant told you that?"

"We had," said the thief, "a brief conversation."

"And then?"

Raffalon sipped his arrack. "Is it possible, do you think, to combine two major spells?"

Glabro's greasy brow contracted. "Unlikely, but it is far from my area of interest."

"How about two major spells plus a third to transport their target to your workroom?"

The wizard's head drew back and his chin tucked itself into his neck. "Impossible!"

"Specifically, Ixtlix's Sprightly Wearaway and Chunt's Descending Flambeau. I don't know the name of the transporter but it involves two syllables and a gesture like this." He struck his knuckles against each other.

"Ridiculous!" said Glabro. "The fluxions are inharmonious. No synergism of—"

"He did it," Raffalon cut him off. He described the kicking, slapping, hair-igniting, vanishing.

"My topiary!" Glabro cried. But then he caught up with what Raffalon had been telling him. "But you did not appear before me!"

"Exactly!"

The wizard had the look of a man who realizes he has missed a clue. "So . . ." he began.

"Tell me," said the thief, "how many planes are there?"

"Wait," said the magician, "we were discussing what happened to you."

"We still are. How many?"

Glabro shrugged. "Nine."

"And does any one of the nine include a formless, featureless void? With neither up nor down nor sideways?"

The wizard's face expressed irritation. "No. Now what about—"

"A void from which one can see any place and go there simply by an act of will?"

"Never mind all th—" This time it was Glabro who interrupted himself. "Wait a moment, you're saying that you were in such a nonplace?"

Raffalon raised his beaker in an ironic toast. "Now you have it."

Later that evening, they were in Glabro's workroom. Raffalon paced nervously as the wizard stood at his lectern, before him a yellow-bound book of the same edition that Hurdevant possessed plus a handwritten parchment scroll, partly unrolled and held down by bric-a-brac.

They had agreed that there had to be a test. And the thief was the only choice for its subject. He had, after all, shown that he could go and return; besides, only Glabro had the wizardly wherewithal to cast the three spells. But now that the moment approached, Raffalon's enthusiasm began to wane.

Glabro looked up. "Ready," he announced. An odor of ozone pervaded the room, but the wizard's eyes were not changing color as Hurdevant's had – instead they alternately bulged and subsided, apparently in rhythm with the man's pulse. The effect was not an attractive sight, the thief thought.

He stood in a clear space where bidden by the other. Glabro took a moment to steady himself, then spoke the words of the jig spell – meaningless to Raffalon – and brought his hand down in the same sweep, ending with the finger-pointing. The high kicks and rump-slapping began. Moments later, what remained of the thief's hair ignited.

Now should come the cantrip that would send Raffalon on his way. They had agreed, in case events did not go as planned, that the third spell should move him no farther than to another clear space on the other side of the room. Glabro could then extinguish the blaze before it could consume him.

But as the fire burnt almost to the roots of the test subject's hair, the wizard went pale and rocked a little unsteadily. Casting two powerful spells in rapid succession had taken much out of him. He had to put a hand on the bench to steady himself, take a deep breath and blow it out.

Meanwhile, the thief capered and burned. The skin on top of his head was becoming uncomfortably warm. Finally, Glabro recollected himself. He uttered two syllables and struck his knuckles together. Instantly, Raffalon was adrift in the void, his limbs still and his scalp tender but unseared.

He rallied his faculties and conjured up an image of the wizard's workroom. As before, a clear view of the place appeared before his eyes. He could see Glabro coming from behind the lectern to examine the spot where he had just been, peering at the air and floor through a hollow tube of brass.

Raffalon willed himself to approach the scene. The image grew larger. Arrayed on the workbench were three objects: a plain wooden cup, a gold candlestick, and a fist-sized, purple crystal. The thief concentrated on the trio, drawing himself closer to them until they were within arm's reach. He put out a hand and again felt resistance, as if a taut membrane separated him from the experimental targets.

Now he left his arm outstretched, just short of the barrier, and willed the limb to pass through it. He had no sense of motion, but felt the same tingling as before, starting at his fingertips and moving at a moderate pace up his arm. But by the time the sensation had reached his elbow, his hand had closed around the cup. Now he willed arm and hand to withdraw from the wizard's workroom. A moment later, he floated in the noneness, and when he opened his hand, a wooden cup hung beside him.

Back in the workroom, he could see Glabro, eyes abulge, staring at the spot where the cup had been. Raffalon readied himself again and repeated the exercise, this time retrieving the heavy metal candlestick. Soon, it too floated beside him in the grayness. He noticed, before he let go of it, that here it had no weight at all.

Then he went for the faceted crystal and drew it smoothly to him. This was a crucial part of the experiment, because it was a receptacle for the storage of arcane power – not a great deal of mana, but neither was it purely mundane – and both thief and wizard were anxious to know if such could pass through the barrier.

It did so without hindrance, Glabro observing with his tube to his eye – then watching again as Raffalon reversed the process, restoring cup, candlestick, and crystal to the bench, before willing himself through the membrane and back into the workroom.

The wizard comprehensively examined the test objects then the man who had moved them. He pronounced them unaffected by any measure he could take. The crystal, when properly handled, delivered a flow of colorful energy that the magician captured as a liquid and poured into an alembic.

"Perfect," he said, holding up the vessel and making the stuff swirl. "Completely unaffected."

"I will rest a little while," said Raffalon, "then you can try the spell that regrows hair. After that, we will make our first foray."

Glabro had placed the Sphere of Diverse Utility on a plinth in his study. It was no longer his most prized possession, but it still deserved pride of place among the wealth of thaumaturgical artifacts that adorned his shelves and lurked within the drawers of his cabinets. His overstocked library would have been the envy of any wizard in the Three Lands – if, that is, he had ever invited a colleague to peruse his collection; but he never would, because any of them would soon discover volumes that had gone missing, under circumstances so mysterious as to be baffling, from their own.

A conclave had been called, at the estate of Yssanek the Paragon, to discuss the scourge of disappearances. The attendees had eyed each other with suspicion, and veiled accusations had been whispered when allies put their heads together. Familiars and gate-guardians had been summoned and grilled – in one case, literally – but all inquiries had led to indefinite conclusions.

Glabro had attended the assembly, but no one had deigned to seek his opinion or invite him to join any cabals. He went home wrapped in secret smiles.

For his part, Raffalon was storing up treasures of a more worldly sort. The wizard paid him in coins, weighty ingots, and sacks of gems. And in that regard Glabro was unstinting, his acquisitions having given him the means to whip up chestfuls of precious goods on demand. The thief bought a small house with strong walls and doors and built an even stronger room in its basement, where he stored his earnings, safe from his fellow Guild members.

He and the wizard had established a "system without a system", as Raffalon put it. They made their strikes at different times of day and night, and never at regular intervals. They chose their victims and their targets randomly, so that no pattern would allow their prey to predict their next raid.

Sometimes the thief would watch from the void as snares and ambushes were prepared for him, then will into being a portal to some other part of the target's manse, where he would stage a noisy diversion. When the defenders rushed there to respond, he would return to his original view of the trap, delicately extract the bait, and be gone before the alarm could be raised.

It was a happy time for the partners. Glabro found that he was perfectly suited to the life of a secret gloater. Raffalon was considering early retirement, perhaps to open an academy to train the next generation of purloiners.

They had agreed to a long hiatus before their next outing, but Raffalon came to the wizard's manse a week before to discuss the intended target – the curio collection of Firondel the Incomparable – and plan a reconnaissance. They made themselves at ease in Glabro's study, where the wizard conjured up a flask of the golden wine of sunny Abrizonth, though that fair land had drowned beneath the invading waters of the Stygmatic Sea 10,000 years before.

The magician sipped from his long-stemmed glass and indicated a well-worn tome that lay open on his table. "I have been researching the phenomenon that is enriching us," he said. "And I have found something of interest."

"Will it put more gold in my strongroom?" said Raffalon. And when the answer was in the negative, he shrugged and drained his glass, then held it out for a refill.

"At first," said the wizard, "I thought we had discovered a tenth plane – such a thing is theoretically possible – but one which the Demiurge left unfilled when he assembled the universe."

Raffalon made a noncommittal noise and looked out the window.

"But then I came upon this" – he indicated the old book – "that we got from the highest shelf of Zanzan's library."

"While he rushed off to see who was trifling with his menagerie of fanciful beasts," said the thief, adding a short, dry laugh.

"I had to summon up a ghost from Old Edevan to help me translate the script."

"Old Edevan?"

"Fourteenth Aeon."

"Never heard of it."

Glabro showed mild irritation at the interruptions to his flow. Raffalon noticed but offered no apology. "In any case," the wizard went on, "it's a record of how the present version of the universe was—"

"There have been others?" Raffalon was not interested in the answer. He liked to goad the magician occasionally; he had not forgotten the touch of Jhezzik.

"Several. Now let me finish. This is interesting."

The thief waved his hand in a somewhat regal manner. "Pray proceed."

"The nub of it is that, for convenience's sake, the Demiurge first built himself a workshop."

"Sensible."

"It was a setting that enhanced his axial volition, which of course was already vast."

Raffalon swallowed the mouthful of Abrizonth he'd been swishing about his teeth. "What's axial volition?"

"The technical term for what you would call 'will'. It's what the universe runs on. If you have enough of it, you can become a wizard. If you don't, it doesn't matter how much studying you put in, your spells will always dissipate like a fart in a fresh breeze."

"Really," said Raffalon, holding out his glass. "A little more, I think."

Glabro handed him the flask and the thief poured for himself. "The thing is," the wizard went on, with enthusiasm, "he seems to have left the workshop still standing after the work was finished."

The thief shrugged. "Perhaps he kept it in case he needed to modify things later."

"I suppose," said the magician. "He might decide to adjust the gravitational constant or add some more colors to the spectrum." He paused to pursue the thought on his own.

"So what about Firondel's curios?" said Raffalon. The flask was now empty, and in a moment, so was his glass.

"If I've got this right," Glabro said, "that thing you call a void is actually the primal chaos from which everything was made."

Raffalon shook his head. "Chaos is busy-busy, everything higgled and piggled together. The void is nothingness."

"No," said the wizard, "chaos is the seeming nothingness from which the four elements of creation – matter, energy, spirit, and gist – are generated."

"Something from nothing?" said the thief, feeling a stir of interest. "By axial whatsit?"

"Exactly." Glabro consulted the tome. "And it may still be workable."

Raffalon sat up straighter. When his brain was engaged, it was capable of cutting through fog straight to wherever profit might be found. "Are you saying that, in the void, an act of will creates something from nothing?"

"I suppose I am."

"What kind of something?"

"Any kind."

"And how much of it?"

"That would depend on the strength of the axial volition. The Demiurge's was powerful enough to generate an entire universe."

Raffalon was thinking now. His will had been powerful enough to show him any place he thought of, and to let him penetrate the barrier between chaos and creation. "Hmm," he said.

"Of course," Glabro was saying, "there might be repercussions . . ."

But the thief was not listening now, though he did say, "Hmm," one more time.

Raffalon hung in the void. Before him, seen as if through a window, was the tabletop on which Firondel the Incomparable kept his remarkable collection: a small cube of immortal flesh said to have been cut from the heart of an incarnate deity; a sextet of ivory figurines that, when brought into proximity with each other, performed simplified versions of a hundred classic dramas; the curved horn of a beast long thought to be mythical; a lens that permitted views of the fifth plane, adjusted to make them comprehensible to third-plane eyes; a thunder-stone found in the belly of a great fish; and several other singular items.

The thief examined the surroundings for traps and defenses. And found one: above the table, concealed by a masking spell, hung a mechanical spider equipped with injector-fangs loaded with a powerful soporific, poised to fall upon any hand that reached for one of the small treasures. But Raffalon had learned that, when viewed from his present vantage, objects or persons supposedly screened by magic were nakedly visible to him.

Having surveyed the scene, as a good thief should, Raffalon now opted to pause before continuing the operation. Since his discussion with Glabro, he had been thinking about what the wizard had revealed concerning the effects of will exercised in the Demiurge's workshop. He now held out one hand in the void, and willed that something should appear in its cupped palm. Nothing happened. He concentrated. For a moment, nothing changed. Then he felt what he could only describe as a ripple pass through the void around him, and through his own being. He felt the sensation go down his arm and exit through his outstretched hand. And when it was gone, in his palm lay a pea-sized globe of purest gold.

Ah, said the thief, and *so*. He tucked the bauble into an inner pocket of his upper garment then repeated the exercise, this time concentrating on a jewel. Again, the ripple passed through him, and when it left his fingers he saw that he held what poets call a gem of purest ray serene, and thieves a nice bit of sparkle.

He put the jewel with the gold pea. The experiment was concluded. Next time, he would make preparations: first he must expand his strongroom to several times its size, so that it could hold all the abundance he intended to will into creation and pass through the membrane. No, better yet, he should buy himself a manse.

But first he had to complete the lifting of Firondel's curios. He adjusted his point of view so that he was now seeing the mechanical spider from above. His eye traced the pattern engraved on its gold-chased back then his hand reached through the barrier and turned its activating screw from energetic to inert. The threat of the spider thus neutralized, he repositioned himself again so that the membrane was just above the tallest item on the tabletop.

The thief had become so skilled at working from the void that he could will the intervening membrane to be mere inches from whatever prize he had come to collect. To anyone observing from the third plane, all that could be seen of Raffalon was his fingers and a portion of the back of his hand – and then only for the moment it took to appear and seize the item.

He reached for the thunderstone, drew it into the void, and popped it into a satchel suspended by a strap from his shoulder. Next he picked up a silver flute known to have been played by the siren Illisandra. Into the satchel it went. Then, one by one, the six thespian figurines.

Methodically, he stole Firondel's treasures. The second-last was the cube of deathless god's heart. But as he reached for it, it moved away of its own accord, crossing most of the tabletop to stop at the farther edge. Raffalon, lulled into a routine, did not think to withdraw his fingers, reposition himself, and try again from closer up. Instead, he merely extended his arm through the barrier until his fingers closed on the wandering morsel of meat.

But when he picked it up, he felt resistance. The cube was on the end of a string that had been used to lure him. Immediately, he dropped it, but immediately was not fast enough. Even as the fragment of godstuff was falling back to the table, a steel manacle was closing around Raffalon's wrist with a fateful *snick*.

He pulled, but the only effect was to make taut a strong chain that connected the ring around his limb to another bracelet – and this one was around the wrist of the man now coming out from under the table: Hurdevant Ironhand, his grim features set into an image of triumphant vengeance.

The wizard pulled, but his strength could have no effect on a man anchored in the Demiurge's workshop, although the steel slid down on to Raffalon's exposed hand and compressed the bones and sinews, causing him pain. Now Hurdevant was moving his free hand in a complicated pattern and speaking a string of syllables – but again to no effect; magic could not trouble the membrane.

That left only one option. If the robber could not be pulled into the world, the wizard must go to where he hid. Hurdevant seized Raffalon's hand and thrust it back toward the barrier.

This suited the thief, whose quick mind had already assessed the situation. Hurdevant no doubt thought that his thaumaturgical arts would serve him well once he had his adversary cornered. But magic had no effect in the void. It was a place where only will mattered.

Hurdevant, as a wizard in his prime, would be equipped with willpower well beyond the ordinary. Raffalon had no illusions that he could match him. But the thief knew the ground, and the magician did not. While Hurdevant was learning that magic was of no avail, Raffalon would be willing a last unpleasant surprise for the man on the other end of the chain.

He focused his will, and the wizard came through the barrier. The thief saw two surprises register on the other man's face: first, at the nature of their surroundings; second, when he recognized Raffalon.

"You!" he said. And now that look of savored revenge was coming back. The wizard lifted his free hand, crooked its fingers in a certain manner, and began to utter a spell.

But Raffalon was already at work. He willed a pair of adamantine shears to appear in his unfettered hand. In an instant, they were there – *I'm getting better at this*, he thought – and a moment later the chain was severed.

He let the shears float and saw that Hurdevant had already digested the meaning of his spell's failure. Now the wizard reached into his robe and came out with a springer, which he deftly cocked with a practiced motion. Raffalon had no doubt that the barbed tip of the missile in the weapon's slot would be coated with poison.

There was nowhere to flee and no time to create an exit; it always took several heartbeats to pass through the membrane, and Hurdevant's dart would make sure that one of those beats would be Raffalon's last. He needed to will something into existence that would change the dynamic of impending events. And he needed to do it now, as Hurdevant raised the springer and aimed it at his belly.

As a boy, Raffalon had been entranced by tales of adventure and derring-do, in which stout-hearted individuals faced down terrors and won through to rewards of great renown. One of those tales had featured a monster that had so frightened the young lad that it came to him several times afterwards in night-mares. The shaggy, brutal creature of some storymaker's imagination remained Raffalon's private definition of the worst thing that could happen.

On impulse, he willed it now into existence, just behind Hurdevant. Thus, as the wizard's finger tightened on the springer's release, a thick, muscular limb, clad in matted gray fur and ending in a paw tipped by two claws like black crescent moons, slid around his waist. The weapon dropped from the wizard's grasp as he was hoisted backwards and upwards – the monster was oversized – and delivered to its serrated fangs.

The thing ate the wizard in two bites. Then its yellow eyes fell upon Raffalon, and the thief remembered that, in the story, the creature's appetite was insatiable – and that, in his worst dreams, it pursued him wherever he fled.

He willed it to disappear – to no effect; perhaps the Demiurge had another workshop for destruction – and so he willed instead the existence of a portal through which he could exit the void and find help.

Only one such place came to mind: Glabro's workroom. As Raffalon appeared out of the air, the wizard looked up from the book he'd been reading and said, "How did it—"

"Coming behind me!" the thief shouted. "Destroy it!"

Then his feet hit the carpet and he ran for the door, seizing the latch and yanking it hard. Behind him, he heard Glabro say, "What's—" and then a sharp intake of breath as the nightmare willed itself through the membrane in pursuit of its next meal.

Unfortunately for Glabro, he was not much talented in the art of wizardly improvisation. While he was assembling a spell in the forefront of his mind, the monster swept aside his study table and sank its cruel claws into his middle. Raffalon, at the other end of the corridor and fleeing down the steps at his best pace, heard the scream and then the sounds of crunching bones.

By the time he reached the bottom of the steps and opened the door into the wizard's back courtyard, he could hear the beast's slobbering vocalizations descending the stairs. He flung wide the gate and bolted into the alley, slamming it shut behind him. Moments later, he heard the *skreek* of its hinges being torn from their posts. He put on more speed. Raffalon had often been pursued – desperate chases were part of being a thief – but never had he run with such conviction.

Glabro's manse was on the crest of a hill that ran down to the city gate and the road to Carbingdon. The thief sped along the cobblestones, leaping down the occasional flights of marble steps, until he came to where the road debouched into a small square. Here customs inspectors examined incoming wagons and mule trains and the watch apprehended ne'er-do-wells. There were always men with weapons about.

As he entered the square, he need not look back; he could hear the ogre's claws clicking on the stones behind him; it was closing on him. He saw the halberdiers clustered near the gate, their faces turning toward him in surprise as he raced toward them, shouting, "A monster! A monster!"

Then he saw their expressions change as the beast came into view. Raffalon had never cared for guards of any kind – their interests and those of thieves were almost always opposed – but he vowed to give a warm thought to these men as they charged their weapons and formed a resolute line – through which he passed by scrambling between their legs on hands and knees.

The halberdiers slowed the nightmare. It reared up on its hindlegs and swatted at their points, roaring and slobbering. Raffalon ran on through the gate, then paused long enough to look back. He saw a team of cannoneers reversing one of the great guns that stood behind the crenellations and depressing it to aim down into the square.

He had not gone another ten paces before he heard the boom of the weapon followed instantly by the crack of its missile exploding. After that, he heard no more roars – only a hubbub of voices as the crowd formed. Raffalon kept going; the incident of the ogre would attract inconvenient questions. He walked some miles out of the city, to where an inn stood at a crossroads, and used his gold pea to buy himself supper and a bed.

In the morning, he walked back to the city, but avoided the gate. Using an entry route and methods known to the Guild, he made his way to the house where he kept his strongroom. He watched from concealment for most of the morning, but saw no signs that the house had become of interest to anyone other than himself.

Finally, he sauntered up the walk. While he was getting out his key, he noted that the almost invisible hair he had pasted across the crack between door and jamb was still in place. He went in and found no trace of an intruder.

Whistling, he hoisted the sack that contained Firondel's curios and descended the hidden passage to his strongroom. He opened the great door and stepped within – to find that the space was empty. Worse, he was plunged into sudden darkness and surrounded by a roaring wind. When the noise stopped and light returned, he was in a place he had only seen from the outside: the headquarters of the Ancient and Worthy Council of Wizards and Thaumaturges.

He looked about him at the figures seated on the tiers of benches and saw no friendly faces. The questions began, and the inducements to give satisfactory answers.

Raffalon stuck to a plausible story: Glabro, resentful of Hurdevant in particular and generally jealous of his worthier colleagues, had planned the entire exercise. The thief had been a mere hireling, and knew nothing of the spells the wizard had woven to defeat their wards and defenses. He did not mention the Demiurge or his workshop.

In the end, if he was not totally believed, he was not totally disbelieved. "What shall we do with him?" said Zhazh Optimus, the current chair of the Council, when the wizards understood that they had gained all the satisfaction they were likely to achieve. Several suggestions were advanced, while Raffalon trembled. After a few moments, he interrupted the argument.

"Whatever you do to me," he said, "please don't let it be what Glabro threatened me with if I did not perform."

Zhazh eyed the thief the way a bird eyes a worm. "And what would that be?" he said.

Raffalon recited, as if by rote, "Ixtlix's Sprightly Wearaway, Chunt's Descending Flambeau, and a spell that would send me into the desert."

"All three together?" said a spectrally thin thaumaturge. "It would never work. No harmony of fluxions."

The thief made a gesture expressing his inability to judge the matter. "I only know what he told me," he said. "He'd done it to someone once. It sounded awful."

"Hmm," said Zhazh. He went to one of the bookcases in the Council chamber and ran his finger along the serried spines, looking for a particular volume. "Hurdevant had a theory about synthesis." He found the tome he was seeking and opened it. "And if Glabro could do it . . ."

He paused, a finger halfway down a page, and smiled a wizard's cruel smile. "Ixtlix's Sprightly Wearaway, Chunt's Descending Flambeau, and a sending spell, you say?"

"Oh, no!" cried Raffalon. "Not that! Anything but that!"

AT THE EDGE OF DYING

Mary Robinette Kowal

Kahe peeked over the edge of the earthen trench as his tribe's retreating warriors broke from the bamboo grove on to the lava field. The tribesmen showed every sign of panicked flight in front of the advancing Ouvallese. Spears and shields dropped to the ground as they tucked in their arms and ran.

And the Ouvallese, arrogant with their exotic horses and metal armor, believed what they saw and chased the warriors toward him. The timing on this would be close. Kahe gathered the spell in his mind and double-checked the garrote around his neck. His wife stood behind him, the ends resting lightly in her hands. "Do it."

Bless her, Mehahui did not hesitate. She hauled back, cutting into his throat with the knotted cord. Kahe tried not to struggle as his breath was cut off. Black dots swirled in his vision, but he could not afford to faint yet.

With each breath he could not take, with each step closer to death, Kahe's power grew. As the tribe's warriors reached the trench and leaped down, he scanned the lava field to make certain none was left behind. Vision fading, he unleashed the spell coiled inside him.

The heat from the firestorm singed the air as it swept out from his trench. Even through his graying sight, the blue flame burned like the sun as it raced toward the Ouvallese battalion. Screams rose like prayer as his spell crisped the men in their armor.

As soon as the spell rolled out, Mehahui released her hold and Kahe fell against the damp red soil. The grains of dirt blended with the dots dancing in front of his eyes, so the very earth seemed to move. Air scraped across his tortured throat as life flooded into him. He gasped as the goddess's gift of power faded.

Beyond his own wrenching sobs, Kahe heard the agonized screams of those Ouvallese too distant to be instantly immolated. He prayed to Hia that his spell had gotten most of them; the goddess of death and magic had rarely failed him. Still, the kings of the tribes would have to send runners out to deal with the burned soldiers; a dying enemy was too dangerous to allow to linger.

Mehahui patted him, soft as a duckling, on the back. Her round face hovered in the edge of his vision. "Stay with me."

Kahe coughed when he tried to speak. "I am." His throat scraped as if it were filled with thorns. He knew she hated seeing him downed by a spell, but flirting with Hia was the only way to get the power he needed for a spell this big. Pushing against the earth wall, Kahe sat up.

His head swam. The dirt thrummed under his hands.

The vibration grew to a roar and the earth bucked. A wall collapsed. Dirt spilled into the trench, as the earth quaked.

No. A sorcerer must have been at the edge of his firestorm and, by almost killing him, Kahe had given him access to Hia's power – only a dying man would have enough power to work magic on the earth itself. As the trench shifted and filled with falling rocks, the spell he needed to counter it sprang to his mind but without power. He turned to Mehahui even while knowing there wasn't enough time for the garrote to work. He fumbled for the knife at his side.

The tremors stopped.

Dust settled in the suddenly still air but he had not cast the counter-spell. Even if he had, it would have been as a rush lamp beside a bonfire.

Around them, men in the earthworks called to each other for aid or reassurance. Trickles of new dirt slid down the wall in miniature red avalanches. King Enahu scrambled over a mound, using his long spear as a walking staff.

"Hia's left tit! You're still alive." He slid down the side of the trench, red dirt smearing his legs with an illusion of blood. "When you stopped the earthquake, I didn't think you could have survived the spell. Not so soon after working the other."

"I didn't stop it." Kahe watched Mehahui instead of the king. Her skin had bleached like driftwood and she would not meet his eyes.

Beside him, King Enahu inhaled sharply, understanding what Kahe meant. "There's another sorcerer in the ranks? Hia, Pikeo, and the Mother! This could be the saving of us. Who?"

Mehahui hung her head, her hair falling around her face like rain at night. "It's me."

Kahe's heart stuttered, as if he had taken makiroot poison for a spell. Hia only gave her power to those on the road to death. "That's not possible."

"I'm dying, Kahe." His beautiful wife lifted her head and Kahe could not understand how he had missed the dark circles under her eyes.

With only a thin blanket covering her, every breeze in the hut chilled Mehahui. She shivered and kept her attention focused on the thatched pili-leaf ceiling while the surgeon poked at her.

Iokua stepped back from the table. "Why didn't you come to me sooner?" he asked.

Clinging to the blanket, Mehahui sat up. "Could you have done anything?"

"I could have tried."

They had studied under the same masters at the Paheni Academy of Medicinal Arts; she didn't need Iokua to tell her that only palliative care was possible. "Are you finished?"

He nodded and Mehahui wrapped her felted skirt back around her waist. Her hands shook when she tucked in the ends of the fabric. "Will you tell Kahe? I can't." She pulled her hair away from her face, securing it with the tortoiseshell pins Kahe had given her for their fifteenth anniversary. She tucked a red suhibis flower behind her left ear so her married status was clear – not that she needed it. Everyone in the united tribes knew Kahe.

Iokua tugged at his graying doctor's braid. "As you wish." He paused to pick up the sandalwood surgeon's mask and settled it on his face. The image of the goddess hid his worry behind her fragrant, smooth cheeks. Carved filigree of whale bone formed the mask's eyes, giving no hint of the man beneath.

He pushed aside the hanging in the door of the hut. Outside, Kahe was pacing on the lanai. He stopped, face tightening like leather as he saw the surgeon's mask, but he came when Iokua beckoned him.

Mehahui could not say anything as she took her husband's hand. The scars on the inside of his wrists stood out in angry relief.

Iokua bowed formally. "Your wife has a tumor in her abdomen." The mask flattened his voice.

"Can you cut it out of her?" Kahe sounded like she was still strangling him.

"No." The surgeon's mask was impassive. "I'm sorry."

Despite her husband's touch, Mehahui felt herself shrink into the far distance.

"How long does she have?"

The mask turned to her, cold and neutral, though the voice underneath was not. "I suspect Mehahui will know better than I."

And she did know. Underneath the constant ache in her belly, the mass hummed with the goddess's power. She had known she was dying, but until today she had been afraid to prove it.

Kahe grasped her hand tighter. "Mehahui?"

Blindly, she turned toward him. "Weeks. Maybe."

As soon as they were alone, Kahe said, "Why didn't you tell me?" When had the soft curves of her face turned to planes?

"You would have tried to heal me."

Hia dealt out the power to kill but was more sparing with her willingness to heal. She would grant a life only in exchange for another. Kahe could have healed Mehahui, could still heal her, but only if he were willing to be taken to Hia's breast himself. And to do that would leave the king without a sorcerer.

He stood and paced the three strides that their tiny house allowed. The pili-leaf walls pressed in on him and his throat still felt tight. After all the times Mehahui had nearly killed him, only now did he feel the impact of death. He went over the list of poisons in his kit. "Makiroot acts slowly enough that I could work spells for the king until it was time to heal you. I'd be stronger than I am from strangling, so—"

"Stop. Kahe, stop." Mehahui clutched the sides of her head. "Do you think I could live with the guilt if you wasted your death on me?"

"It wouldn't be a waste!"

"Will you look beyond me? Paheni is being invaded. The South Shore Tribe have allied with the Ouvallese and we are overwhelmed. Hia has given us this gift and—"

"A gift!" If the goddess presented herself right then, he would have spit in her face.

"Yes, a gift! It's like Hia and Pikeo's Crossroads all over again. Can you imagine a better meeting of death and luck? It's not as if I am a common housewife – I've worked at your side; I know all the spells but I've never had the power to cast them. Hia gave me this so we can win the war." Mehahui held out her hands to him. "Please. Please don't take this from me."

Kahe could not go to her, though he knew she was right. Her power would only grow, as his mentor's had at the end of his life. In short order, she would surpass what he could do, and the tribes needed that to turn the tide in their favor.

But he needed her more. "How long do you have? Think deeply about it, and Hia will tell you the time remaining."

Mehahui's gaze turned inward. He watched her, sending a prayer to Pikeo for a little bit of luck. Hia's brother could be fickle, but Kahe no longer trusted his patron goddess.

"Eighteen days." Those two words shook Mehahui's voice.

But a tiny seed of hope sprouted in Kahe. "That might be enough."

"What? Enough for what?"

"To get you to Hia'au." Pilgrims from every tribe went to the goddess's city to die and sometimes – sometimes Hia would grant them the power to heal with their dying breath.

Mehahui looked at him like he had lost his senses. "But we lost Hia'au to Ouvalle."

Kahe nodded. "That's why we have to win this war quickly."

*   *   *

King Enahu's great house, despite the broad windows opening on to a terraced lanai, felt close and stifling with the narrow thoughts of the other kings who had gathered to meet with him. Kahe's knees ached from kneeling on the floor behind Enahu.

King Waitipi played with the lei of ti leaves around his neck, pulling the leaves through his fat hands in a fragrant rattle. "We are sorry to hear of your wife's illness, but I fail to see how this changes any of our strategies."

Kahe bent his head before answering. "With respect, your majesty, it changes everything. Mehahui will be stronger than me in a matter of days. What's more, she can cast spells at a moment's notice. We can take the battle right to the Ouvallese ships and handle anything that they cast at us."

"I'll admit it's tempting to retake Hia'au." The bright-yellow feathers of King Enahu's cloak fluttered in the breeze. Across his knees lay the long spear he used in battle as a reminder of his strength.

King Haleko said, "I, for one, do not want to subject our troops to another massacre like Keonika Valley."

"I understand your concern, your majesty. But the Ouvallese only have one full sorcerer from their alliance with the South Shore tribe. With Mehahui's power added to mine, we can best them."

"Of course I do not doubt your assessment of your wife's power" – King Waitipi plucked at a ti leaf, shredding it – "but it seems to me that the South Shore tribe is making out much the best in this. Should we not reconsider our position?"

So many kings, so few rulers.

King Ehanu scowled. "Reconsider? The Ouvallese offered to let us rule over a portion of *our* land. A portion. As if they have the right to take whatever they wish. I will *not* subject my people to rule by outlanders."

"Nor I." King Haleko nodded, gray hair swaying around his head. "But this does raise some interesting possibilities." King Haleko's words raised hope for a moment. "Would the infirm in our hospices offer more sorcerers?"

"You would find power without knowledge. Hia's gift only comes to those who study and are willing to make the sacrifice of themselves."

"But your wife—"

"My wife . . ." Kahe had to stop to keep from drowning in his longing for her.

In the void, King Enahu spoke. "The lady Mehahui has studied at Kahe's side all the years they have been in our service."

Kahe begged his king, "This war could be over in two weeks, if you let us go to the South Harbor. It would not divert troops; only a small band need come with us. No more than ten to protect us until we reach the South Harbor where the Ouvallese are moored. We could wipe them out in a matter of minutes." And then, though he would not say it out loud, he could take Mehahui to the Hia'ua and pray that one of the dying in the goddess's city would heal her.

King Enahu scowled. "Pikeo's Hawk! You're asking me to bet my kingdom that your wife is right about how long she has to live. What happens if we extend ourselves to attack and are cut off because she dies early? Everything is already in place to stop Ouvalle's incursions into King Waitipi's land. I need you there, not at the South Shore."

"Well." King Waitipi let the lei fall from his hand. "You've convinced me this merits more discussion and thought. Let us consider it more at the next meeting."

Kahe slammed his fists on the floor in front of him, sending a puff of dust into the air. "Eighteen days. She has eighteen days. We don't have time to wait."

The men in the great hall tensed. Kings, all of them, and disrespect could mean a death sentence.

Half-turning, Enahu let his hands rest on the spear across his knees. "Kahe. You are here on my sufferance. Do not forget yourself."

Trembling, Kahe bit his tongue and took a shallow breath. He bowed his head low until it rested on the floor. "Forgive me, your highness."

King Waitipi giggled like a girl. "You are no doubt distraught because of your wife's condition. I remind you that she will find grace with Hia no matter the outcome of our meetings."

Kahe knew that better than any king could.

But to wait until they made up their mind was worse than trusting Mehahui's life to the hands of Hia's brother god, Pikeo – luck had never been his friend.

If they did not decide fast enough, he would take Mehahui and go to the goddess's city without waiting for leave. He tasted the chalky dust as he knelt with his forehead pressed against the floor. Leaving his king would mean abandoning his tribe in the war.

Surely Hia could not ask for a higher sacrifice. Surely she would spare Mehahui for that.

Mehahui could not remember the last time she had seen a crossroad instead of the usual roundabout. Most people went out of their way to avoid invoking the gods with crossed paths, connecting even forest tracks like this with diagonals and circles.

She half expected Hia and Pikeo to materialize and relive their famous bet.

A cramp twisted in her belly. Mehahui pressed her fist hard into her middle, trying to push the pain away. It was clear which god would use her as a game piece if they appeared. Doubling over, a moan escaped her.

She tried to straighten but Kahe had already returned to her. "Are you all right?"

Mehahui forced a laugh. "Oh. Fine. Hia's gift is being a talkative one this morning." She unclenched her fist and patted him on the arm. "It will pass."

"Can I do anything?" He caught her hand and squeezed it. Every angle of his body spoke of worry.

"Just keep going." Mehahui wiped her face. Her hand came away slick with sweat, but she smiled at her husband. "See. It has already passed."

She pushed past him on to the main road to Hia'ua.

As if she had said nothing, Kahe took her hand and pulled her to a stop in the middle of the crossroad. "You should take something for the pain." He knelt and fished his sorcery kit out of his pack.

Amid the ways of dying lay the remedies. Some spells needed a long slow death and he had poisons for that. Others needed the bright flash of blood flooding from the body, and he had obsidian knives, bone needles and sinew for those. But all of the deaths brought pain. Mehahui had nursed him back from all of them. The painkiller had been one of the most faithful tools in her arsenal.

She held out her hand to accept one of the dark pills from him. "Thank you."

A drumming sounded on the main road, heading toward the harbor.

She dropped the pill. A queasy tension in her belly held Mehahui rigid. Three creatures came into view – men whose bodies were twisted into something like massive storks with four legs. Her fear raced ahead of her mind and she had already begun to back away from the road before she recognized them as men riding horses, the exotic animals the Ouvallese had brought with them from overseas.

Warriors, clearly, and wearing the green and black Ouvallese colors – outriders, returning to the main band. If the gods were replaying their age-old game, then this unlucky chance was clearly Pikeo's move.

Which had more influence on mortal lives: Death or Luck? Would Hia win again in her battle against her brother?

The man in front saw them and shouted. She could not understand his words, but his intent was clear. Halt. Kahe placed his hand on his knife.

In moments, the three riders had cut them off, pinning them in the middle of the crossroad. The one who had shouted, a small effete man with blond curls showing under the bottom of his black helm, pushed his horse in closer. He pointed at Kahe's knife.

"Not to have!" His Pahenian was slow as if he spoke around a mouth of nettles.

Kahe glanced at the other riders. "I don't understand."

The blond pointed to the ground. "There. Put!"

Kahe nodded and reached slowly for the tie of his knife belt.

Despite the shade of the trees, heat coursed through Mehahui. The knot in her stomach throbbed with her pulse. Hia could not have brought them to this crossroad only to abandon them.

She looked around for an answer. The soldier closest to her lifted a bow from his saddle. Without giving Kahe time to disarm, he pulled an arrow from his quiver. Aimed it at her husband. Drew.

"Kahe!"

Her husband flinched and turned at her cry. Before he finished moving, the arrow sprouted from his cheek.

Mehahui shrieked. The soldier turned to her, bow raised.

Kahe flung out his hand and a palpable shadow flew through the air to engulf the soldier. His face was visible for a moment as fog in the night, then he vanished.

Blood cascaded from Kahe's mouth down his chest. He staggered but raised his arms again.

Spooked by its rider's disappearance, the soldier's horse reared and came down, nearly atop Mehahui. She danced back and grabbed at the dangling reins, trying to stop the bucking animal.

Ignoring her, the other two soldiers closed on Kahe. She flung the same spell she had seen him use, sucking a living night into being.

In that moment of inattention, the horse crashed into her, knocking her down. A hard hoof slammed against her belly.

Mehahui rolled, frantic to get away from the horse's plunging feet. Fetching up against a trunk at the side of the road, she struggled to get air into her lungs. Dear goddess, was this what Kahe felt when she strangled him?

The hard crack of metal on obsidian resounded through the forest. Kahe somehow had drawn his knife and met the remaining soldier's blow, but the glass shattered on the steel.

Mehahui pushed at the ground, but her arms only twitched. The bright pain of Hia's gift flared in her belly, almost blinding her. Her thighs were damp and sticky.

The soldier raised his sword again to bring it down on Kahe's unguarded neck.

Mehahui cried out, "Stop!"

It was not a true spell, but the soldier stopped. His arm, his horse, everything froze in mid-motion.

Kahe shuddered. Then, he slipped sideways and fell heavily to the ground.

The soldier, a statue in the forest, did not move.

Mehahui crawled across the dirt road to her husband. The pain in her stomach kept her bent nearly double. Her skirts were bright with blood.

Something had broken inside when the horse had knocked her down.

No matter now, Kahe needed her. During the years of aiding him, she had seen almost every form of near-death and learned to bring him back. She grabbed the smooth leather sorcerer's kit. With it in her grasp, Mehahui set to work to save him.

The arrow had entered his cheek under his right eye, passing through his mouth and lodging in his jaw opposite. Kahe was bleeding heavily from the channel it had cut through the roof of his mouth, but she knew how to deal with that.

Shaking, Mehahui turned him on his side, so he would not drown in his own blood. She broke the arrow and pulled the shaft free. Then with a pair of forceps, she tried to pry the arrowhead out of his jawbone. The forceps slipped off it. She gripped it again, but her hands shook too much to hold it steady and his mouth open. If she could not get it out, the wound would suppurate and Kahe would die despite all her efforts. Again, she tried and gouged his cheek when the forceps slipped.

Mehahui looked at the sky, tears of frustration pooling in her eyes.

The frozen soldier still stood in arrested motion. His cape stood away from his body showing the bright gold seal of the Ouvallese king on the field of dark green. A bead of sweat clung to the edge of his jaw in unmoving testament to her power.

She did not need the forceps. She had Hia. Praise the goddess for giving Mehahui power when she needed it most.

Mehahui focused on the arrowhead and sent a prayer to Hia. Channeling the smallest vanishing spell possible, she begged the arrowhead to go. For an instant, a new shadow appeared in Kahe's mouth and then blood rushed from the hole where the arrowhead had been.

"Praise Hia!"

The other wounds would answer to pressure. From the kit she took pads of clean cloth, soaked them in suhibis flower honey and packed them into the wounds. When all was tied and tight, Mehahui looked again at the soldier. There was no time to let Kahe rest.

She held smelling salts under his nose and braced herself for the next task.

Kahe retched and his world exploded with pain. Every part of his head, his being, seemed to exist for no reason but to hurt.

He tried to probe the pain with his tongue and gagged again. Cloth almost filled his mouth.

"Hush, hush . . ." Mehahui's gentle hand stroked his forehead.

Kahe cracked his eyes and tried to speak, but only a grunt came out. Bandages swaddled his head and held his mouth closed.

"You have to get up, Kahe. The rest of the warriors will be coming."

Battalion. He had to get up. Kahe could barely lift his head and somehow he had to stand. With Mehahui's help, he rolled into a sitting position.

A soldier stood over them. His sword was raised to strike.

Kahe tried to push Mehahui away from the man and fell face forward in the road. All the pain returned and threatened to pull him back into Hia's blessed darkness.

"It's all right! He's – he's frozen." Mehahui helped him sit again.

He looked more carefully at the soldier. The man's cloak had swung out from his body, but gravity did nothing to pull it down. Kahe did not know of a spell that could do such a thing.

He looked at Mehahui. The shadows under her eyes were deeper. In the hollows of her cheeks, the bone lay close beneath her skin. Blood coated her skirts and showed in red blotches at her ankles.

He tried to ask, but his words came out more garbled than a foreigner's.

Still, Mehahui understood enough. "Hia granted my prayer." She stood, the effort clear in her every movement.

Kahe grabbed her skirt and gestured to the blood. What price had Hia demanded for this power?

She pushed his hands away. "You have to hurry. I think the main road is the fastest way back, yes?"

Kahe forced a word past the cloth in his mouth. "Back?" They could go around the battalion in the forest.

"Yes. Back." Mehahui stood with her hands braced on her knees, swaying. "You have to go to King Enahu."

He shook his head. "Hia'au."

"I am not going to Hia'au. The goddess gave me the power to save Paheni, not myself. I am staying here."

She could not mean that. Kahe clambered to his feet. The forest tipped and swayed around him, but long practice at being bled kept him standing. He had to make her understand that going to Hia'au would save both her and Paheni. No possible good could come from her staying here.

As if in answer to his thoughts, Mehahui said, "Look at the soldier, Kahe. Do you see the badge on his shoulder?"

Kahe dragged his eyes away from her. The coiled hydra of Ouvalle shone against a field of green. Where the necks sprouted from the body, a crown circled like a collar.

"That's their king's symbol, isn't it? He's landed. It's not a single battalion, but his army." Mehahui beckoned him. "Please, Kahe."

He would not leave her here. Kahe clawed at the bandages surrounding his head. If he could only talk to her, she would understand.

"Please, please go. Hia—" Her voice broke. Tears wiped her cheeks clean of dirt. "Hia has given me more power, but I only have until this evening before she takes me home. I want to know you are safe while I meet the King of Ouvalle."

Thunder rumbled in the distance.

Kahe had freely dedicated himself to the goddess but she had no right to demand this of his wife. Mehahui was his wife. His. Hia had no right to take her from him. Not now. Not like this.

Death combined with Luck showed the hands of Hia and Pikeo and they stood square in the middle of a crossroads. The Mother only knew what else the gods had planned.

"Hate her."

"No. No! Do you think this is easy for me? The only comfort I have is that I am serving a greater good. That this is the will of Hia and Pikeo and the Mother. You will *not* take my faith from me."

How could he live without her? The thunder grew louder, discernible now as the sound of a great mass of men marching closer.

Mehahui limped to his side and took his hand. She raised it to her lips and kissed his knuckles tenderly. "Please go."

Belling through the trees, a horn sounded.

Kahe cursed the goddess for cutting their time so short and leaned in to kiss his wife. The pain in his jaw meant nothing in this moment.

The sound of approaching horses broke their embrace. Kahe bent to retrieve his sorcery kit; if he took one of the faster poisons, then he could match Mehahui's power and meet Hia with his wife.

Mehahui put her hand on his shoulder. "No. I don't want you to go to the goddess. Someone must bear witness to our king."

He shook his head and pulled out the tincture of shadoweve blossoms.

"I have spent our entire marriage helping you die and knowing I would outlive you. Have you heard me complain?" She spoke very fast, as the army approached.

Kahe glanced down the road. The first of the men came into view. It seemed such a simple thing to want to die with her.

A mounted soldier separated from the company and advanced, shouting at them until he saw his immobile comrade. Moments later, a bugled command halted the force a bowshot away.

Men crowded the road in the green and black of Ouvalle. Scores of hydras fluttered on pennants, writhing in the breeze. Rising above the helmets of the warriors were ranks of bows and pikes. In the midst of them were towering gray animals, like horses swollen to the size of whales, with elongated, snaking noses that reached almost to the ground and wicked tusks jutting from their mouths. Each whale-horse glimmered with armor in scales of green lacquered steel. The black huts on their backs brushed the overarching trees. What spell had they used to bring these monsters across the ocean?

Mehahui squeezed Kahe's shoulder. When she stepped away from him, the absence of her hand left his shoulder cold and light.

She spoke; a spell amplified her voice so the very trees seemed to carry her words. "Lay down your arms and return to your homes."

Involuntarily, the closest warriors began to unbuckle their sword belts. Their sergeant shouted at them and looks of startled confusion or bewildered anger crossed their faces.

Then, at a command, the front rank of archers raised their bows.

Kahe reached for what little power was available to him. A rain of arrows darkened the air between them and the army. Kahe hurled a spell praying that Hia would allow him to create a small shield. As the spell left him, the air over them thickened, diverting the leading arrows but not enough.

Mehahui wiped the air with her hand; arrows fell to the ground. Their heavy blunt tips struck the road creating a perimeter around them. Designed to bludgeon a sorcerer to unconsciousness, without risking a wound that would bring more power, these arrows meant the Ouvallese army had recognized what the two of them were.

How long would it take them to realize that *he* was without power? Kahe turned to his kit when the air shuddered. A spell left Mehahui and the trees closest to the road swayed with a breeze. A groan rose from their bases. The trees toppled, falling like children's playthings toward the road.

Horses and men screamed in terror. Trumpeting, the tall whale-horses were the first to feel the weight of the trees.

On the lead whale-horse, the cloth curtains of the black hut blew straight out as a great wind pushed the trees upright.

The curtains remained open. An ancient, frail man stood at the opening, supported by two attendants – Oahi, the South Shore king's sorcerer. Another spell left the traitor king's sorcerer, forming into a bird of fire as it passed over the warriors' heads.

Screaming its wrath, the phoenix plummeted toward them. The counter-spell formed in Kahe's mind and he hurled it, creating a fledgling waterbird. The phoenix clawed the tiny creature with a flaming talon and the waterbird steamed out of existence.

Moments later, Mehahui hurled the same spell. Her water-bird formed with a crack of thunder. The roar of a thousand waterfalls deafened Kahe with each stroke of the mighty bird's wings.

As it grappled with the phoenix, dousing the bird's fire in a steaming conflagration, Kahe saw the power of the goddess. *This* was why Hia wanted them both there; Mehahui had the power and the knowledge, but not the instincts of a sorcerer.

Without waiting for her waterbird to finish the phoenix, Kahe attacked the Ouvallese. The pathetic spell barely warmed the metal of a whale-horse's scales. But when Mehahui copied him, the animal screamed under the red hot metal, plunging forward in terror. Its iron shod feet trampled the warriors closest to it.

On its back, the attendants clutched Oahi, struggling to keep him upright as he worked the counter-spell. Even though he cooled the scales, the panicked creature did not stop its rampage. A blond, bearded man, with a gold circlet on his helm staggered forward in the hut to stand next to the old man. What would the King of Ouvalle do when all his animals panicked?

Kahe croaked, "Others."

Mehahui nodded, and heated the scaled armor of the whale-horse next to the first.

As quickly as she heated it, the Ouvallese sorcerer cooled it, but the frightened animal turned the disciplined ranks around it to chaos. Mehahui turned to the next one as the king shouted to a hut behind him.

Kahe drew in his breath as the front whale-horse plunged into the wood, letting him see the one behind it clearly for the first time. In this hut rode a half dozen men and women. Though of differing ages, each wore a simple gray skirt with the white flame of Hia – these passengers were some of the dying of Hia'au. The Ouvallese did not have one sorcerer, they had a half dozen, and in battle, Hia's only chosen people were the dying. Kahe could expect no favors from her, unless he paid her price.

Clutching the upright post in the corner, a priest of Hia spoke quickly to the woman closest to him.

Kahe grunted and pointed at them. Mehahui had to destroy the sorcerers before the priest finished explaining the spell he wanted the woman to cast.

Mehahui nodded and threw the spell to heat their whale-horse's scaled armor, but Oahi anticipated her and cooled it before the animal panicked. Kahe shook his head. "No. People."

Squinting her eyes in confusion, Mehahui refined her spell and released it. The magnitude of the spell staggered Kahe as it passed him. It came from someone on the threshold of death. Mehahui's face was gray. She swayed on her feet. They had to finish this now, before she went home to Hia.

The warriors of Ouvalle screamed as one, ripping their helms from their heads. Some threw themselves on the ground in their efforts to get away from armor that began to take on the dull cherry red of heat.

Even the king wrenched his circlet from his head before Oahi cooled the metal.

It was a mighty spell, but the wrong one. Hia's dying wore no metal. Kahe grabbed Mehahui's arm and pointed at the hut of the dying. He threw a cloud of dark, hoping to absorb the priest in that veil of nothing.

Mehahui nodded. Staggered and threw the same spell. The world groaned at the immensity of the void she created. As it flew forward, it unfurled to the size of the road. In the moment when it engulfed the first row of warriors, the woman in the hut unleashed her spell as well, dying as it left her. Small and arrow-bright, the spell flew past the void without pausing. Its shape seemed familiar, but Kahe did not recognize the form. He tossed a general defensive spell and prayed to Pikeo for luck that it would be enough to counter this attack.

The void continued eating its way through the ranks of Ouvallese warriors. Those closest to the edge of the road threw away their weapons and ran for the woods. The old sorcerer in the hut produced the counter-spell for the void, but it only reduced the girth of the dark cloud.

Kahe looked at his wife, at her gray and bloodless lips, at the bright red staining her skirts and ankles; Hia, Pikeo and the Mother – she had surpassed the ancient man in power.

The dying woman's narrow spell struck Mehahui in the belly. Light as white as Hia's fire flared around her. She convulsed.

Kahe leaped to catch her as she collapsed. Seeing her fall, the Ouvallese king shouted a command to the few remaining archers. They raised their bows and fired at Kahe and Mehahui. Kahe welcomed the speeding arrows, but they too were consumed by the void Mehahui had created.

It roiled forward.

The handler for the king's whale-horse frantically turned the animal, trying to outrun the void.

Created in the moment before her death, it was the strongest spell Kahe had yet seen.

Seeming to recognize this, the sorcerer in the king's hut grabbed a knife from his side and plunged it into his own heart, throwing the counter-spell again. It struck the void, undoing it, as the whale-horse plunged into the trees. The archers again raised their bows.

In Kahe's arms, Mehahui stirred and opened her eyes.

She gulped in air. "Oh, Hia. No!"

Her skin was clear and flushed with life. Kahe took her face in his hands, feeling the warm vitality of her flesh. "How?"

"They healed me," she groaned. "The goddess has left." She looked past him at the archers. Her eyes widened.

They had no more blunt arrows. A field of sharp points sprang toward them.

"Pikeo save us!" Kahe threw himself across her, turning to cast a shield at the deadly arrows. It stopped most of them.

A familiar pain tore open his cheek. Another arrow plunged into his left shoulder and the third went through his right arm and pinned it to his thigh.

But none of them hit Mehahui.

Kahe waited for Hia's power to come to him, but the wounds were too slight. So he sent a prayer to Pikeo begging for good luck. They were in a crossroads, if ever Luck were going to play fair with him, it would be here and now.

And this would be the moment to strike. Oahi sagged in the arms of his escort, already gone home to Hia, but Kahe lacked the power for any large spells. He tried to reach for his dagger but, by unlucky chance, the arrow bound his right arm to his leg.

His left arm hung limp. This was how Pikeo answered his prayer?

Mehahui pushed him off of her and got to her knees. He saw her prep for a spell with a sense of despair. Flush with life, she had even less power than he.

The spell fluttered from her, almost dissipating by the time it reached the army. She had thrown an unbinding spell. It was a simple childish spell, good only for causing a rival's skirt to drop.

One tie on the king's hut came undone.

Kahe held his breath, praying that Pikeo would notice that chance and play with it.

As the animal lurched on to the road, the king's hut slid off and toppled among the remnant of the Ouvallese army. The hut splintered as it crushed the men unlucky enough to be caught underneath it. As the debris settled, Kahe gasped at what the hand of Pikeo had wrought: the pike of one of the Ouvallese had impaled the king like a trophy of war.

He convulsed once and hung limp.

At the sight of their dead monarch, a rising wail swept through the remaining warriors. Those closest to Mehahui and Kahe backed away. Others, seeing their decimated ranks, threw down their arms and ran.

Mehahui leaned her head against Kahe's back. Then she patted him, soft as a hatchling. "Stay with me."

Kahe coughed as he tried to speak, gagging on the mass in his mouth. She knelt in front of him.

Looking at his wife's fair and healthy face, Kahe sent a prayer of thanks to both gods.

"The arrow in your cheek appears to have followed the same path as the other did; it is lodged in your bandages. I'd say we have Luck to thank for our survival today." Mehahui picked up the sorcery kit. "And now, my love, I intend to keep you out of Hia's hands."

She placed a hand against his cheek and Kahe had never felt anything so sweet as his wife's touch, proving they were both alive.

VICI

Naomi Novik

"Well, Antonius," the magistrate said, "you are without question a licentious and disreputable young man. You have disgraced a noble patrician name and sullied your character in the lowest of pursuits, and we have received testimony that you are not only a drunkard and a gambler – but an outright murderer as well."

With an opening like that, the old vulture was sending him to the block for sure. Antony shrugged philosophically; he'd known it was unlikely his family could have scraped together enough of a bribe to get him let go. Claudius's family was a damn sight richer than his; and in any case he could hardly imagine his stepfather going to the trouble.

"Have you anything to say for yourself?" the magistrate said.

"He was a tedious bastard?" Antony offered cheerfully.

The magistrate scowled at him. "Your debts stand at nearly 250 talents—"

"Really?" Antony interrupted. "Are you sure? Gods, I had no idea. Where *does* the money go?"

Tapping his fingers, the magistrate said, "Do you know, I would dearly love to send you to the arena. It is certainly no less than you deserve."

"The son of a senator of Rome?" Antony said, in mock appall. "They'd have you on the block, next."

"I imagine these circumstances might be considered mitigating," the magistrate said. "However, your family has petitioned for mercy most persuasively, so you have an alternative."

Well, that was promising. "And that is?" he said.

The magistrate told him.

"Are you out of your mind?" Antony said. "How is that mercy? It's twelve men to kill a dragon, even if it's small."

"They did not petition for your life," the magistrate said patiently. "*That* would have been considerably more expensive. Dragon-slaying is an honorable death, and generally quick, from my understanding; and will legally clear your debts. Unless you would prefer to commit suicide?" he inquired.

Dragons could be killed, guards might be bribed to let you slip away, but a sword in your own belly was final. "No, thanks anyway," Antony said. "So where's the beast? Am I off to Germanica to meet my doom, or is it Gaul?"

"You're not even leaving Italy," the magistrate said, already back to scribbling in his books, the heartless bugger. "The creature came down from the north a week ago with all its hoard and set itself up just over the upper reaches of the Tiber, not far from Placentia."

Antony frowned. "Did you say its *hoard*?"

"Oh yes. Quite remarkable, from all reports. If you do kill it, you may be able to pay off even your debts, extraordinary as they are."

As if he'd waste perfectly good gold in the hand on anything that stupid. "Just how old a beast are we talking about, exactly?"

The magistrate snorted. "We sent a man to count its teeth, but he seems to be doing it from inside the creature's belly. A good four to six elephantweight from local reports, if that helps you."

"Discord gnaw your entrails," Antony said. "You can't possibly expect me to kill the thing alone."

"No," the magistrate agreed, "but the dragon hunter division of the Ninth is two weeks' march away, and the populace is getting restless in the meantime. It will be as well to make a gesture." He looked up again. "You will be escorted there by a personal guard provided by Fulvius Claudius Sullius's family. Do you care to reconsider?"

"Discord gnaw *my* entrails," Antony said bitterly.

* * *

All right, now this was getting damned unreasonable. "It breathes *fire*?" Antony said. The nearest valley was a blackened ruin, orchard trees and houses charred into lumps. A trail of debris led away into the hills, where a thin line of smoke rose steadily into the air.

"Looks like," Addo, the head of the guards, said, more enthusiastically than was decent. Anyone would've thought he'd won all the man's drinking money last night, instead of just half. There hadn't even been a chance to use it to buy a whore for a last romp.

The guards marched Antony down to the mouth of the ravine – the only way in or out, because the gods had forsaken him – and took off the chains. "Change your mind?" Addo said, smirking, while the other two held out the shield and spear. "It's not too late to run on to it, instead."

"Kiss my arse." Antony took the arms and threw the man his purse. "Spill a little blood on the altar of Mars for me, and have a drink in my memory," he said, "and I'll see you all in Hell."

They grinned and saluted him. Antony stopped around the first curve of the ravine and waited a while, then glanced back: but the unnaturally dedicated *pedicatores* were sitting there, dicing without a care in the world.

All right: nothing for it. He went on into the ravine.

It got hotter the further in he went. His spear-grip was soaked with sweat by the last curve, and then he was at the end, waves of heat like a bath-furnace shimmering out to meet him. The dragon was sleeping in the ravine, and *merda sancta*, the thing was the size of a granary. It was a muddy sort of green with a scattering of paler-green stripes and spots and spines, not like what he'd expected; there was even one big piebald patch of pale-green splotchy on its muzzle. More importantly, its back rose up nearly to the height of the ravine walls, and its head looked bigger than a wagon-cart.

The dragon snuffled a little in its nose and then grumbled, shifting. Pebbles rained down from the sides of the ravine walls and pattered against its hide of scales lapped upon scales, with the enameled look of turtleshell. There was a stack of bones heaped neatly in a corner, stripped clean – and behind that a ragged cave in the cliff wall, silver winking where some of the coin had spilled out of the mouth, much good would it do him.

"Sweet Venus, you've left me high and dry this time," Antony said, almost with a laugh. He didn't see how even a proper company would manage this beast. Its neck alone looked ten cubits long, more than any spear could reach. And breathing fire . . .

No sense in dragging the thing out. He tossed aside his useless shield – a piece of wood against this monster, a joke – and took a step towards the dragon, but the shield clattering against the ravine wall startled the creature. It jerked its head up and hissed, squinty-eyed, and Antony froze. Noble resignation be damned; he plastered himself back against the rock face as the dragon heaved itself up to its feet.

It took two steps past him, stretching out its head with spikes bristling to sniff suspiciously at the shield. The thing filled nearly all the ravine. Its side was scarcely arm's length from him, scales rising and falling with breath, and sweat was already breaking out upon his face from the fantastic heat: like walking down the road in midsummer with a heavy load and no water.

The shoulder joint where the foreleg met the body was directly before his face. Antony stared at it. Right in the armpit, like some sort of hideous goiter, there was a great swollen bulge where the scales had been spread out and stretched thin. It was vaguely translucent and the flesh around it gone puffy.

The dragon was still busy with the shield, nosing at it and rattling it against the rock. Antony shrugged fatalistically, and taking hold of the butt of his spear with both hands took a lunge at the vulnerable spot, aiming as best he could for the center of the body.

The softened flesh yielded so easily the spear sank in until both his hands were up against the flesh. Pus and blood spurted over him, stinking to high heaven, and the dragon reared up howling, lifting him his height again off the ground before the spear ripped back out of its side and he came down heavily. Antony hit the ground and crawled towards the wall choking and spitting while rocks and dust came down on him. "Holy Juno!" he yelled, cowering, as one boulder the size of a horse smashed into the ground not a handspan from his head.

He rolled and tucked himself up against the wall and wiped his face, staring up in awe while the beast went on bellowing and thrashing from side to side above, gouts of flame spilling from its jaws. Blood was jetting from the ragged tear in its side like a fountain, buckets of it, running in a thick black stream through the ravine dust. Even as he watched, the dragon's head started to sag in jerks: down and pulled back up, down again, and down, and then its hindquarters gave out under it. It crashed slowly to the ground with a last long hiss of air squeezing out of its lungs, and the head fell to the ground with a thump and lolled away.

Antony lay there staring at it a while. Then he shoved away most of the rocks on him and dragged up to his feet, swaying, and limped to stand over the gaping, cloudy-eyed head. A little smoke still trailed from its jaws, a quenched fire.

"Sweet, most-gracious, blessed, gentle Venus," he said, looking up, "I'll never doubt your love again."

He picked up his spear and staggered down the ravine in his bloodsoaked clothing and found the guards all standing and frozen, clutching their swords. They stared at him as if he were a demon. "No need to worry," Antony said cheerfully. "None of it's mine. Any of you have a drink? My mouth is unspeakably foul."

"What in stinking Hades is that?" Secundus said, as the third of the guards came out of the cave staggering under an enormous load: a smooth-sided oval boulder.

"It's an egg, you bleeding *capupeditum*," Addo said. "Bash it into a bloody rock."

"Stop there, you damned fools, it stands to reason it's worth something," Antony said. "Put it in the cart."

They'd salvaged the cart from the wreckage of the village and lined it with torn sacking, and to prove the gods loved him, even found a couple of sealed wine jars in a cellar. "Fellows," Antony said, spilling a libation to Venus while the guards loaded up the last of the treasure, "pull some cups out of that. Tomorrow we're going to buy every whore in Rome. But tonight, we're going to drink ourselves blind."

They cheered him, grinning, and didn't look too long at the heap of coin and jewels in the cart. He wasn't fooled; they'd have cut his throat and been halfway to Gaul by now, if they hadn't been worried about the spear he'd kept securely in his hand, the one stained black with dragon blood.

That was all right. He could drink any eight men under the table in unwatered wine.

He left the three of them snoring in the dirt and whistled as the mules plodded down the road quickly: they were all too happy to be leaving the dragon-corpse behind. Or most of it, anyway: he'd spent the afternoon hacking off the dragon's head. It sat on top of the mound of treasure now, teeth overlapping the lower jaw as it gradually sagged in on itself. It stank, but it made an excellent moral impression when he drove into the next town over.

The really astonishing thing was that now, when he had more gold than water, he didn't need to pay for anything. Men quarreled for the right to buy him a drink and whores let him have it for free. He couldn't even lose it gambling: every time he sat down at the tables, his dice always came up winners.

He bought a house in the best part of the city, right next to that pompous windbag Cato on one side and Claudius's uncle on the other, and threw parties that ran dusk until dawn. For the daylight hours, he filled the courtyard with a menagerie of wild animals: a lion and a giraffe that growled and snorted at each other from the opposite ends where they were chained up, and even a hippopotamus that some Nubian dealer brought him.

He had the dragon skull mounted in the center of the yard and set the egg in front of it. No one would buy the damn thing, so that was all he could do with it. "Fifty sesterces to take it off your hands," the arena manager said, after one look at the egg and the skull together.

"What?" Antony said. "I'm not going to pay *you*. I could just smash the thing."

The manager shrugged. "You don't know how far along it is. Could be it's old enough to live a while. They come out ready to fight," he added. "Last time we did a hatching, it killed six men."

"And how many damned tickets did it sell?" Antony said, but the bastard was unmoved.

It made a good centerpiece, anyway, and it was always enter-taining to mention the arena manager's story to one of his guests when they were leaning against the egg and patting the shell, and watching how quickly they scuttled away. Personally, Antony thought it was just as likely the thing was dead; it had been sitting there nearly six months now, and not a sign of cracking.

He, on the other hand, was starting to feel a little – well. Nonsensical to miss the days after he'd walked out of his step-father's house for good, when some unlucky nights he'd had to wrestle three men in a street game for the coin to eat – since no one would give him so much as the end of a loaf of bread on credit – or even the handful of times he'd let some fat rich lecher paw at him just to get a bed for the night.

But there just wasn't any juice in it anymore. A stolen jar of wine, after running through the streets ahead of the city cohorts for an hour, had tasted ten times as sweet as any he drank now, and all his old friends had turned into toadying dogs, who flattered him clumsily. The lion got loose and ate the giraffe, and then he had to get rid of the hippo after it started spraying shit everywhere, which began to feel like an omen. He'd actually picked up a book the other day: sure sign of desperation.

He tried even more dissipation: an orgy of two days and nights where no one was allowed to sleep, but it turned out even he had limits, and sometime in the second night he had found them. He spent the next three days lying in a dark room with his head pounding fit to burst. It was August, and the house felt like a baking-oven. His sheets were soaked through with sweat and he still couldn't bear to move.

He finally crawled out of his bed and let his slaves scrub and scrape him and put him into a robe – of Persian silk embroi-dered with gold, because he didn't own anything less gaudy anymore – and then he went out into the courtyard and collapsed on a divan underneath some orange trees. "No, Jupiter smite you all, get away from me and be quiet," he snarled at the slaves.

The lion lifted its head and snarled at him, in turn. Antony threw the wine jug at the animal and let himself collapse back against the divan, throwing an arm up over his eyes.

He slept again a while, and woke to someone nudging his leg. "I told you mange-ridden dogs to leave me the hell alone," he muttered.

The nudging withdrew for a moment. Then it came back again. "Sons of Dis, I'm going to have you flogged until you—" Antony began, rearing up, and stopped.

"Is there anything more to eat?" the dragon asked.

He stared at it. Its head was about level with his, and it blinked at him with enormous green eyes, slit-pupilled. It was mostly green, like the last one, except with blue spines. He looked past it into the courtyard. Bits and chunks of shell were littering the courtyard all over, and the lion— "Where the hell is the lion?" Antony said.

"I was hungry," the dragon said unapologetically.

"You ate the lion?" Antony said, still half dazed, and then he stared at the dragon again. "You ate the *lion*," he repeated, in dawning wonder.

"Yes, and I would like some more food now," the dragon said.

"Hecate's teats, you can have anything you want," Antony said, already imagining the glorious spectacle of his next party. "Maracles!" he yelled. "Damn you, you lazy sodding bastard of a slave, fetch me some goats here! How the hell can you talk?" he demanded of the dragon.

"*You* can," the dragon pointed out, as if that explained anything.

Antony thought about it and shrugged. Maybe it did. He reached out tentatively to pat the dragon's neck. It felt sleek and soft as leather. "What a magnificent creature you are," he said. "We'll call you – Vincitatus."

It turned out that Vincitatus was a female, according to the very nervous master of Antony's stables, when the man could be dragged in to look at her. She obstinately refused to have her name changed, however, so Vincitatus it was, and Vici for short. She also demanded three goats a day, a side helping of something sweet, and jewelry, which didn't make her all that different from most of the other women of Antony's acquaintance. Everyone was terrified of her. Half of Antony's slaves ran away. Tradesmen wouldn't come to the house after he had them in to the courtyard, and neither would most of his friends.

It was magnificent.

Vici regarded the latest fleeing tradesman disapprovingly. "I didn't like that necklace anyway," she said. "Antony, I want to go flying."

"I've told you, my most darling one, some idiot guard with a bow will shoot you," he said, peeling an orange; he had to do it for himself, since the house slaves had been bolting in packs until he promised they didn't have to come to her. "Don't worry, I'll have more room for you soon."

He'd already had most of the statuary cleared out of the courtyard, but it wasn't going to do for long; she had already tripled in size, after two weeks. Fortunately, he'd already worked out a splendid solution.

"Dominus," Maracles called nervously, from the house. "Cato is here."

"Splendid!" Antony called back. "Show him in. Cato, my good neighbor," he said, rising from the divan as the old man stopped short at the edge of the courtyard. "I thank you so deeply for coming. I would have come myself, but you see, the servants get so anxious when I leave her alone."

"I did not entirely credit the rumors, but I see you really have debauched yourself out of your mind at last," Cato said. "No, thank you, I will not come out; the beast can eat you, first, and then it will be so sozzled I can confidently expect to make my escape."

"I am not going to eat Antony," Vici said indignantly, and Cato stared at her.

"Maracles, bring Cato a chair, there," Antony said, sprawling back on the divan, and he stroked Vici's neck.

"I didn't know they could speak," Cato said.

"You should hear her recite the *Priapea*, there's a real ring to it," Antony said. "Now, why I asked you—"

"That poem is not very good," Vici said, interrupting. "I liked that one you were reading at your house better, about all the fighting."

"What?" Cato said.

"What?" Antony said.

"I heard it over the wall, yesterday," Vici said. "It was much more exciting, and," she added, "the language is more interesting. The other one is all just about fornicating and buggering, over and over, and I cannot tell any of the people in it apart."

Antony stared at her, feeling vaguely betrayed.

Cato snorted. "Well, Antony, if you are mad enough to keep a dragon, at least you have found one that has better taste than you do."

"Yes, she is most remarkable," Antony said, with gritted teeth. "But as you can see, we are getting a little cramped, so I'm afraid—"

"Do you know any others like that?" Vici asked Cato.

"What, I suppose you want me to recite Ennius's *Annals* for you here and now?" Cato said.

"Yes, please," she said, and settled herself comfortably.

"Er," Antony said. "Dearest heart—"

"Shh, I want to hear the poem," she said.

Cato looked rather taken aback, but then he looked at Antony – and smiled. And then the bastard started in on the whole damned thing.

Antony fell asleep somewhere after the first half-hour and woke up again to find them discussing the meter or the symbolism or whatnot. Cato had even somehow talked the house servants into bringing him out a table and wine and bread and oil, which was more than they'd had the guts to bring out for *him* the last two weeks.

Antony stood up. "If we might resume our business," he said pointedly, with a glare in her direction.

Vincitatus did not take the hint. "Cato could stay to dinner."

"No, he could *not*," Antony said.

"So what was this proposition of yours, Antony?" Cato said.

"I want to buy your house," Antony said flatly. He'd meant to come at it roundabout, and enjoy himself leading Cato into a full understanding of the situation, but at this point he was too irritated to be subtle.

"That house was built by my great-grandfather," Cato said. "I am certainly not going to sell it to you to be used for orgies."

Antony strolled over to the table and picked up a piece of bread to sop into the oil. Well, he could enjoy this, at least. "You might have difficulty finding any other buyer. Or any guests, for that matter, once word gets out."

Cato snorted. "On the contrary," he said. "I imagine the value will shortly be rising, as soon as you have gone."

"I'm afraid I don't have plans to go anywhere," Antony said.

"Oh, never fear," Cato said. "I think the Senate will make plans for you."

"Cato says there is a war going on in Gaul," Vincitatus put in. "Like in the poem. Wouldn't it be exciting to go see a war?"

"What?" Antony said.

"Well, Antonius," the magistrate said, "I must congratulate you."

"For surviving the last sentence?" Antony said.

"No," the magistrate said. "For originality. I don't believe I have ever faced this particular offense before."

"There's no damned law against keeping a dragon!"

"There is now," the magistrate said. He looked down at his papers. "There is plainly no question of guilt in this case, it only remains what is to be done with the creature. The priests of the Temple of Jupiter suggest that the beast would be most highly regarded as a sacrifice, if you can arrange the mechanics—"

"They can go bugger a herd of goats," Antony snarled. "I'll set her loose in the Forum, first – no. No, wait, I didn't mean that." He took a deep breath and summoned up a smile and leaned across the table. "I'm sure we can come to some arrangement."

"You don't have enough money for that even now," the magistrate said.

"Look," Antony said, "I'll take her to my villa at Stabiae—" Seeing the eyebrow rising, he amended. "Or I'll buy an estate near Arminum. Plenty of room, she won't be a bother to anyone—"

"Until you run out of money or drink yourself to death," the magistrate said. "You do realize the creatures live a hundred years?"

"They do?" Antony said blankly.

"The evidence also informs me," the magistrate added, "that she is already longer than the dragon of Brundisium, which killed nearly half the company of the Fourteenth Legion."

"She's as quiet as a lamb?" Antony tried.

The magistrate just looked at him.

"Gaul?" Antony said.

"Gaul," the magistrate said.

"I hope you're happy," he said bitterly to Vincitatus as his servants joyfully packed his things, except for the few very unhappy ones he was taking along.

"Yes," she said, eating another goat.

He'd been ordered to leave at night, under guard, but when the escort showed up, wary soldiers in full armor and holding their spears, they discovered a new difficulty: she couldn't fit into the street anymore.

"All right, all right, no need to make a fuss," Antony said, waving her back into the courtyard. The house on the other side had only leaned over a little. "So she'll fly out to the Porta Aurelia and meet us on the other side."

"We're not letting the beast go spreading itself over the city," the centurion said. "It'll grab some lady off the street, or an honorable merchant."

He was for killing her right there and then, instead. Antony was for knocking him down, and did so. The soldiers pulled him off and shoved him up against the wall of the house, swords out.

Then Vincitatus put her head out, over the wall, and said, "I think I have worked out how to breathe fire, Antony. Would you like to see?"

The soldiers all let go and backed away hastily in horror.

"I thought you said you couldn't," Antony hissed, looking up at her; it had been a source of much disappointment to him.

"I can't," she said. "But I thought it would make them let you go." She reached down and scooped him up off the street in one curled forehand, reached the other and picked up one of the squealing baggage-loaded pack mules. And then she leaped into the air.

"Oh, Jupiter eat your liver, you mad beast," Antony said, and clutched at her talons as the ground fell away whirling.

"See, is this not much nicer than trudging around on the ground?" she asked.

"Look out!" he yelled, as the Temple of Saturn loomed up unexpectedly.

"Oh!" she said, and dodged. There was a faint crunch of breaking masonry behind them.

"I'm sure that was a little loose anyway," she said, flapping hurriedly higher.

He had to admit it made for quicker traveling, and at least she'd taken the mule loaded with the gold. She hated to let him spend any of it, though, and in any case he had to land her half a mile off and walk if he wanted there to be anyone left to buy things from. Finally, he lost patience and started setting her down with as much noise as she could manage right outside the nicest villa or farmhouse in sight, when they felt like a rest. Then he let her eat the cattle, and made himself at home in the completely abandoned house for the night.

That first night, sitting outside with a bowl of wine and a loaf of bread, he considered whether he should even bother going on to Gaul. He hadn't quite realized how damned *fast* it would be, traveling by air. "I suppose we could just keep on like this," he said to her idly. "They could chase us with one company after another for the rest of our days and never catch us."

"That doesn't sound right to me at all," she said. "One could never have eggs, always flying around madly from one place to another. And I want to see the war."

Antony shrugged cheerfully and drank the rest of the wine. He was half looking forward to it himself. He thought he'd enjoy seeing the look on the general's face when he set down with a dragon in the yard and sent all the soldiers running like mice. Anyway it would be a damned sight harder to get laid if he were an outlaw with a dragon.

Two weeks later, they cleared the last alpine foothills and came into Gaul at last. And that was when Antony realized he didn't know the first damn thing about where the army even was.

He didn't expect some Gallic wife to tell him, either, so they flew around the countryside aimlessly for two weeks, raiding more farmhouses – inedible food, no decent wine, and once some crazy old woman hadn't left her home and nearly gutted him with a cooking knife. Antony fled hastily back out to Vincitatus, ducking hurled pots and imprecations, and they went back aloft in a rush.

"This is not a very nice country," Vincitatus said, critically examining the scrawny pig she had snatched. She ate it anyway and added, crunching, "And that is a strange cloud over there."

It was smoke, nine or ten pillars of it, and Antony had never expected to be glad to see a battlefield in all his life. His stepfather had threatened to send him to the borders often enough, and he'd run away from home as much as to avoid that fate as anything else, nearly. He didn't mind a good fight, or bleeding a little in a good cause, but as far as he was concerned, that limited the occasions to whenever it might benefit himself.

The fighting was still going on, and the unmusical clanging reached them soon. Vincitatus picked up speed as she flew on towards it, and then picked up still more, until Antony was squinting his eyes to slits against the tearing wind, and he only belatedly realized she wasn't going towards the camp, or the rear of the lines; she was headed straight for the enemy.

"Wait, what are you—" he started, too late, as her sudden stooping dive ripped the breath out of his lungs. He clung on to the rope he'd tied around her neck, which now felt completely inadequate, and tried to plaster himself to her hide.

She roared furiously, and Antony had a small moment of satisfaction as he saw the shocked and horrified faces turning up towards them from the ground, on either side of the battle, and then she was ripping into the Gauls, claws tearing up furrows through the tightly packed horde of them.

She came to ground at the end of a run and whipped around, which sent him flying around to the underside of her neck, still clinging to the rope for a moment as he swung suspended. Then his numb fingers gave way and dumped him down to the ground, as she took off for another go. He staggered up, wobbling from one leg to the other, dizzy, and when he managed to get his feet under him, he stopped and stared: the entire Gaullish army was staring right back.

"*Hades me fellat,*" Antony said. There were ten dead men lying down around him, where Vincitatus had shaken them off her claws. He grabbed a sword and a shield that was only a little cracked, and yelled after her, "Come back and get me out of here, you damned daughter of Etna!"

Vincitatus was rampaging through the army again, and didn't give any sign she'd heard, or even that she'd noticed she'd lost him. Antony looked over his shoulder and put his back to a thick old tree and braced himself.

The Gauls weren't really what you'd call an army, more like a street gang taken to the woods, but their swords were damned sharp, and five of the barbarians came at him in a rush, howling at the top of their lungs. Antony kicked a broken helmet at one of them, another bit of flotsam from the dead, and as the others drew in he dropped into a crouch and stabbed his sword at their legs, keeping his own shield drawn up over his head.

Axes, of course they'd have bloody axes, he thought bitterly, as they thumped into the shield, but he managed to get one of them in the thigh, and another in the gut, and then he heaved himself up off the ground and pushed the three survivors back for a moment with a couple of wide swings, and grinned at them as he caught his breath. "Just like playing at soldiers on the Campus Martius, eh, fellows?" They just scowled at him, humorless *colei*, and they came on again.

He lost track of the time a little: his eyes were stinging with sweat, and his arm and his leg where they were bleeding. Then one of the men staggered and fell forward, an arrow sprouting out of his back. The other two looked around; Antony lunged forward and put his sword into the neck of one of them, and another arrow took down the last. Then, another one thumped into Antony's shield.

"Watch your blasted aim!" Antony yelled, and ducked behind the shelter of his tree as the Gauls went pounding away to either side of him, chased with arrows and dragon-roaring.

"Antony!" Vincitatus landed beside him, and batted away another couple of Gauls who were running by too closely. "There you are."

He stood a moment panting, and then he let his sword and shield drop and collapsed against her side.

"Why did you climb down without telling me?" she said reproachfully, peering down at him. "You might have been hurt."

He was too out of breath to do more than feebly wave his fist at her.

"I don't care if Jupiter himself wants to see me," Antony said. "First I'm going to eat half a cow – yes, sweetness, you shall have the other half – and then I'm going to have a bath, and *then* I'll consider receiving visitors. If any of them are willing to come to me." He smiled pleasantly, and leaned back against Vincitatus's foreleg and patted one of her talons. The legionary looked uncertain, and backed even further away.

One thing to say for a battlefield, the slaves were cheap and a sight more cowed, and even if they were untrained and mostly useless, it didn't take that much skill to carry and fill a bath. Antony scrubbed under deluges of cold water and then sank with relief into the deep trough they'd found somewhere. "I could sleep for a week," he said, letting his eyes close.

"Mm," Vincitatus said drowsily, and belched behind him, sound like a thundercloud. She'd gorged on two cavalry horses.

"You there, more wine," Antony said, vaguely snapping his fingers into the air.

"Allow me," a cool patrician voice said, and Antony opened his eyes and sat up when he saw the general's cloak.

"No, no." The man pushed him back down gently with a hand on his shoulder. "You look entirely too comfortable to be disturbed." The general was sitting on a chair his slaves had brought him, by the side of the tub; he poured wine for both of them, and waved the slaves off. "Now, then. I admired your very dramatic entrance, but it lacked something in the way of introduction."

Antony took the wine cup and raised it. "Marcus Antonius, at your command."

"Mm," the general said. He was not very well favored: a narrow face, skinny neck, hairline in full retreat and headed for a rout. At least he had a good voice. "Grandson of the consul?"

"You have me," Antony said.

"Caius Julius, called Caesar," the general said, and tilted his head. Then he added thoughtfully, "So we are cousins of a sort, on your mother's side."

"Oh, yes, warm family relations all around," Antony said, raising his eyebrows, aside from how Caesar's uncle had put that consul grandfather to death in the last round of civil war but one.

But Caesar met his dismissive look with an amused curl of his own mouth that said plainly he knew how absurd it was. "Why not?"

Antony gave a bark of laughter. "Why not, indeed," he said. "I had a letter for you, I believe, but unfortunately I left it in Rome. They've shipped us out to . . ." he waved a hand, "be of some use to you."

"Oh, you will be," Caesar said softly. "Tell me, have you ever thought of putting archers on her back?"

ABJURE THE REALM

Elizabeth Bear

Captain, d'ye see the banners brave
Floating on the wind?
Fire and folly fear, me boys,
Hail and hell they'll send.

Riordan limped down the parapet to the next guard post, the soft sole of his left boot hissing on black granite as he hitched along in pursuit of the High-King. A cloak of tatters in colors gleaned from half a thousand fiefdoms swung from the bard's shoulders, but he had left his lute and his harp behind this afternoon. He was unarmed.

Aidan, called the Conqueror, glanced over his shoulder. The High-King frowned when a midsummer breeze lifted Riordan's lovelocked hair and blew it across the bard's face, revealing silver at the temples and the nape of his neck. "You should bind that back," Aidan commented, returning his attention to the amorphous smudge staining half of the eastern horizon, distant beyond the steep gabled roofs of the town. The guard stepped courteously aside to give his liege a clearer view, and one of the white-robed wizards the King kept always in attendance stood inconspicuously nearby.

Riordan followed the gaze. The enemy converging on the caer reminded him of ravens gathering when slaughter was on the wind. In fact, he saw a drift of shapes like leaves swept up in a wind spiraling over the enemy ranks. *The harbingers of battle.*

A long way off, but coming.

"I've been in wars before, Your Majesty." But Riordan produced a scrap of thong from his sleeve and twisted it through metal-red curls, obedient to the will of the King.

Aidan's lips curled slightly in a sneer as the bard's gesture revealed a half-dozen golden earrings. The King turned back to the encroaching army, resting his elbows on a stone crenellation. "Do you know what that is, Harper?"

Riordan too leaned against the rough-hewn wall, taking the weight off his malformed foot. "An army, Your Majesty." *Never tell a King he's dull.*

Aidan bent forward and spat off the parapet. "The army of my bastard half-sister the sorceress, master bard. The undead army of Maledysaunte, the Hag of Wolf Wood."

"Aye, Your Majesty."

Aidan shoved himself upright. "The gates of Caer Dun have never been breached. But odds are very good that something will die here today. An old blood debt. And with luck, a wicked woman. I look forward to your songs."

With a final stiff nod, the King turned and stalked away, leaving the crippled bard to struggle after if he cared to.

> *Captain, d'ye see yon maiden fair*
> *That all in black do ride?*
> *That iron sword in her white hand, me lads,*
> *An iron heart does guide.*

The Hag of Wolf Wood laid a gentling hand on the neck of her immense black stallion, noticing with amusement that the dirt from her cabbage patch still discolored her nails. She rode bareback and without reins, her steed restrained only by the sound of her voice and the grip of her thighs. Necromancer snorted and tossed his head, his broad dazzling blaze flashing in the sunlight. Murders of carrion birds – corpse-crows black as Maledysaunte's straight, shining hair; enormous whiskery ravens; white-vested hooded crows – wheeled overhead, drawn by the rotting stench of the sorceress's undead army.

Maledysaunte herself wore sachets of lavender and pennyroyal about her neck, the little pouches dangling over the whitework embroidery on her laced bodice. The rest of her robes

– voluminous homespun lawn – were dyed black with sloes, giving her the look of one of her attendant magpies. She crushed one of the sachets, rolling the bag between her fingers to release the scent as she turned her head to survey the army of corpses.

Caer Dun, home of her childhood, loomed on the horizon. The gates were not yet closed for siege, and she smiled despite the colorful wardsigns, invisible to the unmagicked, that were written on the air above it. *I'll see you yet avenged, Ygraine, though I damn my soul to do it. See how the old bastard lives in fear of me now? Those are the workings of ten wizards at least.*

She sighed, and shifted her sore bottom on the stallion's back. She scrubbed her hands on her thighs as if they were sticky. *I've tried, Ygraine. But even I could not breach those defenses. Without a distraction. Without having come here myself.*

I never wanted to come back here, or to pay these prices.

Necromancer shook his head hard, shying backward as a rotting wolfhound trotted too close to his feet. *What a wand cannot master, the hand must undertake. At least I gave them enough warning to get most of the townspeople away.*

"Sorry, old boy," she said to the horse. "I know, they don't exactly reek of sanctity. But they're all we have."

Patting his withers one-handed, she reached over her shoulder and touched the hilt of the black iron dagger that hung between her shoulder blades, concealed under the fall of a mantle of deepest green. *Well, if I fail this time, I won't get another chance.*

The thought cheered her.

She touched Necromancer with her small bare heels and he pranced forward, displeased slaver dropping from his lips. His head came up as she turned him south and west, away from the stinking vanguard. She nudged him into a gallop, clinging with a hand knotted in his mane and trusting him not to throw her. He left the dead willingly behind.

She guessed they were about to find out.

> *Captain, d'ye hear the trumpets brash*
> *Sounding the battle call?*
> *We'll charge to the rolling drums, me boys,*
> *To the rolling drums we'll fall.*

Riordan could have caught Aidan, limp or no limp, but the bard did not hurry as much as he might have. Nigh on fifty years he'd reigned, and he didn't look a day over thirty-five. And after a fortnight in the High-King's court, Riordan was ready to concede that the Hag had a point. Her half-brother was anything but charming.

Still, he was King, and the finest King the realm has ever seen. Witness the peace he enforced from sea to sea.

If Kings were charming they wouldn't need Harpers.

The bard watched the High-King's glossy black curls and cloth-of-gold surcote recede along the battlement, then returned his attention to the field. Teamsters and farmers, wainwrights and coopers and goodwives streamed in through the gates of the caer. A broader river of people fled west across the plains, who perhaps had not truly believed in the Hag's grave-stolen horde until they smelled it.

Riordan shook his head. If he'd a lick of sense, he'd be with that refugee train. Not trapped in a tyrant's summer castle while his evil half-sister rode down.

The warm wind from the east brought a stench of rot. Riordan covered his mouth with one string-callused hand and shaded his eyes with the other, trying to make out some detail of the enemy. Other than the clouds of carrion birds surrounding the advancing ranks, the curious silence and the lack of banners, he could see nothing. There must be a bard here, to tell the truth of it.

It had all the markings of a bleak and epic history, though Riordan had not been born when Aidan and his sister became enemies. The fresh-created King had married his bastard half-sister's half-sister, daughter of another branch of the same royal line. That bastard, a half-hour older than the legitimate Prince and touched with the evil eye, had been made a pawn of other factions, and the King's wife had smuggled her sister out of the caer and been burned for her pains.

But the bastard with the yellow eye had lived.

Maledysaunte, Riordan thought. *The Hag of Wolf Wood, from whom no knight escapes.* For nearly half a century, the sorceress had sent their corpses home to her half-brother on biers woven of greenwood and roses, even in the dead of winter. Every so often another of her treacherous gifts had arrived as well, disguised as tribute from a conquered king – a poisoned cloak, a pretty girl slave with a dagger concealed in her hair. Legend had the witch bent and ragged, one eye green as poison and the other naught but a rotting sore with snakes writhing behind it. There was supposed to be a beautiful princess as well, imprisoned in the witch's dank tower.

Every sticky mark of a good story. And here he was, caught in it.

Riordan's teeth grated together. He drew his gaudy cloak tighter over his shoulders, mindful of the brilliant scrap-work twisting on the breeze. He wouldn't place a bet on the snakes.

That sounded the sort of touch Henri of Canton would add to a ballad. Besides, if her brother so belied his age, why should she look any older?

Riordan smiled privately. *Because she's wicked, of course.*

And then the wind brought him putrescence again. The polite soldier gagged, averting his streaming eyes and using the hem of his royal-blue tunic to muffle his face. In sympathy, Riordan clapped his shoulder.

The soldier coughed again before he straightened, and rewarded the Harper with a grateful glance. *He's just a boy*, Riordan thought, and was ashamed of it as soon as the soldier said, "Don't worry, Harper. The King's men will take care of you, and this caer has never fallen to a siege."

Words were already taking shape in the bard's mind, and he was only half-listening. *All under the Lion Banner / On a clear warm day in June* . . . "What's your name, lad?"

He drew himself up proudly and touched a bronze badge pinned over the tartan on his shoulder. "Captain Dunstan, Harper." A stinking wind ruffled his ash-blond curls.

Dunstan rode to the battle / and the drummers called the tune. "Have you ever fought an army like this one, then?"

The young soldier's face blanched behind his bravado, but he did not look down. The bard noticed a signet ring on the lad's finger when he lifted it to scratch his beardless chin. One of the King's many bastards, then. That's why he had the command so young. Aidan had married only the once, and gotten no legitimate heirs before burning his young wife for treason.

Riordan suspected the experience had soured him.

Dunstan spoke. "She's never come out of Wolf Wood before. Nor ever sent an army."

"Sort of makes you wonder what's changed, doesn't it?" Riordan followed after the High-King, already humming the first verse of a ballad and thinking about the words he would put to it, after the battle was won.

> *Captain, d'ye hear the clash of blades*
> *And the battle cries so fierce?*
> *We'll cry the more this night, me boys,*
> *If her blade our hearts does pierce.*

Maledysaunte would have lowered her green mantle from her head and paused inside the gates of the caer, pinioned on girlhood memories, but the press of refugees bore her forward. Dust rose in a plume around them, stirred by many feet; the once-familiar high walls, hung with blue and gold, oppressed her.

She had left Necromancer concealed in the sprawl of the town, and now she limped as if footsore and weary. *So many people.* She wanted to gag on the stench of them, like the stench of the dead. The press of bodies assaulted her from all sides. The dull-colored flagstones were rough under her feet.

She refused to look too hard at the children, at a young couple hand in hand, the woman leaning on her husband's arm. At an old man who crouched in the shade out of the flow of traffic, a book – *a book!* – balanced on his knee. At the stout brown-haired woman who smiled and stepped out of Maledysaunte's path with a friendly nod to the weary-looking girl.

Too late. The deal was already struck: blackest necromancy. There was an irony there, that Maledysaunte's inability to get to Aidan had driven her to the very crimes he accused her of.

Debts must be paid.

Permitting the river of townsfolk to sweep her past the guards, Maledysaunte turned into the bailey. The burden of wizardry pressed over her like sodden blankets, and had the encroaching revenant army not already triggered every magical ward on the caer, alarms would have shrilled her presence. She smiled – more a grimace of pain – and closed her eyes to feel her way. And almost ran down the rag-cloaked figure of a bard.

"Pardon!" The sorceress tried to squeak like a terrified townswoman, but her voice was rusty with disuse. She couldn't remember the last time she'd spoken to a man. She never bothered to introduce herself to the knights who came to kill her anymore, instead permitting the forest to murder them while she sat at her loom or dug in her garden. They hadn't offered much entertainment at best: invariably stalwart and of limited imagination.

"No pardon required. If only pretty lasses would walk into me more often. I'm Riordan." He picked up her hand, which hung at her side, and swept a bow over it. His right foot dragged.

I could have healed that when he was born. A bitter thought, made bitterer by history. *But thou shalt not suffer a witch to live. Much less a bastard daughter of the lord who's a half-hour older than the son and heir, and has the misfortune to know how to talk to animals.*

Wizards are all right, though. Although they never seem to heal anybody. She kept her eyes downcast, working her mouth around the taste of dust. If he noticed she had one eye green and one amber, he'd find her memorable, and she did not wish to be remembered. "I . . . Y . . . Ygraine, master bard." As she stammered over the name, she wondered why she had chosen it.

"A lovely name, if out of favor these days."

"My parents were from the provinces," she lied, extemporizing wildly. "They did not know the name of the King's first wife, nor had they heard the story . . ."

"A piercing irony that you should find yourself here, girl – besieged by the very sorceress that infamous queen aided in her escape. Let us hope that your name is not a portent, shall we?"

"Let us hope," she said, and curtsied lower when it seemed as if the bard would reach out and lift her chin to see her face the better. "I must . . . my husband is waiting, Harper. Thank you for your kindness."

Infamous. A kinder word than many would have chosen. Still, her teeth hurt from grinding them. She caught herself scouring her hands against her gown and twisted them in the black cloth of her skirts instead.

She turned and scurried toward the keep itself, chafing under the weight of innocent humanity all around her and the itch of the iron dagger hungry between her shoulders.

> *Captain, d'ye smell the smoke of war*
> *And the stench of burning men?*
> *Aye, and I hear the screaming, lads,*
> *In the keep which we defend.*

Riordan watched the girl with the mismatched eyes hurry across drab red and grey flagstones, the spill of hair from under her mantle catching blue highlights in the dusty sun. *Husband.* Something about the word nagged in his mind. *Ygraine. Husband.*

She was gone from sight before he jerked upright and turned to follow her, limping toward the tower keep as fast as he could drag his crippled foot. *Husband. And wearing her hair down on her shoulders like a maiden? Not likely!*

"Dunstan! Captain!" The bard pitched his voice to carry, wishing he had more at his belt than an eating knife only so long as the span of his palm. He caught sight of the Captain leaning against a paneled divider and lurched toward him.

The blue-eyed lad turned his head sluggishly when Riordan clutched his arm. "Master bard." He blinked twice, as if struggling to focus.

"Did a girl go by here?"

The young Captain shook his head, but it wasn't precisely denial. "Everything swims in my vision."

"Bewitched." *Or poisoned.* But he couldn't see a wound. Riordan gulped and dragged at Dunstan's arm. "Hurry. The Hag is in the castle!"

"The King!"

"In his study. Go!"

Dunstan all but carried the bard up the spiraling stairs, until Riordan knocked his hand away. "Go. Hurry. I'll follow."

Dunstan nodded and drew his sword, bolting up the uneven stair. Riordan followed more slowly, hauling himself along by means of handholds on the sloppily dressed stone wall. Faster. Faster. He was halfway there when he heard the hiss of blades drawn, only a few steps from the top and able to see over the landing when steel rang on steel and he glimpsed Dunstan, cursing, engaged with another soldier in the livery of the King – a soldier who fought dead-eyed and with inhuman quickness.

Dunstan fought well, Riordan granted. But the lad was a lad, and half-weeping in frustration at dueling his comrade. He was pulling his blows, fighting defensively. The bard lurched higher, catching the shin of his bad leg on the step.

Beyond the combatants, Riordan could see the slight girl in the green mantle, a wicked little dagger clutched in her hand. The body of Aidan's attendant wizard lay at Maledysaunte's feet, blood a banner across the white bodice of her gown. The King faced her, a half-step up on the little platform his gilded desk stood on, his broadsword drawn. The spines of priceless books framed his aquiline profile. Arrogant confidence could have dripped the length of his blade.

Swords chimed together like hammers striking the anvil. Dunstan cursed again and parried. Out of the corner of his eye, Riordan saw blood streaming down the inside of the Captain's arm.

"Surrender," Maledysaunte said to the King, as Riordan attained the landing.

Aidan laughed, loud and true. "I should be saying that to you, little sister." He extended the massive sword in his hand, holding it as if it were light as a willow wand.

"I never would have opposed you. I never cared who sat on your father's throne. I was a *bastard*, Aidan. But half a century ago, on a day like today, you burned a girl."

Riordan took a step closer, transfixed. A grunt and the unmistakable slick hiss of steel into flesh interrupted his concentration. He glanced aside to see Dunstan drawing his blade out of his comrade's belly and flicking the blood from it in a long, spattering arc.

The King turned his head and spat. "Your witchery won't avail. This is your last mistake."

Maledysaunte smiled, a long, cool smile that went into Riordan sharp as the dagger in her hand. "You don't understand, Your Majesty. Even if you kill me, my army is coming. And blood was the price of their raising. Your blood." Her throat worked as if she swallowed bile. "They're coming to collect."

Dunstan staggered forward, weaving across the distance to the girl, his blood spattering the floor. He stumbled.

The sorceress reversed her dagger in her hand and spread her arms wide, as if inviting the High-King to strike her down. "More so than empire, I am your finest creation, High-King. Look at what you've made!"

He looked. Long and steadily, unflinching, he met his sister's gaze. He stepped forward, hand unwavering on his sword.

Riordan dragged himself painful steps closer. Dunstan went to his knees and planted his sword as a prop, trying to haul himself upright. His hand slipped in his own blood. He fell.

Maledysaunte hurled the dagger as Riordan lunged. His sound foot skittered on blood-slick stone and he went down hard, catching himself on the palm of one hand. Aidan had only begun raising his sword to parry when the blade went into his eye.

Riordan shoved himself into a crouch before he froze, unbelieving. His hand went to his mouth. The High-King fell ponderously, like an oak, and Maledysaunte had turned her back on him and stepped over Dunstan's unconscious form by the time he slumped unmoving. His sword was still ringing on the stones when she passed Riordan.

She hesitated. And did not glance back. "I've had time to learn skills other than magic," she said in chill even tones.

Not knowing what he did, he reached out and caught the edge of her mantle. "You're the princess. Not the Hag."

She stopped at the top of the stairs, cloth stretched between them like a flag to be folded. She did not turn her head. "Are the two so different, then?"

A great tingling numbness seemed to have fallen over him. Outside, he could hear the bustle of the refugees, the neighing of horses. Words spilled from his throat. "Are we conquered, then? Will you rule?"

Her laugh was a humorless, gasping thing. "The King has many bastards to duel over his throne." She turned back to the bard, and came up close, her mantle furling like a wing. She smelled of lavender and mint, and blood.

The sorceress Maledysaunte raised her thumb to her mouth and bit down on it, blood coloring her sharp white teeth. She smiled pitilessly and reached out, crimson wound like ribbons around the whiteness of her hand.

"The dead must be fed for their labors, but someone should live to tell the tale." She touched him between the eyes with her own red blood. "I won't be back. Let darkness fall."

> *Captain, the women scream and cry*
> *And the walls are breached at last*
> *The Captain can make no reply, me boys,*
> *And the dark is falling fast.*

Maledysaunte's army attacked at sunset, but the sorceress was not among the ranks. Kingless, Captainless, Caer Dun was taken in an hour. By moonrise, all that was left within her walls was the wandering bodies of the dead . . . and a staring, green-eyed bard whom no revenant would touch, for he was marked by their mistress.

The Hag's army fell to ash at the first touch of the sun.

> *She stands in her chamber*
> *Weaving her summer*
> *In threads green and golden*
> *Under eaves hung with winter.*

Winter lay thick on the ground around her tower, snow white on her ebony window ledge. A chime like a glass bell resounded on frosty air as the water in a silver basin clouded and then cleared. Maledysaunte looked up from her weaving, brushing a strand of hair still glossy black behind her ear.

She hadn't heard that sound in fifteen years or longer, since Caer Dun, since her brother's death. She had almost believed herself forgotten.

Curiosity almost moved her to thrust the shuttle through the warp and walk across the tapestry-carpeted floor to the scrying bowl. Almost. She had become what they said she was, and now they feared her enough to trouble her no longer.

There was a moral there.

After a moment, she shrugged and selected a red handful of threads. *The trees will take care of it for me.* But she glanced back over her shoulder nonetheless.

> *True Tam dismounted at the greenwoodside*
> *Tied his mare's reins up to the pommel*
> *He slapped her flank and he stepped inside*
> *And she went home with an empty saddle.*

Riordan shuffled painfully along a deer-trail packed through the snow, leaning on a hewn rowan staff. Pausing at the very edge of the wood, he pulled his many-layered cloak around his shoulders, feeling the winter like ice in every joint. It had been a long few years. He regarded the trees warily, wondering if the branches really were reaching after him.

His mount trotted three steps away and stopped, staring after him as if she could not believe what he meant to do. Her breath frosted on her whiskers, and she nickered softly, as if to say, *Get back on, Man. We can still go home.*

"There's a lady in there with a story to tell, Gracie," the old Harper said, with good humor. "Besides, she didn't kill me last time. And her mark is on me still. Her creatures should leave me alone."

Should. You never knew. But if one took no chances, there would be no stories.

Riordan took a breath and stepped into the wintry wood.

> *All in green did my lady go*
> *All in green went riding*
> *Among the barrows of the silent dead*
> *On a white mare, she went riding.*

THE WORD OF AZRAEL

Matthew David Surridge

At the edge of the battlefield of Aruvhossin grew an elm tree. Half its branches were covered in orange leaves. Half were bare and dead. In its shadow, upon a patch of sere grass, sat a man named Isrohim Vey.

Beyond the grass the earth had been bloodied and churned to mud.

Naked to the cold sun were dead men and dead horses and those slowly dying, and scavengers and carrion creatures flitting from one to another. Isrohim Vey sat under the elm, spine against the trunk, a sword driven into the turf by his side, and watched them all. He drew one leg up, as though protecting guts and groin with his thigh-bone. There was a distant terrible pain in his stomach where he had been wounded. Seven kings lay dead on Aruvhossin nearby, and all their armies with them.

The battle had been a day and a night and half a day again. Witchfires had circled Aruvhossin in the darkness, raised by goblinkin slaves of one army or another, burning blue and green and indigo. Dizzy, Isrohim Vey shut his eyes and thought he saw again the stunted things that danced as they died, thought he saw knights charging into a storm of arrows, thought he saw the lipless one-eyed giants whose clubs made the ground tremble, and saw the cloaked Dominies alone or in circles calling on the storms and the powers beyond the storms, and saw his captain die, and saw the last stand of the Anochians, and saw men in armor he'd killed, the Westlander, the kilted Elavhri, and saw necromancers commanding the dead to rise again and whirl about the field to slay and slay and slay; all the world slain on the field of Aruvhossin, the greater part may be mercenaries like him, brutal and who can say but they deserved this, all this.

Isrohim Vey opened his eyes, and it was noon on the second day of the battle of Aruvhossin, and he was (so he imagined) the only living thing that had seen the battle from the beginning and remained alive; and then Isrohim Vey saw the Angel of Death.

The angel was beautiful and smiled on him, and Isrohim Vey was helpless to tell the depths of that smile or its breadth; if it was a man's smile, or a child's, or if it was large as the field of Aruvhossin, or as all the world. Only that the meaning in it was beyond expression and that the power which moved the sun and the other stars lurked in it and rent his heart.

He did not know what the angel was about on that battlefield.

He neither perceived nor understood anything of it, or little, beyond the smile. But in that smile was all it was and all he was and all he ever would be. His right hand moved, seeking his sword, finding it. It was a fine sword. He had found it fallen on the field of Aruvhossin late on the first day of the battle. It had served well. Now he felt only the sharpness of its edge cutting his hand.

The Angel of Death smiled on Isrohim Vey, and said a Word.

After the angel had gone Isrohim sat under the elm tree and stared past the field of Aruvhossin. Shafts of sun fell through distant clouds. He was no longer dizzy. He was no longer in pain. He sat, clutching inside himself at the last dregs of the feeling he had been taught when he had seen the angel and the angel had looked on him. He knew he would live. For a time. Live to seek the Angel of Death; live till he saw it once more, and forever.

Live till he knew again the smile and could tell its meaning within his own soul. Just so long, and no longer.

The Dominie peered into the heart of the circlet of amber and crystal.

"The sword is special," he said. "It has a destiny. Be wary; many will seek to take it from you."

"The sword is not my concern," said Isrohim Vey.

The Dominie crossed his study, silver threads glittering in his green cloak, and set the circlet in its space on a shelf between an eggshell painted with a map of the world and a small stoppered glass jar, which held an ink elemental splashing and sulking inside its prison. "Yes; your angel," said the Dominie. "Angels are powerful things. Some say, more powerful than all the gods of men. They move the spheres of the sky and rule the houses of the days and the nights. They are beyond both destiny and freewill. They hold the keys, you know; the keys."

"I have seen one."

"Azrael," said the Dominie. "You saw the Angel of Death, whose name is Azrael."

"What do I do now?" asked Isrohim Vey.

The Dominie shrugged. "Go forward, and be blessed."

"Not enough."

"What more will you have, then?"

"I want to see the angel again."

The Dominie sighed. "When you die."

"I have watched men die. They see no angel. Sometimes, maybe; more often, not."

"Hum," said the Dominie. He asked: "What is death, then, to you?"

"Freedom," answered Isrohim Vey. He looked away from the Dominie. The wizard's study was close and warm. Though it was day, colored candles burned and cloying scent reeled through the air. "I've gone back to the wars since Aruvhossin. I have seen men die, and women, in numbers. I have haunted places of slaughter. But I have not seen the angel again."

The Dominie tilted his head back and drew a breath through his nostrils.

"Who can divine the ways of angels?" he asked, and half his mouth turned up in a grin. "I cannot say where you should look. Only I suggest this. Go to the Free City of Vilmariy for the Grand Masque at midsummer. On that night all things are upended; the people fill the streets in their guises, and I have heard it said, and do well believe, that their costumings on that night reveal hidden and inadvertent truths."

"Are there angels in Vilmariy?" asked Isrohim Vey.

"There are angels everywhcre," answered the Dominie.

★   ★   ★

It has been said that on the night of the Grand Masque in Vilmariy the veils between the country of the dead and the country of the living weaken; as though the two were never separate at all, but two nations in their solitudes interpenetrating.

Isrohim Vey came to Vilmariy for the first time on that carnival night, and walked among the people in costume and the things in no costume and searched for a sign of truth.

He found a bazaar where witches sold candles and silver jewels; where vampires haggled for spices with goblinkin; where clergymen kept assignations with bejewelled succubi; where a half-mad prince bought, from an old man with a long-stemmed pipe and moonstone eyes, a map to the legendary Fount of All out of which proceeds every created thing. In a park he came upon an elegant dance under faerie lights, where stag-headed men partnered green women crowned with garlands of red leaves, and children of the Ylvain in fashions of old time fenced with blunt copper swords stolen from human barrows. In a cemetery he found a frenzy where the white queen of winter copulated with the red king of war in an open grave, and a flockless shepherd pawed the unlikely breasts of a pirate captain, and skeletons danced a lecherous reel with red-eyed hags.

None of these things, to him, was a sign.

Not long before dawn he saw, leaving the grounds of a rich estate where noblewomen in the guise of constellations mingled with Svar Kings from under the earth, a woman dressed as an angel. This was high up the triple-peaked hill on which Vilmariy is built. Isrohim Vey followed the woman down into the heart of the city, along thoroughfares where dukes and outlaws and satyrs lay drunk in the gutters, and then into a maze of alleys. Nor was he the only one who followed her.

Behind him he knew there were others. When the angel slipped in the dark, and kicked at a man with a hyena's head asleep in his own piss, that was when they rushed forward. For a moment Isrohim Vey was caught up in a storm of devils.

Then they were past him, and had reached the angel. Three men dressed as devils to her one. The devils fought with sword and dagger while the angel had only a slim steel rapier. But she was swift as wrath, and they could not touch her. Isrohim Vey drew the sword he had found on the field of Aruvhossin. With his first strike he broke a devil's back. His second thrust threw another against a wall. Then he had to parry; and again; and again. A dagger entered him. Then the devil facing him fell and the beautiful blood-drenched angel smiled at him.

It was not the smile he had looked for. But, he thought, dazed, it will do for now.

"Who are you?" Isrohim Vey murmured, as his legs gave way and he fell to his knees.

"I am Yasleeth Oklenn," said the angel, "the greatest duelingmaster of this or any other time; and, sir, you have aided me, and for this I owe you a favor; the which I shall discharge now, in saving your life."

"That is well done," agreed Isrohim Vey.

Three years later, with much having passed between them, he prepared to leave Yasleeth.

At the very end, she said to him: "You're the greatest student I ever had. You've learned all I have to teach of the cunning old man called death. Why go, when you might stay with me, and be rich?"

"Because there is more to know of death," he said, "and I must find it out."

"Death is simple," she said.

He could not argue. He went, nevertheless.

So Isrohim Vey wandered the wide world. He had to fight, often, either to earn his way or simply to survive the bad bandit-haunted roads between cities and fortresses.

Sometimes men sought him out to fight him and take his sword. Sometimes, before he killed them, they mentioned that they had been sent by Nimsza, a Bishop of the Empire Church.

Eventually Isrohim Vey went to the land of Marás, where, in the nave of the Obsidian Cathedral, he slew the Black Bishop called Nimsza; and, taking up Nimsza's ring, spoke with the demon Gorias that Nimsza had commanded in life.

"It may be true," Gorias purred, "that demons know something of the ways of angels." Gorias held Nimsza's soul between its claws, and was content.

"Tell me of the Angel of Death," said Isrohim Vey.

"Azrael cannot be evaded," the demon said.

"I do not want to evade the angel," said Isrohim Vey. "I want to find him."

"It is, of course, an error to refer to an angel or demon as male or female," observed Gorias thoughtfully. The soul it held wailed a tiny shriek that never ended nor wavered. "However, language on these planes is crude, and incapable of suggesting our essence. I will tell you this: understanding of the Death Angel will come with the right death, when the world turns upside down."

"Explain."

"I cannot. My understanding is not as yours, filtered through reason. Like angels, demons know only what they know. Order me to come with you, if you like. Command me to aid you. With your nameless sword, and my aid, you can become the conqueror that the Black Bishop dreamed of becoming. We will topple empires and you will crush the nations of the world beneath your boots. I have power to do that."

"No."

"Otherwise, pain will come to you. Through me the way to a life of ease. You have the ring that is my weakness; command me."

"No."

"I can give you to Azrael," said Gorias. Isrohim Vey said nothing. "You will know the smile you seek," said the demon. "Command me."

"Then you will have my soul," said Isrohim Vey.

"But you will have your angel," said the demon Gorias.

"I will say this to you," said Isrohim Vey, and spoke the Word of Azrael.

Gorias shrieked and fled to the thirteen hells.

Theologians have since debated the fate of Nimsza's soul. As is the case with most souls, however, its destiny remains unclear.

Excommunicated by the Empire Church for slaying the Black Bishop, Isrohim Vey travelled to the Valley of Rhûn that had been the heart of the Dominion of the Lohr when that mighty and cunning people had ruled half a continent. Centuries before the Valley of Rhûn had been overrun by goblinkin who had come in a swarm out of the north; the Lohr now were gone, and the goblins warred with each other among the ruins.

In the fallen Lohr capital of Opallios Isrohim Vey found libraries of ancient unreadable script guarded by Ylvain warring against the goblinkin, and small gargoyles who glared after him with garnet eyes and bellowed out proclamations of might, and carrion birds with old man's heads, and a kind of large bone-white spider which seemed clever in the way that foxes are clever and which wove webs that wailed gently in the wind. He also found wands of light and darkness, and bell-shaped diamonds holding frozen songs, and a whip that commanded the flood and the eclipse, and the ashes of a book which had held the Seven Secret Words to Command Love and War, and, finally, ghosts.

He spoke to the ghosts one by one in the broken streets and other places, saying, "I seek the Angel Azrael." And none of them had intelligence of the angel to give him.

Some said to him, "Be happy and do not drive yourself through the warm life with your eyes upon the next."

These ghosts Isrohim Vey ignored.

He found sometimes ruins of the temples of the twelve gods of the Lohr and the God of All Other Things. In these places the ghosts of priests served the ghosts of gods, and Isrohim Vey spoke to them.

A priest of Ikeni, goddess of Names, said this to him:

"Your name is Isrohim Vey, and your sword has no name. Your identity is this: like any seeker of any kind, you are what you look for. To find it will be to destroy yourself."

"The sword has a name," said Isrohim Vey. "It is called Azrael's Word." And he left Opallios.

Sometime after, the excommunicate Isrohim Vey was seen in the castle-city of Tíranin, which is the capital of Yriadriú, the First Empire.

Tíranin is very old, and no one now remembers whether it began as a castle which grew into a city, or as a city which built itself up into a single castle.

Isrohim Vey was soon known and feared in the great halls that house bardic contests, in the hole-in-the-wall taverns, in the sordid side passages where thieves swindle each other and whores keep appointments in rooms filled by the ratgnawed finery of long-gone dynasties. There is very much dust, everywhere in Tíranin.

Isrohim Vey, soon after his arrival, became involved in a labyrinthine conspiracy against the ruling line of Yriadriú. By the time events worked themselves into History's chosen pattern, five towers were set afire, the Bronze Duke committed suicide, a hatmaker who ran a shop on a high balcony near Parliament Keep had an emerald pin stolen, Queen Jael met her own reflection walking in a chapel maze, a brief but violent battle flared among the Dominies of the High Thaumaturgical Council, an enslaved unicorn was freed from the flesh-marts, Isrohim Vey changed sides, the strange secret of the Leader of the Parliamentary Opposition was revealed, and a mad priest who worshipped the Red Gods of a people long thought extinct raised a forest of oaks to crack the stones of Tíranin, and in so doing revealed an army of ghouls lurking in old secret places within the walls preparing to fall upon the living who were their descendants.

In the end, it was Isrohim Vey who led the search for the Hidden Necropolis, and then led the battle against the Ghoul Lords in their tombs. Finally, facing over the point of his sword the King-That-Was-And-Would-Be-Again, Isrohim Vey heard the name of the Angel of Death once more.

"I know," said the dead King, "that you came to Tíranin seeking knowledge of Azrael. But the libraries of the Dominies have not helped you, nor have all the histories of the ages of the world."

In his hands the King-That-Was-And-Would-Be-Again held a skull. The skull said: "Murder and maim, torture and slay, long the path of Isrohim Vey."

Isrohim Vey said: "Tell me about Azrael."

The King-That-Was-And-Would-Be-Again said: "I can tell you nothing, for death has sealed my lips. But this is my counselor and prophet, who may speak as he will."

And the skull said: "Thou grim unfearing restless soul! Walk alone, no clue to your goal."

Then Isrohim Vey knew his time in Tiranin had been useless; and Queen Jael came riding through a mirror on a unicorn, and stabbed the King-That-Was-And-Would-Be-Again through his unbeating heart with an emerald pin, and the dead King fell to dust.

The skull fell to the ground and said: "One and all have their fates interlaced. Death's grin your end; all else is waste."

Leaving Tiranin, for some time Isrohim Vey wandered the north of the world. He established a society of outlaws in Thursegarth Gianthome; further east, he organized villages of the Mistborn tribes in a defense against incursions of the Nekrûl. Eventually the Nekrûl came in force, with their wicked beasts warped by chaos, their companies of toad-troopers, their priests of old and unclean dogmas.

They captured Isrohim Vey, and he was sent to Illullunor in the Clawline.

The Clawline had been carved upon the face of the world before Time began by one of the Elder Gods the Nekrûl worshipped; sunlight never came there, and fungi grew in mutated forms like wind-shaped snowdrifts, and the ground had been made brittle and false by the ages-long gnawing of subterranean acids. Illullunor, the Hideous Prison, was set in the sides of a great rift in the earth; the base of the rift, never seen, birthed cold mists that drained will and strength from the prisoners even as they were made to mine the bitter ores of the Clawline.

Iä Quis, Master of Illullunor, spoke with Isrohim Vey three times.

The first time, he said: "I know who you are. I know what happened at Aruvhossin. I know the things you've done since; and why. I know your sword has a destiny, and that is why I have learned these things and brought you here. I am an initiate of the Old God Ophion, and I know Its rites and mysteries and theurgies. I will take your destiny from you. Do you understand? I will penetrate into it and defile it. You must understand. That is how it begins."

The second time Iä Quis spoke to Isrohim Vey was some while later.

Numerous tortures had been inflicted upon the swordsman by that point.

Another prisoner, a youth named Valas, had become his guide and ally. This was not known to Iä Quis, and at that time was not relevant.

"Nothingness precedes existence, and is therefore logically superior to it," said Iä Quis. "The Old Gods of Nekrûl come from the void that was before all things. To return to the gods, all things must be erased. Destiny must be, not simply changed or negated, but turned back on itself. Nihilism, to be perfect, must be universal. But your sword remains a mystery. You yourself have not uttered a word since you arrived in Illullunor, excepting your screams. Speak now; explain yourself, and the history of the sword, and be released." Isrohim Vey said nothing, and Iä Quis was not sure if the swordsman understood him or if pain had driven him mad.

The third time Iä Quis spoke to Isrohim Vey, the Master of Illullunor had a fever's sweat, and his flesh was pale, as though his blood had dripped out of him. "Ophion is the Old God who first drew the distinction between *those who have* and *those who have not*; who invented power and weakness, and the lust for power, and the idea of murder for power's sake, and all the science of oppression. For power is nothingness . . . but this, the sword," and the hand of Iä Quis shook as he indicated Azrael's Word, "this I cannot unriddle . . . Only, I find always the same answer . . . that is, death. Can death, and only death, be your destiny? But that is the destiny of every living thing."

Then Isrohim Vey spoke to Iä Quis for the first and last time, and said, "The meaning of these things is that you will die by Azrael's Word." Then it so happened that the youth Valas caused a carefully planned collapse in the mine tunnels, and all Illullunor shook, and in a moment Isrohim Vey proved his words to be true.

There was, after that, much murder done in Illullunor the Hideous Prison. Perhaps all of those who died deserved their fates.

When it was done, and the former prisoners victorious and all the corpses thrown into the mists below Illullunor, the youth Valas asked to accompany Isrohim Vey on his travels.

"I am looking for the smile of the Angel of Death," said the swordsman.

Valas, expressionless, nodded.

"He frightens me," said Valas to the blind bard. "I know there was a woman, once, in Vilmariy. He loves her, but will not go back to her. Or he doesn't love her. He left her in order *not* to love her. How can a man do that?"

The old man nodded, very slow; meaning nothing. In a corner of the inn room the bard's three daughters watched, wordless. "You met him in a place which scarred many men," said the bard. "And he, you say, suffered more than most."

"There's more to it," said Valas. "I know what Illullunor did to men: You learn ways of surviving, how to gnaw dirt to cure yourself of the taste for food, which of the guards have a taste for rape, how to hide yourself away inside your head and how to find your way back to the world. But when he came and when he left was much the same. Partly it's that which frightens me."

The bard shifted on his bench, and scratched at his bristly beard. From outside the thrum of summer rain came, beating against the lush forest beyond the inn. "You've travelled with him three years? Four? – I've heard stories of the death-bound swordsman for some time, and it seems to me stories of the boy at his side began about so long ago . . . have you been afraid of him all that time?"

"No. Or, yes, but I thought it would ease over time. Lessen. It hasn't."

"Why stay?"

"One and all have their fates interlaced." Valas looked away from the bard, toward the inn's hearth. "That's something he says. At night, while he sleeps. But in a normal voice."

"What does it mean?" asked the blind bard.

"Well," said Valas. "I don't believe in fate." He propped his chin in his hand and stared into the coals of the fire. "But I have seen a great deal of the world with him. I'm learning something, I feel, though I don't know what. You say you've heard the stories."

"I'm a King among bards," said the blind man. "For what that's worth. Of *course* I've heard the stories. The amber stairs and the salamander's daughters. The white gold tears of the desolation of Thamycos. The battle with the ice of Grandfather Hiberius. The assassins sent by the House of Quis—"

"Yes, and he doesn't care," said Valas. "*That's* what frightens me. In the end. Glories, treasures, deaths, they don't . . . *touch* him."

The blind bard tapped a finger on the table as though playing an unseen instrument. "Then he's wrong. These things have become legend. Tales of Isrohim Vey are told across all the lands north of the Inheritors of Kesh. And all we are, are tales we make of ourselves. This I know to be true, as I am King of Bards; I swear it by the Fount of All, source of all things and all tales."

"Maybe," said Valas, his head bowed. He flicked his eyes to the three daughters of the old man; two of them stared back, while the third watched her father lovingly. "But what if there's something more, or what if those tales are shaped by something beyond us?"

All through this talk, Isrohim Vey sat staring out a window at a crippled dog drowning in a puddle of water. He did not move, and it was impossible to say if he had heard Valas and the blind bard, or what his thoughts were if he had.

The wanderings of Isrohim Vey took him at last to sea, and Valas with him. Far from land, their ship was attacked by pirates of the Nahor Islands.

The ship, the *Crone of Keys*, was swarmed by pirates and Isrohim Vey slew them as they came. There were half-a-dozen pirate vessels, and more and more of them were forced to send their crew aboard the *Crone of Keys* as Isrohim Vey killed and killed. The *Crone of Keys* began to burn, and he fought on. The decks were washed with blood, and the air tasted of salt. Every crewman aboard the ship had been slain, but Isrohim Vey continued to battle with Azrael's Word, and with Valas at his side.

Then the leader of the pirates came forward and shouted to Isrohim Vey, "We must fight, you and I. I am Reivym Shoi, who came from the mainland to rule these wicked crews."

Isrohim Vey nodded, and the two of them fought for a long while under the sun.

"You're going to die on this ship," said Reivym Shoi. He had a deep cut in his off-hand.

"Maybe," said Isrohim Vey, who was bleeding down one side of his face.

"I have a hero's fate," said Reivym Shoi. He began a long series of slashes and thrusts, elegant and precise; he had been schooled. Isrohim Vey blocked many of them, but not all. "I am going to wield the Nameless Sword and strike down the Angel of Death. What is fated to be must be. But this is not why you are going to die. You are going to die because I'm a better swordsman than you."

Isrohim Vey said nothing. But a moment later Reivym Shoi's sword had cut his right wrist, and he dropped Azrael's Word. Remorseless, Reivym Shoi dealt his concluding stoke. Isrohim Vey threw up his left arm to block it. The blade's edge bit deep, and struck into the bone, and stuck there. Isrohim Vey twisted his arm back and wrenched the sword from Reivym Shoi. Then he drew the sword from his arm-bone and ran the pirate through. The wound was not fatal, but Reivym Shoi staggered back against the rail of the ship as Isrohim Vey picked up Azrael's Word.

Then Reivym Shoi said "Ah, that is the Nameless Sword which was used against me."

"It is Azrael's Word," said Isrohim Vey.

"I know you," said Reivym Shoi. "The death-bound swordsman. Isrohim Vey, you and I are the only two men to have survived the battle of Aruvhossin."

Isrohim Vey lashed out with Azrael's Word. The pirate fell from the deck of the *Crone of Keys* into the deep sea. He was not seen to resurface.

Valas, who from infancy had lived in the Hideous Prison Illullunor, discovered he was the heir to a lost kingdom when the Princess Elidora Byth of Kethonin was abducted by Ûr Quis, patriarch of the House of Quis, Duke of the Tyranny of Nekrûl, whose grandson Iä Quis had been delivered to the Angel of Death at the ruin of the Hideous Prison Illullunor. The King of Kethonin sent agents to Isrohim Vey to tell him that the leader of the clan of his enemies was abroad and engaged in some evil plan. So Isrohim Vey and Valas climbed into the mountains of what had been the kingdom of Dys in search of Ûr Quis. And this was as Ûr Quis had planned.

They found him in an ancient temple of the Nekrûl hidden deep in a cave; the mountains of Dys are within sight of the Clawline, and the Nekrûl had long ago infiltrated the countries of their neighbors. Ûr Quis had returned to this forgotten place to raise an aspect of the Old God called Ophion. Isrohim Vey slew Ûr Quis and the avatar of Ophion, a lamprey-jawed serpent thick as a man.

Valas desecrated the altars of Ophion and shattered Princess Elidora Byth's manacles.

When they returned to Kethonin, the King had it announced that Valas was the rightful heir of Dys, captured by the Nekrûl when he was a baby, and of a status to marry the Princess Elidora Byth. These things were supported with all relevant proofs and testimony from those who remembered the stolen infant prince. Princess Elidora, who was noted for her fierceness and who had sworn an oath to Halja of the Keys to make the marriage bed a place of war and poisons for any husband forced upon her, proclaimed herself pleased by this revelation, as was the young hero Valas. As for the King of Kethonin, whose subjects in the province of Dys had been restless of late, and whose daughter was noted among noblemen's sons for her troublesome spirit and her bloodthirstiness, he was himself quite satisfied at how events had fallen out. The wedding would be a great festival for all the lands nearby.

The night before it took place, Valas spoke to Isrohim Vey.

"Will you stay with us, in Kethonin?" he asked. "You'll have much honor."

He was afraid as he said this.

Isrohim Vey said nothing for a long time, staring at the stars. Then he looked at Valas. For the first time Valas realized that Isrohim Vey, who was most alone when with other people, could not frame in words things that he felt; and that therefore there were many things he did not know about himself.

"All right, then," said Valas. "But will you give us your benediction?"

Isrohim Vey nodded, and on the next day before the nobility of seven kingdoms he blessed the marriage of Prince Valas and Princess Elidora Byth by speaking the Word of Azrael.

Many years later Isrohim Vey came to Lugbragthoth the University City at the time of its sack by the armies of Ettra, headman of the Non.

The Non, who were barbarians, were laying siege to the rocky spires of the Thirteen Colleges. The Lower City was mostly ruins and ashes. Some fires burned. There were corpses, the stink of death and roasting flesh, rubble and offal. There were raw screams; these came mostly from women and girls. The males who were not at war were all dead.

Lugbragthoth had been built, not long after the beginning of the current Age of the world, upon the jagged mountain called Tavish. Each of the thirteen high narrow peaks housed a College dedicated to a branch of learning, and each of the Colleges had high old walls and many guardsmen. They also held books, which were rare things, and being books they were held to be magic, and were therefore objects of hate and lust. Around the Colleges, spreading down the sides of the mountain, was the Lower City. It seemed like a counter-attack was underway against the Non as Isrohim Vey walked toward the Dire Stairs leading to the College of the Seven Saints; anyway men in livery battled Ettra's men here and there through the city. Isrohim Vey ignored them and ignored the screaming and walked on up the hillside. Blood flowed past him, the streets became rivers flowing downhill to unimaginable oceans.

Once three Non tribesmen came upon him, and attacked chanting their war-songs. Two he slew quickly; the largest gave him a minute's battle, and that was mostly due to a tough hide the big man wore. Otherwise, he climbed to the Dire Stairs and up in silence.

The Dire Stairs branch off, then the branches cross and recombine in a diagonal labyrinth. Isrohim Vey did not know the quickest way to the College of the Seven Saints and had no skill with mazes, but he was patient. He tried every branch and turn, and retraced his steps when he needed to, which was often.

Sometimes the stairs led up to and then down from outcroppings, lookout points. At one of these places he saw the Aureate College collapse in flames. At another he met a howling old man with the corpse of a young woman in his arms; Isrohim Vey noticed that the old man's eyes were milk-white, and took his arm to guide him along the stairs.

"She's dead!" screamed the old man. He seemed not to notice the swordsman's touch. "She's dead!"

"You're alive," said Isrohim Vey.

The old man quieted at once and turned, seeking after the sound. "Your voice," he whispered. "Are you there? *You?*"

"Do you know me?"

"I heard your voice, once," said the old man. "I have echoed it for a long time since."

Isrohim Vey did not understand this, but he presumed the man was mad.

"This place is not safe. I will guide you away from here."

"Ah," said the blind old man. "I know where you'll lead me."

"I will lead you to Saints' College."

"No. You've changed with the years, but not so much."

"I have nothing to do with this war. I've come only to speak with the wise men of Lugbragthoth, who I have heard are philosophers who think and write of life and also of death."

"Oh, but you, you are Isrohim Vey," said the blind man. "I know you, better than I know myself. I've told tales of you, long years I've told the tales. I know you from the inside. You will lead me to death. That's your tale, and we are every one trapped in empty tales of ourselves told by fools."

"Would you rather be free?" asked Isrohim Vey. The blind old man took a deep breath.

"I am King of Bards," he said, "and my one faithful daughter is dead." He stepped off the stairs, and fell a long way and then died.

There are stories of Isrohim Vey at the Sack of Lugbragthoth and how he led the defense of Saints' College. How by his skill and strength he threw back the invaders. Some stories say that he slew Ettra, leader of the people of the Non, in single combat, and burned his legendary gryphon-skin armor. Other stories say Ettra was killed before Isrohim Vey arrived, in a chance scuffle in the Lower City. Many of the stories are contradictory, but none has died for lack of telling.

Isrohim Vey learned to read and studied for a while in the Colleges of Lugbragthoth. Then for a time he disappeared from the known lands. Travelers to the deep forests of the stag-headed Ceridvaen races claimed to hear of a silent swordsman haunting the standing stones of an Age gone by. Eventually he was seen in Zimri, that curious city of popes, poisoners, and patrons of the arts, where he was involved in the spate of odd deaths surrounding a curious moonstone icon dedicated to Halja, Matriarch of Keys. After the destruction of the icon by lightning, Isrohim Vey travelled south past the Inheritors of Kesh to Ulvandr-Kathros the Confederate Empire, where the seasons are reversed and the stars different. Following a riot in the slave marts of the Empire's capital of Carcannum, Isrohim Vey returned to the north of the world and visited the witch-kingdom of Wyrddh, where without explanation he was taken prisoner and bound by a crossroads in a cage of yellow bone and black iron. A Duke of Cats was set to watch him and given Azrael's Word for a plaything, and so Isrohim Vey was left for dead.

Then Valas came, and he distracted the Duke of Cats with riddles and took the sword and rescued Isrohim Vey.

Valas told Isrohim Vey that the dragon Umbral had burnt most of Kethonin and abducted the Queen Elidora Byth. "I know where the dragon's lair is," said Valas. "But Umbral is very powerful. I need your help to kill him."

"I will help you," said Isrohim Vey, and they set out.

They went a very long way, across North Ocean to the Cauldron Lands where the savage goblinfolk churn in endless warfare. They crossed fields of ice and snow-storms and passed under curtains of light in the nighttime skies.

The dragon's lair was a glacier of black ice worked into spires and curves.

Four rivers crusted with half-frozen poisons flowed away from it to every point of the compass. Valas and Isrohim Vey approached as carefully as they could. They passed into a great hall, all of ice, and a chamber of black ice mirrors, and through the empty pathways of the glacier; until at last they descended into the pits below, and discovered Umbral in a fountain arising from the earth, his black scales fouling the waters at their source.

"Give me back my wife," Valas demanded of the waiting dragon.

"She's dead," said Umbral. "I killed her some time ago." Valas screamed and drew his sword and Umbral breathed a black flame and killed him. The dragon turned its old head to the other man.

"Why did you take Elidora Byth?" asked Isrohim Vey.

"Perhaps I wanted to bring you to me," said Umbral. "It worked for Ûr Quis."

"Ûr Quis is dead."

"Yes," said the dragon. Then it leaped at Isrohim Vey, huge as night.

Isrohim Vey drew Azrael's Word and in a moment the sword was buried in Umbral's heart.

"This is my death," said the dragon. "I have known all the Ages of the world; it is enough. I am slain by the Nameless Blade forged by Einik of the Svar; and that too is enough. It is a fitting death. I have made my end."

Then Umbral died, and Isrohim Vey took back Azrael's Word and set off for the south.

Traveling to the Dweorgheorte Mountains, Isrohim Vey descended into the subterranean tunnels called Chthonia or Domdaniel. In these tunnels he made his way to the Svar kingdom of Vâlain.

The Svar are half the height of a man, until they choose to be otherwise, when they can grow tall as a giant. They do not eat or drink, and do not age or die unless violence is done to them. Isrohim Vey made his way through their halls under the earth by the light of their eyes, which are burning lamps.

"Where is the smith named Einik?" he asked, and every time he asked he was given the same answer:

"Further down."

But however far down into Domdaniel Isrohim Vey travelled, he found that Einik was always further, beyond Vâlain itself, in the tunnels of the Deep Dark where only the mad and the visionary among the Svar dared to go.

It was one of these, a prophet, who finally came to Isrohim Vey and promised to lead him to Einik. Isrohim Vey went with the Svar prophet to the Deep Dark, and the prophet led him past great white bats and the cities of the grim peoples under the earth and a seer of the goblinfolk raving of a human boy who would come to be king of Domdaniel and lead his folk to victory over the armies of the surface. Then the Svar stopped and told Isrohim Vey how to proceed and the swordsman walked the last distance to the forge of Einik alone.

Einik, the legendary smith, worked at fashioning a Svar child while Isrohim Vey spoke to him.

"The truth of your sword," said Einik, "is that it is the product of a deal I made, a very long time ago. I'd realized that whatever I made would, in the end, break. Nothing was perfect. Nothing lasted. I disliked that. I made a deal; I would make a thing, a sword, the greatest thing I would ever make, and that sword would last forever through all the Ages of the world."

"Who did you make this deal with?" asked Isrohim Vey.

"Father Stone?" suggested the smith. "The One Above All? The Jack-of-all-Ills? I don't know. I don't need to know. But it was done."

"How old is the sword?"

The smith considered this. "Old," he decided.

"How did it come to the battlefield of Aruvhossin?"

"I don't know," said Einik. "I don't keep track of its whereabouts."

"Why not?"

Einik smiled without looking away from his work. "I don't need to," he said. "It's perfect. It will last. Somewhere, in the world, is the perfect thing that I made, which will outlive me. That's enough."

Isrohim Vey thought about this, too, and watched as Einik finished his work.

"Does the sword have a destiny?" he asked.

"I don't know," said Einik. "I made it; that's enough. I suppose either everything has a destiny, or nothing does."

"I have given it a name," said Isrohim Vey. "It's called Azrael's Word."

"It's been called many things," said Einik. "It outlasts names." He turned the infant Svar over in his hands. It did not move and its eyes were dark.

"What did you give in exchange for the making of the sword?" asked Isrohim Vey; and then for the first time Einik of the Svar locked eyes with him, and the swordsman saw that a white heat burned in him with a hard gem-like flame.

"I will tell you," said the smith, "but you must do a thing in exchange."

Isrohim Vey nodded.

"In exchange for making one perfect thing," said Einik, "I had to accept that every other thing I made would be less than perfect. That I would never again reach the height of the Nameless Sword. Now: reach into my forge and take out a burning coal, and put it in the mouth of the child."

Isrohim Vey reached into the fire with his left hand and did as the smith demanded. As he screamed, the eyes of the Svar baby lit up.

After leaving the Dweorgheorte Mountains, Isrohim Vey returned to the city of Vilmariy and was caught up in a struggle between two noble houses which resolved itself in a duel by proxy; Isrohim Vey was one proxy, and the other was the greatest fencer in all the Free Cities, Yasleeth Oklenn. Isrohim Vey slew Yasleeth and left Vilmariy, swearing a great oath upon his soul never to return again.

The people of the hamlet of Mun-at-Tor go about their work each day in silence, unsmiling. To the north, east, and south of Mun-at-Tor are quarries of fine stone, and it is to these places that the people go. No one goes west, past the three heavy stone churches, to the high forested hill; no one passes under the old stone arch built over a gully in the hillside, where the greenery grows richest. No one follows the music that comes from the arch at dawn and twilight. At least, no one from

Mun-at-Tor; sometimes a wild-eyed traveler comes to the grey quarry town and strides up the hill and through the arch and is, most often, not seen again.

Isrohim Vey came to Mun-at-Tor from Vilmariy and, arriving at dusk, walked under the old stone arch into the Faefair of the Ylvain.

Stalls were scattered across the face of the darkening hillside. The stalls were made of rare white and golden and crimson woods and carved into fantastic shapes, from which sprigs of holly and mistletoe sometimes grew. Pale musicians played inhuman sounds on skin drums and beetle-shell flutes and harps strung with cat's whiskers. The faerie folk were everywhere, buying and selling, some of them with foxes' heads, some half-a-foot high, some bent and bony as gargoyles, and some of them of the noble houses of the Ylvain.

Like their enemies the Svar, the Ylvain are immortal; but the Ylvain are tall and fair, and live in magic and forestlands, and their skin is bright as dawn, and in their veins is neither blood nor ichor but fine white mist, and it is their curse that everything they touch turns to beauty.

Isrohim Vey strode into the Faefair. He ignored the slender peddlers in green with pointed brows and wolf's fangs, selling trinkets like unbreakable chains of flowers and an elixir that was the essence of music. He passed cobblers selling boots that could walk between the moments of the clock; he passed drinking-booths selling beer that tasted of summers past; he passed stalls selling rare fruits, oranges and indigos, passionfruit and repentancefruit, firstfruits and lastfruits; he passed no blacksmiths or ironmongers. He didn't know what he was looking for.

He came to a high wagon; doors in the back were open, and inside there was paper: books, scrolls, and maps. More paper than Isrohim Vey had ever seen outside of the libraries of Lugbragthoth or the archives of Tíranin, and both of those were closely guarded. An old man in faded robes sat on a step leading into the wagon, smoking a long-stemmed pipe. He seemed human, but for his eyes, which were moonstones. He nodded to Isrohim Vey as the swordsman stepped into the wagon.

"You're mortal," said Isrohim Vey.

"I'm old. That's near to mortal."

"I don't know how old I am," said Isrohim Vey. "Fifty, I think. Close. Most men in my way of life don't live as long."

"What are you looking for at the Faefair? Youth?"

"Truth," said Isrohim Vey.

"I can sell you truth. But there will be a price."

"I'll pay it."

"So sure? You don't know what it is."

Isrohim Vey said nothing.

The old man sighed and refilled his pipe. "This is the truth: fifty years ago, give or take, the Nameless Sword hung above the bed of the Duke of Eblinn. Beneath its point a child was conceived, and nine months later was born. The Nameless Sword had been in the family of the Duke of Eblinn for centuries by this time. At the birth of the boy-child, a Dominie predicted firstly that he would meet death on a field named Aruvhossin; but also that if he evaded this death, he would go on to kill death itself. This boy was named Reivym Shoi. You met him once."

"Did I?"

"It was a long time ago. But he was at Aruvhossin, commanding his father's armies; you were at the same battle, having joined a company of Naranthi mercenaries fighting under the standard of the King of Anoch. Reivym Shoi bore the Nameless Sword in battle, believing that its destiny would keep him safe to pursue his own."

"What is the destiny of the sword?" asked Isrohim Vey.

"It is a sword. Its destiny is death. More than that no created being has ever been able to tell. Perhaps it will slay all the world. It kept Reivym Shoi safe and living until late on the first day of the battle, when he was attacked from behind by a Panjonrian soldier and left for dead. The Panjonrian took the sword, but was soon slain himself. You took the sword from his dead hand. With it, you survived the rest of the day, and through the night, and through to the end of the battle."

Isrohim Vey thought about this. Then he nodded, slowly. After some time he asked: "What do I do now?"

"Go forward, as you like. But I will tell you this. If you still wish to see the Angel of Death, then look for Reivym Shoi, who will meet the angel before he dies."

"Where's Reivym Shoi?"

"Reivym Shoi has been looking for you. He has gone to the one place you returned to, in all your time of wandering. He has gone to Vilmariy, and he has sworn a great oath upon his soul not to leave until you come a third time to the city."

Isrohim Vey said nothing. He sat on the step of the wagon and laughed.

The old man watched him.

"Now come with me," said the old man, "for you promised to pay my price."

"What must I do?"

"Fight, and kill, and perhaps die."

The old man took Isrohim Vey to a high tower in the Oneda Mountains that looked out over all the world. "I am the Dominie Segelius," the old man told Isrohim Vey, "and you are in the Demesne of Starry Wisdom and Golden-Eyed Dawn, which is the true home country of every wizard. Rest; tomorrow you begin to fight."

On the next day, Isrohim Vey fought and killed a gray-skinned warrior with a dog's head. The battlefield was a giant's outstretched palm, a thousand feet above deep forest broken by a single plume of smoke marking out an isolated inn.

The day after that, he fought and killed a pack of feral children. The battlefield was the high side of a cloud, under a sky lit by three full moons and a thousand constellations, each exerting its pull upon human destinies.

The day after that, he fought and killed a troll with three eyes and three mouths; no mouth spoke a comprehensible language, though each gibbered all through the fight. The battlefield was, or appeared to be, the Dire Stairs.

After each of these battles, and after every battle on every day that followed, Isrohim Vey found himself in the Dominie's tower, where he healed over the course of a night. On occasion the Dominie Segelius would speak with him.

What the Dominie said might be quite brief, as when he observed "wizardry is to witchcraft as art is to madness". Or he might speak at length, as when he explained to Isrohim Vey the true nature and relationship of all the gods of every mortal people, from the One Above All and the Jack-of-all-Ills of the Empire Church to the Great Gods of the Holy Dominion to the Twelve Gods and the God Of All Other Things of the Lohr to the Red Gods to the Unwritten Book to the Old Gods to Time, who was worshipped as a god in the far country of Knutherizh; and then on to the hundreds of gods of the Faefolk, and to Father Stone of the Svar, and to the gods of dragons and giantfolk and goblinkin, and how all these gods served to mortal understanding as giving to life a meaning in the face of death.

"Which is not to say," the Dominie then observed, "that they are unreal, or do not serve other purposes as well; but such purposes remain unknown, as the gods themselves are ultimately unknown. It is only the angels who can mediate between the human and divine spheres, being beyond gods as they are beyond destiny. The Dominion goddess of death, for example, is Halja; but she does not separate the soul from the body. No more does the hand of the One Above All. You know these things."

Isrohim Vey said nothing to this, and the next day he fought and killed two warriors of the shape-strong race of the Mirator, one of whom took the form of Valas as a youth while the other took the form of Valas as a king. The battlefield was the fountain of Umbral.

It was not so many days later that the battlefield was a deep dungeon, from which Isrohim Vey had to escape by defeating again the King-That-Was-And-Would-Be-Again.

The Dominie Segelius came to the aging swordsman after that fight, and Isrohim Vey asked: "Will I have to fight other figures of my past? Grandfather Hiberius, or Yasleeth Oklenn?"

"Does it surprise you that we know your history?" asked the Dominie. "We are wizards."

"Do you know everything there is to know?" asked Isrohim Vey.

The Dominie shrugged. "I know how scared you were when you faced the demon Gorias. I know you were not scared at all when you faced Umbral; but I don't know why not."

"Neither do I," said Isrohim Vey.

The Dominie nodded.

"Give me the worst of it," said Isrohim Vey.

The next day was a running battle across the field of Aruvhossin where seven armies lay dead. In that place Isrohim Vey killed his selves that might have been. He killed Isrohim Vey, the bloodthirsty mercenary captain. He killed Isrohim Vey, lecherous sybarite and drunk. He killed Isrohim Vey, devout chaplain of the Empire Church. These and many others he killed. Savage black dogs came to eat the entrails of the dead men. They scented the living Isrohim Vey, and chased him. There were too many to kill. Isrohim Vey was brought to ground. His muscles were torn from his bones and the tongues of dogs lapped at his blood. There was no angel. Only the quiet dissolution of all the world.

To his surprise, Isrohim Vey woke up in the Dominie's tower.

When the Dominie Segelius came to visit him, the swordsman said: "I died."

The Dominie shrugged.

"Why bring me back?" asked Isrohim Vey. Before the Dominie could answer, he asked also, "Why make me fight? Why do these things to me?"

"Wizards have their reasons. Perhaps we wanted to know how long it would be before you began to ask 'Why?' Perhaps we wanted to see what you would do now."

"What do you mean?"

"You're free to go," said the Dominie Segelius. "You should leave the Demesne. But other than that, you may go wherever you like. Do what you will."

After a long while, Isrohim Vey asked, "Why did you wait so long to find me? Why did you wait until I was so old?"

The Dominie shrugged.

Isrohim Vey travelled south from the Demesne of Starry Wisdom and Golden-Eyed Dawn, a long way south until the stars changed. He travelled through Ulvandr-Kathros the Confederate Empire until he reached its southwest coast, and then across the harsh seas until he reached the island of

Thættir. The people of Thættir were, and are, solitary and grim, fisherfolk and pirates, often foul of temper, overall seasoned by the salt of the sea and the bitter winds that lash the island of volcanic rock and ice fields; but they work together without complaint, are very brave, and love freedom. Isrohim Vey was soon voted by them to be Lawspeaker, which meant in essence to be their king.

For several years Isrohim Vey governed the people of Thættir wisely and well. Also in these years he organized their defenses. The Empress Adara XI had come to power in Ulvandr-Kathros; she was mad and lusted for conquest. For these reasons she looked westward, to Thættir, which had always before been too distant from the mainland to attract conquerors; it was that which had led men and women to settle on Thættir, and be free from rulers.

Isrohim Vey led raids against the mainland, sinking ships at harbor; he concluded alliances, with other island-folk and with the races under the ocean; and he sent agents northward to Opallios to recover that whip which commanded the flood and the eclipse, along with other treasures he had discarded decades before. When all these things had been done he made further preparations, but those were for his own future.

The night before the navies of Ulvandr-Kathros were to battle the ships of Thættir, Isrohim Vey went to the Dawn Tower, a lighthouse on the far eastern end of the island; with him was Ida, whom he trusted most on Thættir. Ida was the one he had chosen to go to Opallios. "We will win tomorrow," Isrohim Vey said to her, looking eastward.

"Yes, we will," said Ida. "The whip will determine it."

"True," agreed Isrohim Vey. "So there is no need of me." He took the obsidian amulet of the Lawspeaker from around his neck. Its chain clicked against itself as he gave it to Ida.

"I don't understand," she said. But she trusted him, and took the amulet.

"I have had some men loyal to me prepare a boat," he said. "I must go north. You will be the Lawspeaker."

"I am too young," said Ida.

"Some old men are wise," said Isrohim Vey. "Others have only lived a long time without meeting death."

"You can stay," said Ida. "Lead us further. If we break the navy of the Confederate Empire, we can raid inland – we could take the Pelian Isthmus, starve the city of Carcannum – you could topple the Empress, rule half the world."

"I could, old as I am. I choose not to."

Ida set the chain about her neck.

Suddenly, Isrohim Vey said: "You can escape destiny. Change your fate. The world's fate. If you choose to. If you know that, then you may not need to."

Below them, the waves of the sea crashed against the mossy black rocks of the island of Thættir, as they always had.

"What will I tell the people?" asked Ida.

"Tell them I have finally gone to the Angel of Death."

"Death. This will be difficult for them to understand."

Isrohim Vey said, "Death is simple."

Isrohim Vey did not know that the night he arrived in Vilmariy for the third and last time in his life was also the night of his sixty-first birthday; nor, if he had known, would it have mattered.

It was the night of the Grand Masque, when all things were upended.

Isrohim Vey walked through the city, past satyrs and devils and Kings of old time.

He asked a watchman for directions to the home of Reivym Shoi; whether this was truly a watchman or not did not matter. The man told the old swordsman where to find the estate of Reivym Shoi, heir to the line of Eblinn, and that was enough.

The house was dark and silent. Isrohim Vey walked to the front door and pounded on the solid wood. When no one came after a minute he pounded again; and then again. And eventually the door opened, and Reivym Shoi stood before Isrohim Vey.

"The servants are gone to the Grand Masque," said Reivym Shoi, who seemed not to see the man before him. "I am the master here. Who are you, and what do you seek?"

"I am Isrohim Vey, the death-bound swordsman. I carry the sword called Azrael's Word, which some say is the Nameless Sword. I seek the Angel of Death."

For a moment Reivym Shoi did not move; then he sprang back into the shadows of the house. Isrohim Vey followed, more slowly, and drew Azrael's Word. Then Reivym Shoi came at him, sword in hand, and the two old men fought.

Reivym Shoi's eyesight had faded with the years, but in the dark of the house Isrohim Vey found this gave him no advantage. But the wound he had given Reivym Shoi years ago on a ship still seemed to trouble him. Isrohim Vey drove him back across an old entrance hall. Then Reivym Shoi ducked into a shadowed archway, and turned and ran. Cautiously, Isrohim Vey gave chase.

He ran through dark room after dark room. Ahead of him, in the moonlight filtering through high windows, was always the form of Reivym Shoi. As fast as Isrohim Vey ran he could not gain ground, and for the first time in his life he felt truly old. Sometimes Reivym Shoi would shout and guards would come.

Isrohim Vey killed them. Reivym Shoi came to a flight of stairs and paused; a light flared, a lantern in his hand. Reivym Shoi ran down the stairs. Isrohim Vey followed.

The diagonal of the stairs ran a long way into the dark. Then there was a landing, a switchback, another long diagonal. Another landing, another switchback. And again. Isrohim Vey would catch up to Reivym Shoi during the long descents; then Reivym Shoi would turn a corner and without the light of his lantern Isrohim Vey was forced to slow down.

The stairs seemed to continue endlessly, past walls of old stone, then past no walls at all, into a vast cavern, then through a close arched shaft of rock carved with old runes. The stairs were pitched at an odd angle, and were of varied heights, as though to fit the strides of creatures with several sets of legs and a variable length of stride. Isrohim Vey and Reivym Shoi were by this time far far below the city of Vilmariy, farther below the earth than the deepest tunnel of the Hideous Prison Illullunor, farther below than the Deep Dark where Isrohim Vey had spoken to the Svar smith Einik.

As they raced down the stairs in their weary old-man's hobble, both men became aware of a third presence with them; and Isrohim Vey remembered the Dominie he had spoken to almost four decades past saying, "There are angels everywhere."

Then they were out of the tunnel, still upon the stairs, but the stairs now circled a curving stone wall; a great circle of stone, like a vast cup or cauldron on a scale fit for gods. Isrohim Vey heard a crashing and a pounding from below, and as he ran downwards he realized there was a fountain at the base of the cauldron, like the fountain under Umbral's glacier, but much larger. He could see the waters seething and frothing, raging and white; could see, at the edge of the light of Reivym Shoi's lantern, a fine mist of spray that seemed to take an infinity of forms. And those forms persisted when the light had moved on, so that in the darkness were all things made.

At the base of the long, long stairs there was a stone path like an isthmus or bridge leading out to an island in the middle of the fountain; like an image of Vilmariy, which was an island city built upon a mountain rising from a great river. Reivym Shoi hastened along the path. Isrohim Vey followed, slowly now as there was no other way off the island.

Finally, deliberately, Reivym Shoi set down his lantern and turned and drew his sword. "Do you know what this place is, Isrohim Vey?" he cried. "This is the Fount of All! Here all things come into the world! Here all things begin! So it must be here that all things end!"

It was at this point that Isrohim Vey understood that the years had taken Reivym Shoi's reason as well as his sight. Nevertheless the man attacked, and Isrohim Vey drew Azrael's Word for the last time in his life.

Isrohim Vey and Reivym Shoi battled for a long time on the island at the heart of the Fount of All.

It seemed to Isrohim Vey that every move he made he had already made, many times before. That his life was a circle and that all things in it had come round again.

Then he battered down Reivym Shoi's sword and kicked it away across the island. And he raised Azrael's Word; and brought it down; and Reivym Shoi's collarbone was crushed as the sword sank into his chest.

And then there was a light on Reivym Shoi's face, and his

eyes were focused on something far away, and Isrohim Vey turned, knowing what he would see.

And there was Azrael, the Angel of Death; and the angel was smiling.

And for the third and last time of his life Isrohim Vey spoke the Word of Azrael.

And, knowing that Reivym Shoi had still several moments of life left, Isrohim Vey deliberately let his sword fall from his hand; and this, the last decision in his life, was made in acceptance of his destiny, which, he understood now and for the first time, was only the beginning of himself and not the summation, just as he was defined not by the nature of that destiny but in how it was met and fulfilled.

And so Isrohim Vey moved beyond both destiny and free will.

And then Reivym Shoi took up the Nameless Sword which Isrohim Vey had called Azrael's Word, and, falling forward, with the last of his life drove the point of the sword through Isrohim Vey's chest and on into the heart of the Angel of Death.

And all Isrohim Vey knew was the smile of the angel. And the smile hurt with a sweet pain that grew until it was all he knew, and he knew everything and nothing. And Isrohim Vey felt his lips curve and pull back from his teeth, and felt his blood surge, and knew a rare warmth.

And Isrohim Vey smiled the smile of the Angel of Death, and all things were upended, and the world turned upside down.

Such is the end of the story of Isrohim Vey, as the Dominies tell it, and the keepers of the truths of angels. And all of them have since debated the fate of the soul of Reivym Shoi, and of the Angel of Death called Azrael, and of Isrohim Vey.

As is the case with most souls, however, their destiny remains unclear.

LADY OF THE GHOST WILLOW

Richard Parks

The remnants of my saké cask, like my sleep, had not lasted the night. Having no further resources to drown my nightmares, I rose, dressed, and went out into the streets of the Capital. The night was at its darkest, lost like me in the time evenly split between dusk and dawn, when ghosts and demons came out of hiding and walked freely about the city. I had no care for that possibility, save that I could have used the distraction.

So when the shining figure with the appearance of a lady approached me, I was more curious than worried.

I stood at the highest point on Shijo Bridge. It was a good spot to view the moon, if there had been a moon to view at that hour. It was a decent tactical location in case of trouble, with only two directions to defend. She came out of the darkness and stood on the eastern end of the bridge in the direction of the place where cremations were done, beyond the city walls and the clustered temples specializing in funerals.

She was not a ghost, though someone less experienced in these matters could easily mistake her for one. The glow around her was very faint but easy to see, and there was a slight flutter in her step that gave her away. Not a ghost. A shikigami, a magical creature with little more reality than the scraps of paper used to create her and no independent will save that of her master, whoever that might be. Still, the person who created her had done a superb job.

I had seen shikigami that seemed little more than poorly manipulated puppets, but this one could easily pass for human. From the number of layers of her kimono down to the precise cut of her hair, she appeared exactly as one would expect of a well-born attendant to a noble family. Not that such a one would ever be abroad this time of night, and certainly not on foot and alone.

I turned my gaze back over the water, though I kept her image in the corner of my eye. "What do you want?"

She bowed to me then. "I am sent with a message for Yamada no Goji. I serve Fujiwara no Kinmei."

The name was familiar. A high-ranking deputy to the Minister of the Right, if I recalled correctly. I had heard Prince Kanemore speak of him, and never disparagingly. Which was remarkable, considering His Highness's general opinion of the Fujiwara. My curiosity was piqued.

"I am Yamada. How did you or your master know I would be here?"

She bowed again. "We did not. I was on my way to your lodgings when I found you here instead."

That was plausible, since a Fujiwara compound was located in one of the southeastern wards not far from Gion. "I will hear you."

"May I approach? I do not wish to share my Master's business with others."

"Very well, but not too close."

The last was simple caution. While this particular shikigami might resemble a delicate young woman, I had dealt with such before and knew better. She could very well have been an assassin, and such a charming one would have very little trouble reaching her intended victim under normal circumstances, but my instincts told me that this was not the case. I trusted my instincts . . . up to a point.

She approached to within ten feet and bowed again. I looked over her shoulder. "You have a companion."

The shikigami frowned. "I came alone."

"I don't think this person bothered to ask permission."

She followed my gaze. A rough-looking samuru was approaching behind her, his hand on the hilt of his sword. I sighed. It was ever thus when more than one or two of the provincial lords and their retinues were in the Capital on business. Many of them kept well-disciplined attendants, but not all. And many of those were not above a bit of nocturnal enrichment or forced pleasure, at opportunity. The shikigami and I must have appeared to represent both potentials. My long dagger was well concealed but within easy reach. I only hoped the ruffian was no more skilled than he appeared.

He spoke to the messenger, though his eyes were on me. "Woman, behave yourself and nothing too unpleasant will happen to you. I must deal with your friend first."

The shikigami smiled at me as the man pushed past her. "Please, my lord. Allow me."

I grunted assent and the samuru's eyes grew wide as he felt himself gripped from behind. In another moment he cleared the bridge railing like a drunken crane who'd forgotten how to fly. I counted to three before I heard the splash. The shikigami held the samuru's sword in her hands.

"What shall I do with this?"

"A poor-quality blade," I said as I eyed it critically. "He may keep it."

Soon there was another, smaller splash. The messenger then turned back to me and spoke as if nothing unusual had happened at all.

"My master wishes your assistance in a rather delicate matter. He believes a friend of his has been cursed. His own arts have proved ineffective, and even the priests have been confounded. My master does not know where else to turn. Will you speak to him?" she asked.

"Yes," I said, "I believe I will."

My surmise about the location of Fujiwara no Kinmei proved accurate. According to the shikigami, he currently held sole possession of the mansion in the southeastern ward, as his uncle Fujiwara no Shintaro was away on a diplomatic assignment to the north. She brought me to the north gate where I stated my business to the old man who kept watch there. I heard a faint rustle beside me and the messenger was gone. All I saw was a piece of folded paper that quickly blew away down the street on a freshening breeze.

The servant escorted me into the compound. He barely spoke at all and made no comment on the disappearance of my companion. I imagined that such sights were not unknown to him.

Lord Kinmei was waiting for me in the main wing of the house. At that hour there was no one else stirring, no doubt part of his intention in sending such a late summons. We had never met before, so we took a moment to study each other. I could only imagine how I must have appeared to him, in my threadbare robes and ungroomed state. For his part he was elegantly but simply dressed. I judged him perhaps thirty years old, handsome, but little else seemed there to read. He offered me saké, which I refused, though it pained me to do so. Considering my reputation, I expected him to be surprised, but if so he didn't show it. He beckoned me to an empty cushion and sat down himself.

"Forgive my late summons, but under the circumstances it seemed best. I trust my servant told you my purpose?"

"In general terms, my lord, but not many specifics. You have a friend who is cursed?"

The man sighed. "I call it that for want of a better word. I would say 'haunted', but that is impossible."

"How so?"

"As you may know, I am a man of some influence. My friend in turn is a man of good family and some wealth. He has had priests and monks alike place spirit wards at all points of access to his home, and I myself have brought in exorcists of great skill to watch over him. Yet despite both our efforts, a spirit has been seen walking his compound at night, apparently with impunity."

"What sort of spirit?"

"A female, as best anyone can tell. At first glance she appears totally unremarkable, yet the witnesses who have encountered her up close swear that she has no face. They see only a blank white mask where the face should be."

"And there are no exorcists on duty when this happens?"

He smiled then. "You must not think me so negligent of my friend's health, Lord Yamada. Twice the spirit has been trapped and banished to whence it came, yet it always returns again on another night as if nothing had happened. After each visit my friend's condition worsens. I have sutras being read at half the temples in the Capital. Nothing seems to help."

That was indeed puzzling. My friend Kenji, though lacking in most other attributes of a priest, was one of the finest exorcists I knew, and I had never known a spirit that he had exorcised fail to *remain* exorcised. I had no doubt those engaged by Lord Kinmei were of equal or greater skill. Besides, any competent priest could create a barrier that would be proof against spirits of the dead or even minor demons. Still, I found myself wishing that Kenji was not currently on a pilgrimage to Mount Hiea. His bursts of actual piety were infrequent but seldom convenient for all that.

"Lord Kinmei, before we go any further, I must ask you a question: why did you send a shikigami to fetch me? Have you no other servants?"

He smiled again. "Many. But none I would send into the streets of the Capital at this demon-infested hour."

"Also, this way, clearly yet without saying a word, you demonstrated that you are not without skill in supernatural matters. So I would understand that your need must indeed be great to seek me out."

Lord Kinmei bowed slightly. "It's true that I am not without my resources, Lord Yamada. Chinese magic is a slightly disreputable pursuit for one such as I, of course, but useful. Yet you can also see that my ... intervention, in this matter, must remain at a discreet level. You have quite a reputation, Lord Yamada."

"For saké?"

A bit blunt on my part, but I preferred honesty in these sorts of dealings, to the degree that was possible. It prevented many a misunderstanding later.

"That as well," Kinmei admitted, "but also for discretion. The saké I do not care about, save that it not interfere with your services."

"It will not. Now, then, is it my aid or my advice you seek?"

"Both. For which I am quite willing to pay two casks of rice from the first harvest of my western farms, plus five bolts of blue silk and one bar of gold to the weight of twenty Chinese coins."

I kept my face blank with an effort. Such would pay off all my current debts plus support me comfortably for an entire year. More, if I were sensible, though of course I would not be.

"Your terms are acceptable. I will require a written introduction to your friend, along with his cooperation. You can start by telling me his name."

"You'll understand that I could not say until we had agreed, but he is Minamoto no Akio. He is a member of the Emperor's guard, though at present he is on leave for his health. All is easily arranged. He will listen to my wishes in this. Do you have any thoughts on the problem at this point?"

The victim was unknown to me, but I felt sure I could find out more from Prince Kanemore if need compelled. That would not be necessary, if Kinmei was being as honest with me as he seemed to be. "A couple. But first I must ask you an indelicate question: to your knowledge, is your friend prone to intemperate love affairs?"

Kinmei smiled again, though I felt that he almost laughed. "Akio has never been prone to intemperance of any kind, Lord Yamada. He is quite likely the most serious, dutiful man I have ever met. He has only one . . . attachment, that I am aware of."

"Do you know her name? Where the lady might be found?"

Kinmei sighed. "I'm sorry, but such is Lord Akio's discretion that I barely know of her existence. Why do you ask?"

"Because of the nature of the attacks. Now, one possibility is that the ghost enters his compound by avoiding the barriers."

"Certainly, but how? The priests are quite diligent, I assure you."

"By the simple expedient of already being *within* his compound. If the grave is located on the premises, even an exorcist would not send her far."

From the expression on Kinmei's face it was obvious that the possibility had never occurred to him. "Far-fetched," he said at last, "but certainly possible. That must be considered."

"The other possibility is that we're not dealing with a ghost in the normal sense at all, which is why I asked about his love affairs, meaning no disrespect. Our creature could be an ikiryo."

He frowned. "Ikiryo? You mean the vengeful spirit of a living person?"

I was not surprised that he had heard of such things, but again it was clear the possibility had not occurred to him before now. No wonder. Such instances were extremely rare, and the most famous one of all never actually happened, unless the lady known as Murasaki Shikibu's account of a feckless prince's life was truer than was commonly believed.

"Even so," he said, "I consider that even less likely than finding a grave on the grounds."

"Jealousy and anger are powerful emotions and can arise even in the best of people. Like the Lady of the Sixth Ward herself, whoever is doing this might not even be aware of it." I made the reference to the *Genji Monogatari* in the full confidence that he would understand it, nor was I disappointed.

"The Lady of the Sixth Ward wrought great harm to the Shining Prince's loved ones all unawares. So. We must consider all possibilities, not only for Akio's sake but the future happiness of our two families. Suzume especially."

I frowned. "Your pardon, Lord Kinmei, but I don't know who you mean."

"Fujiwara no Suzume. My younger sister, Lord Yamada. Once Akio has recovered his health, he and Suzume are to be married."

It occurred to me that, if Lady Suzume had been the "attachment" to which Lord Kinmei referred, he would know more of the matter than he was telling. Again, my instincts spoke against that. Which left the matter of Lord Akio's lover a question that would need answering.

It took a little while for the introductions and arrangements to be made, so by the time I arrived at Akio's family compound on the sixth avenue south of Gion, his condition had worsened and he was unable to receive visitors. Akio had been placed in the east wing of the mansion, and I could plainly hear the drones of the priests reciting sutras. No expense had been spared, though so far to no good effect.

As evening fell again, I toured the grounds in the company of an aged senior priest named Nobu. I told him of my suspicions, and he considered them in silence for several moments.

"A burial in a place meant for the living would be most unusual," he said. "One that would occur only in circumstances that were themselves . . . unusual."

I smiled then. I was beginning to like the old priest. "We must speak frankly to one another," I said. "You mean either a burial from ancient times . . . or a murder."

"Lord Akio's family have long been patrons of my temple. I would not accuse this great and noble house of such a thing," Nobu said.

"Nor would I. It's possible the grave exists without their knowledge. So it would be in their interest that we find it and remove it, if that grave does in fact exist."

In some ways Nobu reminded me of Kenji, at least in the sense that I always got when watching a master at work. In a very short span of time I saw that Lord Kinmei's confidence had not been misplaced. Nobu worked the area of the compound with his tools, and I with mine. He counted the beads on his prayer necklace while keeping up a steady chant as he paced off the length and breadth of the grounds like a water-diviner. For my part I kept a close watch for rising miasmas and the blink of corpse lights. When we met back near the front gate, we had both come to the same conclusion.

Nobu sighed. "Nothing, Lord Yamada. I can find no grave here."

"I agree. Which is a shame, really. A grave would have been easier to deal with."

"A proper cremation. A proper funeral ritual and reburial with respect. Even someone torn from this world by violence could be appeased on that score," he said. "Pity."

"So that leaves us with the second possibility that I mentioned."

"My wager," the old priest said, "would have been on the grave. Lord Yamada, I've known young Akio all his life. It simply makes no sense to me that anyone would harbor this level of ill-feeling towards him, consciously or not. He's as decent a man as I've ever known."

"Someone clearly does . . . and that someone is here!"

I spotted the faintly glowing figure only a moment before Nobu did. I sprinted toward the veranda of the east wing, with the priest, for all his years, barely three paces behind me.

The creature was exactly as had been described. It was dressed in flowing white robes, as for a funeral, though it was hard to make out any specific details of the garb. The ghost's long, unconfined black hair twisted and flowed in the freshening breeze as if it were a separate thing with its own will, framing a face of no features. No eyes, nose, mouth, just a white emptiness that was more chilling than the most ferocious devil-mask.

I put myself between the thing and the house with no clear idea of what I was going to do. I had amulets for protection against ordinary spirits, but I wasn't sure they would serve here. I never got the chance to find out, for in another moment Nobu was beside me. I expected him to begin the rite of exorcism, but instead he produced a strip of paper and slapped it directly on to the creature's empty face. In another moment it had vanished, and only then did Nobu sink slowly to the ground, his chest heaving.

"Are you all right?" I asked. I started to help him up, but he waved me off.

"I think I will live, Lord Yamada, but one of my age should not run so much. Give me a moment."

I waited until Nobu's breathing – and my own – had returned to something closer to normal, then I helped him to stand again. "What did you use on that thing?"

"A seal more appropriate for a powerful kami rather than a simple ghost. Which, if you are correct, this thing is not. After seeing the result, I'm inclined to agree. Do you think I destroyed it?"

So my suspicions were confirmed. A powerful spirit but a ghost of the living, not the dead. Ikiryo. I shook my head. "A friend of mine once helped me contain a shape-shifter's power with something similar, but more likely you banished it temporarily, much like the previous exorcisms. I believe it will return."

"I can replace the wards on Akio's room with these," he said. "I have just enough left. But he can't stay in that room forever. I'll send to Enryaku Temple tonight for more seals, but I'm not sure how long these will last. The wards are strongest when first used. Their power fades over time."

"If I can find the source of the ikiryo that will be a moot point," I said. "And to do that, I have to learn more about who Lord Akio's unseen enemy might be. I may need to search his private quarters."

Nobu hesitated. "Lord Kinmei trusts you and thus so must I, but I would be remiss in my duties to the family if I allowed you to riffle through Akio's belongings without supervision."

I had no argument with that condition. I waited while the priest changed the defenses of Lord Akio's sickroom. When he returned he looked relieved.

"Lord Akio is sleeping peacefully. Whatever the creature meant to do, I believe it was thwarted tonight."

"Then let us hope I find something that will help keep it away permanently."

I allowed Nobu to escort me to the young master's private rooms and remain with me as I searched. I opened and closed several chests, but most contained extra clothes and such and were of little interest. In truth, very little that was obvious to me on first inspection was of interest. I stopped, considering what I might have missed.

"It might help if you told me what sort of thing you're looking for," Nobu said.

I sighed. "The only way I could tell you would be if I'd already found it."

I took another long look around the room. Like a tiny insect crawling on my arm, a thing scarcely noticed save for the itch, something was bothering me. Something was . . . missing.

"Your master is of the royal court and yet not literate?"

Nobu scowled. "Illiterate? Nonsense! Even the Emperor has remarked on Akio's skill as a poet."

"Then where is his writing table?"

Nobu's scowl deepened, then suddenly cleared away. "Oh! It was brought to his sickroom. I think its presence was meant to comfort him."

"I need to see it, but I do not wish to disturb the young man's sleep."

"We should be able to bring it out for you. Come with me."

Akio's quarters were in the west wing of the mansion. We made our way through the corridor, into the main house, then out into the east wing. There were few servants about, mostly women, and they moved silently on their own errands with barely a glance at us. As we grew closer to the sickroom, the chanting of the monks grew louder, though the sound remained somewhat muted in order to not awaken Akio.

Nobu left me where three priests sat in prayer, and a female attendant slid the screen aside for him to enter the room. In a few moments he returned, bearing the writing table.

It was of fine make, lacquered and painted with scenes of mountains and rivers and set at the perfect height for a kneeling man to use. There was a small chest attached for his inkstones and brushes, and a separate drawer for paper. All was in good condition and in order, though it was also clear that the table and its implements had seen heavy use.

There were also several cubbyholes containing scrolls. Nobu looked unhappy but said nothing as I pulled each out in turn and examined it. Drafts of poems, mostly completed. I read a few and silently agreed with Nobu's opinion – Lord Akio clearly was a talented poet and could no doubt hold his own or better at court, where nearly all written communication of importance was in poetic form. I soon found a common reference in several completed poems and a few drafts. I showed them to Nobu.

"Lord Akio uses the expression 'Lady of the Ghost Willow' more than once. There's also a few references to a 'Lady of the Morning Iris'. Do you know who he meant?" I asked, but Nobu just shrugged.

"I'm afraid the references have no meaning to me," he said.

"The poems I showed you *are* Lord Akio's work, are they not?"

"Of course. Why do you ask?"

I held a piece of paper which, as the wrinkles and creases clearly showed, had been folded into a thin strip and tied into a knot. "To be certain." I showed him the bit of writing on that paper. "Is this your master's calligraphy?"

Nobu was looking decidedly uncomfortable. "No. I don't recognize the hand, though I think I've seen it before. What is it?"

"A letter . . . or rather, a poem."

"Lord Yamada, this is all really improper. These poems are private correspondence."

"I agree. Yet I'm afraid that this is my main virtue, for the missions I've undertaken: I'm willing to be improper as the need arises. And in this case, the need is that I read these private communications on the chance that they will tell me something that can help Lord Akio."

Nobu's scowl deepened, but he did not object further. I flattened out the paper as much as possible and read what was written there:

> *The humbled swordsman*
> *Once proud, a blade cut his sleeve*
> *Now wet with the dew.*

The tanka was written in a delicate, refined script and was incomplete. Normally the one who received such a poem would write two lines to complete the form and return it to the sender. I had no way of knowing if the poem had been intended for Akio or whether he had replied.

I had little talent for poetry, but my instruction in the classic metaphors was probably no less extensive than Akio's. The poem was both an entreaty and a question; that much was clear. But what was the answer? One who might be able to tell me was beyond speech now and might be for some time, if not forever. I wondered if there was anyone aside from Akio who might know.

"Lord Akio is safe for the moment. I must leave now and get a little sleep before I return to Lord Kinmei's house tomorrow. Please return this table to its rightful place."

Nobu looked at me. "Tomorrow? But it's my understanding that Lord Kinmei left for Enrakyu Temple to pray for Lord Akio's health this very morning. He won't be back until the day after. And even then he plans to stay here, rather than at his own home. He wishes to be present if . . . when, his friend awakens."

"Perfect, since it is Fujiwara no Suzume I need to speak with."

"His sister? May I ask why?"

"Because it's possible that she knows more about this matter than her brother does."

It was mid-morning before Fujiwara no Suzume was ready to receive me. I was ushered into the main reception hall. There was a low dais on which a translucent curtain of silk had been hung. Lady Suzume kneeled on a cushion behind that curtain, with two female attendants flanking her at a discreet distance. I could see the outlines of her small form but few details. It would have taken a far more intimate connection than the one I had to be allowed to see her face.

"My brother left instructions to the household that we refuse no reasonable request from you," she said without preamble. "What do you wish of me, Lord Yamada?"

Straight to the point. I know she was trying to be rude, but at the moment such directness served my needs admirably.

"Please forgive my intrusion, but there are some questions I need to ask you, for Lord Akio's sake."

"Akio? What can I tell you that would be of help?"

Was that actual concern in her voice? I had to admit that it at least sounded that way. "I understand that you were promised to Lord Akio."

"I am still promised to Lord Akio," she replied, with some of the coldness I had originally felt returning to her voice. "And if it be the will of Heaven that promise will be honored. Akio's father and my uncle have both approved the match."

"Is that your will as well?"

There was a long silence. Thanks to the curtain I couldn't tell if she was shocked or merely trying not to laugh.

"What has that to do with the matter, Lord Yamada? You know the law as well as I."

"Of course, my lady. But that was not my question."

There was an even longer silence, then she turned to her two attendants. "You are both to withdraw to just beyond the doorway. Keep us in sight, as is proper, but no more."

They both bowed and obeyed, though without a great deal of enthusiasm. When they were clearly out of earshot,

Lady Suzume beckoned me closer. She then pulled the two halves of the curtain apart, only a little, but it was enough that I could finally see the woman kneeling behind the curtain, and the sight was very familiar. Easily explained: her resemblance to her brother was quite striking. She was, in her own way, as beautiful as he was handsome. She also seemed to be his model for the shikigami who had served as his messenger earlier.

"I had to see your face, Lord Yamada. Forgive me, but some matters cannot be judged by words alone through a veil."

I had of course seen the veil as a hindrance to myself, but now I understood that hindrance worked both ways. "I am honored."

"Not by my own inclination. Your reputation is unsavory at best, but I want you to understand that I will do anything I can to be of service to Lord Akio. Anything, and that includes answering your rather impertinent question, Lord Yamada – yes, it is my will. Akio and my brother grew up together and were inseparable, and so Lord Akio in turn was like an older brother to me. My affection for him has only increased over the years. He is the kindest, gentlest man I have ever known."

"So you are . . . content, to be Lord Akio's wife?"

She did laugh then, demurely covering her mouth with her fan. "'Content'? Lord Yamada, I have lived in *terror* of some of the marriages my family contemplated for me. Yet when my uncle gave me the news that I was for Akio instead, I counted myself thrice blessed! He is a good man, a friend, and will treat me well. I cannot believe the gods would be so cruel as to offer me such happiness and then snatch it from me before I have even touched it."

I, on the other hand, had no trouble at all believing that they would do such, and worse besides. I had seen it, and not from nearly as far a distance as I would have liked. Which was another reason I did not want to follow my current path but did not see much in the way of alternatives. I did note that Lady Suzume never said that she loved him, but perhaps in her view that was entirely beside the point.

"Forgive me, Lady Suzume, but you do know that he has other attachments?"

For the space of a dozen heartbeats, there was almost absolute silence. "What of it?" she asked, finally, and I could not imagine the snows of Hokkaido containing any more chill than the one in her voice.

"So you did know."

"Of course I knew! It was my business to know. What I do not know is why you're asking me this."

"Again I must beg your indulgence, but I did ask for a reason."

She closed the curtain again. "I am not curious about that reason. If there is more to the matter, I suggest you consult the so-called 'Lady of the Ghost Willow' for yourself."

So she even knew her rival's poetic euphemism. I should have been surprised, but I was not. "No one seems to know who she is."

I thought she was going to laugh, call me an idiot, or both. "I assume you've seen Lord Akio's poems, or you wouldn't be asking me about this woman. I believe he also refers to her as 'Morning Iris'. Put it together, Lord Yamada."

I frowned. Morning Iris? Ghost Willow? For a moment I just stared at her. Then I almost called *myself* an idiot. "The tree called the ghost willow is 'yanagi', and it's also a family name. Iris is 'ayame', a flower and also a woman's name. 'Lady of the Ghost Willow.' I'm looking for a woman named Yanagi no Ayame."

I couldn't see her smile, but I knew it was there. "So you're not a complete fool. That's good to know, since you seem to be our only hope for Lord Akio's deliverance. You *will* find a way to save him, Lord Yamada. I hope there is no misunderstanding between us on this."

At that point I did not think there was. "Everything I do now is in the service of Lord Akio's deliverance, Lady Suzume."

"Then I humbly suggest you stop wasting my lord's time. The woman you seek lives in the Fifth Ward. If you need answers, she's more likely to possess them than I."

The Yanagi family compound had seen better days. The walls had been patched in several places; the gate swung uneasily on rusty hinges. Yet the patching was of fine workmanship, and if the hinges were rusted the gate itself had been recently repaired. An old woman, whom I soon learned was the only retainer remaining, closed the gate behind us and led me through the dilapidated garden. A very old willow, the sort with long, trailing limbs and commonly known as a "ghost willow", had pride of place there, such that it was, doubtless due to its family association. Such trees were often the haunts of yokai and ghosts, and considered unlucky. When I saw the state of the Lady of the Morning Iris's home, I was inclined to agree.

Whatever lowly condition the family had come to, etiquette itself had not been abandoned. I was led to an audience with Yanagi no Ayame that, at least so far as the procedures and forms were concerned, was little different than the one earlier with Lady Suzume. Only this time, the curtains were not opened. Yet their threadbare state did give me a glimpse of the woman on the opposite side of the veil from time to time.

She was about Suzume's age or perhaps a bit younger. Her kimono and green Chinese overjacket were of fine quality, and if the kimono was a little worn, the overjacket was obviously new. Ayame herself was a lovely, delicate woman, though with little of the serenity of Lady Suzume.

"Thank you for receiving me. I am Lord Yamada."

Yanagi no Ayame was worried, and she didn't bother to conceal it. "I apologize for our current surroundings, Lord Yamada, but as you see, maintenance has been impossible until recently."

"That is of no consequence. Thank you for receiving me under these circumstances."

"Your messenger barely preceded you within the hour, so I must ask you: is there any further news of Lord Akio?"

"He yet lives, but his health is grave. Surely you knew of this before my messenger arrived?"

"I only knew . . ." Her voice trailed off. "That is . . ."

I didn't want to embarrass her, but I didn't have the time to dance around the matter all evening. Nor, I was certain, did Lord Akio. "You only knew that he had not visited or written to you in the last several days, yes?"

"Yes," she said, so softly I barely heard her. "In my loneliness I was afraid he had forgotten me."

Attachments among the nobility tended to follow set protocols: in the case of a formal alliance, the man would visit his love openly, and any children produced would be immediately acknowledged. If there was no formal understanding, the visits would of course be more discreet, whatever the outcome, including children. I was fairly certain that Lord Akio's relationship with the "Lady of the Ghost Willow" fell into the informal second category, whatever their feelings toward each other might be.

"I realize it is both painful and indelicate to speak of such things, so I must ask your forgiveness in advance. I have Lord Akio's welfare at heart."

"As do I, Lord Yamada. He has been very kind to me in my troubles, and if I can be of service to him now, I will. But I don't know what I can tell you that may be of help."

"Perhaps we may discover something together. Now, then: you say you did not know of Lord Akio's condition. Did you also not know that he is engaged to Lady Fujiwara no Suzume?"

She sighed. "That I did know. He told me himself some weeks ago."

That got my attention. "If I may ask, what was his purpose in telling you?"

She frowned slightly. "It may surprise you, Lord Yamada, considering the differences in circumstances between me and my lord, but we had . . . *have* few secrets between us. He told me of his father's decision because he thought I had the right to know."

I was beginning to wonder how the ikiryo was managing to harm Lord Akio in the first place. The more I heard of the man, the more I expected him to be surrounded by the divine protective glow of saintly purity. I dismissed the thought as unworthy, and wondered if I was beginning to feel jealous of the man.

"I could understand one being angry at such news," was all I said.

Through one of the rips in the curtain, I clearly saw Ayame frown. "Why should I be angry? It is a good match; I know he has always been fond of Lady Suzume and her brother. He often spoke of them. They've been friends since they were children."

"And you had no ambitions of one day occupying the place that Lady Suzume will soon take by his side?"

Ayame was silent for several heartbeats. "That was always impossible," she finally said, her voice barely audible.

"I can see how your current circumstances would be a hindrance, but are you certain? Did Akio never speak to his family on your behalf?"

Silence again. Then, "Lord Yamada, you misunderstand. When I refer to 'my circumstances', it is not my obvious poverty that is the obstacle. It is the fact that my father and brother were both carried off by a demon of disease when I was fifteen. I have no other brothers or male cousins."

As with Lady Suzume, again I felt like a complete fool. Under both law and custom, Ayame was unable to speak for herself in these matters. Only her father or any surviving male relative of age could grant her permission to marry. And there was none.

"You are the last of your family, aren't you?"

"Do not think me despairing, Lord Yamada. I may yet have children, so in some fashion the Yanagi Clan may survive. But I can never formally marry. When the time came, I couldn't even offer myself to Lord Akio freely. I had to beg him to force me, so that I would not offend my father's spirit by usurping his prerogative."

"I'm sorry," I said, though the word seemed like nothing.

"I do not need your pity, Lord Yamada. I need for you to understand me. If Lord Akio did not marry Suzume, he would marry another. If the gods will that this be the end of our love, then it will be so. But I do not think that will be the case. Perhaps that hope is an illusion, but I will cling to it. Now. Is there anything else?"

"No, Lady Ayame."

"Then this audience is at an end."

On the evening of the third day I found Nobu pacing the perimeter of the mansion, his prayer beads out. "I'm glad you've returned," he said. "I think we'll need all the aid we can find."

"Did the creature return last night?"

"Yes, but the seals held. It didn't get in. But I warned you that the seals were losing potency, and my messengers have not yet returned from Enryaku Temple. If they don't come after tonight we'll be back to bare exorcism."

"You have no seals at all?"

He grunted. "Only two that I still trust, but that's not enough to secure the chamber where Lord Akio is being tended."

I breathed a silent prayer of thanks to whoever might be listening. "Two may be just enough. Has Lord Kinmei returned?"

"Yes, though he was weary from his journey. I believe he is asleep in Lord Akio's chambers. Shall I awaken him?"

"No, but I would like to check on him. First give me one of the wards, just in case I meet the creature before you do. You take the other and keep watch. I'll be back shortly."

There was an attendant at the door. I ordered him to go join the guard around the room where Lord Akio was being kept, and then I slipped inside the room where Lord Kinmei was sleeping. I tarried there for a few moments but was careful not to awaken him, and then I left as quietly as I could and returned to where the others kept watch. On my way back I saw the ghostly figure floating across the ground in the courtyard.

"The ikiryo is coming," I said.

In an instant Nobu had the spirit ward in his hand. "You saw it? Where?"

"Close by. Be prepared."

The ikiryo manifested just beyond the veranda, in manner and appearance exactly the same as I had seen it two nights before. It floated toward Lord Akio's sickroom as if it didn't even notice us. I wondered if perhaps that was indeed the case. I leaned close to Nobu.

"Once the seal is placed, be prepared to move quickly."

He started to ask me something, doubtless to inquire what I was talking about, but there was no time. He stepped into the spirit's path and placed his last remaining ward.

"Hsssss . . ."

I have no idea how the creature hissed like a cat with no visible mouth, but then I halfway expected the thing to be stronger than before. Nonetheless, Nobu's spirit seal performed its duties admirably, and the creature began to fade. I turned to the other priests and attendants nearby as I took a torch out of the hands of one startled servant. "Stay here. Make sure no one approaches Lord Akio until we return. Master Nobu, follow me!"

I saw the confusion on the old man's face but he didn't hesitate. I sprinted down the corridor, across the main wing and back into the west wing of the mansion with Nobu close behind.

"Is Lord Kinmei . . . in danger as well?" he managed to gasp.

"Extremely so!"

There was a bewildered attendant at the door to Lord Akio's quarters where Lord Kinmei was sleeping. I sent him off to join the guard around Lord Akio.

"Why did you send him away?" Nobu asked as I slid the door aside.

"So he wouldn't see this," I said.

Lord Kinmei lay on his bedding right where I'd left him, still fast asleep, only now the ikiryo hovered above him, its no-face mere inches from his face. Nobu grabbed his prayer beads and immediately began a rite of exorcism, but I stopped him.

"If you value Lord Kinmei's life, wait," I said.

Nobu stared at me, uncomprehending, but there wasn't time for questions. I darted forward and slapped Lord Kinmei awake.

"What—?"

He started to scramble to his feet but I held him down. "Look, Lord Kinmei. Look at it."

Despite his obvious fear, he did as I commanded, and comprehension finally came. "Is this . . . ?"

"Yes, my lord. It is."

"I-I swear I didn't know. I didn't mean . . ."

"I know."

I reached forward and plucked Nobu's last remaining spirit seal, the one he'd given me earlier, from Lord Kinmei's chest where I'd left it after I saw the ikiryo emerge from Lord Kinmei only a few minutes before. With the barrier dissolved, the ikiryo returned to its rightful place as Lord Kinmei began to weep.

★   ★   ★

I joined the guard surrounding Lord Akio until Nobu returned to fetch me later in the evening. "He's ready to receive you now."

"How is he?"

"Devastated, as one might expect. He wants to become a monk."

"Do you think that's a wise decision?"

He smiled. "As a rule? Yes. But he's in no condition to be making that choice now. Besides, his father requires heirs to the clan line and would never allow it. He's in negotiations for an arranged marriage even as we speak."

"That would be what's expected."

"Lord Yamada, I have been a spiritual counselor to both families for a long time. Do you think I didn't know of Lord Kinmei's inclinations? This does not change the fact that he is a loyal son and will do what is expected of him. But the ikiryo? That I did not know, or even suspect, but at least I understand now why you halted my exorcism."

I sighed. "I've often asked you to trust me during this time, but now it seems that I must trust you, Master Nobu. You are quite correct. With the 'grave' of the spirit blocked, an exorcism might have worked too well, and Lord Kinmei would have lost that part of himself forever. I've seen that happen once before, and I'd call the result an improvement. But in this case? I think we would have done irreparable harm."

"Perhaps we already have. Is this really necessary?"

"'A poisoned wound never heals.' Lord Akio will recover. Now we must make sure Lord Kinmei does the same."

Lord Kinmei was waiting for us in Akio's quarters. Upon first glance, I'd say "devastated" was an understatement. At that moment Lord Kinmei had to be the most miserable human being I'd ever seen, and that included my own reflection. There were cushions there on the floor by the bedding and he motioned for Nobu and me to sit.

"I will never forgive myself, Lord Yamada," he said without preamble. "When I think of what I almost did . . . but I didn't know. How did you?"

"In order to answer that, I must ask you a question or two yet. Are you prepared?"

He took a long breath and then indicated assent. I recited the unfinished poem I'd found in Lord Akio's writing table. "That was yours, wasn't it?"

"Yes, Lord Yamada."

"The allusion to the cut sleeve was obvious, a reference to shared love between men that has been used in poetry since ancient times. But Lord Akio did not return your affections, did he?"

There were tears in Lord Kinmei's eyes. "Lord Akio has great regard for me, as one might a brother. My feelings for him were . . . are, deeper. No, Lord Yamada, he did not share those feelings."

"There is much I don't understand," Nobu said, "but I realize now that the attacks began only after Akio's engagement to Suzume was formalized. Why was she not attacked instead?"

I smiled then. "Obviously, because Lord Akio's upcoming marriage was an accident of timing, not the cause. Would you agree, Lord Kinmei?"

He looked at the floor. "I had no reason to resent my sister. If Akio had truly returned my affections, the technicality of a wife would not prevent our relationship, just as it does not for other men and women whose affections are elsewhere, whatever their inclinations."

I nodded. "In truth, even after the poem, I tended to suspect that Suzume might be the real culprit. The appearance of the spirit was . . . ambiguous, and the death of the groom is one sure way to prevent an undesired marriage."

Kinmei sighed. "May I ask how Suzume convinced you of her innocence?"

"At the end of our audience she told me to find a way to save Lord Akio," I said.

Now Nobu scowled. "You believed her? Just because of a plea?"

I almost laughed. "Plea? No, Master Nobu – it was a *command*. With, I might add, implied consequences for failure."

Kinmei managed a weak smile. "Even as a child, Suzume was never easily nor lightly thwarted."

I bowed. "Thus your sister thoroughly squelched any suspicion that the match was undesirable in her eyes. With that fact established, the nature of the ghost itself argued against her involvement. If the ikiryo had awakened within Lady Suzume, it would certainly have gone after the Lady of the Ghost Willow, not Lord Akio."

"You found her?" Nobu asked. "Then how did you know that *she* was not the culprit?"

"Suzume's innocence argued for that of Lord Akio's lover as well. An ikiryo is a very special sort of assassin, conjured in a moment of great emotional upheaval, which by then I was certain that Suzume only experienced *after* the first attacks, not before. The Lady of the Ghost Willow knew about the marriage arrangement long before Lord Akio was attacked, which likewise removed the heat of passion as an issue. I'm afraid, Lord Kinmei, that left only you."

"I want to die," he said.

Nobu glared at me, but I just smiled again. "Why? For saving Lord Akio's life?"

Lord Kinmei stared at me as if I'd slapped him. "For . . . ? I almost killed him!"

I shook my head. "No, my lord. Your resentments, your jealousy, those powerful emotions that sometimes get out of our control almost killed him. But you? That part that is and always remains Fujiwara no Kinmei felt nothing but love and concern for your friend. You almost certainly prevented his death as if you'd shielded him with your own body."

Tears were streaming down his face now. "How? How did I do this?"

"You summoned *me*. With all due respect to Master Nobu and his associates, if you had not done so, Lord Akio would likely be dead now."

"That is no more than simple truth," Nobu said ruefully.

Lord Kinmei would not meet my gaze. "You are kind," he said.

I shook my head. "No, my lord, I am not. As Master Nobu just pointed out, I have told you the truth, no more and no less. If there is any kindness here, you must find it for yourself."

"But what must I do now? Akio remains in danger so long as I live!"

Nobu bowed. "With respect, I rather doubt that."

I nodded. "Again, Master Nobu speaks truly. An ikiryo feeds on repressed resentments, unacknowledged emotions. That was why I sealed you off, so it could not return to you without your full awareness. Now, you *know*, and that changes everything. I do not believe the creature will return. If you can make peace with yourself now, I guarantee it will not."

"I will speak to your father," Nobu said. "I'm sure he will approve a time of retreat at Enryaku Temple. You will not be taking the tonsure, mind, but you can rest and recover and, most of all, satisfy yourself that there is no danger. If anything were to happen, we would be prepared."

"What do you think, Lord Yamada?" Kinmei asked.

I grunted. "I think you should listen to a man who understands spiritual matters better than I do, and that man is sitting beside me."

I took my leave of Nobu and Lord Kinmei then. My duties were at an end, but for someone like Master Nobu, theirs had just begun. I rather thought he had a more difficult mission than mine, but then perhaps his rewards were, eventually, greater.

It wasn't very late. I looked up into the clear evening sky, and then smiled and headed toward Shijo Bridge while there was still time. Lord Kinmei was a man of his word, and I had no doubt that my payment would arrive soon, and then there would be saké.

Right now, there was a lovely moon.

THE SINGING SPEAR

James Enge

To drink until you vomit and then drink again is dull work. It requires no talent and won't gain you fame or fortune. It's usually followed by a deep dark stretch of unconsciousness, though, so it had become Morlock Ambrosius's favorite pastime.

In a brief lapse from chronic drunkenness he had invented a device which intensified the potency of wine many times. Because he had no use for gold (he could make it by the cartful if he needed it), he gave the device to Leen, the owner of the Broken Fist tavern. Leen proceeded to make gold by the cartful, through the more mundane method of selling distilled liquor. By his order, Morlock's cup was never to be left empty when he entered the Broken Fist. Morlock entered the Broken Fist on a daily basis thereafter and stayed until the disgusted potboys tossed him, snoring, into the street. In another time and place, Morlock might have been called an alcoholic. In the masterless lands east of the Narrow Sea, he was simply a man drinking himself to death – and not quickly enough for those few who had to deal with him.

One evening, as Morlock was just settling down to work, a man came up to him and asked, "Is it true that you're Morlock the Maker?"

If Morlock had been a little more sober, he would have just denied it. If he'd been a little drunker, he would have embarked on an elaborate series of lies to make the questioner suspect that he himself might be Morlock the Maker. And if Morlock had been very much drunker, he wouldn't have been able to answer at all. But, as it happens, he was at that precise state when he was able to know the truth and not care. Apart from actual oblivion, it was the state of mind he enjoyed the most.

"I'm Morlock," he said, lifting his slightly crooked shoulders in a shrug. "What's your poison? They have to serve you for free if you drink with me, you know. Drink with me, get served for free – that's practically a song, isn't it?"

"I don't want a drink," the questioner said, sitting down at Morlock's table. "I want help."

"I'm not in the help business. I'm in the drinking business."

"That's not a business."

"Not with your lacka . . . lacka . . . lackadaisical attitude, no. But I take these things more seriously."

Morlock drank several cups of distilled wine while the other told him a long, involved story and then concluded, "So you see, don't you, that you have to help?"

"I might, if I'd been listening," Morlock admitted. "Thank God Avenger, I wasn't."

"You useless bucket of snot!" the other shouted. "Didn't you hear me tell you that Viklorn has the singing spear?"

"I heard you that time. Who's Viklorn – some juggler or carnival dancer?" Morlock could see how a singing spear might be useful in a carnival act. Almost involuntarily, his mind began to envision various ways to make a spear sing on cue.

"Viklorn!" shouted the other man. "The pirate and robber! He's been using the singing spear to kill and rob all along the coast of the Narrow Sea. And now they say he's killed his own crew with it and is coming inland with Andhrakar."

"Wait a moment."

"And you sit there sucking down that swill—"

"You're telling me that this 'singing spear' is the weapon called Andhrakar?"

"Yes. And if you—"

"Just who was stupid enough to take the spear and start using it?"

The other looked at Morlock almost pityingly. "Viklorn. A pirate and robber."

"Moron, you mean. Well, it's no skin off my walrus."

"You mean you won't help?"

"I knew you'd catch up eventually. Drink? No? Mind if I do?"

"You made the damned thing! It's your responsibility to do something about it!"

"I made the weapon called Andhrakar," Morlock admitted. "Arguably, I also damned it. I didn't make Viklorn, though. Perhaps you'll have better luck if you consult *his* creator."

The other stared at Morlock for a while, then got up and walked off without a word. He rode away west that night to fight Viklorn, and was killed by the weapon called Andhrakar. It was also called "the singing spear" because, before it killed someone, it began to emit a faint musical tone, which grew louder and deeper until it sank into a human body and was satisfied with blood and life.

That's how it was with Morlock's questioner. He came upon Viklorn in the night, hoping to surprise him. But Viklorn did not sleep, could not sleep, remembering the things he had seen and done, and watching the visions that Andhrakar put in his head. He heard the man approaching stealthily through the brush and leapt up from his bedroll. Andhrakar, the singing spear, was ready in his hand – in fact, he could not let go of it now. Through Andhrakar's magic, his fingers were oak-hard, growing into the wooden shaft of the spear, bound in an unbreakable grip on the damned weapon he had chosen to wield.

Viklorn fought the man who longed to kill him, silently in the dark, until both men heard the spear begin to sing (faint and high at first, but then stronger, deeper, louder), and both men groaned (the one with fear, the other with anticipation). Soon Andhrakar split the attacker's torso and grew still. Viklorn left the corpse unburied in the dark and lay back down on his bedroll, next to the spreading pool of blood. Thus died the man Morlock would not help, a brave man but not very shrewd. No one remembers his name.

Morlock was shrewd, on occasion, but he didn't think of himself as brave. Some drunks, perhaps, display courage, but Morlock wasn't that type. He drank because he was afraid, of life and of death. It hadn't always been that way. Once Morlock had been a hero, at least in the eyes of some – in any case, he'd been a more useful sort of person than he was now. But that part of him was used up. So he jeered at himself: only a coward would drink and drink because he was afraid of the pain life held.

Viklorn continued to rob and kill throughout the region. You had to call it robbery, for he took stuff and destroyed what he couldn't take. But he was likely to leave what he took by the roadside or in an open field. He stole because part of him was still Viklorn, a robber. But there was not enough of the man left to remember what robbers robbed for, what use they made of the things they took. Increasingly, he simply killed and killed, destroying with fire what he could not kill with Andhrakar.

"Why did you make that damn spear?" the barkeep asked Morlock one night, before he was too drunk to answer sensibly.

"I had my reasons," Morlock answered sensibly.

Later that night, Leen, the owner of the Broken Fist and the man to whom Morlock had entrusted the invention of the still, sat down beside him. Now that Leen was wealthy, he never stood behind the bar himself; he was so short that he had trouble seeing over it. Back in the days when he couldn't afford to hire help, he'd kept a series of boxes behind the bar, and it had been fun to watch him deftly leaping from box to box. And if he ever needed to climb over the bar to take care of an unruly customer, he saw to it that the customer would never be a problem again. Morlock rather liked him, although he understood that to Leen he was just another gullible drunk.

"Morlock," Leen began.

"Leen."

"Morlock, what do you think you can do about Viklorn and Andhrakar?"

"Leen," Morlock answered sensibly (but just barely), "what do *you* think I can do about Viklorn and Andhrakar?"

Leen stood up and walked away. The faces scattered around the barroom, never friendly, turned to Morlock afterward with especial distaste. Morlock, never sensitive, was uncomfortable enough to leave while he was still conscious, an unusual event.

He was back at the usual time the next day, but the Broken Fist was closed. Closed permanently: the door and window-shutters of the inn were nailed shut. He asked a passing townswoman, who told him that Leen had packed up in the night.

"People say he's moved north to Sarkunden," she said. "I'm going south, myself. People say Viklorn's already been there: why would he go back?"

Morlock brushed aside people and their concerns and stuck to the essential point. "Leen went to Sarkunden – a *thousand* miles away?" he shouted. "Is he insane? What am I supposed to drink?"

The townswoman made a suggestion. Morlock declined (the fluid she mentioned was not an intoxicant), and went back to his cave.

For a day or so, Morlock suffered the delirium that comes sometimes at the end of a drunken binge. Finally he fell asleep and dreamt a prophetic dream. (Among his other wasted talents, Morlock was a seer.)

In the dream, Morlock saw himself confronting Viklorn and Andhrakar. Viklorn was a tall pirate with eyes as red as a weasel's. He wore dirty, pale, untanned leather with golden fittings, and a gold clip kept his shaggy blond hair out of his face. He said nothing; they fought silently, except for the sound of Andhrakar's deadly unbreakable blade clashing against Morlock's sword. Andhrakar dripped with fresh blood, but it was still hungry for life, and soon it began to sing, faintly at first, but then louder and louder. Viklorn laughed, excited and pleased, and Morlock awoke with a curse in his mouth.

This was bad, he thought, sitting up. Never in a thousand years would he have chosen to fight someone armed with Andhrakar. But, although he might be *not especially brave* (a phrase Morlock preferred, when sober, to the franker *coward*), he wasn't stupid. He would fight Viklorn: so the vision told him. He needed to act swiftly if the meeting was to be on his own terms.

He consulted a crow he knew in the neighborhood, who promised to locate Viklorn for him. He spent that day and the next doing exercises to bring his agility and wind closer to what they once had been. When the crow came and told him that Viklorn was at Dhalion, a day's walk north and west, he thanked it and fed it some grain. Then he threw his backpack on his shoulders, belted on his sword, and started loping with a long, uneven stride northeast on the old Imperial Road. The chances were he would run into Viklorn, if Viklorn was moving eastward from the Narrow Sea.

The road was bad. The old Empire of Ontil had been out of business for centuries, and its roads were returning to nature. Often Morlock walked next to the "pavement" of shattered rocks, dense with tree-roots and overgrowth. But he made pretty good time going on foot. He had a serenely unpleasant feeling he was headed straight for his destined meeting with Viklorn, and it turned out he was right.

It happened this way. Morlock topped a ridge and, looking downward, he saw a wagon overturned beside the road. This was not uncommon. The road was the only route through the masterless lands, but it was terrible for carting goods. Morlock found with surprise, though, that he recognized the man standing beside the cart: it was Leen. He'd had at least three days' head start on Morlock, but his property must have slowed him down. Morlock saw some people running away from the cart, farther up the road. Perhaps they were going for help, although there was little help to find along this road. Then Morlock saw a man approaching Leen. Morlock knew this man also, but not from seeing him in his waking life. It was the hulking blond man in his dream, the man who carried Andhrakar: Viklorn the killer.

"Leen!" shouted Morlock, lifting his leaden feet and running down the hill. "Run away, you fool! Leave your stuff! I'll make you a new still! I'll make you new gold! Run like hell!"

But Leen didn't run. He turned to face Viklorn the killer, with a piece of wood in his hand and no hope in his face. Against Viklorn, he was like a squat mountain peak, impinging on the great golden face of a rising moon. He didn't seem to hear Morlock, and as Morlock ran closer he heard what Leen must have heard before: the sweet musical tone of the singing spear, growing deeper and stronger as the foredestined moment of death approached.

Leen had stayed behind intentionally, Morlock realized – stayed to confront Viklorn, knowing he would die, giving the others a chance to run for their lives. Leen struck out at Viklorn with his makeshift club. The killer easily evaded his blow; Andhrakar slashed twice and Leen fell in three pieces on the ground. Viklorn laughed a high-pitched, weary, hysterical laugh. So Leen died – a shrewd man and brave, though that didn't save him.

"You son of a bitch!" Morlock shouted, tears stinging his eyes. "You've killed my bartender!"

Viklorn turned to face him. His eyes were red as a weasel's – as red as the fresh blood dripping from the spear. He pointed at Morlock with the dark blade – crystalline, unbreakable, fashioned by the greatest magical craftsman the world had ever known – and smiled.

Morlock shrugged his backpack off on to the broken road behind him and drew his sword. Viklorn's smile dimmed as he saw the blade, kin to the spearhead on his own weapon: dark, crystalline, unbreakable. Morlock demonstrated the latter fact by passing the sword through a broken pillar beside the road. It fell obligingly to pieces, raising a great cloud of dust. Morlock leapt through the cloud, lunging at Viklorn.

If the fight had been between Morlock and Viklorn, Morlock would have won easily. True, Morlock was a drunk rather badly in need of a drink, not at all the man he had been. But Viklorn was not well either: his face was the face of a dying man; God Sustainer knew when he had last slept, or if he ever ate or drank.

But the fight was really between Andhrakar and Morlock. Viklorn looked on in bemusement as his dark blade feinted and lunged at the man who had made it. Andhrakar didn't need sleep, or food, or water, or air. All it needed was human life; all it hungered for was the savor of dying men and women. Though it still dripped with fresh blood, it was clearly thirsty for more; it began to sing, faintly at first, but then louder and louder. Viklorn laughed, excited and pleased, and Morlock cursed. The singing tone rose and fell and rose again, like a bell, like the baying of a dog. Andhrakar would kill again, and soon.

The spear lashed out. Morlock ducked away from the spearhead and grabbed the shaft just above Viklorn's lifeless hand. Morlock brought down his dark blade and slashed off Viklorn's spear-hand at the wrist. The severed hand still clutched the shaft of the spear in an unbreakable grip. The spear still sang, louder than ever now, drowning all other noises. Morlock spun the business end of the spear about. As Viklorn stood there, blinking at the gushing stump of his arm, Morlock buried the dark shining spearhead in his neck. Viklorn fell backward to the ground and the singing spear fell silent, slaked by his death.

Morlock! The voice of the demon Andhrakar sounded in his head. *Will you free me now from this prison you made for me?*

Morlock laughed harshly as he cleaned and sheathed his dark blade. "Hope springs eternal in the demonic breast. Learn despair, Andhrakar: I won't free you to hunt human souls. I can't understand how you caught this one. I bound you in the spearhead, then buried you in a crypt full of traps, and then posted a warning outside the crypt. How did you get free?"

Warning – or advertising? the demon whispered in his mind. *Generations of heroes died seeking the lost treasure left by Morlock the Maker. Finally one succeeded. His people would be making songs about him now – if I hadn't persuaded him to kill them all.*

Morlock scowled and turned away to bury Leen. He laid him in the ground and put the still and a few gold pieces beside the butchered corpse, then covered him up. He broke some boards from the wagon and made a grave-sign for the dead innkeeper. He supposed the people that Leen had died to save would come back eventually, so he wrote the grave-message to them, in the great, sprawling runes of Ontil: LEEN DIED HERE. WHERE WERE YOU?

He returned to the dead body of Viklorn. He kicked it furiously several times, then grabbed the shaft of Andhrakar and drew it from the wound. Morlock let the dead pirate's hand stay where it was, gripping the shaft, as he carried the spear away. He looked back once from the ridge: a few carrion birds were already circling the pirate's unburied body.

Will you at least keep me and use me? the demon whispered. *I am a powerful weapon. If you feed me human lives, I can give you vengeance on your enemies.*

Morlock said nothing, but carried Andhrakar back to the village where the Broken Fist stood. He found the town abandoned: everyone had fled to escape Viklorn and Andhrakar. Morlock broke into the blacksmith's shop, kindled a fire in the forge, and assembled a set of tools at the anvil.

You cannot destroy my prison in a primitive smithy like this, the demon said, sounding somewhat uneasy.

"You don't know what I can do," Morlock disagreed. "Nor have you guessed what I'm going to do."

He fashioned a spearhead, exactly like Andhrakar in form. He even managed to give its surface a glassy basaltic glaze, something like the dark crystalline surface of Andhrakar. He tempered it, hammered it, let it cool, and polished it. He unfixed Andhrakar from its shaft and put the new spearhead on the shaft, with Viklorn's severed hand still attached. Then he took the greatest hammer in the smithy and he struck the new spearhead until it lay in fragments.

Morlock took a chisel and carved on the side of the anvil: HERE I, WHO MADE ANDHRAKAR, DESTROYED IT, BECAUSE IT KILLED MY FRIEND LEEN. FORGIVE ME AND REMEMBER ME: MORLOCK AMBROSIUS.

Liar! the demon screamed inside his mind.

Morlock shrugged. "The world thinks I made you, which is a lie. I only imprisoned you. If I could have imprisoned you in a spittoon, or a wooden doorstop, or something not obviously deadly I would have done so. The magical laws which govern imprisoning demons limited me. But I can negate one lie with another. These fragments of the accursed spear Andhrakar will become cherished heirlooms, perhaps to be reforged as a new weapon someday—"

They'll know! They'll know it's not me!

"—not as effective as the old weapon, of course, but they don't make anything like they used to. And no one will go looking for Andhrakar, since everyone knows where it is. There will be no advertising for your new resting place. You will wither and die in the dark and you will eat no more human souls."

I am immortal.

"You say so, but I never believed it. You eat things; I think you'll starve to death if you never eat again. Anyway, we'll try the experiment. I'll stop by in a few hundred years to see how you're doing."

He threw the accursed spear-blade imprisoning the demon Andhrakar into the pit under an outhouse. Then he shoveled a hundredweight of soil atop it.

At last, he wanted a drink rather badly. He broke into the Broken Fist and availed himself of Leen's left-behind stock. At least, he poured himself a cup of wine and stood at the bar, preparing to drink it. He stood there for a moment, watching his distorted reflection in the smooth, dark surface of the wine.

When people returned to the town, they found the inscription on the anvil, and the fragments of the spearhead, and they reacted much as Morlock had anticipated. They also found the broken door of the Broken Fist, and they saw the wine cup, full to the brim, standing untouched on the bar. But they did not see Morlock, then or ever again.

SO DEEP THAT THE BOTTOM COULD NOT BE SEEN

Genevieve Valentine

Anna woke up knowing the last narwhal had died.

It was a note in the air as she dressed; when she opened her door, the wind sighed it into her face, across her fingers.

(She didn't bother with gloves anymore. Winters weren't what they used to be.)

It was still dark as she walked over the dirt flats to the observation post, her shadow dotted by the fence that marked the last four acres of protected Inuit territory.

Nauja Marine Observatory had been a three-room school, back when. After the new state schools had swallowed up all the students, the government cleared out the building for Anna ("A gesture of goodwill," the representative said with a straight face). Now it housed third-hand equipment gifted from the territorial government.

The observatory was on the water's edge. When Anna went down the embankment in summer, she could look past the electric-green shallows to where the shore fell into the sea and left nothing but fathomless black water and slabs of milky ice. The sheet ice was already turning greasy and breaking, rotting through as it melted.

The creeping spring made Anna ill; she didn't look.

Inside, she pulled up the computer and was registering the date of death when the knock came.

The man at the door was in a parka and gloves and a hat and was still shivering.

"Anna Sitiyoksdottir?"

Her State name.

After a second, she said, "Sure."

This seemed to cheer him up. He checked his handheld. "Miss Sitiyoksdottir, my name is Stephens. I'm here to invite you to the First International Magical Congress."

She snorted.

He glanced at his handheld to find his place. "The United Nations has called a task force of magic-users to discuss our rapidly changing magical and environmental climate, and to begin cooperation on future initiatives. As a shaman with natural magic, your input will be invaluable. The conference begins tomorrow and goes for two days."

"No," she said.

He smiled and went on as if she hadn't spoken. "I will be your escort and aide while you're a delegate. We can go now, if you're ready. I'll wait while you pack."

"I'm not a shaman," she said. "And when the last one was alive, spellcasters and the UN didn't find her input valuable in the least. Pass."

His smile thinned out. "Miss Sitiyoksdottir, you're the last Inuit with any shaman status on record, and the government of the Northern States insists you be present. Please reconsider. I have authorization to involve the police if necessary."

So it was the usual sort of government invitation.

"I need an hour," she said finally. "Narwhals became extinct last night. I have to find the body on radar and send a report in to the Wildlife Council."

He blinked. "How do you know they're extinct if you didn't see anything?"

She looked at him and didn't answer. After a moment, he had the good manners to blush.

The narwhal had thrown itself on to the shore to die. Anna saw that the sand around it was undisturbed – it hadn't fought to get back to the water, hadn't so much as tossed its head to call out.

"Are you going to move it?" Stephens was breathing heavily from the scramble over the rocks. When he pulled off his cap to fan his face, she saw that his hair was thinning.

Narwhals, like winters, weren't what they used to be, but the carcass still weighed 600 kilograms.

"No," she said, then added, "It's right that the birds have it."

"Oh," he said slowly, as if he was in the presence of great and terrible magic.

She wished the sea would swallow him.

The whale's skin was pale grey and utterly smooth, like a pup, even though it was adult. Anna knew it meant something, but she couldn't sense what. She stepped forward and touched it with a flat hand, waiting. Listening. She rested her forehead on the cool, clammy hide.

Talk to me. Talk to me. What should I do?

"Miss Sitiyoksdottir, if you're not planning to move the animal, we should get you to the airport."

It was an answer of sorts.

So Anna went. It wasn't like narwhals would be less extinct in two days.

Her mother, Sitiyok, had moved to Umiujaq as soon as the rest of the province began to fill up with refugees from the Southern States.

Everyone thought Sitiyok was a worrier and a coward to go. She was the shaman; how could she leave them? The land had been given to them; the land was theirs. Nothing would happen. Just because the Southern States were warming up didn't mean anything. Let some people move north. Who wanted to live in the south anyway, if they could help it?

Sitiyok had smiled at them all, and had moved as far north as she could.

It was not a comfort to know, years later, that she had been right. Her parents' cities were concreted over to make room for newcomers from the south.

Most Inuit tried to live off the new landscape as they had tried to live off the old one. They gave up hunting and waited tables; they gave up tanning hides and minded stores. They became government workers, or hotel managers, or pilots. Around them the air got warmer; winter was carved away from the land a little more each spring, and Southerners filled in the cracks like a rockslide.

In Umiujaq, Sitiyok took dogs out on to the ice to hunt for seal. She sold the skins she could spare; eventually she sold the dogs. When the sea warmed up and the seals didn't return, the others in Umiujaq moved inland to find work, one family at a time.

"You can't stay," they said. "Come with us."

Sitiyok smiled, and stayed where she was.

She and a few others remained in the ghost town, slowly starving out on their homeland. Sitiyok learned how to hunt rabbit; how to snare fish; how to go hungry.

One winter, she had a child, and named her Annakpok – the one who is free.

The Congresse Internationale du Magique was held in the Amphitheatre at Aventicum, in Switzerland; it avoided any question about the host country unduly influencing the proceedings.

As they left the hotel and the morning hit her, Anna frowned against the baking sun. "And we're meeting in the Amphitheatre because?"

"For the magic," Stephens said, waving one hand vaguely before he caught himself. "No disrespect. It's just – my faith is in science. I studied biology."

She said, "So did I."

He coughed. "Here's our car."

The Amphitheatre was ringed with police. Under a sign that read PLEASE KEEP ALL AMULETS VISIBLE, two security guards were peering at talismans, necklaces, and tattoos. Inside the Amphitheatre, food stands and souvenir booths had been set up, and the vendors were shouting over one another in their attempts to reach the milling crowd.

The tiers above the gladiatorial floor were marked off by country. She saw signs for Kenya, Germany, the Malaysian Republic, Russia. (She wondered if the Nenets still had real winter.)

"How long did it take to find enough natural magicians to fill the quota? Are there decoys? You can tell me."

Stephens said, "Please keep your voice down."

Her name was at the Canadian United Republic table, beside a man whose nameplate read James Standing Tall. He was older – as old as her mother would have been – and when he saw her approaching he blinked.

"I didn't know there were still shamans in the Northern States," he said by way of greeting.

"There aren't," she said as she sat. "They'll take anyone these days."

The sorcerer Adam Maleficio, Greater Britain delegate, was the last of them to arrive – under a suddenly dark sky, in a single crack of lightning and a plume of smoke.

Several of the spellcasters stood and pointed their wands, canes, and open palms at the source of the disruption.

"Hold!" one shouted, and another cried, "Pax!"

Adam Maleficio held up his hands. "Friends, hold back your spells! I come among you as a brother, to speak with you of future friendship." Absently, he brushed off his cape and his lapels. "*Absit iniuria verbis*, no?"

A handful of sorcerers laughed. He laughed as well, his eyes glinting red, his teeth glinting white.

From behind Anna's chair, Stephens leaned forward and translated, "May our words not injure."

Anna said, "We'll see about that."

The Congress Director called for comments before the floor opened for debate.

Maleficio stood up with great ceremony and said, "I have been elected to deliver a statement on behalf of all users of magic."

James Standing Tall looked at Anna. "Too late to opt out?"

"Eight hundred years too late," she said.

Maleficio delivered an erudite and lengthy Statement of Brotherhood to the assembled. (There was no telling who had elected him to speak, since some spellcasters' wands stayed pointed at him the whole time he read.)

After the first twenty minutes, Anna and James wrote notes to each other on their programs.

She learned he was Cree, one of the last of his nation. He had remained in the Southern States even after Canada had annexed them. He would come home to a spring of 130 degrees.

I can call the wind with prayer, he wrote. *It's better than leaving.*

She didn't question why he stayed. Anna had no questions to ask about where people dug the trenches for their last stands.

Instead she wrote, *Why did you come?*

He wrote, *I wanted a voice.*

What are you fighting for? she wrote.

He wrote, *Everything. We will have to fight everything, if we are to have any power.*

After a moment she wrote, *My mother was the shaman, not me. I have no real magic.*

On the floor of the Amphitheatre, Adam Maleficio was saying, "Unity is more important now than ever, when magic-users are taking a unique and visible position in a changing world. Let us not forget this is a place we made. This is a place of magic. This is a place *for* magic. And without unity, we weaken."

James wrote, *As long as you can fight.*

Maleficio was still going, enjoying the podium and trying to drown out the translators for good measure. "This is a place for those who know true magic to meet with respect and understanding, to come together with a single vision, and, *conjunctis viribus*, we shall succeed in all we try to do on this sacred ground."

"With united powers," Stephens translated.

"May this be a milestone of a new era," Maleficio finished.

He crushed the pages in his hands and threw his arms wide; the paper turned into six doves and flew away.

The day was boiling hot and fruitless, and during the Magic-Assisted Environment Preservation referendum Anna decided she would leave. There was no reason for her to pretend she had a voice in a council full of wand-wavers.

Then one of the delegates from Japan stood up to address the assembly.

She was wrapped in a fox stole so long that half a dozen fox heads knocked against one another as she stood. Under the stole her suit was the grey of rotting ice; the grey of the narwhal.

Anna sat up in her chair.

"While I can't speak for all natural magicians," the woman said, her voice carrying over the hum of translation, "I know my own magic has already been compromised by the problem that you ask us to solve. Without a natural world for us to call upon, we are powerless."

Maleficio called, "Don't pretend you're powerless, foxwitch!"

Her stole rippled as the six fox heads lifted and hissed at the crowd.

"No magic, *no* speaking out of turn," called the Congress Director. "Delegate Hana, thank you, you may sit down – no magic, ladies and gentlemen, *please!*"

The woman sat, amid a chorus of derisive laughter from the spellcasters.

James said, "If they had to call their spells from the grass, they wouldn't be laughing."

"If they had to call their spells from the grass," Anna said, "we'd still have grass."

The first thing Annakpok had done as shaman was build a bier for her mother's body and sing as it burned down to ashes.

It was still cold enough that Annakpok walked out on to the sea, scattering the ashes around the holes in the ice where her mother had hunted – a gift to the seals, in return for what they had given.

(It was an empty gesture; there were no more seals.)

There would be a feeling of light, her mother had told her. Annakpok would take a breath and know her purpose as shaman, and her power would move through her blood.

The closest Annakpok had come to feeling like a shaman was when she was twelve, and a government agent came to get her mother's blood sample and register Sitiyok as a natural magician.

The deep-winter sun had already set, and without her mother Annakpok was alone in Umiujaq. Besides the moon on the empty ice, there was no light at all.

The wind stole the ashes from the bowl as she walked; when Annakpok reached land again, she was empty-handed.

That was the last thing Annakpok had done as shaman.

*　　*　　*

Anna put herself in the Japanese woman's way as everyone filed out of the theatre at sunset. The woman didn't look surprised to see her.

("Kimiko Hana," Stephens told her. "*Tsukimono-suji.* They hold power over magic fox familiars. It's inherited."

"Is that spellcasting or natural magic?"

Stephens shrugged.)

Anna watched the fox heads watching her. "Do you kill them to get their power?"

The fox heads shrank back and hissed; Kimiko rested her hand on the stole to quiet them.

"No," she said, when they were still again. Her voice was carefully neutral. "It's to remember them after they leave our family. Their children are close to us." She looked askance at Anna. "Do you . . . have a familiar?"

Anna wondered if a dead narwhal counted. "No," she said, and then, recklessly, "I don't even have magic."

Kimiko raised an eyebrow, kept walking.

Anna followed her down the stairs and across the Amphitheatre, waiting for a reciprocation that never came.

Finally she asked, "What sort of magic have you got?"

"It serves me better not to explain," Kimiko said. Her dark eyes flashed red. "If you don't have power, pretend otherwise. If you *do*, pretend otherwise."

She stroked the foxes' heads; under her hand, they sighed.

"What is your power?" Kimiko asked.

Anna said, "I'm great with funerals."

A woman outside the hotel was selling amulets from a card table.

"Magicked by the sorcerers from the Congress," she called, holding out a stamped clay bead on a string. "Talismans and charms! Witch-blessed! Shaman-approved!"

Anna didn't know what the symbols meant, but she could tell they were empty of power. The seller had dusted them all in cinnamon; the smell choked the air.

As Anna passed, the woman thrust it at her brightly. "Need a little magic, miss?"

Yes, Anna thought, and kept walking.

* * *

Anna dreamed of the narwhal, stark and pale against the black rocks. When she walked across the ice to meet it (she was so far away, she should not have wandered), she slipped. She remembered the ice was rotten, and was afraid. She stood where she was, too frightened to move another step and risk falling through the ice and into the water.

On the beach, the narwhal had turned to face her. Its mouth gaped open, revealing Sitiyok inside, standing and waving, gesturing to the shore.

Annakpok could not move, she was so frightened – even when the ice she was standing on sank under her, she stayed where she was. She looked down at the water lapping at her knees – so cold she couldn't feel herself drowning, so deep that the bottom could not be seen.

The ice gave way under her, and she tilted her face upwards, fighting for her last breath. The sun above her gleamed fox-red.

As the water swallowed her, she opened her hands and felt something slip from them; she had been holding tight to something she could not see.

There is always more than we can see, her mother said.

Her mother was unafraid.

Her mother was waving.

"You look horrible," Stephens said as they took their seats. "Didn't you sleep? The papers will think you're a refugee."

"And *that's* why they recruited you into the Diplomatic Corps," Anna said.

The environmental referendum ended with spellcasters insisting that they could not possibly be to blame for a weakening of natural magic they did not even use.

"We make a study of the art," said Maleficio. "Our magic is the result of scholarship. If anything, we begin at a disadvantage, because natural magic rarely chooses us. We are powerless, though we may pretend otherwise."

Anna looked up. The tips of her fingers itched as if she were stroking fur.

Maleficio threw his arms wide. "Natural magicians have the authority of the ages – they have inherited magic!"

"We have to register like livestock!" someone from the Kenyan delegation called.

Maleficio ignored him. "We spellcasters have to read and practice, and must make the best we can of lesser circumstances, to create what power we can."

The spellcasters nodded sadly. Anna and James exchanged a look.

Kimiko said, "Then in your infinite scholarship and wisdom, suggest a solution that will enable natural magicians to find enough magic for ourselves without robbing powerless, impoverished spellcasters of all their hard work."

"No magic!" cried the Congress Director, as a dark rumble spread through the Amphitheatre.

The air crackled, and heat rose from the dozens of angry sorcerers. Adam Maleficio seemed angriest of all, his arm trembling, the air rippling around him.

For a moment, his blue eyes glinted fox-red.

There is always more than we can see.

In the pause between debates, Anna slid into place behind Maleficio. Across the Amphitheatre she could see James and Stephens frowning at her. She ignored them and leaned in. This close, Maleficio smelled of sulfur.

"Tsukimono-suji," she whispered.

He startled, stiffened. "Who are you?" he asked without looking.

"I'm natural magic. And so are you, foxwitch."

"I'm a sorcerer," he hissed. Around them, people were caught up in arguments over who was responsible for making natural magic possible for those who practiced it; no one heard him. "I studied at Stonehenge. I *spellcast.*"

"You have a fox at home," she said. "The rest is party tricks."

She felt, rather than saw him, flinch. "What do you want?"

"Force a vote," she said. "In our favor."

He sniffed. "Forget it. I'm not about to switch sides. Besides, the others won't care if I'm foxblood. I put in the work on spellcasting."

"Oh sure," she said. "It's heartwarming. We'll wrap up with that story, then," and she moved as if to rise.

He flailed one arm behind him. "Stop, stop, come back, you horror. What am I putting to a vote?"

In a surprise turnaround, Adam Maleficio made an eloquent case for the responsibility of the magical community to support its own.

"Natural magic was the earliest magic," he said. "It deserves our respect, our support, and our devotion. I, for one, will be voting to create a coalition that will work to discover a magic strong enough to shield the natural from the ravages it has suffered, and shame, *shame*, on those who do not join me!"

The spellcasters drew wands, and voted (barely) yes.

As Anna walked the ring of the Amphitheatre back to her seat, she passed the Japanese table. Kimiko caught her eye and beckoned her over.

"What did you do to him? You must have more power than you thought."

Anna smiled. "I had no power," she said. "I just pretended otherwise."

One of the fox heads looked up and grinned.

When she got back to her seat, the notepaper was waiting for her. James was looking straight ahead; he didn't even acknowledge she had come back.

Under *I have no real magic*, James had drawn a question mark.

She folded the paper carefully, rested both hands on it like a talisman.

At home, she waited for dark to go down to the water.

A hundred yards out, in the dim moonlight, she could still see that the narwhal was gone.

She ran.

As she lurched over the rocks, she saw it was not really gone; it hadn't sprung to life again and swum out to sea (as she had half-hoped).

It was devoured.

The narwhal was eaten clean down to the bones (impossible for birds to manage in three days), and the bones themselves were intact, despite the wind (impossible, impossible). The ribs rose sharply white against the green-black sky, the skin curling like parchment against the black ground as if the wind itself had pulled it gently from the flesh.

Annakpok looked in the sand for tracks. No animal tracks (she expected none), but she was surprised that only her own footprints came out this far.

She walked slowly, tracing the edge of the laid-out hide with her feet as she went, trying to still her pounding heart. She had to listen; she needed to see.

There was no flesh left on the bones at all; she would have suspected that she had been trapped in time, at the summit for a hundred years, except that the bones had not yet begun to dry. They were pearl-white still, the ribs like joyful hands, the tailbones pointing mournfully to the sea.

Anna knelt and plucked the smallest tailbone from the hide. It was the length of her palm, and hollow. She slid it over one finger.

She made rings out of ten vertebrae. They warmed against her skin; when she curled her hands they shifted against one another like she wore gloves of bone.

The ice under her feet was slippery, rotten, but she stepped where the moon reflected thickest. The bones in her hands thrummed as she breathed.

She walked across the sheet ice, out and on, past the light from shore, past her mother's old hunting grounds, to the edge of the ice-veiled sea. There she stopped, and trembled. The ice rocked gently under her feet, and she knew if she slipped here the sea would swallow her.

It might swallow her in any case. (She thought of her mother inside the mouth of the narwhal, beckoning her home.) It was great magic, what she was attempting. It was beyond her power.

She would be the sacrifice.

Around her the world was flat and black; the wind slid mournfully against her face.

Annakpok held out her open hands before she could be afraid. If she was a shaman, the sea would bring them back to her as narwhals. She had only to wait, and be worthy.

(*What are you fighting for?*
Everything.)

The bones fell into the water, ten white sparks that disappeared into a black so deep that the bottom could not be seen.

When she turned for the shore, the narwhal's bones looked like a doorway, like an open hand waving her home.

WARRIOR DREAMS

Cinda Williams Chima

Russell's new home under the abandoned railroad bridge was defensible, which was always the first priority. Secluded, yet convenient to the soup kitchens downtown. It offered a dry, flat place for his sleeping bag, and some previous occupant had even built a fire ring out of the larger rocks.

The bridge deck kept the snow and sleet off, and because the bridge wasn't in use, he didn't have to deal with the rattle-bang of trains. Any kind of noise still awakened the Warrior – the dude born in Kunar Province, in Korengal, in the Swat Valley – even in places like Waziristan, where he never officially was. Any sudden noise left him sweating, heart pounding, fueled by an adrenaline rush that wouldn't dissipate for hours.

Best of all, the bridge was made of iron – a virtual fortress of iron, in fact, which should've been enough to win him a little peace. That and the bottle of Four Roses Yellow Label he'd bought with the last of this month's check.

But Russell was finding that, for an out-of-the-way place, his new crib on Canal Street was in a high-traffic area for magical creatures. The river was swarming with shellycoats – he heard the soft chiming of their bells all day long. Kappas lurked around the pillars of the bridge, poking their greenish noses out of the water, watching for unwary children. The carcasses of ashrays washed up on shore, disintegrating as soon as the sunlight hit them.

Where were they all coming from? Was there some kind of paranormal convention going on and nobody told him?

The first night, he'd awakened to the adrenaline rush and a pair of red fur boots, inches from his nose.

"Hey!" Russell said, rolling out of danger and grabbing up the iron bar he always kept close. The creature screeched and scrambled backwards, out of range. It was the size of a small child, with a long beard, burning coal eyes, and a ratty red and black fur coat. Like a garden gnome out of a nightmare.

"Listen up, gnomeling," Russell said, "you sneak up on a person, you're liable to get clobbered."

The creature struck a kind of pose, lips drawn back from rotten teeth, one hand extended toward Russell.

"Je suis le Nain Rouge de Detroit," it began.

Russell shook his head. "En Anglais, s'il vous plait. Je ne parle pas français."

It scratched its matted beard. "You just did."

"Did what?"

"Spoke French."

"Maybe," Russell said, "but now I'm done." He leaned back against a bridge pillar and lit a cigarette with shaking hands. At one time, he'd been fluent in five languages, but he'd forgotten a lot since the magic thing began.

The gnomeling let go a sigh of disgust. "I am the Red Dwarf of Detroit," it repeated. "Harbinger of doom and disaster."

"I hate to break it to you," Russell said. "But this isn't Detroit. It's Cleveland. Detroit's a little more to the left." He pointed with his cigarette. "Just follow the lake, you can't miss it."

The dwarf shook his head. "I may be the Red Dwarf of Detroit, but my message is for you." And then it disappeared.

Way to ruin a good night's sleep.

The second night, it was the dog. Russell woke to find it snuggled next to him, its huge, furry body like a furnace against his sleeping bag. He nearly strangled it before he realized what it was. He was definitely losing his edge. No way any animal that size should've been able to sneak up on him

"Hey," Russell said, sitting up. "Where'd you come from?" After holding out his hand for a sniff, he scratched the beast behind the ears. It was immense, probably a Newfoundland, or a mix of that and something else.

Russell liked dogs. They accepted a wide range of behavior without question, and they believed in magic, too.

The next morning, Russell shared his meager gleanings from the dumpster behind the Collision Bend Café, and the dog elected to stay with him another night. Russell's rule was, if a dog stays two nights, it gets a name.

"Is it all right if I call you Roy?" Russell asked. The dog didn't object, so Roy it was. That night Russell fell asleep, secure in the belief that old Roy had his back.

He awoke to six nixies tugging on his toes with their sinuous fingers. Yanking his feet free, he said, "Ixnay, nixies."

They swarmed back into the water and commenced to squabbling about what, if anything, they should do with him.

"He sees us!"

"He will tell!"

"We must drown him!"

"Some watchdog you are," Russell said, glaring at Roy. The Newfie stretched, shook out his long black coat, and trotted off to anoint the bridge for the hundredth time.

After shooing away the nixies, Russell kindled a fire. He hadn't lost the knack since he'd been chaptered out of the Army. Like riding a goddamn bike. He curled up and tried to go back to sleep, but he couldn't shake a sense of imminent danger. The nixies kept muttering, and that didn't help. He tossed and turned so much that Roy growled, got up, and found a spot on the other side of the fire.

It was no use. Russell sat up. As he did so, the wind stung his face, bringing with it the stench of rotten flesh.

Stick with Lieutenant MacNeely. It's like he can smell danger.

He searched the embankment that ran down to the water. There. He caught a flicker of movement along the riverbank. The lights from the bridge reflected off a pair of eyes peering out of a tangle of frozen weeds. The eyes disappeared and the weeds shifted and shook, a ribbon of motion coming toward him. Something was creeping closer, stalking him. Something big. Was it plotting with the nixies or was it here on its own?

Warrior Russell planted his feet under him, reached down and gripped his trusty iron bar.

Know your weapon.

You are the weapon.

With a roar, the creature burst from the underbrush, its claws clattering over the concrete as it bounded forward. It was incredibly tall, cadaverously thin, with long, snarled hair. Coming to his knees, Russell waited until it was nearly on top of him, then jack-knifed upward, swinging his iron bar, slamming it into the creature in midair. It screamed, a sound as lonely as a train whistle at night. Then burst into shards of ice that rained down on the riverbank until it looked like his campsite had been hit by a localized hailstorm.

"What the hell was that?" Russell muttered, brushing slush off his parka.

The nixies looked at each other, chattering excitedly, pointing at Russell. One of them slipped beneath the river's surface and disappeared.

"Where'd she go?" Russell demanded, glaring at them. He stood, cradling the iron bar. "If she went for reinforcements, well, then bring it. I'm Russell G. MacNeely, and I'm not giving up this crib."

The nixie reappeared a few minutes later, with reinforcements. A reinforcement, rather. The newcomer – a girl – surfaced with scarcely a ripple, regarding Russell with luminous green eyes. Her skin was ashy white, with just a hint of blue, and her long red hair was caught into a braid just past her shoulders.

She raised one pale hand, and waved at him, a tentative flutter of fingers. Russell waved back.

She flinched back, eyes wide. "So you *can* see us."

"I'll pretend I can't, if that makes you feel better," Russell said. "I'm used to it. It helps me fit in better in the world."

"You killed the Wendigo," she said, her voice the sound of moving water over stone. "I'm impressed. They aren't easy to kill, one on one."

"I killed the *what?*"

She scooped up a handful of ice. Tilting her hand, she let it fall, glittering in the lights from the bridge, clattering on the concrete.

"Uh, right. Wendigo," Russell said. "Don't they usually hang out further north?"

"Usually," she said, with a sigh. "Not these days." Sweeping bits of ice out of the way, she boosted herself on to the bank.

She wore a skimpy dress of what looked like seaweed, and a necklace of water lilies and freshwater mussel shells. She was sleek and fit, her arms and legs well muscled, as if she worked out. Though her skin was pale as permafrost, she was probably the loveliest thing Russell had ever seen.

Just stop it. You always get like this when you're off your meds. There's just no point in that kind of thinking for someone like you.

Truth be told, he hated being on meds. He hated living in a black-and-white world, blinders over his eyes, cotton stuffed in his ears. Sleepwalking. Sitting at the bottom of a well of sadness, unable to climb out.

He needed to stay alert. He needed to be able to defend himself.

I am not a violent person, but I will defend myself.

"I'm Russell, by the way," he said. No reason he couldn't be friendly.

"I'm Laurel," she said. With nimble fingers, she unraveled her braid. Then rewove it – tighter.

Russell cast about for something else to say. "Um – you're not as green as most nixies," he said, hoping that would be taken for a compliment.

She shook her head. "I'm not a nixie. I'm a kelpie." She'd been focused on her braid, but now she raised her eyes to Russell's face, as if to assess his reaction. "A limnades kelpie, to be specific."

The word was familiar, but all he could think of was seaweed. Kelp. The other Russell – the pre-deployment Russell – would have known. The other Russell was good with words.

"Nixies, kelpies – what's the difference?"

"I'm a shape-shifter," Laurel said.

Ah, Russell thought. A shape-shifter. In the years since the TBI, he'd become familiar with many magical creatures, but there always seemed to be more to learn.

"And a warrior," she added. "I'm the last remaining guardian of the lakes."

"A warrior." Russell resisted the temptation to roll his eyes, and bit the insides of his cheeks to keep from smiling. A small victory for the old social filters. And the new role of women in combat.

"The nixies are debating whether to kill you." She said this matter-of-factly, like she was interested in Russell's opinion on it.

"I'd like to see them try." Russell scooped up the iron bar and rested it across his knees. "I'm not a violent person, but I will defend myself."

He'd said that, over and over, in therapy.

Laurel watched him handle the iron staff with something like jealousy. "I can see that you have some skill with weapons," she said.

"I should," Russell said. "That used to be my job. Killing people." When Laurel's eyes narrowed, he added, "Don't worry. I only killed the bad guys – or at least that's what I thought. Then I got RFS'd out of the Rangers for misconduct, along with a bad case of TBI and PTSD."

"You sure have a lot of letters," Laurel observed.

"My point is, I'm not considered competent. So nobody is going to believe a thing I say. Your secrets are safe with me."

Laurel cocked her head. "What is this 'TBI' and 'PTSD'?"

"I got blown up a lot when I was in the military," Russell said, stretching out the kinks in his back. "So now, my brain doesn't work like other people's. For instance, I can see and hear you. No offense, but that ain't normal in my world, so I'm crazy. They claim I was crazy before I enlisted. Not their fault."

She thought about this for a moment. "I can see and hear *you*," she pointed out.

"I didn't make the rules," Russell said. "Anyway, what are you doing so far upriver? You're surrounded by steel mills, and it's all iron bridges and what-not. Your kind don't tolerate iron, right? You're gonna make yourself sick."

"It wasn't our idea," Laurel said. "We've been forced into the rivers, because the lake is no longer safe. But you're right – we can't survive here for long. The rivers are cleaner than they used to be, but still not healthy enough to live in perma-nently. Plus, as you said, there's the metal."

"There's the metal," the nixies sang.

Laurel wrapped her arms around her knees. She was completely dry now, and looked like any other half-naked girl you'd meet at a bodybuilder's convention. More at home in her body than most girls.

"Our time is up, Russell," Laurel said. "You and I – we are doomed."

"We are doomed," the nixies sang.

"You've seen the omens," Laurel continued, "both the Red Dwarf of Detroit and the Black Dog of Lake Erie."

"The black dog of—" Russell swung around. Roy was sound asleep again, snoring and farting by turns. "You mean Roy? He's just a stray."

"Call him whatever you like, a Black Dog has signaled doom on the lakes for centuries."

"So you're saying that *I'm* doomed, if he's hanging out with me?"

"I'm afraid so," the kelpie said. "I give you another day, maybe two."

Russell thought on this a moment. "Can you tell how I'm going to die?"

Laurel shook her head. "From all appearances, I'd say you'll get drunk and fall in the river." She nudged the bottle of Four Roses with her foot.

"Well, thanks for the heads up, but I don't get whether you're warning me to be careful, or telling me to do whatever the hell I want because I'll end up dead either way."

"I'm here to offer you a warrior's death," Laurel said.

The warrior? That guy's already dead, Russell wanted to say. That guy doesn't exist anymore. But of course he didn't, because it wasn't true. "What do you mean?"

"I told you that I'm the last remaining guardian of the lakes. When I am gone, the lakes will run with the blood of the gifted."

Russell rubbed his stubbly chin. "What's the mission? Do you want me to slaughter all the people who're dumping crap into the lake?"

Laurel shook her head. "Pollution *is* a problem, but our immediate concern is the storm hag of the lake."

"The storm hag of the lake," the nixies sang.

"What – what – what – wait a minute," Russell said. "Storm hag?"

"You've not heard of her?" Laurel tilted her head, perplexed. "She is famous. All the Lake Erie sailors know about her."

"I don't know any sailors," Russell said. "I'm not from around here. I just came in on the bus."

"I've known a lot of sailors," she said.

Russell put up both hands. He had a feeling he didn't want to know about the sailors. "Never mind. Tell me about this hag."

"Her name is Jenny Greenteeth. She roams the lakes, riding on an enormous lake sturgeon. She foments storms, then pulls ships underneath the water and drowns the sailors."

"I can see where that's a problem for the sailors, but how is that a problem for you?"

"It's not just sailors," Laurel said, fingering her necklace. "Jenny has lived in the lakes since the dawn of history, but she has recently developed a voracious appetite for magic. We think *that* might be the result of phosphates. Or hormones. We've fought back, but none of us can stand against her. Many of us have died – not just nixies and kelpies, but grindylows and water-sprites, snallygasters and selkies and hippocamps."

"No offense," Russell said. "But that sounds like a catalog of the world's most obscure magical creatures. Creatures nobody but me will even miss." Not that anybody would miss *him*, if he disappeared.

Laurel snorted softly. "Most of the original creatures of faerie are already extinct. Those that call attention to themselves were the first to go. Elves and unicorns, griffins, centaurs, and dragons – humans loved them to death. We may be all but invisible, but that's why we've survived."

That's how I survive, Russell thought. By being invisible. "I'm sorry," he said. "I didn't mean to imply that you aren't important."

"I'm used to it," Laurel said. "Magical creatures persist in those places in the world that are hard to get to. That are still relatively free of iron and pollution. There are pockets of dryads in the deep forests of South America, sea serpents and mermaids in the great oceans of the world. Once the Great Lakes were large enough to shelter us, too. These days, not so much. Think about it – it's the tiny magics, like hexes and charms and lutins, house elves and brownies and wood-sprites that add color and texture to the world. That keep it from being all metal and glass and right angles. Can we really afford to have less magic in the world?"

"Well, when you put it that way," Russell began, "I guess I—"

"With every creature she destroys, Jenny grows larger and hungrier and more dangerous. Soon the lake will be completely barren of magical creatures. Except, of course, for her. Then, I believe, she will turn her attention to the land."

"Can't you gang up on her?" he asked. "Couldn't all of you together take her down?"

"We have tried. Every time we've gone against her, we've suffered huge losses. I am the sole survivor of my squadron."

How'd it happen, MacNeely? How is it that you're the only survivor?

"What do you mean, your squadron?"

"There used to be scores of us, patrolling the Great Lakes from Superior to Ontario. Now there's just me. You see, the only weapon that works against her is iron, and none of us can wield it." She raked back her red mane of hair. "We need a champion."

"We need a champion," the nixies sang.

"A champion?" Russell frowned, perplexed.

"We need someone who can partner with us. Who can wield iron on our behalf. We need a warrior." She looked Russell in the eyes, and then down at the iron bar beside him in the snow. "We need you."

"What? No!" he said. "Oh, no. Don't look at me. You've got the wrong guy."

But she *did* look at him, a mingling of eagerness and challenge.

"Don't you get it?" Russell said, his anger rising. "I'm done with that. Heroes get killed. If they're lucky."

He should know. He was a bona fide hero, with the medals to prove it. And the wounds that nobody saw, that nobody wanted to see.

"You've proven that you can wield iron – can kill with it, if you have to. You've experienced magic, so you know what we stand to lose. You are unique in the world, Russell G. MacNeely."

"Yeah, well, you try and be unique for a while, and see how it works out for you," Russell growled.

"I *am* unique," Laurel said, "in these lakes, at least. My entire family – my mate, my birth family, and my children have been killed. I'm the only one left."

"I'm sorry to hear that," Russell blurted, as regret sluiced over him. "I know what it's like to lose a child."

"Son or daughter?" Laurel asked.

"Daughter," Russell said, wishing he hadn't brought her up.

"How did she die?" Laurel asked.

"Oh, she's not dead," Russell said. "I stay away from her. It's better that way. Safer."

Know your weapon.

I am the weapon.

Laurel cocked her head. "But if – if she's still alive, then . . . ?"

"Look, back to business," Russell said. "Even if you found a champion, how would he hope to go after this hag? Wouldn't she just swim away? And if he swam after her, even if he caught her, he'd be too exhausted to fight."

"We have a plan," Laurel said, as if she'd just invented the wheel. "We'll set a trap."

"You have this all worked out, don't you?" Russell laughed bitterly. "Now all you have to do is find somebody to do it. Somebody else. You can't expect me to fight your magical battles for you."

"You don't understand, Russell," Laurel said. "I'm not asking you to fight for me. I'm a warrior, too. We'll fight together."

Russell looked her up and down. "Right. Now, I'm going to bed. With any luck, I'll get some sleep."

Turning his back on Laurel, Russell ducked under the bridge, took another hit of the Four Roses, and crawled into his sleeping bag.

"Whether you help me or not, your fate is sealed," she called after him.

He didn't sleep well. All night long, the nixies sang of battles and valor, invading his dreams. The soft tinkling of bells from the river told him the flow of refugees was continuing.

He dreamt he galloped through the waves astride a white horse, bursting through spray, his sword held high over his head. Just ahead, Jenny Greenteeth rose out of the waves, rose and rose and rose until she blotted out the sky. He swung his blade with a two-handed stroke and—

A faint noise woke him. Gripping his weapon, heart thumping, that metallic taste of fear on his tongue, he searched the darkness.

"It's me, Russell," Laurel said, sounding amused. "Put away the iron. I won't hurt you."

He heard a soft rustle of fabric. Then she sat down next to him, unzipped his sleeping bag, and slipped in beside him. She was very clearly naked.

"What are you doing?" Russell said, rolling on his side to face her.

"Isn't it obvious?" she said. "Please say yes." And then she kissed him, which awakened sensations he thought he'd forgotten.

With every ounce of resolve that was in him, he gripped her shoulders and pushed her to arm's length. "Why?" he demanded.

She regarded him, perplexed. "Because I want to?" She poked him playfully. "It seems you do, too."

"Why?" Russell repeated, bringing up his knees in defense.

Laurel let go an exasperated sigh. "Well, it's kind of a tradition for warriors on the eve of battle to – you know – in case it's the last time."

"I told you," Russell said. "I'm not going to fight. No matter what you—"

"Russell." Laurel put a finger over his lips. "Silly. I wasn't talking about you," she said. "I was talking about me. I just need a little cooperation."

And so, after a bit more persuasion, Russell cooperated.

After, they lay, looking up at the sky. Or they would have, if the bridge wasn't in the way. Laurel fingered Russell's dogtags. "What are these? Amulets of some kind?"

"It's ID. So, if you're killed, they can figure out who to notify."

"What about this one?" She read the inscription aloud.

"I will always place the mission first. I will never accept defeat. I will never quit. I will never leave a fallen comrade."

"That's the Warrior Ethos," Russell said. "It's something they make us memorize, but they don't believe in themselves." He sighed. "All I ever wanted to be was a soldier."

In the morning, he awoke alone. Hungry and sore and worn out, like he'd been doing battle all night. Laurel was a warrior, for sure. He smiled, remembering.

"Laurel?" he said. No answer beyond the howling of the wind, blowing down the river.

He quickly yanked on his clothes, shivering in the cold. Laurel's seaweed dress still lay where she'd dropped it, dried and disintegrating.

Crawling out from under the bridge, he saw that black thunderclouds were piling up in the northwest. An unusual sky for February. Something bad was brewing.

The area around his campsite was deserted, not a nixie nor a pixie to be seen. After the tumult all night long, it was a little unnerving. And, truth be told, a little lonely.

"That was a strange dream," he said aloud.

Roy lifted his head and whined when Russell spoke. "Guess I didn't dream you up, boy." He'd been half-convinced the dog would be gone in the morning, too. Gently, he gripped the dog's ruff to either side and looked at him, nose to nose. Roy's eyes glowed like red coals, like in all the stories about hell-hounds.

"Are you really the harbinger of doom?" Russell asked. "Is my number really up?" Would the harbinger of doom leave piss-marks all around the camp?

In answer, Roy unfurled an impossibly long tongue and licked him in the face. Pulling away, he pawed at a bundle, lying in the snow. A long bundle wrapped in seaweed, a squarish package next to it. Russell knew what it was before he ever picked it up.

"You forgot something, Laurel!" he called. "Come get this stuff! I don't want it."

Nobody answered.

He couldn't help himself. He was a warrior, after all. Picking free one edge of the seaweed shroud, he unrolled it.

It was an iron sword in a leather baldric, a massive blade with dragons on the hilt. As he drew it out, he saw that it was freshly oiled and free of rust and incredibly sharp, as Russell found out when he tried his thumb on the edge.

"Ow!" he said, sucking on his thumb. "You call this a weapon? Where's my M110?" he called out. "How 'bout an M4?" No answer.

Unwrapping the other bundle, he pulled out a circular shield and a silver helm.

He picked up the shield in his right hand, the sword in his left. Dancing around on the riverbank, thrusting and parrying, he fought an invisible opponent to surrender.

He'd taken fencing lessons, back in the day. It was an up-close, intimate dance that seemed appropriate to a warrior. His muscles remembered what his unreliable mind had forgotten.

A soft whickering drew his attention back to the river. A horse stood there, dripping wet, having just climbed out of the water. Her coat shone white with a faint tinge of blue, translucent as stillwater ice. Water streamed from her red mane and tail. She wore no saddle or bridle, only a necklace of water lilies and freshwater mussel shells. The luminous blue eyes were hauntingly familiar. Recognition pinged through Russell.

"Laurel?" he whispered.

"I told you," she said, tossing her head and pawing at the earth with her hoof. "You won't be alone. We're in this together."

He took a step back, shaking his head weakly, the tip of his massive sword dragging in the snow. "No," he said.

She came forward, twitching water from her tail, her eyes fixed on Russell. When she was close enough, she reached out and butted him gently with her head. He stroked her velvety soft nose. Pulling back her lips, she exposed fearsome sharp teeth. Gripping his parka, she dragged him forward a few steps, toward the river's edge. Then knelt, to make it easier for Russell to climb on.

Russell looked back at Roy, hoping for direction. Roy sat in the snow, his tail beating on the ground, his red-coal eyes fixed on Russell.

"Is this it, Roy?" Russell asked. "Is this how it all ends?"

Roy said nothing.

"I can't believe I'm asking advice from a dog I've only just met," Russell muttered.

He looked back at his crib under the railroad bridge, the meager campsite he'd defended like a junkyard dog, knowing it was the best he could hope for. He could stay here, and eke out a living, dumpster-diving and haunting the soup kitchens. He could go back to the world and start taking his medicine again. Or he could do this thing. He could be a warrior, one more time. It was the one thing – the only thing – he'd ever wanted to be.

Laurel had her head twisted around, looking at him.

"Where is everyone?" Russell asked.

"They're down in the harbor, waiting for you."

"You said you had a plan?" Russell said.

"The nixies will lure her inside the breakwall," Laurel said. "That will prevent her from taking advantage of the sturgeon's speed. We can either run her aground or trap her against the breakwall. Then it's up to you."

It's up to you, MacNeely. Somebody has to take out that gunner or we'll never get out of here.

Russell picked up the helm and slid it on to his head, strapped the baldric on to his back, and slid the sword into it. He retrieved his shield and strode to the kelpie's side. Swinging his leg over, he twined his fingers into her mane. "Let's do this thing," he said.

The next thing he knew, they were flying over the concrete barrier at the water's edge and plunging into the icy river. It was a good thing he was holding on tight, or he would've been pitched right off. The water was just as cold as Russell expected, but Laurel gave off heat like a furnace, warming his entire body. He could feel her muscles under him, extending and bunching, extending and bunching as she swam with the current, following the switchbacks of the crooked river toward the lake. The shoreline blurred by, faster than Russell could focus. Fleetingly, he wondered whether Laurel was in a hurry to act before he had second thoughts.

They swept under the Shoreway, under another railroad bridge, past Wendy Park on their left-hand side.

They burst out of the mouth of the river like a log out of a chute. At that point the wind hit them, a furious pounding from the northwest, whipping up whitecaps even within the breakwall. Laurel kept swimming, angling across the flow of water to a spot just inside and to the east of the passage through the break into the greater lake. There she hovered, constantly swimming just to keep from being swept out into the lake.

"We'll wait here," Laurel shouted, but Russell could barely hear her over the howling of the wind and the thunder of the waves crashing over the wall.

Just beyond the wall, the lake water seethed with swimming bodies – nixies and grindylows, water-sprites, and selkies. This was the bait that was meant to lure the storm hag.

She was on her way, if the weather was any indication. Sleet hissed into the water all around them, found its way under Russell's collar, and bit into his face like a thousand tiny knives. If not for Laurel between his knees, he'd be frozen solid already. Swiping ice from his lashes, he peered into the distance, where the black horizon melted into the turbulent lake.

Then he saw it, something that looked like a massive tidal wave heading for the breakwall, higher than any other wave. Ahead of it, magical creatures peeled off to either side, desperate to escape.

"Is that something?" he asked Laurel.

"That's her," she said, and dove.

Russell clung desperately to her back, squeezing his eyes tightly shut. Pressure built in his ears until it seems like they might pop. He held his breath as long as he could, then tried to let go, so he could kick his way to the surface. He stuck to her back like a burr on Velcro, unable to free himself. He breathed in – he couldn't help it – and to his surprise, it was fine. He reached up to his neck and found gills there – deep slits on either side. He was breathing underwater.

That's when he knew he was having some kind of a major breakdown.

When you see things, MacNeely, what do you see?

Russell's head broke the surface, and then Laurel's, and he saw she'd come up just inside the breakwall. Russell turned to look just as the storm hag burst through the passage from the lake, driving a cryptozoological menagerie before her.

Russell gaped at Jenny Greenteeth, pawing through his mental thesaurus of words for huge. Like colossal. Humongous. Statuesque. Immense. She was as tall as the thunderclouds piling up behind her, and she rode a fish the size of a freight train.

Her skin was the color of verdigris, like copper after years of exposure to seawater and sunlight. Her hair was chartreuse, with jewels, shells, pearls, and other glitterbits woven into it. She wore what looked like a fortune in bling – pearls, diamonds, opals, and other gemstones roped around her neck. She controlled her steed with reins that looked to be made of moray eels.

Her eyes were the mustard yellow of a sulfur spring, her teeth grass-green, and she wore a kind of armor made of brass plates.

"Shipbuilder's plaques," Laurel explained. "One for each ship she's foundered."

"Shit," Russell said, looking down at his puny shield, then back up at his opponent. And laughed. "She's colossal. We're totally fucked."

"Courage, Russell," Laurel said.

The sturgeon surged forward, plowing into the school of fleeing lake creatures, magical and not. The storm hag sluiced her fingers through the water on either side, straining them out. She crammed fistfuls of nixies, kelpies, carp, and walleye indiscriminately into her mouth.

Even astride the fish, she towered over buildings on the shore.

And then, she began to sing.

> *Come into the water, love,*
> *Dance beneath the waves,*
> *Where dwell the bones of sailor lads*
> *Inside my saffron caves.*

"What's that all about?" Russell asked.

"It's her thing," Laurel said briskly. "Kind of a tradition. She likes to sing before a kill. The others are going to draw her this way, into the closed end of the breakwall, so she's trapped. Then we're going in. Just be careful – her claws are deadly poisonous."

"*Now* I'm worried," Russell said, grinning. What the hell did he have to lose?

That MacNeely? He's crazy brave.

There was a time when being crazy served a soldier well.

The surviving decoys made a sharp right turn past where Laurel and Russell lurked, making speed toward a small opening in the breakwall at the west end – too small for the sturgeon to fit through. When Jenny saw where they were headed, she yanked her reins hard right, digging in spurs made of oyster shells. She lashed her mount with a small whip, screeching, "Don't let them get away!"

Like a lake freighter, the sturgeon made a wide turn to follow, its wake slopping over the shoreline like water sloshing out of a bathtub. It put on speed, blood staining the water from the wounds in its sides. It reached the breakwall at ramming speed just as the last of their quarry slipped through the hole. The sturgeon slammed into the opening, ramming halfway through, and then stuck there, its tail flailing, sending tidal waves on to the shore.

Outside the breakwall, the nixies cheered.

But Jenny Greenteeth wasn't done yet. Howling in fury, she stood astride the breakwall like a colossus at the gate. Truth be told, Russell thought she might indeed be a little bigger than she started out.

"Russell," Laurel said. "I think it might be time to draw your sword."

"Not yet," he said, leaning forward to whisper into Laurel's ear. "I'm going to need both hands. Bring me in close to the fish," he said.

"He'll smash you against the rocks," Laurel protested, swimming closer just the same. They followed the breakwall in, avoiding the lashing tail, until they were all but bumping up against the sturgeon's side. The eel reins were dangling in arm's reach. Russell gripped the reins and ran up the slippery side of the fish, coming up underneath Jenny's position on the wall.

Russell reached over his shoulder, gripped the dragon hilt of the sword, and pulled it, hissing, from its baldric. It was all he could do to hold the blade steady with his trembling arms. Balancing lightly atop the sturgeon, he slashed into the storm hag's ankle with a two-handed swing. Then slid down, flattening himself against the sturgeon's side, pressing his face into its leathery skin, clinging to the eel harness as if his life depended on it. Which it did.

Jenny screamed, a scream that could have been heard in Canada. Crouching, she scanned the area around her feet for the culprit.

"Hey! Greenteeth!" Laurel shouted. "Over here!"

Turning, she spotted Laurel, hovering between the sturgeon's tail and the wall. Flopping down on the sturgeon's back, she reached for Laurel while the kelpie swam furiously for open water. Seizing hold of the water horse, Jenny lifted her, dripping, while Laurel struggled in the hag's massive hand, shifting from horse to girl to slippery fish.

"What's this?" Jenny snarled. "Did you sting me?"

Russell ran lightly up the hag's spine, using the braids in her hair to climb to the top of her head.

He stood there, sword in hand, and his eyes met Laurel's. She nodded, once, then sank her razor teeth into Jenny's fleshy palm. Enraged, the storm hag flung Laurel away. The kelpie landed, broken, on the rocks of the shoreline and lay there without moving.

Russell rappelled down the front of the hag's face. Bracing his feet on either side of her nose, a hair's breadth above her gaping mouth, he plunged his sword into one of her sulphur-pool eyes.

The storm hag exploded, covering Russell head to toe with yellow goo and launching him far out into the lake. He hit the water hard and sank, a helpless bag of broken bones in the churning waves. Drowning's not a bad way to go, he said to himself as he spiraled down.

Then multiple hands were supporting him, lifting him back toward the surface. He saw it coming toward him, so brilliant it hurt his eyes, and then his face broke through, into the sunlight.

Incredibly, the storm was over, the waters lapping calmly

against the breakwall, the sky that brilliant blue that sometimes happens on rare days in autumn.

"Laurel," Russell gasped. "Where's Laurel?"

"Don't worry," the nixies said. "You go together."

"Good," Russell said. And closed his eyes.

An honor guard of six nixies laid the two warriors side by side in a small boat filled with water lilies and sea glass and some of the sea hag's ropes of pearls, since she wouldn't be using them anymore.

Followed by a retinue of nixies and grindylows and shelly-coats and water dragons and brook horses, they towed the boat far out into the lake, to a place where the sunlit waves glittered all the way to the horizons. The mourners commenced to diving, bringing up pebbles and stones from the bottom of the lake and piling them into the boat until it sank beneath the surface.

The nixies scattered flowers over the warriors' watery grave and chanted,

> *I will always place the mission first.*
> *I will never accept defeat.*
> *I will never quit.*
> *I will never leave a fallen comrade.*

Every one of them knew that a new Lake Erie legend had been born.

"This is it?" Margaret MacNeely ducked under the metal infrastructure of the bridge. "This is just as you found it?"

Sergeant Watson nodded. "Yes," she said. "Except, you know, for the personal effects we've already given you. The medals and like that. We were afraid somebody would take them, if we left them there."

There wasn't much. A sleeping bag, left unzipped, gaping open. The charred remains of a fire. A US Army backpack.

Margaret knelt and poked through the backpack. A few flannel shirts, socks, underwear, an extra pair of jeans. The e-reader she'd given him last Christmas, carefully protected in a plastic bag. She flicked it on, scanning through the book-shelves. They held the books she'd pre-loaded it with, nothing more. Before his four deployments, he'd been an avid reader. These days, he had trouble concentrating long enough to read a book.

On the ground next to his sleeping bag lay some shreds of dried vegetation. It looked like seaweed.

Margaret slid the straps of the backpack over her shoulders and returned to the riverbank. "But you didn't find a body?"

"Sometimes it takes months for a body to surface, especially this time of year," Watson said. "Sometimes they never do."

Margaret walked along the rocky beach. "Why would he come here?" she muttered, kicking driftwood out of the way, shivering in the November wind.

"Does he have friends in Cleveland?" Watson asked. "Has he ever been here before?"

Margaret shook her head. "Not that I know of. But, I guess it's possible. I haven't seen much of him since his discharge from the service." Looking down the shoreline to the west, she saw a small flotilla of boats bobbing just inside the breakwall. And more people on the wall itself.

"What's going on over there?" she said.

Watson rolled her eyes. "This giant fish got caught in the passage there. The biggest lake sturgeon anyone has ever seen. So there's a lot of talk about sea monsters and like that. *Weekly World News* has been and gone. If you ask me, it's a big stinky mess. I'm just glad they didn't give me the cleanup job."

Just then, Margaret noticed something caught in the rocks by her feet. Reaching down, she pulled it free.

It was a necklace made of freshwater mussel shells. Bits of rotting flowers fell away as she lifted it.

"What did you find?"

"Looks like somebody dropped a necklace," Margaret said. She sighed, and blotted away tears with the backs of her hand. "I appreciate your bringing me down here and all," she said. "It just helps to see where my father died."

"I'm glad to do it, ma'am. See, I was in the military myself." He paused. "They said he won the Silver Star."

"Yes. He did," Margaret said, her voice low and bitter. "And the Distinguished Service Cross."

"That's something."

"Yes," Margaret said. "That's something. Being a soldier was everything to him."

Pulling out the bag of effects they'd given her at the station house, she surfaced the velvet case that contained her father's medals. Lifting the Distinguished Service Cross from its nest, she weighed it on her palm.

"Ma'am?" Watson put her hand on Margaret's arm. "What are you doing?"

"I'm going to give it back to him," Margaret said. Cocking back her arm, she threw it. It flew in a high arc over the lake, glittering like a meteor in the sun until it disappeared into the waves.

THE MAGICIAN AND THE MAID AND OTHER STORIES

Christie Yant

She called herself Audra, though that wasn't her real name; he called himself Miles, but she suspected it wasn't his, either.

She was young (how young she would not say), beautiful (or so her Emil had told her), and she had a keen interest in stories. Miles was old, tattooed, perverted, and often mean, but he knew stories that no one else knew, and she was certain that he was the only one who could help her get back home.

She found him among the artists, makers, and deviants. They called him Uncle, and spoke of him sometimes with loathing, sometimes respect, but almost always with a tinge of awe – a magician in a world of technicians, they did not know what to make of him.

But Audra saw him for what he truly was.

There once was a youth of low birth who aspired to the place of King's Magician. The villagers scoffed, "Emil, you will do naught but mind the sheep," but in his heart he knew that he could possess great magic.

The hedge witches and midwives laughed at the shepherd boy who played at sorcery, but indulged his earnestness. He learned charms for love and marriage (women's magic, but he would not be shamed by it) and for wealth and luck, but none of this satisfied him, for it brought him no nearer to the throne. For that he needed real power, and he did not know where to find it.

He had a childhood playmate named Aurora, and as they

*approached adulthood Aurora grew in both beauty and cleverness.
Their childhood affection turned to true love, and on her birthday
they were betrothed.*

*The day came when the youth knew he had learned all that he
could in the nearby villages and towns. The lovers wept and
declared their devotion with an exchange of humble silver rings.
With a final kiss Emil left his true love behind, and set out to find
the source of true power.*

It was not hard to meet him, once she understood his tastes. A
tuck of her skirt, a tug at her chemise; a bright ribbon, new
stockings, and dark kohl to line her eyes. She followed him to a
club he frequented, where musicians played discordant
arrangements and the patrons were as elaborately costumed as
the performers. She walked past his booth where he smoked
cigarettes and drank scotch surrounded by colorful young
women and effeminate young men.

"You there, Bo Peep, come here."

She met his dark eyes, turned her back on him, and walked
away. The sycophants who surrounded him bitched and
whined their contempt for her. He barked at them to shut up
as she made her way to the door.

Once she had rejected him it was easy. She waited for his
fourth frustrated overture before she joined him at his table.

"So," she said as she lifted his glass to her lips uninvited,
"tell me a story."

"What kind of story?"

"A fairy tale."

"What – something with elves and princes and happily-
ever-after?"

"No," she said and reached across the corner of the table to
turn his face toward her. He seemed startled but complied, and
leaned in until their faces were just inches apart. "A real fairy
tale. With wolves and witches, jealous parents, woodsmen
charged with murdering the innocent. Tell me a story,
Miles . . ." she could feel his breath against her cheek falter as
she leaned ever closer and spoke softly into his ear ". . . tell me
a story that is true."

★   ★   ★

Audra was foot-sore and weary when they reached the house at dawn. She stumbled on the stone walk, and caught Miles's arm to steady her.

"Are you sure you don't need anything from home?" he asked as he worked his key in the lock.

At his mention of *home*, she remembered again to hate him.

"Quite sure," she said. He faced her, this time with a different kind of appraisal. There was no leer, no suspicion. He touched her face, and his habitual scowl relaxed into something like a smile.

"You remind me of someone I knew once, long ago." The smile vanished and he opened the front door, stepping aside to let her pass.

His house was small and filled with a peculiar collection of things that told her she had the right man. Many of them were achingly familiar to Audra: a wooden spindle in the entryway, wound with golden thread; a dainty glass shoe on the mantle, almost small enough to fit a child; in the corner, a stone statue of an ugly, twisted creature, one arm thrown protectively over its eyes.

"What a remarkable collection," she said and forced a smile. "It must have taken a long time to assemble."

"Longer than I care to think of." He picked a golden pear off the shelf and examined it. "None of it is what I wanted." He returned it to the shelf with a careless toss. "I'll show you the bedroom."

The room was bare, in contrast with the rest of the house. No ornament hung on the white plaster walls, no picture rested on the dresser. The bed was small, though big enough for two, and covered in a faded quilt. It was flanked by a table on one side, and a bentwood chair on the other.

Audra sat stiffly at the foot of the bed.

The mattress creaked as Miles sat down beside her. She turned toward him with resolve, and braced herself for the inevitable. She would do whatever it took to get back home.

She had done worse, and with less cause.

He leaned in close and stroked her hair; she could smell him, sweet and smoky, familiar and foreign at the same time. She lifted a hand to caress his smooth head where he lingered above her breast. He caught her wrist and straightened, pressed her palm to his cheek – eyes closed, forehead creased in pain – then abruptly dropped her hand and rose from the bed.

"If you need more blankets, they're in the wardrobe. Sleep well," he said, and left Audra to wonder what had gone wrong, and to consider her next move.

Aurora was as ambitious as Emil, but of a different nature. She believed that the minds of most men were selfish and swayed only by fear or greed. In her heart there nestled a seed of doubt that Emil could get his wish through pure knowledge and practice. She resolved in her love for him to secure his place through craft and wile.

Aurora knew the ways of tales. She planted the seed of rumor in soil in which it grew best: the bowry; the laundry; anywhere the women gathered, she talked of his power.

But word of the powerful sorcerer had to reach the King himself, and to get close enough she would need to use a different craft.

The hands of guards and pikemen were rougher than Emil's; the mouths of servants less tender. She ignited the fire of ambition in their hearts with flattery, and fanned it with promises that Emil, the most powerful sorcerer in the kingdom, would repay those who supported him once he was installed in the palace.

And if she had regrets as she hurried from chamber to cottage in the cold night air, she dismissed them as just a step on the road toward realizing her lover's dream.

Audra woke at midday to find a note on the chair in the corner of the room.

In deep-black ink and an unpracticed hand was written:

"Stay if you like, or go as you please. I am accountable to only one, and that one is not you. If that arrangement suits you, make yourself at home. – M."

It suited her just fine.

She searched the house. She wasn't sure what she was looking for, but she was certain that any object of power great enough to rip her from her own world would be obvious somehow. It would be odd, otherworldly, she thought – but that described everything here. Like a raven's hoard, every nook contained some shiny, stolen object.

On a shelf in the library she found a clear glass apothecary jar labeled "East Wind". *Thief*, she thought. Audra hoped that the East Wind didn't suffer for the lack of the contents of the jar. She would keep an eye on the weather vane and return it at the first opportunity.

Something on the shelf caught her eye, small and shining, and her contempt turned to rage.

Murderer.

She pocketed Emil's ring.

Miles seemed to dislike mirrors. There were none in the bedroom; none even in the washroom. The only mirror in the house was an ornate, gilded thing that hung in the library. She paused in front of it, startled at her disheveled appearance. She smoothed her hair with her fingers and leaned in to examine her bloodshot eyes – and found someone else's eyes looking back at her.

The gaunt, androgynous face that gazed dolefully from deep within the mirror was darker and older than her own.

"Hello," she said to the Magic Mirror. "I'm Audra."

The Mirror shook its head disapprovingly.

"You're right," she admitted. "But we don't give strangers our true names, do we?"

She considered her new companion. The long lines of its insubstantial face told Audra that it had worn that mournful look for a long time.

"Did he steal you, as well? Perhaps we can help each other find a way home. The answer is here somewhere."

The face in the Mirror brightened, and it nodded.

Audra had an idea. "Would you like me to read to you?"

Emil traveled a bitter road in search of the knowledge that would make his fortune. By day he starved, by night he froze. But one day Luck was with him, and he caught two large, healthy hares before sunset. As he huddled beside his small fire, the hares roasting over the flames, a short and grizzled man came out of the forest, carrying a sack of goods.

"*Good evening, Grandfather,*" Emil said to the little man. "*Sit, share my fire and supper.*" The man gratefully accepted. "*What do you sell?*" Emil asked.

"*Pots and pans, needles, and spices,*" the old man said.

"*Know you any magic?*" Emil asked, disappointed. He was beginning to think the knowledge he sought didn't exist, and he was losing hope.

"*What does a shepherd need with magic?*"

"*How did you know I'm a shepherd?*" Emil asked in surprise.

"*I know many things,*" the man said, and then groaned, and doubled over in pain.

"*What ails you?*" Emil cried, rushing to the old man's side.

"*Nothing that you can help, lad. I've a disease of the gut that none can cure, and my time may be short.*"

Emil questioned the man about his ailment, and pulled from his pack dozens of pouches of herbs and powders. He heated water for a medicinal brew while the old man groaned and clutched his stomach.

The man pulled horrible faces as he drank down the bitter tea, but before long his pain eased, and he was able to sit upright again. Emil mixed another batch of the preparation and assured him that he would be cured if he drank the tea for seven days.

"*I was wrong about you,*" the man said. "*You're no shepherd.*" He pulled a scroll from deep within his pack. "*For your kindness I'll give you what you've traveled the world seeking.*"

The little man explained that the scroll contained three powerful spells, written in a language that no man had spoken in a thousand years. The first was a spell to summon a benevolent spirit, who would then guide him in his learning.

The second summoned objects from one world into another, for every child knew that there were many worlds, and that it was possible to pierce the veil between them.

The third would transport a person *between* worlds.

If he could decipher the three spells, he would surely become the most powerful sorcerer in the kingdom.

Emil offered the old man what coins he had, but he refused. He simply handed over the scroll, bade Emil farewell, and walked back into the forest.

★　　★　　★

Audra filled her time reading to the Mirror. The shelves were filled with hundreds of books: old and new, leather-bound and gilt-edged, or flimsy and sized to be carried in a pocket.

She devoured them, looking for clues. How she got here. How she might get back.

On a bottom shelf in the library, in the sixth book of a twelve-volume set, she found her story.

The illustrations throughout the blue cloth-bound book were full of round, cheerful children and curling vines. She recognized some of her friends and enemies from her old life: there was Miska, who fooled the Man-With-The-Iron-Head and whom she had met once on his travels; on another page she found the fairy who brought the waterfall to the mountain, whom Audra resolved to visit as soon as she got home.

She turned the page, and her breath caught in her throat.

"The Magician and the Maid", the title read. Beneath the illustration were those familiar words, "Once upon a time."

A white rabbit bounded between birch trees toward Audra's cottage. Between the tree tops a castle gleamed pink in the sunset light, the place where her story was supposed to end. Audra traced the outline of the rabbit with her finger, and then traced the two lonely shadows that followed close behind.

Two shadows: one, her own, and the other, Emil's.

Audra was reading to the Mirror, a story it seemed to particularly like. It did tricks for her as she read, creating wispy images in the glass that matched the prose.

She had just reached the best part, where the trolls turn to stone in the light of the rising sun, when she heard footsteps outside the library door. The Mirror looked anxiously toward the sound, and then slipped out of sight beyond the carved frame.

The door burst open.

"Who are you talking to?" Miles demanded. "Who's here?" He smelled of scotch and sweat, and his overcoat had a new stain.

"No one. I like to read aloud. I am alone here all day," she said.

"Don't pretend I owe you anything." He slouched into the chair and pulled a cigarette from his coat. "You might make yourself useful," he said. "Read to me."

The room was small, and she stood no more than an arm's length away, feeling like a schoolgirl being made to recite. She opened to a story she did not know, a tale called "The Snow Queen", and began to read. Miles closed his eyes and listened.

"Little Kay was quite blue with cold, indeed almost black, but he did not feel it; for the Snow Queen had kissed away the icy shiverings, and his heart was already a lump of ice," she read.

She glanced down at him when she paused for breath to find him looking at her in a way that she knew all too well.

Finally, an advantage.

She let her voice falter when he ran a finger up the side of her leg, lifting her skirt a few inches above her knee.

She did not stop reading – it was working, something in him had changed as she read. Sex was a weak foothold, but it was the only one she had, and perhaps it would be a step toward getting into his mind.

"He dragged some sharp, flat pieces of ice to and fro, and placed them together in all kinds of positions, as if he wished to make something out of them. He composed many complete figures, forming different words, but there was one word he never could manage to form, although he wished it very much. It was the word 'Eternity'."

He fingered the cord tied at her waist, and tugged it gently at first, then more insistently. He leaned forward in the chair, and unfastened the last hook on her corset.

"Just at this moment it happened that little Gerda came through the great door of the castle. Cutting winds were raging around her, but she offered up a prayer and the winds sank down as if they were going to sleep; and she went on till she came to the large empty hall, and caught sight of Kay; she knew him directly; she flew to him and threw her arms round his neck, and held him fast, while she exclaimed, 'Kay, dear little Kay, I have found you at last.'"

His fingers stopped their manipulations. His hands were still on her, the fastenings held between his fingertips.

She dared not breathe.

Whatever control she had for those few minutes was gone. She tried to reclaim it, to keep going as if nothing had happened. She even dropped a hand from the book and reached out to touch him. His hand snapped up and caught hers; he stood, pulling hard on her arm.

"Enough." He left the room without looking back. She heard the front door slam.

Audra straightened her clothes in frustration and wondered again what had gone wrong.

It took only a moment's thought for Audra to decide to follow him. She peered out into the street: there he was, a block away already, casting a long shadow in the lamplight on the wet pavement.

Her feet were cold and her shoes wet through by the time he finally stopped at a warehouse deep in a maze of brick complexes. He manipulated a complex series of locks on the dented and rusting steel door, and disappeared inside.

So this was where he went at night? Not to clubs and parlors as she had thought, but here, on the edge of the inhabited city, to a warehouse only notable for having all its window glass.

The windows were too high for her to see into, but a dumpster beneath one of them offered her a chance. The metal bin was slick with mist, and she slipped off it twice, but on her third try she hoisted herself on top and nervously peered through the filthy glass of the window.

In the dim light she could just make out the shape of Miles, rubbing his hands fiercely together as if to warm them, then unrolling something – paper, or parchment – spreading it out carefully in front of him on the concrete floor. He stood, and began to speak.

The room grew brighter, and a face appeared in front of him, suspended in the air – a familiar face made of dim green light; Audra could see little of it through the dirty glass. She could hear Miles's voice, urgent and almost desperate, but the words he shouted at the thing made no sense to her.

She shifted her weight to ease the pain of her knee pressing against the metal of the dumpster, and slipped. She fell, and cried out in pain as she landed hard on the pavement.

She didn't know if Miles had heard, but she did not wait to find out. She picked herself up – now wet, filthy, and aching – and ran.

When she reached the house she went straight to the library. Audra shifted the books on the shelf so that the remaining volumes were flush against each other, and she hid her book in the small trunk where she kept her few clothes.

The Mirror's face emerged from its hiding place behind the frame, looking worried and wan.

"It's my story, after all," she told it. "I won't let him do any more damage. What if he takes the cottage? The woods? Where would I have to go home to? No, he can't have any more of our story."

The language of the scroll was not as impossible as the little man had said – while it was not his own, it was similar enough that someone as clever as Emil could puzzle it out. He applied himself to little else, and before long Emil could struggle through half of the first spell. But when he thought of arriving home after so long, still unable to execute even the simplest of the three, the frustration in him grew.

Surely, he thought, he should begin with the hardest, for having mastered that the simpler ones will come with ease.

So thinking, he set out to learn the last of the three spells before he arrived home.

When Miles finally returned the following evening at dusk, he looked exhausted and filthy, as if he had slept on the floor of the warehouse. She met him in the kitchen, and didn't ask questions.

He brooded on a chair in the corner while she chopped vegetables on the island butcher block, never taking his eyes off her, then stood abruptly and left the room.

The hiss and sputter of the vegetables as they hit the pan echoed the angry, inarticulate hiss in her mind. She had been here for days, and she was no closer to getting home.

The knife felt heavy and solid in her hand as she cubed a slab of marbled meat. She imagined Miles under the knife, imagined his fear and pain. She would get it out of him – how to get home – and he would tell her what he had done to her Emil before the miserable bastard died.

Sounds from the next room were punctuated with curses. The crack of heavy books being unshelved made her flinch.

"Where is it?" he first seemed to ask himself; then louder, *"Where?"* he demanded of the room at large; then a roar erupted from the doorway: *"What have you done with it, you vicious witch?"*

A cold wash of fear cleared away her thoughts of revenge.

"What are you talking about?"

"My book," he said. "Where is it? What have you done with it?"

He came at her hunched like an advancing wolf. They circled the butcher block. She gripped the knife and dared not blink, for fear that he would take a split second advantage and lunge for her.

"You have many books."

"And I only care about one!" His hand shot out and caught her wrist, bringing her arm down against the scarred wood with a painful shock. The knife fell from her hand.

He dragged her into the library. "There," he said, pointing to the shelf where her book had been. "Six of twelve. It was there and now it's not." He relaxed his grip without letting go. "If you borrowed it, it's fine. I just want it back." He released her and forced a smile. "Now, where is it?"

"You're right," she said, "I borrowed it. I didn't realize it was so important to you."

"It's very special."

"Yes," she said, her voice low and hard, "it is."

And with that, she knew she had given herself away.

Miles shoved her away from him. She fell into the bookcase as he left the small library and shut the door behind him. A key turned in the lock.

It was too late.

She rested with her forehead against the door and caught her breath. She tried to pry open the small window, but it was sealed shut with layers of paint. She considered breaking the glass, and then thought better of it; she could escape from this house, it was true, but not from this world. For that, she still needed Miles.

She watched the sunset through the dirty window, and tried to decide what to do when he let her out. She heard him pacing through the house, talking to himself with ever greater stridency, but the words made no sense to her. It gave her a headache.

The sound of the key in the door woke her. She grabbed at the first thing that might serve as a weapon, a sturdy hardcover. She held it in front of her like a shield.

Miles stood in the doorway, a long, wicked knife in his hand.

"Who are you?" he finally asked, his eyes narrowed with suspicion. "And how did you know?"

"Someone whose life you destroyed. Liar. Thief. Murderer." She produced Emil's ring.

He seemed frozen where he stood, his eyes darting back and forth between the ring in her hand and her face. "I am none of those things," he said.

"You took all of this," she gestured around the room. "You took him, and you took me. And what did you do with the things that were of no use to you?"

She had been edging toward him while he talked. She threw the book at his arm and it struck him just as she had hoped. The knife fell to the floor and she dove for it, snatching it up before Miles could stop her.

She had him now, she thought, and pressed the blade against his throat. He tried to push her off but she had a tenacious grip on him and he ceased his struggle when the knife pierced his thin skin. She felt his body tense in her hands, barely breathing and perfectly still.

"You still haven't told me who you are."

"Where is he?" she demanded.

"Where is who?" His voice was smooth and controlled.

"The man you stole, like you stole me. Like you stole all of it. Where is he?"

"You're obviously very upset. Put that down, let me go, and we'll talk about it. I don't know about any stolen man, but maybe I can help you find him."

He voice was calm, slightly imploring, asking for understanding and offering help. She hesitated, wondering what threat she was really willing to carry out against an enemy who was also her only hope.

She waited a moment too long. Miles grabbed a heavy jar off the shelf and hurled it at the wall.

The East Wind ripped through the room, finally free.

Fatigued and half-starved, Emil made his way slowly toward his home, and tried to unlock the spell. Soon he had three words, and then five, and soon a dozen. He would say them aloud, emphasizing this part or that, elongating a sound or shortening it, until the day he gave voice to the last character on the page, and something happened: a spark, a glimmer of magic.

He had ciphered out the spell.

Finally, on the coldest night he could remember, with not a soul in sight, he raised his voice against the howling wind, and shouted out the thirteen words of power.

As weeks turned into months the stories of Emil the Sorcerer grew, until finally even the King had heard, and wanted his power within his own control.

But Emil could not be found.

The angry vortex threw everything off the shelves. Audra ducked and covered her head as she was pummeled by books and debris. Miles crouched behind the trunk, which offered little protection from the gale.

There was a crash above Audra's head; her arms flew up to protect her eyes; broken glass struck her arms and legs, some falling away, some piercing her skin.

The window broke with a final crash and the captive wind escaped the room. The storm was over. Books thumped and glass tinkled to the ground.

Audra opened her eyes to the wreckage. Miles was already sifting through the pages and torn covers.

"No," he said, "no! It has to be here, my story has to be here . . ." He bled from a hundred small cuts but he paid them no mind. Audra plucked shards of dark glass out of her flesh. The shards gave off no reflection at all.

A cloud drifted from where the Mirror had hung over the wreckage-strewn shelves, searching. On the floor beside

Audra's trunk, the lid torn off in the storm, it seemed to find what it was looking for. It slipped between the pages of a blue cloth-bound volume and disappeared.

"Here!" Audra said, clutching the volume to her chest. He scrambled toward her until they kneeled together in the middle of the floor, face to face.

Smoke curled out of the pages, only a wisp at first. Then more, green and glowing like a sunbeam in a mossy pond, crept out and wrapped itself around both them.

"The Guide you sought was always here," a voice whispered. "Your captive, Emil, and your friend, Aurora." Audra – Aurora – looked at the man she had hated and saw what was there all along: her Emil, thirty years since he had disappeared, with bald head and graying beard. Miles, who kept her because she looked like his lost love, but who wouldn't touch her, in faith to his beloved.

Emil looked back at her, tears in the eyes that had seemed so dead and without hope until now.

"Now, Emil, speak the words," the voice said, "and we will go home."

So should you happen across a blue cloth-bound book, the sixth in a set of twelve, do not look for "The Magician and the Maid", because it is not there.

Read the other stories, though, and in the story of the fairy who brought the waterfall to the mountain, you may find that she has a friend called Audra, though you will know the truth: it is not her real name.

If you read further you may find Emil as well, for, though he never did become the King's Magician, every story needs a little magic.

ABOUT THE CONTRIBUTORS

Jay Lake (1964–2014) lived in Portland, Oregon, where he worked on numerous writing and editing projects. His books include *Kalimpura, Last Plane to Heaven* and *Love in the Time of Metal and Flesh*, and his short fiction appears regularly in literary and genre markets worldwide. Jay was a winner of the John W. Campbell Award for Best New Writer, and a multiple nominee for the Hugo, Nebula and World Fantasy awards. He blogged regularly about his terminal colon cancer (www.jlake.com).

Chris Willrich's stories have appeared in *Asimov's, Beneath Ceaseless Skies, Flashing Swords, Lightspeed* and *Fantasy and Science Fiction*, where his characters Gaunt and Bone first appeared. Chris has also written the Gaunt and Bone novels *The Scroll of Years* (2013) and *The Silk Map* (2014) as well as *Pathfinder Tales: The Dagger of Trust* (2014).

After a brief career in the legal profession, K. J. Parker took to writing full time and has to date produced three trilogies, five standalone novels, five novellas (two of which won the World Fantasy Award) and a gaggle of short stories. When not writing, Parker works on a tiny smallholding in the west of England and makes things out of wood and metal. K. J. Parker isn't K.J. Parker's real name; but even if you knew K. J. Parker's real name, it wouldn't mean anything to you.

Tanith Lee was born in London in 1947. She began writing at age nine. Her science fiction and fantasy has been published since 1974–5, beginning with *The Birthgrave*. Since then she has published over ninety books and more than 300 short stories, and written two TV scripts (*Blake's 7*) and four broadcast radio plays. She has won many awards, was made Grand Master of Horror in 2009, and given a Life Achievement Award in 2013. She lives with her husband, writer/artist John Kaiine, and two black and white cats in Sussex, near the sea.

Bradley P. Beaulieu is the author of the critically acclaimed epic fantasy series *The Lays of Anuskaya*. Along with fellow author Gregory A. Wilson, Brad runs the science fiction and fantasy podcast Speculate (www.speculatesf.com). He continues to work on his next projects, including a Norse-inspired middle-grade series and *The Song of the Shattered Sands*, an Arabian Nights-inspired epic fantasy (www.quillings.com).

Aliette de Bodard lives and works in Paris, where she has a day job as a systems engineer. She writes speculative fiction, including the Aztec noir trilogy *Obsidian and Blood*. Her short stories have appeared in *Clarkesworld*, *Asimov's Science Fiction* and the *Year's Best Science Fiction*. She has won Nebula, Locus and British Science Fiction Association awards, and been a finalist for the Hugo, Sturgeon and Tiptree awards (www.aliettedebodard.com).

Benjamin Rosenbaum lives near Basel, Switzerland, with his wife and children. His stories have appeared in *Harper's*, *Fantasy and Science Fiction*, *Asimov's Science Fiction*, *McSweeney's*, *Strange Horizons* and *Nature*. His work has been nominated for the Hugo, Nebula, World Fantasy, BSFA and Sturgeon awards, and has been translated into over twenty languages. His stories are collected in *The Ant King and Other Stories* (www.benjaminrosenbaum.com).

Alex Dally MacFarlane is a writer, editor and historian. When not researching narrative maps in the legendary traditions of Alexander III of Macedon, she writes stories for

Clarkesworld Magazine, Strange Horizons, Beneath Ceaseless Skies, Phantasm Japan, Solaris Rising 3, Heiresses of Russ 2013: The Year's Best Lesbian Speculative Fiction, The Year's Best Science Fiction & Fantasy: 2014 and other anthologies. Her poetry can be found in *Stone Telling, The Moment of Change* and *Here, We Cross*. She is the editor of *Aliens: Recent Encounters* (2013) and *The Mammoth Book of SF Stories by Women* (2014).

Saladin Ahmed's poetry has earned fellowships from several universities, and has appeared in over a dozen journals and anthologies. His short stories have been nominated for the Nebula and Campbell awards, have appeared in numerous magazines and podcasts, and have been translated into five languages. He has also written nonfiction for the *Escapist, Fantasy Magazine* and *Tor.com*. His first novel is *Throne of the Crescent Moon*.

Scott Lynch was born in St Paul, Minnesota, in 1978. His first novel, *The Lies of Locke Lamora*, was released in 2006 and launched the ongoing Gentleman Bastard sequence. His latest novel, *The Republic of Thieves*, reached the *New York Times* and *USA Today* bestseller lists. Scott has been a volunteer fire-fighter since 2005. He lives mostly in Wisconsin and occasionally in Massachusetts, the home of his partner, SF/F writer Elizabeth Bear.

Carrie Vaughn is the author of the *New York Times* bestselling series of novels about a werewolf named Kitty. She's also written a handful of standalone fantasy novels and over seventy short stories. She's a graduate of the Odyssey Fantasy Writing Workshop, and in 2011 she was nominated for a Hugo Award for best short story. She's had the usual round of day jobs, but has been writing full-time since 2007. An Air Force brat, she survived her nomadic childhood and managed to put down roots in Boulder, Colorado, where she lives with a fluffy attack dog and too many hobbies (www.carrievaughn.com).

Tony Pi is a Taiwanese-Canadian writer whose childhood memories of a sugar sculptor inspired this story. His works appear in many places such as *Clarkesworld Magazine*, *InterGalactic Medicine Show*, *The Mammoth Book of Steampunk Adventures* and *The Dragon and the Stars* (www.tonypi.com).

N. K. Jemisin is a Brooklyn author whose short fiction and novels have been multiply nominated for the Hugo, World Fantasy and Nebula awards, shortlisted for the Crawford and the Tiptree awards, and won the Locus Award. Her latest novel is *The Shadowed Sun* (2012) and she is working on her next trilogy (www.nkjemisin.com).

Benjanun Sriduangkaew enjoys writing love letters to cities real and speculative, and lots of space opera when she can get away with it. Her works can be found in *Clarkesworld*, *Beneath Ceaseless Skies*, *The Dark*, *The Mammoth Book of Steampunk Adventures*, *Upgraded* and *Solaris Rising 3*. They are also reprinted in *The Best Science Fiction and Fantasy of the Year Vol. 8*, *The Year's Best Science and Fantasy 2014* and *The Mammoth Book of SF Stories by Women*.

Yoon Ha Lee's fiction has appeared in *Clarkesworld*, *Lightspeed*, *Beneath Ceaseless Skies*, *Fantasy and Science Fiction* and other publications. Her collection *Conservation of Shadows* came out in 2013. She lives in Louisiana with her family and has not yet been eaten by gators, books or dolls.

Matthew Hughes writes science fiction and fantasy. His novels are: *Fools Errant* and *Fool Me Twice*, *Black Brillion*, *Majestrum*, *The Commons*, *The Spiral Labyrinth*, *Template*, *Hespira*, *The Damned Busters*, *The Other*, *Costume Not Included* and *Hell to Pay*. His short fiction has appeared in *Asimov's Science Fiction*, *Fantasy and Science Fiction*, *Postscripts*, *Storyteller*, *Interzone* and a number of anthologies. His short story collection, *The Gist Hunter and Other Stories*, was published in 2005. Formerly a journalist, he spent more than twenty-five years as a freelance speech-writer for Canadian corporate executives and political leaders. His works have been short-listed for the Aurora, Nebula, Philip K. Dick, A. E. Van Vogt and Endeavour Awards (www.matthewhughes.org).

Mary Robinette Kowal is the author of the *Glamourist Histories* series of historical fantasy novels. In 2008 she received the Campbell Award for Best New Writer and, in 2011, her short story "For Want of a Nail" won the Hugo Award for Short Story. Her work has been nominated for the Hugo, Nebula and Locus awards. Her stories appear in *Asimov's Science Fiction*, *Clarkesworld* and several anthologies. She is a professional puppeteer and performs as a voice actor, recording for authors such as Elizabeth Bear, Cory Doctorow and John Scalzi. She lives in Chicago with her husband Rob and over a dozen manual typewriters (www.maryrobinettekowal.com).

Naomi Novik is the *New York Times* bestselling author of the *Temeraire* series and winner of the Campbell, Locus and Compton Crook awards. She was born in New York in 1973, a first-generation American, and raised on Polish fairy tales, Baba Yaga and Tolkien. Her next fantasy novel, *Uprooted*, will be published in 2015. Naomi lives in New York City with her husband Charles Ardai, daughter Evidence and many purring computers (www.naominovik.com).

Elizabeth Bear was born on the same day as Frodo and Bilbo Baggins, but in a different year. When coupled with a childhood tendency to read the dictionary for fun, this led her inevitably to penury, intransigence and the writing of speculative fiction. She is the Hugo, Sturgeon, Locus and Campbell award-winning author of twenty-five novels and almost a hundred short stories. Her dog lives in Massachusetts; her partner, writer Scott Lynch, lives in Wisconsin. She spends a lot of time on planes.

Matthew David Surridge is a Montreal-area writer. He has an ongoing fantasy serial at www.fellgard.com and writes about fantasy fiction at www.blackgate.com.

Richard Parks has been writing and publishing science fiction and fantasy longer than he cares to remember . . . or probably can remember. His work has appeared in *Asimov's Science Fiction*, *Realms of Fantasy*, *Lady Churchill's Rosebud Wristlet* and several annual anthologies. His second print novel, *To Break the Demon Gate*, was published in 2014. He blogs at "Den of Ego and Iniquity Annex #3" (www.richard-parks.com).

James Enge lives with his wife in northwest Ohio, where he teaches classical languages and literature at a university. His first novel, *Blood of Ambrose* (2009), was nominated for the World Fantasy Award. He is also the author of *This Crooked Way*, *The Wolf Age*, *A Guile of Dragons* and *Wrath-Bearing Tree*, as well as short fiction mostly focusing on Morlock Ambrosius (www.jamesenge.com).

Genevieve Valentine's first novel, *Mechanique*, won the 2012 Crawford Award. Her second is called *The Girls at the Kingfisher Club*. Her short fiction has appeared in *Clarkesworld*, *Strange Horizons*, *Journal of Mythic Arts* and *Fantasy*, and the anthologies *Federations*, *Running with the Pack*, *After*, *The Way of the Wizard* and more. Her nonfiction and reviews have appeared at NPR.org, *The A. V. Club*, *Strange Horizons* and *io9* (www.genevievevalentine.com).

Cinda Williams Chima grew up with talking animals and kick-butt Barbies. She nearly failed first grade because she was always daydreaming instead of listening. By junior high, she was writing novels in class, which were often confiscated. She was also caught reading *a very racy novel* in Problems of Democracy class. Cinda believes in the magic of books. Books took her from first-grade failure to first-generation college graduate to college professor to *New York Times* bestselling author of *The Heir Chronicles* and the *Seven Realms* quartet (cindachima.com).

Christie Yant's fiction has appeared in anthologies and magazines including *Year's Best Science Fiction & Fantasy 2011*, *Armored*, *Analog Science Fiction & Fact*, *Beneath*

Ceaseless Skies, *io9*, *Wired.com* and China's *Science Fiction World*. She lives on the central coast of California with two writers, an editor and assorted four-legged nuisances (Twitter @christieyant).

ACKNOWLEDGEMENTS

SMALL MAGIC © 2006 by Joseph E. Lake, Jr. Originally appeared in *Weird Tales*. Reprinted by permission of the author.

KING RAINJOY'S TEARS © 2002 by Chris Willrich. Originally appeared in *Fantasy and Science Fiction*. Reprinted by permission of the author.

A RICH FULL WEEK © 2010 by K. J. Parker. Originally appeared in *Swords & Dark Magic*, edited by Jonathan Strahan and Lou Anders. Reprinted by permission of the author.

THE WOMAN IN SCARLET © 2000 by Tanith Lee. Originally appeared in *Realms of Fantasy*. Reprinted by permission of the author.

FLOTSAM © 2004 by Bradley P. Beaulieu. Originally appeared in *Writers of the Future 20*, edited by Algis Budrys. Reprinted by permission of the author.

A WARRIOR'S DEATH © 2006 by Aliette de Bodard. Originally appeared in *Shimmer*. Reprinted by permission of the author.

A SIEGE OF CRANES © 2006 by Benjamin Rosenbaum. Originally appeared in *Twenty Epics*, edited by David Moles and Susan Marie Groppi. Reprinted by permission of the author.

FOX BONES. *MANY USES*. © 2012 by Alex Dally MacFarlane. Originally appeared in *Beneath Ceaseless Skies*. Reprinted by permission of the author.

WHERE VIRTUE LIVES © 2009 by Saladin Ahmed. Originally appeared in *Beneath Ceaseless Skies*. Reprinted by permission of the author.

THE EFFIGY ENGINE: A TALE OF THE RED HATS © 2013 by Scott Lynch. Originally appeared in *Fearsome Journeys*, edited by Jonathan Strahan. Reprinted by permission of the author.

STRIFE LINGERS IN MEMORY © 2002 by Carrie Vaughn. Originally appeared in *Realms of Fantasy*. Reprinted by permission of the author.

A SWEET CALLING © 2010 by Tony Pi. Originally appeared in *Clarkesworld Magazine*. Reprinted by permission of the author.

THE NARCOMANCER © 2007 by N. K. Jemisin. Originally appeared in *Helix SF*. Reprinted by permission of the author.

GOLDEN DAUGHTER, STONE WIFE © 2014 by Benjanun Sriduangkaew. Originally appeared in *Beneath Ceaseless Skies*. Reprinted by permission of the author.

EFFIGY NIGHTS © 2013 by Yoon Ha Lee. Originally appeared in *Clarkesworld Magazine*. Reprinted by permission of the author.

WEARAWAY AND FLAMBEAU © 2012 by Matthew Hughes. Originally appeared in *Fantasy & Science Fiction*. Reprinted by permission of the author.

AT THE EDGE OF DYING © 2009 by Mary Robinette Kowal. Originally appeared in *Clockwork Phoenix*, edited by Mike Allen. Reprinted by permission of the author.

VICI © 2009 by Naomi Novik. Originally appeared in *The Dragon Book*, edited by Jack Dann and Gardener Dozois. Reprinted by permission of the author.

ABJURE THE REALM © 2007 by Elizabeth Bear. Originally appeared in *Coyote Wild*. Reprinted by permission of the author.

THE WORD OF AZRAEL © 2010 by Matthew David Surridge. Originally appeared in *Black Gate*. Reprinted by permission of the author.

LADY OF THE GHOST WILLOW © 2010 by Richard Parks. Originally appeared in *Beneath Ceaseless Skies*. Reprinted by permission of the author.

THE SINGING SPEAR © 2010 by James Enge. Originally appeared in *Swords & Dark Magic*, edited by Jonathan Strahan and Lou Anders. Reprinted by permission of the author.

SO DEEP THAT THE BOTTOM COULD NOT BE SEEN © 2010 by Genevieve Valentine. Originally appeared in *The Way of the Wizard*, edited by John Joseph Adams. Reprinted by permission of the author.

WARRIOR DREAMS © 2013 by Cinda Williams Chima. Originally appeared in *Once Upon a Time: New Fairy Tales*, edited by Paula Guran. Reprinted by permission of the author.

THE MAGICIAN AND THE MAID © 2010 by Christie Yant. Originally appeared in *The Way of the Wizard*, edited by John Joseph Adams. Reprinted by permission of the author.

808.838766 M265

The mammoth book of
warriors and wizardry /
Central NONFICTION
12/14